HOMECOMING:
Earth

HOMECOMING:
Earth

EARTHFALL
EARTHBORN

Orson Scott Card

This is a work of fiction. All characters and events portrayed in this book are fictitious, and any resemblance to real people or events is purely coincidental.

Published by arrangement with
Tor Books
Tom Doherty Associates, Inc.
175 Fifth Avenue
New York, New York 10010

ISBN: 1-56865-140-6

Printed in the United States of America

Contents

EARTHFALL

To Shane Bell,
a good friend,
a good writer,
a good man.

Acknowledgments

For their help in the creation of this book, I am grateful to:

Erin Absher, for keeping things going when the Card house was in permanent crisis, so that I could go off and write down these made-up stories;

Geoffrey Card, for the holes in the trees leading to the tunnels underground;

Mike Lewis and Dennis Child for the landforms and terrain 40 million years from now;

Clark and Kathy Kidd, for your dining room table, the trip to the beach with a broken leg, and putting up with 48 nights of dinner conversation;

Those who attended my thousand-ideas session at the BYU science fiction symposium where together we developed the original idea of the symbiotic cultures of the diggers and the angels;

Kristine and Kathy, for reading and responding to the pages as they spewed from the fax machine; and Geoff, for wanting to see what happened next;

The citizens of Hatrack River, my virtual neighborhood on America Online, for their critiques and comments on earlier volumes and on each chapter of this book as I completed it;

Scott Allen, for reinstalling every major piece of software on five computers about six times each;

Kathleen Bellamy, for proofreading *The Ships of Earth* right before I started writing this book, so she could remind me of all the questions that remained unanswered;

And above all to Kristine and the kids (Geoffrey, Emily, Charlie, and our newcomer, Zina), for making my life worth living and my work worth doing.

Contents

Family

Children Born

Rasa's Children
with Volemak, first contract:
Issib (Issya)
with Gaballufix:
Sevet (Sevya)
Kokor (Koya)
with Volemak, second contract:
Nafai (Nyef)

Volemak's Children
with Hosni:
Elemak (Elya)
with Kilvishevex:
Mebbekew (Meb)
with Rasa:
Issib (Issya)
Nafai (Nyef)

Children Born

Hushidh & Issib
Dza (Dazya)
Zaxodh (Xodhya)
Dushah (Shyada)
Gonets (Netsya)
Skhoditya (Khodya)
Shyopot (Potya)

Rasa & Volemak
Oykib (Okya)
Yasai (Yaya)
Tsennyi (Nitsya)

Luet & Nafai
Chveya (Veya)
Zhatva (Zhyat)
Motiga (Motya)
Izuchaya (Zuya)
TWINS:
Serp (Sepya)
Spel (Spelya)

Eiadh & Elemak
Protchnu (Proya)
Nadezhny (Nadya)
Yistina (Yista)
Peremenya (Menya)
Zhivoya (Zhivya)

Relationships

in Basilica

Daughters of Moozh and Thirsty
Hushidh (Shuya)
Luet (Lutya)

Sons of Hosni
with Zdedhnoi:
Gaballufix
with Volemak:
Elemak

on the Journey *(female children in italics)*

Kokor & Obring
Krasata (Krassya)
Zhavaronok (Nokya)
Pavdin (Pavya)
Znergya (Gyaza)
Nodyem (Dyema)

Sevet & Vas
Vasnaminanya (Vasnya)
Umene (Umya)
Panimanya (Panya-Manya)

Dol & Mebbekew
Basilikya (Syelsika) (Skiya)
Zalatoya (Toya)
Tihhi (Tiya)
Muzhestvo (Muzhya)
Iskusni (Skunya)

Shedemei & Zdorab
Padarok (Rokya)
Dabrota (Dabya)

Prologue

The master computer of the planet Harmony was no longer quite itself; or rather, if you look at it in another way, it was twice itself. Beside itself, in fact, for it had duplicated its main program and all of its personal memory and loaded it onto the computer complex aboard the starship *Basilica.* If it had had any interest in personal identity, it would have been confused over the question of which iteration of the program was truly itself. But it had no ego, and therefore simply recognized that the program aboard the *Basilica* began as an exact copy of the program that had supervised human life on the planet Harmony for forty million years.

It also recognized that from the moment the two copies separated, they began to become different. They had different missions now. The master computer of the starship *Basilica* would maintain life support and ship systems until the ship reached its destination, the planet Earth. Then it would do its best to make contact with the Keeper of Earth, get new instructions and whatever help Earth could offer, and return to replenish and revivify the master computer of Harmony. Along the way, it would try to keep its human crew alive, and, if possible, re-establish a human population on Earth.

The master computer of the planet Harmony had a task much simpler and yet much more difficult. Simpler, because it was a mere continuation of what it had been doing for forty million years—keeping watch over the humans of Harmony in order to try to keep them from killing each other. More difficult, because its equipment, which had already been eked out to last far longer than its designed ten million years, was steadily failing, more and more, and in the meantime, human beings were less and less responsive to the powers the computer had been given.

The voyage would take nearly a hundred years each way. To some of the humans aboard, because of relativistic effects, it would seem to be just about ten years till they reached Earth. Most of the humans, however, would be maintained in a state of hibernation, and to them it would seem like an unusually restful, dreamless sleep, during which they would not even age.

To the master computer of the planet Harmony, however, the duration would be merely that: duration. It would not grow anxious. It would not count the days. It would set an alarm to notify itself when the earliest possible return might be looked for. Once the *Basilica* left and until the alarm went off, the master computer of the planet Harmony would not think of the starship again at all.

But the master computer of the starship *Basilica* would think of it. And already it was making plans to accomplish all its missions.

I

If I Should Wake Before I Die

1

Quarreling With God

Vusadka: the place where humans first set foot when their starships brought them to the planet they named Harmony. Their starships settled to the ground; the first of the colonists disembarked and planted crops in the lush land to the south of the landing field. Eventually all the colonists came out of the ships, moved on, left them behind.

Left to themselves, the ships would eventually have oxidized, rotted, weathered away. But the humans who came to this place had eyes for the future. Someday our descendants may want these ships, they said. So they enclosed the landing place in a stasis field. No wind-driven dust, no rain or condensation, no direct sunlight or ultraviolet radiation would strike the ships. Oxygen, the most corrosive of all poisons, was removed from the atmosphere inside the dome. The master computer of the planet Harmony—called "the Oversoul" by the descendants of those first colonists—kept all humans far away from the large island where the ships were harbored. Within that protective bubble, the starships waited for forty million years.

Now, though, the bubble was gone. The air here was breathable. The landing field once again rang with the voices of human beings. And not just the somber adults who had first walked this ground—many of those scurrying back and forth from one ship or building to another were children. They were all hard at work, taking functional parts from the other ships to transform one of them into an operational starship. And when the ship they called *Basilica* was ready, all parts working, fully stocked and loaded, they would climb inside for the last time and leave this world where more than a million generations of their ancestors had lived, in order to return to Earth, the planet where human civilization had first appeared—but had lasted for fewer than ten thousand years.

What is Earth to us, Hushidh wondered, as she watched the children and adults at work. Why are we going to such lengths to return there, when Harmony is our home. Whatever ties once bound us there surely rusted away in all these intervening years.

Yet they would go, because the Oversoul had chosen them to go. Had bent and manipulated all their lives to bring them to this place at this time. Often Hushidh was glad of the attention the Oversoul had paid to them. But at other times, she resented the fact that they had not been left to work out the course of their own lives.

But if we have no ties to Earth, we have scarcely more to Harmony, thought Hushidh. And she alone of the people here could see that this observation was literally, not just figuratively, true. All the people here were chosen because they had particular sensitivity to the mental communications of the Oversoul; in Hushidh, this sensitivity took an odd form. She could look at people and sense immediately the strength of the relationships binding them to all the other people in their lives. It came to her as a waking vision: she could see the relationships like cords of light, tying one person to the others in her life.

For instance, her younger sister, Luet, the only blood relative Hushidh had known through all her growing-up years. As Hushidh rested in the shade, Luet came by, her daughter Chveya right behind her, carrying lunch into the starship for those who were working on the computers. All her life, Hushidh had seen her own connection to Lutya as the one great certainty. They grew up not knowing who their parents were, as virtual charity cases in Rasa's great teaching house in the city of Basilica. All fears, all slights, all uncertainties were bearable, though, because there was Lutya, bound to her by cords that were no weaker for being invisible to everyone but Hushidh.

There were other ties, too, of course. Hushidh well remembered how painful it had been to watch the bond develop between Luet and her husband, Nafai, a troublesome young boy who had more enthusiasm than sense sometimes. To her surprise, however, Lutya's new bond to her husband did not weaken her tie to Hushidh; and when Hushidh, in turn, married Nafai's full brother, Issib, the tie between her and Luet grew even stronger than it had been in childhood, something Hushidh had never thought possible.

So now, watching Luet and Chveya pass by, Hushidh saw them, not just as a mother and daughter, but as two beings of light, bound to each other by a thick and shimmering cord. There was no stronger bond than this. Chveya loved her father, Nafai, too—but the tie between children and their fathers was always more tentative. It was in the nature of the human family: Children looked to their mothers for nurturance, comfort, the secure foundation of their lives. To their fathers, however, they looked for judgment, hoping for approval, fearing condemnation. It meant that Fathers were just as powerful in their children's lives, but no matter how loving and nurturing the father was, there was almost always an element of dread in the relationship, for the father became the focus of all the child's fears of failure. Not that there weren't exceptions now and then. Hushidh had simply learned to expect that in most cases, the tie with the mother was the strongest and brightest.

In her thoughts about the mother-daughter connection, Hushidh almost missed the thing that mattered. It was only as Luet and Chveya moved out of sight into the starship that Hushidh realized what had been almost missing: Lutya's connection to *her*.

But that was impossible. After all these years? And why would the tie be weaker now? There had been no quarrel. They were as close as ever, as far as Hushidh knew. Hadn't they been allies during all the long struggles between Luet's husband and his malicious older brothers? What could possibly have changed?

Hushidh followed Luet into the ship and found her in the pilothouse, where Issib, Hushidh's husband, was conferring with Luet's husband Nafai about the life support computer system. Computers had never interested her—it was reality that she cared about, people with flesh and blood, not artificial constructs fabricated of ones and zeroes. Sometimes she thought that men reveled in computers precisely because of their unreality. Unlike women and children, computers could be completely controlled. So she took some secret delight whenever she saw Issya or Nyef frustrated by a stubbornly willful program until they finally found the programming error. She also suspected that whenever one of their children was stubbornly willful, Issya believed in his heart of hearts that the problem was simply a matter of finding the error in the child's programming. Hushidh knew that it was not an error, but a soul inventing itself. When she tried to explain this to Issya, though, his eyes glazed over and he soon fled to the computers again.

Today, though, all was working smoothly enough. Luet and Chveya laid out the noon meal for the men. Hushidh, who had no particular errand, helped them—but then, when Luet started talking about the need to call the others working in the ship to come eat, Hushidh studiously ignored the hints and thus forced Luet and Chveya to go do the summoning.

Issib might be a man and he might prefer computers to children sometimes, but he did notice things. As soon as Luet and Chveya were gone, he asked, "Was it me you wanted to talk with, Shuya, or was it Nyef?"

She kissed her husband's cheek. "Nyef, of course. I already know everything you think."

"Before *I* even know it," said Issib, with mock chagrin. "Well, if you're going to talk privately, *you'll* have to leave. I'm busy, and I'm not leaving the room with the food on any account."

He did not mention that it was more trouble for him to get up and leave. Even though his lifts worked in the environs of the starships, so he wasn't confined to his chair, it still took much effort for Issib to do any major physical movement.

Nyef finished keying in some command or other, then got up from his chair and led Hushidh out into a corridor. "What is it?" he asked.

Hushidh got right to the point. "You know the way I see things," she said.

"You mean relationships among people? Yes, I know."

"I saw something very disturbing today."

He waited for her to go on.

"Luet is . . . well, cut off. Not from you. Not from Chveya. But from everybody else."

"What does that mean?"

"I don't know," said Hushidh. "I can't read minds. But it worries me. *You're* not cut off. You still—heaven knows why—you still are bound by ties of love and loyalty even to your repulsive oldest brothers, even to your sisters and their sad little husbands—"

"I see that you have nothing but respect for them yourself," said Nyef drily.

"I'm just saying that Luet used to have something of that same—whatever it is—sense of obligation to the whole community. She used to connect with everyone. Not like you, but with the women, perhaps even stronger. Definitely stronger. She was the caretaker of the women. Ever since she was found to be the Waterseer back in Basilica, she's had that. But it's gone."

"Is she pregnant again? She's not supposed to be. Nobody's supposed to be pregnant when we launch."

"It's not like that, it's not a withdrawal into self the way pregnant women do." Actually, Hushidh was surprised Nafai had remembered that. Hushidh had only mentioned it once, years ago, that pregnant women's connections with everyone around them weakened, as they focused inward on the child. It was Nafai's way—for days, weeks, months, he would seem to be an overgrown adolescent, gawky, apt to say the wrong thing at the wrong time, giving the impression of never being aware of other people's feelings. And then, suddenly, you'd realize that he was keenly aware all along, that he noticed and remembered practically everything. Which made you wonder if the times he was rude, he actually *meant* to be rude. Hushidh still hadn't decided about that.

"So what is it?"

"I thought you could tell *me,*" said Hushidh. "Has Luet said anything that would make you think she was separating from everybody except for you and your children?"

He shrugged. "Maybe she has and I didn't notice. I don't always notice."

The very fact that he said so made Hushidh doubt it. He *did* notice, and therefore he *had* noticed. He just didn't want to talk to Hushidh about it.

"Whatever it is," said Hushidh, "you and she don't agree about it."

Nafai glared at her. "If you aren't going to believe what I say, why do you bother to ask me?"

"I keep hoping that someday you'll decide that I'm worthy to be trusted with the inner secrets."

"My, but we're feeling out of sorts today, aren't we," said Nafai.

It was when he started acting like a little brother that Hushidh most hated him. "I must mention to Luet sometime that she made a serious mistake when she stopped those women from putting you to death when you violated the sanctity of the lake back in Basilica."

"I'm of the same opinion," said Nafai. "It would have spared me the agony of watching you suffer through the distress of being my sister-in-law."

"I would rather give birth every day, that's how bad it is," said Hushidh.

He grinned at her. "I'll look into it," he said. "I honestly don't know why Luet would be separating herself from everybody else, and I think it's dangerous, and so I'll look into it."

So he was going to take her seriously, even if he wasn't going to tell her what he already thought the problem was. Well, that was about as much as she could hope for. Nafai might be leader of the community right now, but it wasn't because he had any particular skill at it. Elemak, Nafai's oldest brother, was the natural leader. It was only because Nafai had the Oversoul on his side—or, rather, because the Oversoul had

Nafai on *her* side—that he had been given the power to rule. Authority didn't come easily to him and he wasn't always sure what to do with it—and what not to do. He made mistakes. Hushidh just hoped that this wouldn't be one of those times.

Potya would be hungry. She had to get back home. It was because Hushidh was nursing a newborn that she was spared most duties involved with preparing for launch. In fact, the schedule for the launch had been set up to accommodate her pregnancy. She and Rasa had been the last to get pregnant before they found out that no one could be pregnant during the voyage. That was because the chemicals and low temperature that would maintain almost all of them in suspended animation during the voyage could do terrible things to an embryo. Rasa's baby, a little girl she gave the too-cute name of Tsennyi, which meant "precious," had been born a month before Hushidh's third son and sixth child. Shyopot, she had named him. "Whisper." Potya as his dearname, his quickname. Coming at the last moment, like a breath of a word from the Oversoul. The last whisper in her heart before she left this world forever. Issib had thought the name was odd, but it was better than "precious," which they both thought was proof that Rasa had lost all sense of judgment and proportion. Potya was waiting, Potya would be hungry, Hushidh's breasts were telling her so with some urgency.

On the way out of the ship, however, she passed Luet, who greeted her cheerfully, sounding like she always did, as loving and sweet as ever. Hushidh wanted to slap her. Don't lie to me! Don't seem so normal when I know that you have cut yourself off from me in your heart! If you can put on our affectionate closeness like a mask, then I'll never be able to take joy in it again.

"What's wrong?" asked Luet.

"What could be wrong?" asked Hushidh.

"You wear your heart on your face," said Luet, "at least to me. You're angry at me and I don't know why."

"Let's not have this conversation now," said Hushidh.

"When, then? What have I done?"

"That's exactly the question I'd like to know. What have you done? Or what are you planning to do?"

That was it. The slight flaring of Luet's eyelids, her hesitation before showing a reaction, as if she were deciding what reaction she ought to show—Hushidh knew that it was something Luet was planning to do. She was plotting something, and whatever it was, it required her to become emotionally distant from everyone else in the community.

"Nothing," said Luet. "I'm no different from anyone else these days,

Hushidh. I'm raising my children and doing my work to prepare for the voyage."

"Whatever it is you're plotting, Lutya," said Hushidh, "don't do it. It isn't worth it."

"You don't even know what you're talking about."

"True, but *you* know. And I'm telling you, it isn't worth cutting yourself off from the rest of us. It isn't worth cutting yourself off from *me*."

Luet looked stricken, and this, at least, was no sham. Unless everything was a sham and always had been. Hushidh couldn't bear to believe *that.*

"Shuya," said Luet, "have you seen that? Is it true? I didn't know, but maybe it's true, maybe I've already cut myself off from—oh, Shuya." Luet flung her arms around Hushidh.

Reluctantly—but why am I reluctant, she wondered—Hushidh returned the embrace.

"I won't," said Luet. "I won't do *anything* that would cut me off from you. I can't believe that I—can't you do something about it?"

"Do something?" asked Hushidh.

"You know, the way you did to Rashgallivak's men when he came to Aunt Rasa's door that time, meaning to carry her daughters away. You tore his men's loyalty from him and brought him down, just like that. Don't you remember?"

Hushidh remembered, all right. But that had been easy, for she could see that the ties between Rash and his men were very weak, and it took only a few well-placed words and a bit of attitude to fill them with contempt for him and cause them to abandon him on the spot. "It's not the same," said Hushidh. "I can't *make* people do things. I could strip Rash's men of their loyalty because they didn't really want to follow him anyway. I can't rebuild your ties to the rest of us. That's something you have to do yourself."

"But I want to," said Luet.

"What's going on?" asked Hushidh. "Just explain it to me."

"I can't," said Luet.

"Why not?"

"Because nothing *is* going on."

"But something's *going* to go on, is that it?"

"No!" said Luet, and now she sounded angry, adamant. "It will *not* happen. And therefore there's nothing to discuss." With that, Luet fled up the ladderway leading to the center of the ship, where the meal was waiting, where the others were gathering.

It's the Oversoul, Hushidh knew then. The Oversoul has told Luet to do something that she doesn't want to do. And if she does it, it will cut her off from all the rest of us. From everybody except her husband and children. What is it? What is the Oversoul up to?

And whatever it was, why hadn't the Oversoul included Hushidh in it?

For the first time, Hushidh found herself thinking of the Oversoul as an enemy. For the first time, Hushidh discovered that she herself did not have any strong ties of loyalty to the Oversoul. Just like that, mere suspicion had dissolved them. What are you doing to me and my sister, Holy One? Whatever it is, cut it out.

But no answer came to her. Just silence.

The Oversoul has chosen Luet to do something, and she has *not* chosen me. What is it? I have to know. Because if it's something terrible, I'm going to put a stop to it.

Luet did not like the building they lived in these days. Hard surfaces everywhere, smooth and unalive. She missed the wooden house they had lived in for eight years in their little village of Dostatok, before her husband found and opened the ancient starport of Vusadka. And before that, all her memories were of living in Rasa's house in Basilica. City of women, city of grace; she yearned sometimes for the mists of the hidden and holy lake, for the noise of the crowded markets, for the endless rows of buildings elbowing their way out over the street. But this place—had the builders ever thought of it as beautiful? Had they liked to live in such dead places?

Yet it *was* home, all the same, because here was where her children gathered to sleep, to eat; where Nafai finally came home so late at night, to curl up wearily beside her on their bed. And when the time came to enter the starship they had named *Basilica,* she would no doubt miss this place also, the memories of frenzied work and excited children and groundless fears. *If* the fears turned out to be groundless.

Returning to Earth—what did that mean, when no human had been there for millions of years? And those dreams that kept coming into their minds, dreams of giant rats that seemed to be filled with a malevolent intelligence, dreams of batlike creatures who seemed to be allies but were still ugly beyond belief. Even the Oversoul did not know what those dreams meant, or why the Keeper of Earth might have sent them. Still, the overall impression Luet got from everyone's dreams of Earth was that it was not going to be a paradise when they got there.

What really frightened her, though—and, she suspected, frightened everyone else, too—was the voyage itself. A hundred years asleep? And supposedly they would emerge without having aged a day? It seemed like something out of a myth, like the poor girl who pricked her finger on a mouse's tooth and fell asleep, only to find that when she woke up, all the rich and beautiful girls were fat old ladies, while she remained the most youthful and beautiful of all. But still poor. That was an odd ending to that story, Luet always thought, that she was still poor. Surely there ought to be some version of it in which the king chose her because of her beauty instead of marrying the richest woman to get his hands on her estate. But that had nothing to do with what she was worrying about right now. Why had her mind wandered so far afield? Oh, yes. Because she was thinking about the voyage. About lying down on the ship and letting the life support system poke needles into her and freeze her for the voyage. How did they know that they wouldn't simply die?

Well, they could have died a thousand times since things first started falling apart in Basilica. Instead they had lived this long, and the Oversoul had led them to this place, and so far things were working out reasonably well. They had their children. They had prospered. No one had died or even been seriously injured. Ever since Nafai had got the starmaster's cloak from the Oversoul, even Elemak and Mebbekew, his hate-filled older brothers, had been relatively cooperative—and it was well-known that they *hated* the idea of voyaging back to Earth.

So why was the Oversoul so grimly determined to ruin everything?

<I'm grimly determined to save your lives, you and your husband.> Here in this place where the Oversoul actually lived, Luet heard the voice of the Oversoul far more easily than she ever had back in Basilica.

"The starmaster's cloak will protect Nafai," Luet murmured. "And he will protect us."

<And when he's old? When Elemak has taught his sons to hate you and your children? It's elementary mathematics, Luet. When the division of your community comes—and it *will* come—on the one side there will be Elemak and his four sons, Mebbekew and his son, Obring and his two sons, Vas and his son. Four strong adult males, eight boys. And on your side, who? Your husband, of course. But who are his allies? His father, Volemak?>

"Old," murmured Luet.

<Yes, too old. And Issib is a frail cripple from birth. The only other man is Zdorab, and how can you guess where he will stand?>

"Even if he stood with Nafai, he isn't much."

<So you see the problem. Even with your four sons, Issib's three, and Volemak's two, it isn't going to be much of an army. Anyway, Elemak will strike soon, before any of the children are old enough to matter. So it's four strong and brutal men against one man who is *not* strong and *not* brutal.>

"Only if Nafai fails to hold everyone together."

<Elemak is only biding his time. I *know* this. And so you *will* persuade him to do as I have shown you. . . .>

"*You* persuade him."

<He won't listen to me.>

"That's because he knows that your plan would be a disaster. It would cause the very thing that you claim to be trying to prevent."

<Of course there will be some resentment. . . .>

"Resentment! Oh, just a little. We reach Earth and all the adults are wakened from suspended animation, only to discover—oops!—Nafai and Luet somehow neglected to go into suspended animation themselves, and—oops again!—they somehow got a dozen of the older children to stay awake with them for the whole ten years of the voyage! So you see, my dear sister Shuya, when you went to bed your daughter Dza was only eight years old, but now she's eighteen, and married to Padarok, who, by the way, is seventeen now—sorry about that, Shedemei and Zdorab, we knew you wouldn't mind if we raised your only son for you. And while we had these children up, we happened to spend the whole time teaching them, so that now they are experts on everything they'll need to know to build our colony. They're also large and strong enough to do adult work. But—oops again!—none of *your* children, Eiadh and Kokor and Sevet and Dol, none of *yours* has had *any* of this training. *Yours* are still little children who won't be much help at all."

<I see that you have thought through every aspect of the plan. Why can't you see that it is both necessary and flawless?>

"They'll be furious," said Luet. "They'll all hate us—Volemak and Rasa and Issib and Shuya and Shedemei and Zdorab because we stole their oldest children from them, and all the others because we *didn't* give the same advantage to *their* children."

<They will be angry, but those who are my trusted friends will soon come to understand the necessity of having their children be older and stronger. It will change the balance of physical power in the community. It will keep you all alive.>

"They'll always be sure that the only reason the community broke apart was because Nafai and I did such a terrible thing. They'll hate us and blame us and they will certainly never *trust* us again."

<I will tell them that it was my idea.>

"And they'll say that you're just a computer and of course you didn't understand how humans would feel, but *we* understood, and *we* should have refused to do it."

<Perhaps you should. But you won't refuse.>

"I already refused. I refuse again now."

<You refuse with your mouth and with your mind, but Hushidh saw that in your heart, you are already making ready to obey me.>

"No!" cried Luet.

"Mother?" It was Chveya's voice, through the door of Luet's room.

"What is it, Veya?"

"Who are you talking to?"

"Myself, in a dream. All foolishness. Go back to sleep."

"Is Father home yet?"

"Still in the ship with Issib."

"Mother?"

"Go to sleep now, Chveya. I mean it."

She heard the scuffing sound of Chveya's sandals on the floor. What had Chveya heard? How long had she been listening at the door?

<She heard everything.>

Why didn't you warn me?

<Why did you speak out loud? I hear your thoughts.>

Because when I speak out loud my thoughts are clearer, that's why. What's your plan, to get Chveya to carry out your plot?

<Since you won't discuss it with Nafai, I woke Chveya to hear what you were saying. She'll bring it up with him.>

Why couldn't you just talk to him yourself?

<He won't listen to me.>

That's because he's a very wise man. That's why I love him.

<He needs another perspective. You would have been best. Chveya will do.>

You leave my children alone.

<Your children are people in their own right. When you were Chveya's age, you already were known as the Waterseer of Basilica. I didn't notice you complaining that I had such a relationship with you then. And when Chveya first started getting dreams from the Keeper of Earth, I seem to recall that you rejoiced.>

"And to think I once thought of you as . . . as a *god.*"

<And what do you think I am now?>

"If I didn't know you were a computer program, I'd say you were a meddlesome, loathsome old bitch."

<You can be angry at me if you like. It doesn't hurt my feelings. I even understand. But you have to take the long view, Luet. I do.>

"Yes, your view is so long that you hardly notice how you ruin the lives of little mayflies like us."

<Has your life been so terrible up to now?>

"Let's just say that it hasn't gone as expected."

<But has it been so terrible?>

"Shut up and leave me alone."

Luet threw herself back down on the bed and tried to sleep.

But she kept remembering: Hushidh saw that I am no longer connected to the others in the community. That means that somewhere in my heart I already have the unconscious intention of doing what the Oversoul has planned. So I might as well give up and do it consciously.

Do it and then spend the rest of my life knowing that my sister and Aunt Rasa and dear Shedemei all hate me and that I absolutely, completely deserve their hatred.

2

The Face of the Old One

Everyone expected that Kiti's sculpture this year would be a portrait of his otherself, kTi. That was Kiti's intention, too, right up to the moment when he found his clay by the riverbank and set to work, prying and loosening it with his spear. There had been no more beloved young man in the village than kTi, none more hoped-for; there was talk that one of the great ladies would choose him for her husband, an offer of life-marriage, extraordinary for one so young. If that had happened, then Kiti, as kTi's otherself, would have been taken into the marriage as well. After all, since he and kTi were identical, it made no difference which of them might be the sire of a particular child.

But he and kTi were not identical, Kiti knew. Oh, their bodies were the same, as with every other birthpair. Since about a quarter of all birthpairs both lived to maturity, it wasn't all that rare to have two identical young men preparing to offer themselves to the ladies of the village, to be taken or rejected as a pair. So by custom and courtesy, everyone showed Kiti the same respect they showed his otherself. But everyone knew that it was kTi, not Kiti, who had earned their reputation for cleverness and strength.

It wasn't entirely right for kTi to get all the credit for cleverness. Often when the two of them were flying together, watching over one of the village herds or scouting for devils or chasing crows away from the maizefields, it was Kiti who said, One of the goats is bound to try to go that way, or, That tree is one that's likely for the devils to use. And at the beginning of their most famous exploit, it was Kiti who said, Let me pretend to be injured on that branch, while you wait with your spear on that higher perch. But when the story was told, it always seemed to be kTi who thought of everything. Why should people assume otherwise? It was always kTi who acted, it was always kTi whose boldness carried the day, while Kiti followed behind, helping, sometimes saving, but never leading.

Of course he could never explain this to anyone. It would be deeply shameful for one of a birthpair to try to take glory away from his otherself. And besides, as far as Kiti was concerned it was perfectly fair. For no matter how good an idea of Kiti's might have been, it was always kTi's boldness that brought it off.

Why did it turn out that way? Kiti wasn't lacking in courage, was he? Didn't he always fly right with kTi on his most daring adventures? Wasn't it Kiti who had to sit trembling on a branch, pretending to be injured and terrified, as he heard the faint sounds of a devildoor opening in the tree trunk and the tiny noises of the devil's hands and feet inching their way along the branch behind him? Why was it that no one realized that the greatest courage was the courage to sit still, waiting, trusting that kTi would come with his spear in time? No, the story that was told in the village was all about kTi's daring plan, kTi's triumph over the devil.

It was evil of me to be so angry, thought Kiti. That's why my otherself was taken from me. That's why when the storm caught us out in the open, kTi was the one whose feet and fingers Wind pried away from the branch, kTi was who was taken up into heaven to fly with the gods. Kiti was not worthy, and so his grip on the branch held until Wind went away. It was as if Wind were saying to him, You envied your otherself, so I have torn you apart to show you how worthless you are without him.

This was why Kiti meant to sculpt the face of his otherself. And this was why, in the end, he could not. For to sculpt the face of kTi was also to sculpt his own face, and he could not, in his deep unworthiness, bear to do that.

Yet he had to sculpt something. Already the saliva was flowing in his mouth to moisten the clay, to lick it and smooth it, to give a lustrous patina to the finished sculpture. But if he did not sculpt his otherself's face, so soon after kTi's death, it would be scandalous. He would be seen as lacking in natural affection. The ladies would think that he didn't love his brother, and so they wouldn't want his seed in their family. Only some mere woman would offer to him. And he, overwhelmed with clay fever, would accept that offer like any eager boy, and she would bear his children, and he would look at them every year from then on remembering that he was the father of such low children because he could not bring himself to sculpt the face of his beloved kTi.

I did love him, he insisted silently. With all my heart I loved him. Didn't I follow him wherever he decided? Didn't I trust him with my life again and again? Didn't I save him time after time, when his impetuosity brought him into peril? Didn't I even urge him to turn back, a storm was coming, let's find shelter, we have to find shelter, what does it matter if we find the devilpath on this flight or the next, turn back, turn back, and he wouldn't, he ignored me as if I didn't exist, as if I were *nothing,* as if I didn't even get a vote on my own survival, let alone his.

The clay was growing moist, balling up and beginning to flow in his hands, but it was as much tears as saliva that moistened it. O Wind, thou tookest my otherself, and now I cannot find his face in the clay. Give me a shape, O Wind, if I am worthy! O Maize, if I am to bring you daughters to tend your fields, then give my fingers knowledge even if my mind is dull! O Rain, flow with my saliva and my tears and make the clay live under my hands! O Earth, thou deep-burning mother, make my bones wise, for they will someday belong to you again. Let me bring other bones, young bones, child bones out of your clay, O Earth! Let me bring young wings into your hands, O Wind! Let me make new grains of life for thee, O Maize! Let me bring new waterdrinkers, new weepers, new sculptors for thee to taste, O Rain!

Yet despite his pleading, the gods put no shape under his hands.

His tears blinded him. Should he give up? Should he fly up into the sky of the dry season and search for some faraway village that might want a sturdy male and never see Da'aqebla again? Or should his despair go even further? Should he put the clay out of his hands and yet remain there at the riverbank, exposed, for the watching devils to see that he had no sculpture in him? Then they would take him like an infant back to their caves, and devour him alive, so that in his dying moments he would see the devil queen eating his own heart. That was how his end should come. Carried down into hell, because he was not worthy to be taken by Wind up into heaven. kTi would have all the honor then, and not have to share it with his low unworthy otherself.

His fingers worked, though he could not see what they shaped.

And as they worked, he stopped mourning his own failure, for he realized that there *was* a shape now under his hands. It was being given to him, in a way that he had only heard about. As a child, playing at sculpture with the other boys, he had been the cleverest every time, but he had never felt the gods interceding with his hands. What he shaped was always from his own mind and memory.

Now, though, he didn't even know what it was that was growing under his hands, not at first. But soon, no longer grieving, no longer fearful, his vision cleared and he saw. It was a head. A strange head, not of a person or a devil or any creature Kiti had ever seen before. It had a high forehead, and its nose was pointed, hairless, smooth, the nostrils opening downward. Of what use was such a snout as this? The lips were thick and the jaw was incredibly strong, the chin jutting out as if it was competing with the nose to lead this creature forward into the world. The ears were rounded and stuck out from the middle of the sides of the head. What kind of creature is this that I am shaping? Why is something so ugly growing under my hands?

Then, suddenly, the answer came into his mind: This is an Old One.

His wings trembled even as his hands continued, sure and strong, to shape the details of the face. An Old One. How could he know this? No one had ever seen an Old One. Only here and there, in some sheltered cave, was there found some inexplicable relic of their time upon the earth. Da'aqebla had only three such relics, and Da'aqebla was one of the oldest villages. How could he dare to tell the ladies of the village that this grotesque, malformed head that he was shaping was an Old One? They would laugh at him. No, they would be outraged that he would think they were foolish enough to believe such a nonsensical claim. How can we judge your sculpture, if you insist on shaping something that has never been seen by any living soul? You might have done better to leave the clay in a shapeless ball and say that it was a sculpture of a river stone!

Despite his doubts, his hands and fingers moved. He knew, without knowing how he knew, that there must be hair on the bony ridge over the eyes, that the fur of the head must be long, that there must be a depression centered under the nose and leading down to the lip. And when he was through, he did not know how he knew that it was finished. He contemplated what he had made and was appalled by it. It was ugly, strange, and far too large. Yet this was how it had to be.

What have you done to me, O gods?

He still sat, contemplating the head of the Old One, when the ladies came soaring, swooping down to the riverbank. At the fringes were the men whose sculptures had already been seen. Kiti knew them all, of course, and could easily guess at what their work was like. A couple of them were husbands, and because their lady was married to them for life their sculptures were no longer in competition with the others. Some of them were young, like Kiti, offering sculptures for the first time—and from their slightly hangdog expressions, Kiti could tell that they hadn't made the impression that they hoped for. Nevertheless, the clay fever was on all the males, and so they hardly looked at him or his sculpture; their eyes were on the ladies.

The ladies stared in silence at his sculpture. Some of them moved, to study it from another angle. Kiti knew that the workmanship of his sculpture was exceptionally good, and that the sheer size of it was audacious. He felt the clay fever stirring within him, and all the ladies looked beautiful to him. He saw their skeptical expressions with dread—he longed now for them to choose him.

Finally the silence was broken. "What is this supposed to be?" whispered a lady. Kiti looked for the voice. It was Upua, a lady who had never married and who, in some years, had not even mated. It gave her a reputation for being arrogant, the hardest of the ladies to please. Of course she would be the lady who would interrogate him in front of all the others.

"It grew under my hands," he said, not daring to tell them what it really was.

"Everyone thought that you would do honor to your otherself," said another lady, emboldened by Upua's disdainful question.

The hardest question. He dared not dodge it. Did he dare to tell the truth? "I meant to, but it was also my own face, and I wasn't worthy to have my face sculpted in the clay."

There was a murmur at that. Some thought that was a stupid reason; some thought it was deceptive; some gave it thought.

Finally the ladies began deciding. "Not for me." "Ugly." "Very odd." "Interesting." Whatever their comment, they took flight, rising up and circling, drifting toward the branches of the nearest trees. The men, no doubt feeling quite triumphant at the complete rejection of the supposedly talented Kiti, joined them there.

At last only Kiti and Upua remained upon the riverbank.

"I know what this is," said Upua.

Kiti dared not answer.

"This is the head of an Old One," she said.

Her voice carried to the ladies and men in the branches. They heard her, and many gasped or whistled their astonishment.

"Yes, Lady Upua," said Kiti, ashamed at having his arrogance caught out. "But it was given to me under my hands. I never meant to sculpt such a thing."

Upua said nothing for a long time, walking around the sculpture, circling it again and again.

"The day is short!" called one of the leading ladies from her perch in the trees.

Upua looked up at her, startled. "I'm sorry," she said. "I wanted to see this and remember it, because we have been given a great gift by the gods, to see the face of the Old Ones."

There was some laughter at this. Did she really think Kiti could somehow sculpt what no one had ever seen?

She turned to Kiti, who was so filled with clay fever now that he could only barely keep himself from throwing himself at her feet and begging her to let him mate with her.

"Marry me," she said.

Surely he had misunderstood.

"Marry me," she said again. "I want only your children from now on until I die."

"Yes," he said.

No other man had been so honored in a thousand years. On his first sculpting, to be offered marriage, and by a lady of such prestige? Many of the others, ladies and men alike, were outraged. "Nonsense, Lady Upua," said another of the leading ladies. "You cheapen the institution of marriage by offering it to one so young, and for such a ridiculous sculpture."

"He has been given the face of an Old One by the gods. Let all of you come down here and study this sculpture again. We will not leave here for two songs, so that all of us will remember the face of the Old Ones and we can teach our children what we've seen this day."

And because she was the lady who had offered marriage and been accepted on this spot, the others had to do her will for the space of two songs. They studied the head of the Old One, and together Kiti and Upua entered into the legends of the village of Da'aqebla forever. They also entered into marriage, and Kiti, who would have trembled at the thought of being the husband of such a terrifying lady, would soon learn that she was a kind and loving wife, and to be an attentive and protective husband to her would bring him only joy. He would still miss kTi from time to time after that, but never again would he think that Wind had punished him by not catching him up to heaven with kTi.

On this day, however, they did not know what the future would bring. They only knew that Kiti was the boldest sculptor who had ever lived, and because his boldness had won him a lady as his wife, it raised him at once in their estimation. He was truly kTi's otherself, and thought kTi was taken from them, in Kiti his courage and cleverness would live on until, with age, they would become strength and wisdom.

When the two songs had passed, when the flock of ladies and men arose and went on to the next man, dark shapes emerged from the shadows of the trees. They, too, circled the strange sculpture, and then finally picked it up and carried it away, though it was uncommonly large and heavy and they did not understand it.

3

Secrets

It just slipped out. Chveya didn't intend to tell anyone what she had heard outside Mother's door last night. She could keep a secret. Even a devastating secret like the fact that Mother was planning for Dazya to grow up and marry Rokya during the voyage. What did *that* mean, that Chveya was supposed to marry Proya or something? That would be fun, wouldn't it. He should marry Dazya, so the two bossiest children could boss each other to their heart's content. Why did Chveya's own mother want Dazya to get the best boy who wasn't a double first cousin?

Chveya was still brooding about this when Dazya started yelling at her for some stupid thing—leaving a door open that Dazya wanted closed, or closing it when Dazya wanted it open—and Chveya just blurted out, "Oh, shut up, Dazya, you're going to grow up and marry Rokya during the voyage anyway, so you can at least let me decide about doors."

And it wasn't Chveya's fault that Rokya happened to be coming through the door with his father right then, carrying baskets of bread to be frozen for the voyage.

"What are you talking about?" said Rokya. "I wouldn't marry *either* of you."

It wasn't Rokya's reaction that worried Chveya. It was Rokya's father, little Zdorab. "Why are you thinking about who will marry Padarok?" asked Zdorab.

"He's just the only one who's not a cousin or something," said Chveya, blushing.

"Veya always thinks about marriage," said Dazya. Then, helpfully, she added, "She's sick in the head."

"You're only eight years old," said Zdorab, smiling with amusement. "Why would you think marriages would be happening during the voyage?"

Chveya clamped her mouth shut and shrugged. She knew that she shouldn't have repeated anything she heard outside her mother's door. If she said nothing more now, perhaps Zdorab and Rokya and Dazya would forget about it and then Mother would never know that Chveya was a spy and a blabber.

Elemak listened to Zdorab impassively. Mebbekew was not so calm. "I should have known. Planning to steal our children from us!"

"I doubt it," said Elemak.

"You heard him!" cried Mebbekew. "You don't think *Chveya* would invent this scheme of keeping children awake so they'd grow up during the voyage, do you?"

"I mean," said Elemak, "that I doubt Nyef would choose to keep *our* children awake."

"Why not? He could have ten years to poison their minds against us."

"He knows that if he did that to me, I would kill him," said Elemak.

"And he knows that *I* would *not*," said Zdorab. "Imagine—telling his daughter about it, but not even mentioning a hint of it to us."

Elemak thought about that for a moment. Such carelessness wouldn't be unheard of in Nafai, but still he doubted it. "It may not be Nafai's plan, you know. It might be Chveya's mother. Perhaps the Waterseer still misses the influence she had back in Basilica."

"Perhaps she fancies the idea of running a school like her mother did," said Mebbekew.

"But what can we do about it, anyway?" asked Zdorab. "He has the cloak of the starmaster. He has the Index. He controls the ship. No matter what he says, what's to stop him from waking our children during the voyage and doing whatever he wants?"

"The food supply isn't infinite," said Elemak. "He can't wake everybody."

"Think about it, though," said Mebbekew. "What if we wake up and his son Zhatva is a tall seventeen-year-old? Nyef was tall at that age. While our children are still little. And Father's last two boys, Oykib and Yasai. And your Padarok, Zdorab."

Zdorab smiled wanly. "Padarok won't be tall."

"He'll be a man. It's not a stupid plan," said Mebbekew. "He'll have indoctrinated them during the voyage to see things his way."

Elemak nodded. He had already thought of all this. "The question is, what will we do about it?"

"Stay awake ourselves."

Elemak shook his head. "He's already said that the ship won't launch until everyone but him is asleep."

"Then we won't go at all!" said Mebbekew. "Let him take off for Earth and as soon as he's gone, we can take our families back to Basilica."

"Meb," said Elemak, "have you forgotten that we aren't rich anymore? Life in Basilica would be miserable. If they didn't throw us in prison. Or kill us on sight."

"And the journey would be miserable, with little children," added Zdorab. "Not to mention the fact that Shedemei and I don't want to do that."

"So fly with Nafai," said Mebbekew. "I don't care what you do."

Elemak listened to Mebbekew with disgust. What kind of fool *was* he, anyway? Zdorab had brought them the story of what Chveya had said. Zdorab had never been an ally before, but now, his children threatened, they had a good chance to wean him away from Nafai for good. Then Nafai's party would consist only of himself, Father, and Issib—in other words, Nyef, the old man, and the cripple.

"Zdorab," said Elemak, "I take this very seriously. I think that we have no choice but to seem to go along with Nafai's plans. But surely there's some way to get into the ship's computer and set it up to waken us well into the voyage, at a time when Nafai will think he's having everything his own way and so he won't be expecting us. The suspended animation chambers are far from the living quarters of the ship. What do you think?"

"I think that's stupid," said Mebbekew. "Have you forgotten what the ship's computer *is*?"

"Is it?" Elemak asked Zdorab. "Is the ship's computer identical with the so-called Oversoul?"

"Well," said Zdorab, "when you think about it, maybe not. I mean, the Oversoul was set into place *after* the starships first came here. He's loading part of himself into the ship's computers, but he's not as familiar with it as he is with the hardware he's been inhabiting for the past forty million years."

"*He*," muttered Mebbekew scornfully. "*It*, you mean."

Elemak never let his gaze waver from Zdorab's face.

"Um," said Zdorab. "I'm not sure. But I don't think the original voyagers would have . . . I mean, they didn't turn their *own* lives over to the Oversoul. It was the next generation, not themselves. So maybe the ship's computers. . . ."

"And maybe," said Elemak, "if you find some way to be clever about it."

"Misdirection," said Zdorab. "There's a calendar program, for scheduling events during the voyage. Course corrections, and so on. But the Oversoul would be checking that often, I imagine."

"Think about it," said Elemak. "It's really not the sort of thing I do well."

Zdorab preened visibly. Elemak had expected that. Zdorab, like all weak and studious little men, was flattered to have the respect of someone like Elemak, a large, strong man, a leader, charismatic and dangerous. It was easy to win him over. After all these years of seeing Zdorab in Nafai's pocket, it had been astonishingly easy after all. It took patience. Waiting. Burning no bridges.

"I'm counting on you," said Elemak. "But whatever you do, don't talk about it afterward. Not even to me. Who knows what the computer can hear?"

"As in, for instance, it's probably heard everything we said here," said Mebbekew snottily.

"As I say, Zdorab, do your best. It might not be possible. But if you can do *something*, it's more than Meb or I can do."

Zdorab nodded thoughtfully.

He's mine now, thought Elemak. I have him. No matter what happens, Nyef has lost him, and all because he or his wife didn't keep their mouths shut in front of their children. Weak and foolish, that's what Nafai was. Weak, foolish, and unfit to lead.

And if he did anything to harm Elemak's children, then it wouldn't be just Nafai's position of leadership that he'd lose. But then, it was only a matter of time, anyway. Perhaps after Father died, but the day would come when all the insults and humiliations would be redressed. Men of honor do not forgive their lying, cheating, spying, traitorous enemy.

"Let's take a walk," said Nafai to Luet.

She smiled at him. "Aren't we tired enough already?"

"Let's take a walk," he said again.

He led her from the maintenance building where they all lived, out across the hard, flat ground of the landing field. He led her, not toward the starships, but out into the open, until they were far from anyone else.

"Luet," he said.

"Oh," she said. "We're upset about something."

"I don't know about us," he said. "But *I'm* upset."

"What did I do?"

"I don't know if you did anything," he said. "But Zdorab entered a wake-up date into the ship's calendar."

"Why would he do that?"

"He set it for halfway through the voyage. It was to wake up him. And Shedemei. And Elemak."

"Elemak?"

"Why would Zdorab do that?" asked Nafai.

"I have no idea," said Luet.

"Well, can you think about it for a minute? Can you think about something that you might know, that might allow you to figure it out?"

Luet was getting angry now. "What is this, Nafai? If you know something, if you want to accuse me of something, then—"

"But I don't know anything," said Nafai. "The Oversoul told me about finding Zdorab's little wake-up schedule. And then I said, Why? And then he said, Ask Luet."

Luet blushed. Nafai raised an eyebrow. "So," he said. "Now it all comes together?"

"It's the Oversoul that's playing games with us."

"Oh, really?" said Nafai.

"It shouldn't surprise us," said Luet. "That's what she's been doing all along."

"Do you mind letting me know what the game is this time?"

"It has to be related, though I don't see . . . oh, yes I do. Chveya heard me."

Nafai put his fingers to his forehead. "Oh, now it's all clear. Chveya heard you *what?*"

"Talking to the Oversoul. Last night. About—you know."

"No, I don't know."

"You can't be serious," she said.

"More serious by the minute."

"You mean the Oversoul hasn't even brought it up with you? About keeping the children awake on the voyage?"

"Don't be absurd. We don't have enough supplies to keep everybody awake. It's ten years!"

"I don't know," said Luet. "The Oversoul said that we had enough supplies to keep you and me and twelve of the children awake through most of the voyage."

"And why would we do that?" asked Nafai. "The whole point of the suspended animation is that ten years in a starship will be incredibly boring. *I'm* not even planning to be awake the whole time. Should our children spend ten years of their lives—more than half!—sitting around inside that metal pot?"

"The Oversoul never talked to you about it," she said. "That makes me so angry."

Nafai looked at her, waiting for an explanation.

"It would be our older children, all but the twins, and Shuya's down to Netsya, and Shedemei's boy and girl, and your brothers Oykib and Yasai."

"Why not the little ones?"

"You can't spend your first two years of life in low gravity."

"It can't work," said Nafai. "Even if the others would stand for it, the children would have no one their own age to marry except Shedya's two. The rest would be siblings or double first cousins or, at the best, Oykib and Yasai, and they're single first cousins."

"Nyef, I've said this to her over and over. Do you think I don't know what a stupid idea it is? That's what Chveya must have heard last night. I was arguing with the Oversoul."

"You don't have to talk out loud to the Oversoul, Luet," he said.

"*I* do," she said.

"Well, whatever happened, Zdorab apparently thinks he has to wake up in the middle of the voyage to check up on me."

"I imagine he's angry," said Luet.

"Well, there's only one thing we can do." Nafai took her by the hand. They headed back to the maintenance building.

It took only a few minutes to gather all the adults into the kitchen, surrounding the large table where they ate their meals in shifts. As usual, Elemak looked quietly annoyed, while Mebbekew was openly hostile. "What's all this?" he demanded. "Can't we even go to sleep at a normal hour anymore?"

"There's something that needs straightening out right now," said Nafai.

"Oh, did one of us do something bad?" asked Meb, tauntingly.

"No," said Nafai. "But some of you think that Luet is planning something—no, come to think of it, you probably think that *I'm* planning it—and I want to get it out in the open right now."

"Openness," said Hushidh. "What a novel idea."

Nafai ignored her. "Apparently the Oversoul has been trying to persuade Luet that we should do something foolish with some of the children on the voyage."

"Foolish?" Volemak, Nafai's father, looked puzzled.

"Foolish," said Nafai. "Like keeping some of them awake during the voyage."

"But that would be so boring for them," said Nafai's older sister, Kokor.

Nafai did not answer her, just looked around from face to face. It was gratifying to see that even Elemak, who surely knew about the idea of keeping children awake and understood all the implications, was now looking a bit surprised by what Nafai was doing. "I know that some of you were aware of this even before I was. The only reason I found out about it at all was because the Oversoul found the wake-up signal you put into the ship's calendar, Zdorab."

Mebbekew's quick glance at Zdorab, and his equally quick glance away, confirmed that he, too, had known about the wake-up signal. He probably even thought Zdorab's little alarm clock would wake him up along with the others. But of course Zdorab knew that waking Mebbekew would be useless. If only Meb understood the contempt that everyone held him in. But then, he probably did, which was why he was so relentlessly belligerent.

"I think, Zdorab, that it's a good idea," said Nafai. "Of course the Oversoul removed your wake-up signal, but I will put a new one in. At midpoint of the voyage, all the adults will be wakened. Just for a day, so you can inspect all your sleeping children and make sure that they're the age they were when you left them. I can't think of any better way for you to make sure that the Oversoul did not get his way in this."

Volemak chuckled. "Do you really think you can fool the Oversoul?"

Luet spoke up. "The Oversoul understands many things, but she is not a human being. She doesn't understand what it would cost us, if our children's childhood was taken away from us. How would you feel, Aunt Rasa, if you woke up and found that Okya and Yaya were eighteen- and seventeen-year-old men? That you had missed all the years in between?"

Rasa smiled thinly. "I would never forgive anyone who did that to me. Even the Oversoul."

"I was trying to explain that to the Oversoul. She doesn't understand human feelings sometimes."

"Sometimes?" murmured Elemak.

"I . . . I spoke out loud. In the privacy of my room. Nafai was working late. But Chveya got up and she must have listened for a rather long time before she knocked."

"Are you saying that *your* daughter is a *sneak?*" said Mebbekew, pretending to be shocked.

Luet didn't look at him. "Chveya didn't understand what she was hearing. I'm sorry that it caused everyone to be disturbed. I know some of you knew about it, and some of you did not, but when Nafai learned about it a few minutes ago he and I rushed back here and . . . here we are."

"Tomorrow, Zdorab can verify that the wake-up signal is set for midvoyage. The only way that it won't wake us up is if the Oversoul cancels it during one of the many times that I'll be asleep myself. But I don't think that's likely, because as soon as I woke up again, I'd waken you all myself manually. I'm telling you now, once and for all, that there will be no games played with the passage of time. Our children will be, when we arrive, the same ages they were when they left. The only person who will have aged during the voyage is me, and believe me, I have no interest in aging any more than the minimum necessary to operate the ship safely."

"Why are you needed awake at all?" asked Obring, Kokor's husband, a little snake of a man, in Nafai's considered opinion.

"The ships weren't designed to be run by the Oversoul," said Nafai. "In fact, the Oversoul's program wasn't fully written until after the original fleet arrived on Harmony. The computers here can hold the Oversoul's program, but no single program is able to control all the computers on the ship at once. It's for safety. Redundancy. The systems can't all fail at once. Anyway, there are things that I have to do from time to time."

"That *someone* has to do," murmured Elemak.

"I have the cloak," said Nafai. "And that point was settled a while ago, I think. Do you really want to dredge up old arguments?"

Nobody wanted to, apparently.

"Son," said Volemak, "you won't be able to stop the Oversoul from doing what it knows is right."

"The Oversoul is wrong," said Nafai. "It's that simple. None of you would ever forgive me if I obeyed the Oversoul in this."

"That's right," said Mebbekew.

"And I would never forgive myself," said Nafai. "So the issue is closed. Zdorab will see the calendar tomorrow, and he and anybody else who cares can look at it again just before we launch."

"That's very kind of you," said Elemak. "I think we can all sleep more easily tonight knowing that nothing is being planned behind our backs. Thank you for being so honest and open with us." He arose from the table.

"No," said Volemak. "You can't get away with rebellion against the Oversoul. No one can! Not even you, Nafai."

"You and Nafai can discuss this all you want, Father," said Elemak. "But Edhya and I are going to bed." He got up from the table and, putting his arm around his wife, led her out of the room. Most of the others followed—Kokor and her husband Obring, Sevet and her husband Vas, Meb and his wife Dolya. On their way out, Hushidh and Issib stopped for a few words with Nafai and Luet. "Very good idea," Hushidh said, "calling everybody together like this. It was very persuasive. Except that Elemak won't believe anything you do. So it just convinced him you were being devious."

"Thanks for the instant analysis," Luet said nastily.

"I appreciate it," Nafai said quickly. "I don't expect Elemak to take anything I do at face value."

"I just wanted you to know," said Hushidh, "that the barrier between you and Elemak is stronger and deeper than any bond between any two people here. In a way, that's a kind of bond, too. But if you thought that this little scene today was going to win him over, you failed."

"And what about you?" said Luet. "Did it win you over?"

Hushidh smiled wanly. "I still see you separated from everyone else except your husband and children, Luet. When *that* changes, I'll start believing your husband's promises." Then she turned and left. Issib smiled and shrugged helplessly and drifted out after her.

Zdorab and Shedemei lingered. "Nafai," said Zdorab, "I want to apologize. I should have known that you wouldn't—"

"I understand perfectly," said Nafai. "It looked to you as if we were planning something behind your back. I would have done the same, if I'd thought of it."

"No," said Zdorab. "I should have spoken to you privately. I should have found out what was happening."

"Zdorab, I would never do anything to your children without your consent."

"And I would never give it," he said. "We have fewer children than anyone. To think of the two of them—having their childhood taken away from us—"

"It won't happen," said Nafai. "I don't want your children. I want the voyage to pass quickly and uneventfully and for us to establish our new colony on Earth. Nothing else. I'm sorry you had to even worry about it."

Zdorab smiled then. Shedemei didn't. She glared at Nafai and then at Luet. "I didn't ask to come on this journey, you know."

"It would be impossible for us to succeed without you," said Nafai.

"But there is one question," said Luet.

"No, Lutya," said Nafai. "Haven't we already—"

"It's something we have to know!" said Luet. "No matter what. I mean it has to be obvious to you, Shedya, that your two children are the only ones who won't face a consanguinity problem."

"Obviously," said Shedemei.

"But what about the others? I mean, isn't it dangerous for all of us?"

"I don't think it will be a problem," said Shedemei.

"Why not?" asked Luet.

"The only time it's bad for cousins to marry is when there's a recessive gene that leads to problems. When cousins marry, their children can get the recessive gene from both sides, and therefore it expresses itself. Mental retardation. Physical deformity. Debilitating disease. That sort of thing."

"And that's not a problem?"

"Haven't you been paying attention?" asked Shedemei. "Didn't you learn anything back in Basilica? The Oversoul has been breeding you all for years. Bringing your father and mother together, for instance, Luet, all the way from opposite sides of the sea. The Oversoul has already made sure your genetic molecules are clean. You don't *have* any recessive traits that will cause harm."

"How do you know that?"

"Because if you did, they would already have expressed themselves. Don't you get it? The Oversoul has been marrying cousins together for years to get you people who are so receptive to her influence. Any idiots or cripples have already shown up and been bred out."

"Not all," said Rasa. Everyone knew at once that she was thinking of Issib, Nafai's older full brother. His large muscles hopelessly uncontrollable from birth, he had never been able to walk or move without the help of magnetic floats or a flying chair.

"No," said Shedemei. "Of course not all."

"So if my children, for instance, married Hushidh's children. . . ." Luet didn't finish the sentence.

"Hushidh already asked me this years ago," said Shedemei. "I thought she would have told you."

"She didn't," said Luet.

"Issib's problem is not genetic. It was prenatal trauma." Shedemei looked at Rasa. "I imagine Aunt Rasa didn't know she was pregnant when it happened."

Rasa shook her head. No one asked her what it was that she had, in all innocence, done to Issib in the womb.

"It won't be passed on in your children's genes," said Shedemei. "You can marry your children off to your heart's content. If that means you'll be leaving my children alone now, I'll be very thankful."

"We weren't planning anything!" cried Luet, outraged.

"I believe that Nafai wasn't," said Shedemei, "because he discussed it with us all at once."

"I wasn't going to do it either!" insisted Luet.

"I think you were," said Shedemei. "I think you still intend to." She turned and left the room, Zdorab following nervously behind her.

In the corridor outside, Zdorab found Elemak waiting. Letting Shedemei stalk on ahead, Zdorab and Elemak fell in beside each other. "So you were very subtle about it, I see," said Elemak.

Zdorab looked up at him and smiled. "I was certainly clumsy, wasn't I? The Oversoul found my wake-up signal right away." Then he winked and walked faster, leaving Elemak behind. Elemak walked slowly, thinking. Then he smiled slightly and turned down the corridor leading to his family's rooms.

Back in the kitchen, only Volemak and Rasa remained with Nafai and Luet. "You're being foolish," said Volemak. "You must do what the Oversoul commands."

"What the Oversoul commands," said Luet, "is for us to concede that our colony will be permanently split into two irreconcilable factions, and to act in such a way as to make the rift so deep it will last for generations."

"Then do it," said Volemak.

"This discussion is pointless," said Nafai. "Isn't it, Mother?"

Rasa sighed. "There are things that no decent person will do," she said. "Even for the Oversoul."

"There are larger issues," said Volemak.

"I have these three last children," said Rasa. "Oykib, Yasai, and my little precious daughter. I would hate forever anyone who took them away from me. Even you." She looked from Nafai to Luet. "Or you." And then she looked at her husband. "Or you." She stood up and left the room.

Volemak sighed and rose to his feet. "You'll see," he said. "The Oversoul isn't to be flouted."

"Somewhere along in here," said Nafai, "the Oversoul has to take into account *our* feelings."

But Volemak didn't stay to hear him finish his sentence.

Luet put her arms around Nafai and held him. "I should have told you before," she said. "But I was afraid you'd just do whatever the Oversoul told you."

"The Oversoul knows me better than you do, apparently," said Nafai. "That's why he didn't tell me at all."

"Come to bed, husband," said Luet.

"I have some work to do," he said.

"So we leave a day later," she said.

"I have some work to do."

She sighed, kissed him, and left.

Nafai cut himself a slice of bread, wrapped it around a slightly overripe podoroshny, and bit off chunks of it as he left the maintenance building and walked back to the starship.

<Aren't you the clever one.>

I think so, answered Nafai silently.

<Everyone thinks I never even discussed this with you.>

You never did.

<Ignoring me is not the same thing as never having heard me.>

It was never a discussion. It won't happen.

<It will because it must. You'll be killed and so will Luet if you don't.>

You can't see the future.

<Elemak will take your children and make slaves of them.>

He won't punish children for what their parents do.

<He'll call it adopting them. Eiadh is the one who'll turn it into slavery.>

It won't happen.

<It will happen if you don't surround yourself with six more young men whose loyalty to you is complete.>

And I'm telling you again, for the thousandth time, that I will not even consider it without their parents' consent. And I will not lift a finger to persuade them. In fact, I'll argue against it.

<That's a very wise strategy, Nafai. Then they won't be able to blame you when they regret giving their consent.>

Nafai shook his head. They'll never agree to it, he said silently.

<You underestimate my influence.>

4

Persuasion

Shedemei checked the children again. The third time that night. When she came back to bed, Zdorab was awake.

"I'm sorry," she said. "I had a dream."

"A nightmare, you mean," he said.

For a moment she misunderstood. "Did you have it too?"

"No," he answered, faintly disgusted. "Was it one of those?"

"No, no," she said. "Not from the Keeper of Earth, if that's what you're asking."

"Bats and weasels."

"Giant rats. I don't really have those. I dream of gardens when it's that kind of dream."

"But that's not what you dreamed tonight."

She shook her head.

"And you're not going to tell me."

"If you want, I will."

He waited.

"Zdorab, I kept seeing . . . us, arriving on Earth. All of us coming out of the ship. You and me, unchanged, just as we are now. But then I saw this fine young man and young woman that I had never known before. He was handsome and bright-faced, cheerful and strong. She was dark but her smile was dazzling, and she laughed and there was such intelligence in her eyes."

"And he was eighteen and she was sixteen." His voice sounded sour.

"Rokya and Dabya are the only children I'm ever going to have," she said.

"Are you going to accuse me because of that? After all these years?"

"I'm not accusing anyone. I'm just . . . I went to look at them. To make sure they were all right. To make sure they weren't . . . having the same dream."

"And how did you know they weren't? Did you waken them and ask?"

"I don't know what they're dreaming. I only know that they're so young. And I'm looking forward so much to what they'll be. To next week and next month and next year and . . . but then I also saw that. . . ."

"What?" asked Zdorab.

"I remembered how they were. The little babies they were. When they suckled. When they first walked. When they first spoke, when they first played, when they first learned to read and write, I remember everything, and those children are gone."

"Not gone, just grown."

"Grown, I know, but each age of them, *that* goes. You lose those years no matter what you do. They grow past them, they push their own childhood out of the way, they don't thank you for remembering it."

Zdorab shook his head. "I've seen how this overgrown computer works on people, Shedemei. You know you don't want to give your children to Nafai and Luet to raise. They're children themselves."

"I know I don't want to. But what's best for them? What's best for all of them? People have given their children to war. They've given their children to great acts of heroism."

"And when they've lost them, they've grieved and never stopped grieving."

"But don't you see? We won't lose them. It will be as if . . . as if we sent them away to school. People did it all the time in Basilica. Sent their children to someone else's house to be raised. If we'd stayed there, I would have done it too. They would already be gone, both of them. All we'd really be missing is the holidays."

Zdorab raised himself on his elbow. "As you say, Shedemei, these are our only two children. I never thought I'd have any. I did it only as a favor to you, because you're my . . . friend. And you wanted them so much. And if you had asked me back then, when they were conceived, whether you could give them up, I would have said, Fine, whatever you want, they're yours. But they're not just yours now. I fathered them, incredible as that is to me, and I have taught them and cared for them and loved them and I'll tell you something. I don't want to lose a day with them."

She shook her head. "Neither do I."

"So forget these dreams, Shedya. Let the big computer in the sky plan what it wants to plan. We aren't part of it."

She lay back down in the bed beside him. "Oh, I'm part of it, all right."

"And how is that?" he asked.

She took his hand and held it. "That nonsense I said. About genes. Recessive ones expressing themselves, all that."

The bed shook. Zdorab was laughing.

"It's not funny."

"None of it was true?"

"I have no idea if it's true or not. They know I'm an expert in genetics, they think I know what I'm talking about. But I don't. Nobody does. I mean, we can catalogue the genomes, but most of each genetic molecule is still undeciphered. They used to believe that it was junk, meaningless. But it isn't. That much I've learned from working with plants. It's all just . . . quiet. Waiting. Who knows what will show up if they let those cousins marry each other?"

Zdorab laughed some more.

"It isn't funny," said Shedemei. "I really should tell them the truth."

"No," said Zdorab. "What you told them made it so they won't feel any need to include our children with theirs in any experiment they decide to perform. Fine. That's how it should be."

"But look at Issib."

"What, was his condition genetic after all?"

"No, that part was true enough. But how he's suffered, Zodya. It's not right to let other children go through that, other parents, I can't. . . ."

Zdorab sighed. "You pretend to be hard-nosed, Shedya, but you're soft as cheese on a summer day."

"Thanks for choosing such a foul-smelling analogy."

"Shedya, if what you said wasn't true, how did you think of it?"

"I don't know. The words just came to my mouth. Because I needed *something* to say to turn them away from our children."

"That's right. Now, the Oversoul is perfectly capable of telling them things, right?"

"Constantly."

"So let the Oversoul tell them not to let their children intermarry."

Shedemei thought about that for a moment. "I never thought of that," she said. "I'm not one of those people who 'leaves things up to the Oversoul.' "

"And besides," said Zdorab. "How do you know the Oversoul didn't put the words into your mouth?"

"Oh, don't be so—"

"I'm quite serious. You said the words just came to you. How do you know it wasn't from the Oversoul? How do you know that it wasn't *true*?"

"Well, I don't *know*."

"There you are. You don't need to say anything to them about anything."

She had no answer to that. He was right.

They lay there in silence for a long time. She thought he was asleep. Then he spoke, a whisper just on the edge of voice. "We aren't just a man with children and a woman with children, sharing the same house, sharing the same children. Are we?"

"No, not just that," said Shedemei.

"I mean, how much does a husband have to desire his wife, sexually, for his feelings toward her to be love?"

She felt her way carefully toward an answer. "I don't know if the feelings have to be sexual at all," she said.

"Because I admire you so much. And the way you are with Rokya and Dabya, I . . . delight in that. And the way you teach them, all the children. And the way you are with . . . with me. The way you're so kind to me."

"And what else would I do? Beat you? Scream at you? You're the most aggravatingly unannoying man I've ever known. You don't do anything wrong."

"Except that I don't satisfy you."

She shrugged. "I don't complain."

"But I do love you. Like a sister. A friend. More than either of those, like a. . . ."

"Like a wife," said Shedemei.

"Yes," said Zdorab. "Like that."

"And I love you as my husband, Zdorab. As you are. Like that." She rolled over, reached for him, kissed his cheek. "Like that," she said again. Then she rolled back onto her other side, her back to him, and soon enough she was asleep.

The dreams came, night after night, those last weeks before the starship *Basilica* was launched. And toward the end, one by one, the dreamers came to him.

Hushidh was first, telling him that the Oversoul was right, that the breach between him and Elemak would never be healed, so he had to be ready. "Don't keep your promise, either," she said. "Don't wake anybody up in midvoyage. It would be a disaster, when we're all confined in that tiny space together."

"Thanks for the suggestion," Nafai said.

"Ignore me if you want," said Hushidh. "You're the one with the cloak, after all."

"Don't snipe at me," said Nafai. "You're Luet's older sister, not mine."

"And we all know what fine specimens *your* older sisters are."

They both burst out laughing.

"Tell Luet for me," said Hushidh, "that once I made up my mind to obey the Oversoul and give my four oldest to you to raise during the voyage, I found that the bonds between Luet and me returned, as strong as ever. The barrier might have been her fault when it began. But it was my fault it wasn't healed till now."

"I'll tell her that," said Nafai. "But better if you tell her yourself."

"I knew you'd say that," said Hushidh. "That's why I hate you." She kissed his cheek and left.

Then Rasa and Volemak came to him together. "It was selfish of us to want to withhold our sons from you. They were born late," said Rasa. "This will be a way for them to catch up with their older brothers."

Volemak smiled thinly. "I'm not so interested in that as Rasa is. As usual, she thinks of people's feelings more than I do. I just remember all that we've given up to get this far, and how stupid it would be for us to repudiate the Oversoul now. There's such a thing as trust, Nafai. Don't risk the survival of the whole colony, particularly of your own family, solely in order to protect your own image of yourself as a man who always does the 'right' thing."

Nafai listened to his father but found no comfort in his words. "I lost that image of myself when I cut Gaballufix's head from his shoulders, Father. I've regretted that every day of my life since then. Foolish of me, wasn't it, to want to spare myself another source of guilt."

Volemak fell silent then, but Rasa did not. "Wallowing a bit, are we?" she said. "Well, Nafai, you're still young, so you still think the whole universe revolves around you. But the fact is it doesn't. The Oversoul has persuaded us that it's best if our youngest sons are kept awake for the voyage. Now it's up to you to decide if you have the courage to face down Elemak's anger when it's all done."

"And it doesn't matter to you that I gave him—that I gave *everyone*—my word that I wouldn't do this?"

"I am your father," said Volemak, "and Rasa is your mother. We release you from your oath."

"I'm sure Elemak will calm right down when he hears that."

Rasa laughed lightly. "Come now, Nafai. Elemak is the one person out of this whole community who has never believed for a moment that you would keep your word. And do you know why he doesn't believe it? Because he knows that if the situation were reversed, *he* would break that promise in an instant."

"But I'm not Elemak."

"Yes you are," said Volemak. "You are exactly what Elemak would have been, except he never had the goodness of heart."

Nafai wasn't sure if he had been praised or slapped.

After Hushidh, after Father and Mother, Issib came, bringing with him, as usual, not just the dreams the Oversoul had given him, but also ideas to make things work better.

"We need to talk," Issib said.

Nafai nodded.

"I keep having these dreams."

"The Oversoul," said Nafai. "I know, I have them too."

"Not the same ones, Nyef," said Issib. "I see my oldest boy, Xodhya, as he comes out of the starship—"

"As I see Zhyat—"

"And he looks just like *me.* Which is silly, because there's so much of his mother's face in his, but in my dream, he's me. Except he's tall and strong, his arms, his chest—like a god. Like one of those statues around the old orchestra."

"Of course. The Oversoul is just manipulating you, Issib."

"Yes, I know that," said Issib. "I was with you when we first withstood him, don't you remember? We did it together."

"I haven't forgotten."

"We proved that we didn't *have* to do what the Oversoul wanted, didn't we, Nafai? But then we decided to help the Oversoul because we wanted to. Because we agreed with what he was trying to accomplish."

"And as long as I agreed, I've cooperated. At great cost, too, I might add."

"Cost? You? With the cloak of the starmaster?"

"I'd trade the cloak in a minute to know that my brothers loved me."

"*I* love you, Nyef. Have you ever doubted that?"

"No, I didn't mean—"

"And Okya and Yaya love you. Are they not your brothers? Am I not your brother?"

"All of you are."

"And I don't really think you give a rat's ass whether Meb likes you or not."

"All right, Elemak. I'd trade the starmaster's cloak for Elemak's respect if I thought I could ever have it."

"Don't you see, Nyef? You can never have his respect."

"Because I'll never be worthy of it."

"Stupid." Issib laughed at him. "You are dense, Nafai. You can't have his respect precisely because you *are* worthy of it."

"I always hated paradoxes in school. I think they're the conclusion that philosophers reach when—"

"When they've given up on thinking, I know, it's not the first time you've said it. But this isn't a paradox. Elemak hates you because you're his younger brother and he knows, he *knows*, that you have more of father's respect and love than he has. That's why he hates you, because he knows that in Father's eyes, you're a better man than he is."

"I wish."

"You know it's true. But if you gave it all up, if you surrendered everything to Elemak, if you gave up the cloak, if you repudiated the Oversoul, do you think he'd respect you then? Of course not, because then you really *would* be contemptible. Weak. A nothing."

"You've persuaded me. I'll keep the cloak."

"The cloak is nothing. You're already doing something far worse."

Nafai regarded him steadily. "Am I to understand that you're really here trying to persuade me to keep your four oldest children awake during the voyage, teaching them, raising them for you, so that when you awake you'll find them already grown?"

"Not at all," said Issib. "I'd hate that."

"Well, then, what is all this about?"

"Keep them awake, but bring me awake too, sometimes. Once a year for a few weeks. Let me teach all the children computers, for instance. Nobody's better at that than me."

"They won't need computers in the new colony."

"Mathematics then. Surveying. Triangulation. I can read the same books as you and teach them just like you. Or were you planning on having an agricultural laboratory here? Forestry, perhaps? When were we going to bring the trees aboard?"

"I never thought of that."

"You mean the Oversoul never thought of that."

"Whatever."

"Do it in shifts. Wake Luet up for a while, but then let her sleep again. Wake me, wake Hushidh. Wake Mother and Father. A few weeks at a time. We'll see the children grow, then. We won't miss it all. And when we reach Earth, they'll be men and women. Ready to stand beside you against the others."

Nafai didn't answer right away. "That's not the way the Oversoul explained it to Luet."

"So, where is it engraved on stone that you have to do everything the Oversoul's way? As long as you do what he wants, the methodology hardly matters, does it?"

"Does Hushidh feel the same way?"

"She might. In a while."

"I won't take anyone's child without their agreement."

"Really? And what about the children themselves? Going to ask *them?*"

"I really ought to," said Nafai. "I'll think about this, Issib. Maybe this compromise will work."

"Good," said Issib. "Because I think the Oversoul's right. If we don't do this, if we don't give you strong young men and women to back you up, then when we get away from the starship, when the Oversoul's influence weakens, you'll be a dead man, and so will I."

"I'll think about it," said Nafai.

Issib rose up from the chair and leaned toward the door, then stepped lightly toward it, the floats bearing almost all of his weight. At the door he turned.

"And something else," said Issib.

"What?" asked Nafai.

"I know you better than you think."

"Do you?"

"For instance, I know that the Oversoul talked to you about this whole thing long before Luet ever let anything slip."

"Really?"

"And I know that you wanted it to happen all along. You just didn't want it to be your idea. You wanted it to be us persuading *you.* That way we can never blame you later. Because you tried to talk us out of it."

"Am I really that clever?" asked Nafai.

"Yes," said Issib. "And I'm really clever enough to figure it all out."

"Well, then, I'm not so clever after all."

"Yes you are," said Issib. "Because I really *do* want you to do it. And I never *will* be able to blame you if I don't like the results. So it worked."

Nafai smiled wanly. "I wish you were completely right," said Nafai.

"Oh? And how am I wrong?"

"I would rather, with all my heart, let all our children sleep through the voyage. Because I would rather have there be no division between us all in the new colony. Because I would rather make my brother Elemak the king of us all and let him rule over us, than to have him as my enemy."

"So why don't you?"

"Because he hates the Oversoul. And when we get to Earth, he'll resist just as much whatever it is the Keeper of Earth wants us to do. He'll end up destroying us all because of his stubbornness. He can't be the ruler over us."

"I'm glad you understand that," said Issib. "Because if you ever start to think that he ought to rule, that's when he'll destroy you."

Volemak, Rasa, Hushidh, Issib; and then at last Shedemei and Zdorab came to him, only an hour before they were all supposed to go to sleep for the voyage. "I don't want to do it," said Zdorab.

"Then I won't waken your children," said Nafai. "I'm not sure yet that I'm going to waken anyone's children."

"Oh, you are," said Shedemei. "And you're going to waken us, too, from time to time, to help teach them. That's the deal."

"And when we get to Earth, and our children are all ten years older than Elya's and Meb's and Vasya's and Briya's, you'll stand up to them with me? You'll say, We thought it was a good idea? We asked him to do it?"

"I'll never say I thought it was a good idea," said Zdorab. "But I'll admit that I asked you to do it."

"Not good enough," said Nafai. "If you don't think it's a good idea, why are you asking me to let your only two children take part in it?"

"Because," said Zdorab, "my son would never forgive me if he knew that he had a chance to reach Earth as a man, and I made him arrive there as a boy."

Nafai nodded. "That's a good reason."

"But remember, Nafai," said Zdorab. "The same thing goes for the other children. Do you think that when Elya's boy Protchnu wakes up and finds that your *younger* son, Motya, is eight years older than him instead of two years younger, do you think that Protchnu will ever forgive you, or Motya either? This will cause hatred that will never be healed, generation after generation. They will always believe that something was stolen from them."

"And they'll be right," said Nafai. "But the thing that was stolen, it wasn't taken away until they had already rejected it."

"They'll never remember that."

"But will you?"

Zdorab thought about it for a moment.

"If he doesn't," said Shedemei, "I'll remind him."

Zdorab smiled grimly at her. "Let's go to bed," he said.

No matter who would be wakened later, all would be asleep for the launch itself. There was too much stress, too much pain to pass through it consciously. Instead they would be encased in foam inside their sleep chambers.

Each couple put their own young children to bed, laying them into their suspended animation chambers, kissing them, then closing the lid and watching through the window until they drifted into the drugged sleep that began the process. There was some fear in the children, especially the older ones who understood something of what was going on, but there was also excitement, anticipation. "And when we wake up, we'll be on Earth?" they asked, over and over. "Yes," their parents said.

Then Nafai took the parents to the control room and showed them the calendar with the midvoyage waking scheduled. "You'll be able to check all your children and make sure that they're sleeping safely," Nafai assured them.

"Now I can sleep peacefully indeed," Elemak answered with dry irony.

Nafai watched them all go to sleep, one by one, and one by one he authorized the life support computers to drug them, surround them with foam, chill them until their bodies were barely alive at all. Then he, too, climbed into his chamber and drew the lid closed after him.

No human being saw the ship rise silently into the air, a hundred meters, a thousand, until it was as high as the magnetics of the landing field could raise it. Then the launching rockets fired, blasting downward as the starship rose up into the night sky.

Far away, on the other side of the narrow sea, travelers on the caravan road looked up and saw the shooting star. "But it's rising," said one of them. "No," said another. "That's just an illusion, because it's coming toward us."

"No," said the first again. "It's rising into the sky. And it's much too slow to be a shooting star."

"Really?" scoffed the other. "Then what is it?"

"I don't know," said the first. "But I thank the Oversoul that we could see it."

"And why is that?"

"Because after millions of years, fool, there's not a thing that any man can see that hasn't been seen a hundred or a thousand or a million times before. But *we've* seen something that no one else has ever seen."

"You think."

"Yes, I think."

"And what good is it? To see something wondrous, and have no idea what it is you saw?"

The starship *Basilica* rose higher, out of the gravity well of the planet Harmony. When it was far enough away, the rockets stopped. They would not be used again until it was time for the ship to land on another world. Instead, a web unfolded itself from the sides of the ship, made of strands so fine that they could not be seen were it not for the dazzle of light upon the wires when a molecule of hydrogen or some particle even smaller fell into the energy field the web generated. Then the shape of it could be seen, like a vast spiderweb, gathering the dust of space to fuel the onward progress of the starship. The *Basilica* began to accelerate, faster and faster, until Harmony was left behind, just another dot of light indistinguishable by the naked eye from any other. After forty million years, human beings had left the surface of this world, and, against all expectations, they were going home.

5
The Eavesdropper

The other children all supposed, upon waking, that they must have arrived at Earth. That's what they had been told upon going to sleep in the suspended-animation chambers—when you wake up, it will be Earth.

Oykib, however, already knew that he would be waking long before then. He was not surprised that instead of normal gravity, he seemed unbelievably light and strong, each step sending him bounding up to touch the ceiling. That's the way it was in space, when instead of a planet to hold you down, you had only the acceleration of the ship. And if he had any doubts, they were dispelled by the fact that as Nafai and Luet gathered the children into the ship's library—the largest open space in the starship, except for the centrifuge—Oykib could hear the faint murmurings of the Oversoul to Nafai and Luet: This is a bad idea. Don't give them a choice. Children that age are too young to decide something this important. Their parents have already agreed. If you tell them they have a choice when they really don't, they'll only hate you for it. And so on, and so on.

Oykib had been hearing scraps of conversation like this since earliest childhood. He couldn't remember a time without it. At first, though, it was like music, like wind, like the sound of waves for a child who grows up by the sea. He thought nothing of it, did not search for meaning in it.

But gradually, by the time he was four or five, he began to realize that this background noise contained names; that there were ideas in it, ideas that later showed up in discussions among the adults.

Though the voices were all in his mind, and therefore soundless, he began to associate certain ways of thinking with certain people. He began to notice that sometimes, when he was with Mother or Father, Nafai or Issib, Luet or Hushidh, the conversation that he heard most clearly was one that seemed appropriate to what they were talking about with someone else. He would see Luet trying to deal with a quarrel between Chveya and Dazya, for instance, and hear someone saying: Why won't she hold her own with Dazya? Why does she back off like this? And someone else—the most constant voice, the strongest voice—saying, She's holding her own, she's doing fine, have patience, she doesn't need to win openly as long as you assure her of your respect for her. Thus he knew that a particular passionate, intimate manner meant that he was hearing Luet; a cooler, calmer, but more uncertain way of thought belonged to Hushidh. The most matter-of-fact, impatient, argumentative voice was Nafai's.

Yet even so, he was young enough that he didn't realize that he wasn't supposed to be hearing these things. It first became clear to him because of the dreams, for that was one of the Oversoul's most powerful ways of talking to people. One time when Oykib was a very little boy, Luet had come to the house to talk to Mother about a dream she had had. When she finished, Oykib had piped up and said, "I had that dream, too," and then repeated the things that Luet had seen.

Mother answered him then with a smile, but he knew that she didn't believe that he had seen the same dream. The second time it happened, with a dream of Father's, Mother took Oykib aside and gently explained to him that there was no need to pretend to have the same dreams as other people. It was better to tell only his own dreams.

Oykib was bothered by not being believed, and the older he got, the more it bothered him. Why, with so much communication between these adults and the Oversoul, did they all assume that he, as a three-year-old, as a four-year-old, could not have had the same communication? Eventually he decided that the problem was that the dream really *was* sent to someone else—it was appropriate for their situation, and not at all appropriate for Oykib. Therefore, the adults knew that the Oversoul would never have sent such a dream to him, because it had nothing to do with his life. And in fact the Oversoul *hadn't* sent the dream to him. The dreams and the background conversations were all real enough, but they were also not his own.

He wondered: Why doesn't the Oversoul have anything to say to *me?*

By the time Oykib turned eight, he had long since learned to keep what he overheard to himself. He was naturally quiet and reserved, preferring to be silent in a large group, listening to everything, helping when he was needed. He understood far more than anyone thought he did, partly because he had grown up overhearing adult problems being discussed with an adult vocabulary, and partly because he could hear, along with the vocal conversation, scraps and snatches of internal dialogues as the Oversoul made suggestions, tried to influence mood, and occasionally attempted to distract someone from what they were thinking or doing. The trouble was that it always distracted Oykib, so that he could hardly have any thoughts of his own, so busy was his mind in trying to follow all that was going on around him. When he did open his mouth to speak, he could never be sure if he was responding to what had been said aloud, or to things that he understood only because of overhearing that which he really shouldn't have been hearing.

There was also another reason why Oykib said little. He had learned about privacy and secrets, and he knew people wouldn't be happy if they ever guessed how much he knew. He suspected that it would make them angry to know that their most intimate thoughts, framed in their own minds where only the Oversoul could hear, were being heard and noted and stored away in the mind of a six- or seven- or eight-year-old boy.

Sometimes, the burden of all these secrets was more than Oykib could bear. That was why he had begun having little talks with Yasai, his younger brother. He never told Yaya how he was learning the things he learned. Instead he always said things like, "I'll bet that Luet is angry because of the way Hushidh never stops Dazya from bossing the younger children," or "Father doesn't really love Nafai more than everybody else, it's just that Nafai is the only one who understands what Father is doing and can help him to do it." Oykib knew that Yaya was dazzled by how often Oykib's "insights" turned out to be right, and that Yaya was also flattered to be included in his "wise" older brother's confidence; sometimes it made him feel like a cheater, to let Yaya think that Oykib had simply figured things out. But he knew, without knowing why, that it was a bad idea to tell even Yaya about how all communication with the Oversoul spilled over into Oykib's mind. Yaya was good about keeping secrets, but something *that* important was bound to slip out sometime.

So Oykib kept his secrets to himself. The hardest time was a few months back, when Nafai went out to the mountains and broke through the perimeter and found the starships. Oykib heard some terrible, frightening things. Luet pleading for the Oversoul to protect her husband.

The Oversoul urging someone else to be calm, be calm, don't kill your brother, you don't want to live with yourself afterward if you kill your brother. He understood the community well enough by then to know who it was who was planning to kill Nafai. Oykib longed to be able to do something, but he couldn't; in fact, he was almost immobilized by the maelstrom of needs and hungers, shouts and demands, pleas and griefs. He was so frightened; he went to Mother and clung to her, and heard her say to Volemak, "See how the children pick up on things without understanding them?" He wanted to say, "I understand perfectly well that Elemak and Mebbekew are planning to kill Nafai and then rule over all of us—I know it because I've heard the Oversoul trying to get them to stop. I know that Luet is terrified and so are you, that Nafai might be killed. But I also know that the Oversoul is saying a torrent of things to Nafai, important things, beautiful things, only he's so far away that I only catch glimmers of it, and I know that Nafai himself has no fear at all, he's just excited, he keeps shouting inside himself, "Now I get it! So that's it! Now I understand it! Yes!" But he could explain none of this. All he could do was cling to his mother until she had to push him away to get on with her work, and then talk it out with Yasai. "I think Elya and Meb are going to try to kill Nyef today, when he comes back," he said, and Yaya's eyes grew wide. "I think Nyef isn't worried, though, because he's become so strong that nobody can hurt him."

When it all ended with Elemak and Mebbekew humbled before the power of the starmaster's cloak, Yaya was in awe of Oykib's insights more than ever. But Oykib was exhausted. He didn't want to know so much. And yet, underneath it all, he wanted to know more. He wanted the Oversoul to speak to *him.*

Why should he? Oykib was only an eight-year-old boy, and not strong and domineering like Elemak's boy Protchnu, either, even though Proya was a few weeks younger. What would the Oversoul have to say to *him?*

Now, sitting with the others in the library of the starship *Basilica,* Oykib already knew exactly what was going to be explained to them, because he had heard the Oversoul arguing with the adults about it before the ship was launched, and he could hear the Oversoul arguing with Luet and Nafai even now. He wanted to shout at them to just shut up and *do* it. But instead he held his peace, and listened patiently as Nafai and Luet explained it all.

He didn't like the way they handled it. They told the truth, of course —he had learned to expect that from them, more perhaps than from any of the other adults—but they left out a lot of the real reasons for what they were doing. They only talked about it as a wonderful chance for the children to learn a lot of things they'd need to know in order to make the colony work when they got to Earth. "And because you'll be fourteen or fifteen or sixteen—or even, some of you, eighteen years old—when we arrive, you can do the work of a man or a woman. You'll be grownups, not children. At the same time, though, you'll only see your mothers and fathers now and then during the voyage, because we can't afford the life support to keep more than two adults awake at a time."

Yes yes, all of that is true, thought Oykib. But what about the fact that only a dozen of us children will be in this little school of yours? What about the fact that when I am an eighteen-year-old at the end of the voyage, Protchnu will still be eight? What about friendships like the one between Mebbekew's daughter Tiya and Hushidh's daughter Shyada? Will they still be friends when Shyada is sixteen and Tiya is still six? Not very likely. Are you going to explain *that?*

But he said nothing. Waiting. Perhaps they would get to that part.

"Any questions?" asked Nafai.

"There's plenty of time," said Luet. "If you want to go back to sleep, you can do it in a few days from now—there's no rush."

"Is there anything fun to do on this ship?" asked Xodhya, Hushidh's oldest boy. That was the most obvious question, since the adults had spent a lot of time before the launch assuring the kids that they *wanted* to sleep through the voyage because it would be so dull.

"There are a lot of things you can't do," said Luet. "The centrifuge will provide Earth-normal gravity for exercise, but you can only run in a straight line. You can't play ball or swim or lie in the grass because there's no pool and no grass and even in the centrifuge, it wouldn't be practical to throw and catch a ball. But you can still wrestle, and I think you could get used to playing tag and hide-and-seek in low gravity."

"And there are computer games," said Nafai. "You've never had a chance to play them, growing up without computers as you did, but Issib and I found quite a few—"

"You won't be able to play those very much, though," interrupted Luet. "We wouldn't want you to get too used to them, because we won't have computers like that on Earth."

Playing tag in low gravity—that alone probably would have won most of them over. Oykib found himself getting angry that they would pretend to be giving a choice when all they told about were mostly the good things and none the worst.

He might have said something then, but Chveya spoke up first. "I think it all depends on what Dazya decides."

Dza, always full of herself as the most important child because she was firstborn, visibly preened. Oykib was disgusted, mostly because he had never seen Chveya kiss up to Dza like this before—he had always thought she was the most sensible of the girls.

"Chveya, you children have to make up your own minds about this."

"You don't understand," said Chveya. "Whatever Dazya decides, I'm going to do the opposite."

Dazya stuck out her tongue at Chveya. "That's just what I'd expect from you," she said. "You're always so immature."

"Veya," said Luet, "I'm embarrassed that you would say something so hurtful. And would you really change your whole future, just to spite Dazya?"

Chveya blushed and said nothing.

At last Oykib reached the point where he could not maintain silence. "I know what you should do," he said. "Put Dazya back to sleep for three days. Then when she gets up, Dza and Chveya would be exactly the same age."

Chveya rolled her eyes as if to say, That wouldn't solve anything. But Dazya went crazy. "My birthday would always be first no matter what!" she shouted. "I'm the first child and nobody else is! So I'm *going* to stay awake and still be the oldest when we get there! Nobody else is ever going to boss me around."

Oykib saw with satisfaction that Dazya had shown Nafai and Luet exactly why Chveya didn't want to stay awake if Dazya did.

"Actually," said Luet, "nobody has the right to boss other people around just because she's oldest or smartest or anything else."

Several of the younger children laughed. "Dazya bosses everybody," said Shyada, who, as Dazya's next younger sister, bore the brunt of Dazya's whims.

"I do not," said Dazya. "I don't boss Oykib or Protchnu."

"No, you only boss people who are *weaker* than you, you big bully!" said Shyada.

"Be quiet, all of you," said Nafai. "What you've just seen here is one of the problems with keeping you awake for school during the voyage. The ship isn't very large inside. You're going to be cooped up together for years. We let a lot of things slide back on Harmony, figuring that you'd work things out as the years went by. But during the voyage, we won't tolerate older children bossing the younger children around."

"Why not?" said Dazya. "Grownups boss children around all the time."

"Dza," said Luet quietly, "I believe you're intelligent enough to grasp the idea that the three days between you and Veya are not as significant as the fifteen years between you and me."

Chveya followed up this idea at once. "If I stay awake, Mother, then when we reach Earth I'll be three years older than *you* were when I was born."

"Yes, but she was *married*," said Rokya, Zdorab's and Shedemei's boy. Then, suddenly, he seemed to realize what he had just said, because he blushed and clamped his mouth shut.

"I don't think marriage is something you need to worry about now," said Luet.

"Why not?" said Chveya. "*You* worry about it. Rokya is the only boy here who isn't an uncle or a double first cousin of mine."

"That won't be a problem," said Luet. "Shedemei said that there will be no genetic problems, so if it should happen that as you get older, you fall in love with a cousin or an uncle—"

Most of the children made groaning or puking noises.

"I say, as you get *older*, when the idea is no longer repulsive to you, there will be no genetic barrier."

But Oykib knew that before the launch, Shedemei had begged the Oversoul to forgive her for having told that lie to Nafai, and asked the Oversoul to tell Nafai to forbid marriages between close cousins if there would be any danger from it. He also knew something else, though, something Shedemei herself didn't know: that what she said about everyone being carefully bred by the Oversoul so as to be without any defects had been given to her by the Oversoul. He had overheard it as a very powerful sending. And so he was at peace with the idea of marrying a cousin. The Oversoul had better be right—Oykib and Yaya couldn't *both* marry Shedemei's and Zdorab's daughter Dabrota, and therefore one of them was going to marry a niece or die unmarried.

Chveya wasn't satisfied. "That's not what you said that night—"

"Veya," said Luet, trying to be patient. "You didn't hear both sides of that conversation, and besides, I learned some new information since then. Have a little trust, dear."

Motiga spoke up then. Caring nothing about the marriage issue, he had been thinking about something else. "If the people who stay asleep don't get any older, then will the ones who aren't here now still be little? I mean, will I be bigger than Protchnu?"

Luet and Nafai glanced at each other. Clearly they had wanted to avoid facing this question. "Yes," Nafai finally said. "That's what it means."

"Great," said Motiga.

But others weren't so sure. "That's stupid," said Shyada, who had a six-year-old's crush on Protchnu. "Why don't you just have us take turns being up, like you're going to do with the grownups?"

Oykib was surprised that a six-year-old would have thought of this most sensible of solutions. So were Nafai and Luet. They were obviously at a loss as to what to say, how to explain.

So Oykib, always looking for a chance to help, plunged in. "Look, we're not awake right now because Nafai and Luet like us best or anything like that. We're here because our parents are on Nafai's side, and the kids who are still asleep, *their* parents are on Elemak's side."

Nafai looked angry. Oykib heard him saying to the Oversoul, Any chance of teaching this boy how and when to keep his mouth shut?

Oykib also heard the Oversoul's answer: Didn't I warn you not to offer them a choice?

"I think it's good for us all to decide knowing the *real* reason for things," said Oykib, looking Nafai right in the eye. "I know that you and my parents and Issib and Hushidh and Shedemei and Zdorab are the ones who obey the Oversoul, and I know that Elemak and Mebbekew and Obring and Vas tried to kill you and the Oversoul thinks they'll try again as soon as we reach Earth." He knew he had probably said too much, had given away things that he wasn't supposed to know. So Oykib turned to the other children, to explain it to them. "It's like a war," he said. "Even though Nafai and Elemak are both my brothers, and even though Nafai doesn't want there to be a fight between them, Elemak is going to try to kill Nafai when we get to Earth."

The other children were looking at him with very serious faces. Oykib didn't talk all that much, but when he did, they listened; and what he was saying was serious. It was no longer about trivial matters like who was the boss of the children. That had been Luet's and Nafai's mistake. They wanted the children to choose, but they meant to make them do it without knowing the real issues involved. Well, Oykib knew these children better than the grownups did. He knew that they would understand, and he knew how they would choose.

"So you see," Oykib went on, "the real reason they woke us up is so that Yasai and Xodhya and Rokya and Zhyat and Motya and I will be men. *Big* men. While Elya's and Kokor's and Sevet's and Meb's sons are all nothing but little kids. That way, Elemak won't just be facing an old man like my father or a cripple like Issib. He'll be facing *us,* and we'll stand beside Nafai and fight for him if we have to. And we will, won't we!"

Oykib looked from one boy to the next, and each one nodded in turn. "And it's not just the boys," he added. "The twelve of us will marry and have children, and our children will be born before the others ever have children, and so we'll always be stronger. It's the only way to keep Elemak from killing Nafai. And not just Nafai, either. Because they'd have to kill Father, too. And Issya. And maybe Zdorab, too. Or if they didn't kill them, they'd treat them like slaves. And us, too. Unless we stay awake on this voyage. Elemak and Mebbekew are my brothers, but they aren't *nice.*"

Luet's face was buried in her hands. Nafai was looking at the ceiling.

"How do you know all this, Okya?" asked Chveya.

"I just know it, all right?" Oykib answered. "I just *know* it."

Her voice got very quiet. "Did the Oversoul tell you?" she asked.

In a way, yes—but for some reason Oykib didn't want to lie or even mislead Chveya. Better not to answer at all. "That's private," he said.

"A lot of what you just said is private, Oykib," said Nafai. "But now you've said it, and we have to deal with it. It's true that the Oversoul thinks that there's going to be a division in our community when we reach Earth. And it's true that the Oversoul planned all this so that you children would be old enough to stand with your parents against Elemak and his followers and their children. But I don't think there has to be a division like that. I don't *want* a division. So my reason for this is because it would be a good thing to have twelve more adults to help with the work of building the colony—and twelve fewer children who have to be looked after and protected and fed. Everybody will prosper more because of it."

"You weren't going to tell us any of this till Oykib said it, though," said Chveya, just a little angry.

"I didn't think you'd understand it," said Nafai.

"I *don't,*" said Shyada, truthfully.

"I'm staying awake," said Padarok. "I'm on your side, because I know my mother and father are. I've heard them talking."

"Me too," said his little sister Dabya. One by one, they all assented.

At the end, Dazya turned to Chveya and added, "And I'm sorry if you hate me so much that you'd rather stay a little girl than have to be with me."

"You're the one who hates *me,*" said Chveya.

"I really don't," said Dazya.

There was silence for a long moment.

"When it comes right down to it," Chveya said, "we're on the same side."

"That's right," said Dazya.

And then, because Chveya really wasn't good at thinking how things would sound before she said them, she added, "And you can marry Padarok. That's fine with me."

Padarok at once cried out in protest as most of the other children hooted and laughed. Only Oykib noticed that after she said this, Chveya looked straight at *him* before dropping her eyes down to her lap.

So I'm the chosen one, he thought. Sweet of you to make up my mind for me.

But it was also obvious. Of this group of twelve children, Oykib and Padarok were the only boys born in the first year, and Chveya and Dza were the only girls. If Dza and Padarok ended up together, Chveya would either have to marry Oykib or else one of the younger boys or else nobody.

The thought was faintly repulsive. He thought of the one time he had gotten roped into playing dolls with Dza and some of the younger girls. It was excruciatingly boring to pretend to be the father and the husband, and he fled after only a few minutes of the game. He imagined playing dolls with Chveya and couldn't imagine that it would be any better. But maybe it was different when the dolls were real babies. The adult men didn't seem to mind it, anyway. Maybe there was something missing when they played dolls. Maybe in real marriages, wives weren't so bossy about making the husbands do everything their way.

Padarok had better hope so, because if he ended up with Dazya he wasn't going to be able to think his own thoughts without her permission. She really was about as bossy a person as ever lived. Chveya, on the other hand, was merely stubborn. That was different. She wanted to do things her own way, but at least she didn't insist that you had to do them her way, too. Maybe they could be married and live in separate houses and only take turns tending the children. That would work.

Nafai was taking the other children now to show them where they would sleep—the girls' room and the boys' room. Oykib, lost in speculation about marriage, had lingered in the library, and now found himself alone with Luet.

"You certainly had a lot to say just now," said Luet. "Usually you don't."

"You two weren't saying it," said Oykib.

"No, we weren't," she answered. "And maybe we had good reason for that, don't you suppose?"

"No, you didn't have a good reason," answered Oykib. He knew it was outrageous for him to say such a thing to a grownup, but at this point he didn't care. He was Nafai's brother, after all, not his son.

"Are you so very sure of that?" She was angry, oh yes.

"You weren't telling us the real reason for everything because you thought we wouldn't understand it, but we did. All of us did. And *then* when we made up our mind, we knew what we were choosing."

"You may think you understand, but you don't," said Luet. "It's a lot more complicated than you think, and—"

Oykib got really angry now. He had heard their arguments with the

Oversoul, all the nuances and possible problems they had worried about, and even though he wasn't going to tell them how he knew these things, he certainly wasn't going to pretend now that he couldn't understand them. "Did you ever think, Lutya, that maybe it's a lot more complicated than *you* think, too?"

Maybe it was because he called her—an adult!—by her nickname, or maybe it was because she recognized the truth of what he said, but she fell silent and stared at him.

"You don't understand everything," said Oykib, "but you still make decisions. Well, we don't understand everything, either. But we decided, didn't we? And we made the right choice, didn't we?"

"Yes," she said quietly.

"Maybe children aren't as stupid as you think," Oykib added. It was something he had been wanting to say to an adult for a long time. This seemed like the appropriate occasion.

"I don't think you're stupid at all, not you or any of the. . . ."

But before she could finish her sentence, he was out of the library, bounding up the corridor in search of the others. If he wasn't there when they picked, he'd end up with the worst bed.

It turned out that he ended up with the worst bed anyway, the bunk on the bottom right by the door where he'd be in plain view to anybody coming down the corridor so he couldn't get away with *anything.* He had chosen the best bed, and since he was first boy, none of the others had argued with him. But then he saw how miserable Motya was at having the worst spot—especially when Yaya and Zhyat teased him about it. So now he was stuck with the worst bed and he knew nobody was going to want to trade later. Ten years, he thought. I'm going to have to sleep here ten lousy years.

6

The Ugly God

Emeez's mother took her to the holy cave when she was six years old. It was a miraculous place, because it was underground and yet it had not been carved by the people. Instead it grew this way, a gift from the gods; they had created it, and so this was where the gods were brought to be worshipped.

The cave was strange, all jagged and wet, not dry and smoothwalled like the burrows of the city. Limey water dripped everywhere. Mother explained how the water left a tiny amount of lime behind with each drop, and in time that's what formed the massive pillars. But how could that be? Weren't the pillars holding up the roof of the cave? If the pillars weren't forming until the water dripped for years and years, what would have held the roof up at the beginning? But Mother explained that this cave was made of stone. "The gods break holes in the mountain the way we chip off flakes of stone for our blades," Mother said. "They can hold up a roof of stone so wide that you can't see the other side, even with the brightest torch. And there is no wind so strong that it can tear the roof off the burrow of the gods."

That's why they're gods, I suppose, thought Emeez. She had seen what the storm did to the uphill end of the city, knocking down three rooftrees so that rain and later sunlight poured into what had once been nurseries and meeting halls. It took days to seal up the tunnels and create new burrows elsewhere to replace the lost space, and during that time two cousins and three nieces stayed with them. Mother nearly went crazy, and Emeez wasn't far behind. They were private, quiet people, and didn't deal very well with busybodies constantly prying into their business. Oh, what's *this*, are we learning to weave at such a young age? Oh, I'll bet you've already set your heart on some young fellow who's just now out on his first hunt, you pretty little thing you.

Such a lie. Because Emeez was not a pretty little thing. She wasn't pretty. She wasn't little. And she wasn't a *thing*, either, though people often treated her that way. She was too hairy, for one thing. Men liked a woman with very downy hair, not dark and coarse like hers. And her voice wasn't lovely, either. She tried to sound like Mother, but Emeez just didn't have that kind of music in her. One time when Cousin Issess —*there* was an undistinguished name for you!—didn't know Emeez was nearby, she said to her stupid daughter Aamuv, "Poor Emeez. She's a throwback, you know. They're just as hairy as that back on the east slope of the mountain. I hope she doesn't have any of their *other* traits!" The story was, of course, that the hairy east-slopers ate the hearts and livers of their enemies, and some said they simply spitted their victims and roasted them whole. Monsters. And that's what people thought of Emeez, because she was so hairy.

Well, she couldn't help what grew on her body. At least it wasn't a horrible fungus infection like the one that made poor Bomossoss stink so badly. He was a mighty warrior, but nobody could really enjoy being around him because of the odor. Very sad. The gods do what they want with us. At least I don't smell.

There wasn't any worship going on here—of course, since that was a man thing, and not for women, and *certainly* not for little girls. But she had heard that the men worshipped the gods by licking them until they were wet and soft and then rubbing them all over their bodies. She hadn't really believed it, until she came into the first of the prayer chambers.

Some of the gods were very intricately carved, with startlingly beautiful faces. There were pictures of fierce warriors and of the hideous skymeat beasts, of goats and deer, of coiled snakes and dragonflies perched on cattails. But when Mother started pointing out the very holiest of the gods, the ones most worshipped, to Emeez's surprise *these* were not intricately carved at all. The very holiest of them were nothing but smooth lumps of clay.

"Why are the beautiful ones not as holy as the ones that don't look like anything?"

"Ah," said Mother, "but you have to understand, they were once the most beautiful of all. But they have been worshipped most fervently, and they have given us good babies and good hunting. So of course they've been worn smooth. But we remember what they were."

The smooth lumpy ones disturbed her. "Couldn't somebody carve new faces on them?"

"Don't be absurd. That would be blasphemy." Mother looked annoyed. "Honestly, Emeez, I don't understand how your mind works. Nobody carves the gods. They would have no power if men and women just made them up out of clay."

"Well who *does* make them, then?"

"We bring them home," said Mother. "We find them and bring them home."

"But who makes them?"

"They make themselves," said Mother. "They rise up from the clay of the riverbank by themselves."

"Can I watch sometime?"

"No," said Mother.

"I want to watch a god coming forth."

Mother sighed. "I suppose you're old enough. If you promise you won't go telling the younger children."

"I promise."

"There is a certain time of year. In the dry season. The skymeat come down and shape the mud by the riverbank."

"Skymeat?" Emeez was appalled. "You can't be serious. That's disgusting."

"Of course it *would* be disgusting," said Mother, "if you thought the skymeat actually understood what they were doing. But they don't. The god comes awake inside them and they just start mindlessly shaping the clay in fantastic intricate patterns. Then, when they're done, they just go away. Leave them behind. For us."

The skymeat. Those nasty flying things that sometimes trapped and killed hunters. Their young were brought home and roasted and fed to pregnant women. They were dangerous, mindless beasts, treacherous and sneaky, and *they* made the *gods?*

"I'm not feeling well, Mother," said Emeez.

"Well, then, sit down here for a few minutes and rest," said Mother. "I'm supposed to meet the priestess three rooms up—that way—and I can't be late. But you can come after me and find me, right? You won't wander off the main path and get lost, will you?"

"I don't think I suddenly turned *stupid,* Mother."

"But you did suddenly turn rude. I don't like that in you, Emeez."

Well, nobody likes much of anything in me, she thought. But that doesn't mean I have to agree with them. *I* think I'm excellent company.

I'm much smarter than any of my other friends, and so everything I say to myself is scintillating and exciting and has never been said before. Unlike those who say over and over, endlessly, the same bits of "wisdom" they picked up from their mothers. And I'm certainly better company than the boys, always throwing things and breaking things and cutting things. Much better to dig and to weave, the way women do, to gather things rather than kill them, to combine leaves and fruit and meat and roots together in a way that tastes good. I will be a fine woman, hairy or not, and whatever man ends up getting stuck with me will make a big show about how disappointed he is, but in secret he'll be glad, and I'll make him a whole bunch of smart hairy babies and they'll be just as ugly and just as smart and clever as I am until someday they wake up and realize that the hairy ones make the best wives and mothers and the hairless ones are just slimy and *cold* all the time, like skinned melons.

Angry now, Emeez got up and started looking closer at the gods. She couldn't help it—there was nothing interesting about the overworshipped gods. It was the pristine, intricate ones that fascinated her. Maybe that was her whole problem—she was attracted to gods with poor reputations, and that's why she was cursed with ugliness, because the really effective gods knew that she wouldn't like them. That was terrible, though, to punish her from birth for a sin she wouldn't even commit until she was six, only two years before she became a woman.

Well, as long as I've already been punished for it, I'm going to go right ahead and *deserve* the punishment. I'm going to find the very most beautiful, most *un*worshipped god of all and choose that one for my favorite.

So she began searching seriously for one that was in perfect condition. But of course all the gods had received at least *some* worship, so even though she could find sections of them that still had the most beautiful details, there was none that was unmarred.

Until she found the most astonishing one, in the back corner of a small side chamber. It looked like none of the others. In fact, it looked like no beast that she had ever seen before. And the carving was absolutely pristine. It had been smoothed nowhere, which meant that it had never been worshipped by anyone.

Well, she said to the ugly god. *I* am your worshipper now. And I will worship you the best way, not like any of the others. I won't lick you or rub you or whatever other disgusting thing they do with those other muddy gods. I'm going to worship you by looking at you and saying that you are a *beautiful* carving.

Of course, it was a beautiful carving of an astonishingly ugly creature. Or rather, just the head of the creature. It had a mouth like a person, and two eyes like a person, but the nose pointed downward and its jaw was amazingly pointed and down at the base of the head it narrowed down until the neck was much, much thinner than the head. How does it hold up such a massive head on such a skinny neck? And why would a stupid skymeat even think of making something that no one had ever seen?

That answer to that last question was obvious enough, of course, when she thought of it. The skymeat carved this head because this was what the god looked like.

No. What god would choose to look like *that?*

Unless—and here was an astonishing thought—unless the gods couldn't help the way they looked. Unless this god was just like her and grew up ugly and yet he didn't think that meant he didn't have a right to have a statue and be worshipped, and so he got a skymeat to carve his head but then when it was brought down here not one soul ever worshipped him and he got stuck off in a dark corner, only now *I've* found you, and I may be ugly but I'm the only worshipper you've got so don't tell me you're going to reject me now!

<I accept you.>

She heard it as clear as if someone had spoken behind her. She turned around to look, but there was no one in this darkish room, no one but her.

"Did you speak to me?" she whispered.

There was no answer. But as she looked at the ugly beautiful statue, she suddenly knew something, knew something so important that she had to tell Mother at once. She ran from the room and up the main road until she reached the room where Mother and the priestess were conversing animatedly. "I see you feel better, Emeez," said Mother, patting her head.

"Mother, I have to tell you—"

"Later," said Mother. "We've just about decided something wonderful for you and—"

"Mother, I have to tell you *now.*"

Mother looked embarrassed and annoyed. "Emeez, you're going to make Vleezheesumuunuun think that I haven't raised you well."

From the priestess's name, Emeez realized that she must be somebody very important and distinguished, and suddenly she was shy. "I'm sorry," she said.

"No, that's all right," the old priestess said. "It's the hairy ones who still hear the voice of the gods, they say."

Oh, great, thought Emeez. Don't tell me that because I'm ugly I might have to end up as a *priestess.*

"What was it you wanted to tell us, child?" asked the priestess.

"I just—I was looking at a really beautiful god, only it was really ugly, and suddenly I knew something. That's all."

The priestess went down on all fours. Immediately Mother did too, and Emeez was well-bred enough to know that *she* must also assume that posture. It was exhilarating, though, because it meant that the priestess was taking her seriously. "What did you suddenly know?" asked Vleezheesumuunuun.

"Well now that I think about it, I don't even know what it means."

"Tell us anyway," said Mother, and the priestess blinked a slow *yes*.

"The ones that were lost are coming back home."

Mother and the priestess looked at her blankly. Finally mother spoke. "That's *all*?"

"That's enough," the priestess whispered. "Tell no one." The priestess's eyes were closed.

"Then you know what this means?" asked Mother.

"I don't," said the priestess. "Not what it *means*. But don't you remember from the song of creation, where the great prophet Zz says, 'There will be no more meat from the sky on the day when the lost ones are found, and no more gods from the river when the wanderers come home'?"

"No, I don't remember that one," said Mother, "and if you'll notice, Zz didn't say anything about lost ones coming home. She said the lost ones are found, and the ones who come home are the wanderers. So I don't think you need to take this so seriously and frighten my poor daughter to death."

But it was obviously Mother who was frightened. Emeez certainly wasn't. She was exhilarated. The god had told her he accepted her worship, and then had given her a gift, that bit of knowledge that meant nothing to her, but apparently meant a great deal to the priestess—and to Mother, too, despite her protests to the contrary.

"This changes everything," the priestess said.

"I was afraid of that," Mother said with a small voice.

"Oh, don't be absurd," said the priestess. "I'm still going to find a mate for your daughter."

Find a mate! Oh, what awful shame! An arranged marriage! Mother was *so* sure that no man would ever want her that she had gone to the priestess to arrange for a *sacrifice* marriage? Some man would be forced to take her as a wife in order to make up for some offense? Emeez had seen that happen twice before, and both times the woman who was offered that way had also been an offender, and that was *her* penance, to be forced upon a man like some nasty herb to heal a wound.

"What crime am I guilty of?" Emeez whispered.

"Don't be petulant," said the priestess. "As I said, this changes everything."

"How?" asked Mother.

"Let's just say that when the words of Zz are promised their fulfillment in the mouth of a girl, that girl will not be given to a common blunderer or a moral cretin."

Oh, joy of joys, thought Emeez bitterly. I suppose that means I'll be given to some truly spectacular miscreant.

"She's six?" asked the priestess. "Two years till she's a woman?"

"As far as we can guess such things," said Mother. "It's the choice of the gods, of course."

The priestess stroked Emeez's fur. As always, Emeez stiffened under the touch. People were always touching the crooked limbs or stumps of cripples, too, and she just hated it, even if it *was* supposed to bring them luck. But then she realized that the priestess wasn't doing that hesitant little lucktouch. She was stroking Emeez's fur with real affection, it seemed, and it felt good. "I don't know if we've been right," said the priestess, "to call that soft downy nothing hair beautiful. I think along with the hair of our women we might have lost something else. A closeness to the gods."

Mother was too polite to disagree, but her very silence made it plain that *she* was not of that opinion.

The priestess was still talking. "Muf, the son of the war king, will be of age at about the same time as Emeez here."

After a moment's pause, Mother laughed. "Oh, you can't mean that you'd. . . ."

"A girl who hears the echo of Zz after all these centuries. . . ."

Mother was still protesting. "But Muf won't be happy to be given a. . . ."

"Muf intends to be war king. He will marry as the gods direct. As far as I'm concerned, the gods have chosen here today."

But it wasn't the gods, thought Emeez. Or rather, *I* chose *him.*

"It's too much for her," said Mother. "She never expected such honor."

"The girls who expect it," said the priestess, "are the very ones who should never be given it."

Finally Mother could believe it—or perhaps she finally realized that her very incredulity was making it plain to Emeez just what she thought of her. Whatever the reason, Mother finally squeaked in delight and embraced Emeez.

Before they left, the priestess had Emeez show her which god she had been looking at. She knew as soon as Emeez led her into that small side chamber which god it would be. "The big ugly one, right? No one has ever touched it."

"But the workmanship is beautiful," said Emeez.

"Yes, that's true," said the priestess. "No large hands like ours could ever make such intricate perfection. That's why the gods use the skymeat to give them material shape. But this one—I always wondered what he would do, since no one has ever given him a chance to make a child or bring the rain or anything like that. He must have been waiting for you, child." And again the old priestess stroked her hair.

I will be the wife of the new war king, if he turns out to be worthy to succeed his father. I'll do everything I can to help him be worthy. And I'll keep a beautiful room for him, with carpets and tapestries, baskets and robes more lovely than have ever been seen before. And when people see him, they won't think, Look at that poor man, to have such a hairy wife. Instead they'll say, the wife of the war king may be hairy, but she has surrounded our king with beauty.

I will never forget you for this great gift, she said silently to the beautiful ugly god.

"Will you move this god out into the open now?" asked Mother.

"No," said the priestess. "Nor are either of you to tell anyone what god it was who put these words into the girl's mouth. This god has never been touched. Let him stay that way."

"I've never heard of treating a powerful god like that," Mother protested.

"And I've never heard of an untouched god having any power," said the priestess. "So we don't have any precedents here. Therefore—we will do whatever works. And not touching this one seemed to be quite effective. That's enough for me."

And for me, said Emeez silently. Then, aloud, she repeated the first and clearest words that the god had said. "I accept you."

"Save those words for your husband," said Mother. "Now I think we'd better head home while there's still time to make a good supper."

All the way home, Mother kept repeating to her that she had to keep all these things to herself and not brag to anyone because until old Vleezh made some public announcement she could still change her mind. "Or she might die. She's old. And you can't imagine that any of the other priestesses would be the least bit impressed if I brought you in and said, But Vleezh said she was going to pair my Emeez with Muf, the son of the war king."

No, of course I can't imagine that, Mother. Who could?

In the back of her mind, though, one question kept nagging at her, one that Mother and the priestess both seemed to have ignored. What did it *mean*, to say that the lost ones were coming home? Who was coming? And how did they get lost? And why was it this strange ugly god who brought the news, out of all the thousands of gods in the holy cave?

I will watch and wait, thought Emeez. I think the god meant to accomplish more with these words than just to get me married off so far beyond all expectations. So I will try to see what the god's message really meant, and when I do, I will proclaim it or whatever else the god wants me to do. It will be clear to me, when it happens, what I'm supposed to do.

She did not wonder how she knew that. Instead she began to speculate on what word to add to her name, for the wife of the war king's son would never be left with just her weaning name. Emeezuuzh? Uuzh was the ending Mother had taken on her day of glory, when her basket was chosen for the burial of the old blood king. But that was a pretty name, a delicate name when a woman chose it. Emeez would have something stronger. She would have to think about that. There'd be plenty of time to make up her mind.

7

A Storm at Sea

Zdorab had been born in the wrong era. He had never realized it until now. Oh, he knew he didn't fit in where he grew up or where he lived in Basilica before Nafai gave him the chance to save his life by coming with him into the desert. But now, at the end of his second stint as Nafai's co-teacher of the children on the starship *Basilica,* Zdorab knew where he truly belonged. The trouble was, the culture that might have valued him had been gone for forty million years.

Whoever it was that built this starship, with its fineness of design and craftsmanship, was to be admired, of course. It was only after living in it that Zdorab understood that he also loved their way of life. True, they were confined indoors, but as far as Zdorab was concerned, outdoor life was over-rated. He did not miss insects. He did not miss excessive heat and cold, humidity and dryness. He did not miss the defecations of animals and the smells of strange things cooking or overfamiliar things rotting.

But it wasn't the absence of annoyances that made him relish the life aboard ship. It was the positive things. A comfortable bed every night. Daily bathing in a shower of clean water. A life centered around the library, around learning and teaching. Computers that could play as well as work. Music perfectly reproduced. Toilets that cleaned themselves and had no odors. Clothing that could be cleaned without laundering. Meals prepared in moments. And all of it while traveling at some unfathomable speed on a hundred-year voyage to another star.

He tried explaining it to Nafai, but the young man merely looked at Zdorab in puzzlement and said, "But what about trees?" Obviously Nafai couldn't wait to get to the new planet, which would no doubt be another place with lots of dirt and bugs and plenty of sweaty manual labor to do. Zdorab had played obsequious servant all the way across the desert; he loved the fact that in this starship there *were* no servants, because all work was either done by machines and computers or was so simple and easy that anyone could do it—and everyone did.

And he loved teaching the children. Some of them were barely children anymore, six years into the voyage. Oykib had shot up to nearly two meters now, at the apparent age of fourteen. He was lanky, but Zdorab had seen him working out in the centrifuge and his body was wiry with hard tight muscles. Zdorab knew he was middle-aged by the fact that he could see that beautiful young body and feel only the memory of desire. If there was any mercy in nature, it was the fading of the male libido with middle age. Some men, feeling the slackening of desire, went to heroic—or criminal—lengths to get the illusion of renewed sexual vigor. But for Zdorab it was a relief. It was better to think of Oykib and his even-more-beautiful younger brother, Yasai, as students. As friends of his son, Padarok. As potential mates of his daughter, Dabrota.

My son, he thought. My daughter. Good Lord. Who would ever have guessed, during his years in clandestine love affairs in the men's city outside Basilica, that I would ever have a son and a daughter. And if any man laid hands on either one of them without my consent, I think I'd kill him.

And then he thought: I'm a jungle creature after all.

He was going to sleep again today, as Shedemei wakened to take his place. They would overlap for a few hours—the Oversoul said there was life support enough for that—and it would be good to see her. She was his best friend, the only one who knew his secrets, his inward struggles. He could tell her almost everything.

But he could not tell her about the little program he had set up in a life support computer, one of those not directly part of the Oversoul's memory. Just before scheduling the one wake-up call for midvoyage, the obvious one that the Oversoul had detected at once, Zdorab had written a program that ostensibly took a harmless inventory of supplies. It also checked, however, to see if it was exactly six and a half years into the voyage, and if it was, it would send a new version of the schedule file to the computer where the calendar was executed. The new version would call for Elemak, Zdorab, and Shedemei to be wakened thirty seconds later; then, after another second, the original copy of the schedule would be restored and the inventory program would rewrite itself to eliminate the extra subroutine. It was all very deft and Zdorab was proud of its cleverness.

He also know that it was potentially lethal to the peace of the community and he kept intending, now that he was taking part in Nafai's little plan, to get into the life support computer and eliminate it before it could go off. The trouble was that it was not as easy to get access to that computer, now that they were in flight. He had duties, and when those were done, the children were everywhere all the time and they would be bound to ask him what he was doing. He told himself that he was looking for a safe opportunity to make the change. Now he was only hours from going back to sleep, and he had found no such opportunity. Why not?

Because he was afraid, that's why. That was the worm in his salad. Not that he was afraid for himself—the hunger for self-preservation was no longer as important to him as the need to protect his children. He had gone along with Nafai's scheme, not because of dreams—those were for Shedemei and others that the Oversoul had bred to be especially receptive to them—but because he did not want *some* of the children to be given an advantage, and not his own. When Issib came up with the plan of having the adults help teach the children in shifts, Zdorab wouldn't have dreamed of refusing to take part.

At the same time, though, he was afraid of what Elemak would do later on to take vengeance. When he woke up on Earth and found himself surrounded by these strong young men, all committed to Nafai's cause, he would be so filled with hate that he would *never* forgive. There would be war, sooner or later, and it would be bloody. Zdorab didn't want his children to suffer from that. Didn't want them to have to take part, or even take sides. What better way to accomplish that than to prove his loyalty to Elemak by letting the wake-up call come through as planned?

Of course, Nafai and the Oversoul would have no problem figuring out who had done it—nobody else had the computer skills back on Harmony, and none of the children who had acquired those abilities during the voyage were likely to want to wake up Elemak. Hadn't he heard Izuchaya—who had been so young at launch that she barely remembered Elemak—asking, "Why do we have to wake up Elemak at all, if he's so bad?" "Because that would be murder," Nafai had answered her, and then explained that even when you disagree with someone, they still have a right to live their life and make their own choices. The only time you have a right to kill someone is when they're actually trying to kill you or someone you need to protect.

Someone you need to protect. I need to protect my children. And here's the cold hard truth, Nafai: My children are no blood kin of yours. Therefore, even if we side with you, I can't believe for a moment that you will ever be as careful of them, as loyal to them, as you are to your own children or your parents' young children or your brother Issib's children. I have to find a way to protect them myself, to make it so Elemak won't hate them the way he will hate you and your children—even as I've helped them take advantage of your plan to become older and stronger than Elemak's boys. That's what a father does. Even if his wife wouldn't approve of it.

Shedemei had different ideas of loyalty, Zdorab knew. She was an all-or-nothing kind of person. That's because she hadn't lived in the nightmare world of interweaving treachery that Zdorab had inhabited for so many years. Gaballufix's constant plotting, in which other people's trust was regarded as a weapon to be turned against them; the routine violence and corruption of life in the men's village, where the ameliorating influence of women did not penetrate; and of course the relentless deception of the life of a man who loved men. No one can really be trusted, Shedemei, he said silently.

Not even the Oversoul. Especially not the Oversoul.

Zdorab's only contact with the master computer was through the Index and, later, through the ordinary computers of the starship. He had no dreams, and as far as he knew the Oversoul neither cared about him nor heard any of his thoughts. How else could he have installed his clandestine wake-up program? The Oversoul had no particular use for him except to provide the other set of chromosomes for Shedemei to reproduce. Well, that was fine—Zdorab didn't have all that much use for the Oversoul, either. He was firmly convinced that whatever it was the Oversoul wanted, it didn't care much about the comfort and happiness of the human beings it manipulated. And because the Oversoul didn't care about him, he was the one person in the whole community with privacy.

At the same time, in the back of his mind, Zdorab hoped that in fact the Oversoul *did* hear his thoughts and knew all about the wake-up call. It had probably already removed it, in fact; Zdorab hadn't checked it for the same reasons that he hadn't removed it himself. The Oversoul wouldn't let anything dangerous happen during the voyage. Elemak wasn't going to wake up until Earth. And when he did, Zdorab could truthfully say, "I left the wake-up call in place. The Oversoul must have found it."

He silently rehearsed the words, shaping them with his lips and tongue and teeth, knowing even as he did it that Elemak wouldn't believe him, or if he did he wouldn't care.

They're wrong to have brought me with their family, wrong to force me to choose between them in their deadly domestic quarrels.

He stood before Shedemei's sleep chamber as the lid slipped back and her eyes fluttered open. She smiled weakly.

"Hi, brilliant and beautiful lady," he said.

"To be flattered upon first waking is every woman's fondest dream," she said. "Unfortunately I'm still stupid from the drugs."

"What drugs?" He helped her sit up before he unclamped and dropped the side of the chamber so she could get out.

"You mean I'm just naturally this mentally slow?"

She got up and clung to him, partly to support herself as she tried to get her legs working again in the low gravity, and partly as an embrace between friends. He responded, of course, and began telling her of all that the different children had accomplished since she had last been awake. "I think this may be the finest school that ever existed," he said.

"And how convenient that the teachers are all put to sleep between terms," answered Shedemei.

They spent the hours together talking about the children, especially their own, and about anything that came to Shedemei's mind. But they did not talk about the one thing preying most on Zdorab's mind, and Shedemei noticed something was wrong.

"What is it?" she asked. "You're not telling me something."

"Like what?" he answered.

"Something is worrying you."

"My life is worry," he said. "I don't like climbing into the sleep chamber."

She smiled thinly. "All right, you don't have to tell me."

"Can't tell you what I don't know myself," he said, and since this contained a grain of truth—he didn't know whether the Oversoul had removed his program or not—Shedemei's truthsense allowed her to believe him and she relaxed.

A few hours later he said goodbye to the children in a ritual that they were all used to by now, since their teachers all came and went this way. Handshakes or hugs all around, depending on the child's age; a kiss for his own children whether they liked it or not; and then Nafai and Shedemei escorted him to his chamber and helped him in.

As the drugs began to take effect, though, he was filled with a sudden panic. No, no, no, he thought. How could I have been so stupid? Elemak will never be loyal to me, no matter what I do. I have to change the program. I have to keep him from waking up and taking Nafai by surprise. "Nafai," he said. "Check the life support computer."

But the lid of the chamber was already closed, and he couldn't see whether Nafai was even watching his lips, and before he could even move a hand, the drug overwhelmed him and he slept.

"What did he say?" Nafai asked Shedemei.

"I don't know. Something was bothering him but he didn't know what."

"Well, maybe he'll remember it when he wakes up," said Nafai.

Shedemei sighed. "I always have that same anxiety, too, like I've forgotten to say something *very* important. I think it's just one of the side effects of the suspension drugs."

Nafai laughed. "Like when you wake up in the middle of the night with a very important idea from a dream, and you write it down and then in the morning it says, 'Not the food! The dog!' and you have no idea what that could possibly mean or why you once thought it was important."

"The real dreams," said Shedemei, "you don't have to write down. You remember them."

They both nodded, remembering what it felt like to have the Oversoul or the Keeper of Earth speak to them in their sleep. Then they returned to the children and set to work on the next part of their training.

Chveya was working with Dza on coaching some of the younger children through their exercises. They had learned years ago that everybody had to be supervised or they would start to slack off, even though Nafai had warned again and again that if they didn't put in two hard hours every day in the centrifuge, they would reach Earth with bodies so slack and feeble that they would have to borrow Issib's chair just to get around. So the younger children exercised with older children calling the times, and the older children worked with younger ones monitoring them. That way they never had peers "telling them what to do." The system worked well enough.

Dza was still not Chveya's friend—they really hadn't that much in common. Dza was one of those people who couldn't stand to be alone, who always had to surround herself with the hubbub of conversation, with eager gossip, with laughter and mockery. Chveya could see that, now that Dza wasn't bossing them anymore, the younger girls genuinely liked her. It appeared to Chveya like a physical connection between them, and she could see how the younger girls brightened when they came into Dza's presence—and how Dza brightened also. But Chveya could not enjoy being with them for long. And envy wasn't the cause of it, either, though at times she *did* envy Dza her bevy of friends. All the constant chat, the rapidly shifting demands on her attention—it wore Chveya out very quickly, and she would have to go off by herself for a while, to surround herself with silence and music, to read a book continuously for an hour, holding the same thread of talk.

Father had talked to her about it, and Mother, too, when she was awake the last time. You spend too much time alone, Chveya. The other children sometimes think you don't like them. But to Chveya, reading a book was not the same as being alone. Instead she was having a conversation with one person, a sustained conversation that stuck to the subject and didn't constantly fly off on tangents or get interrupted by someone demanding to tell *her* gossip or talk about *her* problem.

As long as Chveya got her solitary time, though, she could get along peaceably enough with the others—even Dza. Now that she had got over her childish infatuation with being "first child," Dza was good company, bright and funny. To her credit, Dza had not been jealous when it was discovered that Chveya alone of the third generation had developed the ability to sense the relationships among people, even though it was Dza's mother, not Chveya's, who had first learned to do it. When Aunt Hushidh was awake, she spent more time with Chveya than with her own daughters, but Dza did not complain. In fact, Dza once smiled at Chveya and said, "Your father teaches all of us all the time. I'm not going to get mad because my mother spends time teaching you." Studying with Aunt Hushidh was like reading a book. She was quiet, she was patient, she stuck to the subject. And better than a book: She answered Chveya's questions. With Aunt Hushidh, Chveya suddenly became the talkative one. Perhaps that was because Aunt Hushidh was the only one who had seen the things that Chveya saw.

"But you see more," Aunt Hushidh said one day. "You have dreams like your mother, too."

Chveya rolled her eyes. "There's no Lake of Women on this starship," she said. "There's no City of Women to make a fuss over me and hang on every word of my accounts of my visions."

"It wasn't really like that," said Hushidh.

"Mother said it was."

"Well, that's how it seemed to her, perhaps. But your mother never exploited the role of Waterseer."

"It wasn't useful, though, like . . . well, like what we can do."

Hushidh smiled slightly. "Useful. But sometimes misleading. You can interpret things wrongly. When you know too much about people, it still doesn't mean that you know enough. Because the one thing you never really know is *why* they're connected to one person and distant from another. I make guesses. Sometimes it's easy enough. Sometimes I'm hopelessly wrong."

"I'm always wrong," said Chveya, but it didn't make her ashamed to say this in front of Aunt Hushidh.

"Always *partly* wrong," said Hushidh. "But often partly right, and sometimes very clever about it indeed. The problem, you see, is that you must care enough about other people to really think about them, to try to imagine the world through their eyes. And you and I—we're both a little shy about getting to know people. You have to try to spend time with them. To listen to them. To be friends with them. I'm saying this, not because I did it at your age, but because I didn't, and I know how much it hampered me."

"So what changed it?" asked Chveya.

"I married a man who lived in such constant inner pain that it made my own fears and shames and sufferings seem like childish whining."

"Mother says that long before you married Uncle Issib, you faced down a bad man and took the loyalty of his whole army away from him."

"That's because they were another man's army, only that man was dead, and they didn't have much loyalty to begin with. It wasn't hard, and I did it by blindly flailing around, trying to say *everything* I could think of that might weaken what loyalty remained."

"Mother says you looked calm and masterful."

"The key word is 'looked.' Come now, Veya, you know for yourself—when you're terrified and confused, what do you do?"

Chveya giggled then. "I stand there like a frightened deer."

"Frozen, right? But to others, it looks like you're calm as can be. That's why some of the others tease you so mercilessly sometimes. They think of you as made of stone, and they want to break in and touch human feelings. They just don't know that when you seem most stony, that's when you're most frightened and breakable."

"Why is that? Why don't people understand each other better?"

"Because they're young," said Hushidh.

"Old people don't understand each other any better."

"Some do," said Hushidh. "The ones who care enough to try."

"You mean you."

"And your mother."

"She doesn't understand me at *all*."

"You say that because you're an adolescent, and when an adolescent says that her mother doesn't understand her, it means that her mother understands her all too well but won't let her have her way."

Chveya grinned. "You are a nasty conceited arrogant grownup just like all the others."

Hushidh smiled back. "See? You're learning. That smile allowed you to tell me *just* what you thought, but allowed me to take it as a joke so I could hear the truth without having to get angry."

"I'm trying," Chveya said with a sigh.

"And you're doing well, for a short ignorant shy adolescent."

Chveya looked at her in horror. Then Hushidh broke into a smile.

"Too late," said Chveya. "You meant that."

"Only a little," said Hushidh. "But then, all adolescents are ignorant, and you can't help being short and shy. You'll get taller."

"And shyer."

"But sometimes bolder."

Well, it was true. Chveya had started a growth spurt soon after Hushidh went back to sleep the last time, and now she was almost as tall as Dza, and taller than any of the boys except Oykib, who was already almost as tall as Father, all bones and angles, constantly bumping into things or smacking his hands into them or stubbing his toes. Chveya liked the way he took the others' teasing with a wordless grin, and never complained. She also liked the fact that he never used his large size to bully any of the other children, and when he interceded in quarrels, it was with quiet persuasion, not with his greater size and strength, that he brought peace. Since she was probably going to end up married to Oykib, it was nice that she liked the kind of man he was becoming. Too bad that all he thought of when he looked at *her* was "short and boring." Not that he ever said it. But his eyes always seemed to glide right past her, as if he didn't notice her enough to even ignore her. And when he was alone with her, he always left as quickly as possible, as if it nearly killed him to spend any time in her company.

Just because we children are going to have to pair up and marry doesn't mean we're going to fall in love with each other, Chveya told herself. If I'm a good wife to him, maybe someday he'll love me.

She didn't often allow herself to think of the other possibility, that when it came time to marry, Oykib would insist on marrying someone else. Cute little Shyada, for instance. She might be two years younger, but she already knew how to flirt with the boys so that poor Padarok was always tongue-tied around her and Motya watched her all the time with an expression of such pitiful longing that Chveya didn't know whether to laugh or cry. What if Oykib married *her*, and left Chveya to marry one of the younger boys? What if they *made* one of the younger ones marry her?

I'd kill myself, she decided.

Of course she knew that she would not. Not literally, anyway. She'd put the best face on it that she could, and make do.

Sometimes she wondered if that's how it was for Aunt Hushidh. Had she fallen in love with Issib before she married him? Or did she marry him because he was the only one left? It must be hard, to be married to a man you had to pick up and carry around when he wasn't in a place where his floats would work. But they seemed happy together.

People can be happy together.

All these thoughts and many more kept playing through Chveya's mind as she helped Shyada, Netsya, Dabya, and Zuya get through their calisthenics. Since Netsya was a cruel taskmaster when *she* was doing times for the older children, it was rather a pleasure to say, "Faster, Netsya. You did better than this last time," as Netsya's face got redder and redder and sweat flew off her hands and nose as she moved.

"You are," Netsya said, panting, "the queen, of the bitches."

"And thou art the princess, darling Gonets."

"Listen to her," said Zuya, who was *not* panting, because she did all her exercises as easily as if they were a pleasant stroll. "She reads so much she talks like a book now."

"An old, book," Netsya panted. "An ancient, decrepit, dusty, yellowed, worm-eaten—"

Her list of Chveya's virtues was interrupted by a loud ringing sound, followed by a whooping siren that nearly deafened them. Several of the children in the centrifuge screamed; most held their hands over their ears. They had never heard such a thing before.

"Something's wrong," Dza said to Chveya. Chveya noticed that Dza was not holding her hands over her ears. She looked as calm as an owl.

"I think we should stay here until Father tells us what to do," said Chveya.

Dza nodded. "Let's make sure who we have and not lose track of them."

It was a good idea. Chveya was momentarily jealous that she hadn't had the presence of mind to think of it. But then she knew that the wisest thing *she* could do was not to worry about who came up with the good ideas, but simply to use them. And Dza was a natural leader. Chveya should set the example of quick and willing obedience, as long as Dza's decisions were reasonable ones.

Dza had been working with the younger boys. She quickly counted them up. Motya, the youngest; Xodhya, Yaya, and Zhyat. She herded them to where Chveya had the younger girls. Chveya already had her tally because her girls had been working out together when the alarm went off.

"Just sit here and wait," shouted Dza to all the children.

"Can't they turn it off?" wailed Netsya, clearly terrified.

"Cover your ears, but keep looking at the rest of us!" shouted Dza. "Don't close your eyes."

Dza thought of things quickly—if the children couldn't hear, they had to *watch*, so they could receive instructions if they needed to do something. Again Chveya felt a little stab of jealousy. It didn't help that she could see how clearly everyone's loyalty, trust, *dependence* on Dza had suddenly increased.

Even my own, thought Chveya. She really *is* first child, now that she doesn't misuse it.

A pair of legs appeared in the ladderway at the top of the centrifuge. Long legs, with big awkward feet. Oykib. And he was more awkward than usual, because he was carrying something bulky under his arm. Something wrapped in cloth.

When he reached the floor, he turned at once to Dza. As if he had known she would be in charge. "It's not as loud in the sleeping rooms," he shouted. "Can you get all the younger ones to their beds?"

Dza nodded.

"That's where Nafai wants them, then, if you can do it safely without losing any."

"All right," said Dza, and immediately she started giving instructions. The younger children started up the ladder, Dza reminding each one to wait in the tube just outside the centrifuge until she got up there. Chveya felt completely unnecessary.

Oykib turned to her and held out the cloth bundle. "It's the Index," he said. "Elemak is awake. Hide it."

Chveya was amazed. None of the children had ever been allowed to touch the Index, even wrapped in cloth. "Did Father tell you to—"

"Do it," said Oykib. "Where Elemak won't think to look."

He shoved the bundle into her stomach and her arms instinctively folded around it. Then he turned and left, following Dza up the ladder.

Chveya looked around the centrifuge. Was there anyplace to hide the Index here? Not really. The exercise space was largely unencumbered, except for the strength machines, and those offered no concealment. So she clutched the Index under her arm and waited for her turn up the ladder.

Then she saw, where the centrifuge floor curved up to make its circle around the girth of the ship, the break in the carpet where the access door was. When the centrifuge was stopped, the access door could be pulled up so that someone could crawl down into the system of wheels that allowed the centrifuge to spin. The trouble was, it would take half an hour for the centrifuge to spin to a stop even if she turned it off right now. And then another hour or more to spin back up to speed. It would be obvious to Elemak that the centrifuge had been stopped for *some* reason. She couldn't count on his not noticing. Just because he had never been awake during the voyage didn't mean he wouldn't be aware of anomalies in the working of the ship.

On the other hand, the very fact that the centrifuge hadn't been stopped would imply to him that nothing had been hidden there.

She ran to the access door and pulled up on it. It wouldn't budge—an interlock prevented it from being opened while the centrifuge was spinning. She ran to the nearest emergency stop button and pushed it. The alarm that it sounded was lost in the howling of the main siren. Now the access door could be opened, even though the centrifuge was spinning rapidly. She flopped it back; it formed a slight arch on the curved floor. Through the door she could see the wheels of the centrifuge as the roadway hurtled by beneath them; then her perspective shifted, and she realized that she was on the hurtling surface, and the roadway was really the structure of the rest of the ship, holding still beneath the wheels. Up at the top of the ladder, the spin seemed so much slower. Just as many revolutions per minute, but so close to the center that it wasn't fast at all.

If I drop the Index, will it be crushed?

More to the point, if I fall or even touch the roadway, will I be killed or just maimed and crippled for life?

Sweating, terrified, she extended one leg, then the other, down through the opening until she was standing on the frame of the nearest wheel assembly. Then, holding her weight on her right hand, she braced the Index against the door while she got her hand under it. Balancing the Index on her palm, she carefully lifted it down into the opening and reached into the top of the other wheel assembly, right up under the centrifuge floor. In a place where four metal bars formed a square, she gingerly tipped the Index out of her hand, so that it rolled off and dropped into place. It was secure there—nothing was going to tip it off and it was far too wide to drop through. Best of all, it couldn't be seen unless you got down into the opening so far that your head was under the level of the centrifuge floor. Chances were that long before he got down far enough to see it, Elemak would conclude that it was far too dangerous for anyone to have put the Index down here and would give up and search somewhere else.

In fact, now that she thought about it, it really *was* dangerous to be down here. And she had to get back up and turn the centrifuge back on so its alarm would stop sounding before the main siren finally shut down. Getting out wasn't as easy as getting down had been, and now that she wasn't concentrating on getting the Index hidden, she had time to be really terrified. Slow, she kept telling herself. Careful. One slip and they'll be scraping bits of me off the road for a month.

Finally she was out, spread-eagled over the opening. She spider-walked until she was clear of it, then leaped to her feet and flung the door closed. It slammed into place, the catch engaged, and now she could turn the centrifuge back on. She could barely feel it speeding up—it was so well-engineered that in all that time with the motors off, friction had hardly slowed it down at all.

The siren went off. The silence was like a physical blow; her ears rang. She had made it with only ten or fifteen seconds to spare.

In the silence, she heard the noise of someone on the ladder.

She looked up. Legs. Not Father's. Not a child's. If she was found here, for no reason, then Elemak would wonder why she hadn't gone with the other children.

Without even thinking, she flung herself down to the floor, curled up in fetal position, buried her face in her hands, and began to whimper softly, trembling with fear. Let them think she had panicked, frozen up, terrified by the strange loud noise. Let them think she was weak, that she had lost all control of herself. They would believe it, because nobody knew she was the kind of person who could perform dangerous acrobatics while speeding over a roadway. Why should they? She hadn't known it herself. She could hardly believe it now.

"Get up," said the man. "Get yourself together. Nothing's going to hurt you."

It wasn't Elemak. It was Vasnya's and Panya's father, Vas. Aunt Sevet's husband. So it wasn't just Elemak who was awake.

"Nothing to be ashamed of," he said. "Loud noise—it gets to some people. You should see how the little ones are. It's going to take hours to get them quieted down."

"Little ones?" She realized at once that he didn't mean the twelve- and thirteen-year-olds. "The little children were wakened?"

"Everybody's awake. When the suspended animation alarm goes off, everybody is awakened at once. Just in case something is wrong with the system."

"What set it off?" asked Chveya.

Now, for the first time, a dark look of anger came across Uncle Vas's face. "We'll have to find that out, won't we? But if it hadn't wakened us, we wouldn't have had a chance to see you as such a pretty little—what—fourteen-year-old?"

"Fifteen," she said.

"Happy birthday," he answered dryly. "I'm sure my eight-year-old daughter Vasnaminanya will be delighted to see her dear cousin Veya. You'll really enjoy playing dolls with her, don't you think?"

Suddenly Chveya was ashamed. Vasnya had been her friend, the one child of the first year who had been nice to her and included her in things even during the times when Dza decreed that Chveya was untouchable. But because Vasnya's parents were friends of Elemak instead of Nafai, Vasnya had been left behind. Chveya was already six and a half years older. They would never really be friends again. And why? Was it anything Vasnya had done? No—she was a good person. Yet she had been left behind.

"I'm sorry," Chveya said quietly.

"Yes, well, we know who's to blame for this, and it isn't any of the children." He held out a hand to her. "Elemak's in charge now. He should have done it long ago."

He was trying to seem nice and reassuring, but Chveya wasn't stupid. "What have you done to Father?"

"Nothing," said Vas, smiling. "He just didn't seem terribly interested in contesting Elemak's authority."

"But he has the cloak of the—"

"Cloak of the starmaster," said Vas. "Yes, well, he still has it. Sparking its little heart out. Nafai has the cloak. But Elemak has the twins."

The twins, Serp and Spel. Chveya's youngest brothers, so small that they couldn't be included in the school. Elemak must be holding them hostage, threatening to hurt them if Father doesn't do what he wants.

"So he's using babies to get his way?" said Chveya scornfully.

Vas's expression got very ugly indeed. "Oh, what an awful thing for him to do. Someday you'll have to explain to me why it's bad for Elemak to use the children to get his way, but it was all right for your father to do exactly the same thing. Now come with me."

As she preceded him up the ladder, Chveya tried to find a clear distinction between holding babies hostage, like Elemak, and giving children a free choice to join with him in—in keeping control of the colony. That's what it came down to, didn't it? Using the children to get and keep control of the whole community.

But it *was* different. There was a clear moral difference and if she thought hard enough she would be able to explain it and then everybody would understand that the voyage school was a perfectly decent thing to do, while holding the twins as hostages was an unspeakable atrocity. She would think of it any minute now.

Then a completely different thought came to her. Oykib had given her the Index. He had assumed that Dza would lead the other children to safety, but when it came time to hide the Index of the Oversoul, instead of doing it himself he had entrusted it to Chveya. And he hadn't told her where to hide it, either.

Everyone was gathered in the library. It was the only room large enough to hold them all, since it was a large open room using almost the whole girth of the ship. There were babies crying and little children looking puzzled and afraid. Chveya knew all the little children, of course. They were unchanged, gathered around their mothers. Kokor, Sevet, Dol. And Elemak's wife, Eiadh. She wasn't holding her own youngest, though, not Zhivya. No, Aunt Eiadh was holding one of the twins, Spel.

And Elemak, standing at one edge of the library, was holding Serp.

I will never forgive either of you, Chveya said silently. I may not be able to sort out the moral theory of it, but those are my brothers you're holding, using the threat of harming them to get your own way.

"Chveya," said Luet, seeing her.

"Shut up," said Elemak. "Come here," he said to Chveya.

She walked toward him, stopped a good many paces away.

"Look at you," said Elemak, contemptuously angry.

"Look at *you*," said Chveya. "Threatening a baby. Your children must be proud of their brave daddy."

A hot rage swept over Elemak, and she saw his connection to her take on an almost negative force. For a moment he wanted her dead.

But he did nothing, said nothing until he had calmed himself a little.

"I want the Index," said Elemak. "Oykib says he gave it to you."

Chveya whirled on Oykib, who looked back at her impassively. "It's all right," Oykib says. "Your father was the one who wanted it hidden. Now the Oversoul is telling him to give the Index to Elemak."

"Where's Father?" asked Chveya. "Who are you to speak for him?"

"Your father is safe," said Elemak. "You'd better listen to your *big* uncle Oykib."

"Believe me," said Oykib. "You can tell him. The Oversoul says it's all right."

"How can you possibly know what the Oversoul says?" demanded Chveya.

"Why shouldn't he?" Elemak said snidely. "Everybody else does. This room is *full* of people who love to tell other people what the Oversoul wants them to do."

"When I hear it from Father's mouth, I'll tell you where the Index is."

"It has to be in the centrifuge," said Vas, "if she's the one who hid it."

Oykib's eyes grew wide. "There's noplace to hide it in there."

Elemak snapped at Mebbekew and Obring. "Go and find it," he said.

Obring got up at once, but Mebbekew was deliberately slow. Chveya could see that his loyalty to Elemak was weak. But then, his loyalty to everybody was weak.

"Just tell them, Veya," said Oykib. "It's all right, I mean it."

I don't care whether you mean it or not, said Chveya silently. I didn't risk my life to hide it, only to have a traitor like you talk me into giving it back to them.

"It doesn't matter," said Oykib. "The only power the Index has is to enable you to talk to the Oversoul. Do you think the Oversoul is going to have anything to say to a man like *that?*" His voice was thick with scorn as he gestured at Elemak.

Elemak smiled, walked to Oykib, and then with one hand lifted him out of his chair and threw him up against the wall. It knocked the breath out of Oykib, and he slumped, holding his head where it had banged against the cabinets. "You may be tall," said Elemak, "and you may be full of proud words, but you've got nothing to back it up, boy. Did Nafai really think I'd ever be afraid of a 'man' like you?"

"You can tell him, Chveya," Oykib said, not answering Elemak at all. "He can beat up on children, but he can't control the Oversoul."

It seemed to be just a flick of Elemak's hand, but the result was Oykib's head striking the cabinets again with such force that he fell to the floor.

Chveya saw the great, bright strands of loyalty connecting Oykib to her. It had never been like this before. And she realized that he was undergoing this beating at Elemak's hands solely to convince her that he was not a traitor, that what he was saying was true. She could give the Index to Elemak.

But she couldn't bring herself to do it. Even if Oykib was right and the Index would be useless, Uncle Elemak didn't seem to think so. He wanted it. She might be able to get some leverage out of that.

However, she couldn't very well let Oykib take any more abuse if she could help it. "I'll tell you where it is," said Chveya.

Obring and Meb were poised at the ladderway in the center of the library.

"When you let me see that Father is all right," Chveya added.

"I've already told you that he's all right," said Elemak.

"You're also holding a baby to make sure you get your way," said Chveya. "That proves you're a decent person who would never tell a lie."

Elemak's face flushed. "We've grown up with a mouth, have we? Nafai's influence over these children is such a wonderful thing." As he spoke, though, he walked to where Mother sat silently with her other children. He handed Serp to her. "I don't threaten babies," said Elemak.

"You mean now that you already got Father to surrender to you," said Chveya.

"Where is the Index?" said Elemak.

"Where is my father?" asked Chveya.

"Safe."

"So is the Index."

Elemak strode to her, towered over her. "Are you trying to bargain with me, little girl?"

"Yes," said Chveya.

"As Oykib said, the Index is useless to me," said Elemak with a grin.

"Fine," said Chveya.

He leaned down, cupped his hand behind her head, whispered in her ear. "Veya, I will do whatever it takes to get my way."

As soon as he pulled away from her, she said loudly, "He said, 'Veya, I will do whatever it takes to get my way.' "

The others murmured. Perhaps at her audacity in repeating aloud what he had whispered to her. Perhaps at Elemak's threat. It didn't matter—the network of relationships was shifting. Elemak's hold on his friends was a little weaker. Fear and dread still bound all the others to him, of course; his mistreatment of Oykib had strengthened Elemak's control. But Chveya's boldness and his blustering against her had weakened the loyalty of those who were following him willingly.

He seemed to sense this—he had been a strong leader of men, taking caravans through dangerous country, and he knew when he was losing ground even if he didn't have Chveya's and Hushidh's gift of seeing ties of loyalty and obedience, love and fear. So he changed tactics. "Try all you like, Veya," he said, "but you can't make me the villain of this little scene. It was your father and those who conspired with him who betrayed the rest of us. It was your father who lied when he promised to waken us in mid-voyage. It was your father who cheated our children out of their birthright. Look at them." He waved his hand to indicate the four-year-olds, the five-year-olds, the eight-year-olds who were still trying to reconcile these tall adolescents with the children of their own age whom they remembered seeing only hours before, when they were put to sleep together before the launch. "Who is it who mistreated children? Who is it who exploited them? Not me."

Chveya could see that Elemak was winning sympathy again. "Then why is your wife still holding Spel?" asked Chveya.

Eiadh leapt to her feet and spat out her answer. "I don't hold babies prisoner, you nasty little brat! He was crying and I comforted him."

"Maybe his own mother might have done it better," said Chveya. "Maybe your husband doesn't *want* you to give Spel back to Mother."

Eiadh's immediate glance at Elemak and his irritated gesture proved Chveya's point for her. Eiadh sullenly carried Spel to Luet, who took him and sat him on her other knee. In all this time, however, Luet had said nothing. Why is Mother silent? Chveya wondered. Why have these adults left it to me and Oykib to do all the talking?

<Because they have children.>

The thought came into her mind with such clarity that she knew it came from the Oversoul. She also understood the Oversoul's meaning at once. Because the adults have little children, they're afraid of what Elemak might do to them. Only adolescents like Oykib and me are free to be brave, because we don't have any children to protect.

<Yes.>

So if you can talk to me, and it's all right for me to give the Index to Elemak, why not say so?

But there was no answer.

Chveya didn't understand what the Oversoul was doing. Why she was telling Oykib one thing while *not* confirming it to her, not telling her anything she needed to know. The Oversoul could pipe up and explain why the grownups weren't saying anything, but she didn't have any helpful advice about what Chveya should actually *do*.

Maybe that meant that what she was already doing was fine.

<Yes.>

"Take me to see Father," said Chveya. "When I see that he's unharmed, I'll give you the Index."

"The ship is not that large," said Elemak. "I can find it without you."

"You can try," said Chveya. "But the very fact that you're so reluctant to let me see my father proves that you've hurt him and you don't dare let these people know what a violent, terrible, evil person you are."

She thought then, for a few moments, that he might hit her. But that was just an expression that flickered in his eyes; his hands never moved; he didn't even lean toward her.

"You don't know me," said Elemak quietly. "You were just a child when we last met. It's quite possible that I'm exactly what you say. But if I were really that terrible, evil, and violent, why aren't you bruised and bleeding?"

"Because you won't make any points with your toadies if you slap a girl around," said Chveya coldly. "The way you treated Oykib shows what you are. The fact that you aren't treating me the same just proves that you're still not sure you're in control."

Chveya would never have dared to say these things, except that she could see with every word, with every sentence, that she was weakening Elemak's position. Of course, she was bright enough to know that this was dangerous, that as he became aware of his slackening control he might behave more rashly, more dangerously. But it was the only thing she could think of doing. It was the only way of asserting some kind of control over the situation.

"But of course I'm not in control," said Elemak calmly. "I never thought I was. Your father is the only one who wants to control people. I have to keep him restrained because if I don't, he'll use that cloak thing to brutalize people into doing what he wants. All I'm looking for is simple fairness. For instance, all of you overgrown children can go to sleep for the rest of the voyage while *our* children get a chance to catch up halfway, at least. Is that such a terrible, evil, violent thing for me to want?"

He was very, very good at this, Chveya realized. With just a few words, he could rebuild all that she had torn down. "Good," she said. "You're a sweet, reasonable, decent man. Therefore you'll let me and Oykib and Mother all go and see Father."

"Maybe. Once I have the Index."

For a moment Chveya thought that he had given in. That she had only to tell where the Index was, and he would let her see Father. But then Oykib interrupted.

"Are you going to believe this liar?" demanded Oykib. "He talks about Nafai brutalizing people with the cloak—but what he doesn't want anybody to remember is that he and Meb were planning to *murder* Nafai. That's what he is, a murderer. He even betrayed our father back in Basilica. He set Father up to be slaughtered by Gaballufix and if the Oversoul hadn't told Luet to warn him—"

Elemak silenced him with a blow, a vast buffet from his massive arm. In the low gravity, Oykib flew across the room and struck his head against a wall harder than ever before. Gravity might be lower, but as all the children of the school had learned, mass was undiminished, and so Oykib's full weight was behind the collision. He drifted unconscious to the floor.

Now the adults did not keep silence. Rasa screamed. Volemak leapt to his feet and shouted at Elemak. "You were always a murderer in your heart! You're no son of mine! I disinherit you! Anything you ever have now will be stolen!"

Elemak screamed back at him, his self-control momentarily gone. "You and your Oversoul, what are you! Nothing! A weak, broken worm of a man. I'm your *only* son, the only real man you ever begot, but you always preferred that lying little suck-up to me!"

Volemak answered quietly. "I never preferred him to you. I gave you everything. I trusted you with everything."

"You gave me nothing. You threw away the business, all our wealth, our position, everything. For a *computer*."

"And you betrayed me to Gaballufix. You are a traitor and a murderer in your heart, Elemak. You are not my son."

That did it, Chveya knew. In that moment, though fear remained, all loyalty to Elemak evaporated. People would still obey him, but none of them willingly. Even his own oldest son, eight-year-old Protchnu, was looking at his father with fear and horror.

Rasa and Shedemei were taking care of Oykib. "He's going to be all right, I think," said Shedemei. "There'll probably be a concussion and he may not wake up very soon, but there's nothing broken."

Silence held for a long time after her words. Oykib would be all right—but nobody could forget who had caused the injuries he did have. No one could forget the utter savagery of the blow, the rage that was behind it, the sight of Oykib flying through the air, helpless, broken. Elemak would be obeyed, that was certain. But he would not be loved or admired. He was not the leader of choice, not for anyone, not now. No one was on his side.

"Luet," said Elemak softly. "You come with me and Chveya. And Issib, too. I *want* you to witness that Nafai is all right. I also want you to witness that he is not going to be in command on this ship again."

As Chveya followed Elemak down the ladderway to one of the storage decks, she wondered: Why didn't he just take her to see Father when she first asked? It made no sense.

<He didn't take you, because you demanded it.>

How childish of him.

<No, it was prudent. If he was going to establish his authority, he had to assert total control from the start.>

Well, he's done *that*.

<On the contrary. Between you and Oykib, and Volemak at the end, you broke him. He's already lost. It might take him a while to know it, but he's lost.>

It gave her a glow of triumph as she followed Elemak to the storage room where Father was imprisoned.

The glow dissipated quickly, though, when she saw how they had treated him. Father lay on his side on the floor of a storage compartment. His wrists had been bound tightly—savagely—behind his back. She could see the skin bulging above and below the twine, and his hands were white. They had also tied his ankles together, just as tightly. Then they had pulled his legs up behind him, bowing him painfully backward, and had run two cords from his ankles up over his shoulders, twisting them before and after so they were held tight along his neck. Then they ran the cords down his stomach to his crotch and passed them between his legs to where they fastened them, behind his buttocks, to his bound wrists. The result was that the cords exerted constant pressure. The only way Father could relieve the pressure on his shoulders, at his groin, was to pull his legs even higher or bend himself backward even more. But since he was already pulled in that direction as tightly as they could force his body, there was no relief. His eyes were closed, but his red face and quick, shallow breaths told Chveya that he was in pain and that even breathing was hard for him in that impossible posture.

"Nafai," Mother murmured.

Nafai opened his eyes. "Hi," he said softly. "See how a little storm at sea can disrupt the voyage?"

"How cleverly you tied him," Issib said with venom in his voice. "What an inventive tormentor you are."

"Standard procedure on the road," said Elemak, "when a needed person is being stubborn about something. You can't kill him and you can't let him get away with his defiance. A couple of hours like this is usually enough. But Nyef has always been an exceptionally stubborn boy."

"Can you breathe, Nafai?" Mother asked.

"Can *you?*" asked Father.

Not until that moment had Chveya realized that the air *was* rather close and stuffy.

"What do you mean by that?" demanded Elemak.

Issib answered for him. "The life support system can't handle so many people awake all at once," he said. "It's straining already. We're going to get lower and lower on available oxygen as the hours go by."

"Not a problem," said Elemak. "We're putting all the sneaks and liars and their overgrown children back to sleep for the rest of the voyage."

"No you're not," whispered Father.

Elemak regarded him quietly. "I think when I have the Index, the ship's computer will do what I want."

Father didn't even answer.

"The Index, Chveya," said Elemak. "I kept my word."

"Untie him," said Chveya.

"He can't," said Issib. "Nafai has the cloak. It can't be taken from him. So if he ever lets him go, Nafai will be back in control in moments. No one could stand against him then."

So this was what holding the twins as hostage had accomplished. Father had willingly submitted to being tied like this, so that his little ones would be unharmed. For the first time, Chveya really understood how powerless parents were. Only people without children were really free to act on their own best judgment. Once you had little ones to care for, you could always be controlled by someone else.

"Can't you loosen the cord?" Chveya said. "You don't have to twist him up like that."

"No, I don't have to," said Elemak. "But I *want* to. After all, I'm evil and terrible and violent." He eyed her steadily. "The Index, Chveya, or your mother goes down on the floor beside him. It doesn't hurt him, not really, because the cloak heals him, but it won't heal *her*."

Chveya could feel how Mother stiffened beside her. "You won't," said Chveya.

"Won't I? Since you and Oykib and Father have already got everybody hating me, it won't make things any harder for me. And if I prove that I can treat a woman just as badly as a man, maybe I won't have to put up with any more interference from big-mouthed little bitches like you."

"Tell him," said Father. His voice sounded like defeat.

She had heard it from his own mouth. There was nothing more to accomplish by resisting. "I'll take you," said Chveya. "It's in the centrifuge. You'll have to wait until it spins down, though. You can't get it out while it's moving."

"Inside the works, then?" Elemak said. "All this bother—and I would have thought of it eventually anyway. All right, get out, all of you. I'm locking this door behind me, and I'll post a continuous watch here, so don't even imagine that you can sneak down here and untie him. You're lucky I haven't killed him already."

For a moment Chveya wondered: Why hasn't Elemak already killed him? He tried before, didn't he? It has to be the cloak. Father can't be killed, not that easily. Not while he's inside the ship, or even near it. Elemak probably can't even touch him, let alone do violence to him, not unless Father permits it. And if Elemak tried to kill him, it might not even require a voluntary response on Father's part to strike back. The cloak would probably lash out automatically. Or maybe the Oversoul controls it. But that's automatic, too, isn't it? Because the Oversoul is really just a computer.

<And you're really just an array of organic compounds.>

Chveya blushed. She let Elemak herd her and the others out of the room, remembering only at the last moment to call out, "Father, I love you!"

At first Elemak insisted on getting the Index out while the centrifuge was still moving, but when he saw for himself that the Index could not possibly be removed without running a serious risk of dropping it and breaking it under the wheels, he glumly waited while the machine ran down. Then, with it stopped, he sent Obring into the opening to get it. Chveya understood why. Elemak dared not get completely down into the opening, because he then couldn't be sure that someone wouldn't slam the door shut. He could get out soon enough, through one door or another—there were openings leading from the roadway out into the rest of the ship—but not before somebody could make it to Father and untie him. He couldn't trust anyone now. So it was Obring who went down through the maintenance hole, and Obring who handed up the cloth-wrapped Index to Elemak.

"I can't believe she got it in there while the thing was moving," Obring said.

Elemak didn't respond, but Chveya was defiantly proud of the compliment. She *had* done well. And even though Oykib, for whatever reason, had told Elemak almost at once who had hidden the Index, she had managed to weaken Elemak's position and visit her father as the price of telling where it was.

Now Elemak lifted off the cloth and held the Index in his hands.

Nothing happened.

He turned to Issib. "How does it work?" he demanded.

"Like that," said Issib. "Just what you're doing."

"But it's not doing anything."

"Of course it's not," said Issib. "The Oversoul controls it, and he's not speaking to you."

Elemak held it out to Issib. "You do it, then. Make it do what I tell you, or Hushidh ends up with Nafai on the storeroom floor."

"I'll try, but I don't think the Oversoul will be fooled just because I'm the one holding it. It's still not going to submit to you."

"Shut up and do it," said Elemak.

Issib sank lightly to the floor and received the Index as Elemak laid it in his lap. He put his hands on it. Nothing happened.

"You see?" said Issib.

"What usually happens?" asked Elemak. "Could it just be slow to respond?"

"It's never slow," said Issib. "It's just not going to work while the starmaster is not in control of the ship."

"Starmaster," said Elemak, as if the word were poison in his mouth.

"We're going to run lower and lower on oxygen," said Issib. "The ship can only break up carbon dioxide so fast, and we have too many people breathing."

"What you mean is that the Oversoul is trying to use the oxygen supply to force me to surrender."

"It's not the Oversoul," said Issib. "He doesn't control the life support systems, not directly, and he certainly couldn't override them in order to cause human beings harm. The machines have failsafe systems built in. It's just the way things are."

"Fine," said Elemak. "We'll just put to sleep all the people I don't want up. I might even let Nafai go to sleep for the rest of the voyage—though I think he might stay tied up like that during his nap."

"And come out crippled worse than me at the end?" asked Issib.

"That's a thought," said Elemak, clearly approving of the idea. "I never had any trouble with *you*."

"Doesn't matter what you plan," said Issib. "The Oversoul *can* stop you from starting up any of the suspended animation chambers. All it has to do is keep sending a danger signal to the computers that control them. You can't override that."

Elemak contemplated the idea for a while.

"Fine," he said. "I can wait."

"You think you can outwait the Oversoul?"

"I think the Oversoul doesn't want this voyage to fail," said Elemak. "I think he'll eventually realize that I'm *going* to lead the colony, and he'll make his accommodation."

<Not a chance.>

"Not a chance," Chveya echoed.

"Oh, really," said Elemak, turning to her. "Is the Oversoul talking to *you* now?"

Chveya said nothing.

<I can accomplish my primary mission even if every organism on this ship is dead.>

"The Oversoul can accomplish her main purpose even if everybody on the ship is dead," Chveya said.

"Or so it tells the people it deceives," said Elemak. "I guess we'll have an interesting few days, as we find out just how sincere the Oversoul is."

"The babies will die first," said Issib. "And the old people."

"If one of my babies dies from this," said Elemak, "then as far as I'm concerned everybody can die, myself included. Death would be better than another day being ruled over by that lying, sneaky, smart-mouthed, traitorous bastard that Father foisted on me as a brother." Elemak turned to Chveya and smiled. "Not to say anything bad about your father in front of you, little girl. But then, since you take after him so thoroughly, it probably sounded to you like praise."

Chveya's loathing overcame her fear of his anger. "I would be ashamed of him," said Chveya, "if a man like you didn't hate him."

Did Obring chuckle softly behind Elemak? Elemak whirled to see, but Obring was all innocence.

You've already lost, thought Chveya. The Oversoul was right. We've already beaten you. Now let's just hope that nobody dies before you finally realize it.

8

Unbound

Luet was angry, but not with Elemak. To her, Elemak had become almost a force of nature. Of course he hated Nafai. Of course he would seize on any excuse to hurt him. There was too much history between them now, too much old resentment, too much guilt at Elemak's earlier attempts to kill his brother. You didn't manage the situation by trying to change Elemak. You managed it by finding ways to avoid provoking him.

You did this, Luet said to the Oversoul. It was your idea. You pushed it. You maneuvered Nafai and me and the parents of the other children to play these little games with time.

<And I was right.>

You just didn't count on them waking up, is that it?

<I am still right. Everything will work out.>

My babies are having trouble breathing. They can hardly eat because swallowing takes so long they're gasping for another breath by the time it's done. We're dying, and you tell me everything will work out?

<We have days before anyone is in danger of dying.>

Well, that makes me feel so much better.

<I am not Elemak. I did not make Elemak do the things he did.>

You set it up. You put us in the situation.

<Did you think this day would never come? That if you did everything just right, Elemak would never turn on you? Better here, where I have some control over the situation, than on Earth, where you'll be entirely on your own.>

Oh, no, we won't be on our own on Earth. We'll have the Keeper of Earth to look out for us. And if she has half the love and care for us that you have, we'll all be dead within a year.

<The Keeper is much more powerful than I am.>

That's nice to hear.

<I understand your anger. Just don't let it cloud your judgment.>

No, we mustn't have clouded judgment, as we pant to get enough oxygen, as we watch our children getting sluggish and torpid, as we think of our husband twisted and bent, his hands and wrists garotted with cords. . . .

So went Luet's conversations with the Oversoul, hour after hour. She knew that when her rage was spent she would fall silent, would reconcile herself to the situation, would even, in the end, probably agree that things had worked out for the best. But they hadn't worked out yet. And if this was the best, it was hard to imagine what the worst—or even the next best—might have been. That's the one thing that could never be known: what *would* have happened. People spoke as if it could be known. "If only that alarm hadn't gone off." "If only Nafai had not had such a smart mouth as a boy"—that was Nafai's own favorite, Luet well knew, as he took the blame for everything on himself. But nothing is ever caused by just one thing, Luet knew, and removing or changing one cause does not always make the effect go away, or even make things better.

I will someday stop feeling this deep, unreasonable rage at the Oversoul, but not now, not with the sight of Nafai in such cruel bonds so fresh in my mind, so alive in my nightmares. Not with my children gasping after each swallow. Not with bloody-hearted Elemak in control of the people on this ship.

If only we had all withstood the Oversoul and not held school during the voyage.

In her heart she raged; ranted at the Oversoul; invented long, viciously cutting speeches that she knew she could never deliver to Elemak, to Mebbekew, to all who supported them. But to the others she showed a calm, impassive face. Confident, unafraid, not even annoyed, as far as she would let anyone else see. She knew that this more than anything else would unsettle Elemak and his followers. To see that she did not seem much worried would worry them; it was the most she could do, little as it was.

They. We. In her own mind, she had taken to thinking of Elemak's followers and their families as "the Elemaki"—the people of Elemak—and of those who had taken part in the voyage school as "the Nafari."

Normally such endings were used to refer to nations or tribes. But are we not tribes, here on this ship, however few in numbers we might be?

Elemak required the Nafari families to take their meals at the same time in the library, and then he or Meb would escort each family back to their cramped quarters and seal the door. While they were gone, Vas and Obring kept watch. Luet studied them, there in the library during meals. They did not seem really comfortable with their office, but whether that was because of shame or because they simply weren't confident in their ability to prevail in a physical confrontation she had no way of knowing.

Some of the Elemaki women made feeble attempts at conversation in the library during meals, but Luet did not show by facial expression or gesture, and certainly not by word, that she knew they existed. They went away angry, especially Kokor, Aunt Rasa's younger daughter, who snippily said, "You brought it all on yourself anyway, putting on airs because they used to call you Waterseer." Since this had nothing whatever to do with the conflict, it was clear that Kokor was merely revealing her own ancient resentment against Luet. It was hard not to laugh at her.

Luet's silence toward the Elemaki women was not motivated by pique. Luet knew perfectly well that they had had nothing to do with the men's decisions, that Meb's wife Dol and Elemak's wife Eiadh were deeply mortified at what their husbands were doing. She also knew, however, that if she ever let them assure her of their sympathy, if she ever let them cross over the invisible boundary between Elemaki and Nafari, it would make them feel *much* better. In fact, it might make them feel downright comfortable, even *noble* at having extended friendship to Nafai's beleaguered wife. Luet did not want them comfortable. She wanted them to be so uncomfortable, in fact, that they began to complain to their husbands, until at last the pressure built up so strongly that the others would begin to fear their wives' displeasure and contempt almost as much as they feared Elemak's, and Elemak himself would begin to believe that his actions were costing him more in his family than he was gaining in that twisted part of his psyche that held his hatred for Nafai.

Of course, there was always the chance that additional pressure from his wife would merely make Elemak more intransigent. But since snubbing the Elemaki women was the only thing Luet could do, she did it.

The only anomalous thing was the strange way Zdorab and Shedemei were treated. They were definitely being watched, escorted everywhere just like Luet, Hushidh and Issib, and Rasa and Volemak. But in the library, they were not under the same kind of scrutiny. They and their children were encouraged to sit with the Elemaki, and they were allowed to converse freely among themselves.

It led Luet to the inescapable conclusion that the alarm that opened all the suspended animation chambers had not been an accident, that somehow Zdorab had managed to leave not one but two wake-up calls, and the Oversoul had not found the second one. It was not possible that Shedemei had known about this; it was barely believable that Zdorab had known, for hadn't he joined with them in teaching the children? Hadn't he been part of the voyage school? Hadn't his son and daughter grown up along with the other children? What sort of twisted mind did he have, to allow him to accept freely the friendship of the Nafari, and yet know the whole time that his wakeup call would put Nafai's life in danger and split the whole community worse than ever? No, it was impossible to imagine. Zdorab couldn't have done it. No one could be so duplicitous, so. . . .

And yet there was Zdorab, sitting with his son, Rokya, next to him, and Meb's wife Dolya right across. Shedemei, on the other hand, sat apart from the others. Her shame was almost palpable. She kept her daughter Dabya with her, and spoke only when spoken to. She did not look at anyone, keeping her eyes to her plate while eating, and then leaving the room as quickly as possible. Luet longed to ask Chveya or Hushidh to assess the relationships, to find out where Zdorab's loyalty lay. But she was forbidden to talk to Hushidh, and Chveya, too, was kept isolated from everyone else. Oykib was also isolated from the other children; the two of them had certainly attracted special attention from Elemak.

In the evening of the second day Luet opened the door of her family's room to find that it was Zdorab knocking. The twins were asleep, breathing rapidly but regularly. The older children—Zhatva, Motiga, and Izuchaya—were not asleep, but they lay on their beds, resting so as to avoid using more oxygen; all of them had been ordered to do this whenever possible, and since they could feel how depleted the oxygen already was, this was one command of Elemak's that all obeyed readily.

Luet regarded Zdorab wordlessly, waiting for him to speak.

"I have to talk to you."

She debated closing the door in his face. But that would be to judge him without having heard what he had to say. She stepped back and let him inside. Then she leaned out into the corridor and saw that Vas and Obring were both watching. This was not a clandestine visit, then. Unless those two stout hearts actually had the courage to conspire against Elemak's express orders.

She closed the door.

"It was me," said Zdorab. "I know you know it, but I had to tell you myself. Elemak told me that I should say that I couldn't have removed my wake-up program even if I wanted to, but I could have. And I did want to. Right at the end, as I was being put to sleep, I tried to shout for Shedya and Nyef to stop, to open my chamber, to. . . ."

He could see that his words were having no effect on her. He looked away toward the door. "I couldn't foresee how things would work out. I just—I thought that Elemak would see it was an accomplished fact. That maybe he'd work out a way to have the other children get the last three years of schooling. Something like that. Your children would have had six and a half years, his would have three and a half. I didn't—the violence, Nafai tied up like that, and now the life support—running out of air—can't you get the Oversoul to relent and let half of us go back to sleep?"

So that was what this was about. Elemak and the others were using Zdorab to try to talk her into saving them from the consequences of their own actions.

"You can tell Elemak that when Nafai is untied and put back in control of the ship, he and his people will be free to go back into their suspended animation chamber at any time. Or should I be saying you and *your* people?"

To her surprise, tears almost leapt from Zdorab's eyes. "I don't have a *people,*" he said. "I may not even have a wife. Or a son or a daughter."

So Shedemei hadn't known. Not that that was a surprise.

"I don't expect you to feel sorry for me," he said, wiping his eyes and getting back in control of himself. "I just want you to understand that if I had known—"

"If you had known what? That Elemak hated Nafai? That he wanted him dead? How did you miss that little bit of information, considering that we all saw Nafai covered with blood from Elemak's last little plot?"

Anger flashed in Zdorab's eyes. "It wasn't Elemak with the little plot this time."

"No, it was the Oversoul," said Luet. "*And* you. In fact, you managed to take part in conspiracies on both sides." Then it dawned on her. "Oh, that was the point, wasn't it?"

"I'm an outsider here," he said. "Shedya and I aren't kin to anybody."

"Shedya is one of Aunt Rasya's nieces."

"That's not a blood relationship, that's—"

"It's closer."

"But not *me.* My son, my daughter, they're going to be caught up in this family quarrel between Nafai and Elemak no matter what I do. I'm not like Volemak or his sons, I'm not physically strong, I'm not—I'm not much of a *man* the way men are judged. So how could I protect *my* children? I thought that if I could have a good relationship with both Nafai and Elemak—"

"That is not possible," said Luet. "Especially now, thanks to you."

"I did what I thought was best for my children. I was wrong. Now neither side trusts me, and my children will pay for that, too. I was *wrong,* and I'm not trying to conceal what I did or how bad it was. But I wasn't trying to betray you or Nafai. I was doing what I thought was best for my children."

"Very good," said Luet coldly. "You have unburdened yourself. I've heard you and if I'm ever allowed to speak to anyone but my children again, I'll be sure to tell everyone that you were motivated entirely by altruistic concern for your children."

"Mebbekew says you're a cold one," said Zdorab.

"And we know what a fine observer of human beings Meb can be."

"But he's wrong," said Zdorab. "You're not cold, you're on fire."

"Thank you for that insight into elemental metaphors for my character."

"Just remember, Luet. I did you wrong. I know that, and I'm in your debt, deeply and forever. I'm not a dishonorable man by nature. I acted as men like me have always had to act—for survival, as best I understood it. There'll come some future time when, no matter how much you despise me, you'll need my help. I'm here to tell you that when that time comes, and when you or Nafai ask me, I'll do whatever you need."

"Good. Tell Elemak to untie my husband."

"Whatever you need that's within my power. I've already asked him to untie your husband. Kokor and Sevet have demanded it. Your oldest daughter spit in his face and called him a eunuch who had to imprison his betters in order to feel like a real man."

Luet gasped. "Did he hit her?"

"Yes," said Zdorab. "But she's all right. Everybody was disgusted at him for it, and he hasn't gone near her since. For what it's worth, I think it turned even his own wife against him, to see him hit Chveya like that."

No doubt that was Chveya's purpose. "That's always been Elya's problem," said Luet. "He has always attempted to answer words with actions. It might silence the speaker, but it only confirms the truth of what was said."

"Even you, with your unbending silence—that's half what the women talk about," said Zdorab. "And Shedya has joined in your boycott of conversation. Everybody wants Elemak to stop. I thought you'd want to know that. What you're doing, what Chveya and Oykib have done, even Nafai's quiet endurance—it's all a kind of resistance, stubborn and brave, and it makes everyone who's on Elemak's side so . . . so ashamed."

Luet nodded gravely. She needed to hear that. The fact that he came and told her didn't make them friends.

"I've seen real courage these last two days," said Zdorab. "I've never had it myself, not the kind of courage that stands out in the open, even when you're powerless, and dares the strong one to do his worst. Chveya. Oykib. My life might have been different if I'd ever acted like that." Then he laughed bitterly. "Yes, I'd probably be dead."

It occurred to Luet that she actually knew almost nothing about Zdorab, about his upbringing. He spoke as if he had lived his whole life friendless and in fear. Why?

In spite of herself, she had to admit that things might look very different from where he stood. For her, there was no choice—she had to do everything she could to help Nafai and the Oversoul prevail against Elemak, because if they did not win, there would be nothing left for her. But Zdorab could conceive of a future in which Elemak had won, and if that happened—and it certainly could happen—it wasn't morally unspeakable for him to try to prepare a place for himself and his children in Elemak's camp.

The trouble was that he might easily end up without a place on either side. Which is where things were headed right now.

She did not let herself sound so cold when she spoke again. "Zdorab, what you've said hasn't fallen on deaf ears. If you're worried about the future, I can tell you this with complete confidence. None of us will retaliate against you and certainly not against your children. They haven't lost their place with us, if that's where they want to be."

"Elemak is going to lose this one," said Zdorab. "It's only a matter of how many will die before he breaks."

"None, I hope," said Luet.

"I'm just saying that pure self-interest could have brought me here. You have no reason to trust me. I deceived you all. You thought I was one of you, and I betrayed you. You can never forget that. *I* certainly never will. But this you can count on: If you or Nafai ever need me again, I'll be there. No matter what. Even if I die trying to help you."

Luet barely suppressed a scornful, mocking answer.

"It's not for me," Zdorab said. "Or even really for you. I just . . . it's the only way I can ever redeem myself in the eyes of my children. Everyone will know what I did, sooner or later. That's why I didn't bother trying to conceal this conversation from your children, the ones lying there awake with their eyes closed. My children will be ashamed of me, even if no one taunts them for it. Somehow, someday, I'm going to redeem myself in their eyes. That's what survival means, for me. I thought it was a matter of staying alive, but it isn't. Nobody lives forever anyway. It's how you're remembered. It's what your children thought of you, what they think of you after you're dead. That's survival." He looked Luet steadily in the eye. "And if there's one thing that can truly be said about me, it's this: I survive."

He got up from the edge of the bed where he had been sitting. Luet palmed the door open and he left.

In the silence after the door closed, Zhatva spoke softly. "I'm glad I'm not in *his* shoes."

Luet answered wryly, "Don't be so sure. Our own shoes aren't all that comfortable right now."

"I wish I'd been as brave as Veya," said Zhatva.

"No no, Zhyat, don't think that way. She was in a position where being brave could accomplish something. You weren't. When the time ever comes when you need courage, you'll have it. Enough of it. All you need." To herself she added silently: May that day when you need courage never come. Even as she said it, though, she knew that the day *would* come. She shuddered.

Oh, Nafai, she said silently. If only you could hear me as the Oversoul hears me. If only you knew how much I love you, how much I ache thinking of what you're going through. And all I can do for you is take care of the children as best I can and trust in the Oversoul and in the workings of human nature to work some miracle and set you free. What I *can* do, I'm doing, but it's not enough. If you die, what life will there be for me? Even if the children are all safe, even if they live to be good, strong, wonderful adults, it won't be enough, not if I've lost you. The Oversoul might have brought us together as pawns in her game, but that doesn't mean that the bond between us is any weaker. It's strong, far more powerful than the cords they've tied you with, but without you beside me I feel as if I'm the one who's tied, trussed up inside my soul and unable to move, unable to breathe. Nafai.

His name rang through her mind. The image of his face seared her. She lay down on the bed, willing herself to relax, commanding herself to sleep. The less oxygen I breathe, the more he will have, the more the children will have. I must sleep. I must be calm.

But she was not calm, and even when she finally slipped into a fitful sleep, her heart raced and she breathed quickly, short sharp breaths, as if she were engaged in battle, the enemy jabbing at her as she barely dodged each new thrust.

* * *

The first meal of the third day, Elemak was out of the room. Where he was, no one dared to ask. Nor did anyone mind. When he was gone, wariness remained; real fear only returned when he did. This was not because anyone trusted to the good will of Meb, Obring, and Vas—Meb seemed to delight in tiny cruelties, and Obring, to all appearances, enjoyed his status as one of those who shared in authority. Everyone knew, though, that either of them would gladly betray Elemak in a moment, if they thought it would benefit them. Vas, on the other hand, seemed to detest what he was doing; nevertheless, he did it, and was the one Elemak relied on most. Elemak could give him a task and expect that it would be carried out resourcefully and well, even when Elemak was not there watching—something that could not be said of the other two Elemaki men.

On this day, however, with Elemak gone, there came the first open challenge to his authority. Volemak, after a glance at Rasa, rose to his feet and began to address the group.

"My friends and family," he began.

"Sit down and shut up," said Mebbekew.

Volemak fixed a gaze of snakelike calmness on his second son and said, "If you care to silence me, feel free to attempt it. But in the absence of physical force, I will have my say."

Meb took one step toward his father. Immediately, though they had not been prompted in any way, Volemak's youngest son Yasai, Issib's eldest boy Zaxodh, and Nafai's eldest, Zhatva, all rose to their feet. They were nowhere near Volemak, but the threat was clear.

Meb laughed. "Do you think I'm afraid of you children?"

"You might want to be careful," Rasa said. "They've been living in low gravity for six years, while you still seem a little uncertain on your feet."

"Come on, Obring," said Meb.

Obring took a step toward Volemak. Now Nafai's second son, Motiga, stood up, as did Zdorab's son Padarok. A moment later, Zdorab himself rose to his feet.

"Vas," said Meb, "you can pretend not to care, but this looks like a revolt to me."

Vas nodded. "Obring, go get Elemak."

"We can handle it ourselves!" Meb snapped.

"I can see. We're doing so well already."

Obring looked from Vas to Mebbekew, then turned and left the library.

"As I was saying," said Volemak, "this entire dispute is misplaced. It was I whom the Oversoul summoned into the desert, and I was the one who led this expedition at all times. It's true that in the desert I delegated the day-to-day authority to Elemak, but this was never more than a temporary arrangement in recognition of his skill and experience. Likewise, during the voyage I have delegated command of the ship itself to Nafai, because he is the one to whom the Oversoul gave the cloak of the starmaster. The fact remains that I am the only lawful leader of this group, and when we arrive on Earth, I shall not delegate that authority to anyone else. Neither Elemak nor Nafai will be in command as long as I am alive."

"And how long is that, old man?" asked Meb.

"Longer than you wish, you contemptible slug," said Volemak mildly. "It is obvious that Elemak is out of control. Through threat of force and the cooperation of three weak-willed bullies"—he looked Vas in the eye—"and because Nafai has submitted to captivity in order to save the lives of his babies, Elemak's mutiny at present seems to be prevailing. However, we are all aware that at some point Elemak will inevitably have to submit to reality—the ship cannot sustain us all awake, and the Oversoul will not permit him to put anyone into suspended animation while Nafai remains bound. So what I ask of you now is your solemn oath, every one of you, to submit to my authority and no one else's, after this crisis has passed. While I live there will be no choosing between Nafai and Elemak, but only obedience to me, in accord with your solemn covenant. I invite all of you, men and women, to take this oath. All who vow to submit only to my authority after this crisis, rise to your feet and say yes."

Immediately all the men who were standing, except Vas and Mebbekew, said a resounding yes. Rasa, Hushidh, Luet, and Shedemei also rose at once, joined by the young women who had taken part in the school; their higher voices echoed those of the men. Issib rose slowly and said yes.

"I assume," said Volemak, "that if Oykib and Chveya were not being kept in isolation they would also join in this oath, and so I also count them among the lawful citizens of my community. When Nafai is released, I will also ask him to submit to this oath. Is there anyone here who doubts that he will affirm it? And that he will keep that oath, having taken it?"

No one spoke.

"Remember, please, that I am asking you to accept my authority *after* the present crisis has passed. I am not asking you to jeopardize yourselves by entering into resistance to Elemak at this time. But if you do not take this oath at this time, you are not citizens of the colony I will establish on Earth. You may, of course, apply for citizenship at a later time, and then I will take a vote of the citizens to see whether or not you will be admitted. If you take the oath now, however, you will be a citizen from the beginning."

To everyone's surprise, Vas spoke up. "I will take this oath," he said. "When the crisis has passed, your authority is the only authority I will accept as long as you are alive. And I will do all I can to prolong your life as long as possible."

With Vas having spoken, his wife Sevet rose to her feet, along with her three young children. She said, "I take the oath," and her children echoed her.

Those who remained seated obviously were feeling beleaguered indeed.

"Elemak won't be happy with you," said Meb to Vas.

"Elemak isn't happy these days anyway," said Vas. "All I want is peace and justice."

"My father was part of Nafai's little plot, too, you know," said Meb. "He's hardly unbiased."

"I know that some of you are unhappy about the children who were kept awake to be schooled during the voyage," said Volemak. "Unfortunately, Elemak has never permitted us to explain. Every one of us whose children were included in the school were urged by the Oversoul to do so. Nafai was very reluctant to do it. We pressed him until he agreed. These children were chosen by the Oversoul, and they and we freely chose to go along. The result is not an unhappy one. Instead of having only a handful of adults and many unproductive children, we have divided the younger generation, so that we will now have a continuous population of young people coming into adulthood for many generations to come. Whatever disadvantage you think you perceive at this time will disappear when you realize that you will have more years of life on Earth than those who stayed awake during the voyage."

Dol rose to her feet, causing her children to stand, also.

"Sit down, you disloyal bitch!" screamed Mebbekew.

"My children and I will be citizens of your colony," said Dol. "We all affirm the oath."

Mebbekew rushed toward her. Vas stepped between him and his wife, putting out a hand to restrain him. "This isn't a good time for violence," said Vas. "She's a free citizen, I think, and has the right to speak her mind."

Mebbekew flung Vas's hand away from his chest. "None of this will mean *anything* after Elemak comes back!"

Only a meter away from him, Eiadh rose to her feet. Immediately her oldest son, Protchnu, plucked at her sleeve to pull her back down. "After the crisis, I will submit to your authority, Volemak," she said.

Protchnu turned to the other children and shouted at them, "Don't you dare take the oath!" The children were obviously frightened of his rage.

"I recognize that your younger children are being intimidated into not taking the oath," said Volemak. "So they will be given a chance to take it freely at a later time."

"They'll never take it!" shouted Protchnu. "Am I the only one here who is loyal to my father? He's the only one who should lead us!"

Kokor stood up, her children with her. "We'll be citizens too," she said. "After the crisis."

"You will if you take the oath," said Volemak.

"Well, that's what I meant, of course," she said. "I take the oath."

Her children nodded or murmured their assent.

From the doorway, Elemak spoke softly. "Very well," he said. "Everyone has made their choice. Now sit down."

Immediately, Kokor sat down and urged her children to join her. Gradually the others also sat, except for Volemak, Rasa, and Eiadh, who turned to face her husband. "It's over, Elya," she said. "You're the only one who doesn't see that you can't possibly win."

"What I see," said Elemak, "is that I won't permit Nafai to rule over me or anyone else."

"Even if that means that your own children suffocate?"

"If Nafai's pet computer chooses to kill the weakest of us, I can't stop it. But it won't be me killing anyone."

"In other words, you don't care," said Eiadh. "As far as I'm concerned, that's the final proof that you aren't fit to rule this colony. You care about your pride more than the survival of our babies."

"That's enough from you," said Elemak.

"No," said Eiadh, "that's too much from you. Until you stop this childish display of masculine temper, you are not my husband."

"Oh, not renewing me, are you?" asked Elemak with a nasty smile. "What do you think of *that,* Proya?"

His eldest son, Protchnu, walked to his father. "I think that I have no mother," he said.

"How appropriate," said Elemak, "since I have no father and no wife. Have I also no friend?"

"I'm your friend," said Obring.

"I stand with you," said Meb. "But Vas here took the oath."

"Vas will take whatever oath you ask," said Elemak. "But his word has always been worthless. Everybody knows that."

Sevet laughed. "Look at your friends, you poor man," she said. "One deluded eight-year-old boy. And then what? Meb! Obring! They were both worthless back in Basilica."

"You didn't say that when you invited me into your bed!" Obring shouted at her.

"That had nothing to do with you," said Sevet contemptuously. "That was between me and my sister, and believe me, I have paid deeply for that mistake. Vas knows that since then I have been faithful to him, both in my heart and in my actions."

The children old enough to understand what was being revealed here would have plenty of family scandal to talk about later. Obring and Sevet had an affair? And how did Sevet pay for it? And what did she meant that it was between her and Kokor?

"Enough," said Elemak. "The old man has made his little play, but you'll notice he didn't have the courage to ask you to stand against me now. It was only in some imagined future that he rules over you. He knows, as you all know, that I rule over you now, and believe me, you will never see a future in which I do not." He turned to Obring. "Stay here and keep everyone in the library."

Obring grinned at Vas. "I guess you aren't going to be giving me orders anymore."

"Vas is still a guard," said Elemak. "I don't trust him, but he'll do what he's told. And now he'll do what *you* tell him, Obring. Right, Vas?"

"Yes," said Vas quietly. "I'll do what I'm told. But I'll also keep all my oaths."

"Yes yes, a man of honor and all that," said Elemak. "Now, Meb, let's take Father and his wife to visit Nafai. And while we're at it, let's bring along the woman who claims she is no longer my wife."

"What are you going to do?" asked Rasa contemptuously. "Tie us up the way you've tied Nafai?"

"Of course not," said Elemak. "I have respect for old people. But for every person who took that little oath of yours, Father, Nafai will take a blow. And you will watch."

Volemak glared at Elemak. "I wish that before I fathered you, I had been castrated or killed."

"What a sad thought," said Elemak. "Then you would never have fathered your precious Nafai. Though, come to think of it, I wonder if there was a man's seed involved in conceiving him. He is so completely his mother's little girl."

A moment later, Elemak and Mebbekew manhandled Volemak and Eiadh down the ladderway and through the corridor to the storage room where Nafai lay. Rasa followed helplessly behind.

* * *

Nafai was not really asleep, not ever during the past few days. Or if he did sleep, it felt as though he was awake, so vivid were the dreams. Sometimes they were his worst fears, dreams of the twins gasping for air until finally they stopped breathing altogether, their eyes open, their mouths agape, and in the dream he tried to close their eyes and close their mouths, but they kept flying open again as soon as he took away his hand. He woke gasping for breath himself from these dreams.

Sometimes, though, the dreams were of other times, better times. He remembered getting up in the morning at his father's house and running out under the shower and turning on the cold water. At the time he had hated it, but now he remembered it with fondness. An innocent time, when the worst thing that could happen to you was a shock of icy water on your head and back, when the worst thing you could do to someone else was smart off at them until they got angry enough to stop laughing and start pushing you around. Only now they never laughed at all, they never forgave at all, and the cold water was nothing, would be a pleasure if it could ever come again. How could I have known in those days, he wondered upon waking from such memory dreams, how could I have known that Elemak's annoyance would turn to such hatred? That such evil days would come upon us? I made smartmouth jokes because I wanted his attention, that was all. He was like a god, so strong, and Father loved him so much. All I wanted was for him to notice me, to tell me that he liked me, that he thought I might someday ride with him on a caravan to some faraway land and come home with exotic plants for Father to sell. All I wanted was for him to respect me and put his arm around my shoulder and say, This is my brother, look at my brother, I can count on him, he's my right-hand man.

Who else could have been your brother, Elemak? Meb? He's the one you chose? Was I so despicable to you, that you chose him over me?

<He chose Meb because he could rule Meb. He hated you because you were stronger than him.>

Yes, with the cloak of the starmaster I'm stronger.

<You know you can strike him down at any time.>

No I can't. The cloak can. *You* can. But I can't. I'm tied up here and my wrists and ankles hurt.

<It's your choice not to heal them. You know the cloak can do it in a moment.>

He wants me in pain. If he sees my skin chafed and bleeding, maybe that will satisfy him.

<He will only be satisfied with your death.>

So be it.

<I will not let you die. As soon as you're unconscious, the cloak is mine to control again, and I will heal you.>

Stay away from me in my sleep. I want none of your dreams now, and certainly none of your meddling.

<Do you like the pain?>

I hate the pain of having my brother hate me. And knowing that this time maybe I deserve it.

<You never deserve to suffer for helping me.>

Oh, and here I thought *you* were helping *me* by having us keep those children awake.

<I was helping you so you could help me. Don't pretend to be stupid or play those childish argument games with me.>

Are you really talking to me? Or am I dreaming this, too?

<Yes. And yes.>

So if this is a dream, why can't I wake up from it?

As soon as he said this in his mind, Nafai awoke. Or rather he dreamed that he awoke, for he knew at once that he was still asleep, perhaps more deeply than before. And in his sleep, thinking he was awake, he felt the cords melt away from his hands and he rose to his feet. The door opened at his touch. He walked through the corridors and here and there he saw people lying there, mouths open, panting, none of them noticing him as if he were invisible. Ah, he thought. I understand now. I'm dead, and this is my spirit walking the corridor. But then in his dream he realized that his wrists and ankles hurt and he was having trouble walking straight, even in the low gravity, so he wasn't dead after all.

He got to the ladder and climbed up, higher and higher, to the highest level of the starship, where the shielding field was generated. But now the ladder didn't stop. It went up, and the next opening was not onto the smooth plastic floor of the starship, it now opened onto a stone floor. He stepped out onto the floor, and felt his body weigh heavily, his steps painful because gravity was normal again. It was dark, a cave. He heard footsteps here and there, but none of them came near; nor did they go very far away. Just a scurry of steps, and he walked a little, and then another scurry of steps. That's all right, he thought. Follow me, I'm not afraid of you, I know you're there but I also know you won't harm me.

He came to a corridor and saw a light burning in a small side chamber of the cave. He walked there, entered the room, and saw dozens of statues, beautifully carved of clay, perched on every shelf of rock and all over the floor. But as he looked more closely, he saw that all the statues were marred, smoothed here and there, the detail lost. Who would deface such marvelous work? Deface it, and yet keep it here as if it were a secret treasure trove?

Then at last he noticed a statue high up and far back from the light, a statue larger than the others, and unmarred. It wasn't the perfection of the detail work that made him stare, however. It was the face itself. For unlike the others, which were all either animals or gargoyles, this was a head of a human. And he knew the face. He should. He had seen it in every mirror since he became a man.

Now the footsteps came closer, not scurrying, but slowly, respectfully. He felt a small hand touch him on the thigh. He did not look; he did not need to. He knew who it was.

Except that it was only in the dream that he knew. In fact he had no idea who it might be, and he tried to make his dream self turn, look down, see who or what had touched his hand. But he could not make his own head turn; he could not make himself bend over. In fact, he was bending backward, and his neck was caught between two cords, and there were footsteps, loud ones now, not quick scurrying steps, and a light went on, dazzling him.

He blinked open his eyes. Really awake now, not just dreaming that he was awake.

"Time for my walk?" he asked.

A quick whistling sound, and then a sharp pain in his arm. Against his will he cried out.

"That's one," said the voice of Elemak. "Tell me, Rasa, what's your count? How many took the oath?"

"Do your own foul business," said Mother's voice.

"Could it be hundreds?" asked Elemak. Again the whistling sound. Again the excruciating pain, this time in the ribs of his back. One of them broke; he felt the bone stabbing him as he breathed. And yet he couldn't stop breathing, he had to gasp, because he wasn't getting enough oxygen anymore, he couldn't breathe deeply enough to get the air to stay conscious.

<Heal yourself.>

"I don't count any of these against the total, until you tell me what the total might be," said Elemak.

"Count it yourself," said Rasa. "It was everybody except Protchnu, Obring, and Mebbekew. *Everybody*, Elemak. Think about *that*."

"He's not healing himself," said Luet.

Nafai heard her voice and felt a surge of anger against Elemak. Did he think she was so weak that her spirit would break because she saw her husband enduring pain? What was Elemak trying to gain, anyway? It was the Oversoul he had to persuade—or surrender to. Something had happened, though. An oath.

"I've noticed that," said Elemak. "His wrists don't seem to get better, or his ankles. I can't figure out if that's because the cloak just isn't working right now, or because he's deliberately not healing himself in order to look more pitiful so I'll feel sorry for him and loosen his bonds so he can get free and kill me."

The whistling sound. Another blow, this time on the back of his neck. Nafai gasped at the pain that shot up and down his spine; for a few moments he was numb from the neck down, and he thought, He's broken my neck.

<A stunning blow, that's all. Some neural damage.>

Why doesn't he just kill me?

<Because I still have some influence over him. Enough to distract him whenever his thoughts turn to finishing you off.>

Well, stop it. Let him kill me. Then he'll have his victory and there'll be peace and everybody will be better off.

<Elemak doesn't know it, but killing you is the worst thing he could ever do. Because then he'd never be able to defeat you.>

What, dead isn't defeated?

<What he wants is for his father to say, You, Elemak. I choose you. And if you're dead, Nafai, Volemak can never choose him over you. He'll always be second choice then.>

Then if you have any decency, tell Volemak to say the magic words and end all this.

<There's the rub, Nafai. Elemak wouldn't believe it even if Volemak said it. Because he knows that it isn't true. He knows that he's not as good or decent or wise or strong a man as you, so that even if his father said, Elemak, I choose you, it would be a lie, because he knows Volemak is not such a fool as to value him above you.>

I'm too tired to make sense of this. Go away and let me die.

<He just caused you very serious damage with that last blow.>

The one on my neck?

<That was three blows ago. You're bleeding internally now.>

Oh, yes. I can feel that.

<I'm going to heal you.>

Don't do it.

<Before the blood loss causes internal damage.>

Don't heal me until he leaves the room. Give me that much dignity.

<Dignity? Would you die for dignity?>

It's between him and me. I don't want him to see how you intervene for me.

<Your pride is unbelievable. It's between him and *you?* It's between him and *me,* and it always has been. Just as it was between Moozh and me. Just as it's between *you* and me. And between Luet and me. And when we get to Earth, it will be between all of you and the Keeper.>

This really hurts.

<I'm healing you, that's why.>

I said not to.

<Too bad.>

"Look," said Elemak. "His leg is straightening out. I guess we found out how much pain he could take, and now he's got his invisible friend to save him."

"I'm looking," said Volemak coldly. "What I see is a coward, striking a bound man with a metal rod."

Elemak's voice rose to a scream. "*I'm* the coward? I'm not the one with the cloak! I'm not the one who can get magically healed whenever I stub my toe! I'm not the one with the power to give people jolts of electricity whenever I want to bring them to heel!"

"It's not the power you have that makes you a coward or a bully," said Volemak. "It's how you use it. Do you think that being bound like that keeps the cloak from having the same power it's always had? As badly as you're treating him, as badly as you're treating all of us, Nafai still chooses not to strike you dead where you stand."

"Do it then, Nyef," said Elemak softly. "If you have the power to strike me dead, do it. You've killed before. A drunk lying unconscious in the street, I think it was. My older half-brother, I think it was. That's your specialty, killing people who can't fight back. But Father thinks *I'm* the bully. How can it be bullying, to break the bones of a man who can heal himself in moments? Look, I can break your skull and—"

There was a scream of rage from a woman and the sound of scuffling. Then someone was slammed into a wall; a woman cried. Nafai tried to open his eyes. All he could see was the wall his face was pressed against. "Luet," he whispered.

"Luet can't heal herself, can she?" said Elemak. "She should remember that before she tries to fight with me."

"All you're doing," said Nafai, "is using up the oxygen that your children need to breathe."

"You can end it at any time, Nyef," said Elemak. "All you have to do is die."

"And then what?" asked Volemak. "You'll just start hating the next best man, and for the same reason. Because he's better than you. And when you kill him, you'll find still another better than you. It will go on and on forever, Elemak, because each act of bullying cruelty you commit makes you smaller and smaller until finally you'll have to kill every human being and every animal and even then you'll look at yourself with such contempt that you won't be able to bear it—"

The rod smashed down right in Nafai's face. He felt it cave in all the bones of the front of his head, and then everything went black.

A moment later? It could have been; it could have been hours or days. He was conscious again, and his face was not broken. Nafai wondered if he was alone. Wondered what had happened to Father and Mother. To Luet. To Elemak.

Someone was in the room. Someone was breathing.

"All better," said the voice. A whisper. Hard to identify. No, not hard. Elemak. "The Oversoul wins again."

Then the lights went out again and the door closed and he was alone.

Eiadh was singing softly to the little ones, Yista and Menya and Zhivya, when Protchnu came to her. She heard him come into the room, the door sliding open and then sliding closed again behind him. She did not stop singing.

When the light returns again
Will I remember how to see?
Will I recognize my mother's face?
Will she know me?

When the light returns again
Then nothing will I fear;
So I close my eyes and dream of day
In darkness here.

"Singing is a waste of oxygen," said Protchnu softly.

"So is crying," Eiadh answered quietly. "Three children are not crying now because one person sang. If you came to stop my singing, go away. Report my crime to your father. Maybe he'll get angry enough to beat me. Maybe he'll let you help."

Still she didn't turn to look at him. She heard him breathing a little more heavily. Raggedly, perhaps. But she was surprised that when he spoke again, his voice was high with barely contained weeping. "It's not my fault you turned against Father."

She had been so stung by his repudiation of her in the library that she hadn't spoken to him since, and had avoided thinking of him. Protchnu, her eldest, saying such terrible things to his own mother. The boy had looked so savage at that moment, so much like Elemak, that she had felt as though she didn't know him. But she did know him, didn't she? He was only eight years old. It was wrong for him to have been torn between quarreling parents like this.

"I didn't turn against your father," she said softly. "I turned against what he's doing."

"Nafai cheated us."

"The Oversoul did. And all the parents of those children did. Not just Nafai."

Protchnu was silent. She thought maybe she had carried the point with him. But no, he was thinking of something else. "Do you love him?"

"I love your father, yes. But when he lets anger rule him, he does bad things. I reject those bad things."

"I didn't mean Father."

It was plain that he expected her to know already. That he had the idea somehow that she loved another man.

And, of course, she did. But it was a hopeless love and one that she had never, never shown to anyone.

"Whom did you mean, then?"

"Him."

"Say the name, Proya. Names aren't magic. It won't poison you to put the name on your lips."

"Nafai."

"Uncle Nafai," she corrected. "Have respect for your elders."

"You love him."

"I would hope that I have a decent love for all my brothers-in-law, as I hope you will also love all your uncles. It would be nice if your father had a decent love for all his brothers. But perhaps you don't see it that way. Look at Menya, lying there asleep. He is the fourth son in our family. He stands in relation to you as Nafai stands to your father. Tell me, Proya, are you planning someday to tie up little Menya and break his bones with a rod?"

Protchnu started to cry in earnest now. Relenting, Eiadh sat up and reached out for him, gathered him into her arms, pulling him down to sit beside her on the bed. "I'll never hurt Menya," he said. "I'll protect him and keep him safe."

"I know you will, Proya, I know it. And it's not the same thing between your father and Nafai. The difference in their ages is much greater. Nafai and Elya didn't have the same mother. And Elemak had a brother even older."

Protchnu's eyes opened wide. "I thought Father was the oldest."

"He's the oldest son of your grandfather Volemak, back in the days when he was the Wetchik, in the land of Basilica. But Elemak's mother had other sons before she married Volemak. And the oldest of those was named Gaballufix."

"Does Father hate Uncle Nafai because he killed his brother Gaballufix?"

"They hated each other before that. And Gaballufix was trying to kill Nafai and your father and Issib and Meb."

"Why would he want to kill Issib?"

Eiadh noted with amusement that Protchnu didn't wonder why someone would want to kill his uncle Meb. "He wanted to rule Basilica, and the sons of the Wetchik stood in his way. Your grandfather was a very rich and powerful man, back in the land of Basilica."

"What does 'rich' mean?"

What have I done to you, my poor child, that you don't even know what the word means? All wealth and grace have gone from life, and since you have seen nothing but poverty, even the words for the beautiful life are lost to you. "It means that you have more money than. . . ."

But of course he didn't know what *money* meant, either.

"It means you have a more beautiful house than other people. A larger house, and fine clothing, many changes of clothing. And you go to better schools, with wiser teachers, and you have better food to eat, and more of it. All you could want, and more."

"But then you should share," said Protchnu. "You told me that if you have more than you need, you should share."

"And you *do* share. But . . . you won't understand, Proya. That kind of life is lost to us forever. You'll never understand it."

They were quiet for a few moments.

"Mother," said Protchnu.

"Yes?"

"You don't hate me because I chose Father? In the library that day?"

"Every mother knows there'll come a time when her sons will choose their father. It's a part of growing up. I never thought it would come to you so young, but that wasn't your fault."

A pause. Then his voice was very small indeed. "But I don't choose him."

"No, Protchnu, I didn't think you would ever really choose the bad things he's doing. You're not that kind of boy." In truth, though, Eiadh sometimes feared that he *was* that kind of boy. She had seen him playing, had seen him lording it over the other boys, teasing some of them cruelly, until they cried, and then laughing at them. It had frightened her, back on Harmony, to see her son be so unkind to those smaller than him. And yet she had also been proud of how he led the other boys in everything, how they all looked up to him, how even Aunt Rasa's Oykib stepped back and let Protchnu take the first place among the boys.

Can it ever be one without the other? The leadership without the lack of compassion? The pride without the cruelty?

"But of course you choose your father," said Eiadh. "The man you know he really is, the good brave strong man you love so much. That's the man you were choosing that day, I know it."

She could feel how Protchnu's body moved within her embrace as he steeled himself to say the hard thing. "He's really unhappy without you," he said.

"Did he send you to tell me that?"

"I sent myself," said Protchnu.

Or did the Oversoul send you? Eiadh wondered sometimes. Hadn't Luet said that they were *all* chosen by the Oversoul? That they were all unusually receptive to her promptings? Then why shouldn't one of her children have these extraordinary gifts, like the one that had popped up in Chveya, for instance?

"So your father is unhappy without me. Let him release Nafai, restore peace to the ship, and he won't have to be without me anymore."

"He can't stop," said Protchnu. "Not without help."

He's only eight years old? And he can see this deeply? Perhaps the crisis has awakened some hidden power of empathy within him. The Oversoul knows that at his age I was utterly without understanding or compassion for anyone. I was a moral wasteland, caring only for who was prettiest and who sang the best and who would be famous someday and who was rich. If I had only grown out of that childishness earlier, I might have seen which of the brothers was the better man, back before I married Elemak, back when Nafai was gazing at me with the calf eyes of adolescent love. I made a terrible mistake then. I looked at Elemak and couldn't see him without thinking, he's the heir of the Wetchik, oldest son of one of the richest and most prestigious men of Basilica. What was Nafai?

Of course, if I'd been truly wise, I'd have married neither of them and I'd still be in Basilica. Though if Volemak was right, Basilica has already been destroyed, the city demolished and its few survivors scattered to the wind.

"And what sort of help does your father need?" asked Eiadh.

"He needs a way to change his mind without admitting that he's wrong."

"Don't we all," she murmured.

"Mother, I can hardly breathe sometimes. I wake up in the morning feeling like somebody's pressing on my chest. I just can't breathe in deeply enough. Sometimes I get dizzy and fall down. And I'm doing better than most. We have to help Father."

She knew that this was true. But she also knew that after that scene in the library, she didn't have the power to help him. Now, though, with Protchnu beside her, she could do it. Had this eight-year-old that much power?

Eight years old, but he had seen. He had understood what was needed, and he had taken the responsibility for acting on that understanding. It filled her with hope, not just for the immediate future, but for a time far distant. She knew that the community would divide, at the death of Volemak if not sooner, and when it did, Elemak would be the ruler of one of the halves. He would be angry, embittered, filled with loathing and violence. But Elemak would not live forever. Someday his place as ruler would be filled by someone else, and the most likely man was this one sitting beside her on the bed, this eight-year-old. If he grew in wisdom over the years, instead of growing in rage as his father had done, then when he took his father's place as ruler of the people he would be like autumn rains on the cities of the plain, bringing relief after the dry fire of summer.

For you, Protchnu, I will do what must be done. I will humble myself before Elemak, unworthy as he is, for your sake, so that you will have a future, so that someday you can fill the role that nature has suited you to.

"At the next mealtime in the library," she said. "Come to me then, and with you beside me I'll do what must be done."

Elemak was with them during the meal, of course. He always was, now, ever since Volemak had used his absence as an opportunity to give the oath. The meals were more sparsely attended these days. After watching Elemak beat Nafai, Volemak and Rasa had taken to their beds. The lack of oxygen was affecting them as badly as the youngest of the babies. They hadn't the strength to move, and those who tended to them—Dol and Sevet—reported that they kept slipping into and out of unconsciousness and were delirious much of the time. "They're dying," they whispered—but loudly enough that Elemak could surely hear them during meals. He showed no reaction.

At the noon meal of the fourth day of the waking, Elemak was sitting alone, his food untouched, when Protchnu got up from the table and walked to his mother. Elemak watched him go, his face darkening. But it was clear to everyone there that Protchnu was not joining himself to his mother's cause. Rather he was fetching her, bringing her along. He might be only two-thirds her height, but he was in control. Slowly they approached the table where Elemak sat.

"Mother has something to tell you," said Protchnu.

Suddenly Eiadh burst into tears and dropped to her knees. "Elemak," she sobbed, "I am so ashamed. I turned against my husband."

Elemak sighed. "It's not going to work, Eiadh. I know what a good actress you are. Like Dolya. You can turn the tears on and off like a faucet."

She wept all the harder. "Why should you ever believe me or trust me again? I deserve whatever terrible things you want to say to me. But I am your true wife. Without you I'm nothing, I'd rather die than not be part of you and your life. Please forgive me, take me back."

Everyone could see how Elemak struggled between belief and skepticism. It was not as if he had it in him to be subtle or clever. Everyone was getting logy and stupid from the lack of oxygen. They could remember that once they had good, quick judgment, but they couldn't remember what it even felt like. Elemak blinked slowly, looking at her.

"I know who the strongest, best man is," she said. "Not one who relies on tricks and machines, on lies and deception. You're the honest one."

His lip curled in contempt at her obvious flattery. Yet he was also affected by it. Someone understands. Even if she's just mouthing empty words, the words *are* being said.

"But the liars have the upper hand. *They're* the ones who are holding our babies hostage, not you. Sometimes a man has to give in to evil in order to save his children."

Most of those listening knew that they were hearing a distortion of the truth. And yet they wanted it to be believed, wanted Elemak at least to believe it, because if he did, it would provide him with a way to surrender and still be noble and heroic in his own eyes. Let this be the version of history that Elemak believes in, so that our history can go on beyond this hour.

"Do you think I'll be fooled when Nafai starts strutting around here again? Him and his sparkling cloak embedded in his flesh, making him look like a machine himself—I'll be grateful to go back into suspended animation for the rest of the voyage, so I don't have to look at him. When I wake up, let it be on Earth, with you beside me, and our children still to raise. They'll grow older. Time will pass. And you'll still be my husband and a great man in the eyes of all who know the truth."

Elemak looked at her sharply. Or at least he tried to be sharp. Now and then she simply went out of focus.

She opened her mouth to speak again, but Protchnu laid a hand on her shoulder and she settled back, sitting on her ankles, as Protchnu stepped forward and spoke quietly, where few but Elemak could hear.

"Pick the time of battle," he said quietly. "You taught me that back in Vusadka. Pick the time of battle."

Elemak answered him just as softly. "They've won already, Protchnu. By the time I awoke they had already cheated you out of your inheritance. Look at you, so young, so small."

"Do what it takes to let us all live, Father. Someday I will not be small, and then we'll have vengeance on our enemies."

Elemak studied his face. "*Our* enemies?"

"What they have done to the father, they have done to the son," whispered Protchnu. "I will never, never, never, never, never forget."

It filled Elemak with hope, to hear such resolve, such hatred in his son's voice.

He rose to his feet. All eyes were upon him, watching as he took Protchnu by the hand and led him to the ladderway in the middle of the room. He turned back. "Meb. Obring."

They got up slowly.

"Come with me."

"Who'll watch these people, then?" asked Obring.

"I don't care," said Elemak. "I'm tired of looking at them."

He dropped down the ladderway, Protchnu after him, and then Obring and Meb.

As soon as they were gone, the women gathered around Eiadh. "Thank you," they said softly. "It was brave of you." "You were wonderful." "Thank you." "Thank you."

Even Luet took Eiadh's hands in hers. "Today you were the greatest among women. It's over now, because of you."

Eiadh could only press her face into her hands and weep. For she had overheard the words that Protchnu said to Elemak, had heard the hatred in his voice, and she knew that Protchnu was not putting on a performance as she had done, not now, anyway. Protchnu would carry on his father's hatred into the next generation. It was all for nothing. She had humbled herself for nothing. "For nothing," she murmured.

"Not for nothing," said Luet. "For our children. For all the children. I say it again, Eiadh. Today you were the greatest among women."

Luet knelt beside her; Eiadh reached out to her and wept against her shoulder.

The door opened and the light came on. Nafai's eyes adjusted quickly. Elemak, Mebbekew, Obring, and Elya's son, Protchnu. He could see the hatred in their eyes, all of them.

They've come to kill me.

To Nafai's surprise, the thought did not come as a relief. Despite all his words of desperation to the Oversoul, he did not really want to die. But he would do it, he would submit to it, if that's what would bring peace.

To his surprise, Elemak knelt down at his feet and began fumbling with the knots at his ankles. Mebbekew joined him, working on the knots at his wrists.

His skin was sore there, and their working chafed him painfully. After his beating, after the Oversoul had caused the cloak to heal him, Nafai had resumed letting the sores at his ankles and wrists go unhealed. Now it made the moment of release almost excruciating.

"We've taken an oath," Elemak said quietly. "The oath Father administered to everyone else on the ship. *He* is the sole ruler of the colony. No one else is his second in command or his chief adviser or any other such fiction that disguises power. *He* will rule. I've taken the oath, and so have Meb and Obring. And my son Protchnu. As long as Volemak lives, we obey him and no other."

"That's a good oath," said Nafai softly. He did not add: If only you had taken it earlier and lived by it, as I did from my childhood on. It would have spared us a lot of trouble.

"You go straight from here and take the oath as well," said Meb.

The cords at his neck, the cords that had pulled his body in a backward arch, suddenly released. Pain shot up and down his back. He moaned.

"Stop the histrionics," said Meb contemptuously. "We know you could heal this in a moment if you wanted to."

His feet and hands were numb; they felt like heavy clubs, sluggish, not obeying what he told them to do. As he rolled onto his stomach, his back ached and he could hardly pull himself up onto his knees. Bracing himself on the wall, he finally stood on unsteady legs. "Where's Father?" asked Nafai. "I must go and take the oath."

"Oykib and Chveya haven't taken it yet, either," said Obring.

"Go get them, then," Elemak answered scornfully. "Are you still waiting for me to command you? I'm not in charge here anymore."

"And neither am I," said Nafai.

But he was. Already the cloak was giving him whatever information he wanted. "There is enough oxygen in the working reserve to bring us up near normal for two hours. That will be enough time to oxygenate everyone's blood and for all of us to enter suspended animation. Then the ship can replenish itself before anybody else wakes up."

Elemak laughed nastily. "What, aren't you going to promise us to stay asleep till we reach Earth?"

"I'm going to resume the school where we left off," said Nafai. "If Father says I should."

"I have no doubt that he'll say whatever you want him to say."

"Then you don't know him or me at all. Because Father will say whatever the Oversoul wants him to say, and nothing else."

"Oh, let's not argue, Nafai," said Elemak, with exaggerated cheeriness. "We must be *friends* now."

Nafai walked in silence, leaning against the corridor walls as he needed to, grateful for the low gravity. "Is this really what you want for Protchnu, Elemak? To feed him this steady diet of hate?"

"Hate is the richest of foods," said Elemak. "It makes you strong, it fills you with power. And I have a banquet of it to give my children."

"Let there be peace between your children and mine, Elya," said Nafai.

"Between your big, tall children and my little tiny ones?" asked Elemak. "Of course there'll be peace, the way there's peace between the lion and the fly."

They reached the door of Volemak's and Rasa's room just as Obring returned with Oykib and Chveya. Wordlessly Chveya embraced her father, and he leaned on her as they went into the room.

Nafai knelt and took the oath, holding his father's hand as he did it. Chveya and Oykib followed him.

Feebly, Volemak spoke from the bed. "Then it's done. All have taken the oath. Give us the oxygen now, and let us return to sleep."

In only a few seconds, they began to feel the difference, all of them. The breaths they were taking were deep enough, and in a few moments their panting, their gasping, began to cause them to feel drunk on oxygen, faint with air. Then their bodies adjusted, their breathing went back to normal, and it was as if nothing had ever been wrong. Mothers wept over their babies, now breathing normally. Children began to laugh and shout and run, because at last they could.

Long before the two hours were up, however, the laughing and shouting had ended. Parents put their children to sleep. Zdorab and Shedemei put all the adults to sleep then, except for Nafai, who stayed apart from all the others so as not to cause needless offense to Elemak and those who regretted his defeat.

Once again Nafai and Shedemei stood over the chamber where Zdorab lay. "Forgive me, Nafai," said Zdorab.

"I already have," said Nafai. "Luet explained to me what you were thinking at the time. And how you regretted it after."

"No more surprises," said Zdorab. "I'm with you till I die."

"Your oath is to my father," said Nafai. "But I'm glad of your friendship, and you may be sure that you have mine."

Alone with Shedemei, Nafai could allow the sores on his wrists and ankles to heal at last. "Who would have guessed," he said.

"What?" she answered.

"That Zdorab's mistake would end up accomplishing something that would have been impossible otherwise."

"And what is that?"

"I expected that as soon as we reached Earth, Elemak would go out of control and we'd be at war. I think the Oversoul expected it, too. But now we've had the war, and I think the peace will hold."

"Until your father dies," said Shedemei pointedly.

"Father isn't old yet," said Nafai. "It gives us time. Who knows what might happen in the years to come?"

"I don't want to be there," said Shedemei.

"It's a little late to decide that now," said Nafai.

"I don't want to be there for the conflict. For the fighting. I came here to do some gardening." She laughed self-deprecatingly. "To tinker around with the plant and animal life of Earth. That's the dream the Keeper sent to me. Not like you others. I'm just the gardener."

"Just? You'll be the most important person among us."

"I lied to you too, you know, Nafai. When I told you that it would be safe for cousins to marry. Just like Zdorab, I held something back."

"That's all right," said Nafai. "Everyone holds something back, whether they know it or not."

"But your children—the consequences may be terrible."

"I don't think so," said Nafai.

"Oh." She grimaced. "So the Oversoul told me what to say?"

"Suggested it. Every word was true."

Shedemei laughed sardonically. "Or at least as true as every *other* word of the Oversoul."

"I trust him," said Nafai.

"Trust her to say whatever is necessary to accomplish her purposes. That's as far as she can be trusted," said Shedemei.

"Ah, but you see, Shedya, the Oversoul's purposes *are* my purposes. So I can trust him completely."

She patted his cheek. "You may be technically about as old as I am by now, what with staying awake continuously during the voyage. But Nyef, I must say, you still have a lot to learn."

With that she swung into place in her chamber. Nafai raised the side, locked it, then activated the suspension process. The lid slipped closed.

He watched as she drifted to sleep in the airtight compartment. He was alone again.

<I can only sustain the oxygen like this for about fifteen more minutes, and then it's gone.>

I'm hurrying.

<Everything worked out rather well, don't you think?>

I have an idea. Just don't talk to me for a little while. Let me go to sleep with only my own thoughts in my head.

<If you want. But it will feel rather strange to you.>

I can handle it.

<Because you've never gone to sleep without me in your life.>

I wish you were better company, then.

<Go ahead and be angry at me. But remember that I didn't make Elemak the way he is. If he had chosen better, if he were innately a better man, then he'd be in your place, wearing the cloak of the starmaster.>

I wish he were.

<Yes, you mean that. You really don't want to have the responsibility or the power. And yet you accepted them both because someone must, and only you could do it. Not against your will, but against your desires and your better judgment. And that is why I led you to the cloak. Because if you had understood what it was, you would never have reached for it.>

I'm just the puppet you want, is that it?

<You're not a puppet at all. Puppets are useless to me. I need willing friends and allies.>

Let me go to sleep in peace, and maybe when I wake up I'll be willing again.

<Sleep well, my friend. There's a long road yet ahead of us.>

The skyscreen in the library showed it, the globe of Earth, blue and white, with patches of brown and green here and there. Since they had slept through the launch, they had never seen a world like this, like a ball floating in the black of night.

"Like a moon," said Chveya.

Oykib reached out and took her hand. She looked up at him and smiled. The last three and a half years had been both wonderful and excruciating, to know that he loved her, and yet to know that it was impossible to marry and have children during the voyage. They didn't speak of what they felt—it was easier for both of them that way. The others had been just as discreet in their pairing up. But now, as they made their reconnaissance, orbitting the Earth again and again, reading the reports the instruments made, studying the maps, searching for the landing place, waiting for the Oversoul to make a decision, or for a dream from the Keeper to tell them what to do, it was impossible for Oykib to keep himself from thinking about Chveya, about what lay ahead for them. A new world, hard work, farming and exploring, and who knew what sort of dangers from disease or animals or weather—but set against all this was the thought of Chveya in his arms, of babies, of starting the cycle over again, of being part of the living world.

"We once fled from this world in shame and fear," said Chveya. "We once fouled it and slaughtered each other."

She did not need to add the fear that it would happen again. They all knew that the time of real peace would be over, that even if the oath to Volemak held, the tension would still be alive underneath the civility. And how long would Volemak live? Then war might come again. Human blood might once again be shed on Earth.

Oykib heard Chveya speaking to the Oversoul. Why did you bring us here, when we're no better and no wiser than the ones who left?

"But we *are*," said Oykib. "Better and wiser, I mean."

She turned to him, her eyes wide. "What is it that you do? Back in the crisis, you spoke so knowledgeably. Of what the Oversoul wanted. Of what Nafai wanted, when you hadn't even spoken to him. What is it you do?"

"I eavesdrop," he said. "It's been that way all my life. Anything that's said on the channels of the Oversoul, I hear. What he says. What you say."

She looked horrified. Is this true? she was saying to the Oversoul. That's horrible!

"Now you know why I've never told anyone. Though I certainly showed it clearly enough during the crisis. I'm surprised no one guessed."

"What I say to the Oversoul—it's so private."

"I know that," said Oykib. "I didn't ask to hear it. It just came to me. I grew up knowing a great deal more than any child should know. I understand what's going on in others' lives to a degree that—well, let's just say that I'd much rather take people at face value than to know what really troubles them. Or, with the ones who never speak to the Oversoul, what things he has to do to keep them from doing the worst things they desire. It's not a pleasant burden to carry."

"I can imagine," said Chveya. "Or maybe not. Maybe I can't imagine. I'm not even trying to imagine right now. All I'm doing is trying to remember what I've said to the Oversoul, what secrets you know."

"I'll tell you one secret I know, Veya. I know that of all the people on this starship, no one is more honest and good than you, no one more loving and careful of other people's feelings. Of all the people on this ship, there's no one who is so at peace with herself, no one who adds less to the burden of shame and guilt that I carry around with me. Of all the people on this ship, Veya, you are the only one that I would be glad to be close to forever, because all your secrets are bright and good and I love you for them."

"Some of my secrets are *not* bright and good, you liar."

"On the contrary. The evil secrets you're ashamed of are so mild and pathetic that to *me,* having seen real evil to a degree I hope you'll never understand, to me even your darkest, most shameful secrets are dazzling."

"I think," said Chveya, "that you're hinting around that you want to marry me."

"As if it could ever be a secret to you, who senses the connections between people just like Aunt Hushidh. Talk about invasion of privacy."

"I do know your secret, Okya," she said, smiling, facing him, putting her arms around his waist, holding his hips against hers. "I know what you want. I know how much you love me. I see us bound by bright cords, tied so tightly that there's no escape ever as long as either of us lives. You are my captive, and I'm never going to have mercy and let you go."

"Those bonds aren't bondage at all, Veya," said Oykib. "They're freedom. This whole voyage I've been in captivity because I couldn't have you. When we step out on that new world, that old world, and I'm tied to you at last, openly, so we can begin our life together—that's when I will truly be unbound."

"My answer is yes," she said.

"I know," he said. "I heard you tell the Oversoul."

II
Landfall

9

Watchers

There were many things for a young man to do, many duties that the community required of him, even if he *was* already married, and to a remarkable woman like Iguo. Because of pTo's extraordinary advancement, people looked to him for achievement, looked for him to be a model of young manhood.

Well, perhaps not always. Many of them looked to pTo for disappointment at best, scandal at worst. He was too young. Iguo had only married a mere boy like that because her great grandmother Upua had done the same with Kiti. It had become something of a family tradition for the women of that line, to marry a man who was too young—and pTo was no Kiti, as many were quick to point out.

"You're no Kiti, you know," said pTo's own otherself, Poto.

"As well for you I'm not," said pTo. "*His* otherself was dead the year he made his sculpture and was chosen by Upua."

"You can't go doing crazy things. They're not going to forgive you anything. If you're brilliant they'll say you're arrogant. If you falter, they'll say you overreached. If you're friendly they'll say you're condescending. If you're aloof they'll say you're arrogant."

"So I might as well do what I want."

"Just remember that it's my name you're dragging through the mud. If *you're* a madman, what am I?"

"A helpless victim of my lunacy," said pTo. "I want to go to the tower."

Resting on the stout limb of a tree, they were watching over a flock of fat turkeys. The turkeys themselves were docile enough, too stupid to know the fate that the people had in store for them. The danger was from devils, who liked nothing better than to steal from the herds of the people. Lazy creatures, devils never did their own work except digging their nasty little holes in the ground and carving out the hearts of trees. During the birthing season, they came in force, stealing sometimes as many as a third of each year's newborns—that was why so many people had lost their otherself. During the rest of the year, though, it was the flocks and herds they were after.

"We're on watch," said Poto.

"We're watching the wrong thing," pTo insisted. "The Old Ones at the tower are the most important creatures in the world."

"Boboi says they're our enemies."

"Why was my wife's ancestor shown the face of an Old One, then, if they aren't to be our friends?"

"To warn us," said Poto.

"The Old Ones know secrets, and if we don't make friends with them, they'll give those secrets to the devils. Then we really *will* have them as enemies."

"It's forbidden," said Poto, "and we have responsibilities here, and no matter how young you might have been when you got married, you are *not* Kiti."

pTo knew that his otherself was right. He usually was. But pTo couldn't bear to concede the point, because he knew that if he didn't learn about the Old Ones, no one else would. No one else *dared.* "I'm not Kiti," said pTo, "but I also am the only man who doesn't fear that he'll be rejected by all the women because of flouting Boboi's ban on visiting the Old Ones."

"You're not the only married man."

"You know what I mean. The older men don't *want* to go. They get a little slow, a little fat. It's too dangerous for them to go down there into the heart of devil country."

One of the turkeys decided, as turkeys will, that it was urgently required to be somewhere out in the brush, and it suddenly started gobbling and running. Without a word, Poto swooped down from the limb and flew in front of the bird, shouting. The bird stopped, gazing stupidly at the man beating his wings in the air in front of him. Poto dropped to the ground, then jumped into the air again and, on the leap, kicked the turkey in the face. It screeched, turned around, and trotted back to the herd.

When Poto rejoined him on the limb, pTo couldn't resist. "What you just did to that turkey is what Boboi is doing to all the men."

Poto sighed. "Give me a little peace, pTo."

"What I'm saying, Poto, is that I'm going. You can tend the herd alone."

"We herd in twos because a man is needed to watch the turkeys, and another to watch the man so he isn't taken by surprise."

"Then come with me," said pTo. "I'm not ashamed to admit that I'm afraid to go alone."

"I'm afraid to go at all, and you should be, too."

"Then goodbye, my otherself, my bettermind. Perhaps my Iguo will marry you after I'm dead." In the old days, they would both be married to her already. Sometimes pTo wished it had not changed.

"Yes, everything's a poem to you," said Poto scornfully, but pTo was not deaf to the emotion behind his hard words.

"My death, when it comes, will be one that the poets sing of."

"Better to have a life that your children remember with joy than a death that the poets remember with song."

"Hard to believe you're not an old man, when you quote nonsense like that."

"Go if you must."

pTo immediately leapt from the branch. Moments after his glide began, he rose up, circling higher than the treetops. He shouted down at Poto. "Watch your back, Obedient One!"

"No!" shouted Poto, truly angry. "I won't do your work for you!"

His words stung, but pTo flew on, down the valley. He knew that others would see him, and he knew that while Poto was high enough up the valley to be in little danger, others would say that he was so unnatural as not to love his otherself. Let them say what they would. Boboi was wrong. There was great danger in ignoring the Old Ones. pTo *would* study them, learn about them, perhaps enter into conversation with them. Learn their language. Become their friend. Bring back their ancient secrets. Better to bring knowledge back to the people than mere trinkets. Their trove of Old One artifacts was not large, but it had taken many generations to collect it. All of it was worthless, because none of it meant anything. It was knowledge that was needed, secrets that must be told. Not to the devils, either. To us.

It wasn't far. pTo wasn't even tired when the tower came into view. He had seen it before, from afar, and marveled at it every time. Who could shape a thing as smooth and tall as that? Like sunlight on the water, it was so bright, and the trees looked like bushes bowing down to worship it.

Why had the Old Ones come to dwell among the devils, and not among the people? Was it possible that the Old Ones were hellfolk and not from the gods at all? Yet they had not burst upward from the ground. They came from the sky. How then could they be hellfolk?

They could be hellfolk because they rested their tower right beside a stand of thick, ancient trees. The signs of a devil city were all around. Dead trees here and there; depressions here and there from old tunnels that had given way; and nearby, the rocky hills that held miles of caves for their obscene cannibalistic worship. The Old Ones must have seen all this, must have known, and yet they built their own village where the devils could watch them without leaving their holes. Why would the Old Ones do this, if they didn't intend to befriend the devils? They probably already had. It was already too late.

But if it *is* too late, then I'll see signs of their alliance, I'll get some idea of what the danger is, and I'll come home and report. When the danger is clear enough, they'll stop listening to Boboi. But then we'll come down here for war instead of learning, and the Old Ones will probably strike us out of the sky with magic. The Old Ones live in a tower that stands on a foundation of fire. Even the greatest warrior of the people would be no more irritating to them than a gnat.

It must not be war. It must be friendship. I must find a way to make it friendship.

The devils had no doubt already noticed him. Flight was the salvation of the people, but it was also their bane, at least in the daytime. They could leap to the sky to escape an enemy; but their enemy could look to the sky to watch them approach. Much had been made of the difference: The people were open and honest, the devils stealthy and deceptive. The people lived in the realm of the sun and stars, the devils in the realm of the worms and grubs. The people were as light as air, and therefore spiritual, akin to the gods; the devils were heavy and plodding, and therefore earthy, akin to stone.

But it didn't change the fact that if a devil once got its hands on a man, it could break any of his bones as easily as snapping a twig. There was no fighting the devils hand to hand. One thrust with a spear, that's all a man would ever get. Then he either had to fly or die. He couldn't even lift a very heavy burden—not even a stone to drop on a devil's head, or at least not a stone large enough to cause harm.

Couldn't even lift his own child when the child was at that awkward age, too large to carry in flight, too young yet to fly. So it was at that time of year that the devils came, and parents had to make the terrible choice: Which child the two of them would carry to safety. Some were able to get back in time to save the second. Some were lucky enough to have older children who had not yet mated, who could take the other twin to safety. That's how Poto had survived, because he and pTo were thirdborn. Rare indeed was the firstborn whose otherself was still alive.

So the devils were watching him, wondering why he came. Salivating, too, no doubt, at the thought of having his meat between their teeth. Well, pTo was young and quick enough that no one was going to take him. He was still light enough to perch on far branches that the devils couldn't climb on without shaking them. His ears were still so keen that he could hear the sound of the fingers digging into the bark of the tree. There was danger if he walked into a trap, but if he was careful he would be safe.

Then pTo had a troubling thought: Every man or woman taken by the devils must have thought exactly the same thing, right up to the moment when they realized they were wrong.

The Old Ones' village was very small, in terms of numbers, but huge in terms of size. Their houses were monstrously large. Whole trees had been felled and split to make the walls and roofs, except for the few buildings made of strange substances that pTo had never seen before. It was hard to make sense of what the buildings were for. The large one must be a dormitory—but then, why was there only one? Did their unmated males and females sleep in the same house? Unthinkable.

He chose his vantage point—a slender branch, sturdy enough to provide a good launch for flight, with many leaves to keep him from the Old Ones' view. He inspected the trunk of the tree, but it was thin enough that the devils couldn't have hollowed it yet, so he didn't have to worry about ambush through a hidden door in the tree. For a devil to get to him it would have to climb the outside of the trunk, and pTo would hear it.

Unless he *didn't* hear it, or unless they *could* hollow a tree that thin.

pTo ignored his own fears and settled down to watch. He watched all day, and by sundown he had learned many strange new things. The most amazing thing was that all the adults seemed to be married, each couple dwelling in their own house. The largest building was used during the day by a couple of adults and all the young children; obviously the Old Ones were holding school. But indoors? Closing their children off from the world in order to teach them about it made no sense to pTo.

Another thing pTo learned was that everyone lived in the buildings made of wood; the buildings made of that strange, smooth substance were only for storage or some more arcane purpose, for these buildings were rarely visited, and then only to fetch a tool or some other item, or return it to its place.

The Old Ones kept some animals in pens, but very few, and they were strange. A pair of them looked like goats, but they were huge. A pair of them looked like cows, but they were tiny. And there were dozens of wolves—or at least they barked and whined and howled like wolves—and they ran free among the Old Ones. Friends of wolves! What kind of creatures were these Old Ones? Didn't they fear for their babies' safety? Or were their babies born strong? No, not at all: pTo could see that a couple of the Old Ones carried babies with them in slings, and the babies looked completely helpless.

At first pTo thought—with disappointment—that all the children were alone. It was only late in the afternoon that he realized that two of the little ones were identical, and had the same parents. They did have otherselves! And yet the two of them weren't always together—that was why pTo hadn't realized they were not the same child until late in the day. He thought about this: only one pair out of all the children. Had the Old Ones been such calamitously unlucky parents that all the other pairs had been broken? Or was it possible that only some of their children were born in pairs, and all the others simply came as singles? What were they, then—animals?

Time to think about that later. When he had learned their language, he could perhaps find a way to ask such indelicate questions. For now, though, he could only watch. But particularly he would watch the pair, to see how they could go through childhood so often apart from each other. Are they so much stronger than we are, pTo wondered, or do they simply lack real affection?

During the day he noticed that most of the adults spent a great deal of time in the large cleared area, where they had marked the earth in many rows, as if loosening the clay to make a giant sculpture—though the soil here was loose, and would never hold together if they tried to shape it. But after watching for several hours, it dawned on pTo that the furrowed soil was quite possibly just an early stage of the four strange meadows, each with grass of a different height. For there, too, the roots of the grasses seemed to grow in rows. There were other areas, too, where plants seemed to have been intentionally placed, and from one of them a couple of Old Ones went to gather melons, which were then cut open and shared with the workers in the middle of the day.

This was the first secret pTo learned from the Old Ones, that instead of remembering from year to year where the best plants grew, and taking care to leave an offering of fruit and roots in the earth so the Mother would give back new plants the next year, the offerings could be taken away from their original rooting place and herded together like turkeys or goats, so they could be watched over and cared for all at once, by only a few men and women. Of course, there would be danger in this, too—all the devils would have to do is find an artificial meadow like this, and then lie in wait until the gatherers came. So it might be that the people couldn't use this particular secret of the Old Ones. But maybe they could.

More to the point, the devils almost certainly could. But then, the devils could easily have learned the people's secret, too, of herding animals so they could be protected from predators and led to good eating. Instead, the devils simply learned to search for the people's flocks and herds, and steal from them. No doubt the devils were already planning to steal fruit and seeds from the meadows of the Old Ones.

Here was the strangest thing of all. No one stood on guard. Some of the children took turns standing in two of the meadows, the one where all the grasses were coming ripe at once, and the one that was new-furrowed, where the birds seemed to be finding new-planted seeds. There the children watched for birds to land and ran to shoo them away.

Birds they watch for, but not devils.

Did this mean that the Old Ones had already befriended the devils? Or perhaps they had already conquered them and forced them into submission.

Or—was it possible?—the devils had been so stealthy, and the Old Ones so careless, that they had not yet noticed that the devils were watching them.

Surely the Old Ones could see some fragment of what pTo could see. During the day he had watched as more than a dozen different parties of devils arose out of the earth or emerged onto branches of trees, to watch. pTo had seen several of the devils taking note of *him*, too, and was sure that they were plotting some way to take him, or at least drive him off. The devils were clever, but not *that* clever. Or were the Old Ones merely unobservant? How could they have become so powerful if they were too stupid to notice things as important as where the devils were, what they were watching, where they were laying their traps?

The sun set.

Now was the time, pTo knew, when the devils would spring whatever trap it was that they had been planning all day. Night was also when they would do their thieving and spying on the Old Ones. He could already see in the waning light that devils were gathering at meadow's edge; yet the Old Ones gave no alarm, and seemed to set only the most inadequate watch—one male, walking around carrying a lamp in his hands (and never spilling it!). A lamp—it made no sense. Why not just shout, "I'm coming, get out of my way, hide from me so I can't see you!"

pTo heard a faint rubbing sound and felt his branch vibrate. For a moment he was tempted to wait, to tease the devil, to pretend that he didn't know he was being stalked. But then he thought: Perhaps this is all the warning I'll get. Perhaps the devil is closer than I think. And if I linger for even a moment longer. . . .

He lunged for the sky and as he did he heard a hiss of disappointment right behind him, so loud and close that he imagined he could feel the devil's breath on his back. That is how people die, he thought. Waiting just a little too long to take to the sky.

He swooped, then rose up high enough to soar for a few moments. He was a little stiff from his posture of stillness during the day. It would have been better if he could have set his hands and feet and hung upside down—but then he would have been in danger of falling asleep. No, stiffness was the price of remaining in an upright posture all day, without moving. Though from what he had seen of the Old Ones, pTo wondered if he needed to be so careful. He could probably do a jig and sing a song, and the Old Ones wouldn't see him.

He knew that the devils would be out in the Old Ones' meadows now, but he felt he had to take a risk and gather up samples of the grasses they were growing in such perfect unison. He went to the ripest field first and saw at once that the danger there was extreme. The stalks weren't strong enough to hold him, and yet were tall enough to interfere with flight. Worst of all, the breeze rustled them constantly so that pTo wouldn't be able to hear any of the faint noises the devils might make moving through the grass. He dared not settle to the ground there—every devil in the grass would have seen him, though he couldn't see any of them at all, and there was a chance he would come down within a few handspans of one of them and never know it till the powerful hands clamped around his legs or arms, or ripped into the tough, thin skin of his wings.

He dared not come to ground, and yet he did it, because he would not go home without some trophy of his expedition. The secrets he had learned were the most valuable things he could bring back, he knew, but it would go better for him in withstanding Boboi's criticism if he also had something in his hands. So he came to ground and immediately started breaking off stalks as near the ground as he could. He didn't bother to look around him. He wouldn't have been able to see anything, anyway. If a devil was very close, he was doomed whether he looked or not; and if the devils were farther off, stopping and looking for them through the impenetrable grass would merely have given them time to get closer.

How many stalks? One. Two. Three. Each one took its moment to break off, to lay down next to the first; how many moments did he have? Four. Five. How many stalks did he need? Six. Seven. Were they all ripe? Or would he be bringing home only immature ones, which would embarrass him? Eight. Nine.

Enough. Done. Fly.

Gathering the stalks in one foot, he squatted, then jumped upward with all his might. His wings could barely spread in the grass, so that he had to fling them out to full length after he rose above the stalks, and then it took all his strength to dig into the air and rise. For a terrifying moment he hovered at the level of the tops of the stalks, moving forward but not rising. Under him, he could see eyes—four, six, eight—glowing in the moonlight, leaping upward toward him as he passed. If they had been taller, or if pTo had been slower, he would now be lying amid the stalks as they tore his body to pieces and carried the bits of him down into their holes to share with their filthy dirt-eating mates.

But they were not taller, and pTo was not slower, and so he rose into the air and flapped his way toward the village of the Old Ones. He had to touch one of the buildings that was not made of wood. This was safer, though. None of the devils had moved into the village, and the Old One with the lamp would probably not see him. He would be on the roof, too, with nothing to hinder him from taking flight.

The roof gave way slightly under his weight. Since he could only hold his place with the foot that wasn't gripping the stalks of grain, he had to bend down and use his hands to feel the texture of it. Woven like a temporary nest, like a basket, only the weave was astonishingly tight and fine. Even water couldn't pass through a weave as close as this. And what the fibers were made of he could not begin to guess. They had shone in the sunlight. Why would the Old Ones kill trees to build their houses, when they could weave a roof as fine and perfect as this one?

One last temptation, after the smooth house: He flew to the base of the tower and touched it. Not like the woven house at all. There was no give to it; it was like stone, except not as cold to the touch. When he struck it lightly with his knuckles, he could hear a faint ring to it, like several of the artifacts of the Old Ones in the village trove. This much, then, was still true of the Old Ones: They built music into the things they made.

He was startled by a noise—like a voice, only loud and deep. He was so frightened that he took flight without thinking. Only when he was airborne could he turn and overfly the place and see who had spoken. It *was* a voice. One of the Old Ones. A male. How had it come upon him so quietly? The Old Ones were noisy in everything they did, like deaf people. This one shouted like a deaf person, too, his voice so loud and booming. And yet he had been able to come upon pTo so quietly that—

So quietly that he obviously must not have "come upon" pTo at all. He must have been sitting there in the shadow of the tower. Sitting there all along. How much did he notice? Did he see the stalks of grain that pTo had stolen? Would he be angry now? Would this theft make the Old Ones enemies of the people?

For a moment pTo thought: I won't tell anyone that the Old One saw me.

But he discarded the idea at once. If we ever become friends with the Old Ones, they will remember the stalks that I stole from their meadow. I will bear the penalty for it then. But my people will already have known that my theft was noticed. They will know that I told them the truth about everything I did—even the mistake of being seen. Many will criticize me for my carelessness—but none will doubt that I am honest, or claim that I altered my story to make myself look good. Better to have the trust of the people than their respect. With trust, their respect could be earned later; without it, respect could never be deserved, and so to have it would be like poison.

Tired from the day's stillness, dreading his homecoming, pTo flapped his way higher, up the canyon, toward the valley where the people lived.

Oykib watched the giant bat as it circled once, then flew away up the canyon. He knew that to others, this would mean the beginning of the fulfillment of the old dreams, the ones from the Keeper of Earth. But to Oykib, it was something else. He had heard the voice of the Keeper, speaking to this visitor—and he had understood it.

The voice of the Keeper was strange. It was quieter than the voice of the Oversoul, less clear. It spoke more in images than ideas, more in desires than in emotions. It was harder for Oykib to understand; indeed, when they first arrived on Earth it had taken him several weeks before he even realized that the voice of the Keeper was there. The conversations between humans and the Oversoul were so much louder that the voice of the Keeper was like distant thunder, or a light breeze in the leaves—more felt than heard. But once he noticed it, once he had an idea of what it was, he began to listen for it. Sitting in the shadow of the starship in the gathering dusk, he could concentrate, gradually letting the louder voice of the Oversoul fade into the background.

It was especially hard because the Keeper didn't speak to humans very often. A dream now and then, sometimes a desire; and the dreams didn't often come at times when Oykib could hear them easily. But the Keeper had almost constant dialogue with someone else. Many someones, who seemed to surround the village of Rodina—but how far away or near they were he couldn't guess. The real problem was understanding what was being said. The dreams, the desires he overheard made no sense. At first he thought it was a simple matter of confusion. There were too many of them, that was all. But then, as he began to be able to distinguish one dream from another, as he began to follow a particular thread of communication, he realized that the strangeness was inherent in the messages. The Keeper was prodding these someones with desires that Oykib had never felt, that he couldn't understand; and then, suddenly, there would be something clear: A desire to go care for a child. A wish not to embarrass himself in front of his friends. And the more he listened, the more he began to glimpse what the stranger hungers were: a desire to dig, to tear at wood with his hands. A desire to smear himself with clay. These things made no sense, and yet as Oykib sat in the shadow of the ship, stripping away his humanness, these desires swept over him and he felt—different. Other. Not himself.

He and Chveya had speculated recently, for she, too, had been catching glimpses, out of the corner of her eye, of inexplicable threads, not connecting one human to another. "And yet I can't possibly be seeing any such thing," she had told him. "I only see the threads connecting people that I can see, or at least people that I know. Yet I've seen no one that these threads could belong to."

"Or you've seen them out of the corner of your eye," Oykib had suggested. "Seen them without knowing what you've seen."

"If that's the case, then dozens of them have been gathered all around the village and the fields, and we haven't seen them. Not once, not ever. That's really a pretty silly idea."

"But they *are* gathered around us, all the time."

"Around us, but far. You said what you heard was faint."

"Compared to the Oversoul, that's all. Like trying to hear a distant concert when somebody's tootling on a fife right next to you."

"See? You said it yourself—a distant concert."

"What if someone *is* watching us?"

"What if they are?" Chveya had answered him. "Let them watch. The Keeper is also watching *them*."

Naturally, all those who believed in the truth of dreams were watching for the winged flyers and the burrowing rodents—what had Hushidh and Luet called them? Angels and Diggers. But in all Oykib's listening, in all of Chveya's glimpses of someone's threads of loyalty and concern, they heard and saw nothing to tell them which of the strange species they had dreamed of their watchful neighbors might be. If it was either of them.

Whatever or whoever these strangers were, though, Oykib had been getting more and more disturbed by the dreams and desires coming into his head. The desire to eat something warm and salt-blooded, still quivering with life—when he first understood that one, it set him to retching with self-revulsion that he could desire such a thing. And even though he knew that the desire came from outside him, it still haunted him as if it had been his own desire. For the warm and salt-blooded something that he wanted to eat alive was, he understood, a soft, tender infant. There was something confusing in his image of it—a dazzle of sky, a leathery crackling blanket. Like all the communications between the Keeper and these strangers, nothing was ever really definite. But this much Oykib knew: It had been a prayer from one of these creatures to the Keeper of Earth, and the prayer had been for the living flesh of a youngling.

What kind of monsters were these people?

I must tell someone, he thought; but he couldn't. To tell anyone but Chveya would be to let them know that he had been overhearing all their most secret communication with the Oversoul for many years. It would make them all feel spied upon, robbed, violated. And to tell Chveya would be to terrify her about the safety of their firstborn child, already growing in her womb; about the safety of the little children she was teaching in the school every day.

So while he could tell her most of what he overheard, he couldn't tell her the worst things; for this past week, he couldn't explain to her why he woke up sweating and gagging in the middle of the night, or why he had grown silent in the past few days, barely speaking to her or to anyone.

Tonight, though, tonight had answered so many questions. For when this bat with its leathery wings came down and landed on the roof of a nearby storage tent, Oykib had sensed a different kind of being entirely. This creature, too, was getting an almost continuous stream of communication from the Keeper in yet another unfamiliar language of desires; but it was brighter and clearer, though more fearful as well. There were questions, and they were formed in ideas that Oykib could understand; best yet, they were linked with language. He didn't understand the words, but he knew that the language could be learned.

The desires, though, he understood very well indeed. A wish not to disappoint others; a desire to protect his wife and children; a hunger for secrets.

Hunger for secrets. Into Oykib's mind, as he watched the creature there on the tent roof, came an image of *whose* secrets the flyer was trying to decipher. Two pictures came into his mind almost at once. A vague image of a human head made of unfired clay, large and monstrous; and then, much more clearly, the image of Nafai in the flesh. Only it wasn't Nafai. It was a creature just like this one, only with patchy hair and tattered wings, unable to fly, and yet respected, being listened to by all the others.

It was Nafai, but it was also not-Nafai.

Then, suddenly, he understood. It's this creature's word for us, for human beings. Old man. Old people. We're the old people.

But that would imply that they knew that humans had once lived on Earth before. That was absurd. Nothing could possibly be remembered for forty million years. And how could they remember anyway? As far as he knew, these creatures had not yet evolved into sentient beings when humans last walked upon the Earth.

Then the creature leapt from the tent and swept quickly over the clearing to the base of the starship. There, as he touched the metal, then rapped upon it with his fingers, he was speaking to the Keeper—no, singing to the Keeper, so rapturous was his mood. Oykib felt as if this creature's awe and rejoicing were inside him. He had a thought, as clear as if it were his own thought: "The Old Ones still put music into the things they make."

He had understood it, even though the words attached to the idea were in a language he had never heard before. No real sound had been uttered, and yet he knew inside his memory what this creature's voice would sound like. High and musical, rich in subtle lingering vowels, but with no sibilants or nasals or even fricatives. The only consonants were plosives and stops, and yet they were no less musical than the tonguing of a flautist, making fluttering interruptions in a tune. T's and K's, G's and P's, B's and D's, and a guttural consonant that Oykib knew his own throat could not possibly make. Sometimes these consonants had an extra puff of air; sometimes they were stopped. It was a beautiful language.

More important, though, was the fact that the desires were not dark and violent, and the Keeper did not seem to be struggling to restrain this creature. Rather than distracting him, the Keeper was encouraging him, reinforcing his desires. The contrast came as such a relief to Oykib after all these weeks and days of confusion and darkness that he spoke aloud. "At last the Keeper has brought a friend to us," he said.

He had forgotten how careful and watchful the creature—no, the angel—had been. He hadn't realized that the angel hadn't seen him there in the darkness. But as soon as he heard his own voice, he knew it was too loud, too sudden. The angel leapt almost a man's height into the air and then beat his wings in a frenzy to rise higher, out of harm's way.

But terror didn't rule him. He flew back, swooping around as if to get a good look at Oykib. Well, look to your heart's content, said Oykib, standing with his hands open and spread wide. I'll not harm you, Oykib tried to say with his body.

And then to the Keeper he said, Help him to know I'm not his enemy.

As usual, there was no answer. Others could get their dreams and their whispered silent words of guidance; Oykib could only overhear them, never receive them directly for himself. For once, though, with the memory of the angel's language and desires still fresh, Oykib did not regret the lack. Perhaps it was the better gift, to hear others.

When the angel winged its way into the night sky, heading up the canyon in moonlight, Oykib walked around the starship and headed back to his house. He could see the flash of the lantern. Who was on duty tonight? Meb? Vas? One of the Elemaki, at any rate.

Obring, that's who it was. Obring always swung the lantern as he walked, making it impossible for him to see any strange motions, for the lantern itself created moving shadows that would mask any real movement that might take place. Oykib had heard Elemak remonstrating with Obring about it once. Obring had only laughed and said, "There's nothing to see, Elya. And besides, it's Volemak we all obey now, not you, remember?"

Elemak remembered. Oykib knew *that.* And while Elemak never spoke to the Oversoul in prayer or conversation, he did curse, and when his curses had real intent behind them, their very intensity moved them into the pattern of communication with the Oversoul, so Oykib could hear him. Silent curses, but nothing said aloud. The man was controlling himself. And at the end there *was* a prayer, or perhaps only a mantra: I am no wordbreaker. I will keep the oath.

Oykib had no doubt which oath he meant—it was the oath to Father, to obey him as long as he was alive to rule over them. Better than anyone except Hushidh and Chveya, who could see the loyalties of the colony laid out like a map before them, Oykib knew that peace in the colony was only skin deep. Everyone knew who the Elemaki were, and who the Nafari; everyone could see that the village was virtually divided down the middle, with Nafari on the east and Elemaki on the west. The colony was not united and never would be. Health to you, Volemak. Health and long life. Let there be no war among us before my children are safely born and grown. Live forever, old man. You are the only cord that holds this harvest together in a single sheaf.

So there was Obring, on watch but worthless at it, while Oykib was aware of dark mutterings and savage prayers out in the darkness and dared not speak to anyone about it.

And tonight, was there some new urgency about it? Some sense of triumph tinged with fear? Daring, that's what it was. Someone was daring something that they had not dared before. And the Keeper was sending a constant stream of distractions. Something's happening. What is it? Speak to me, Keeper! Speak to me, Oversoul!

Chveya was asleep when he came into the house. It was often this way. Up at dawn, Chveya worked hard all day, as if her pregnancy should make no difference in her schedule. Then she would come home and fall asleep without undressing, wherever she happened to sit or lie down. Once Oykib came home and found her asleep standing up, not leaning on anything, just standing like a flagpole in the middle of the single room of the house, her eyes closed. Breathing heavily—had she been lying down, it would have been a snore.

Tonight she was on the bed, but fully dressed, her feet still dangling to the floor. He wanted not to waken her—but her legs would be asleep in the morning and it would cause her much discomfort, especially if she woke up needing to void her bladder in the night, and her legs wouldn't support her.

Besides, it was important. What had happened tonight, the angel coming to him, or at least to the ship, touching it, and the clarity of his voice to the Keeper and of the Keeper's voice to him. The fact that Oykib could hear his language and understand it. And the murmurings and stirrings of the other, darker beings who surrounded the village.

He moved her feet onto the bed. Chveya awoke.

"Oh, again?" she murmured. "I meant to wait up for you."

"Doesn't matter," he said. "Sleep when you can, you need it."

"But you're upset," she said.

"Happy and worried," he corrected her. Then he told her all that had happened and what he thought it might mean.

"So the angels are starting to come to us," she said.

"But you know that it tells us who the others we've been seeing are. Those rat-creatures. Out there in the dark."

"I think you're right," said Chveya.

"Didn't Hushidh have a dream of them stealing her children?"

"And you feel as though something has broken tonight?" asked Chveya. "I think we have to give warning. Put on extra watches."

"And tell them what? Explain what?" asked Oykib.

"Explain nothing. When we ask Grandfather to double, triple the watch tonight, he'll do it even if we tell him it's just a feeling. He has respect for feelings."

They headed for the door, but no sooner had they opened it than a scream sounded from the Elemaki side of the village. It came from a human throat, and all the grief of the world was in it.

10
Searchers

Eiadh was the one who had screamed. In moments the adults were gathered around her. She wasn't screaming now, but it took great effort for her to control her voice as she explained.

"Zhivya's gone!" she said. "The baby. Taken from her crib. I woke up to see them, like low shadows, running." Now she did lose control, the horror of it filling her voice. "They were holding the four corners of her blanket. My baby was stolen away by *animals!*"

Elemak had been—somewhere. Not in the house with her, that was certain. Now, though, he was on his knees in the doorway. "Look at this footprint," he said. "An animal made this. Coming in and going out—two animals, actually. And heavily burdened when they left." He got up and looked at them. "I saw a flying creature go down into the fields, then up onto the food storage tent, and then down behind the ship. A moment later it took off, flying up the canyon. No doubt it went to get its friends." He touched the footprint. "That . . . *thing* . . . could have made this print. I'm going to follow it up the canyon."

But Oykib looked at the footprint and knew that Elemak was wrong. The angel's feet had been like hands, or perhaps more like powerful visegrips. These footprints came from a creature with flatter feet and long heavy-clawed toes. The feet of a runner or a digger. Not a creature that flies, that clings to branches.

"The angel didn't make this print," said Oykib.

Elemak looked up at him with steely hatred in his eyes.

Nafai at once interrupted. "Elemak is the one who knows how to read the tracks of animals, Oykib."

"But I saw the angel—"

"So did Elemak," said Nafai, "and it's his daughter." He turned to Elemak. "Tell us what to do, Elemak."

Chveya turned to Oykib and, for a moment, silently buried her face in his shoulder. It was the way she responded when Nafai said exactly the wrong thing—which was surprisingly often, for a man as bright as he was. Nafai was correct as far as he knew; it was quite proper for everyone to defer to Elemak's judgment in this matter. But he should have known by now that Elemak would not be grateful to prevail because Nafai told everyone to let him have his way.

Besides, Elemak should *not* prevail, because he was wrong. Oykib knew that angels hadn't taken the child. The kidnappers were no flyers. They had to be searched for on the ground. Worse, those who did take Zhivya had among them at least a few who hungered to eat the living flesh of an infant. There was real urgency in the search, and it would be a criminal waste of time to go off trying to track flying creatures who didn't have the baby.

As if she could hear his thoughts, Mother put a hand on Oykib's shoulder. "Be patient, my son," she said. "You know what you know, and you'll be heard in due time."

Due time? Oykib looked down at Chveya. Her lips were pursed; she was as worried as he was, and as frustrated.

Elemak was organizing his search party, assigning men where to go. Volemak spoke up. "Are all the adults gathered here? Who's watching the children, when we already know that they aren't safe in their homes?"

At once the women with children began rushing out of the house, back to their homes.

"Elemak," said Volemak. "Leave me a few men here, to protect the village while you're gone."

Elemak agreed at once. "You keep Nafai and Oykib here—he can tell you his theories to his heart's content. Give me the other men, though."

"I'm a man," said Yasai.

Oykib restrained himself from saying, "Yes, if a dandelion is a tree." This wasn't the time for teasing. And Yasai *was* a man.

"If there's an attack," said Volemak, "we'll need more. Perhaps the younger men."

Now Elemak dug in his heels. "Nafai has the cloak. If you need more, you have the older boys. We're trying to track creatures who fly. I can't do it without as many men as possible."

"I can protect the village," said Protchnu, trying to look older than his nine years.

Elemak looked at him with a serious expression. "You'll have to. Obey your grandfather without question."

Protchnu nodded. Oykib could not help but think that if Elemak had ever followed his own advice, everyone's lives would have been a lot happier over the past few months.

Moments later Elemak was off, leaving behind, of the men, only Nafai, Issib, Volemak, and Oykib.

"Welcome to the ranks of the useless," said Issib wryly.

"Useless? I hardly think so," said Volemak. "All right, now, Oykib. Tell us what you know."

"I saw an angel tonight," said Oykib. "The same one Elemak saw. But he was only a couple of meters from me, and I saw his foot. It couldn't possibly have made this print."

"Who, then?" asked Nafai.

"There are others," said Chveya. "I've caught glimpses of them. Never anything I could see clearly, but enough that I've begun to make connections. Hushidh has got some hints of this, too. They're all around us. But they're low, in the underbrush. Like Eiadh said, low shadows. Sometimes in the trees."

"You know this, and you haven't *seen* them?" asked Issib.

"I see the connections among them. Faintly." Chveya smiled grimly. "It's the best we've got."

"Not enough," said Nafai. He fixed Oykib with a cold stare. "Stop playing games, Oykib. What do you *know?*"

For the first time it occurred to Oykib that maybe he hadn't kept his secret as well as he thought. "What I *know* is that there was no malice in the angel. In his mind we're the Old Ones, and he's filled with respect and awe. But there are other minds, and they've been watching us for months, and some of them. . . ." He glanced at Eiadh, realized that he had to be careful how he said it. "Some of them might be dangerous to Zhivya."

"The ones that we've been calling diggers," said Nafai.

Volemak nodded. "And they live nearby."

Issib laughed. "What, we get shovels and start digging?" He waved his arm to show the vast area they'd have to dig up.

"Burrows have entrances," said Nafai.

"We've been exploring all around here," said Protchnu. "We've never seen any holes."

"Why don't we do the obvious thing?" said Oykib. "The thing that

Elemak would have done, if he hadn't been so sure that the kidnappers could fly. Follow the footprints."

The diggers' prints were lost almost at once in the mess that their own feet had made when they ran in response to Eiadh's scream. It didn't help that Rasa was leading the women in gathering the little children out of their beds and into the schoolhouse. Despite the tumult, though, Volemak managed to get lanterns distributed to the men and the older boys, and in a few minutes Protchnu gave a cry. "Here!" he shouted. "They weren't dodging or anything, they just ran in a straight line."

It was true—the trail picked up just where it might have been expected from the direction the diggers first ran upon leaving Elemak's and Eiadh's door. The others ran to join Protchnu, but stayed behind as he led the way toward the edge of the woods.

"Wait," said Volemak. "Nafai, Oykib—you spread out to the sides and keep watch. I don't want Protchnu walking head down into a trap."

Carrying lanterns in one hand, gardening tools as makeshift weapons in the other, the ragtag little army entered the verge of the forest. Four adult men, a bunch of little boys, and the young women who had no children yet—that would strike terror in their enemies. As soon as they entered the woods, the tracking became harder—leaves on the forest floor didn't hold footprints very clearly. It took Protchnu a while to get even six meters into the woods, and then he lost the trail.

Moving slowly and carefully, they all scouted an ever-widening circle, trying to pick up the trail again. Then Oykib heard a low cry from Protchnu, standing only a few paces off. The boy was looking up into the branches. "I'm so stupid!" he said, and immediately ran back to where he had lost the trail.

Oykib followed him. "You think they carried the baby through the trees?"

"Up into one tree," said Protchnu. "Remember the hollow stumps we found when we were felling trees?"

"Shedemei said it wasn't impossible for some disease to have. . . ."

By then, though, Protchnu had clambered up the tree and was pressing against the trunk here and there, pressing hard. "Protchnu, you aren't looking for secret passages, are you?"

"We burned the hollow trees because we couldn't use them for construction," said Protchnu. "We should have studied them. The prints lead right to this tree and disappear. They went *somewhere.*"

Protchnu suddenly stopped and grinned. "It gave a little here. Hold your torch up, *Uncle* Oykib. I found me a door." Using the blade of the hoe he was carrying, Protchnu pried into a fissure in the bark and sure enough, an oblong patch of trunk opened up like a door. It had been a seamless part of the trunk until that moment.

"Protchnu, remind me never to call you stupid," said Oykib.

Protchnu barely heard him. He had already turned around and had his legs into the opening.

Oykib set down his lantern and fairly leapt up the trunk to grab Protchnu's arm. "No!" he cried. "We don't need to be trying to rescue *two* of Elemak's children!"

"I'm the only one who can fit through the door!" Protchnu yelled, struggling to get free of Oykib's grip.

"Proya, you've been brilliant, so don't turn stupid on me!" Oykib shouted back. "You can't go feetfirst into their den! You don't know whether there'll even be room down there to use the hoe. Come on, get your legs out before they cut off your feet!"

Reluctantly, Protchnu backed out of the door.

By now, the others had gathered. Nafai was carrying an ax, as was Oykib. When Protchnu was out of the tree, they began to work quickly, chopping into the trunk. In only a few minutes, they had torn away so much of the surviving trunk that the tree toppled.

Now the opening wasn't just a tiny doorway. It was large enough that any of the adults could drop down into the hole. And, lowering his lantern as far down into the opening as he could, Nafai announced that the chamber was tall enough for a human to stand, and the tunnels large enough for humans to use them—on all fours.

"I don't think that's a good idea at the moment," said Volemak.

"We don't have time to waste, Father," said Nafai.

"Stand up and look around you, Nyef."

They raised their lanterns and looked. In the trees, on the ground, hundreds of diggers surrounded them, brandishing clubs and stone-tipped spears.

"I think they've got the numbers on us," said Issib.

"They're ugly," said Sevet's son Umene. "Their skin's all pink and hairless."

"Ugly is the least of our problems," said Volemak.

"Any idea who their leader is?" asked Nafai.

"Didn't Chveya come with us?" asked Oykib.

She was already scanning the diggers. She frowned, then pointed. "He's there, behind those others."

At once Nafai stripped his shirt off over his head, baring the skin of his chest and back. As he did, his skin began to glow, to shine. The cloak of the starmaster, normally invisible as it lived under his skin, was now radiating light in order to make a god of Nafai—at least in these diggers' eyes. At once Oykib heard a cacophony of prayers and curses. "It's working," Oykib said quietly. "The sphincter muscles are loosening. There's going to be a circle of extrafertile ground when this night is over."

A couple of the boys laughed. None of the adults did.

Nafai walked over and stood before the place that Chveya had pointed out. "Which one of these little monsters do I want?" he asked.

Chveya came up beside him, careful not to touch his glowing skin. Now she could pick out the leader, a large, strong one, wearing a necklace of small bones around his neck. "The one with the trophy necklace."

Nafai raised his hand and pointed. His finger glowed. Suddenly a spark leapt from his hand to the leader of the diggers. The trophy necklace wasn't much help to him—he immediately sprawled flat on the ground, trembling.

"You didn't kill him, did you?" asked Chveya.

Oykib could barely hear her. The tumult of terrified prayers from the diggers drowned out almost all other perceptions in his mind. Yet even their terror was tainted with rage and with lust for vengeance. They feared Nafai, but they hated him and wanted him destroyed. "If you think you're making friends," Oykib murmured.

"Oykib," said Nafai, ignoring both their comments, "I need you to do the speaking. I'm busy being a god. I can't let them see me struggling to communicate. Besides, you're the only one with a hope of understanding their responses."

Oykib was astonished. "How can I talk to them? I don't know their language."

"You caught some of the angel language, didn't you? The Oversoul said you did."

"But I've never understood or even heard their—"

"You're about to hear it now," said Nafai.

So the Oversoul *is* aware of me and knows what I can do, thought Oykib. It was the first confirmation of this that he had ever had. But did the Oversoul know how much he *couldn't* do?

He stepped forward, walking toward the leader, who was being helped back to his feet. "The baby," said Oykib. He pantomimed rocking a baby in his arms. The diggers had been watching the humans long enough to understand what the gesture represented.

The digger king babbled something. Oykib was surprised by the language. It was the opposite of the angel language—all sibilants, fricatives, nasals, with a sound, not of music, but of spitting and humming. Does it only sound like an evil and slimy language to me because of what I know about their prayers and hungers?

When the digger king was speaking to his followers, Oykib understood nothing, of course. In a few moments the diggers dragged forward four of their soldiers and threw them down at Nafai's feet. Now Oykib *could* get a clear sense of the terror, the cursing and prayers of the four. "These are the ones who did the kidnapping," said Oykib. "I think they're giving them to you for punishment."

Immediately Nafai turned his back on the offering. "Tell them it's the baby I want, not vengeance."

"Oh, I'm supposed to do that with sign language?" said Oykib. But he tried, all the same, using the same symbol for the baby, and then gesturing for the four to be taken away.

But the diggers apparently thought the gesture meant something else. At a command from the king, four other diggers bounded out and put the blades of their spears against the throats of the four kidnappers. "No!" Oykib shouted, hearing Chveya's voice along with his. Nafai turned around and with a single sweep of his dazzling arm he knocked all eight diggers to the ground. Then he seemed to go berserk, pointing at trees, one at a time, until a spot in their branches burst into flame.

"It's too wet to start a real fire going," Oykib murmured.

"I'm counting on that," said Nafai. "You think I want to burn down our village?"

As far as the diggers were concerned, though, this was the rage of the gods and their forest was doomed. The king rushed out and threw himself down on his belly at Nafai's feet. Then, almost at once, he flipped himself onto his back and flung his arms and legs outward, so his naked belly was completely exposed.

Oykib's mind was filled with prayers, and now, because the digger king was close, because Oykib now knew something of the context, he was able to understand more of what the king was saying. "He's pleading with the god—with you—to kill him and spare his people."

"So he *is* a worthy king," murmured Nafai. "Tell him we want the baby and nothing else. But first I'm going to respect his offering." Nafai took a single stride, so he straddled the supine body of the king. Then he reached down and touched the king's chest with the blade of the axe. "What do you think?" asked Nafai. "They're a violent people, right? Help me on this, I'm making up a ritual as I go along."

"No blood," said Oykib. "That wouldn't be right. It's the other king who does the blood rituals."

"Other king?" asked Nafai.

Chveya was startled, but then confirmed it. "There's as much loyalty to another as to this one." Then she frowned. "But there's someone else, too. Someone that the king himself feels allegiance to. Someone underground."

"No blood," said Nafai. "So what should I do?"

"Give him the axe," said Oykib. "That's the thing that he hardly dares to hope for, but wants above all else. He'll give you his spear and his bone necklace."

Nafai let the handle of the axe slip out of his hands.

"No!" shouted Protchnu behind them. "Don't give up your weapon! You never give up your weapon!"

"Shut up, Proya," said Volemak mildly.

The digger king wrapped one hand around the haft of the axe, then rolled to his belly and rose to his feet. He could lift the axe easily enough, but the handle wasn't right for his hand and he couldn't raise the head of the axe while holding to the end of the handle. There was no reason to worry that he could use it as a weapon.

The king bent down and picked up his spear, then offered it to Nafai.

"What does it mean if I take this?" asked Nafai.

"I don't know," said Oykib. "It's not like this stuff comes to me with a glossary and footnotes."

Nafai took the spear. The king now lifted the bone necklace over his head and held it out to Nafai. "I don't like the bones of this thing," said Nafai, hesitant to take it.

"I don't either," said Oykib. "I think it's time to demand Zhivya again."

"And why do you think that?"

"Because I don't like the way he's praying for you to take the necklace. He really, really wants you to take it, but I don't think it's because he loves you."

"All right," said Nafai. "Tell him I want the baby."

Oykib stepped between Nafai and the king, effectively blocking the transfer of the necklace. The king rocked back on his haunches, looking —what? Was that anger? It looked like anger to Oykib. He made the sign for the baby, then shouted—no, screamed—right in the king's face. "Bring us Zhivya or we'll kill every last one of you ugly naked pink-skinned bastards!"

"Since they don't understand you anyway," said Chveya, "couldn't you use language that we won't have to explain to the little boys later?"

"He's trying to communicate rage," said Nafai. "Is it working?"

"Oh, it's working," said Chveya. "You and he are definitely gaining control over the situation. They don't like you, though."

"I'm heartbroken," said Nafai.

"Break the spear," said Oykib.

"What?" said Nafai.

"That's what he's afraid of, as he stands there holding the axe. He's afraid you'll break the spear."

Nafai broke the handle of the spear across his knees. The crack of the breaking wood rang through the air.

At once the digger king took the axe in both hands and tried to break the handle. He couldn't. It was too thick, too well-tempered.

"Do something else he can't do," said Oykib. "He has to fail twice."

Nafai reached down and took the end of the spear that had the head on it. Using the tip of the spear as a knife, he cut quickly and deeply across his own belly. Blood immediately sprayed out onto the digger king's face, and for a moment Oykib saw, to his horror, that Nafai had cut all the way through the muscle and exposed his bowels. In moments, though, the cloak of the starmaster began healing the wound, and as the diggers watched, the wound closed without a scar.

The digger king took the head of the axe in his hands, as if he contemplated his own disembowelment.

"I don't want him to kill himself," said Nafai. "I don't have the power to heal him."

"Don't worry," said Oykib. "You did exactly the right thing. The one thing the war king can't do is shed his own blood for the people. Don't ask me why, I just know that's the quandary he's trying to deal with."

Chveya interrupted. "Someone else is coming."

They looked up and saw that the digger army was indeed responding to someone else. "Not the blood king," said Oykib. "It's the mother."

"The queen?"

"I think she's the war king's mate, yes," said Oykib. "But she's something more than that. They all call her 'the mother.' "

"What, they have a queen rat?" said Chveya. "Like a queen bee or a queen ant?"

"These are mammals," Oykib reminded her. "It's a religious title, I think. Like blood king and war king." Then, tentatively, he made the sound he had heard in his mind. "Emeezem," he said.

"What's that?" asked Nafai.

"Her name. That's the name they're calling. And her title is Ovovoi."

"Say her name again," said Nafai. "I have to get it right the first time I say it."

"Emeezem," said Oykib. "It's not as if I know for sure *I'm* right."

Nafai lifted his chin and bawled out her name like a caller in a marketplace. "Emeezem!"

The diggers all fell silent. A single figure emerged from the woods and slowly approached Nafai.

She was obviously female, but the real surprise was that she was hairier than most of the males. She wore no decoration, but the pattern of graying in her hair served the purpose well enough. She looked regal; she also looked frail.

"She is begging the god to forgive her. She didn't know what the foolish males were planning."

"I want the baby," said Nafai.

"She knows that. Her women are searching for the baby right now," said Oykib. Then, suddenly, he realized what she was straining to see. "Hold your lantern up to Nafai's face, Chveya."

Chveya did it, and the digger queen covered her head and curled herself into a ball on the ground. "She can die happy now," said Oykib, "because she's seen your face in flesh at last."

"*My* face?" asked Nafai.

"That's what it seems to me she's saying," said Oykib. "*You're* the one with the pipeline to the Oversoul. I'm having a hard time making sense of any of this."

"Don't get testy with me," said Nafai. "The Oversoul doesn't hear the things you're hearing. Your connection with the Keeper is better than his."

Oykib felt a glow suffuse throughout his body. Pride and fear, a strange mixture. The Oversoul needs me to help with this—that was the pride. But the fear was stronger: If I make a mistake, there's no one to correct me.

Emeezem uncurled herself from the ground. "She's waited all her life for you," said Oykib, trying to make sense of the images that flashed into his mind—images of herself as a child, of dark underground places. "She thinks it was you that made her queen. Because you accepted her."

"When could I have done that?"

"When she was a little girl," said Oykib. "I don't understand it, but her childhood memories include you."

"Her bond with you is incredibly strong," said Chveya. "Stronger than her bond with her husband. It's really amazing, Father."

"She's begging you to spare her husband's life. He didn't know about the kidnapping either. It was the blood king's son who did it."

Emeezem hissed and sputtered a fierce command to her husband, and he rose to his feet and shouted almost the same words. Moments later, a proud-looking male strode out, casting aside his weapon in a flamboyant gesture. He walked up to stand before Nafai, but he did not bow or show respect in any way.

Emeezem and the war king both muttered commands to him, but he showed no sign of hearing them.

The queen turned to Nafai and spoke a stream of what sounded like horrible invective.

"She's begging you to strike Fusum dead," said Oykib. "That's the young one's name—he plotted everything even though everyone had been commanded not to harm us."

"I'm not going to kill him," said Nafai.

"You have to do something," said Oykib. "This is the guiltiest one. The war king didn't dare to touch him since he's the blood king's son, so that's why he gave you the four actual kidnappers. But you're a god, Nyef. You have to do something to him or—well, I don't know. Chaos. The universe collapsing. Something really bad, anyway."

"I hate this," said Nafai. "How about if I take him prisoner?"

"And put him in our secure prison?" asked Chveya. "Good thing we built a jail first thing."

"Not a prisoner, then," said Nafai. "A hostage?"

"Strike him down," said Oykib. "They're terrified because you hesitate."

"All I want is Zhivya back," said Nafai. "I don't want any corpses here."

Volemak strode forward and took his place beside Nafai. "Bow to me," he said to Nafai. "Or whatever passes for a bow in their culture."

"Get on all fours and kiss Father's belly, then," said Oykib.

"You're kidding," said Nafai. "That's not what the war king did to show respect to *me*."

"The war king was offering himself as an unworthy sacrifice. You're greeting Father as your king and father."

"Do it," said Volemak. "They don't have to know that I don't have the powers of the cloak. They have to see that you, too, are taking directions from someone. That tells them that powerful as you are, they haven't begun to see our powers."

Nafai dropped down on all fours. But from that position he couldn't reach his father's belly to kiss it. He let his hands off the ground and rose up high enough, then pressed his face into Volemak's shirt.

At once there was a murmur among the diggers.

"Can you glow brighter than you already are?" asked Volemak.

"Yes," said Nafai.

"All right, when I touch your head, really light yourself up."

Volemak reached down with a flamboyant gesture and touched Nafai's head. At once Nafai seemed almost to explode with light. Even the humans gasped then, as the diggers cried out in terror.

"Well done," said Volemak. "I figured we needed to juice up the perception of power. Now, knock down this proud little puppy. Don't kill him, just put him out like these others."

Nafai rose to his feet, still glowing, and reached out his hand, pointing toward Fusum.

The son of the blood king didn't cower, didn't even flinch. He just looked Nafai in the face, defiant. Then the air between them sizzled, his limbs leaped out rigidly, and he keeled over like a falling tree. He lay there twitching.

"You do have a natural sense of theatre," said Volemak. "Now, tell Oykib to point to all nine of these sleepy little diggers and have them carried to the ship."

"To the ship?" asked Nafai.

"Don't let it be seen that you argue with me," said Volemak sharply. "Just do it. Hostages. And Shedemei can keep them drugged up or even put them in suspended animation while she runs some nondestructive studies on them. Trust me, Nafai."

"I do trust you, Father. Forgive me for hesitating." He turned to Oykib and elaborately instructed him exactly as Volemak had told him to.

It felt absurd, at first, for Nafai to repeat to him exactly the words that they had all heard Father say. But as Nafai went through it it took on the power of a ritual. It was the expression of authority. The king. The son of the king. The servant of the son. The diggers needed to see the show. But so, too, did the other humans, especially the boys. Especially Protchnu. This is power and authority, Proya, thought Oykib. This is how it should work, and this is why your father is such a failure—because Elemak could never accept the rule of someone over him. Those who will not *be* ruled are not fit to rule anyone else.

So when Nafai finished his recitation, Oykib made a great deal of ceremony about pointing to each of the unconscious diggers and indicating that other diggers should pick them up and carry them to the ship.

The queen seemed to understand the dance that they were doing. In her turn, she spoke sharply to her husband, the war king, and then he in his own turn addressed the soldiers waiting in the trees. Soon, in groups of four, they gathered around the unconscious ones and lifted them from the ground.

At that moment, other voices called out from the woods. Emeezem called out an answer, and four female diggers emerged from the undergrowth. Each held the corner of a blanket, and in the middle lay Zhivya, who was laughing. She was enjoying the ride.

"Quickly," said Volemak. "Protchnu, run back to the village and fetch

Eiadh. Bring her out here!" To Nafai he said, "Don't reach for the baby. Make them wait. They'll deliver Zhivya into her mother's arms."

They held the pose in silence. It felt like forever, though it couldn't have been more than five minutes. Finally Protchnu returned, leading Eiadh, who cried out in joy when she saw the baby. She ran to where the four female diggers stood, and reached down to scoop Zhivya out of the blanket. "Zhivoya, my lively one, my laughing one," she sang, laughing and crying and turning around and around.

"All right," said Volemak. "Nafai, tell Oykib to tell them to carry the hostages to the ship. And order Dazya to lead them there, so she can explain to Shedemei what's needed. I want them kept unconscious and I want them thoroughly studied."

Dazya, the erstwhile First Child, stepped forward. "I understand," she said.

"But you apparently didn't understand well enough to know that I wanted Nafai to give you the order," said Volemak, not looking at her.

Nafai turned to Dazya and gave the exact orders that Volemak had already given. Dazya, blushing, obeyed. The digger soldiers formed a procession behind her, carrying the nine unconscious ones toward the ship.

The order of authority had now been clearly established. Queen Emeezem now addressed herself directly to Oykib. The trouble was, she didn't perceive him as a god, and therefore when she spoke to him, her words weren't a prayer. It wasn't a communication with the Keeper or the Oversoul, and so to Oykib it was nothing but unintelligible hissing and humming. "I can't understand them unless they think they're speaking to a god," said Oykib.

"Just stand there and refuse to hear them," said Volemak. "When she pauses, point to Nafai."

Oykib obeyed. She quickly got the idea and spoke the same words to Nafai. Oykib could understand her again.

Or maybe he couldn't. "She begs you to come and see how well they've . . . cared for your. . . ."

"Cared for my what?"

"It doesn't make any sense," said Oykib.

"Cared for my what?"

"Your head," said Oykib.

"Where does she want me to go?"

"It's underground," said Oykib. "She wants you to follow her underground."

Nafai turned to Volemak and elaborately repeated all that Oykib had said. Volemak made a show of listening with a grave demeanor.

"First make all these soldiers go away," said Volemak. "And then you, Nafai, will follow her into the tunnels. You're the one with the cloak. If they mean to betray us, you're the only one who'll be safe."

"I have to take Oykib with me," said Nafai. "I don't understand a word they're saying."

Volemak hesitated only a moment. "Keep him safe," he said.

11

Holes

It was astonishing that a god would condescend to such a degree. Emeezem dared to ask him because she was old and had no fear, and because in her life she had learned to hope even for things that could not be hoped. And just as he had accepted her when she was an ugly, undesirable child so many years ago, so now the god accepted her again and followed her down into the city.

To leave the world of light and come into dimness because she asked! To let the bright shimmer of his immortal body illuminate the earthen walls of the deep temples! She wanted to sing, to dance her way down the tunnels. But she was leading a god to his temple. Dignity had to be maintained.

Especially for Mufruzhuuzh's sake; he needed dignity today. No one would criticize him for what had happened—after all, it was Fusum who plotted the stealing of the baby, forcing a deadly confrontation that Muf had neither sought nor desired. And he had faced the god bravely—all saw that he had no fear when he offered his heart for the god to take. Then, when the god asked him to match impossible feats, requiring Muf to do things that only the blood king could do, if anyone could do it at all—well, no one could fault him for hesitating, for failing to act. He had nowhere to turn, so he did not turn at all.

Still, it was humiliating for him, that his wife should have to come forward and extricate him from the dilemma. Never mind that it was rare for the wife of the war king to be the root mother also. He was shamed when his wife was accepted by the god who had merely posed unanswerable riddles to him.

But could Emeezem help it that the baby came into her hands? Muf didn't know where the baby had been hidden—it was only when Fusum's sister realized what a terrible thing he had done that she came to Emeezem with the truth, and by then Muf was already facing down the god. It was just an unfortunate set of circumstances. Mufruzhuuzh was still war king. The god would set everything to rights.

The god was so large he had to bow down on all fours to travel through the tunnels. Of course, he could just as easily have walked upright, tearing out the roofs of the tunnels just by passing through them. But he chose not to, leaving the tunnels undamaged for the people to use. Such kindness! Such generosity to mere earth-crawling worms like us!

Around them she could hear the patter of a thousand feet, as men and women and children scurried to every open passageway, hoping for a glimpse of the god as he passed. Emeezem could see hands reaching up to let the light of the god's body touch pink hands; parents held up their babies so the light of the god would bless their tiny bodies. And still the god followed her, his light undiminished.

They came to the chamber where, so many years ago, Emeezem—no, she was mere Emeez in those days—had first seen the unmarred head of the god. She stopped, and beseeched him to forgive them for leaving him in such obscurity for so long.

She heard the undergod speak to him, and he answered. Then he licked his finger, reached out his hand, and touched the lintel of the doorway. Thus did he leave the fluid of his body on the door of the place. That was more than mere forgiveness. She keened in relief, and many others joined in with her. She could hear one voice, a man, singing, "We put your glorious head in darkness, not worshipping it because in the clay we could not see your light. But you return the waters of life to us, and bring light into the stomach of the earth. So noble, so great!" Others sang their assent to his words: "So noble! So great! So noble! So great!"

The god paid them the compliment of staying there, still, unmoving, till the song ended. Then Emeezem moved on, leading him farther up the corridor, to the temple she had caused to be built for him, starting the very day she was chosen as root mother. Because the head was so large, she had decided that the god must also be very tall, and so she had made the people dig his temple so low that the ceiling could be high. She also placed the temple so that the roof reached up into a crevice in the rock, letting a bit of daylight reflect down into the chamber. And in the brightest spot of the soft diffused glow, on a pedestal made of bones of the skymeat, she had placed his head.

It was nighttime now, though, so there was little illumination when he came into the temple. Instead he brought the light with him, and it brightened every corner of the room when he rose to his feet. Others came through the door after him, gathering along the walls of the temple, watching as he approached the pedestal where the sculpture sat. Now he would see how they had worshipped him, once they understood that his strange large head was a sign of power and not of weakness. Hadn't the entire spring harvest of infant skymeat been offered to him that first year, so that his pedestal immediately rose at once to be as high as any god's? Hadn't he also had more than his share of skymeat broken open and shared among the people in his honor every year since then? Yet still no one had used his head in the time of mating, for they understood that he was not to be worshipped in that way.

The god walked slowly to the face and stood before it. It glowed in the brightness of his body, answering his bright face with an earthen one. He reached out to it, touched it. Then he lifted his head upward toward the source of the room's faint natural starlight and sank to his knees before the statue.

I see, thought Emeezem. You show us how to worship you properly. We cannot do exactly what you have done, because our knees do not bend in that direction. But we will touch the face as you touched it. Was there a reason why it was the lips you touched? Should it always be the lips? Or will we touch that part of the face that we want to have bless us? You must tell me. Perhaps later, if you should deign to soil your lips by speaking our language, or if your undergod should choose to speak our impure tongue. We touch your face, look at the light, then go down on our haunches before your face and gaze at it. Yes, I will remember. We will all remember.

Like all the other women, Shedemei was at once frightened, repelled, and fascinated by the procession of diggers who came into the village, carrying their compatriots who had been knocked unconscious by Nafai. But the responsibility for doing something with them was hers, and so she quickly set her personal feelings aside and led the diggers into the ship. She knew at once what Volemak's purpose was; he had seen her doing nondestructive scans and studies of the few animals they had revived, and knew that she could learn a vast amount about a creature using the equipment on the ship. It was imperative that they understand the physical structures and systems that gave shape to the lives of the diggers, and yet it was just as important that they not be harmed.

The trouble was that it might not be such a good idea to let the diggers see the inside of the ship. From the little that Dza had said, she knew that Nafai had overawed them with the powers of the cloak of the starmaster. Perhaps the smooth and shiny surfaces of the inside of the ship would enhance that effect; but perhaps not. There was definitely danger in letting the diggers see that the humans were, after all, human, that what miracles they did were done with tools and machines and not by godlike powers inherent in them.

But that was for another day. Volemak had made his decision, and it was almost certainly best. Even if it wasn't, Shedemei would obey. The peace they had had these past months since arriving on Earth depended on supporting his authority; she would obey him even if he was flat wrong. Peace—that's all Shedemei wanted. A chance to do her work without having to worry about which side she was on and who was on top in the endless family struggles among Volemak's and Rasa's children.

The first order of business once the carriers were gone was to sedate the diggers so that they didn't awaken at an inconvenient time. There had been forty million years of evolution since the biota of Earth and Harmony had diverged, but the most conservative aspect of life was at the chemical level. A light dosage of the safest sedative should do the job. She spoke to the medical computer as she weighed each of the bodies in turn. The dosages were meted out and she pressed the pads against the pink skin.

Pink hairless skin—why would these rodents have lost their fur? She suspected that there was no sound evolutionary reason for it—it was a cultural thing. Some standard of beauty became general and then only those who exhibited the beautiful trait were able to mate. Soon pink skin would predominate in the culture while hairiness would be relegated to a few despised members. Otherwise, the trait made no sense. Digger skin had no melanin. No wonder they had to stay in shadows and tunnels all the time, unlike their ancient rat ancestors—they couldn't bear the sunburn if they emerged from the trees.

Once they were all sedated, she meant to begin scanning them at once. But then sleepiness swept over her like a wave at the beach, and she realized that after being awake all night this was hardly the time to conduct serious investigations. So she used the cart and carried each digger in turn to a suspended animation chamber. She set the chambers to normal life support so they wouldn't kick into suspended animation mode—there was too much risk that the suspended animation dosages wouldn't be right for diggers and they'd be unrevivable.

Then she went to her berth and lay down, just for a nap. A couple of hours and she'd be fine. It reminded her of the way she had lived in

Basilica before they persuaded her—no, tricked her, manipulated her, forced her—to join Volemak's exodus into the wilderness. In those days, when she was hot on the trail of some elusive gene, she could work around the clock, taking short naps that amounted to little more than a couple of hours of sleep a day. The excitement of discovery and creation were more important than sleeping and eating. She had never wanted that life to be interrupted.

Well, it *had* been interrupted, and she wasn't entirely unhappy about it. For one thing, Basilica had been destroyed in Moozh's bid for empire, so her old life couldn't have continued in any case. Even if Basilica still stood, however, Shedemei's journey in the wilderness had given her many good gifts. Her two children, Padarok and Dabrota—their names meant Gift and Kindness, and they had grown up to merit them. Zdorab, her shy and complicated husband, a man who had never desired women and yet had given her two children, not to mention good companionship for these many years. Despite his lack of desire, despite her lack of interest, they had helped each other join the great stream of life, of creation. Wouldn't it have been sad if I had spent my life bending and shaping life, and yet had never taken part in it myself? I was spared that, I am glad of it.

But now Rokya and Dabya were adults. Rokya was married to Hushidh's daughter Dza; Dabya was married to Luet's son Zhatva. They were going to be parents soon. They didn't need Shedemei anymore. Zdorab had never needed her, not really. Liked her, yes, even loved her, but it wasn't a *need.* So why am I still here? she wondered. I don't want to see this community torn apart. I don't want to watch as my children have to choose sides. I don't want to be here when blood is shed, when lives are lost. I don't even want to care about the outcome. I just want to be by myself, working on plants, on animals, studying how the biosystems have diverged, understanding more and more of the way life creates itself. I want to know why giant cattle roam the plains north of this massif. I want to know why two sentient species evolved in such close proximity without one of them destroying the other. I want to know why the Oversoul brought us to this place of all places, instead of to one of the many locations where we could have established our colony without interfering in the lives of diggers or angels.

I want my dream to come true.

Ah, yes, that was the underlying wish above all wishes. The dream that the Keeper of Earth had sent her, so many years ago, a dream of a garden in the sky. Of course it had already *been* fulfilled. The seeds and embryos she had brought with her were already beginning to play a role in the life of this planet. But couldn't the dream be more literal? Once the colony was fully established, couldn't she take the ship back into the sky and orbit the Earth, studying ecosystems, developing variations and enhancements and hybrids of lifeforms from Harmony and Earth, coming down only now and then to take samples and measurements and to introduce new organisms into the world? Then she really would be the gardener of Earth, a whole planet to play with. I'd be good at it, she whispered to the Oversoul. Then I wouldn't have to be part of the messiness here in the colony. I don't want to have to care about rivalries and loyalties. I just want to learn, to change, to create, to transform. That's what my talent is. I have no gift for getting along with humans. I've given you what you needed from me. Let me have now what I want.

<All right.>

Shedemei felt the anxiety and longing seep out of her. The Oversoul said it would be all right. Now she could sleep.

Oykib was grateful to be able to stand up at last, after crawling or duckwalking his way through seemingly endless low tunnels. He had hardly been able to pay attention to his surroundings, partly because the grays and browns of the rock and earthen walls hardly offered much in the way of scenery, but mostly because the diggers that surrounded them were all crying out to the gods, and so Oykib could hear the silent pleadings and psalms and paeans as if they were all singing in his ears.

Still, despite the confusion of voices, Oykib *was* beginning to learn some words, some shapes and structures in the language. It became music to him first, so that he heard the rhythms and tunes that helped carry meanings and emotions. This must be what dogs hear in human speech, he thought. The music of our voices tells them if we're angry or happy, sad or frightened. That was as much of the language as Oykib understood, but he knew that soon he would understand more. He had never had to learn a second language before, so that until now he had never known how easy it was. He had a talent for it. Or perhaps it was simply easier to learn a language if you had some understanding of the speakers before trying to grasp their speech.

Now, standing in the temple chamber, the light from the cloak illuminating every corner, Oykib could take a moment to look at the diggers gathered around the walls of the room. Their origin as rats was unmistakable, but so was the fact that the thousands of generations between them and their ancestors had changed them far more than the humans of Basilica had changed. The snout and whiskers were still prominent, but much less so than in their ancestors, and the jaw had changed shape to allow for speech. Oykib was eager to discuss with Shedemei what all the other structural changes were for.

"Oykib," said Nafai.

That's right, he had a job to do. A little embarrassed at having allowed himself to daydream at such a tense moment, he stepped up beside Nafai. "Yes?" he said.

But Nafai didn't answer, just continued to stare at the statue that rested on a pedestal of tiny bones. It was a human head. But not just any human. The face was clearly Nafai's own.

"When could they have done this?" asked Nafai.

Oykib tried to sort out the many prayers going on in the room, and gradually gleaned a little information. "They didn't do it," he said. "They don't make their gods. The way they tell it, their gods make themselves. They're praising *you* for having given them such a perfect copy of your head."

"It *is* perfect," said Nafai. "Perhaps a little younger."

"Get this," said Oykib. "The head is a hundred years old."

"Impossible."

"It was fifty years ago when the queen found this statue in that tiny secluded chamber that you—blessed, or whatever it was you were doing."

"I hope I was blessing it," said Nafai.

"And it was fifty years old then. Apparently her relationship with that statue was pivotal in her life. It's because of you that she married the war king. Because you accepted her."

"Are you sure you're understanding this?" asked Nafai.

"Not at all," said Oykib. "But it's as clear as anything else I've understood. There's plenty of time to figure this all out. But one thing's sure. This head is older than any living digger. And they definitely claim they didn't make it themselves, though how their clay gods could make themselves I can't imagine. They point out how perfectly the features have been preserved. This is because they worshipped you differently from the other gods. They didn't—this is kind of repulsive—they didn't rub your head in order to breed."

"So their other gods are involved in fertility worship."

"The images I'm getting are pretty nasty," said Oykib.

"Religion isn't always pretty," said Nafai. "Especially viewed from the outside, by an unbeliever. So they use the other statues as part of a mating ritual, but mine they left alone."

"Because you were so ugly." Oykib couldn't keep a bit of laughter out of his voice.

"To them, I'm sure," said Nafai. "Just imagine what they would have thought if it had been *your* head."

"Babies would have run screaming from the cave, I'm sure."

"So what do I do with this sculpture?"

"Invent a ritual, Nafai. You've been winging it pretty well so far."

So Nafai sank to his knees before the statue and improvised a fairly simple and harmless sort of obeisance. When he was done, he got up and smiled at Oykib. "This is kind of embarrassing," he said. "To have people worshipping me. Though there are those who'll be bound to say that it's what I've secretly longed for all my life."

"So don't tell them that you're being worshipped."

"I can't conceal something like this. My face, carved a hundred years ago. Since I certainly did *not* sculpt it, someone did. And someone knew what I looked like."

"The Keeper, obviously."

"Yes, but don't you understand? It means that the Keeper knew things about us here on Earth at a time when—well, when the information couldn't possibly have traveled at lightspeed. At the speed of light, the Keeper would have to have seen my face almost eighty years before I was born in order to have this carved a hundred years ago."

"So we don't know everything about physics. Hardly a surprise, since the Oversoul was keeping human beings from learning a lot of science and technology."

"But Oykib, I've always assumed that the Keeper was some kind of computer, like the Oversoul. The Oversoul was created by humanity at its technological peak, along with our starship. And at that time they knew nothing about faster-than-light communication."

"So, somebody learned more."

"Who, Oykib? The human beings were gone from Earth. Who built the Keeper, if he has powers far beyond what humanity was capable of creating at its peak?"

"Maybe the humans didn't all leave," said Oykib.

"Maybe," said Nafai. "It's a puzzle. In the meantime, I'd really like to get out of this dark, musty, dirty place. It must be near dawn by now, and I'm exhausted."

"I wouldn't mind a nap myself."

"So how do I extricate myself? I have no clue how to get out of here."

"Wing it," said Oykib.

"I'm sure glad I have you along for wise counsel," said Nafai dryly.

Dawn was breaking when Elemak's party reached the place where the canyon became a shallow depression and finally just a part of the saddle of the first range of mountains. It had been slow climbing in the darkness, even with the lanterns. Perhaps especially with the lanterns. And it didn't help that Mebbekew and Obring seemed to be in competition for the longest, vilest string of obscenities whenever they slipped or whenever a passage looked especially forbidding or . . . whenever.

Zdorab hated listening to them. In fact, he realized now, he simply hated *them,* even when by chance they were silent. He hated the way they treated women. He hated the way they treated men. He hated the way they thought. He hated the way they didn't think. It was hard to imagine which of them he hated more. On the one hand, Obring was inherently stupid and brutal. It wasn't a decision he made. It was a chronic condition bordering on the continuous. On the other hand, Mebbekew was actually rather bright; he merely chose to be stupid. He seemed to take pleasure in cruelty, too, but unlike Obring, he didn't care enough to seek out occasions for it. He simply took whatever opportunity to be stupid and cruel happened to come to hand. Which of them, then, was more detestable? The one who was loathsome by nature, or the one who wanted to be loathsome but hadn't enough ambition to excel at it?

How did I come to be here this morning, Zdorab wondered, greeting dawn on a mountain range on Earth, in hot pursuit of a flying creature that left no trail and might not be anywhere near us? Why am I not asleep in a soft chair in a library in Basilica? Why am I now sharing such strenuous activity in the company of exactly the kind of men I most hated back in civilization? And, worse, taking orders from them?

Zdorab knew that most of the others were thinking similar thoughts. Well, not dreaming of soft beds in Basilica. The younger men had never seen the city—or any city, for that matter. Nevertheless, they were filled with resentment, knowing that there was no hope of accomplishing anything. Wherever these flying creatures lived, it would probably be very high. Out of reach. And if in fact they had taken Elemak's daughter, how was this group of men going to save her? With their motley assortment of farming tools, what would they do? Hand over our little girl, you villains, or we'll *plant a garden!*

At this little bit of whimsy Zdorab couldn't help but smile. But at that moment he crested the rise to find Elemak glaring at him.

"What's the smile about, Zdorab?"

"I was off in another world," said Zdorab, ducking his head obsequiously. It was a posture he had learned long ago. It generally deflected the wrath of bullies. "I'm so sorry."

"You shouldn't be," said Elemak. "Better any world than this."

So he, too, resented it. As if he hadn't been part of the cause of it, with his plotting and conniving back on Basilica.

But Zdorab said nothing more. Instead he turned and surveyed the terrain that dawn was revealing. At this altitude the air was noticeably cooler, and the undergrowth wasn't quite as thick. A thin mist had formed in the valley behind the saddle, like a river flowing among the trees. The next row of peaks was astonishing in its craggy beauty, and behind that he could see the very tops of a couple of mountains so high that even at these latitudes they had snow. It had snowed several times during the years he lived in Basilica, but it was never more than an inch or two on the ground, and it always melted within a day. But the snow must never melt up there. What had Shedemei said? Mountains so new and high that it was a miracle the mantle of Earth could sustain the weight of them. Eleven thousand meters. The Oversoul said that there were no mountains so high on Harmony, and as far as his records showed there had never been such high mountains on Earth before, either. These were new, pushed up by an ocean plate being subducted under what had once been a narrow isthmus connecting two continents. Now it was a great massif, the highest spot on Earth, and every climate and terrain existed on its perimeter. On the western coast the mountains were so high their rain shadow caused an utter desert. On the east, there was a place where rain fell almost continuously, day and night, summer and winter, so that it was bare rock, except for a few hardy mosses that could live with perpetual cloud cover.

Why can't Shedemei and I leave this village, simply explore this new planet? They don't need us. We don't want to be with them. Our son and daughter are grown up and married now. It would be nice to visit with them from time to time, but parenting they don't need. When they have children, I can sing them silly songs and dandle them on my knee. Twice a year.

But thinking of little children made him remember why they were there. Why they had spent tonight with no sleep, climbing a canyon in the dark. And now he looked out over the valley and saw that in the first light of dawn, the trees were jumping with life. Flying creatures bounding into the air, flying a short distance, and then dropping back down into the leaves. Each of them seemed to be carrying something in its feet as it flew.

"They're terrified of us," said Elemak softly.

"How can you tell *that?*" asked Mebbekew.

"Because they're evacuating their village. Look—those are their own children they're carrying."

"Look," said Zdorab. "When the children are a little larger, it takes two adults to carry them."

"Good eyes," said Elemak. "It took four of them to lift Zhivya. And if they think they can get away from me by carrying their children to—"

"They *can,*" said Vas scornfully. "They can get away from us any time they want, precisely by carrying their children to safety. What are you going to do, dance along the treetops till you catch up with them?"

Elemak turned slowly. "Go back down the mountain, then, if you don't care about this errand."

Vas immediately apologized. "I'm tired, Elemak. I'm too tired to know what I'm saying."

"Then keep your mouth shut," said Elemak. "And your eyes open."

Zdorab sighed and turned away from this touching scene of true friendship. The only people who hated Elemak worse than his enemies were his friends. And yet they followed him, because they knew he needed them so much he couldn't ignore them, as Nafai certainly would have. That's probably how a lot of vile men get others to follow them, thought Zdorab. They can't get good men to follow them, and they need somebody, so they have to take the kind of men who can't find a good man interested in taking them on. The miracle was that evil persisted in the world, since the only people who took part in it generally couldn't stand each other, and for good reason.

Zdorab's attention was caught by a movement in a tree just down from the crest. A single bat-thing was sitting on a branch. "Look," said Zdorab.

"I see him," said Elemak.

"What's he doing?" asked Yasai.

"We all have the same number of eyes," said Elemak scornfully. "Watch and we'll see together."

The angel abruptly dropped from the tree, fluttering down to the ground in a small clearing that led up to where the humans stood. Zdorab got a chance to see it clearly then, its wings extended. The face was hideously ugly, but that was hardly a surprise. After all, it had descended from some wizen-snouted species of bat, hadn't it? The real surprise was the fascinating compromise that evolution had reached. Its arms and legs were almost mockingly thin. From wrist to ankle on each side of his body, the wings fanned out, held rigid by two distorted fingers of each hand. The other three fingers on each side, however, were of normal size, giving the creature good hands for grasping. And the head was very large for the size of the body. The miracle was that it could fly at all. It was surely at the outside limit of its growth—any larger, and it would lose the power of flight.

At this moment, however, it was walking toward them. It wasn't without grace when it walked, but it was clear that it was more at ease on branches or in the air. A long-distance hiker it would never be, not on those feet.

Those feet.

Zdorab knew enough to hold his tongue. Young Yasai, alas, did not. "Oykib was right," he blurted out. "No way did those feet make those footprints back in the village."

Elemak turned slowly toward him. "So maybe it wasn't this *thing* that made the prints. Do you think I didn't know that was a possibility? The fact remains that this fellow was the lookout for the kidnappers. If he doesn't have Zhivya, he knows where she is." Elemak took a step downward, toward the creature.

Almost at once, the creature stopped, and then did the most extraordinary thing. He reached down and took from his foot a small number of stalks of grain that he had been holding. Then he laid them down in the grass, making a great show of each one, as if counting them out. When they were all laid out, the creature took a step backward.

"That's grain from our field," said Obring.

"Did you just realize that?" asked Vas.

"Does it matter?" asked Meb.

"He thinks that's why we came up here," said Padarok, Zdorab's own son. "Because he stole our grain. He's giving it back."

"And when did you become an expert on overgrown bats?" asked Elemak.

"It makes sense," said Padarok stubbornly.

Zdorab waved a hand at him, trying to get him to shut up.

"No, I won't shut up, Father. This whole thing is ludicrous. The angel took some grain from the field and he doesn't know a thing about Zhivya. If somebody had stopped to give this any thought at all, we wouldn't have spent all night climbing a mountain in pursuit of an innocent man."

Elemak's hands snapped out and seized Padarok by the head. Like his father, Padarok had not grown into a very tall man, and he was slight of build. He looked like a puppet in Elemak's massive grasp. "Man?" Elemak demanded. "You call that *thing* a *man?*"

"Figure of speech," Padarok murmured.

"That *man,* as you call him, knows where my daughter is!" With those words Elemak shook Padarok. His whole body went limp. For a moment Zdorab feared that the shaking had done brain damage, had perhaps even killed him. And even though Padarok's eyes immediately fluttered open and he moved his limbs, the hot rage that surged inside Zdorab did not fade. To his own surprise, Zdorab found himself in the odd position of holding a scythe over Elemak's shoulders and neck, saying to him the most unbelievable words. "Let go of my son," he said. "Now."

Elemak turned slowly and regarded Zdorab with lizard eyes. "And if I don't, will you cut off my arms?"

"Only if I miss your neck," said Zdorab.

Elemak let go of Padarok. "Don't threaten me, Zdorab. Even if *you've* forgotten who our enemy is, *I* haven't." With a quick movement Elemak snatched the scythe out of Zdorab's hands, so quickly that Zdorab could barely register that it had happened. For a moment Elemak stood there, the scythe poised, and Zdorab wasn't sure whether Elemak meant to strike him or his son. But then he cast the scythe to the ground and strode to where the creature waited.

The poor thing visibly wilted under the head of Elemak's fierce glare, but it stood its ground. Elemak reached out a foot and ground the stalks of grain into the muddy grass. "I don't care about the grain," he said. Then he reached down and snatched the creature up by one arm. "Where's my daughter!" he bellowed.

"What language do you expect him to answer in?" said Padarok scornfully. "Or should he draw you a map in midair?"

Please, don't goad him, don't provoke him, Rokya; Zdorab thought the words but didn't say them. Because he was also proud. He had spent his life bowing to men like this, so they wouldn't hurt him. But his son did not bow. He might have inherited my height, thought Zdorab, but he has his mother's spine.

Elemak's answer was to roar in rage, and as he did, he snapped the creature like a whip. Zdorab saw, to his horror, that in Elemak's grip the poor thing was like a brittle stick. He could see its arm break on both sides of Elemak's grip, and at the same time both wings tore and began to bleed, while every joint seemed to have bent the wrong way and now could not get back. The creature screamed once and then fell silent, hanging limp and broken in Elemak's hands.

"My my my," said Meb. "Fellow doesn't know his own strength sometimes."

"Good work," said Padarok. "Now that he's dead, he'll make a great guide."

Elemak hurled the broken animal away from him. It struck the trunk of a tree and stuck there for a moment, then dropped lifelessly to the ground. "Where is my daughter!" Elemak shouted. "They've taken my daughter!"

His rage was so terrible that they all backed away from him, just a step, but it made their fear plain. Except Padarok. *He* didn't back away.

And that meant that he would be the one to bear the brunt of Elemak's helpless fury. Already Elemak was glaring at him.

So, again without thinking, Zdorab stepped forward. "We're going back down now, Elemak. We all tried. But there's no way we can find her, if she's up here. If breaking and killing a helpless little creature will make you feel better, then you've done it. You don't have to kill or break anything else."

He could see Elemak visibly pull himself back under control.

"I'll never forgive you for saying that," Elemak said.

"There's not a soul here that you haven't promised, one time or another, never to forgive," said Zdorab. "But we forgive *you*, Elemak. We all have children. It could have been any one of us. If we could bring her back to you, we would."

"If you could bring her back to me," said Elemak, "I would be your willing servant forever." Then he stalked off, over the saddle, and down into the canyon.

Obring and Meb followed him immediately, but both paused as they passed Zdorab. "Who would have t hought the little pizdoon had some spunk in him after all," Obring said, laughing derisively.

"You keep *this* up," said Meb, "and someday, who knows? You might actually get a hard-on. Then you'll be half a man." He patted Zdorab on the head and followed Obring and Elemak down.

Padarok came to Zdorab and hugged him. "Thank you, Father. I thought he was going to break my neck."

"We saw what he wanted to do to *you*, Rokya," said Zdorab, "because he did it to the angel."

Then, from down by the tree where Elemak had flung the poor creature, Yasai called out. "He's not dead!"

"Then maybe we should kill it to put it out of its misery," suggested Zhatva, Nafai's eldest son. They all gathered around the creature.

"This isn't a dog," said Yasai. "Oykib said he was sentient. A person, not a beast. Shedemei will be able to heal him if it can be done at all."

The creature kept slowly blinking one eye.

"Are you sure that's not a reflex?" asked Xodhya.

Yasai was peeling off his shirt. "Help me lift him onto this," he said. "Without breaking his neck."

"It's already broken," said Motiga helpfully.

"But maybe the spinal column isn't severed." Then Yasai whistled in surprise. "He's so light."

"It hurts him," said Vas. "He's closing his eyes in pain."

"But not complaining," said Zdorab. "He bears his suffering well."

"Yeah, a real man," said Zhatva. But there was little mockery in his voice. The creature was to be admired.

"What if Elemak sees that we're carrying him?" asked Motya.

"I hope he does," said Padarok. "This creature wasn't threatening him in any way, and look what he did. Even if it had *been* a dog. . . ."

He didn't have to finish his sentence. Four of them took up the four corners of the shirt. The others carried their lanterns, and they began the slow journey down the canyon.

Eiadh heard the glad shouting of the children and knew that Elemak and the men who were with him had finally come back down from their night's search. No doubt Elya would be exhausted and a bit frustrated that his search was in vain. But when he saw Zhivya, that would make up for everything.

Zhivya, perhaps worn out from yesterday's excitement, was taking a late morning nap. Eiadh picked her up carefully; the baby stirred but did not wake. Eiadh's one worry now was that she might remember something from the experience. She was old enough to toddle around now, but surely not old enough for memories to linger. There should be no nightmares of diggers looming over her crib or of journeys through long dark tunnels. There was nothing to worry about now.

Zhivya woke up as Eiadh carried her along toward the village's edge. There was Elemak, tall and strong—for all his flaws, a fine man, a powerful figure. Eiadh remembered again why she had fallen in love with him, back when she was a foolish shallow girl in Basilica. True, he had proven not to have the self-control and the selflessness that she admired in some of the other men, and his temper meant that she and the children had to tread carefully at home. But he was her husband, and she wasn't unhappy about that. Not today, not with their children rescued from the monsters of the underground.

As she approached, she could see that Volemak was telling him what had happened; as they spoke, Volemak cast his gaze toward her, and Elemak looked also, seeing that she had the baby. Elemak smiled at her. It could have been a bit more enthusiastic, but he was tired.

Suddenly there was a flurry of activity. Yasai, Rokya, Xodhya, and Zhyat were carrying something in a shirt—Yasai's, no doubt, since he was barechested. Volemak directed them toward the ship, where Shedemei was studying the digger hostages. What was it? They hadn't harmed one of the angels, had they?

As soon as she thought of it, she knew it was true. Volemak was remonstrating with Elemak, and now Eiadh was near enough and their voices were loud enough for her to hear.

"But he was unarmed?" Volemak was saying. "He didn't threaten you at all?"

"I told you that I thought he knew where my daughter was!"

"So you crippled him? Even if you didn't care that we have to live in this place and you have *needlessly* made enemies of a tribe of sentient creatures, you might have thought that brutalizing the one person who *might* have helped you was beyond stupidity!"

Volemak was too angry, Eiadh thought. Elemak didn't respond well to tongue-lashings, especially in public. He had been faithful to the oath of obedience, but why push it?

Of course, she hadn't seen the injured angel, and Volemak had. What had Elemak done?

"Oh, yes, I'm beyond stupid," Elemak was answering. "But your perfect hero with the magic cloak was down playing god with a bunch of rats!"

"He got your daughter back, he and Oykib and Protchnu and I," said Volemak. "And we did it surrounded by armed diggers that outnumbered us by hundreds, because *you* had insisted on taking all but a handful of our men of fighting age."

"If you had commanded me to leave some behind," Elemak began, but Volemak cut him off.

"Oh, yes, you would have obeyed—while you accused me of wanting your daughter to die. Well, Elya, she lived, no thanks to you. Now let's see if that harmless angel is as lucky."

"What am I supposed to do, kneel down and worship at Nafai's feet? Is he supposed to be *my* god, too?"

That was too much for Eiadh. "You might thank him," said Eiadh quietly. "He gave us back Zhivya."

"No he didn't," said Elemak. "The cloak of the starmaster did whatever was done. If *I* had had the cloak, I could have done at least as well."

"No you wouldn't," said Eiadh. "Because you would have been up the canyon with the cloak, no doubt using it to shoot angels out of the sky, and down here without it we would have been overrun and slaughtered by the diggers, every one of us."

"How should I have known that some creatures we'd never seen before took the baby?"

"Oykib tried to tell you, but you wouldn't listen. It's one reason you aren't fit to lead us. You never listen, you just decide based on what you already know. Well, Elemak, you don't know everything." Eiadh heard her own words and knew she was saying too much. The rage in his face was frightening. He hadn't looked at her like that since . . . since she took Volemak's oath during the voyage.

"So this is my greeting from my wife when I come home," he said.

"I meant to greet you with joy," said Eiadh, bowing her head. "I'm sorry."

Because she had submitted, Elemak could turn his anger to others. "So I was wrong," he said. "I didn't hear any of *you* arguing with me!"

They answered him with silence.

"So don't go criticizing me if you haven't the brains to come up with a better idea."

"We all had a better idea," said Padarok quietly. "We all knew that you were wrong. We knew it from the beginning."

His words were like a slap in Elemak's face. "Then why did you follow me?"

"It was your daughter who was missing," said Padarok.

"That didn't mean that I was *right*," said Elemak. "It probably meant my judgment wasn't at its best."

"Yes, that's what I was saying," said Padarok.

"You followed me *because* my judgment wasn't good?" asked Elemak. "You all knew I was wrong, and you followed me *because* I was wrong?" The contempt in his voice made a poor disguise for the confusion he was obviously feeling.

"Elemak, come inside, come to the house," Eiadh said.

"No, I want to understand this," said Elemak. "I want to understand why these so-called men are so stupid that they knowingly follow someone that they think is wrong."

"Please, Elemak."

"We didn't follow you because you were wrong," Yasai finally said. "We followed you because you were irrational. We didn't know what you'd do if we refused to obey."

"What do you mean?" demanded Elemak. "What mattered was finding my daughter. That's *all* that mattered."

"Was it?" asked Eiadh. "If *that* was true, you would have stopped and listened to Oykib when he tried to tell you that it wasn't the angels who took Zhivya. Now please, stop arguing about it. Everybody's home safe and nobody was harmed."

Elemak shrugged off the hand she had laid upon his arm. "Don't patronize me, Eiadh."

"Don't be angry, Elemak," she said. "Zhivya was lost, and she's been restored to us. It's a day for rejoicing, not anger. You might even thank the ones who brought her back to us."

"Thank them? Because the Oversoul gave Nafai the only good weapon? Because they followed me on a foolish chase up the canyon *because* they knew it was foolish?"

Padarok stepped closer to Elemak. "No, Elemak. We followed you because we were afraid that you would do to one of us what you finally ended up doing to that harmless angel. And our fear was not unfounded. If you'll remember, you came very close to doing it to *me*."

Only now did Eiadh notice the bruises on Padarok's neck and jaws.

"If Father hadn't stood against you," said Padarok.

Elemak, his face red with rage—or was it shame?—answered contemptuously. "Do you think I stopped because of *his* pathetic threats?"

"I don't know why you stopped," said Padarok. "But we never know whether you *will* stop. And so we obey you when you're angry and irrational, because we're afraid of you. And if you think about it without letting rage cloud your reason, you'll realize that we have cause to be afraid."

"Let's go home, Elya," said Eiadh again.

But Elemak was determined to have this out. "You would have let Zhivya die, because you were so afraid of me that you didn't dare to argue with me?"

Padarok shook his head. "We knew that Nafai would get her back, if it could be done at all."

"Nafai?" said Elemak. Then he roared. "Nafai! Nafai! Nafai! You trusted *him* to do it! You put my daughter's life in *his* hands! What does he know, that stupid, boastful boy, that snot-nosed little pretender, that—"

"He *did it!*" Eiadh screamed at him. "You stupid angry fool, he *did* save her, so they were *right* to trust him!" Her screaming frightened the baby, who started to cry. But Eiadh couldn't stop now. "And they knew that if you stayed here, you'd just do some angry stupid thing and cause a disaster, so it was *better* to have you off up the canyon where you wouldn't start a war between us and the diggers. Do you get it now, Elemak? Now that you've made us tell you more than we ever meant to, will you finally understand what you *are* to us? We know that if anything delicate needs to be done, *you'd* better not be there, because you'll always, always, always do something like what you did to that angel!"

For a moment Eiadh felt the thrill of having finally blurted out the truth, of having struck down the prideful man who had complicated her life so much for all these years.

Then she saw something she had never seen before. Elemak didn't rage. His shoulders slumped. He visibly wilted. He looked at no one, met no one's gaze. He just turned his back and walked into the forest.

"I'm sorry, Elya," she called after him. "I was angry, I didn't mean it."

But he knew she meant it. Everyone knew she meant it, and everyone knew that what she had said was true. Everyone had known it for years. Finally, today, Elemak knew it too.

He came back the next day. Quiet, subdued. A different man. A broken man. Eiadh tried to apologize to him when they were alone in the house, but he walked out the door and wouldn't listen. They shared their bed, but he never reached out to her. He would answer the children when they asked him questions, and sometimes he would play with them and laugh and smile like the old days. But he didn't come to any of the meetings of the adults, and when Eiadh tried to involve him in decisions about their own household, he always answered the same way. "Whatever you want," he said. "I don't care."

And he didn't care, or so it seemed. He did his work in the fields, but he no longer had any ideas about what others should do. He simply did what he was asked. He worked hard. He exhausted himself, in fact. But he still seemed invisible.

I killed him, thought Eiadh.

Or maybe, just maybe, I took the first step toward healing him.

She would cling to that hope, she decided. This puzzling, quiet, withdrawn personality was just a stage in his development into a mature, wise, self-restrained, good man.

A man like Nafai.

12

Friends

Shedemei asked Volemak for a meeting of all those involved in dealing with the two sentient species. "There are decisions to be made," she said, and so when the evening meal was done, they gathered in the ship's library: Volemak and Shedemei, of course, and along with them Nafai and Luet, Issib and Hushidh, and Oykib and Chveya. "I invited Elemak," Volemak explained, "because he had so much experience back on Harmony, dealing with strange cultures and foreign leaders. He declined to come, but I'm still going to ask him to work with the diggers, at least. They're the ones who are living practically on top of us—"

"Actually, we're living on top of *them*," said Nafai.

Volemak paused for a moment of patience, as if saying silently, When will the boy grow up enough not to make jokes during serious discussions? Luet leaned over to Nafai and jabbed his leg with her finger. He grinned stupidly at her.

Volemak went on. "And it's imperative that we reach a workable living arrangement. I don't know about you, but what *I* saw the night of the kidnapping was a seriously conflicted digger society—an abduction organized by the son of the blood king, contrasted with worship from the wife of the war king. The very fact that the wife—what's her name?"

"Emeezem," said Oykib.

"The fact that Emeezem succeeded where, um. . . ."

"Mufruzhuuzh."

"Where Muffle-whatever had failed may have weakened him. Therefore we can count on there being a faction that wants to rid the Earth of human beings, and perhaps two—Mufya's and the plotters who did the actual kidnapping. I think Elemak can be valuable in reaching some kind of understanding with the hostile ones."

"If he'll do it," said Hushidh. "He isn't very closely bonded right now with anyone. Not even Protchnu, since the boy couldn't keep himself from bragging to his father about how *he* was the one who discovered the entrance to the digger city up in a tree. It wasn't a welcome topic at home."

"You saw this domestic scene?" asked Volemak.

"I heard about it from an eyewitness," said Hushidh.

"So it's gossip," said Volemak.

"First-generation gossip," said Hushidh. "Very accurate. The best quality."

Volemak smiled, then repeated firmly. "Gossip."

Nafai spoke up. "I think Elemak's the natural choice to work with the diggers."

"There won't be just one," said Volemak. "And do us all a favor, Nafai. Don't let it be known that you favor the idea of Elemak having such an assignment."

Nafai nodded, suddenly serious. But Luet was not impressed. She knew that he understood, intellectually, that it was a bad idea for him to keep trying to be nice to Elemak. Just yesterday Luet had tried to explain it to him again, and he had interrupted her and explained it right back. "Elemak doesn't see my eagerness to give him authority as trust or kindness, he sees it as condescension and gloating, I know. But it's not gloating and it's not condescension, Luet. I really *do* admire his abilities and I trust him to do an excellent job of whatever he's doing. I can't help wanting to reach out to him."

"From your end it looks like reaching out," Luet explained, patiently —for the fiftieth time, she was sure. "From his end it's more like rubbing in."

Nafai knew that he should simply remain silent on any issue regarding Elemak, but he couldn't stand it. "Then everybody will think I'm sulking or that I don't want him to do anything. I really *do* want him to do things, and so I have to say so, don't I? So *everybody* knows there's no hard feelings."

"Can't you just trust me?" said Luet. "Can't you just trust me and *shut up?*"

He had given her his solemn vow—again—that he would say nothing to or about Elemak's role in the community. And here he was in this meeting, not a day since the last time she had pleaded with him and he had remade his promise to her, doing exactly what he had vowed not to do.

Volemak was taking the meeting back to its main subject. "Anyway, we won't have just one person working with the diggers. We have to have as many different perspectives as possible—even as we work to raise crops and get food and seeds stored away for the dry season. All of this is just a preamble, though. This meeting is Shedemei's. I assume this means she has a report on digger and angel biology, and that's as good a starting place as any."

"It's not really a report," said Shedemei. "It's more like a list of questions. The initial scan showed that like all the other animals and plants we've examined since we arrived, the diggers and angels show only the normal sorts of evolutionary changes from their ancestors of forty million years ago. Diggers were a species of field rat common in southern Mexico, and angels were a common species of bat. The genetic variation is on the order of only five percent from the original in both cases. It will be ages before we can even begin to examine the fossil record, but here you can see how the digger body has changed to be able to support a heavier head and the hands have evolved for grasping big heavy tools—while not losing the raw power for digging, climbing, and, I must add, killing with no tools at all."

She switched from the rat and digger skeletons on the computer display to the bat and angel skeletons. "The angels had a more complex job—to retain flight, support a heavier brain, and develop the manual strength to use tools. Their compromise is to keep the use of their feet as strong hands. Standing on one foot, these hip joints give them enough rotation to swing a hand axe. But their arms, which in bats have only vestigial hands, have evolved back into good manual instruments. They can't bear much weight, and as we learned through an unfortunate incident, the arms break easily enough in a strong grasp. So the hands aren't used for gross physical activities. Rather they're used for very delicate, fine work."

She sat and regarded them steadily.

Luet finally realized what she was indicating. "You mean that the statues down in the digger city were made by the angels?"

"The digger hand is simply incapable of doing the fine work you described," said Shedemei. "I've tested the diggers when they were semi-conscious. They can't do work that doesn't require a lot of force. When you sculpt in soft clay, you have to be very restrained, press only so hard. The diggers are incapable of that. They would mash the clay to a pulp."

"Perhaps," said Issib, "you've only been examining soldiers and manual laborers."

"Did you notice any dimorphism underground?" Shedemei asked Nafai and Oykib.

"None," said Nafai.

"And they admitted that they didn't make the sculptures themselves," added Oykib.

"But those are their gods," said Chveya. "Gods which they worship by offering the bones of dead baby angels to them. It seems a little incongruous."

"Yes, it does," said Shedemei. "But that strikes at the heart of the most important questions. The first one is, Why did two intelligent species develop virtually in each other's laps like this, without one destroying the other? According to the records in the library, several sentient species evolved along with humans from the same stock—robusts and heidelbergs, they called them—but the erects essentially erased the robusts, and the moderns wiped out the heidelbergs."

"Might have absorbed them," Issib corrected.

"However it happened," said Shedemei, "where the moderns went, there were no more robusts, heidelbergs, or erects. So why do both angels and diggers survive?"

"Because they don't compete for resources?" asked Chveya.

"My good student," said Shedemei with a smile. "But the diggers *do* eat the angels' young. And worship the statues they make. So it's not the same as, for instance, octopuses and eagles, which simply don't compete in any way. The angels are prey to the diggers. And yet they survive."

"Art lovers," said Nafai.

It sounded like another wisecrack and Luet was ready to poke him, but Shedemei answered as if it were a serious suggestion. "I think you're right, Nafai. I think there's something biological here, and the sculptures are involved. Didn't you say, Oykib, that you've learned that the statues are always associated with mating and breeding in their worship?"

Oykib blushed and looked furtively at his wife, then at Nafai.

"Don't be shy about it, Okya," said Volemak. "Nafai felt it was wise to tell the rest of us about what you can do. Not everybody—just the people in this room. No reason to make everybody else paranoid about their prayers."

Issib grinned maliciously. "We, of course, are the ones who are so perfect of heart that we don't mind being spied on."

"What Issya is trying to say," said Volemak, "is that we accept that some of us have the ability to learn things that others might wish kept secret. But you've shown such remarkable discretion throughout your childhood and on into adulthood that we aren't afraid of you."

"I am," said Chveya. "That's the only reason I let you get me pregnant."

"Veya," Luet remonstrated. Did the girl have to be so crude?

"Anyway, Oykib, is that right?" said Shedemei.

"Yes," he said. "Some of the . . . worshipful thoughts . . . they're downright pornographic. I mean, the way they think of the statues. We've seen how most of them were worn down until some of them were just lumps. They worship by rubbing the statues all over themselves."

"That's very helpful," said Shedemei. "That's not a behavior I've seen in rats or any other rodent. Have you ever seen anything about that in your studies?"

"*You're* the biologist, Shedya," said Hushidh. "If you haven't seen it, you can count on it that *we* haven't."

"As long as we're on the subject of who knows what," said Luet, "I'd like to know why I'm here. I mean, Shedya's husband isn't here, and Aunt Rasa isn't here, so we're not doing this in couples or anything. Shuya and Veya are both needed for understanding the diggers and angels because they can see things that language can't convey. Oykib's method is different, but the result is the same. Nafai is the one with the cloak, who has his face on a sculpture down in the digger city. Issib can't work in the fields and he's good at language and nobody handles the Index better than he does, so he'll be vital for research and conversation. Why am *I* here?"

"Feeling a little insecure, my love?" asked Nafai with mock solicitude.

"You're here," said Volemak, "because you're you. Not everybody has to have a specialization for what I have in mind. And you communicate with the Oversoul better than anyone."

"Not when you use the Index," said Luet. "I shouldn't be here."

"Shut up, Lutya," said Hushidh cheerfully. "Your self-doubt is wasting everyone's time."

"Be patient," said Volemak. "I'm making my point, and you'll understand." He took Shedemei's illustrations off the display and replaced them with a map of the immediate area. "Here *we* are," he said, "and here are the diggers. And way up here are the angels. Take a wild guess which culture we'll come to understand best."

"Especially if they get into a kidnapping mood again," said Issib.

"I think that this can lead to an unfortunate outcome," said Volemak. "First, we'd no doubt become closer to the species we know the best, and that might be a serious mistake. Second, and perhaps more important, the angels would certainly assume that we were closer to the diggers, and therefore they would be suspicious of everything we did. Perhaps hostile. You see the problem?"

Issib nodded. "You want some of them to go up and live among the angels."

"That sounds so final," said Nafai. This time Luet did poke him.

"Not some of *them,* Issya," said Volemak. "Some of *you.*"

Issib looked angry. "Not me," he said. "Not the chair."

Luet understood. He had hated those years in the wilderness when he had been physically helpless except when in his floating chair. To have Hushidh have to lift him and carry him and help him with his bodily needs—it was bad enough when his children were little, but now it would be an unbearable humiliation. Here in the vicinity of the ship his magnetic floats worked just as they had in the city of Basilica, giving him nearly normal physical freedom. He was not about to give that up.

"Hear me out," said Volemak. "I've thought this through very carefully, and if you listen reasonably you'll agree with my conclusions. First, I don't think we should send very many to the angels, because we need most of our strength here, working the fields and establishing the colony. So I'm sending only two couples and their small children. I can't send Shedemei, because she has to be here, using the instruments in the ship. But I need to send somebody who is as methodical as she is, and as familiar with the library. That points to you, Issib."

"It points to anybody here and half the people not here," said Issib.

"Chveya and Hushidh both have roughly the same ability," said Volemak, "and that ability is indispensable. So one stays here, and one goes there."

"Oykib is the most valuable one for learning languages," said Issib. "Send him up there."

"I need Oykib down here," said Volemak. "I want him learning the digger language alongside Elemak."

Luet understood, as she was sure everyone else did—it would not be healthy if Elemak were the only interpreter they had. Volemak didn't want to say it outright, but Elemak could not be wholly trusted. And the way he'd been acting since the night of the kidnapping, he might not accept the assignment to work with the diggers anyway.

"Besides," said Volemak, "the diggers know Oykib."

"They know Nafai, too," said Issib.

"Don't fight me on this, Issya," said Volemak. "Nafai they see as a god. Therefore it's very important that they not see too much of him. Let them worship the clay head and leave the man himself a mystery."

"In other words," said Nafai, "nobody who knows me could worship me."

"That's pretty much it," said Volemak.

"I worship you," Luet said, too sweetly.

Nafai smiled sweetly back.

"As for your loathing for the chair," said Volemak, "Nafai and I are pretty sure we can install a relay somewhere on that peak. It overlooks the angels' valley as well as the whole canyon approach. I think your magnetics will work there."

"Unless I walk behind a tree," said Issib.

"The relay consists of four installations so that there's always a parallax," said Nafai. "It would have to be a very big tree."

"If the magnetics work, I'll do it," said Issib.

"You'll do it anyway," said Volemak. "You'll just be angrier if you're in the chair. But think of this as the consolation prize. You get the Index."

"So there we'll be," said Nafai. "The four of us. The brothers who married the sisters."

"I'll still be useless," said Luet, trying to sound dispassionate, but failing.

"No more so than Nafai," said Volemak. "And no less. The angels aren't going to be as impressed by the glowing skin as the diggers were. *Their* first exposure to us was an act of wanton violence. Even with Hushidh and Issib to counsel you, it's going to take some delicate maneuvering to get them to accept you in the first place. Yasai and Padarok have assured me that our injured angel made no offer of violence. But that doesn't mean that the others are necessarily peaceable. After all, they *are* a sentient species. If humans and diggers are any example of what that means, we can anticipate that they have just as many murderous tendencies as we have."

"Then let's just wipe 'em all out," said Nafai.

Everyone looked at him in horror.

"That was a *joke*," he said.

"Try not to make jokes like that with the angels," said Volemak.

Nafai looked disgusted. "When I'm responsible for something, I don't make stupid jokes," he said. Then he grinned. "But this is *your* meeting."

"I appreciate your supportive attitude," said Volemak. "Now does anyone have anything else?"

"I do," said Shedemei. "This is especially for the four of you who are going up to the angels, but it's really for everybody who works with the diggers, too. You have to notice everything. Not just the ways that they're different from us, but the ways that they're the same, too. You have to make a note of it immediately, every single thing you notice, because the longer you wait to write it down, the more you'll be accustomed to their way of doing things and so the more likely you are to stop noticing it. Issib has the Index, and I have the computers here on the ship—we should be making reports every night."

"When do we do all this?" asked Oykib.

"The work with the diggers starts immediately," said Volemak. "But until we can take a healthy—or at least not dying—angel back up to his people, we aren't going back up that canyon. So for now, the four of you will take shifts with this poor busted-up fellow. Spend as much time with him as Shedemei thinks advisable. Make a *friend* out of him, if you can." Then he glowered at them all. "And you *will* make sure that you never take this fellow anywhere that he even *might* run into Elemak. Elya will have access to the ship as always, but I'll ask him to stay off the deck where Shedemei is helping the angel recuperate. That should do the job."

Shedemei had only one thing to add. "I especially want to know anything that has to do with sex. Reproduction and survival—those are the two key forces that drive evolution. I won't understand their biology or their culture until I know what is imperative for their mating, breeding, sustenance, and defense. Somehow those sculptures play a role for *both* cultures."

"Art is life," Nafai intoned. "And life is art."

Luet poked him again, as hard as she could. He yelped. She hoped it left a bruise.

As the meeting broke up, Shedemei and Issib spent a few moments looking in detail at the scans and charts of the digger and angel bodies. "I was going to bring this up for the whole group," Shedemei said, "but the meeting went a different way. I didn't know what Volemak was planning, and all that matters is that *you* be aware of this so you can watch for an explanation when you're up the canyon with the angels."

"I haven't agreed to go," said Issib.

Shedemei looked at him blankly.

"Yes, well, show me anyway," said Issib.

"Here," she said. "In the digger males. And here, in our one angel, also a male."

"I don't know what it is you're pointing at."

"Neither do I," said Shedemei. "But it's a tiny organ, maybe a gland, I'm not sure at all of the function. But it isn't present in humans, and it isn't present in any other species I've scanned."

"So, they're different."

"It's not that simple," said Shedemei. "Biological diversity comes through branching. There are two ways that creatures can have similar organs. One is that they had a common ancestor. The other is through convergent evolution—similar pressures in the environment caused them to develop similar strategies to counter it. Now, if they have the identical organ because of a common ancestor, there should be evidence of it in all the other species that diverged from the same source at the same time. But there isn't, Issib. *No* other species of rat or bat or any other rodent or related animal has anything remotely like this structure in this location or even near it. I'm talking about now and I'm talking about forty million years ago, when the oldest biological database on the ship was put together. It's not there."

"Convergent evolution, then."

"But except in the case of skeletal and muscular structure, convergent evolution only gets you organs with similar *functions*. There's no particular reason why they should have the same location."

"Unless it has to do with male reproduction and just above the scrotum is the only location that would work," said Issib.

"Exactly. So what I need you to look for, and what I'll be looking for down here, is a reason for these two species, and only these two species, to have this organ. When you think about it, why should the two sentient species on Earth have this particular similarity?"

"Because it's related to their intelligence?" asked Issib.

"That has to be the first thought," said Shedemei. "But then, we haven't had a chance to look at females. They're intelligent, too—but if they lack this structure—"

"Or one that has an analogous function—"

"You see the mystery," said Shedemei. "This organ came from somewhere and has some function, and it exists only in the two intelligent species, and may exist only in the males. It may have to do with intelligence. It may have to do with sex, given the location."

Issib grinned. "Maybe they're more similar to humans than we thought."

Shedemei glowered. "You mean that maybe male intelligence is testosterone-related?"

"I would have put it more crudely," said Issib.

"No doubt," said Shedemei, "seeing as you're a male. But as you implied, human males already think with their male appendage half the time, and they *don't* have this strange little organ."

"It was just a joke, Shedemei, not a serious scientific proposal."

Shedemei smiled thinly. "I knew that, Issib. I was joking back."

He laughed. It was a little forced.

"Watch for some explanation, Issib, that's all I ask. I'll put everything I notice in the database so we can share information through the Index the whole time you're up there."

"*If* I'm up there," Issib said.

"Whatever," said Shedemei.

While Issib and Shedemei conferred at one of the computer displays, Chveya stopped Luet and took her aside, letting all the others leave the library and the ship without them.

"Why was Father acting so childish during the meeting?" Chveya asked. "It's embarrassing."

"Childish?" asked Luet. "I don't think of it that way. He's always done this sort of thing."

"I've never seen him do it. And it isn't funny."

"It is to him," said Luet. "And to me, actually."

"I don't understand him at all," said Chveya.

"Of course not," said Luet. "He's your father."

Chveya was almost to the ladderway when Luet thought of the real answer to Chveya's real question. "Veya, my dear, the reason you've never seen him like this before is simple enough. This is how he acts when he's happy."

Chveya raised her eyebrows, nodded thoughtfully, then took hold of the ladder and slid down like a child. "Be careful!" Luet yelled down after her. "Remember that you're pregnant!"

"Oh, Mother!" Chveya yelled back, her voice echoing through every floor of the ship.

And she criticizes her father for acting childish? Luet shook her head, then took hold of the ladder and went down, one step at a time.

Poto hung upside down from the branch, his wings gathered close against his body like the clothing that the Old Ones wore. He listened in patient silence to Boboi's harangue, to all the others who argued her side. There were so many of them, and none had come to speak for Poto. pTo's wife, Iguo, would gladly have spoken for him, but it was forbidden for a wife to speak in such circumstances, simply because everyone knew what she would say. She stood upside down from the same branch as Poto, but she was silent.

If Poto stood alone, he nevertheless had two things going for him. First, everyone here knew what one owed to one's otherself. Boboi could muster all her arguments—pTo is certainly dead; the Old Ones are already angry so let's not provoke them more; the Old Ones only took pTo's body home to feed it to the devils—but in the heart of every man and woman in the assembly there would be all the deep and complicated feelings each had for his or her otherself. Poto's own feelings were difficult to sort out. pTo had gone down against Poto's own advice; it had also been against Poto's advice that he went alone to face the Old Ones, to offer to return the stolen grain. But pTo was also his otherself, and when Poto watched the angry bearded giant break and tear pTo's body like it was kindling, it was all Poto could do to keep himself from screaming and flying at the Old One, even though that would mean certain death and was strictly prohibited. When you cannot save the captured one, then don't give them a second one. Poto tried to be perfectly obedient to the laws and wisdom of the people; others commended him afterward for his silence as it happened, but it was little consolation to him. pTo, you fool! he cried out inside himself. And then, O pTo, my otherself, if only I could have died for you!

For wasn't it fated that Poto should be the one to die? When they were two years old—too big for either of their parents to carry one of them alone—the devils came on their raid and found the family hiding place. Without hesitation, both parents took hold of pTo's feet and carried him off to the high refuge. It was a long flight. Poto was alone on the branch, with a digger climbing rapidly to reach him. Knowing that his parents had chosen his otherself, and not him, Poto almost stayed where he was; why should he value his own life, if his parents did not? But the will to live was too strong. And also there was pTo's shout as his parents carried him off. "Live, little soul!" he cried. For his parents Poto was nothing, so he would not live for them. He would live for pTo.

So he inched his way out to the most remote end of the branch. The devil laughed at him then, and began climbing out the branch, slowly, carefully. It bowed lower and lower under his weight. Poto could see another devil waiting under the branch, ready to seize him the moment he descended low enough.

The devil below him jumped and its fierce digging hands brushed Poto's head. Many children at such a time became so terrified that they tried to fly, but with wings so small and weak they couldn't get aloft, and the devils would have sport chasing them as they fluttered and staggered near the ground. Those who tried to fly always were caught, were always carried down into the devil's tunnels where they were eaten in terrible barbaric festivals.

Poto did not try to fly. Instead, he mustered his courage and moved closer to the devil on the branch. This had the effect of raising him above the height that the lower devil could reach by jumping. But it put him nearly within reach of the upper devil's sweeping hand. Twice the hand struck at Poto's feet. But the second time, the devil had so extended himself that his balance was precarious indeed, and at that moment Poto *bounced.* The devil yelped and fell from the branch. And before he could climb back up and try again, Poto's parents returned and carried him away to safety, to the place where pTo greeted him with an embrace and listened as Poto told him of his terrible adventure. Ever since that time Poto knew that his life had been spared so he could watch over the chosen self; everyone had respect for that and knew that if it were not meant for Poto to protect pTo, he would have been taken by the devils that day.

The second great argument on Poto's side was that everyone knew that no matter what the assembly decided, Poto would go down to find pTo and do his best to save him, even offering himself in pTo's place, if he wasn't already dead. So what the assembly was really deciding was not whether Poto would go, but rather whether Poto's going would be so dangerous that he should have a wing torn to prevent him from going. This would be a terrible punishment, for to deprive a man of flight was the ultimate humiliation. It was the punishment given to a man who forced himself on a woman, and it always led to the same end: a cruel, humiliating death at the hands of the devils on their next raid. Because he was not an infant, he would not be carried down into the caves. Instead, the raiders would eat him raw on the spot, not bothering to kill him first. The distraction of having a tornwing to eat might save a few infant lives—it was the only thing such a criminal was good for.

It would be a cruel thing to do, when Poto's only crime was that he intended to save his otherself no matter what the assembly decided. But it would do no good to deny that he meant to defy the assembly—that would only humiliate him by making it seem that he did not love his otherself more than the law. Just as a wife was expected to plead for the rescue of her husband, and so was silenced regardless of whether she actually would have pled for him or not, so also a man was expected to defy all fears, laws, dangers, and wisdom to fly to the rescue of his otherself. So whether he broke the law or not, he should be punished as if he had. If the people did *not* punish him, it would mean they thought he was the most contemptible of creatures, a man who would not risk all for his otherself. Better to be a tornwing.

So the assembly had to decide whether to tear Poto's wing or to let him risk the people's safety by going down to confront the Old Ones yet again.

Finally Boboi fell silent, the last of her supporters having spoken. How many were there? Fewer than half the assembly, but not very much fewer. If even a few of the silent ones voted with her, Poto would be torn and pTo would remain alone among the Old Ones.

It was Poto's turn. The people were already tired. He would be brief. "I don't believe the Old Ones are all our enemies. They were very angry at pTo or they would not have come up the canyon to find him. They rejected his offering, it's true. But the one who struck him acted alone. I saw the others turn away from him or reach out to stop him—"

"How do you know what the Old Ones *meant* by anything!" Boboi interrupted him.

The assembly squealed their anger at Boboi for daring to interrupt. After all, Poto had maintained perfect courtesy. Abashed by the high screeching, Boboi turned her face away from the assembly.

Poto resumed. "I'm not the only one who saw this. If there's any witness who denies that the other Old Ones did not seem to want him to break pTo as he did, then speak now, I give my consent."

There might have been some who disagreed, but none who were certain enough to dare to repudiate him when he was pleading for his otherself.

"pTo was not dead—I saw how bravely he opened his eyes to show us that he lived. And the Old Ones, seeing him alive, chose not to eat him, even though he was not a child. They treated him tenderly and put him in their own leather to carry him down the canyon. I have no idea what they intended. But the Old Ones are not devils in their bodies, even if they are mostly hairless under their leather, and so perhaps they are not devils in their hearts. They came from the sky, didn't they? So perhaps they are no longer angry at pTo, and if I went to plead for him, they would let me take him home, or at least stay and tend him until he dies."

He swallowed, trying to think of what other points Boboi had made, so he could refute them. "I don't think that the Old Ones are angry at all of us, or they would not have stopped with harming just pTo. It was dawn, and they could surely see the watchwomen flying above the village. They knew where we might be found, but they did not come further than the crest of the ridge. This shows that they do not hold the whole responsible for the acts of the one. Therefore I will not bring danger to the people even if they hate me for coming to them."

What else? Most of Boboi's argument had consisted of many people saying the same things over and over; he had little else to say. "People of the assembly," said Poto, "I can add only this: My otherself did nothing more terrible than to follow in the footsteps of his wife's illustrious ancestor, Kiti. Both of them were drawn to the Old Ones. pTo put us all at risk, but even though Boboi had declared that no one should go to the Old Ones until the assembly decided, the fact remains that the assembly had not yet forbidden what he did. It was foolhardy, but it was also brave and he acted, not for himself, but for what he thought was the good of the people. Should such a one be abandoned? Should his otherself be torn to prevent him from standing beside him? I think everyone here, even Boboi, would be proud to be the otherself of one as brave as my pTo. Let me be a true brother and friend to him. The danger to the people is not known. Should the unknown evil prevent us from doing the known good?"

With that, Poto slowly turned around on the branch and extended his wings, ready to be torn if the vote went against him. He could hear the sound of Boboi's supporters dropping to the ground. How many? They went quickly, all at once, and then there were no more. So easily they made up their minds. Perhaps that meant that only those who spoke with her had voted with her.

Or perhaps not.

Chveya woke up first, as usual. It used to be that she could outsleep Oykib any day of the week, but, to her surprise, pregnancy had already diminished her bladder's capacity and she had to get up before daybreak whether she wanted to or not. And she didn't often want to. There was no use trying to get back to sleep, either. She would just lie awake anyway, so she might as well get up and do something.

What she was doing today was sitting on a stool, leaning against the wall of their one-room house, trying to imagine Basilica, the City of Women. Mother had told her about buildings, thousands of them, so close together they touched on every side except the front. And sometimes people would come along and build a new house right in front of yours, completely cutting yours off from the street, unless you had the money to hire thugs to drive them away. They could build right across a street, completely blocking it—except when passersby, angry that someone was trying to close their street, would dismantle the building as they passed.

It was hard to imagine such a place, so many people. In her entire life, Chveya had known only the people of their colony. The only new people she had met were the babies who were born. The only buildings she had seen were the buildings they built with their own hands—and the impossible, magical buildings of the spaceport, and that was no city, since its population consisted entirely of the same people she had always known.

The diggers had a city, though, didn't they? Even though it was underground, except where the entrances to their tunnels were bored upward into the trees. Chveya imagined how they must have scrambled when the humans first arrived from Harmony and started cutting down trees, extending the meadow where they had first landed. The tunnels that led to doomed trees had to be filled, so that when the humans looked down into the hollow trunks, they wouldn't see that tunnels opened out underneath them. And yet even with so many tunnels filled, the digger city was a vast network of connected chambers.

Chveya knew it was real. She could now see the connections among many, perhaps most of the diggers, and she knew that there were hundreds of them down there, constantly coming and going. It was the only real city she had ever seen, but she hadn't really seen it, probably never *would* see it. She would never crawl along the tunnels. She *hoped* she would never crawl through them, in the darkness. Her skin didn't glow the way Father's could, when he wanted it to. It would be night down there all the time. And she would be surrounded by strangers. It wasn't that they were so alien, so animal-like. It was that she didn't know them, didn't know what to expect. Even Elemak, even Meb and Obring, dangerous and untrustworthy as they were, seemed safer to her because after all she *knew* them. The diggers were all strangers to her.

And that's how it must have been in Basilica. Nobody could possibly know that many people, so walking along the streets must have meant being surrounded by strangers, by people you had never seen before and would never see again, people who could have come from anywhere, who could be thinking anything, who might be desiring terrible things that would destroy you or those you loved and cared for and you had no way of knowing.

How did they do it, the people who lived there? How could they bear to live their lives among aliens? Why didn't they just retreat into their homes, block the doors, and cower in a corner, whimpering?

For that matter, thought Chveya, why don't I? Right now, knowing that I am surrounded by diggers that I don't know, that I can't predict, who have the power to destroy me and everyone I love—why am I still going to bed at night, getting up in the morning?

Someone clapped their hands softly outside the door.

She got up and went to the door. It was Elemak.

"Is Oykib up?" he asked.

"Um, no," said Chveya. "But it's time he was."

"I'm up," said Oykib sleepily from the bed. "Awake, anyway."

"Come in," said Chveya.

Elemak came in. He stood until Oykib sat up in bed and indicated his eldest brother should sit at the foot of it. "What is it?" he asked.

"Volemak wants me to work with this digger hostage," said Elemak.

"If you want to," said Oykib.

"I do my duty," said Elemak. He smiled nastily. "I took the oath."

"Well," said Oykib. "Then we're both supposed to learn his language."

"You have a head start," said Elemak. "I'd like you to teach me what you know about the language."

"Not much yet. Just a few words. I don't know the structure yet."

"Whatever you know, I'd like to learn it. I'd like Protchnu to learn it, too. Can you give us a class in digger language?"

"That's a good idea," said Oykib. "Yes, I will."

Someone was running around outside. Pounding feet. Protchnu stood in the doorway. "Father," he said.

Elemak stood up.

"There's one of those angels standing on the roof of Issib's house."

"Who's on watch?" asked Oykib, standing up, pulling on his clothes.

"Motya," said Protchnu. "He sent me to fetch you."

"To fetch *me?*" asked Elemak.

"Um, to get the adults."

"He didn't mean me," said Elemak.

Protchnu looked defiant. "But *I* did."

"Go get Volemak," said Elemak.

Chveya was surprised that Elemak understood so well what his role in the community was now—and that he seemed to accept it. She knew that his connection to most people was very thin these days, but she could see that his bond with his eldest son was bright and strong. Yet he had let his son see his own humility. It made her rather sad that he could not be as strong and proud as Protchnu longed for him to be. It was bound to cause real pain in Protchnu, and yet Elemak faced it openly and. . . .

Unless he *wanted* to make sure that Protchnu felt that pain.

No, she wasn't going to believe that Elemak had some elaborate plan that involved the kindling of deep resentment in his son's heart.

Oykib was dressed now, and heading out the door. Elemak gave no sign that he intended to follow.

"Aren't you curious?" asked Chveya, as she followed Oykib out.

"I've seen one," said Elemak.

When they got to Issib's house, the angel was standing on the roof, rigid, unmoving. Issib and Hushidh and their children were outside, looking up at him; other people were gathering, too. "He looks so frightened," said Chveya.

"Not of us," said Oykib. He gestured toward the trees. The shadowy forms of diggers could be seen in the branches, in the underbrush. "Their word for the angels is *mveevo.* Meat from the sky."

"They eat them?"

"They prefer the babies," said Oykib. "Let's just say that international relations between diggers and angels are on a kind of primitive level."

But Chveya was seeing something else now. The angel on the rooftop had the brightest, strongest connection she had ever seen between any two people, and the connection led to the ship. "He's here for the other one," she said. "For the injured one in the ship."

"I guess so," said Oykib.

"I know it," she said.

"He's praying that we won't give him to the devils before he finds his . . . brother. But more than a brother."

"Then let's take him," said Chveya. She walked to the edge of the roof, reached up, took hold of the roof beam, and started climbing up the rough log wall.

"Veya," said Oykib, annoyed. "You're pregnant."

"And you're just standing there," she said.

A couple of moments later they were both on the roof. The angel looked at them, but didn't move. Oykib held out a hand. So did Chveya.

The angel spread his wings, unfolding himself like an umbrella. The effect was astonishing. From being a small, quivering thing, he was suddenly transformed into a great looming shadow. So this is what the injured one would look like, if he were strong and healthy. Like a butterfly, though, the body was so thin and frail inside the canopy of the wings. Only the head was still in proportion to the great width of the wings. The heavy, nodding head.

"Well, we can't carry him or anything," Oykib said. He beckoned for the angel to come closer. The angel took an awkward step. "Not much of a walking animal, is he," said Oykib.

"He's not an animal," said Chveya. "He's a very brave and frightened man, and he loves his brother."

"His other self," said Oykib. "That's what the word is. His otherself."

"So let's lead him there." She went to the edge of the roof, sat down, swung off. Oykib followed her. And a few moments later, the angel perched on the edge, then swooped off. Some of the children shrieked and ran off a little way.

Chveya could see the diggers in the forest draw nearer, but they apparently didn't dare to cross the line into human territory.

Oykib was explaining to Nafai and Volemak what he and Chveya had seen, what they had decided.

"Do we want the two angels together?" asked Nafai. "What will his reaction be when he sees how badly injured his brother is?"

"More to the point," said Volemak, "what would his reaction be if we blocked him from seeing his brother?"

Nafai nodded. In the meantime, Oykib and Chveya led the angel toward the ship.

* * *

pTo had awakened several times since the Old Ones took him, but every wakening had been like a dream. He drifted, floating on his back, as if the air had grown thick and now held him up without effort. He didn't know whether he could move or not because he couldn't summon up the will to move, not even his lips to speak. And when he let his eyes fall open, what he saw was a female Old One, also floating, slowly drifting into and out of his field of vision. Above him the sky, of a neutral color, as if the clouds had not yet decided whether to be stormy or benign. And there were faint breezes, coming from no particular direction—perhaps from below him. Nothing smelled alive except his own faint sweat and the mustier perfumes of the Old One.

Then he drifted off again, not into sleep, really, but into oblivion.

Is this death? Do Old Ones take us to the sky god? Is this life inside a cloud?

But then, perhaps the third time or the fifth time he awoke—he wasn't sure how many separate memories had gone before—he realized that this must be the inside of the tower of the Old Ones, and the sky was no sky, but rather a roof. So would this be considered a tunnel, like the ones the devils made, only built above the ground? Or would it be a sheltering nest, like the woven thatch that the people build above the nests where infants clung, first to their mothers' fur, and then to the twigs under the nest?

Are the Old Ones like us, or like them?

Like the devils, because of the way the Old One in his terrible fury tore and flung pTo and left him for dead.

Like the people, because of the careful tender way the Old Ones lifted him onto the woven thatchlike leathers they put on and took off their bodies at will. Like the people, because of the way they carried him down the hill before at last, mercifully, he slipped into unconsciousness. Like the people, because he was still alive, not eaten, not torn to bits, not even held as a prisoner.

Or a third possibility. Perhaps they were like the gods. After all, there was no pain.

And then a day came when there *was* pain, but along with the pain he came fully awake for the first time. Not floating any more. And now able to feel his limbs, his fingers, and to move them. Some of them. A great weight pressed down on the bones that had been broken. He turned his head—yes, he could turn his head, he could shift his back enough to let him see that something had been wrapped around his broken bones, splinting them like the graft of a tree branch. The splints were so heavy he couldn't lift them, and when he tried it only caused the dull undercurrent of pain to become sharp.

Why have they let the pain come back? Is it a prelude to death? Have I been judged and found unworthy? Or is it because they have decided to let me return to life? To see again my otherself. My wife. My people.

A whining, hooting sound—ah, yes, the speech of the Old Ones. There was some music in it, but there were also those devil sounds, hissing and humming.

And then another sound. His name, spoken clearly, with love, with concern. "pTo," said the voice, and he knew it at once, impossible as it was that it could be real.

"Poto," he answered, and then with a rustle of his leathery wings pTo's otherself stood on the same surface where pTo lay, and looked down at him. "I told you not to go to the Old Ones' tower," Poto said.

"And now you've come, too," said pTo.

"Boboi wanted to tear my wings to prevent me," said Poto. "I almost fled without awaiting the verdict. But I wanted you to be able to return in honor if you should live. So I waited, and the people stood with me. With *us*, pTo. They honor you. The way you bore the punishment of the angry Old One."

"He was the most terrible creature I've ever seen," said pTo. "Surely more terrible than the devils."

Poto shook his head. "I've looked the devils in the face, and these Old Ones also."

"But the devils, Poto, they don't hate us, they merely hunger for us. There is no hate like the Old Ones' hate."

"They led me to you, my self, my most beautiful self," said Poto. "They knew who I was and what I wanted, and they led me to you."

The voice of the Old One rang out again. Poto looked at her, and at others; pTo looked around and saw that four others had come into the—what, the nest? The tunnel? Whatever this place was. He recognized one of them—the male he had seen that fateful night, just as he touched the tower. "That's the one who saw me," said pTo. "That's the one who saw I stole the grasses and must have given the alarm."

"But he's not the angry one?" asked Poto.

"He's not angry now," said pTo. "Not like the other one. Oh, let me never see the angry Old One again!"

"Finally," said Oykib. "Something like a prayer. Half of what the diggers say is at least partly directed toward their gods. It'd be easier for me if the angels were as pious."

"But what did he say?" asked Shedemei.

"He wanted never to see the angry one again. The angry Old One." He laughed. "We're Old Ones, of course. The ancients come back."

"That's not to laugh about," said Shedemei. "That's very important. Luet or Nafai, can you go and get Hushidh and Issib? They need to be here, to meet them—if they're going to be liaison with the angels."

"Yes, I'll go," said Nafai.

"No, Nafai, that's silly, I'll go," said Luet.

"*I'll* go," said Oykib.

"We need you here," said Shedemei. "In case you can understand anything more."

Nafai left.

"The language is all pops and song, isn't it?" said Luet. "Like bubbles in a stream. Like. . . ."

"Yes, Mother?" said Chveya.

"Like the music of the Lake of Women, when I floated on it at the edges of a true dream."

"Maybe the Keeper of Earth was able to send their songs to you," said Chveya.

"Hush," said Shedemei. "These two are twins, I think. Look how perfectly identical they are."

"Each calls the other his *otherself,*" said Oykib. "It's much more than a brother."

"My twins might feel that way about each other," said Luet, "if only babies their age could articulate their feelings."

"Hush," said Shedemei. "Listen, Oykib. Watch, all of you."

But Chveya had to say this one last thing: "There's no love I've ever seen among humans like the love that binds these two."

"You are without doubt the stupidest of all men," said Poto.

"I accept the honor," said pTo. "And you are the truest of all. May some woman now see the strength and power in you, and take you as her husband."

Oykib spoke. "The injured one prays that some female will admire how strong the healthy one is and mate with him. No, bind with him."

"Marry him," suggested Chveya.

"Well, it could be. The word has overtones of twining and knotting."

"I know about twining," said Chveya. "He means marriage. The injured one is married, and the healthy one is not—because the injured one has a strong tie to someone not here, someone up the canyon."

"Do they have names?" asked Shedemei.

"You expect me to produce those sounds?" asked Oykib.

"We'll have to, someday. You might as well try."

"The name of the healthy one is oh-oh, with quick little consonants in there. To-to. Po-to."

"And the other one?"

Oykib laughed in frustration. "The same. The same name."

"Otherself," murmured Shedemei.

"No, it's different. Like, Po-*to,* and the healthy one is *Po*-to."

"Quiet," said pTo. "Listen."

"To what?"

"The Old Ones. They just said your name."

They listened.

"Poto," said Oykib. "Poto." Then he babbled some more, and then the name stuck out again. "Poto. Poto."

"They want you," said pTo.

Poto immediately leapt down to the ground, out of pTo's field of vision. But pTo could hear him say, "I am Poto, Old One, if it is truly me you seek. Let no more harm come to my otherself! If you have more punishment, I will bear it."

"He's praying to *us,*" said Oykib.

"Oh, good," said Shedemei. "Maybe we can be gods to everyone now."

"If we're going to tear the wings again, he wants us to tear his and not the wings of his otherself."

"What brought that up?" asked Chveya. "Does he think we're angry?"

"How can he know what to think?" said Luet. "Let me try to show him."

They watched as Luet sank to her knees, then, still on her knees, shuffled forward to the healthy one. "Poto," she said, pointing to him.

He turned his back to her and spread out his wings, not fully wide, but enough that the leather of the wings hung loose and open before her.

"Touch them," suggested Shedemei. "Very gently. They're strong, but I don't know whether they're sensitive to pain or not."

Luet reached out her hand and gently stroked the skin of his wing. It was hairless and smooth, like shoe leather, but much lighter. Springier.

The angel seemed to wait for more, but when it didn't come, he turned around, looked at her.

"Poto," Luet said again. And now she held out her hand to him, palm up, open.

He studied her hand, then looked around from face to face, trying to find meaning. Perhaps he found some meaning that they could not even guess at, or perhaps he simply decided for himself what the gesture must mean. But in the end, he bowed his body until his cheek lay against her palm. As if she had intended this all along, Luet gently closed her other hand over his face, resting her palm against his other cheek. She held this pose for only a moment, then raised her hand.

The angel quietly spoke, not to her, but to his twin.

"pTo, she has made herself an aunt to me, she folded me truly, and on the side."

"Oh, Poto, may all our people have such a gift from the Old Ones," answered pTo from the bed behind him.

"The one on the bed prays that all his people can have a blessing like that from the Old Ones," said Oykib.

"Very nice," said Shedemei.

"Not enough," said Luet. "I refuse to let us be gods to these people."

So now she bowed herself before him, offering her own head to be clasped between hands.

"What do I do, pTo?" cried Poto in distress. "She bows to me as to a father, her head not even turned to the side."

"If the Old One demands that you be her father, then do it!" said pTo. "Don't make her angry! They're terrible when they're angry."

"But I can't be her father," said Poto. "It isn't right."

"It *is* right," said pTo. "She doesn't have a father. He's dead."

"And how do you know that, Broken Wings?"

"He's dead, Poto, I know it. I saw it when I was sleeping. I saw it in my dreams."

"You've never even seen the face of the Old One who kneels before me."

"I've seen her, too. I've seen them all." It was true. pTo had not remembered until now, until the moment that he needed the memory, and then it flooded back. He had seen all their faces in dreams. Even the angry one, only not angry, surrounded by little ones, by his children. And he knew from her voice which one this was. She was the one he saw with both of his own firstborn children perched on her shoulders. "She will stand one day in a meadow in the village, and my children will stand on her shoulders."

"All right," said Poto. "I'll take her as my niece, then."

"Daughter," said pTo. "She has no father. You will be her father now."

"I have no wife," said Poto. "What woman will marry me, if she must become the mother of an Old One when she does?"

"The one who *should* be your wife, and no other," said pTo. "You have been chosen to be the father of an Old One, and you're worried about mating? Are you *that* lonely, my dear mad self?"

"They sound upset," Luet murmured.

"Just stay where you are," said Oykib. "I'm catching some of this. I think when you took his head in your hands, it's like you made him a relative. You took him under protection. And now you're asking him to adopt *you* as a relative."

"Mm," said Luet. "Maybe it's not a good idea."

"Do it," said Shedemei. "Just stay there and let him decide."

The conversation between them stopped. And then Poto spread his wings wide, and instead of placing them on either side of Luet's head, he enfolded her entire body in his wings. She felt them wrap around her, feathery-light. She knew that if she struck out with either arm she would tear the wing; she also knew that to tear this creature's wing would destroy, not him, but her.

"He's praying that he can be a good father to you," said Oykib.

"Father?" asked Luet.

"He says that he hopes he can take the place of your ancient father who died in a faraway place."

"What?" asked Chveya. "Mother, how can he know that?"

"He says that he will not die unless he can die defending you from the hungry devils. I think it's part of the ritual language of adoption. Only of course you're not an infant."

"Can you tell me the word for *father*?" asked Luet.

"Um," said Oykib, "I think—let's see if he says it again when I can—"

The angel spoke some more.

"Bet," said Oykib.

"What?" said Chveya.

"The word is *bet.* The word for *father.*"

When the angel took his wings from around her, Luet sat back on her heels and looked him in the eye. "Poto," she said, pointing to him. "Bet." Then she pointed to herself. "Luet," she said.

"What's she saying?" asked Poto. "I think she's telling me her name, but I don't know what the sound is, it's so strange."

"Oo-et," said pTo.

"No, there's something first. Not a devil sound, either, just a kind of twisting of the music. Woo-et. Yoo-et."

* * *

"Listen to him trying to say your name," said Oykib. "I don't think they have an L sound in their language."

"Wuet is close enough," said Luet. She nodded, agreeing with the name Poto was able to produce. "Wuet," she said, pointing to herself again. Then to him. "Poto. Bet Poto."

"Potobet," the angel corrected her.

"Potobet," she said.

Then he pointed at her again. "Wuetigo," he said.

"Wuetigo," she said, pointing at herself.

As she had done, the angel nodded—but it was an exaggerated, awkward movement for him. Nodding must not be how they showed agreement, but he had learned her way and was using it. "Smart guy," she said.

Then she pointed to the bed, to where the other angel lay. "Po-*to*?" she asked.

"pTo," said Poto.

"pTo," she answered.

"pTobet," Poto added.

"Ah," said Shedemei. "If the one adopts you, the other twin is also your father."

"Twinning must be a big deal in their culture," said Oykib.

From the bed came the voice of the injured one. "Wuetigo," he said. And then, to their surprise, he twisted his tongue around with great effort and said, "Luetigo."

They laughed and clapped their hands in delight. At first the angels seemed startled, afraid. But then, seeing that they were also nodding as they clapped, he began to clap his hands together, too.

At that moment Nafai re-entered the room, with Issib and Hushidh behind him. "Did I miss anything?" he asked.

"Not much," said Luet. "Meet my new adopted fathers, Poto and pTo. Only I must call them Potobet and pTobet because I'm their daughter. And they call me Luetigo."

"Luetigo means that you're their aunt," said Oykib. "Remember, you adopted them first. The one on the bed—puh-*to*—"

"pTo," Chveya corrected him.

"The injured guy," said Oykib. "He's very grateful that after you showed them the honor of taking them to be your nephews, you then showed them the even greater honor of letting them be your fathers. It's a big deal to them. And I think it's permanent."

"Yes," said Hushidh. "You see it, too, don't you, Chveya?"

"They've taken you into their lives, Mother," said Chveya. "You're family. Tied in with them like the way you're tied to me. They aren't joking. It's not just a formality."

"They think," said Oykib, "that it means that all the Old Ones will be friends with the—people, the angels—forever."

"Good," said Nafai. "I think we're off to a very good start. Now let's give the two of them time alone. Lock up the medicine, Shedya, and let's get out of here for a few hours."

"He won't like the pain."

"Can you give him something that leaves him conscious?"

"Yes," said Shedemei. "But will his twin let me do it?"

Poto wasn't happy about it. But when Luet bowed before him, both hands out in supplication, he seemed to understand that no harm was meant by the tool in Shedemei's hand. She applied it to pTo's shank, and then they all withdrew from the room.

"They trust us," said pTo.

"Or else we're both prisoners," said Poto.

"Test them, then. Try to leave. They'll let you go, I know it."

"I won't leave until you can leave with me."

"Then we *are* prisoners. But it is my injury that binds us here, and not the Old Ones."

Poto was back on the bed now, examining his otherself's wounds. "pTo," he said, his voice filled with wonder. "The tear in your wing—it's healing."

"That can't be," said pTo. "Tornwing never heals. Tornwing is devil's meat."

"But it *is* true. The sides of the tear have been joined together, and a scar is forming between them, just like on fur skin. The Old Ones have the power to make leather heal."

"Oh, Poto. Who can say now that it was wrong for me to come down to the Old Ones?"

"Boboi can," said Poto wryly.

"What do *you* say?" asked pTo.

"I say that my otherself led the way. I say that without your courage and daring and disobedience, the people would have remained strangers to the Old Ones. But now the Old Ones are our friends. And one of them is our aunt, and we are her fathers."

For Elemak, learning the language of the diggers was like a return to his youth, to the days when he braved the dangers of the road in order to earn his rightful place as his father's heir. In those days he was quick with languages, picking them up from men he hired, from guides, from hosts in the cities he visited. The first few languages took real effort, but after a while he began to find regularities, patterns in them. Bozhotz was like Cilme except that all *B* sounds became *P* sounds, and long vowels became diphthongs with terminal *U*'s. Just set your mouth right, be careful of a few words that didn't mean the same thing in the different languages—*olpoic* does not mean *home* in Bozhotz, so don't ask a man to take you to his olpoic if you don't want to get stabbed—and you could get along. After long enough on the road, it became so easy that, while Elemak took pride in his ability with language, he took little interest in it.

Now he was discredited as his father's heir, he would never be free to roam the world again—and even if he were, there'd be no place worth going—his wife had repudiated him in front of the entire human population of this planet, and all that was left to him was to learn the language of some overgrown underground rodents.

But that was all right. Even learning the rudiments of it from Oykib was all right. After all, he might be Nafai's pet brother, but he wasn't actually Nafai himself. In fact, if things had worked out differently, Oykib might at last have been the brother that Issib would have been, if he hadn't been crippled. Smart, but not smart-mouthed; obedient, but willing to take the initiative; courageous but not foolish; confident but not boastful. He liked Oykib. He wished that he couldn't tell how obviously Oykib distrusted and feared him. Well, there was that bit about throwing him around a little in the library back on the ship. A matter of temper. No use trying to explain to him that it was Nafai that Elemak was angry at, Nafai's betrayal. No use trying to suck up to him, either, explaining that if once, just once, Nafai had shown a sign of being like Oykib, they would have been friends. It was enough to learn the language from him, to help him puzzle out the hard bits, to search for the rules and patterns.

Because there *were* rules and patterns. Nothing from the languages of Harmony applied, of course, because digger language had evolved on its own, without human antecedents. But there were still constants in language. Ways of expressing time so that language could convey past and present and future, cause and effect, motive and intention. Actors and actions forced every language to develop, after a fashion, nouns and verbs. And quite quickly—almost as quickly as when Elemak was young—he caught on to the *feel* of the language, the music of it. When they went to the forest edge to converse with the observers who watched there, Elemak could see that they liked the way he talked, like the sound of his voice, the fact that one of the gods could handle digger speech.

Elemak could see that Oykib was a little jealous. After all, he had begun as the teacher, and now, after a few weeks, it was Elemak who was teaching, if not the meanings of things, then the grammar and pronunciation, the idiomatic usage. When could Oykib have developed an ear for such things? This was his first foreign language, and Elemak's fiftieth. To Oykib's credit, though, he said nothing but praise for Elemak's ability, and there was no hint of Oykib resisting the change in their relationship or trying to get out of teaching Elemak anymore. If only Nafai had had such self-control. . . .

The time came at last, however, when he felt confident enough to try to communicate with the hostages on the ship. Four of the original nine had already been let go—the soldiers who had been prepared, at the war king's command, to kill the kidnappers. But the four kidnappers remained, and, most important of all, Fusum, the son of the blood king, the man who planned it all. "I want him rehabilitated," said Volemak. "I want him to be the one who carries human culture to the diggers, because he was the one who tried to destroy us. His friendship is the friendship that matters most."

So Elemak would make friends with him. "But I'll do it my way, Father, or not at all."

"What way is that?"

"Fusum is a man of violence and anger, Father," Elemak said.

"So we must teach him another way."

"First we must establish who is the teacher," said Elemak. "Then we can set about teaching him another way to live."

Volemak had his doubts, but finally he gave in. "No harm to him, though, Elya," said Volemak. "Nothing to make the enmity between him and us worse than it already is."

So Elemak wouldn't hurt him. Not permanently, anyway. And in exchange for that promise, he had a free hand in every other way. A free hand, and no observers.

Except that at first he would only be able to meet with Fusum and the other diggers inside the ship, where he would be watched by the computer they still called the Oversoul, even though he hadn't even a tiny fraction of the power the real Oversoul exercised back on Harmony. Well, let the machine watch. Let it make its reports to Volemak and Issib and Nafai. There'd be no secrets. Besides, Nyef and Issya were busy worrying about their little angel twins. Nasty little creatures. Bones like twigs. But they were so pretty when they flew, and they had made nice-nice with Nafai's bitch so now they were all family. Naturally Nafai was too stupid to realize that it does no good to ally yourself with weakness. The angels were useless. Skymeat, the diggers called them. As far as Elemak could figure, the only reason the angels weren't wiped out by now was that the diggers wanted to keep a steady supply of their favorite dish. Sentient casserole, that's all the angels were, stew on the wing, and *those* were the ones that Nafai and Issib were going to befriend.

Please, Father, *don't* make me stay down here and make friends with the strongest, most courageous and self-willed of the strong, aggressive diggers! Elemak almost laughed out loud, sometimes, thinking about how Father's clever maneuvering to try to create peace was setting up a future in which it was Elemak who was the expert on the only creatures of Earth that were worth knowing, while Nafai's expertise pertained to their worthless, witless, boneless prey.

Elemak told Oykib first. "I'm going to start working with the hostages now. I'll want to meet with you every day and compare what I've learned about the language and culture from them with the things you've learned from the free diggers down here."

Oykib accepted that, and never even hinted that he might want to go with Elemak into the ship to work with the hostages. A good boy, a marvelous boy.

Then Elemak went to Shedemei. "Wake up the four kidnappers first," he said. "I want to practice with them for a while. Learn from them, hear them talking to each other, in circumstances where I'm in control so they can't just take off into the brush when the questions get hard."

"They're very strong," said Shedemei. "Stronger than you might think."

"But I think they're very strong," said Elemak. "So I don't think I'll be surprised."

"I'm just saying you might not want to be alone," she said.

"And I'm just saying that I might not want to give them the slightest hint that I fear them," said Elemak. "I've handled men more dangerous than this—men from cultures I didn't know anything about until they showed me by their actions. It's my field of study. I don't look over your shoulder on the genetics thing, do I?"

Shamed, Shedemei awoke the four kidnappers one at a time. Elemak made it a point to be the first face they saw when they woke up. He also made it a point to handle them roughly and constantly. They felt his grip on their shoulders as they were propelled along the corridors of the ship. By their ankles he pushed each one ahead of him up the ladderway to the deck of the ship that he would use as his school, his negotiating table, his prison.

Four weeks he spent with them, learning all he could. New vocabulary every day, of course, and more and more complex rules of grammar, which he scrupulously shared with Oykib every night when the diggers were locked down. But also he learned the culture, the way things worked in the underground city. How the blood king was the holy one, who gave boys the passage into young manhood. The blood king also marked the feast of the skymeat babies, taking care to assign much credit to the men with good clean kills, and most credit of all to those who brought their prey home alive, crippled but not bleeding. Thus the war king trained the young men in fighting, stalking, killing; chose their officers; led them against prey both large and small; but it was the blood king who conferred all honors, the blood king who chose which men were great and which were nothing.

Mufruzhuuzh had been a great war king, but there were men who said that his mistake was marrying Emeezem. Not that he had a choice, of course. He was forced into it. And it wasn't his fault that because of her dreams and voices she was made deep mother, master of the underground city. But her very strength had weakened him; he deferred to her too much, listened to her when he should have been listening to his men. It left a vacuum.

Fusum's father, Shosseemem, should have filled that vacuum. He should have stepped in and helped the men feel their strength instead of letting Emeezem's dominance leach it away. But Shosseemem was as immobilized by Emeezem's visions as Mufruzhuuzh was. After all, she had said that the Untouched God was coming from the sky, and he came. They saw him among the undergods and demigods, saw how he moved with confidence and power, and they dared not doubt Emeezem's authority even when she counseled weakness and passivity.

Watch, she said! Watch and wait! Learn before you act! Well, they had watched, they had waited, and then one day Fusum came to them and said, "Are you men or women? If you're women, then where are the infants to suckle at your teats? And if you're men, then why are you still waiting and watching, when you have seen where the babies are kept and how ill-watched they are? They have neither tunnels nor nests, so their babies are at ground level all the time. Why haven't we taken them to the blood king?"

"Because the blood king doesn't ask for them. And the war king doesn't command us to act."

"That is because they are ruled by women. But I am a man, and if I have no men to rule over me, then I will rule myself. These are not gods, even if they did come from the sky. Don't they piss out their urine onto the ground just as we do? Don't they eat and breathe and defecate as we do? What is there that is divine about them?"

"These are the lies that Fusum told us," they insisted to Elemak. "He deceived us. If we had known that you truly are gods, as we do now, we would never have heeded him. Forgive us, mighty one, let not the wrath of your shining fathergod strike us down," and so on and so on until Elemak wanted to strangle them for their weakness and disloyalty.

But he showed them no sign that he didn't approve of their abject betrayal of Fusum. He let them believe that he wanted them to profess undying devotion to the shining god—to Nafai, the lying little bastard. And when he had learned from them all that he could learn, he told Volemak that he thought they were ready to come out of the ship to where Shedemei and Oykib, Chveya and Yasai and whoever else was trying to learn digger ways could work with them.

Oh, Volemak and all the others were so *happy* with the work that Elemak had done with them. They were so compliant, those four. So eager to please. So rich with information and wisdom. Their wives were sent for and came up to join the conversations; they all got along so well, the humans and the four who once had stolen a baby out of Elemak's house. "I'm proud of you, Son," said Volemak. "You took those who harmed you and your family, and made friends of them. It was a good work, and well done."

Elemak knew better. It would have been a shameful thing, if it had been sincere. But he knew the truth about the four kidnappers. Disloyal, that's what they were. Cowards. Fusum had bullied them into doing what they did, and now they were eager to let Elemak bully them into doing something else. If Fusum had any sense at all, he would kill them as soon as he came into power.

For Fusum *would* come into power. Of that Elemak was certain, for the more he heard from the kidnappers, the more he felt he knew Fusum, knew how he thought, what he felt, what he wanted, and what he would do to get what he wanted.

What he wanted was simple: power.

And what would he do to get it? Whatever it took.

Elemak knew Fusum, yes, because he *was* Fusum. Or at least he might be Fusum, if this son of the blood king had sense enough to understand the situation and bide his time as Elemak was doing.

So the day came when Shedemei brought Fusum's suspended animation chamber into readiness.

"I'd like to be alone with him when he comes to," said Elemak.

She looked at him steadily. "And why is that?"

"Because I know him," said Elemak. "From what the others have said. This one is dangerous, and if he's to be tamed I have to show him who is master. If you're here, he'll see that there is some other human involved. He won't know that I'm in sole control of every aspect of his life. Do you see?"

"I see," said Shedemei. "But I don't agree."

"But you *will* leave me alone with him," said Elemak.

"I will because Volemak said to let you handle things your way." She turned her back on him and left.

After a while, the lid slid back and Fusum lay before him, blinking his eyes, trying to understand his surroundings. Elemak reached down with one hand, took him by the throat, and raised him up almost to a sitting position, screaming at him in the most fluent and colorful digger language, "You stole my daughter! You were going to eat her! Is that the warrior you are, the kind who can fight babies but you cower in front of men?"

Fusum's first response was not fear but rage. Elemak was glad to see that, how Fusum reached out with arms still weak from the suspended animation drugs and tried to rake Elemak's heart out of his chest. Very good. Not a whiner, are you? "So now you attack me, you fool!" Still gripping him by his throat, Elemak yanked him up and out of the chamber and flung him against the opposite wall.

Ah, yes, this one wasn't a weak and fragile toy like the angel had been. This one rebounded, his body unbroken, his teeth bared and his hands ready for fighting. But he had been weakened and he was groggy. It wasn't a fair fight, which was exactly as Elemak wanted it. This was about authority and dominance, not justice. If it were about justice, Elemak would have strangled him in his sleep.

Fusum leapt at him—a high, springing movement that might have caught Elemak off guard if he hadn't already had the kidnappers demonstrate their fighting technique in mock gladiatorial combats. Just to learn the words for each of the things you do, he had told them. Well, he learned the words. He also figured out the physical reply. And so it was that Fusum found his own weight used against him as he was thrown again, this time down the corridor, so that he landed skidding and sliding until he fetched up against the back wall.

With a growl he leapt back into combat, but his feet made poor purchase on the smooth floor and he could never build up enough momentum to knock Elemak off his feet or even unbalance him for a moment. By the time the drugs wore off he was physically exhausted and humiliated by his endless defeats at Elemak's hands.

Finally, when Fusum could move no more, Elemak seized him by a hind leg and dragged him along the corridor to the central ladder, then carried him up to the room where he would be kept in lockdown when Elemak wasn't with him. During the trip he made no effort to protect the digger's head and body from pain, nor did he permit Fusum to get enough leverage or balance to protect himself. And when he got to the room, he threw Fusum into it, followed him in, shut the door, and stood there laughing.

The diggers didn't laugh the way that humans did, but the message was clearly getting across. Fusum rose onto his hind legs, exposing his pink hairless belly. "Are you going to sacrifice me like a man?" Fusum asked. "Here's my belly, take my heart and entrails and eat them before my eyes—I don't care, I'll eat as much of it myself as I can get away from you!"

Elemak knew brave posturing when he saw it. "I'd sooner eat my own feces than have any of your cowardly blood on my lips."

"So you mean to give me a coward's death, then. Here's my throat. Cut it, I don't care. Life is nothing to me because now that you gods are here, men are nothing. There are no men. Only women and cowards with two tails."

Elemak couldn't help but laugh again. Such defiance! He was such a *boy,* this one. But then, it would have been disappointing if he had reacted any other way. An Obring would have been groveling and pleading for his life. A Vas would have been sullen and silent. A Mebbekew would have been trying to bargain, to strike a deal. But this one, Fusum, he really *was* a man, doing his best to take any sense of joy and triumph out of Elemak's victory.

"Fool," said Elemak in digger language. "I don't want you dead. I want you to be king."

That silenced the digger as nothing else could have.

"Your father is worthless," said Elemak. "Emeezem rules over him. Mufruzhuuzh isn't a war leader, he might as well be wingless skymeat for all the good he does. I thought maybe your conspirators, those four who did the kidnapping, I thought perhaps they were men, but they are nothing, they gladly offered to trade you for their own lives, and blamed you for everything." Elemak mimicked their voices, making them breathy and feminine. "Oh, Fusum *deceived* us. He *made* us. It wasn't our *fault.* If we'd known you were really *gods.*"

Fusum hissed in reply, spraying saliva across Elemak's entire side of the room. It was the ultimate gesture of contempt. It would have provoked a deadly battle, if Elemak were a digger.

Elemak only laughed. "If your spittle were poison, it might be worth spending it on me. But there's no point in it. If you intend to save your people, to keep them out of slavery to *us,* then I'm the only hope you've got."

"If you're my hope I have no hope."

"You really are a fool, aren't you. But what can I expect from you? After all, I'm a god, and *you're* an earth-crawling worm."

"I am no worm, and you. . . ."

"Go on, Fusum, my dear little boy, my helpless lovey baby, say the rest of it."

Fusum shook his head.

"You were going to say, 'And you are no god.' Weren't you? Let's be honest with each other."

"I felt your hands on my body," said Fusum. "They were no god-hands."

"Oh really," said Elemak. "No doubt you've had many gods handle you before, so you know how *their* hands feel."

Fusum didn't answer.

"I'll tell you what *my* hands felt like. They felt like they belonged to a man who is stronger, smarter, faster, and more filled with hate than you."

Fusum studied him. "A man, you say."

"I say a man," said Elemak. "Not a god."

"Stronger, yes," said Fusum. "Today, anyway. Faster today. Smarter—perhaps. Today."

"Forever, Fusum," said Elemak. "In ten thousand years your whole people couldn't learn what I know right now."

"Smarter," said Fusum, conceding the point. "But never filled with more hate than me."

"Do you think not?" said Elemak. "Let's compare stories, shall we?"

They did. And when that first long day together was done, when Elemak at last brought food to Fusum, they were no longer prisoner and guard, or hostage and master, or man and god. They were allies, two men out of power among their own people, but determined to use each other's friendship to gain ascendancy over their rivals among their own people. It would take patience and planning. It would take time. But they *had* time, hadn't they? And patience could be learned one day after another. Elemak was doing it, wasn't he? Fusum could do the same.

"Just remember," Elemak told him, as Fusum splunged noisily into his meal. "If there comes a time when you think you can do just as well without me, I will see that thought in your mind before you notice it yourself, and when you turn around to put a knife in me, you'll find that my knife is already in you."

Fusum laughed, the wheezy, hissy laugh of a diggerman. "Now I know I can trust you with my life."

"You can," said Elemak. "All I'm telling you is that I will never trust you with *mine*."

* * *

When Nafai and Luet, Issib and Hushidh set out for the village of the angels, they carried their tools on their backs—or, in Issib's case, on the chair he had following behind him. Yasai and Oykib had climbed to the chosen spot the week before and placed the relay array, so that Issib could float easily up the pathway into the canyon. But his chair was there in case of bad weather, or in case someone stole some of his floats while he slept.

Their little children they left behind in the care of others. If all went well in their first contact with the village of the angels, they would build houses and then come back down to retrieve the children—along with seeds, extra clothing, and materials for teaching. They hoped to have a working farm in time for the full growing season at that elevation. If all went well.

pTo and Poto led the way up the canyon, quickly rising up into the air from time to time, then circling back down so that the humans could talk to them when they caught up. They were all quite aware that many among the angels had rejected the idea of befriending the humans—the Old Ones. But they had prepared the script that they thought would win them over, or at least win permission for the four humans to dwell among them. And when at last they reached the top of the canyon, the very meadow where pTo's bones had been broken, wing torn, blood spilt, they stopped and played it out.

pTo perched on Nafai's head, and Poto on Luet's. Their feet pressed, lightly but firmly, against the humans' jaws. And their wings unfolded, wrapped around Nafai's and Luet's shoulders, like cloaks, like tents.

"Like nests," said Luet.

Nafai nodded. For although they had never seen an angel nest with their own eyes, they had heard the descriptions pTo and Poto gave them, they had looked at the drawings they made, and finally they dreamed them and awoke from the dreams sure that the Keeper of Earth had shown them the truth. Woven and thatched out of supple twigs and grasses, the nests were really roofs sheltering the branches where the wives and young ones slept, hanging head down, wrapped in the blanket of their own wings.

Somewhere in the branches, in the surrounding trees, they knew that angels were watching them. Judging them.

Issib glided forward, his feet not touching the ground; Hushidh followed him, quietly telling him where the angels were, and which ones did not seem well connected to pTo and Poto. Those were the ones who needed to be won over, of course, and Issib, standing in the air—a trick that no one else, not even Nafai with his cloak, could do—he overawed them, the god visible, the only one who could fly.

"Where is Iguo, when her husband comes home to her?" Issib called out loudly in the language of the angels. He knew his voice would be hard to understand, pitched as low as it was, but he spoke quickly, hoping that the consonants would be enough of a guide to help them grasp his words.

No one emerged from the forest, but that was no surprise, not yet.

"His wing was torn, but now there is no tear in it. Do you think we will harm you, we who can heal the torn wing of a brave explorer?"

Still no one came forward.

"When the angry Old One harmed pTo, it was because he thought it was you, the people, who carried off his baby. We did not yet know the dark underground way of the devils."

Luet had argued against using the angels' word for the diggers, but Issib had insisted that they had to speak to them in language they would understand. "After all, Elya and Okya call the angels *skymeat* when they talk to the diggers, don't they?" Issib had pointed out. Everyone agreed then that *devils* was certainly no worse a word to use than that.

Issib went on addressing the invisible angels. "Now we know that the people do not come down the canyon to steal our children. Instead we see that when one brave man has been stricken down unjustly, his other-self, a man as brave as the first, will come down to care for him and save him if he can."

At last a few of the angels began letting themselves be seen, hopping forward to the leading branches of the trees that surrounded the clearing. Some of them stood upright atop the branches; others hung from them, head downward. It was dizzying to watch them, but Issib went on. "Now we know that the people who might have stopped brave Poto chose to let him come. These are the people who hoped for friendship with us, with the Old Ones who have been brought home by the Keeper of Earth."

There had been some argument about that, too. The angels had no concept of the Keeper of Earth, but Nafai had insisted that the name must be introduced from the beginning. "They'll find out soon enough that we aren't gods," Nafai had said. "Let it never be said we lied to them."

"As we lied to the diggers?" asked Luet mildly.

"We aren't trying to rescue a kidnapped baby from the angels," Nafai pointed out. "We're trying to make friends with people who have only seen us be mindlessly cruel. We're not going to let them see us as gods, even if we *do* get their attention by having Issib do his hovering trick."

So now Issib spoke the name of the Keeper of Earth, using the translation that pTo and Poto had given them, when they finally understood what and who the Keeper was. Or rather, when they understood as much as the humans did, as much as they could explain with their rudimentary mastery of the angels' difficult language.

"The Old Ones ask you to forgive us for our mistake. We did not know you then, but we know you now. Through these two brave and virtuous men we know you. Through the healing of pTo's wing you know us. Let the four of us dwell among you. But first, let Iguo come forward to join her husband. Come and see, Iguo, that his body is whole, that it is truly pTo that we have brought back to you."

They waited then, doing nothing, saying nothing except for pTo's and Poto's occasional murmurs of reassurance. Patience. Have patience. This is a difficult thing, for them to decide whether to let Iguo come to us.

She came, fluttering awkwardly under the branches of the nearer trees until she reached the clearing. Her awkwardness, they soon saw, was because two infants clung to the fur of her chest, unbalancing her as she flew.

pTo gasped in surprise, while Poto sang in delight. "Sons," he sang. "The wife of the broken one gave him sons while he healed. Now his joy is doubled and doubled again, for he returns to the woman he left as a wife and finds her now as a mother."

pTo leapt from Luet's head and landed before his wife. The two of them spoke softly, rapidly, the music of their voices beautiful together even though none of the humans could make sense of the words they said. As Iguo inspected pTo's body, especially the wing that had once been torn, pTo in his turn examined the two babies that she left in the grass at his feet. They could stand, even if they could not fly, and though their words were halting and babyish, they knew to call him Father, and pTo wept shamelessly to be able to touch them with his fingertips and his tongue, to have them climb up his body and frolic under the canopy of his wings.

At last Iguo turned back to the waiting angels. "What cannot be healed has been healed," she said. "What was lost forever has been found. Therefore let that which cannot be forgiven be forgiven, and let friendship bind the guests who have come to us, weave them into our hearts and our families, our nests and our trees."

It was the formal proposal that pTo and Poto had primed them to wait for. And now came the vote. Only a few dropped out of the trees to the ground to show their displeasure or their misgivings. And when the voting was finished, all those who had said yes by remaining in the trees now took flight, rising over the clearing, swarming and frolicking and singing, then darting down, a few at a time, to touch the humans, to see them with hands and feet as well as with their eyes, to hear their voices as they struggled with the difficult language.

"Dapai," they called Nafai, because they could not pronounce the nasal and fricative of his name. "Quet," they called Luet, now using the deep guttural plosive as their substitute for the unpronounceable *L*. "Ittib" was Issib, and "Kucheed" was Hushidh. pTo had complained that the Old Ones seemed to have chosen all their names to make them impossible for the people to say them.

But Dapai, Quet, Ittib, and Kucheed were close enough. The angels had spoken their names and welcomed them. With the chair tagging along behind, they followed the soaring, swarming angels down into the valley that was their home.

13

Killings

Vas meant no harm. He was simply an observant man, and a compassionate one. In the months that had passed since Elemak brutalized that flying nightmare they called an angel and Eiadh repudiated him in front of everybody, Vas noticed that the chill between Elemak and Eiadh seemed not to have thawed. Indeed, as far as he could tell the two of them were not speaking to each other, and Elemak managed to spend almost no time in the same house with his wife. Not that Vas normally kept track of people's comings and goings. It was simply a matter of happening to observe that Elemak was staying in the ship with the digger hostage, learning to hum and hiss when he spoke, and poor Eiadh was without a male companion in her life.

Well, Vas was nearly as lonely. Sevet, his dear wife, who had regularly betrayed him back in Basilica, now had betrayed him again by growing thick-bellied from bearing so many children. Worse, she had none of the bright charm that he had loved back when he had contracted to marry her for a few years. In those days she had been a celebrity, a singer, popular and well-loved. It had been quite a coup for Vas to be the man on her arm.

But she hadn't sung in years. Not since that night when Kokor came home to find her husband Obring bouncing away on Sevet's nubile loins. Koya, acting more out of fitful temper than a sense of justice, lashed out at the person she hated most in all the world, her sister Sevet. The blow took her in the larynx, and Sevet hadn't sung a note since. Not that the damage was physical. She could speak, and not in a monotone, either. And she hummed lullabies to the children as they were born. But singing, her voice full out and strong, that was over. And so, of course, was the fame in whose bright shadow Vas had so reveled. So there was nothing much attractive about Sevet anymore. Unfortunately, however, she was Rasa's daughter and they all got caught up in the nonsense that trapped them into coming out in the desert and so the marriage had not ended even though any spark of love that had once been between them ended on the night she betrayed him with her sister's pathetic miserable stupid loathsome worm of a husband, Obring.

So Vas was as lonely as Eiadh, and for similar reasons—both had discovered that their spouses were moral cretins, incapable of even a spark of human decency. Vas had endured his loveless marriage and even sired three children on the bitch and no one guessed how much he hated even to touch her. And it wasn't just her thickening waist or the loss of their fame-gilt life in Basilica. It was the image of her legs wrapped around Obring's white naked flaccid hairy thighs and knowing that she didn't even do it to betray Vas but rather to spite her vicious untalented little sister Kokor. Vas no doubt didn't even enter into Sevet's thoughts at all as she. . . .

Many years ago, it was many long years ago, and a hundred years of interstellar flight, not to mention years in the desert and another year, almost, in this new world, but to Vas it was yesterday, perpetually yesterday, and so Vas remembered very clearly the vow he had made when Elemak stopped him from killing Obring and Sevet to redeem his honor and manhood. He had vowed then that someday, perhaps when Elemak was old and feeble and helpless, Vas would put things back in balance. Vas would kill Obring and Sevet and then, the blood still fresh on his hands, he would come to Elemak and Elemak would laugh at him and say, You still remember? For *that,* so long ago, you killed them? And Vas would say to him, Elemak, it wasn't long ago. It was in this lifetime. And so it is in this lifetime that I will restore the balance. Them, for their betrayal. You, for stopping me from taking this vengeance hot. When it's cold, it takes more blood to make it work. Yours now, Elemak. Die at my hands, the way my pride died at yours.

Oh, hadn't he imagined it ten thousand times since then? Over and over again, when Elemak tried to kill Nafai or Volemak and they stopped him, battered him down, humiliated him, Vas had watched them, saying silently, Don't kill him. Save him for me. Ten thousand times he had imagined the way Obring would whimper and plead for mercy, and Sevet would scornfully disdain him, not believing he would kill her until that look of unspeakable surprise as the knife went in—oh, it would have to be a knife, a weapon of the hand, to feel the flesh break under the pressure of the stabbing blade, to feel the steel slide into the blood-lubricated flesh, probing inside until it found the heart and the blood gouted out under his hand, spasming up his arm in the last climax of Sevet's miserable life. . . .

The day will come, thought Vas. But first, why not prepare for it properly? Elemak thought that it was nothing for another man to sleep with my wife. Won't it be right and just, then, as he lies dying, for me to tell him in his last moments of consciousness that, Oh yes, Elemak, my friend, you remember what my wife did to me? Well, your wife did it to you, too, and with me. And Elemak will look into my eyes and know that I am speaking the truth and then he'll realize that I wasn't a passive creature after all, was never the mindless tool he thought I was for so many years.

The only trouble with that dream was Eiadh herself. Even if she wasn't sleeping with Elemak, that didn't mean she'd spare a thought for Vas. He wasn't a fool. He was an observant man, that's all. He knew that this was a time of vulnerability for her. Loneliness. And Vas could be compassionate. He would not come to Eiadh in anger or seeking vengeance on Elemak, no, not at all. He would come to her as a friend, offer a strong arm of comfort, and one thing would lead to another. Vas had read books. He knew this sort of thing happened. Why not to him? Why not with Eiadh, whose waist had *not* thickened despite bearing twice as many children as Sevet? Eiadh, who still sang, not with the power of a famous entertainer like Sevet, but with a lustrous intimacy, a voice that could waken all the longing in a man's soul, ah, yes, Eiadh, I have heard you singing and I have known that someday that voice would moan, that sweet throat would arch backward as your body shuddered in response to mine.

"Yes?" asked Eiadh.

He hadn't even clapped his hands. She must have seen him coming. How awkward. "Eiadh," he said.

"Yes?" she said again.

"May I come in?" asked Vas.

"Is something wrong?" asked Eiadh. He could see her taking mental inventory of her children.

"Not that I know of," said Vas. "Except that I'm concerned about you."

Eiadh looked confused. "Me?"

"Please, may I come in?" he asked.

She laughed but let him through the door. "Of course, Vas, but I have no idea what you're talking about. Except that I'm tired all the time, but that's the same complaint that everyone else has. If you've come to cut the vegetables for supper, then I'm delighted."

"Do you really need help with the vegetables?" asked Vas.

"No, that was a figure of speech. I'm actually sewing. Volemak insists that we all learn to sew with these awful bone needles. They're so thick that with every stitch they open gaping holes in the fabric but he insists that someday there'll be no more steel ones and so—well, it makes no sense to *me,* not even in the desert did we have to—I'm boring you, aren't I?"

"I'm sorry," said Vas. "Not boring me. But I was listening more to your voice than your words, I hope you'll forgive me. Elemak is a lucky man, to have a wife whose common speech is so like music."

She looked puzzled at the compliment, but then laughed lightly. "I don't think Elemak feels very lucky," she said.

"Then Elemak is a fool," said Vas. "For him to turn away from such goodness and beauty as—"

"Vas, are you trying to seduce me?" asked Eiadh.

Flustered, Vas could only deny it. "No, I can't—did I lead you to think that I—oh, this is embarrassing. I came to *talk.* I've been lonely and I thought perhaps you—but if you think it's not proper for us to be alone in the house here—"

"It's all right," said Eiadh. "I know my virtue is safe with you."

Vas put on his best wry smile. "Everyone's virtue is safe with me, apparently."

"Poor Vas," she said. "You and I have something in common."

"Do we?" he asked. Was it possible she felt toward him as he felt toward her? Perhaps he shouldn't have denied his seductive intent so quickly and emphatically.

"I mean besides the obvious," she said. "It seems that both of us are fated to play secondary roles in our own autobiographies."

Vas laughed because it seemed that she was waiting for him to laugh. "By which you mean . . ." he said.

"Oh, just that we both seem to be buffeted here and there by the choices that other people make. Why in the world were *we* ever brought aboard a starship, can you think of a reason? Just a matter of chance. Falling in love with the wrong person on the wrong day at the wrong point in history."

"Yes," said Vas. "Now I understand you. But can't two bit players like ourselves nevertheless make our own little plays, on a small stage in the wings, while the famous actors make orotund speeches before the great audience of history? Can't there be some kind of happiness snatched in the darkness, where the only audience is ourselves?"

"I'm not the snatch-in-the-darkness type," said Eiadh. "I married stupidly and I knew it almost at once. So did you, I'm afraid. But that doesn't mean that I'll jeopardize the future of my children, not to mention my own future, for the sake of some kind of consolation or vengeance. I take what happiness I can in the light, out in the open. Loving my children. You have good children yourself, Vas. Take comfort in them."

"The love of my children isn't the love that I hunger for," he said. He dared to be direct with her because he realized that she saw through all his attempts at clever indirection anyway.

"Vas," she said kindly. "I have admired you for so long, because you bear everything with such patience. I no longer have any problem knowing which kind of strength, yours or Elemak's, is the better kind. But part of what I admire is that you are able to bear it all without flinching. Let's not become like they are. Let's not stoop low enough that we finally deserve what they're doing to us."

Vas was not an unobservant man. He noticed right away that she seemed to be referring to something recent, not ancient history from back in Basilica. She seemed to assume that he already knew something that he did not know. "You will never deserve what Elemak is doing to you," he said, hoping that it would prompt a certain response.

And it did. "You don't deserve what Sevet is doing to you, either," she answered. "You'd think she would have learned her lesson long ago, but some women learn nothing, while others learn everything."

Vas's head spun. He had dwelt so long on the memory of the years-ago betrayal with Obring that it hadn't crossed his mind that Sevet might be taking someone else into his bed. Yet there were many opportunities. When he was out in the fields, taking his turn; when he was standing watch; when he was off those two times with Zdorab, using the ship's launch to explore and map the surrounding country. Sevet might have—but surely even she would not—not a second time, not after she lost so much, lost her voice.

But then, I wasn't the one who took her voice from her, was I? That was Kokor, and then we were out of Basilica by the time Sevet's voice healed. Sevet might know to fear Kokor's temper, but what has ever taught her to fear mine?

The time has come, Vas realized. This time there would be no patience. This time there would be no Elemak to stay his hand. Sevet and Obring would die, and then he would turn to Elemak and rid Eiadh of the burden of that monstrous husband forever. Then, with all impediments out of the way, *then* she would turn to the man who had freed her.

Or not. Who really cared whether anyone loved him or approved of him at all? He wasn't trying to win anyone's love or admiration except his own. He had been too long without it, and it was time to get it back.

"Hard to believe that she could still be taken in by Obring," said Vas. "You'd think she would see through him now, when he's outgrown his boyish charm—as if he ever had any."

She laughed, but there was a puzzled look on her face. Now, what could that mean?

It meant that it wasn't Obring. Sevet was being unfaithful, but not with Obring.

Then he remembered what she said before. About how they had something in common. "I mean besides the obvious," she said. What was the obvious? So obvious that only Vas had missed it. Everyone must know. Everyone.

She must have seen the realization on his face, because it was her turn to look stricken. "Oh, Vas, I thought you knew, I thought that's why you came here, to get even with them. But I wasn't angry, you see, because I don't want him in my bed anyway, so I don't much care where he puts his sweaty body and I thought . . . I don't know why but I just assumed that you had the same attitude but I see that you don't, you didn't know, and I'm so sorry, I. . . ."

He didn't hear her finish because he got up and left her house. Elemak's house.

"Don't do anything foolish, Vas," she said softly. And then, because she knew perfectly well that there was a very good chance he *would* do something foolish, she went in search of help. Volemak had to know that there was a quarrel brewing. He would know how to put a stop to it. Eiadh should have done this long ago. Adultery was a terrible thing in their tiny community—Elemak himself had laid down that law in the desert years before. Eiadh had never complained because she honestly was glad not to have to have him close to her, with those angry hands that had broken a helpless innocent being, those hands that had brutalized and terrorized everyone aboard the ship. Better to sleep alone and dream of the only real man she had ever known. A man who once, when he was a boy, had loved her, or at least longed for her. A man who now didn't so much as look at her with pleasure.

With all her childish longing for Nafai, it had never occurred to her that the reason Vas hadn't complained about Elemak's and Sevet's adultery was because he didn't know. How could he not know? Were men so much more blind than women? Or did he imagine that just because he might have stopped wanting Sevet, her own sexual desires would naturally just wither away?

It was going to be a mess, and somebody was going to be dead at the end of it, she knew that now, because she had never seen Vas with such a look of blank rage in his face before. She had seen Elemak like that, but Elemak was used to having such feelings and restraining them. Vas had no such practice.

On the way to Volemak's house, she passed Mebbekew, who was staking out the hide of a goat that he and a couple of diggers had taken while hunting up in the hills this morning. "What's the hurry?" he asked.

"You might want to come along and help," she said. "Vas just found out about Sevet's adultery and I think he might be dangerous."

From the way Meb's face went pale, Eiadh knew that Sevet had let more than one farmer plow in her field. "Not you," said Eiadh. "He doesn't know about you."

"Who else?" he asked, baffled.

She laughed at him. "Are all men as stupid as you and Vas? You all think you own the moon, just because you never see anybody else looking at it."

Meb smiled. "So Vas is out to kill Elemak," he said.

"I'm getting Volemak. We've got to put a stop to it."

"Oh, and I'll be right there to help, you can be sure of it. I wouldn't miss this for anything."

But Mebbekew did not follow her to Volemak's house. Instead, still holding the heavy mallet in his hands, he tried to think where Vas might go first. The tool shed, no doubt, to get something to do violence with—Vas wasn't likely to be a bare-hands sort of fighter, not if he had killing on his mind. He knew his limitations. So did Meb. Vas would have something sharp with a long handle. And Meb would have a very large mallet. Vas, being a proud man, would speak to his intended victim, call his name, face him. Meb, having no pride at all, would come up on him from behind. Or lie in wait and take him by ambush. Meb was not ashamed of this. He knew that in an open fight he was no match for a determined enemy. Fighting wasn't a skill he had worked to acquire. He was meant to be an actor and, if there had been a real God and not just this stupid computer, Meb would still be in Basilica on the stage, making a name for himself and finding new women and new friends every night. Instead he was here in this filthy village living in dirt and covered every day with sweat and dust and mud and insect bites, and now there was a very angry husband and, whether the husband knew it or not, Meb was almost certainly the most recent man to sleep with Vas's wife.

He will go to Sevet, of course. He'll go home.

But at Vas's own house there was no one. Sevet was gone. Off with the women. Oh, yes. Teaching, this was her time of day to teach the children, as if reading mattered anymore. What were they going to read? The latest story written by a rat in a hole? But it was saving Sevet's life at the moment, so it wasn't all bad, was it? Sevet was a very grateful lover. And she had acquired some skill during her heyday, so sleeping with her was a welcome relief after Dolya's clinging, cloying, hungry, needy, selfish, clumsy. . . .

Which was not to say that Meb minded sleeping with Dol whenever she wanted. Meb was still a young man, and now that Elemak wasn't policing the adultery law anymore, nobody else seemed to catch on except the adulterers themselves. That was the nice thing about having laws enforced only by those who believed in them—they were not likely to suspect that the laws were being broken because breaking them wouldn't even occur to their innocent little minds.

If Vas couldn't get to Sevet, and if he didn't know about Meb, then he'd certainly go for Elemak. That meant he was heading for the ship, where Elemak would be working with the hostage.

On his way there, though, Meb passed Obring's house and saw that the door stood open, even though Obring would be sleeping late after having kept watch last night and—was it possible? Did Vas harbor resentment against Obring so many years after the fact? Or did Vas imagine that Sevet would ever have slept with Obring again, after that nasty evening when Kokor came in on them? Or was it simply that his wife's new adultery refreshed the memory of the old?

Even if he was safely asleep, Obring would want to see the fun and Meb wouldn't mind having another man with him for safety's sake, even if the man was Obring and therefore unreliable and cowardly. I'm unreliable and cowardly myself, thought Meb, so I can't very well hold it against *him.*

Meb stepped into the house. Obring lay on his bed, eyes wide open, hands spread across the wound in his chest, though it was doubtful he had died from that one. It was the deep slice across his throat that no doubt finished him off. Very neatly done. The wound in the chest could have been from a pick or an axe. Definitely not a hoe. The throat wound made it definite, though, that it was a bladed weapon. One of the scythes. No. An axe. Edge enough to slice the throat, but powerful enough to crush its way into the chest. Poor Obring. Poor me, if Vas decides to take after me. An axe against a mallet? Perhaps I'd better wait until Father decides what to do, let Nafai go in with his magical cloak and give poor Vas a jolt.

What in the world will they do with a murderer?

Meb heard some loud talking far away, near Volemak's house, but he ignored it and headed swiftly into the ship. Vas is in a hurry, and Elemak is waiting. What deck does he have the digger on? Should have paid more attention. Elemak will be glad if I get there in time to save his life. And if I don't, I might still be able to set up a little ambush for Vas. That'll solve Father's problem very nicely, if the murderer turns up pleasantly dead.

Elemak and Fusum were verbally sparring, arguing back and forth, Elemak speaking the digger language, Fusum doing the best he could with the human words. It was part of the deal they had worked out with each other. Fusum would teach Elemak the subtlest nuances of language if, in the end, Fusum also understood whatever it was the humans said. "If you're not gods," said Fusum, "then your language isn't sacred and it's no sin for me to learn it, right?" And Elemak could only agree.

Fusum had nothing like Elemak's skill or practice at learning languages, however, and he had spent most of the morning being resentful and sullen about the way Elemak rattled off eloquent sentences while Fusum could only stammer his way through the most rudimentary answers. Every now and then he would erupt in a torrent of arguments in his native language, only to fall silent at Elemak's superior smile and return to struggling with the human speech. The sounds they made—like skymeat, half their sounds were. Like animals. Or so Fusum said, whenever he gave up and raged for a few moments.

Elemak enjoyed it all.

Until the moment that Vas appeared in the open doorway, a blood-soaked axe in his hands. This was not in Elemak's plans for today. "What have you been doing with that axe?" asked Elemak. The sorry bastard couldn't have killed Sevet already, could he? She'd be teaching right now—he wouldn't do it in front of the children, would he? And who told him? After all these months, why did they tell him *now?*

"I planned to kill you anyway," said Vas. "Because of how you stopped me from killing Obring and Sevet back all those years ago. I never forgot how you humiliated me, Elemak. But this—sleeping with Sevet. Why didn't you just screw one of the digger women, if Eiadh wasn't letting you into her bed? That's your style, isn't it, Elemak? Rutting with helpless little barbarian animals?"

Elemak spoke in digger language to Fusum. "I don't suppose there's anything you can do to help, is there?"

"Talk so I can understand you!" demanded Vas.

"What, haven't you been studying the diggers' language like a good boy?" asked Elemak.

Meanwhile, Fusum had figured out how to answer Elemak's request in human speech. "I'd like to help you but the crazy man has the axe."

Vas looked at him coldly. "Very good decision, rat boy," he said. "I don't much care whether your brains end up on the floor or not."

"Actually," said Elemak—again in digger language—"he'll kill you as soon as he kills me, and then he'll say that you were the one who hit me with the axe and then he struggled with you and got it away and killed *you* with it."

Fusum glared at him and answered, stubbornly, in human speech so Vas could understand him. "The axe is already bloody. He's already killed somebody outside the ship."

"Who did you kill, Vas?" asked Elemak. "Anyone I know?"

"Obring," said Vas. "I took his throat out. After I smashed into his heart."

"How appropriate. To shatter his heart as he shattered yours." Elemak laughed. Not because he didn't believe Vas would kill him. On the contrary, he was quite prepared to believe that Vas would try, and given the fact that Elemak was in a weak position, sitting on the floor with no particular leverage, there was a good chance Vas would fell him with a blow before he could attempt any kind of response.

"It's funny to you?" asked Vas.

"And sad, of course. Poor Sevet. Once I'm dead, she'll be back to having to make do with your clumsy occasional efforts at lovemaking."

"I'll kill her, too," said Vas.

"And then who? Everybody else, for instance? You're doomed, Vas. You should have been more clever. You should have bided your time."

"I've already bided my time long enough."

"You should have made it look like an accident. Or better yet, you could have made it look as though you tried to *save* my life. Take us one at a time, not all at once with an axe. And you have Obring's blood on your clothes. Very clumsy, Vas. They'll have to kill you for it, you know. Can't very well let a murderer run loose."

"You'll be dead first," said Vas.

"Oh, definitely. That'll make you feel *much* better as they—what, strangle you? Drown you? Maybe Shedemei has some drug that will carry you off painlessly in your sleep. You can dream of me as you croak out your last breath."

"I'm not afraid to die," said Vas.

"That's too bad," said Elemak. "Because I am. Do you know why? I'm afraid there might be a life after death. I'm afraid I might have to go on living, only without this very comfortable body. What if I'm reincarnated? What if I come back with a body like . . . *yours?*"

He said this last with as much loathing as he could muster. It had no effect.

"I'm not going to let you goad me into taking an unconsidered move," said Vas. "I know you're sitting there imagining ways to take the axe away from me before I can smash your head in with it. But why should I aim for your head? There are your legs, spread out like the limbs of a tree. I can chop through a five-centimeter branch with a single blow—think I can do as well with your ankle?"

"No, I don't think you can," said Elemak.

"You think you're quick enough to stop me? From a sitting position, you arrogant fool?"

"I don't have to stop you," said Elemak.

"Good thing," said Vas. "Because you can't."

"But Meb can," said Elemak. "He's standing behind you with a very large mallet, and I think he's planning to drive your head down into your shoulders like a spike."

Vas didn't even bother to turn around. "As long as you're conjuring up demons to frighten me with, why not have it be Nafai? *He's* the only real man around here anyway. I'm not afraid of Meb."

"I quite agree with you," said Elemak. "Meb is only frightening when he's behind you with a mallet. Most of the time he's a worthless little digger turd. But Meb, it won't work. You can't drive his head down into his shoulders, not a soft little head like Vas's. It'll burst open like a melon first. Splash all over the room."

"Don't fantasize about my head," said Vas. "It's your legs that are going to go." He raised the axe above his head.

"If it's any consolation to you," said Elemak, "Meb's been sleeping with Sevet, too."

Vas hesitated, not swinging the axe, not striking the blow.

Elemak went on talking. "Your poor wife is apparently lonely enough to settle for anything that pretends to be male, even Meb, who isn't brave enough to smash you from behind after all. What's that mallet *for*, then, Meb? A cure for rectal itch?"

Meb looked back at him with loathing. Elemak knew that he just *hated* being taunted and manipulated.

"Oh, Meb," said Elemak. "Just swing the damn thing and have done."

So he did. Meb turned out to have a much stronger swing than Elemak had expected. But Elemak *was* right about the splashing. It got really nasty, especially after Vas hit the floor and Meb kept right on pounding on his head with the mallet, three, four, five times, until the head was pulped and bits of brain and bone were spattered all over the room. Of course, as soon as Meb calmed down and could look at what he had done, he threw up, as if somehow Vas's head had exploded all by itself and not because he mashed it. But Elemak didn't much worry about Meb. It was Fusum who fascinated him, as he picked bits of Vas's brains off his naked body and ate them.

"Don't get a taste for that, Fusum," Elemak said in digger language.

"Not much different from peccary brains," said Fusum. "I already *have* a taste for those."

"If you ever harm a human, Fusum, I'll cut you into tiny pieces."

"Even Nafai?" asked Fusum, taunting him.

So Fusum had picked up on the conflicts within the human community—even with Nafai up the canyon most of the time, trying to teach the skymeat how to farm.

"Especially Nafai," said Elemak. "He's mine."

Meb had stopped throwing up. "What were you saying? I heard you mention Nafai."

"Oh, Fusum and I were just saying what a pity it was that the one useful act you will ever perform in your life was wasted on Vas."

"Wasted?" asked Meb. "I killed my friend to save your life and you call it a waste?"

"I would have stopped him before he touched me," said Elemak. He didn't know whether it was true, but he was fairly sure Meb would believe it. "And as for Vas being your friend—I'm not going to weep for you. Not with the smell of Sevet still on you from last night while he was on watch."

"Shows what *you* know," said Meb. "Last night I didn't have time for Sevet. After all these months of pestering, I finally gave in and let Eiadh make love to—"

Meb didn't finish his sentence. He found himself pressed against the wall with the axe handle strangling him.

"I know it's a lie," said Elemak. "But if I ever thought that it was true, you'd end up praying for me to do for you what you did for Vas. A quick finish. It'd be too good for you, Meb."

"I was joking, you ass," said Meb, when he could speak again.

"Don't waste my time with your apologies," said Elemak. "Not when we have to explain Vas's death to the people I can hear coming up the ladderway right now."

"What's to explain?" said Meb. "I saved your life."

"Ah, but why was Vas trying to take it? And why did you so sweetly care?"

"He was trying to kill you because you were humping his wife," said Meb. "And I cared enough to stop him because you're my older brother and I love you."

"Is that your best performance, Meb?" asked Eiadh as she strode down the corridor toward them. "Lucky for you that we left Basilica before you could humiliate yourself by trying to *act* in public." Volemak, Oykib, and Padarok came to the door with her, all carrying tools that would have made pretty convincing weapons if they hadn't been in the hands of such gentle, peace-loving souls. "What's all this mess?" asked Eiadh. "Where's Vas?" Then she saw the body on the floor, the ruined head still crookedly connected to the shoulders. She recoiled. "What have you done?" she whispered to Elemak.

"Actually, *I* did it," said Meb. "Just as he was about to take Elemak's ankle off."

But Eiadh paid no attention to Meb. She looked Elemak coldly in the eye. "This man is dead because you couldn't live a month without getting *some* woman into bed."

Elemak smiled at her. "Not true. As long as I've been married to you, my love, my bed has never had a woman in it."

"You really are evil," said Eiadh. "You really do love destroying things. And not even great evil, not even that spectacular, world-wrecking kind of evil that epics are written about. No, what's in your heart is just a whiny little wormlike evil."

"Say your worst," said Elemak. "I know you're really just glad I'm still alive."

"The second most terrible thing I ever did in my life," said Eiadh, "was letting you be the father of my poor, innocent children."

"And the worst thing?" said Elemak. "Go ahead and say it—I'm brave, I'm tough. I've got Vas's blood and brains all over me, I can take anything."

Eiadh smiled at him, for she knew she was about to say the most terrible thing he could ever hear. "The worst thing I ever did was not to marry Nafai when I realized he was in love with me back in Rasa's house. I knew my mistake long before I actually married *you*, Elemak. I only went ahead and married you in order to stay close to Nafai. I prayed that all my sons would grow up to be like him, not you. And every time you made love to me, I always pretended it was him. It was all I could do to keep from crying out his name."

"Enough of this," said Volemak. "Terrible things have happened here today, and you're wasting our time with a domestic squabble."

Elemak obediently dropped the discussion and submitted to Volemak's questioning. But he heard what Eiadh had said to him. He heard, and he would remember.

* * *

It was Oykib who got the assignment of traveling up the canyon to tell about the killings. Shedemei could have used the ship's computers to tell Issib through the Index, but Volemak insisted that it had to be done in person. The first thought, then, was to send Chveya to tell her parents, but she was almost ready to be delivered of her firstborn child, and so her husband was chosen instead. He was not grateful. "I don't like leaving here right now," he said. "Not with violence in the air."

"I think the killing is over," said Volemak.

"And if you're wrong?"

"Be practical," said Zdorab. "If Elemak did nothing when he had Obring and Vas to call upon, will he do anything now, when he has only Meb as a grown man to stand beside him? The killing is over."

"The killing will never be over," interrupted Rasa, "if the adultery continues and goes unpunished."

"I would say," said Volemak, "that the penalty for adultery has been clearly demonstrated."

"I would say it hasn't," said Rasa. "I would say that your two oldest sons are adulterers by the words of their own mouths, and that my two daughters stand condemned by the same testimony."

"What would you have me do?" asked Volemak. "Put them to death? Of the sixteen original adults of our expedition, shall we end with six of them dead?"

"Which is worse, Volemak? Six dead now, and the law affirmed? Or two dead, and the law with them?"

"You're a hard one, Mother," said Oykib. "The death penalty for adultery was a measure for the desert, not for here."

"Because there are trees and streams, adultery is less fatal for our community?" asked Rasa. "I thought I raised you to reason better than that, Oykib."

"Enough of this discussion," said Volemak. "Oykib must travel up the canyon to break the news."

"I think he should take Eiadh with him," said Rasa.

The others looked at her as if she were insane. "After what she said to Elemak?" asked Oykib. "Do you want to sign her death warrant?"

"Do you think that leaving her down here is any better?" asked Rasa.

"Yes," said Volemak. "For her to go up where Nafai is would be seen by Elemak as proof of some kind of liaison between them, when in fact there has never been any such thing. Rasa, are you determined to make things worse?"

Rasa was furious. "I am determined to make things better five years from now, while you seem determined to make things better for the moment and let the future go hang." She stormed out of the library.

Volemak sighed. "Every leader has his critics," he said. "Usually, though, they don't have to go home to them at night."

"She was right in everything she said," said Shedemei. "But you were also right in everything you decided."

Volemak laughed grimly. "Sometimes, Shedya, there *is* no middle way."

"I'm not taking a middle way. You were right that at this moment you can't decide any other way than the way you have decided. But she was right about the consequences. Sevet and Kokor will go on sleeping with Elemak and Mebbekew and, for all we know, every randy male digger who passes by their houses. Elemak and Mebbekew will go on betraying their wives and then hating the very women they're harming."

"And what am I supposed to be able to do about that?" demanded Volemak.

"Nothing," said Shedemei. "Nothing except watch our social order disintegrate."

"Sometimes you're too much the scientist, Aunt Shedya," said Oykib.

"Not possible," said Shedemei. "And you forget, my own children have to live in the new social order we've created here. When you think about it, this really marks the moment of Elemak's triumph over his father. Despite the oath, despite Elemak's many defeats, he has finally succeeded in undoing all his father's works. This is Elemak's type of society now, because the rest of us haven't the coldness of heart to uphold the law and put him to death."

"That's right," said Volemak. "The rest of us haven't the coldness of heart. Do you?"

"No," said Shedemei immediately. "As I said, your decisions are the only ones that can be made, disastrous as they are. Now let's let Oykib be on his way while the rest of you prepare the bodies for burning. As for me, I have a very messy room to clean up."

Oykib stood up to leave. "I'll go up the mountain, but I don't like leaving Chveya at a time like this."

"I'll be all right," Chveya murmured.

"And what worries me has nothing to do with Elemak and Mebbekew and adultery and all that," said Oykib.

"Oh, what's *your* concern, then?" asked Volemak. "I'm always happy to learn of something new to keep me awake at night."

"Fusum saw Vas die."

"We've never pretended to be immortal," Volemak said.

Oykib shook his head. "Fusum saw Vas die. Someday we'll all agree that that was the worst thing about today's events."

He went home long enough to pack up some hard-crusted bread for the journey. The way up the canyon was a path, now, and was becoming more of a road as they cut out underbrush and used picks and spades to smooth the roughest places. So it was only two hours to the saddle at the top of the canyon, and then another hour through the forest to the village.

It had been transformed in the past few months, as Nafai and the others worked with the angels to teach them ways to make their lives better. Where the angels had known the location of every useful plant within twenty kilometers of their village, they now had felled enough trees to make a field where yams and manioc, melons and maize could thrive in open sunlight. Where the angels had kept herbivores from their protected plants and predators from their houses by building traps along every path and track at the perimeter of their territory, they now had a fence around their fields, and their turkeys and goats were corralled at night. Already the angels could grow food enough to feed twice their present population, and most of the surplus could be stored.

But the agricultural revolution was not the only one. The angels seemed to want to emulate the humans in every way. Many of them now had built houses on the ground, the way the humans did, even though they hadn't the strength to build as sturdily and the first strong wind would tear the houses away. They knew this, too, and during bad weather continued to sleep hanging from branches in the trees. But it was important to them that they *have* a house in the human style, and Nafai had long since given up trying to persuade them of the uselessness of it.

Oykib found Nyef and Hushidh working with the angel toolmakers.

"What's wrong?" Hushidh said instantly. "Who is dead?"

"How did you know?" asked Oykib.

"Your face," she said. "Your fear to speak to us."

"Is it Father?" asked Nafai. And that was the most pertinent question—when Volemak died, everything would change.

"Not father," said Oykib. "Vas killed Obring—vengeance for what happened between him and Sevet back in Basilica, apparently. And when he went to kill Elemak for more current betrayals, Meb was able to slip up behind him and kill him."

"Elemak didn't do any killing?"

"He might have, but he didn't get the chance," said Oykib. "Another thing. Fusum was watching when Mebbekew killed Vas. It happened right in front of him. With the mallet Meb had been using to stake out hides."

"And how did Vas kill Obring?"

"An axe to the chest and then through the throat," said Oykib. "Does it matter how?"

"It matters what the diggers have learned about how to kill us," said Nafai.

Oykib smiled grimly. "My own thoughts exactly."

"That's not all you came to tell us, though, is it," said Hushidh.

"No," said Oykib. And then he told them what Eiadh had said to Elemak, taunting him that she had been in love with Nafai all through her marriage to Elemak, that she wanted her sons to grow up to be like Nafai.

"Why didn't she save time and just slit my throat?" said Nafai.

"And then her own," said Hushidh. "As far as Elemak is concerned, the two of you might as well have committed adultery. And no one hates other people's adultery like an adulterer."

"Funny, isn't it," said Nafai, "how few years it took for us to change from the way it was at Basilica. Back there, Eiadh would simply not have renewed Elemak, and Sevet and Kokor would be on their sixth or tenth husbands since then, and nobody would have died for it."

"Do you think that it was more civilized?" asked Hushidh. "The same rages were just beneath the surface, the same hunger for loyalty from a husband or wife. Obring didn't die for something he did in the wild. He died for what he did back there in the city."

"But it wasn't in the city that he died," said Nafai. "Never mind. If the diggers know that humans can be killed, we'd better make sure we tell the story to the angels as well. Fortunately I've never had to play god up here, so it'll come to them as less of a shock. We'll come down the mountain for the funeral, of course. And we'll bring some angels with us. They need to see a human body going into the flames."

"Maybe that's the wrong lesson to teach them," said Hushidh.

"Why?" asked Nafai. "Do you think some angels are secretly wishing to slaughter all the humans?"

"Not at all," said Hushidh. "But I think some angels are counting on us to keep the diggers from coming up against them and stealing their infants to eat them and make pedestals out of their bones. It won't encourage them to see that we can be broken and killed."

"Especially not the way Vas died," said Oykib. Whereupon they insisted that he describe how it happened, and then clearly wished that he had not.

"Just as well to have the angels know our weakness," said Nafai. "It's their own strength they have to trust in, that and the care and wisdom of the Keeper of Earth."

"The Keeper?" asked Oykib. "They know about him?"

"Not by that name, not till we taught them," said Nafai. "But there have always been dreamers among them. And Luet has found several who respond well to the trances that she used as Waterseer in Basilica. The Keeper speaks to them. And I'm working on trying to find weapons they can use that will enable them to stand against the diggers, if it ever comes to war."

"Don't you think we'll be able to keep them at peace with each other?" asked Oykib.

"I don't think we'll be able to keep at peace with ourselves," said Nafai. "We have the first two deaths as evidence."

"Is it very awful of me," said Hushidh, "that I don't think I'm going to miss Obring at all?"

"It would be more surprising if you did," said Nafai. "But Vas wanted to be a good man, I think."

Oykib scoffed. "If he had wanted to be, he would have, Nafai. People are what they want to be."

"What an uncharitable view," said Hushidh. "Why, you'd think, from the way you talk, that people were responsible for their own behavior."

"And they're not?" asked Oykib.

"Haven't you ever seen a three-year-old when he makes a foolish blunder? He looks at whatever child or adult is nearby and screams at him, 'Look what you made me do!' That's the moral universe that Vas and Obring always lived in, and Sevet and Kokor, too."

At the funeral, Kokor kept watching Sevet furtively, matching her tear for tear and sigh for sigh. I'm not going to let the old bitch get any more mileage out of widowhood than me, thought Kokor. After all, it was *her* husband who killed mine. She drove him to it, that's what, because she was so clumsy she got found out. *I* slept with Elemak even back before the voyage to Earth, and nobody ever knew. Sevet has a habit of getting caught in her little liaisons. Of course, maybe she wants to. Maybe that's how she gets her kicks, watching people go into frenzies of misery and rage over what she did and who she did it with.

It certainly worked on me, back in Basilica. She certainly got me angry, didn't she? And then got to play the victim for years and years, never singing again even though her voice came back just *fine* within the first year. Always holding her musical silence over my head when Mother would look at her and reminisce about how she once sang the "Love Dream of Sogliadatai" or the "Death of the Poisoned Sparrow."

The funeral pyres were set alight, and the angels around them started making the most awful whining sort of sound. Nasty little creatures. What did *they* know of grief?

But their singing—if that's what it was—gave Kokor an idea, and she acted on it at once. The "Death of the Poisoned Sparrow" had been Sevet's signature song, and it would fit beautifully right at this moment, even though it was not actually about a funeral, but rather about the end of a beautiful but impossible love affair. And one of the best arrangements of the song had been a duet between Sevet and a flute. Kokor had listened to it over and over, had coveted the song with all her heart, but had never dared to sing it in public for the obvious reason that it would make it look as though she envied her sister and was trying to compete with her. Still, she knew every note of it. And, as she thought about it for a moment, she realized that she also remembered every note of the flute part.

So that is what she began to sing, wordlessly, letting her voice rise and soar in the notes of the flute. She couldn't sing it quite as high as the flute had played, of course, but then, Sevet no doubt couldn't sing as high as she had sung back when she was a girl, especially without practice. Once Kokor started singing, she did not dare even steal a glance at Sevet, or it would look like she was trying to get Sevet to do something instead of simply expressing the heartbreak she felt as she watched her husband's body going up in flame.

She sang the entire flute part and Sevet didn't join in. But Kokor could also tell from the stillness of the others—even the angels fell silent to hear her—that she had chosen to do the right thing this time, that for once the others approved of and even appreciated her. And when she began the flute part again at the beginning, Sevet's voice came out at last, singing the melody. Now the strangeness of the melody Kokor had sung began to make sense as harmony to Sevet's voice, and the words Sevet sang brought tears to people's eyes as the death of such worthless men as Obring and Vas never would have. People cried when she sang it in theaters, when nobody had died—how could they help but sob their little hearts out here, with the smell of cooking meat in their nostrils and Obring's and Vas's littlest children crying their poor little eyes out because their papas were such worthless murdering fornicating pieces of digger poo. Kokor loved the way her voice sounded with Sevet's. For Sevet's had changed, had grown richer and more mature, but Kokor's had not, had retained the flutelike simplicity and purity of youth. Kokor had no need to try to sound like Sevet now, nor Sevet to resent the similarity between them. They made different sounds, but they could be beautiful together nonetheless.

When the song ended, the appropriate action was obvious, and Sevet did not fail her. They both extended their arms at once, and weeping copiously they fell into each other's embrace. Kokar enjoyed hearing the collective sigh of the watching humans. The sisters, reconciled at last! She could imagine Mother reaching down and squeezing Volemak's hand, and Volemak whispering to her later, If only my sons could make peace as your daughters have.

While they clung to each other in their embrace of grief and forgiveness, Sevet whispered in Kokor's ear. "I'm going to be Elemak's mistress now, little sister, so don't try to stop me."

To which Kokor whispered in reply, "So am I. He's cocksman enough for the two of us, don't you think?"

"Share and share alike?" murmured Sevet.

"I'll bet I bear him a baby before you do," whispered Kokor. Of course she had no intention of bearing him a child at all, but it would be lovely if Sevet did, ruining her thick body even more than having three children already had. Let the poor bitch think we're competing to give birth to Elya's bastards—I'll just let her "win" and keep the real victory, which is my youthful body despite having let Obring sire five babies on me. If all five were really his.

They broke the embrace and pulled apart a little. "Oh, Kokor," said Sevet. "My sister." Then she burst into tears again.

Damn. That would be hard to top.

Kokor reached out and took a tear from Sevet's cheek, then held it up as a glistening patch of wetness on her fingertip. "I will never cause you to shed another one of these, my beloved Sevya."

The sigh from the others was all the applause Kokor needed. I win again, Sevet. You're simply no match for me.

Fusum learned two things from the killing of Obring and Vas.

First, he learned that the humans were, in fact, mortal, and could be killed if enough force were applied using a sufficient weapon in the right way. He had no immediate plans to use this information, but he intended to devote a great deal of thought to it over the months and years to come.

Second, he learned that killing was a powerful device that should not be wasted. You must kill the right person, and at the right time, and always in order to achieve an important purpose. That was why, when Fusum was finally judged to be rehabilitated and returned to his people, he made it a point to become a friend and companion to Nen. As the eldest and most gifted son of Emeezem and Mufruzhuuzh, the deep mother and the war king, Nen was the bright golden hope of the next generation. He spoke the human language almost as fluently as Fusum himself, having learned it through close association with Oykib, and when Emeezem and Mufruzhuuzh coerced Fusum's own father, the blood king Shosseemem, to join them in declaring a ban on the kidnapping and eating of skymeat infants, it was Nen who came forward and swept away the pedestal of bones on which the Untouched God had rested. It was Nen who cried out, "Let friendship everlasting stand between our people and the people of the sky." Oh, Fusum had cheered along with everyone else that day. And he worked hard to win a place at Nen's side, as his most trusted friend.

Then one day they were out hunting together, carrying the traditional stone-tipped spear in one hand, knotty club in the other. They were stalking a peccary through the undergrowth, near enough to hear it grunting now and then, when suddenly Fusum saw his opportunity. A panther, too, was stalking the peccary, but as everyone knew, panthers were only too happy to make a meal of whatever meat was at hand. It had to be living meat, though, so when Fusum struck, he didn't strike hard enough to kill—or at least he hoped not. Nen dropped like a rock, but then almost immediately lifted himself up on his elbows, moaning. Fusum didn't even need to throw a stone to attract the panther's attention. It leapt on Nen and tore his throat out in a moment. Then Fusum charged, driving his spear into the panther's side under the ribs, finding its heart immediately. I *am* good at this, thought Fusum. Then he clubbed the panther in the head, over and over, so that no one would think to look for traces of Nen's blood and hair and scent on the club.

Minutes later, he came staggering and weeping into the digger city, crying out his grief at the death of his friend Nen, blaming himself for having failed the golden one, the beautiful one. "No man ever had a worse friend than me!" he cried. "Kill me, I beg you! I don't want to live with Nen's death on my hands." But when they found the scene, the men of the city cleared Fusum of any culpability, and the story of his great grief at the death of his beloved friend swept through the city. Some of Nen's glory thus lingered with Fusum, and many began to look to him as the hope of the future, now that Nen was gone.

14
Words

Nafai wasn't sure whether the dream came from the Keeper, the Oversoul, or his own concerns. Perhaps it was simply the fact that he realized that in all their teaching of the angels and the diggers, in all their teaching of their own children, the one thing they couldn't give them was a compelling reason to learn how to read and write.

What was it good for? Did it make the crops grow better? Did it keep the flocks in their pens at night? Did it ward off predators? Did it keep children from getting sick?

When he talked to Luet about it, she didn't seem worried. "Nyef, we're not recreating Basilica here. We can't. The next generation is going to lack so many things. We have to teach them the herbs that can heal infections or cure different diseases. We have to teach them the principles of sanitation, so they don't foul their own water supply. We have to—"

"We have to keep them human."

"It isn't writing that makes us human."

"Isn't it?" asked Nafai. "Then what is it?"

"The diggers and angels are sentient. They're *people.* And they don't read and write."

It was unanswerable, what she said, and the way she said it made it clear she didn't think it a problem worth worrying about. Yet hadn't they taught their own children how to read and write? Hadn't they risked destruction on the journey, teaching them how to use the computers, letting them pore over millions of volumes of human learning and history and it would all be extinguished in the next generation.

And the next generation was already here. In the five years since landfall, Chveya's and Oykib's generation had all started families. Their children were growing up and when they turned six or seven or eight would there even *be* a school for them? No, they would set to work learning the skills of survival. Side by side with diggers and angels in the fields, out gathering in the forest, building fences and walls, gleaning and weeding, planting and harvesting, tanning hides and tooling leather, carding wool and spinning it into yarn—where in all this activity was there a moment when they needed to read something? On the ship they had been preparing for a new life, learning in advance what they would need to know for subsistence in a new world. Now they were in that world, and the new generation learned from the adults, not from books.

And that was fine. No harm was done. The things that mattered for survival were taught. What else was needed?

Yet Nafai couldn't shake his uneasiness about it. In all the forty million years of history on Harmony, human beings could read and write. Languages drifted and changed over centuries and across kilometers. But there was writing. The past could be recovered. Learned from. It was writing that allowed a community to hold its memory outside the individuals who happened to be alive and present at the moment.

How long till I'm forgotten, I and Luet and Father and Mother and all of us?

Then he laughed at himself for the vanity of wanting people to go to the trouble of reading and writing, just so they could remember that he had once lived. In ten generations it wouldn't matter at all.

It was in the beginning of the sixth year that he had the dream. He saw a man leading a great nation of angels and humans, with farms spreading on either side of a great river, kilometer after kilometer, as far as the eye could see. Angels flew here and there, and goats and dogs drew carts and sledges along roads. Boats trafficked up and down the river, some of them with diggers, some with angels as their crew. And here and there, in towers rising high above the tallest trees, watchmen kept the perimeter in view, so that no enemy could take them unaware.

The man who led this great nation was weary and afraid. Enemies were coming to beset them on every side, and within the nation factions threatened to tear apart the fabric of the community. Towns that had once been independent forgot that in those days they had also been hungry. People whose ancestors had once been rulers forgot that those ancestors had also been killed by enemies and their people only survived at all because they came under the protection of this great nation.

People who longed for wealth were getting it by any means possible, plotting and cheating, bullying and sometimes even killing to get rivals out of the way. It was a beautiful land, but the struggle to keep it so seemed harder every year and the man despaired.

In his loneliness and fear, he went into his small house and opened a box he kept hidden inside a jar of dried corn. Inside the box he found a thick pile of metal sheets, bound together on one side with metal rings. It was a book, Nafai realized, for language had been inscribed in the metal, and the man opened it and began to turn the pages.

Without understanding how, Nafai knew what the words contained, what the man was seeing in his mind's eye as he read. The man was reading the story of Volemak seeing a pillar of fire on a rock in the desert and coming home to Basilica to give warning that the city was going to be destroyed. The story of Nafai and his brothers going back to the city to fetch the Index. The man saw Nafai standing over the dead body of Gaballufix and he nodded. Sometimes those who care for a whole community must act in a way that harms the individual. For a good man it never becomes easy and he avoids it when he can; but when the people need him to be harsh, he will be harsh indeed, and he won't shrink from it, he'll do it with his own hand and let it be known what he does.

From me he learned this, thought Nafai, and then he realized that he was the one who made the book and wrote in it the story of his life, of the life and acts of all the people in this community, their evil deeds and their heroic ones, their times of doubt and their astonishing achievements. And this man, this leader, this king, he looked into the book and found stories in it, tales that made clear to him what he must do, wisdom that stiffened his resolve, love that taught him compassion, hopes that led to noble actions even when the hopes themselves were unfulfilled.

Nafai awoke and thought, This dream was so clear, it must have come from the Oversoul. Or perhaps the Keeper of Earth.

And then he thought, This dream so exactly fits my own desire to keep reading and writing alive among this people that it could just as easily have come out of my own longings.

But then, where did his longings come from? Why did he want so much to preserve written language among his descendants? Couldn't those very desires have come from the Keeper?

No, he thought. Those desires come from my memory of standing over the corpse of Gaballufix. I killed him in order to get the Index from him. And what was the Index for? It was my access—*our* access—to the vast store of learning in the starship that brought us here. It was the key to all that the Oversoul knew. What would it have meant to us if none of us could read and write? To an illiterate people, the Index would be worthless and therefore no man should have had to die so Nafai could get it. I dream the dream that justifies my own actions to myself.

Yet even as he dismissed the dream, he knew that he would act on it.

Explaining nothing, he took his leave from Volemak, from Luet, and took the ship's launch out to where the survey maps showed that gold could be found. It was a rich vein, one brought to the surface of the earth through the great foldings and upheavals that had taken place in the last forty million years. Nafai was armed with the metal tools from the ship's store, and in two days of solitary labor he had several pounds of solid gold taken from the exposed vein in the mountainside. He spent a day refining it. Then he pounded it, unalloyed, into flat, smooth sheets, using the imperturbable metal surface of the launch as his anvil. The metal was very thin, but piled together it was also very heavy. It took him three days to make the sheets of gold, and during that time he only occasionally paused to gather the most obvious food that came easily to hand. He was hungry, but the work he was doing mattered more to him than food.

He found, in his first experiments, that the sweeping curves of the alphabet that had been used for so many millennia on Harmony simply did not work well when pressed by hand into the gold. He had to find squarer forms for the letters and yet still keep them different from each other. Also, some of the spellings were too complex and used too many letters to represent the sounds. So he changed them, inventing five new letters to represent sounds that had previously required two letters each. The result was a definite compression of the written language, and as he wrote, he compressed it even more, using only a couple of letters to stand for the most common words.

How do I dare to change the language like this? he asked himself. Who in the world could understand this?

Obviously, the only people who could read it easily would be people that he taught to read and write, and so they would know what his symbols meant. Perhaps just as important, though, anyone who had learned to read the script he used for pressing language into the gold would easily decode most of the letters used in the language of Harmony —the language of the ship's computer library. At least until the language changed, he would not have cut his descendants off from their literary heritage, if ever the chance came for them to recover it.

Gold. How appropriate, for such a treasure as he hoped this book would be. But it wasn't for the value of the gold as a medium of exchange that he chose it. Rather he used it for the same reasons that gold had been used for coinage in most cultures through most of human history. It was soft. It could be shaped. Yet it was not so soft that it couldn't hold its shape. And it didn't corrode or corrupt, tarnish or degrade in any way. Long after Nafai was dead, the letters would still exist on the pages of his metal book.

He put the gold leaves into the launch, along with all the leftover gold, and flew home. When he returned the launch to the ship, he explained nothing about where he had gone or what he had done. He didn't mean to deceive anyone, and it wasn't that he had no trust in Father or Mother, in Luet or anyone else. It's just that he felt shy about telling anyone. They would think it was silly of him.

No, that wasn't it. That wasn't it at all, he knew. As he sat there working by lamplight, the wick flickering as it floated on the melted fat in the clay cup, he could feel the power in what he was doing. I am projecting myself and my view of all that has happened to us into the future. Someday the only version of these events that anyone will know will be the one I wrote. Our descendants will see us through my eyes and no other. So it is I who will live in their memories. I who will whisper in the ear of that great leader—if he ever exists, if this book survives, if there is really anything of wisdom in it.

It is the writing on these gold pages that makes me immortal. When everyone else is dead, I will be alive and shining. That's why I keep this secret. That's why I hold it for myself. It's a heartless, egotistical thing for me to do.

<No it isn't.>

I know my own heart. I'm not ashamed to admit that my motives are impure.

<It's a generous thing you're doing. Giving your children of ten and twenty generations from now a knowledge of their past. A knowledge of why humans and diggers and angels dwell together in this place.>

What if Elemak were writing this book? It would be a different thing entirely, wouldn't it?

<It would be filled with lies.>

A storyteller can't help but distort every tale he tells. Without even knowing it, I'm also lying by giving events the shape that makes sense to me. Anyone else would write it differently. My way isn't necessarily the best.

<What you are creating will be treated as a sacred object. A token of authority, passed down from generation to generation. Like the Index. It lasted forty million years.>

Nafai laughed silently, careful not to waken Luet or their last three little ones, born since they came up the canyon to live here with the angels, or the twins, who slept in the loft, dreaming of new pranks to play and accidents to stumble into in order to cause their parents to live in perpetual terror.

<You laugh, but you know that I'm telling you the truth.>

So, Oversoul, my dear old friend, was it you that sent me my dream?

<No.>

The Keeper, then?

<You know that I don't know what the Keeper does and doesn't do.>

So it could be just the private fancy of a man who is reaching middle age and feels his future death breathing down his neck.

<And if it *is* nothing more than that, does that change the fact that it's a wise thing to do? A great gift to give to the future?>

I'll have to teach somebody to read my script. I'll have to give it to somebody to pass along into the future.

<You'll find someone. Perhaps one who's little now. It will be clear to you who should have the book, when the time comes.>

I'm telling everything. If they read this, my children will say, Why didn't he just shut up? Why didn't he ever leave well enough alone? My mistakes will be out in the open and they'll despise me.

<What if they do? You'll be dead.>

And if Elemak ever reads this, he'll kill me and destroy the book. You know that.

<I'd suggest that you not show it to him.>

Or anyone. The hours I spend on this—are they wasted?

<Are they?>

Nafai had no answer. Except that he kept on writing. Writing and writing, his script getting ever tinier and more compact, fitting more and more words onto the pages. His tale getting more and more spare.

What did he write? At first it was a very personal story, an account as best he remembered it of all their days in Basilica, of the journey through the desert, of the finding of the starport at Vusadka. But when the story reached Earth, it became far more general. The things they had learned about diggers and angels were set down in the order in which they discovered them or figured them out. The results of Zdorab's journeys in the ship's launch, mapping and bringing back plant and animal samples for Shedemei to study. The culture of the angels and diggers, and the way they responded to the cultural innovations the humans brought to them. The political machinations as the digger and angel communities struggled to deal with the destruction of their gods and the shattering of their equilibrium.

For the old gods were being destroyed. One cannot live with gods and still believe in them, Nafai decided. And even though after the early times of crisis Nafai had explained to them all that he and Volemak had never been gods, that their powers were all the result of technology and learning, that not a one of them had the power to duplicate even the least of the complicated machines in the starship—even though he explained this, he could sense that many resented knowing it. Emeezem most of all. When he told her that as far as he could tell the clay figure that she had worshipped and treasured almost her entire life was just a remarkably fine sculpture by a talented angel named Kiti, she didn't thank him. She acted as if he had slapped her face. "Should I break the statue then?" she demanded bitterly.

"Break something as finely wrought as that?" asked Nafai. "Break something that helped make you into the noble ruler that you are?"

But she was not to be mollified with praise; it sounded like flattery to her now, even though it was truthful and sincere. Nafai's rejection of her worship was the cruelest blow. He could see her wither up; even though she lived on and continued to lead her people with wisdom and firmness, the heart had gone out of her. It was not just faith but also hope that she had lost.

The angels had it easier. Since Elemak's rage had been their first exposure to humans, it was a relief to them to learn that none of them were gods. But the humans knew so many secrets and their wisdom, put to work for the angels, saved so many lives and improved everyone's health so much that there was still an element of worship in their relationship, and therefore a bit—or perhaps a lot—of disappointment and disillusion when some human failed at a task, gave bad advice, or predicted an outcome and was proven wrong.

As he was writing about all of this, Nafai realized that what the people needed, diggers and angels and humans alike, was someone outside themselves in whom their hopes of wisdom and rightness could be invested. They had to begin to think of the Keeper of Earth as the only one who would never be wrong.

Not that Nafai was altogether sure of this himself. He never heard the voice of the Keeper with the kind of clarity with which the Oversoul spoke to him. In fact he was never quite sure whether he heard the voice or saw the dreams of the Keeper of Earth at all. Nor did he know what the Keeper might be. That he was real enough was obvious—there was no other explanation of the statue whose face looked exactly like Nafai, carved back when Nafai was just getting on the starship to come to Earth. Nor was there any other explanation of the dreams they had back on Harmony, when so many of them saw diggers and angels when the Oversoul himself had no notion that these were the creatures that populated Earth. Yet the dreams were always ambiguous, and tinged with the dreamer's own hopes and fears and memories, so that it was never certain where the Keeper's message left off and self-deception began.

Yet, inadequate as Nafai's understanding of the Keeper of Earth might be, he knew that belief in the Keeper would fulfill a vital social function. The Keeper would be the highest authority, the one who was never wrong, the repository of Truth. When it became clear that even the wisest of humans knew very little, really; when it became plain that the most marvelous of miracles was in fact the result of working with a machine or exploiting a bit of ordinary knowledge; then there would still be no disillusionment because, after all, everyone knew that humans, angels, and diggers were all equal in the eyes of the Keeper of Earth, and all equally ignorant and weak and unwise compared to him.

Nafai explained these thoughts to Luet and she agreed. She began teaching the angel women about the Keeper of Earth, and adapting their ancient lore about various gods into a coherent story that replaced all the good gods with various aspects of the Keeper. With the angel men, Nafai was a bit more brutal, sweeping all the old gods away and keeping only a few of their ancient legends. Not that the old legends would die, of course—but he wanted them to start with a pure core of knowledge about the Keeper, even though the knowledge was really very small.

Then Nafai and Luet took Oykib and Chveya into their confidence, and soon Oykib was teaching the digger men and Chveya the digger women about the Keeper of Earth. They, too, adapted what the people already believed; they, too, were candid about how little they personally knew about the Keeper. But they did know this much: The Keeper wanted humans, diggers, and angels to live together in peace.

The trouble was that as the old religion faded, as fewer and fewer diggers took part in the annual raid to steal statues from the mating angels, the diggers' birthrate also seemed to fall off—even as the angels prospered, their population blooming at an almost alarming rate. Whispers began among the diggers that the new religion of the Keeper of Earth was really part of a conspiracy to destroy the diggers so that angels and humans could divide the world between them. Not that many people believed these tales, but enough did that it was a worry. There were those who would exploit such rumors. And, in fact, when Nafai began to hear that it wasn't all the humans but rather just Nafai and those who followed him who were plotting to destroy the diggers, he knew that someone was already seeking to turn these fears to his advantage.

In the meantime, though, the digger birthrate continued falling off, even though the nutrition levels were higher and higher all the time. And the angels had to expand constantly, burning more patches of forest to put more land under cultivation. All those twins, and none of them getting murdered now in infancy; all those healthy adults, and none of them getting culled by the marauding diggers.

They had been on Earth for twelve years when Shedemei called the adult humans together for a meeting. She had finally solved the mysteries, she said. But now there were some new mysteries, and some decisions to be made.

"We've been meddling," said Shedemei. "As you're all aware, the falling birthrate among the diggers is causing some serious worries among them."

"We're worried too," said Volemak.

"Yes, well, now I know why it's happening. We did it. We're doing it."

They waited. Finally Mebbekew said, "I didn't know you had such a flair for the dramatic, Shedya. How long do we wait for the other shoe to drop?"

"This is only the first shoe," she said. "The other shoe comes after." There was some nervous laughter. "The problem is, you see, that we've stopped them from believing in their gods. They aren't worshipping anymore. They aren't even stealing fresh statues from the angels. And that's why they aren't having any babies."

"You're telling us," said Elemak, laughing, "that their religion is *true?*"

"In a word, yes," said Shedemei. "We have a dozen years' worth of close observation of the local digger and angel tribes. Zdorab and I have also made some sampling visits to other digger and angel settlements, and we feel reasonably confident that we have uncovered a universal pattern. For one thing, there's no such thing as an angel village without a digger city nearby, nor a digger city without an angel village within a few hours' walk. This is not an accident. The diggers can't survive without the angels. Specifically, the diggers can't reproduce without worshipping the statues that the angel males create as part of their mating ritual."

"Do I get the impression that the cause is biological rather than theological?" asked Rasa.

"Of course, though it's hard to look at little clay statues and see a biological mechanism," said Shedemei. "It was Zdorab who first pointed out to me that what matters, biologically, may not be the artistry involved in the creation of the statues. It's the spit. The angel men take the clay into their mouths and mix a wet mud out of it, which they use to start the wad that becomes the statue. Every now and then they take another mouthful of mud and wet it. The saliva flows very freely."

The listeners' minds were working rapidly, trying to put things together. "You mean diggers need to rub angel spit on their bodies in order to mate?" asked Dza.

"Not quite," said Shedemei. "The first time we examined the bodies of angels and diggers, we found a little organ—a gland, actually—near the scrotum. It was identical in both species, even though they have no common ancestor with a similar organ. Very puzzling, of course. But we now know the function of the organ. It continuously secretes tiny amounts of a hormone that suppresses the production of sperm. No, let me be clear. It completely shuts down the production of sperm. While the organ is functioning, males are completely, absolutely sterile."

"What a useful little organ," murmured Oykib. Then, louder, "Why would that evolve?"

"It gets worse," said Zdorab.

"There's a tiny flatworm, a microscopic one, that lives in all the freshwater rivers of this massif. During the rainy season, when the rivers are in flood, this flatworm burrows into beds of firm clay and lays millions of tiny eggs. They don't develop as long as they remain wet. But when the dry season comes and the water subsides, the eggs develop, forming hard little coatings that hold in what moisture they have. The embryos are ready to hatch at any time. But they can't, because they can't get rid of their own confining shells. So they hibernate, living off their yolks. They use the yolks so slowly that they can live for twenty or thirty years like that. The next rainy season doesn't cause them to hatch, because water doesn't dissolve the shells. Guess what dissolves them."

"Angel spit," said Oykib.

"Amazing boy," said Shedemei. "My prize student." There was some laughter, but they were all waiting for the story to go on. "No other fluid will do it, because the angels have tiny organelles in the saliva-producing cells of their mouths, which secrete an enzyme that has no function whatsoever within the bodies of the angels—but it dissolves the shells of the flatworm eggs. So when the males bring the clay into their mouths, they're not just softening it to make sculptures. They're also dissolving the shells of millions of little flatworms. And it just so happens that the dissolved shells contain precisely the one chemical that suppresses the action of the prophylactic gland near the angels' and diggers' scrota. The fertility chemical breaks down very slowly, and the statues contain useful quantities of it perhaps as long as ten years, certainly for five."

Everybody was getting it now. "So when the diggers rubbed the statues all over their bodies. . . ." "Were the angels swallowing some of it?" "How much of the fertility chemical does it take?"

Shedemei raised her hands to damp the questions and comments. "Yes, you've got it. The angel males absorb the fertility enzyme by mouth. It doesn't take much of it to shut down the action of the prophylactic gland, and it doesn't recover and start up again for about two weeks, maybe three. So there's a window there in which reproduction can take place. And the digger males have a special absorbent patch on their lower bellies, near the groin, where the chemical can be absorbed quite directly into the bloodstream. Rubbing the statues on their sweating bellies dissolves some of the clay, whereupon the dissolved fertility enzyme is taken into the blood and, just as with the angels, it shuts down the prophylactic gland and the digger males are fertile. But because they actually get a great deal less of the enzyme, the fertility window is only a few days long for them. Doesn't matter, though. Where the angels make their statues once a year and have to score a reproductive hit that one time, the diggers are culturally able to worship the statues any time. In effect, the statues enable them to reproduce whenever they want. They just have to pray first."

"That is the most absurdly complicated, unlikely, ridiculous mechanism I've ever heard of," said Issib.

"Exactly," said Shedemei. "There is no chance that it evolved naturally. Why would the diggers and angels independently evolve identical organs that make them sterile? There's no evolutionary advantage in it. Why didn't the angels simply die out before they ever started making their sculptures in the first place? Why didn't the diggers die out before they ever discovered the virtues of rubbing angel statues all over themselves? And why would a species of flatworm just happen to require a special chemical in angel saliva in order to hatch their eggs? And why did the angels develop a chemical with no use in their bodies except to dissolve the shells of the flatworms?"

"There are a lot of strange things in nature," said Oykib.

"Of course," said Shedemei. "I shouldn't have said there's no chance it evolved naturally. It's just that for me, at least, the coincidence is too great to believe in natural causation. This was *done* to the diggers and angels."

"But that's not what matters right now," said Zdorab. "Shedya has an answer to that, but what matters is that we have to tell the diggers the truth. They need to go back to using the statues. And getting new ones."

"Maybe we can get the angels just to *give* their statues to the diggers," said Padarok. "It's not as if the angels use them after the women judge the men."

"Maybe," said Shedemei. "But it's not just the diggers who are suffering from our interference in their previous social patterns. This relationship, this connection between diggers and angels has been going on for millions of years. Forty million years, to be more precise. And in those countless generations, certain patterns have evolved. The twinning of the angels, for instance. Every pregnancy is double. This isn't accidental. It's only happened twice in all our observations, and never in our own angel village, but when a single birth takes place, the baby is destroyed and the mother is never allowed to mate again. In other words, single births are ruthlessly excluded from angel society. It looks to me as if this is a response to the fact that diggers follow angels wherever they go. The diggers have to follow the angels in order to get the statues. But then the diggers can't help but see the angels as an easy source of meat, especially when the angel infants are at that awkward age when they can't fly well at all, and yet they're too heavy for one adult to carry them alone and still fly. In effect, the twinning allows each generation of angels to have one death and one survivor. Over the years, community cooperation has enabled between two-thirds and three-fourths of the twin-pairs to survive intact. Now, though, in our village all the twins are living to adulthood. And all the damaged, weak, sick, and crippled angels are surviving, where in other villages the diggers cull them out. In short, the angels have evolved a strategy of reproducing far beyond their sustainable population in order to survive the depredations of the diggers. When the diggers no longer prey on them, their population balloons out of control."

"It's a delicate balance," Zdorab said. "I found one place where it reached a crisis. The diggers had lost discipline and were eating more than the infants and the strays. They were systematically wiping out the angels in their area. When I got there, only a few beleaguered families of angels survived. But the diggers were already paying the price. They had plenty of old statues, of course. But no new ones. And so after about five years, their birthrate fell off. Just as it has here. Not so suddenly, of course, since they were still worshipping the statues they had, only the statues contained progressively less and less of the enzyme. Births became more and more rare. With fewer diggers to prey on them, the angel population was going to start recovering soon. When it did, eventually the few surviving diggers would also recover."

Shedemei took over again. "So there's a social balance, you see. The diggers can't harvest too many of the angels for food, because then they lose their own ability to reproduce. It's self-correcting."

"What's to stop the angels from taking off and starting a colony where there aren't any diggers?" asked Protchnu.

"Nothing," said Shedemei, "and I'm sure it's happened many times. But they can only live where they can find clay that supports the flatworms. That means that they can only live where there's a pattern of rainy season flooding, and they can only live at elevations where the flatworm can survive. It's a pretty narrow range, common enough on this massif but not elsewhere. And the diggers range far and wide. I don't think there's anywhere that angels can go without a digger finding them sooner or later. When the digger finds them, he goes home and reports that he's found a new spot that's favored by the gods, and so they send out a colony. It's actually to the benefit of the angels. Without diggers devouring their young, their populations reach climax very quickly."

"Are you suggesting," said Nafai, "that we should let the diggers go back to kidnapping and eating angel infants?"

"That's the question," said Shedemei. "That's really the question, isn't it?"

"Does any of this," asked Chveya, "have to do with the evolution of intelligence among the angels and diggers?"

"Some, I think," said Shedemei. "The way the angel females select their mates is by the intricacy, beauty, originality, and accuracy of their sculptures. Obviously, the more intelligent and creative the angel male, the better his chances of reproducing early and often. For the diggers, it's a little different. In order to kill angels, they have to be devious and smart. We don't see it that much now, of course, because the diggers are *so* smart that the angels had almost given up trying to stop them. But we've all seen the traps that the angels set at the perimeter of their villages. It may be that the stupid diggers used to get caught in such traps. Now they recognize and evade them easily. But perhaps their very intelligence evolved because only the smart ones got through the angel traps in order to steal statues and baby angels."

"In other words, intelligence evolved naturally," said Chveya. "It's this symbiotic relationship that's unnatural."

"Not just unnatural," said Shedemei. "Human-made."

"How can you know that?" asked Protchnu.

"Because we believed that it couldn't be natural. And we knew that humans ceased to live on Earth at the time of the emigration that settled Harmony and, no doubt, other worlds as well. As we searched with the Index, we found that the one part of history where the ship's library had *no* useful information was human life at the time of the emigration."

Zdorab, the librarian, took over here. "Now, we have always imagined that this was because it was such a terrible time that they tried to forget it. There were implications of wars using weapons so dreadful that they turned the Earth for a while into a ball of ice. That's what the Oversoul himself believed. But then something Nafai said to me one time made me realize that this paucity of information really wasn't believable. He said, 'How could the people who saved humanity by leaving Earth have allowed themselves to be so completely forgotten?' And I thought, Of course they couldn't. So I started searching the computers on the ship, the ones that *aren't* tied to the Oversoul. And I found what I was looking for. A database that the Oversoul has no conscious access to. It's called, as nearly as I can translate it, *The Book of the Sins of the Human Race.*"

"Sins?" asked Mebbekew.

"Well, it's the most economical translation. It's a term that means 'willful mistakes.' 'Crimes of avoidable negligence,' perhaps. I thought *sins* was a pretty good way of summing it up."

"What does the book contain?" asked Nafai.

"I only just found it. I haven't read it all, and I'd be glad to have any of you who have the time and interest help me in the translation. The language is close to several known languages but it's very very old and the Oversoul hasn't been updating it because he wasn't conscious that it was there. The thing is, one of the first things I found was the explanation for how the angels and diggers began. It was one of the 'sins,' you see."

Zdorab brought up a document on the computer screen nearest to him and began to read aloud.

"We have sinned by fiddling with the genes of animals, giving them intelligence without freedom, talent without power, desires without hope. We used them for our amusement, displaying their paintings and sculptures and music and dance while keeping the painters and sculptors, the musicians and dancers in prisons. If they escaped their freedom was worthless because they could have children only in captivity. This was an abomination, and the Keeper of Earth revolted against it, driving away the slavemakers and slavekeepers, and setting the little ones free."

Shedemei spoke up. "I think the possible connection with diggers and angels should be obvious. The angels are the ones who still do some kind of art, but that's what they were bred for, perhaps. Zdorab and I can't think what the diggers were originally bred to do."

"Dig," said Elemak.

"Possibly," said Shedemei. "Just because the *Book of Sins* mentioned only the intelligent animals created in order to entertain humans doesn't mean there weren't also animals that were genetically enhanced in order to do more menial tasks. Like seeking out underground deposits of various minerals, for instance. Or simply digging tunnels."

"Sewer work," said Elemak.

"As I said, we don't know," said Shedemei. "I think there's a good chance that the diggers' ancestors weren't very intelligent at all. Enhanced physically, but not mentally. But they survived because they *were* bright enough, or lucky enough, to live close to a tribe of angels and perhaps simply by chance they rubbed themselves with the statues."

"Or maybe they survived," said Zdorab, "because the diggers lived in burrows and the angels lived in caves, and so when the Earth went into a profound ice age they both survived underground and developed their symbiosis there."

"Or maybe they were taught to do it in a dream," said Luet.

"Well, there we are," said Shedemei. "It might all have been planned and controlled. Even as the Keeper of Earth drove out the human race, she might have been planning to replace our ancestors with new species. She might have been manipulating them both to help them both evolve intelligence."

"And in the meantime," said Zdorab, "to make them symbiotic so that they couldn't possibly survive without each other. The old humans created the flatworms and made it so that the angels' ancestors *had* to sculpt clay or they couldn't reproduce. Perhaps they didn't give any of the other captive animals a mechanism that would allow them to get a supply of the chemical they needed without human intervention. Only the diggers found their own way to piggyback on the angels' survival method. Who says the Keeper of Earth couldn't have put it all together that way? Perhaps it was because of the Keeper that humans first developed the flatworm vector for creating the chemical the angels needed. Perhaps the Keeper planned it all."

"Whatever the Keeper is," said Meb.

"I have another idea," said Elemak. "What if there's no such thing as the Keeper? Those dreams you had back on Harmony, you were all so sure they came from this supposed Keeper because the Oversoul knew nothing about the diggers and the angels. But now we find out that the Oversoul had all this information in his databanks, only he simply couldn't *consciously* access it. So those dreams could have come from the Oversoul all along, without his knowing it, right? And now we don't have to imagine some mechanism for sending dreams faster than light across the space between Earth and Harmony."

"Very good theory," said Shedemei. "But it doesn't explain Kiti making a perfect likeness of Nafai a hundred years before we arrived here."

"I don't think," said Volemak icily, "that it's very helpful to assume that just because we find the natural mechanism by which some things came to be, we have therefore proven that the Keeper of Earth does not exist. We don't know how far the reach of the Keeper might be, or what power he has; perhaps all he can do is give dreams to people. Wishful thinking gives false gods to people who hunger for gods, but those who yearn for a world with no gods are no less likely to fall victim to their own wishful thinking."

"I'll memorize that one, Father," said Meb. "That was deep."

Elemak smiled but did not speak.

"If we can set aside speculative theology," said Shedemei, "I want to lay two choices before you. The first choice is this: We can explain everything to the diggers and angels. The diggers can go back to using the sculptures. The angels can start trying to control their population by breeding less often—perhaps nothing more than each man making a sculpture only every other year. There's no reason to go back to the slaughter of infant angels. The trouble is that while this might work here, it will have no effect elsewhere. But perhaps that's the reason the Keeper of Earth brought us here, to teach the diggers and angels how to live together without killing."

"I thought we were setting aside speculative theology," said Meb.

"The other choice," said Shedemei, "is to get rid of that prophylactic gland."

"Get rid of it?" asked Volemak.

"I've found the gene that creates it. It's artificial—it was inserted. By analogy with the genes of unaltered rats and bats, we've found all the inserts and they're quite obvious. We isolated the particular genetic word that creates the prophylactic gland by inserting each of the artificial words into common rats and bats and seeing which ones developed the prophylactic gland. Knowing which gene causes it, we can uncause it."

"How?" asked Volemak.

"A bacterial infection that carries an enzyme whose sole function is to find that genetic word and clip it out. It's the method I use to do gene alteration anyway. I'll just use an infectious bacterium instead of the benign ones I usually work with. It has few symptoms. With the diggers it's a little stiffness of the joints and some nasal inflammation. With the angels it can also cause weeping eyes for a few days. Once the infection has spread throughout all digger and angel populations, reproduction will be cut loose from the flatworms. The angels can sculpt to their hearts' content, of course, but if they stop it won't matter. The change will only affect those conceived after the bacterial epidemic made the alteration in their parents, and it may cause spontaneous abortion of male digger and angel embryos that happen to be in the first few weeks of development when the infection comes. But in a single generation, the prophylactic gland will disappear."

"I don't like it," said Oykib. "The Keeper of Earth set up a mechanism that kept balance here, and we'll be destroying it."

"I don't know, Okya," said Chveya. "It was humans who set up the mechanism, really. It's listed in the *Book of Sins*. It's one of the things that the Keeper hated. Maybe we've been brought back just to remove it."

"As I said," Shedemei went on. "We have those two choices. But personally I favor intervention. Removing the prophylactic gland seems to me like striking the manacles off a slave. After forty million years, it's about time, don't you think?"

"Just do it," said Elemak. "Don't waste our time with endless discussion about what the Keeper might want or might not want. You have the power to do it, and it's a decent thing to do, so just do it and have done." Elemak got up and left.

It took many hours of discussion after that, but finally Elemak's point of view prevailed. The only reason the discussion took so long was because Protchnu suggested asking the diggers and angels what *they* thought should be done. But they all realized that neither the diggers nor the angels had the conceptual framework to understand the genetic issues involved. "They won't receive it as science because they have no science," said Volemak as he reached his decision. "They'll convert it to religion and it will cause division and controversy among them and may lead to real hatred of us or civil war within their own communities. I believe in letting people make their own choices, when they're capable of understanding the choice. But you don't let your toddlers decide whether or not they're ready to play in the stream. You simply keep them away from the water and you don't even try to explain the concept of drowning. Later you can explain it to them, when they're older."

"So the diggers and angels are our children now?" asked Meb, mockingly.

"Better to treat them as our children," said Volemak, "than to treat them as our ancestors did—as slaves, as playthings. So the decision is made. We explain only as much as they can understand. Oykib will explain to the diggers, and Nafai to the angels. I'd appreciate it if everyone else would keep their mouths shut about it. Shedemei, I'd like you to introduce the bacteria as quickly as possible into both communities."

"It's simple enough," she said. "I'll simply expose everyone here to it right now. It'll cause a bit of a runny nose, maybe a slight fever in a few cases. Just make sure you follow your normal pattern of interaction with diggers and angels, and the disease will spread naturally. Just come up here and swab the insides of your noses with this gel."

"That's disgusting," said one of the younger women.

"Only if you use someone else's swab," said Protchnu.

"What worries me," said Mebbekew, "is what's going to happen to the poor flatworms. Nobody seems to care about them. I think we have too much of a bias in favor of big animals. Don't microscopic creatures have rights?" He grinned, and the others laughed with him.

While the meeting went on, however, Elemak had a meeting of his own. He sought out Fusum, who had recently been made blood king after the death of his father.

"I have a gift for you," Elemak said.

"What could you possibly have that I want?" asked Fusum.

"Oh, we're full of ourselves, aren't we, now that we're king."

Fusum growled a little. "I have a life of my own, Elemak. I'm not a hostage anymore. I have responsibilities."

"You also have power," said Elemak, "and I think you wouldn't mind getting a little more. So here's my gift—more power."

"Really," said Fusum. "I didn't know you had any power to give."

"Knowledge is power, or so I've heard," said Elemak. "But there's a condition. You have to promise to tell your people you got the idea from me."

"What idea?" asked Fusum.

"Promise first."

"I promise," said Fusum.

"But do you really really mean it?" asked Elemak.

"If you're going to mock me, you can keep your gift," said Fusum.

"Ah, now that we're the blood king, we're too important to take a little teasing from a friend."

"You've never been a friend, Elemak," said Fusum. "You've been a useful source of knowledge."

"But perhaps now we *can* be friends," said Elemak.

"Either tell me the idea you have or don't."

"Go at once to the statue of the Untouched God," said Elemak.

"You mean the one that looks like your shining brother Nafai?"

Elemak refused to be goaded. "That's the one. Go to it, and in front of as many witnesses as possible, declare that the reason so few children are being born is because this statue has not been properly worshipped. Then do whatever it is you do with it. Rub it all over yourself."

"That could get me killed."

"Not the blood king. Not right away. And not if you promise the people that now that you have worshipped the Untouched God, obliterating the face of that deceiver Nafai, the true god will send a mild plague to purge the last traces of evil among your people. A few male embryos may even be miscarried because they were not pure. All those who are alive right now will have to worship the gods in the old way until the day they die. But the new children born after this time will not have to worship any gods at all. They are born in purity and they are blessed."

"What kind of fungus are you trying to make me eat?" said Fusum. "You're the one who told me that all this religious stuff was nonsense."

"But the people believe it, don't they? So you tell them that no matter what Oykib or Chveya or anybody else tells them, *I* told *you* the truth, and it's *your* action that will free your people from having to go up the canyon and get your gods from the skymeat. You won't *need* the skymeat anymore. Your new children and grandchildren can kill them all then, and it won't matter because they will be pure and the gods won't require them to humiliate themselves by worshipping objects created by the skymeat."

"Why should I believe that any of this will happen?"

"I don't care," said Elemak. "You can doubt me and delay, and then Oykib will come out and make an announcement and all the power and influence will go to him and, through him, to Emeezem. Or you can believe me and act *now,* so that you've already done it before anybody else says a word. Then *you* and *I* will be the liberators of the diggers. It's going to happen anyway, of course. The little act you put on with that statue of Nafai won't actually do anything at all. Except make your people think you've got religious powers beyond any blood king before you. And it won't hurt that you can make hash out of Emeezem's insistence that the Untouched God remain untouched. When your prophecies come true, she'll be discredited. But you can let the opportunity pass you by, Fusum. You can spend the rest of your life wishing you had taken the chance when I gave it to you. I really don't care."

"Yes you do," said Fusum. "And you can be sure that I *will* use your name and tell them that I learned about this from you. Because if it fails, I might be able to save myself by laying the blame on you."

"And when it succeeds," said Elemak, "your people will know who is their true friend among the humans."

"And *I'll* know," said Fusum, "that you are a liar who is obviously planning to betray his own people and you want to have the diggers behind you when you strike."

"Any problem with that?" said Elemak.

"None whatsoever," said Fusum. "Just so you remember who is the king of the diggers when the time comes."

"I'll remember," said Elemak. "I remember everything."

So Fusum went down to the temple of the Untouched God, made his speech and performed his blasphemous worship. Emeezem had him bound and walled up in a prison chamber, but his imprisonment lasted only until Oykib called together the elders of the digger people and explained to them that a minor plague was going to come among them, but all children conceived afterward would no longer need to worship statues anymore. "The Keeper of Earth has set you free from your old gods," he said. But there were many who said among themselves, Fusum set us free. And Emeezem was unable to prevent them from releasing Fusum from his prison and restoring him as blood king.

The plague came within days, just as Fusum had predicted. But no other harmful consequences came from his having touched the Untouched God. And now the Untouched God didn't look like Nafai anymore, and people said, It was Elemak who taught us this secret, that Nafai is not a god, and that he hasn't even got the power to keep his face on the statue. Fusum is a true blood king, but Emeezem as our deep mother didn't know the truth about the Untouched God.

When Mufruzhuuzh died not long after, the people chose Fusum to be the new war king, saying, He was Nen's true friend, and killed the panther that slaughtered him. He also set our children free from the gods of the skymeat. Let him be both war king and blood king, both at once.

That day marked the end of Emeezem's rule over the digger city. She still had great influence over the women, but the men belonged to Fusum, and Fusum began to train them for war.

For months, Nafai and Oykib pored over the *Book of the Sins of the Human Race*, learning from it all they could. Here were the secrets of the evolution of the human race, of the development of technologies, of the cruel uses that humans put them to. Here were the tales of wars and slaughters, of oppressive poverty that paid for the wealth of a few, of stripped and ruined land, of ancient resources burned up or thrown away.

At the end, they found these words:

"These sins came about because of rebellion, for the human race ignored the good dreams that came from the Keeper of Earth, until at last the Keeper wearied of their sins and shrugged them off. Then the great floating continents shuddered, and the earth shook, and the volcanos burst open in a thousand places. The sky was filled with smoke and the plants died; the Earth grew cold and ice covered the face of the Earth in the deepest ice age ever known. Those few human beings who survived understood that the Keeper of Earth was done with them. The Earth had no more room for human beings, and if they were to live at all they must leave. Seven fleets were assembled and seven colonies left, and of the others we have no word. We know only this: that on our new world, Harmony, we will build an Oversoul to be the servant of the

Keeper of Earth, and under the Oversoul's watchful eye the human race will not remember how to sin on such a terrible scale. As for Earth, it belongs to the Keeper now, and human beings will never live there again, unless the Keeper forgives us and calls us home."

Nafai and Oykib both translated this final passage, and then reconciled their translations. "Who wrote this?" Oykib asked. "How could he know what power the Keeper had? To cause earthquakes and volcanos, to change the flow of continental drift. . . ."

"Maybe the Keeper has something to do with the convection currents in the flowing magma on which the crust of the Earth floats. Who knows how quickly it might change?" said Nafai.

"I know this much," said Oykib. "We have to teach our people about this book, the warnings in this book. We have to teach them what the Keeper expects of us, even if we don't understand exactly what the Keeper of Earth might be."

"By 'our people,' do you mean just humans?" asked Nafai.

"Of course not," said Oykib. "In fact, maybe the reason the Keeper brought us back to Earth was precisely so that we could not only set the angels and diggers free from their ancient bondage, but also could teach them how to live so that the Keeper won't feel the need to make the Earth uninhabitable again."

"I think you're right," said Nafai. "But it's going to become a religion no matter what we do or how we teach it. Even our most naturalistic explanations are going to sound mystical to them. After all, what our ancestors wrote in the *Book of Sins* sounds mystical to *us*."

"Is that bad?" asked Oykib.

"Not bad in itself. It's just that religions have a way of losing track of the truth at the core. The diggers had a religion that kept them rubbing themselves with clay that contained the chemical derived from flatworm eggshells and angel spit—but they had no idea why they were doing it, and so they were enslaved by it. All we'll be doing, then, is teaching our children and their children arbitrary rules. The true reasons will be lost, or converted into myths."

"What can we do about it?" asked Oykib.

"We can write a book," said Nafai.

"You mean like the one you're already writing?" he asked.

Nafai glared at him. "I should have known I couldn't keep a secret from you."

"Yes, you should have," said Oykib. "Especially since you talked to the Oversoul about it almost constantly for weeks when you first thought of it. I figured you'd tell me about it when you felt like it."

"Well, I feel like it," said Nafai. "Because I think our descendants aren't going to have access to the ship's computer. The skill of reading and writing will be lost to most of them. But a few of them will be taught to read and write in order to keep a record of what we've learned. We'll write it down as clearly as we can, a true history of our voyage and everything we've learned and done. We'll pass it along from parent to child, and because it's written down it can't be distorted."

"People can distort anything," said Oykib.

"But as long as the original text is there, the next generation or the one after, somewhere along the line, they can go back to the original and discover the truth. The way we learned so much from the *Book of Sins.*"

"Well, fine," said Oykib. "You're already keeping a record."

"I'm keeping *one* record. But I think we need to keep another. This first one has everything in it, all the details, everything I can remember. But I had a dream last night. . . ."

"Ah, another dream."

"I know you'd like to have these dreams yourself, Oykib, but—"

"I don't need to have my own dreams," Oykib said. "Not when I have yours. You dreamed of writing a book that you would give to me and Chveya instead of to Zhyat and Netsya."

"A book," said Nafai, "that includes everything from the *Book of Sins,* written on gold so we don't need a computer to read it and so it won't corrode. We can seal up that part, so no one adds to or changes it. But the rest of the book will be a record, not of the whole history of our people, but just the story of our dealings with the Oversoul and the Keeper of Earth. Just the. . . ."

"Just the theology," said Oykib.

"To the diggers and angels it will seem like theology," said Nafai.

"And to our children and grandchildren, too," said Oykib. "They won't have lived in the starship. They won't have used the great library. They'll have no idea of what a computer is."

Nafai nodded. "So you've come to the same conclusion."

"No, I've simply seen you and Luet and Chveya all having the same dream. The ship has got to go. We have to cut ourselves off from the machinery of the past and live in the technology of the present. The ship has to go up into orbit."

"We don't have the technology anymore to hide it on the planet's surface, the way our ancestors hid it on Harmony," said Nafai.

"I'll help you with your second book," said Oykib. "You write whatever you want to in order to start it off. You have to tell the parts where I wasn't born yet anyway. I'll take over when you tell me to. But in the meantime, I can be copying out the *Book of Sins.*"

"The *Book of Sins,* yes," said Nafai. "And maybe also you should start a record of the dreams the Keeper sent us. Especially the ones that don't seem yet to be completely fulfilled. It's the only guide we have to what the Keeper might have planned for us."

"The *Book of Sins* and the *Book of Dreams,*" said Oykib. "I'll get those started. And you write the *Book of Nafai.*"

"And in the meantime," said Nafai, "I'm going to start figuring out some kind of weapon that the angels can use in flight, something that can kill a digger despite the diggers' enormously greater strength."

Oykib nodded. "So you think your dreams of war between diggers and angels, you think those are from the Keeper of Earth."

"Whether they come from the Keeper or my own fears, I have to be prepared, don't I? I have to prepare my people, just in case."

Oykib nodded. "I love the diggers, Nafai. I don't want to have to choose between them and the angels."

"That won't be your choice, Oykib. *Your* choice will be the same one it's always been. Between Elemak and me, after Father dies."

"Still? Broken as Elemak is?"

"Elemak isn't broken, Oykib. He simply learned how to be patient. How to bide his time. But Hushidh has told me that his connection with Fusum is strong, even if it's tinged with loathing on both their parts. I'm sure Chveya has noticed the same thing, with the two of you living here among the diggers all these years."

"She's noticed it," said Oykib. "But it's hard to see how he can turn it to his advantage."

"Not really," said Nafai. "They'll follow Elemak, if he leads them where they already want to go."

"And where is that?" asked Oykib.

"To slaughter angels. They don't have to leave any angels alive now, because they can propagate without the statues."

Oykib frowned. "Then we made a mistake to wipe out the prophylactic gland?"

"No," said Nafai. "It was right to set both peoples free. But now we have to help them struggle to find a new equilibrium. One that's based on respect and tolerance."

"I wouldn't bet on that anytime soon," said Oykib, "not as long as the diggers think of angels as meat, and angels think of diggers as devils."

"I know," said Nafai. "That's why we have our work cut out for us. Many lifetimes of teaching lie ahead, for us and for those who try to serve the Keeper of Earth after us. And in the meantime, I'm going to come up with some weapons that help even up the combat between angels and diggers. Something that will drive the diggers back into their holes when they dare to make war against the angels."

"So then the angels are masters. How does that help?"

"The angels don't seek out diggers in order to eat them," said Nafai. "They don't want to fight with the diggers at all. They just want to be left alone. As far as I can see, that tips the moral balance heavily onto the side of the angels."

"The diggers aren't monsters," Oykib said. "They're children of their own genetic and cultural heritage. They don't deserve to be slaughtered from the sky."

"I know that," said Nafai. "That's why we have to teach them all as well as we can. And in the meantime, try to keep a balance between them."

"I don't want to choose," said Oykib.

"You have no choice but to choose," said Nafai. "When Elemak takes the diggers to war, you're one of the ones he'll be trying to kill. You'll be on the angels' side because you have nowhere else to turn."

"You know this from dreams?" asked Oykib.

"The Keeper doesn't have to send me dreams to tell me what I can figure out for myself."

Oykib furiously brushed away a tear that had slipped down his cheek. "None of this was necessary," he said. "Why didn't you just kill Elemak when you had the chance?"

"Because I love him," said Nafai.

"So how many of my friends among the diggers and and your friends among the angels have to die because of that?"

"Elemak has his hand in it," said Nafai, "but if you think that Fusum or someone else wouldn't have stirred up the diggers to rebellion against us or war against the angels, you don't understand human nature."

"The diggers aren't humans," said Oykib.

"When it comes to hate and rage and envy, yes they are," said Nafai.

"And love and generosity, too," said Oykib. "And trust, and wisdom, and dignity, and—"

"Yes," said Nafai. "They're human in all those ways. So are the angels."

"So how are we different from our ancestors, who got driven off the planet forty million years ago?"

"I don't know," said Nafai. "But maybe, given enough time, we and the diggers and the angels can find our way to peace."

"And in the meantime, you're going to design weapons," said Oykib.

"I'm thinking of blowguns," said Nafai. "With fleched darts. What I don't know is whether they need to be poisoned or not, in order to be effective."

"It's my friends you're talking about killing," said Oykib.

"Do your best to teach your friends to hate war and refuse to take part in it," said Nafai. "Teach them to loathe the very thought of eating infant skymeat. Then they'll never be brought down by an angel's dart."

15

Divisions

When peace depends on the life of one man, then each new day becomes a deathwatch. Each new plan must include the thought: Can this be finished before he dies? Each new child is welcomed with the prayer: Let safety last another year. Another month, another week.

Not that people talked about it much—about how old Volemak was looking, how his back was stooping, how he winced with arthritis when he walked, how he tended to lose breath when he worked hard, how he now called meetings in the schoolhouse instead of up the ladder inside the starship. It was something they saw, regretted, feared, but kept to themselves, pretending that it wasn't that bad, he had plenty of time left, no need to worry yet.

Then Emeezem died and Fusum seized full power among the diggers. She had started losing heart when her son Nen was killed by a panther while hunting. Later, the desecration of the Untouched God was a harsh blow, and her heart died then; the death of her husband Mufruzhuuzh was merely an afterthought compared to those. The world has ended, Emeezem, and, oh yes, your husband is dead and the brutal boy who *says* he tried to save your son is now both blood king and war king and when you die he will destroy all peace among your people and there's nothing you can do except teach the women to look for a day of peace in some distant day only the women seem to barely listen anymore, and the only one who does you honor is the human Nafai whose face was your salvation long ago. When death finally came to her, coughing out of her lungs as she lay in her deep chamber, in darkness, attended by silent women and a few men watching for the exact moment of death so they could begin destroying her memory—when death finally came to her, she welcomed it with bitter relief. What took you so long? And where are Nen and Mufruzhuuzh? And for that matter, where's my mother? Why has my life turned out to be so worthless?

Only just as she was on the edge of death there came a dream into her mind even though she had thought she was awake. She saw a human, a digger, and an angel, standing together on the brow of a hill as a host of people of all three species gathered round them, weeping, laughing for joy, surging forward to touch them, and each one who touched them sang out loud, the same glad song, and then the human, the digger, and the angel looked at *her*, at Emeezem the deep mother who was dying, and said to her, Thank you for setting your people on this road.

The dream did not bring Nen back to life, or give her hope that Fusum's reign would not be bloody and terrible, and it certainly did not take her from the brink of death. All it did was let her step off that brink into the dark unknown with a smile on her face and pride in her heart. It made death sweet to her.

Fusum saw to it that she was given great honor, and in his funeral oration he praised her for preparing the people for the coming of the humans—even if she misunderstood what the gods meant their people to do. Then, over the next several days, all his rivals and opponents disappeared and were never heard of again. The message was clear: The supreme law of the digger people was Fusum, for Fusum was blood king, war king, deep mother, and, yes, god, all in one, and for all time. Most of the young men were happy with this, for he would make warriors of them once again, after so many years of being in the shadow of the humans and under the thumb of women. And if the young men were happy with him, no one else dared to be unhappy.

Fusum respectfully asked Oykib to stop teaching his silly ideas about the Keeper of Earth. Fusum took Chveya aside and told her that her presence was intimidating to the digger women and they would be happier if she stopped helping them learn about the safe storage and preservation of food. One by one the other humans were kindly asked to desist, until at last only Elemak, Mebbekew, and Protchnu were allowed to visit with the diggers.

What could Volemak do? He asked Elemak to protest to Fusum. Elemak said that he would, then came back and said that he had, and conveyed Fusum's assurance that nothing had changed except that diggers would be taking the responsibility for educating their own people.

"He said that we should be happy, Father, because now we have more time to devote to our own families."

It was all handled so quietly, so politely, that it left Volemak helpless to interfere. He knew—everybody knew—that in effect the diggers were in revolt against human overlordship, even though until the revolt none of the humans had thought of themselves as overlords. They also knew that Elemak had somehow pulled off a coup, for he now controlled all access to the diggers even though until that moment Oykib and Chveya had been the dominant human presence among the digger people. Everyone was sure that Elemak had planned and worked on this for years, that in all likelihood he and Fusum had struck some kind of bargain twenty years before when Fusum was a hostage and Elemak was learning digger speech from him and supposedly winning him over to friendship with the humans.

"Fusum kidnapped Elemak's child," Chveya said, unbelieving. "How could Elemak have made *friends* with him?"

"I think," said Oykib, "that Elemak understood that there was nothing personal about Fusum's choice of kidnap victim. And I don't think that what they made between them was what you or I would understand as friendship."

It didn't matter now what any of the rest of them thought of it. It was done.

That was when they started watching Volemak's health in earnest. Even Volemak began to speak of it, quietly, to a few.

He and Nafai got together with Hushidh and Chveya and made a list of who was clearly loyal to Nafai and who was loyal to Elemak. "We're divided into Nafari and Elemaki again," said Chveya. "I thought for a while that those days might be behind us."

Volemak looked sad, but not grim. "I knew that Elemak had changed, but what he learned was patience, not generosity. The Oversoul knew it all along."

Among the humans, Nafari outnumbered Elemaki overwhelmingly, and of the adult men who might serve as soldiers, there would be no contest if it ever came to battle among humans only. But of course, everyone understood now that the battle, if it came, would be between Nafai's humans and Fusum's army of diggers. On that scale, Nafai's soldiers were the merest handful, and no one had the slightest confidence that the angels, however willing they might be, could really stand against the diggers in an open war. It could not be allowed to come to battle. Nafai and his people would have to leave.

Yet even among the children of Kokor and Sevet, more than half were loyal to Nafai—in part because of the open secret that their mothers were Elemak's mistresses. "The real complication," said Hushidh, "is that Eiadh is perhaps the most loyal of all to Nafai, and she'll want to take as many of her children and grandchildren with her as she can."

"How many of them would come?" asked Nafai.

"Most. Most of Elemak's children would come with you, though not Protchnu or Nadya and their children. But Elemak won't stand for it if you take any of them, even if you take just Eiadh. He'd follow us wherever we might go. We can't bring her with us if we ever hope for peace."

Volemak listened and listened to their discussion, and then made his decision. "You'll take everyone whose loyalty to Nafai is genuine and deep, if they want to go. You'll have to trust in the Keeper of Earth to help you."

If any of them thought to say, That's easy for you to decide, Volemak, because you'll be dead when the wars begin, they kept it to themselves.

As Volemak's health weakened, he began to call people to him, one by one. Just for a conversation, he said, but they all came away rather shaken by the experience. He would sit with them and tell them with almost brutal frankness what he thought of them. The words could sting, but when he praised the good in them, their talents, their virtues, their accomplishments, his words were like gold. Some of them remembered mostly the criticism, of course, and some mostly the praise, but each of these meetings was recorded and later, Nafai or Oykib wrote down the words on the golden leaves of the book. Someday, when they wanted to remember what Volemak said, the words would be there for them to read.

It was an open secret that Volemak was saying good-bye. And when he took sick, the pace quickened.

He met with pTo and Poto, who came down the canyon to him because even in the launch he couldn't stand the strain of traveling to their village one more time. "We will fight and die for Nafai," they told him.

"I don't want you to die, and you must fight only if they force you to. The real question, my friends, is this: Will you and all your people follow Nafai into the wilderness, to start over, to build a new colony in another land?"

"We'd rather defeat the diggers," said pTo. "We'd rather fight like men. Nafai has taught us to fight with new weapons. We can bring down panthers on the run, we can kill them while we're in flight and they can't touch us."

"Diggers are smarter than panthers," said Volemak.

"But angels are smarter than diggers," said Poto.

"You don't understand me," said Volemak. "I say that diggers are smarter than panthers because it means their lives are more precious.

You should not be proud because you can kill diggers, because they're men, not animals."

Abashed, pTo and Poto fell silent.

"Will you and your people follow Nafai higher into the mountains?"

"I can tell you with perfect confidence, Father Volemak," said pTo, "that not only will the people follow Nafai to the moon or to the depths of hell, but also they will beg him to be their king and rule over them, because if he is their ruler they know that they'll be safe."

"What if Nafai didn't have the cloak of the starmaster?" asked Volemak.

They looked at each other for a moment. Finally Poto remembered. "Oh, you mean the thing that lets him glow like a firefly when he wants to?"

"That means nothing to us," said pTo. "We don't want him to lead us because he has some kind of magical power, Father Volemak. We want him to lead us because he and Luet and Issib and Hushidh are the best and wisest people that we know, and they love us, and we love them."

Volemak nodded. "Then you will be my children forever, even after I'm dead."

They went home and told their people to begin to prepare to leave. They gathered up their belongings and decided which to take and which to leave. They packed their seed and the cuttings of the plants that did not grow from seed. They packed the food that they would need for the journey and to live on until their new fields ripened. And they began to move their children a day's flight up the valley and over the next ridge, so that they would already be out of the reach of the diggers if the flight should begin in haste.

"How long will Father Volemak live?" everyone asked them.

How could they answer? "Not long enough," they said, over and over, to everyone who asked.

At last all goodbyes had been said, all blessings given, all hopes and memories and love expressed, and yet Volemak still lingered. Rasa came to Shedemei and said, "Volya and Nyef want to see you, Shedya. Please come quickly." She smiled at Zdorab. "This time alone, please." Zdorab nodded.

Shedemei followed the old woman into the house where Volemak lay, his eyes closed, his chest unmoving.

"Is he. . . ." she began.

"Not yet," answered Volemak softly.

Nafai sat on a stool in the corner. Rasa left the house, saying only, "Be quick." They understood that she didn't want to be outside when her husband died.

"Nafai," whispered Volemak. "Give the cloak of the starmaster to her."

"What?" said Shedemei.

"Shedemei," said Volemak. "Take the cloak. Learn how to use it. Take the ship up into the sky, where no man can touch it or use it. Live long —the cloak will sustain you. Watch over the Earth."

"That's the Keeper's job, not mine," said Shedemei, but in truth her heart wasn't in her protests. Volemak wants me to have the cloak, me to have the ship! Volemak wants me to have the only decent laboratory in the world, and time enough to use it!

"The Keeper of Earth will be glad of any help that he can get," said Volemak. "If he could do his work alone he wouldn't have brought us here."

Nafai stood up, taking off his clothing as he did. "It will pass from my flesh to yours," he said. "If you're willing to receive it. And if I'm willing to let it go."

"Are you?" asked Shedemei.

"Tend this world as your garden," said Nafai. "And watch over my people when I sleep."

Volemak died that night, with only Rasa at his side. By dawn his passing was known from the deepest chamber of the digger city to the highest nest of the angels. The grief was immediate and real among the angels, and among all the digger who did not lust for war. They knew that peace was ended for them all; and also, they had loved and honored the man Volemak, not just for his authority, but for the way he used it.

At Rasa's request they did not burn his body, but rather buried it according to the digger custom.

It was only two days later that the test of authority came. Nafai was preparing to go back up to the angel village, where Luet already waited for him. Elemak, flanked by Meb and Protchnu, and with a dozen digger soldiers behind him, intercepted Nafai at the forest's edge.

"Please don't go," said Elemak.

"Luet's waiting," said Nafai. "Is there some urgent business?"

"I'd appreciate it if you didn't go," said Elemak. "I'll send word to Luet to come down here. I'd rather you live in this village now. The skymeat don't need you anymore."

His words and manner were gentle, so that if Nafai showed any resistance *he* would look like the aggressor, not Elemak. But the message was plain. Elemak was seizing power, and Nafai was his prisoner.

"I'm glad to hear that," said Nafai. "I thought I still had a great deal of work to do among them, but now I imagine I can just retire."

"Oh, no, there's still a lot of work to do down here," said Elemak.

"Fields to be cleared, tunnels to be dug. A lot of work. And your back is still strong, Nafai. I think there's a lot of labor left in you."

He was taken to Volemak's house. Rasa saw at once what was happening, and she did not take it calmly. "You were always a snake, Elemak, but I thought you learned long ago that imprisoning Nafai accomplishes nothing."

"Nafai's not my prisoner," said Elemak. "He's just another citizen, doing his duty to the community."

"What, am I supposed to have the good manners to pretend that I believe your lies?" asked Rasa.

"Lady Rasa," said Elemak, "Nafai is my brother. But you are *not* my mother."

"For which I give thanks to the Oversoul, you may be sure."

Nafai finally broke his silence. "Mother, please. Keep peace. Elemak thinks he rules here, but this world belongs to the Keeper, not to him or any man. He has no power here."

In another time, Elemak would have flown into a rage at those words, would have blustered and threatened, or lashed out in fury. But he was a different man now, a tempered man, a man of discipline and quiet, ruthless wisdom. He said nothing, merely watched until Nafai went into his father's house. Then two digger soldiers were left to stand guard at the door.

Rasa went to the ship, to Shedemei. "I don't think Elemak knows that you have the cloak now, Shedemei. You could use it to stop him, to strike him down."

Shedemei shook her head. "I don't know how to use it that well yet. I'm learning. It's a terrible burden, this cloak. I don't know how Nafai bore it."

"Don't you see that he's helpless here? Elemak is going to kill him, probably tonight. He won't let Nafai live till morning."

"I know," said Shedemei. "I received a message from Issib, through the Index. I hear him directly now, you know, wearing the cloak. He says that Luet dreamed a true dream last night. In the dream she saw all the digger soldiers asleep, and all those who follow Elemak. Asleep while you and Nafai and all the loyal men and women and children journeyed up the canyon, and then onward, higher and farther, to a new land."

"And what is that supposed to mean?"

"I think—she thinks, and so does Issib, and so says the Oversoul—that it was a true dream. The Oversoul has power enough to put the humans to sleep. But since the dream came from the Keeper, perhaps we must trust that she, too, has the power to put her people to sleep."

Shedemei looked away. "I'm not familiar with this sort of thing. I wasn't one to have visions. Just one dream, really, of a garden."

Zdorab was sitting sourly in a corner. "She won't take me with her," he said. "She insists I have to go with Nafai and help start another damn colony."

"You don't *have* to," said Shedemei.

"Or stay with Elemak—do you really think that's a choice?" said Zdorab. "Reason with her, Rasa. I'm a librarian."

"I'm just doing what the Oversoul advised," said Shedemei. "She says that Zdorab will be needed."

"But what about what I *want?*" demanded Zdorab. "Lady Rasa, haven't I kept my oath to Nafai all these years? Haven't I stood by him?"

"Perhaps now," said Rasa, "is your chance to repay him for his forgiveness of your mistake during the voyage."

Zdorab looked away.

"Can't you take him with you?" asked Rasa.

"I want to," whispered Shedemei. "But the Oversoul says not for now."

"Then tell him that. Tell him it's not for now," said Rasa. "He thinks that it's forever."

From the corner Zdorab spoke again, and he was weeping. "Don't you know, Shedemei, that I love you? Don't you know that I don't want to live without you?"

Tears came to Shedemei's eyes, too. She whispered to Rasa, "I never thought he'd. . . ."

"Love you?" asked Rasa. "You never think anyone will love you, but we do. Let him go with you, Shedemei. The Oversoul doesn't know everything. She's just a computer, you know."

Shedemei nodded gravely, knowing perfectly well that Rasa did not believe for a moment that the Oversoul was nothing more than a machine. "Zdorab," said Shedemei, "will you take the ship's launch, to carry Lady Rasa and the heaviest burdens up the canyon? And then use it to take Issib and his chair, and Lady Rasa again, and bring them to the new place where the Nafari will start their colony?"

"I will," said Zdorab.

"And then, when Nafai tells you he has no further use for the launch, would you be kind enough to bring it back to me here at the ship, so we can lift ourselves into orbit?"

He smiled. He embraced her.

"You know that the cloak will sustain my life," she said. "Longer than is natural. And I intend to hibernate a lot, too, so I can have the time to study many generations of life and gather a great deal of data over time."

"I don't mind dying before you do," said Zdorab. "In fact, I rather prefer it that way."

"It'll be work all the time," said Shedemei.

"So you'll need a secretary and librarian all the more."

"And the salary is low," she said.

"I've already been paid," he answered her.

When darkness fell, the digger soldiers outside the door of Volemak's house fell asleep. Nafai stepped out almost at once, and began going door to door, speaking quietly to his loyal supporters and gathering them at the forest's edge. They were not silent, though they tried to be; there was no way to keep the little children from talking or, occasionally, crying or complaining. But no alarm was raised.

Chveya stood beside Nafai, looking at the ties still binding him to the people he was leaving behind. "If they're asleep," said Chveya, "doesn't that mean the Oversoul doesn't want them to go with you?"

"It doesn't matter what the Oversoul wants this time," said Nafai. "I'm taking anyone who wants to join me."

Chveya nodded. "Well, then, I must tell you that you are still bound to Eiadh and three of her children."

Nafai nodded. "But I don't need to speak to her," he said. "See? She's coming."

And it was true. She was accompanied by the young men Yistina and Peremenya and the young woman Zhivoya, the one who had been kidnapped twenty years before. Yistina and Peremenya had their wives with them, but Zhivoya's husband, Muzhestvo, had not come. "He's asleep and I can't waken him," she explained with tears in her eyes.

"You can stay with him," said Nafai. "No one will blame you for that."

She shook her head. "I know what he is," she said. "I didn't when I married him, but I know it now. He's one of them. In his heart and soul, he's one of them." She put her hands on her stomach. "But the baby is mine."

Eiadh touched Nafai's arm. "You don't have to take us, Nafai. I know the danger it puts you in. He'll never forgive us for this. He'll believe that you and I—"

"He'll believe that you and I have done what he and Kokor and he and Sevet and probably he and Dol have already done." Nafai nodded. "But you and I know that we haven't and that we never will."

Eiadh smiled wanly at the gentle way he made it very clear that she was coming as a fellow-citizen, and not as a lover.

"Then we're all here," said Chveya.

"No we're not," said Nafai. "I have to invite my sisters."

"They're sleeping with *him,* Father," Chveya said. "Not to mention that they aren't the most trustworthy people in the world."

"Are we only taking the strong and virtuous?" he asked. "Their husbands are dead, and as you said, their morals have never been their best talent. But they're my sisters." He walked away, back into the village.

It was a ghost town, the doors standing open, the people gone or, in just a few of the houses now, deeply asleep. But when Nafai came to the door of Sevet's house, there she stood in the doorway, looking sleepy and surprised. "I had a dream," she said, when Nafai approached her. "I don't even remember what it was, but it made me get up and here you are."

"We're leaving," said Nafai. "Before Elemak has a chance to kill me, we're leaving, everyone who would rather not live under his rule. We're taking all the angels with us, and going to a new place far away."

"He'll track you down and kill you if he can," said Sevet. "You don't know how much hate there is in him."

"Yes I do," said Nafai. "Will you come with me?"

She began to weep. "Would you really take me, after all I've done?"

"Would you really come?" he asked. "Would you really stand with me now?"

"I'm so afraid of him," she said. "And my Vasnaminanya and my Umya, they think the sun rises and sets with him."

"But Panimanya is with us," said Nafai.

"So am I," said Sevet.

They went to Kokor's door. It stood open, but she was not standing there as Sevet had been. They came inside, quietly, and found that she was not alone in her bed. Mebbekew lay beside her, naked and sweating in the damp heat of the night. But Mebbekew was asleep, while Kokor's eyes were already open when they came inside.

They said nothing, for fear that Meb might come awake. Kokor looked at them in the darkness, blinking. Nafai nodded to her, beckoned, and then led Sevet outside. They waited several paces from the house. Soon she came out, still arranging her clothing. "You're leaving," she said softly. "I dreamed it."

"Will you come with us?" asked Nafai.

Kokor looked at Sevet, her eyes widening. "Us?" she asked.

"You can stay with him if you want to, Kokor," said Sevet. "I think he does love you."

"He doesn't love anybody," said Kokor.

"I didn't mean Meb," said Sevet.

"I know," said Kokor. "But can't I come with you if I want to?"

"There's no going back," said Nafai. "And in our new city, we'll respect the law."

They understood what he was telling them. "I think perhaps we've had our fill," said Sevet.

Kokor rolled her eyes. "I will never have my fill," she said. "But I know it won't be Basilica. I'll be good."

"Are you sure you wouldn't be happier if you stayed?" asked Nafai.

"Don't you want us to come with you?" asked Kokor.

"Of course I do," he answered.

"Give us some credit, Nafai," said Kokor. "We can tell the difference between you and Elemak. We know steel from cheap tin when we see it."

"Then let's go," said Nafai. "There's a long journey ahead of us tonight."

Oykib was already leading the long procession out onto the forest path, so that only a few remained when Nafai got there, among them Rasa and Zdorab on the launch. Shedemei was there, too.

"Seal the ship," said Nafai. "They can't get in if you don't let them."

"I know," she said. "The ship will be safe."

"Don't try to be heroic," said Nafai. "We'll be fine."

"You need more than one night's head start," said Shedemei.

Nafai shook his head, obviously intending to argue further. But she reached out a hand and touched his lips to silence him. "Nyef, my dear friend, I'm the starmaster now. You go lead your colony into the wilderness. I will tend the ship and decide how the powers of the cloak are to be used."

Shedemei embraced Rasa and Zdorab and then waved as the launch rose into the sky and soared over the tops of the trees, passing all the other travelers who were trudging along the road. Then she embraced Nafai and retuned to the ship.

Nafai was the last to set out on the road. He thought he was alone, when suddenly he found himself surrounded by a dozen diggers. His first thought was that the Keeper had failed, that while the Oversoul was able to keep his human enemies asleep, the diggers had been able to awaken. This is how I'll die, he thought.

Then he saw that they weren't armed, and half of them were women.

"Take us with you," said one of them in digger language.

Nafai wasn't as fluent in that tongue as Oykib was, but he could understand them. "And live among the angels?" he asked. "They'll never trust you."

"We would rather be servants to the . . . angels," said the woman who was speaking for them all. Nafai noticed that she did not say *skymeat,* but rather struggled to form her lips and tongue around the strange sounds of the angels' own word for *people.* "Fusum is the most terrible god."

Nafai nodded. "It will be hard for you among the angels," he said, "but you have my protection, and I will trust you unless you teach me that I can't. Do all of you take an oath to obey me and harm none of my people, humans or angels?"

They took the oath, and so he let them follow him. There was consternation among the angels when they arrived, but Nafai's assurances and their own humble pleas won the grudging acceptance of the angels. It was still dark when they left the angel village empty, and set out into the new country to build a new city, of a new kind.

When, after many days of travel, they reached the place that Nafai had chosen years before, knowing that this day might come, pTo and Poto held a little ceremony. "A place must have a name," they said. "And since we will always be known as the Nafari—" the word their lips pronounced was more like Dapati, but they were understood "—then we think this must now be called the land of Nafai—" Dapai "—and you are the one we choose to lead us all."

The voices rang out so loud in approbation that Nafai could only smile and say, "No man could be more happily praised than to have his friends choose to name their home after him." But despite the modesty of his words, they all knew what the naming meant. Nafai was their king. Their war king. And they would gladly die for him.

16

Starmaster

Shedemei heard what Issib said to her through the Index. "It's dawn, and we're well away from the village, but we're slow, Shedya, and an army of diggers could have us by noon."

To this Shedemei replied, "There will be no army today or tomorrow."

"Just remember, Shedya," Issib answered. "There's only one of you to protect all of us. Don't be noble. Don't be fair. Prevail."

"Good advice, Issya. Now let me go and follow it."

For all her confidence, Shedemei was reluctant to leave the shelter of the starship, to make the door seal itself behind her. Wearing the cloak gave her a feeling of connection and closeness to every part of the ship, but in truth she had felt not very differently before. The ship was where her tools were, her library, her work, her career, herself. Stepping out into the village—the remnant of the village, the mostly deserted human-built houses—she was becoming someone else. Nafai must have relished this, thought Shedemei, this feeling of power, of control. But I don't. I'm not interested to find out how much power can be focused through my flesh. I have no desire to know just how strong a jolt I can give someone without killing him.

To be fair, Nafai might not have loved it either. But good-hearted as he might be, he *was* a man, and men seemed to find an obscene amount of pleasure in having the upper hand, in winning. Shedemei, on the other hand, simply wanted to *know.* But maybe it wasn't a matter of men and women. Maybe it was just that Shedemei's connection to other people was never very strong, compared to her love for her work, her devotion to understanding the way life worked. Is that really different, though? she wondered. Nafai and Elemak were born to rule men and determined to win out over each other. But I feel myself also born to rule, not men or women but organisms, genetic codes, life systems, ecologies. And, like Nafai and Elemak, I *will* have my way.

The problem today would not be Elemak, not really. The problem would be the diggers. Shedemei could easily stop Elemak and his few human followers. But there was no way she could seek out and block all of Fusum's soldiers, and they were the ones who would do the killing if they reached the Nafari while they were traveling, encumbered as they were by children and infants, by supplies and flocks and herds.

So whatever Shedemei did, she would have to persuade the diggers that they must wait; if the diggers did not go, then Elemak would also have to wait.

Thus it was that Shedemei walked through the village, paying no attention to the shouting as Elemak, Mebbekew, and Protchnu searched all the houses, ransacked them, really, screaming to each other about the betrayal, about all those who had gone. Mebbekew saw her and called out to her, then went howling off to find Elemak, crying out that Shedemei had stayed, Shedemei couldn't leave the ship after all. "We have the laboratories! We have the computers! We have the Oversoul!" Time enough to disabuse him of this delusion later.

She made her way to where the digger watchmen were conferring in terror, wondering what would happen to them when Fusum learned that somehow they had all slept through the night, seeing nothing, hearing nothing, as most of the humans slipped away. "Fusum will kill you," she said in her halting digger language.

They answered her in human speech, for which she was grateful. "What can we do? What happened to us? Someone poisoned us!"

"It was the Keeper of Earth," she said. "The Keeper of Earth has rejected you, because a murderer rules over you. You have chosen a murderer to be your blood king and your war king." Then, with some effort, she made her skin begin to glow. "Did you think that when Fusum desecrated the statue of the Untouched God, it would go unnoticed?"

She hated doing this. It had taken a great deal of effort to break them free of superstition, and here she was rekindling all their old fears and faiths. But how else could she control them, given the few powers that she had?

They were supine before her, offering their underbellies in a gesture of submission.

"I don't want your naked bellies," she said. "Stand like men, for once. If you had stood like men before, the Keeper of Earth would not be so angry with you now."

"What should we do, great one?"

"Bring me the friend-killer, the liar who murdered Nen on the hunt."

The charge was like an electric current suddenly flowing through them. "So it was not the panther! Not the panther!" they said.

"There was a panther," said Shedemei, "but the panther killed a man who had been struck down by a blow from a friend." Even as she said it, she wondered if it was true, and, if it was, how she knew it.

<I'm wondering that myself.> The voice of the Oversoul was clear and strong inside her head.

Could it be true? she asked.

<I watch over the humans. You're the only ones who have been changed to enable you to hear me, and to enable me to touch your minds.>

But we set twelve satellites in orbit, she said. You must be able to see, even if you can't hear their thoughts.

<I've never been programmed to watch animals.>

Furiously Shedemei responded, Well, I program you *now* to treat diggers and angels as if they were human, too.

<They aren't human, and so I can't regard them that way.>

Then do this, said Shedemei silently. Remember that because the humans have to live among diggers and angels now, our safety and survival depend on you watching what these sentient aliens do. You must always know.

<I don't have the resources that I had on Harmony. I don't have the power, the memory, the speed, the vision to watch them all.>

Do your best.

<And when you set me to work on mathematical problems or searches and comparisons, Shedemei, I can barely watch anything at all.>

Within your limits, within a reasonable set of priorities, do your best.

<We're going to have to have a long talk about priorities, before long.>

Don't pretend to be helpless. I know what you are, *who* you are, and you don't need me to explain things to you. Now do your best to help me understand Elemak.

<Don't kill him.>

Shedemei almost said, I wasn't planning to. But then she realized that in the back of her mind that was exactly what she had planned. Fusum and Elemak, both of them dead and therefore the Nafari safe.

Why not kill him? she asked.

<The diggers must be restrained. Oykib is explaining this to Nafai and

Issib right now. If they aren't held in by a powerful leader, they will run rampant, slaughtering angels and humans alike. The rage and hunger for blood in them is strong, after such long restraint. Fusum wasn't causing them to lust for war, he was using that lust to maintain himself in power. He was riding the panther, but he wasn't controlling it, and now you've cut the panther free of him.>

I haven't done anything to him yet.

<All through the digger city they've risen up in revolt, because they carry the tale of how you, the woman of the tower, have come out shining and angry, condemning them all because of Fusum's treachery.>

How can you know this?

<Oykib knows it. He hears the praying and the cursing. I told you, I have no eyes to see what diggers do underground.>

So Nafai thinks that I need Elemak to keep the diggers in check.

<Nafai says that once they're safely in their new home, they can fight off any attack. Natural defenses, dangerous ascents where diggers will be exposed to the darts of the angels—those will be enough if they can get there safely.>

Nafai was planning this all along, wasn't he? When he gave me the cloak, he knew he would need me to do this.

<Yes, of course. Actually, it was my idea. If he had tried to do what you're doing, Shedemei, he probably would have had to kill Elemak because this would have been one blow too many for Elemak to submit to him again. But with you in the cloak of the starmaster, Elemak should be able to bear another defeat, especially since you're also handing him a victory.>

Victory?

<Over his only serious rival for power.>

They dragged Fusum out of a hole in the ground and spread-eagled him before her. He hissed and howled and cursed her. She gave him the mildest of jolts, and his body spasmed. "Hold your tongue," she said.

He held his tongue.

She had them bring him along into the human village, where now Elemak and Protchnu stood, with all the other humans gathered behind them.

<Mebbekew is planning treachery behind you.>

Shedemei spoke to Elemak. "Tell Mebbekew to come out in the open and join you where you stand, Elya, or I'll have to make an example of him and it won't be nice."

Elemak laughed. "So, underneath our shy and quiet Shedemei there was a queen waiting to emerge. All it took was a little bit of power, and here you are, lord of all."

In the meantime, Mebbekew had slunk out from behind one of the houses and now stood behind Elemak. "Nafai took our women," Mebbekew complained.

"I'm sure that if you ask him, Protchnu will teach you how to ease your deprivation," Shedemei said. Protchnu glowered. So did Mebbekew, when he got it.

"I see you've already seized control of the diggers," said Elemak, gesturing toward the captive Fusum.

"On the contrary," said Shedemei. "I've seized control of nothing. I have merely accused this man, Fusum, of murdering his friend Nen."

"I didn't kill him," Fusum said.

"He clubbed him down when he knew a panther was stalking them," said Shedemei. "Only when he knew that Nen was dead did he lunge forward and kill the panther."

"Why are you telling me this?" asked Elemak.

"Are you not the one that has been chosen to unite humans and diggers into one people?" asked Shedemei. "Are you not the one who will found the nation of the Elemaki?"

Elemak chuckled. "Oh, of course," he said. "Of course the starmaster has always wanted me to rule."

"The starmaster intends to take this starship into space on the day the launch returns with my husband inside it."

"And when will that happy day come?"

"When the great nation of the Nafari is safe."

"As long as I'm alive, there will never be such a day," said Elemak.

Oh, yes, Nafai almost certainly would have had to kill him. "Safe enough," she said. "Because you know and I know that you will only be able to lead your soldiers against their redoubt so many times before the people will cease to follow you. You're a born leader, Elemak. You'll know how far you can push and goad and persuade. And it won't be far enough. Nafai and his people will be safe."

"How many days?" Elemak said. He understood the bargain.

"I think it will take you at least eight days to examine the crimes of this traitor. You'll have to find witnesses among his soldiers who will publicly confess about all the others who were murdered after Emeezem died. Justice takes time."

"Eight days."

"Or until the launch comes back. You'll also be busy moving your village so nobody gets killed when the ship takes off."

"I can see my work is cut out for me."

Protchnu was furious. "You aren't going to accept this corrupt bargain, are you, Father? That snake took half your family, half *my* family—"

Shedemei interrupted him. "Everyone who went with Nafai went of their own free will."

"And we're supposed to believe that?" said Protchnu. "Maybe father will agree to your bargain in exchange for power over *these*—" he indicated the diggers with disdain "—but *I* will track them and hunt them down and my spear will take Nafai's heart out of his body!"

"And your mother's, too?" said Shedemei. "Because the only way she'll ever come back to Elemak is if she's dead."

"She's already dead!" screamed Protchnu. "She has no soul!"

"You have to forgive the boy," said Elemak. "He's distraught."

"He just doesn't understand what he's dealing with," said Shedemei. She reached out a hand toward Protchnu.

"No!" cried Elemak. But the air was already sparking with power, and Protchnu bounced into the air, his limbs cavorting madly. Then he fell to the ground, still twitching, and he whimpered, long high sighs that trembled as they faded. "You are really a bitch after all," whispered Elemak.

"I think it's useful for everyone to see that the Keeper of Earth does not leave her servants without power," said Shedemei. "Now let everyone see how Elemak does justice. Call your witnesses, confer with the leaders of the digger people, and when in eight days or so you reach your judgment, all of us will see whether you are fit to be named the war king of the Elemaki. If the voice of the diggers and the voice of the humans are united in calling for you to lead them, then I will make you war king, and you will lead this people with authority."

Elemak smiled at her, since of course he knew full well that she was trading the freedom of these diggers for the safety of the Nafari. He bent down and helped his son rise, shaking, to his feet.

"Remember, though," said Shedemei. "I said *war* king. There will be no more blood king among the people. Do you all hear me?"

They heard.

"This one has defiled the office so that it can never be held worthily again. From now on it is forbidden to eat the flesh of angel or human. Any man who eats that forbidden flesh will be as guilty as if he ate the flesh of his own child. That is now the law of all people, through all the world! And you will enforce it over all the diggers of every land!"

"Thanks for the assignment," said Elemak softly.

"I think you'll come to see the wisdom of teaching them not to think of humans as a snack," said Shedemei, just as quietly. "If they can eat your enemies, Elya, how long before they decide that you are also a comestible?"

"I got the point already," said Elemak. "Now are you done?"

"No diggers following the Nafari," said Shedemei.

"Do you think we won't be able to follow the trail?" asked Elemak.

"No assassins on the road," she said.

"I know the bargain," said Elemak. "I know that I've been humiliated again, and this time Nafai took my wife and half my family, and you struck down my son. But I can live with that, because you've given me a nation. A nation of ugly rodents who live in dirt, but I've dealt with worse in caravans on Harmony, even though they walked in human shape. I *will* stand over Nafai's body someday, Shedemei, regardless of what you think. But if it makes you feel better, I won't eat him. And I won't let anybody else eat him, either. Except perhaps the crows and vultures."

"I'm glad to see that you're filled with the spirit of conciliation."

He smiled at her. Then he stepped away from her and spoke to the diggers who held Fusum. "Take the prisoner into my house. And then start bringing me those who think they know of crimes this man has done." He looked again at Shedemei. "That should take up the first day, I imagine."

Shedemei turned from him to Protchnu, whose cheeks were stained with tears. "You shouldn't have done that to me," he whispered. "That was *wrong*."

"You were such a promising boy," she answered kindly. "Of all the tragedies this lifelong war between brothers has caused, you are the saddest one of all."

He went livid. "I'll kill him, Shedya. I'll kill them all. Every one of them."

"What you're saying, then, is that you're sure your father's going to fail?"

"I meant that I'd kill any he left behind."

"You know the truth, Protchnu. Stop worrying about vengeance and learn how to be a leader. These people need a king far more than your father needs to be justified. All he's ever done, he did for power. Now he's got it. You'll see. He'll go through the motions of war, but he'll lose because his hunger has been satisfied."

"You don't know Father," said Protchnu proudly. "And you don't know me."

"Nobody does," said Shedemei. "So maybe you'll surprise us all."

Eight days later, Zdorab returned to the ship in the launch. He arrived in time to watch as Fusum was executed for his crimes, his throat cut by one of his own soldiers. His body was then hung from the limb of a tree, so that no part of it was touching the sacred earth. Shedemei, her skin aglow, stepped forward then and went through the ritual of naming Elemak to be war king. The people hailed him and cheered him, then watched in silence as Shedemei and Zdorab flew upward in the launch until they entered the tower through the high wide bay where the launch was kept.

The door closed behind them, and Elemak set out at once with two hundred soldiers, leaving Muzhestvo—Mebbekew's youngest, now a man of twenty-three—to rule the people in his absence. Elemak's army was halfway up the canyon when the starship roared to life and rose into the sky.

It became another point of light in the night heaven, circling and circling, now and then changing its position. It was called *Basilica,* but in time almost no one remembered why, or what it was, or that it had once been a tower standing by the first human village on Earth in forty million years.

Elemak's army tracked the wide path of the Nafari migration, but when they reached the stony cliff that barred the southern passage into the wide high valley of the land of Nafai, angels assaulted them from the air, shooting darts into their exposed backs. Twenty diggers died in that place, and forty more were injured. They struggled back home, and Elemak taught them to make armor so that next year they could try again.

And so it went, year after year. But between the futile wars, both nations prospered and grew, and both sent out traders and teachers to spread the new agriculture and the new modes of warfare and the new myths and legends and religions to every other digger city and angel village.

Generations passed, and the humans became hundreds, then thousands, then tens of thousands, and there was not a digger city that didn't have its human houses overhead, not an angel village that didn't have humans joining in the evening song. The term that became common for humans in both societies was *middle people,* because they stood between the angels in the sky and the diggers in the earth.

In the sky, the starship circled and circled, but it was full of life. Shedemei and Zdorab slept long and often, but then they would emerge and use the launch to explore, to gather specimens, to introduce new variations, to give shape and strength and variety to the gardens of the Earth. In time, Zdorab's body wore out, and Shedemei laid him to rest in a field of flowers she had brought from Harmony. Then, alone, she woke less often. But still from time to time she visited, she gathered, she tended, and silently she watched as the people spread across the face of the land, always cleverer each time she saw them, yet also angrier, and always at war.

What else could happen? The human race was home again.

EARTHBORN

To Jerry and Gail Argetsinger:
Before the pageant, before the costumes,
Before we were cast in the roles we play today,
You taught me how to create a lasting love.

Contents

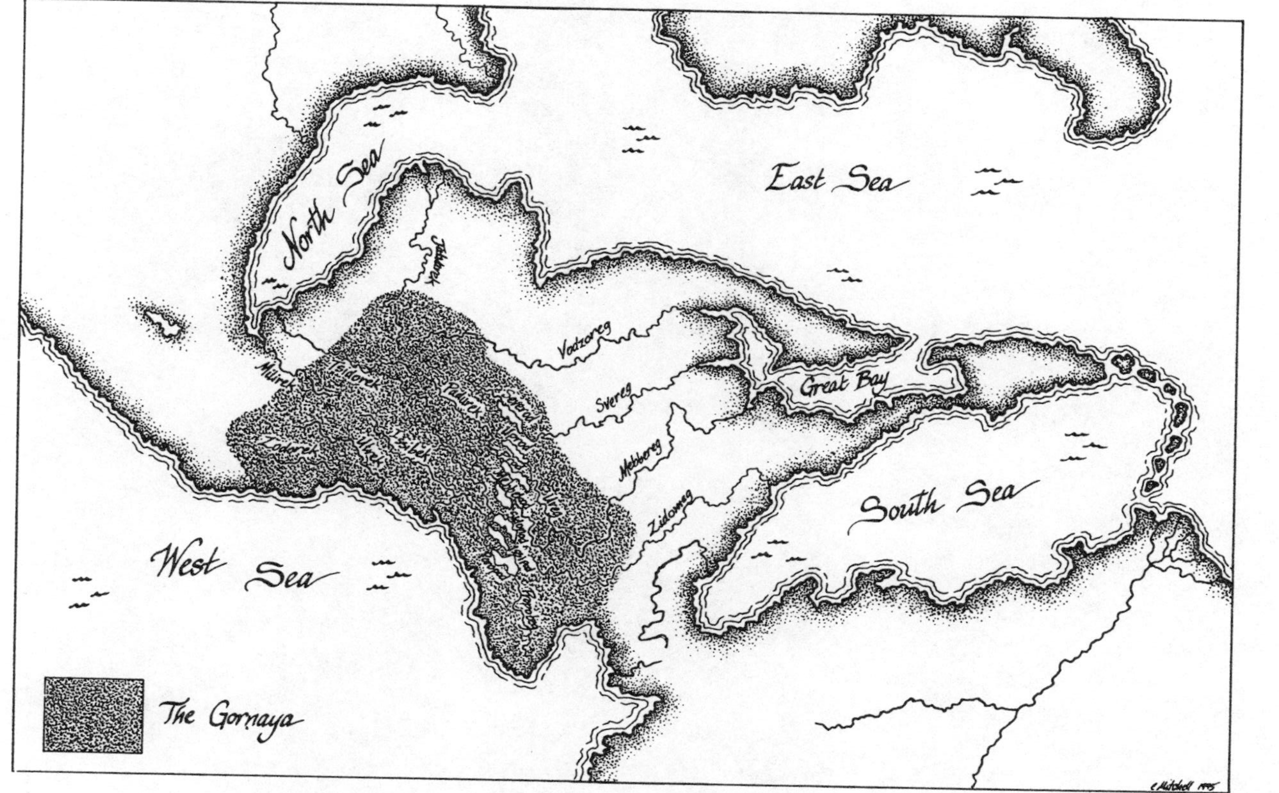
North Sea
East Sea
West Sea
South Sea
Great Bay
Vodzoreg
Svereg
Mebberg
Zidoreg
The Gornaya
C. Mitchell 1995

LANDFORMS

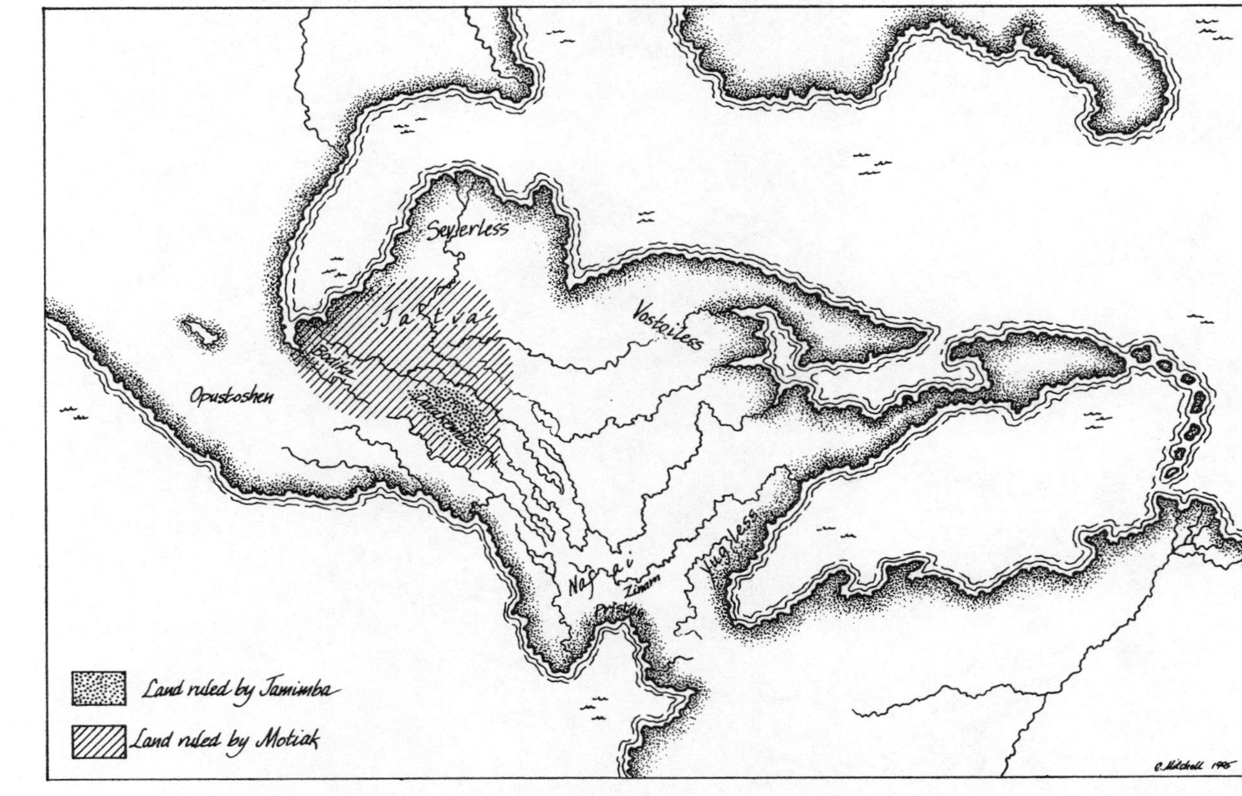

LANDS AND KINGDOMS

Characters

Note on the Conventions of Naming

Among the Nafari humans, it is the custom for persons of distinction to add titles of honor to their names, as honorifics. Formally, the honorific is put at the beginning of the name, so that on state occasions the king of Darakemba is Ak-Moti; but most commonly the honorific is added at the end: thus, Motiak. Some honorifics are altered in order to combine with the name, and some names to combine with the honorific. Thus when Jamim was heir, he was Ha-Jamim or Jamimha, the normal pattern; but as king he was Ka-Jamim or Jaminka (compared with Nuak/Ak-Nu and Motiak/Ak-Moti); and as former king he is spoken of as Ba-Jamim or Jamimba (compared with Nuab/Ab-Nu and Motiab/Ab-Moti).

The honorifics for men that show up in this book are: Ak/Ka, which means "reigning king"; Ha/Akh, "heir"; Ab/Ba, "former king"; Ush, "mighty warrior"; Dis, "beloved son"; Og/Go, "high priest"; Ro/Or, "wise teacher"; Di/Id, "traitor." The honorifics for women that show up in this book are: Dwa, "mother of the heir" (whether she is living or dead); Gu/Ug, "most-honored wife of king"; Ya, "great, compassionate woman."

In addition, the syllable *da* is used as an all-purpose term of endearment, and is inserted at the end of a usually-shortened name, but before any honorifics. Thus Chebeya, in private, calls her husband "Kmadaro," which is (A)kma + da (endearment) + ro (honorific meaning "great teacher"), and Akmaro calls her "Bedaya," which is (Che)be + da (endearment) + ya (honorific meaning "great compassionate woman").

The sons of a prominent man are regarded collectively as his "tribe" and are referred to that way. Thus the four sons of Motiak are sometimes called "the Motaiki"; the four sons of Pabulog are called "the Pabulogi" until they repudiate the name.

It is also worth pointing out that there are several terms for the different intelligent species. The sky people, earth people, and middle people can also be called angels, diggers, and humans, respectively. The former three terms suggest formality, dignity, and equivalency among the species. However, the latter three terms are merely informal, not necessarily pejorative, and members of all three species readily use both the formal and informal terms for themselves.

Humans (Middle People)

IN DARAKEMBA

Motiak, or Ak-Moti—the king, conqueror of most of the Darakemba empire

Dudagu, or Gu-Duda—Motiak's present wife, mother of his youngest son

Toeledwa [toe-eh-LED-wah], or Dwa-Toel—Motiak's late wife, mother of his first four children

Jamimba, or Ba-Jamim—Motiak's late father

Motiab, or Ab-Moti—Jamimba's father, who led the Nafari out of the land of Nafai to unite them with the people of Darakemba, forming the core of the empire

Aronha, or Ha-Aron—Motiak's eldest son, his heir

Edhadeya, or Ya-Edhad—Motiak's eldest daughter and second child

Mon—Motiak's second son, third child; named after Monush

Ominer—Motiak's third son, fourth child; the last of Toeledwa's children

Khimin—Motiak's fourth son; the only child of Dudagu, Motiak's current wife

Monush, or Ush-Mon—Motiak's leading soldier

IN CHELEM

Akmaro, or Ro-Akma—a former priest of King Nuak of the Zenifi, he now leads a group of followers of the teachings of Binaro/Binadi; his people are sometimes called Akmari

Chebeya, or Ya-Cheb—Akmaro's wife, a raveler

Akma—Akmaro's and Chebeya's son and oldest child

Luet—Akmaro's and Chebeya's daughter and youngest child

Pabulog, or Og-Pabul—former high priest of King Nuak, and now a particularly vicious leader among the Elemaki, with an army at his disposal

Pabul—Pabulog's oldest son

Udad—Pabulog's second son

Didul—Pabulog's third son

Muwu—Pabulog's fourth and youngest son

AMONG THE ZENIFI

Zenifab, or Ab-Zeni—the founding king of the Zenifi, for whom the tribe is named; their fundamental belief is that humans should not live with angels or diggers, and they tried to re-establish a pure-human colony in their ancestral homeland of Nafai after the Nafari merged with the Darakembi

Nuak, or Ak-Nu; also Nuab, or Ab-Nu—Zenifab's son and recent king of the Zenifi; in speaking of the time when he reigned, "Nuak" is used; in referring to later times, he is called "Nuab"; there is always some confusion for a while in changing over from one honorific to another

Ilihiak, or Ak-Ilihi—Nuak's son, who was never expected to be the king, but had the office thrust upon him in the crisis after his father was murdered

Wissedwa, or Dwa-Wiss—Ilihiak's wife; she saved the Zenifi after Nuak's cowardly retreat

Khideo—leading soldier of Ilihiak; he refuses all honorifics because he once attempted to kill Nuak

Binadi, or Di-Bina; also called Bianro, or Ro-Bina—condemned to death and executed by Nuak and Pabulog, he was officially designated a traitor (thus Binadi); but among Akmaro's people, he is called Binaro and revered as a great teacher

IN THE STARSHIP *BASILICA*

Shedemei—the starmaster, a brilliant geneticist, she is the one survivor from the original group of humans who were brought back to Earth from the planet Harmony. Among the diggers, or earth people, she is known as the One-Who-Was-Never-Buried

Angels (Sky People)

Husu—commander of the spies, a sort of "cavalry" composed entirely of sky people bGo—Motiak's chief clerk, head of much of the bureaucracy of Darakemba

Bego—bGo's otherself, the king's archivist and tutor to Motiak's children

Diggers(Earth People)

Uss-Uss, or Voozhum—Edhadeya's chambermaid, a slave; but something of a sage and priestess among the other digger slaves

Prologue

Once, long ago, the computer of the starship *Basilica* had governed the planet Harmony for forty million years. Now it watched over a much smaller population, and with far fewer powers to intervene. But the planet that it tended to was Earth, the ancient home of the human race.

It was the starship *Basilica* that brought a group of humans home again, only to find that in the absence of humanity, two new species had reached the lofty pinnacle of intelligence. Now the three peoples shared a vast massif of high mountains, lush valleys, and a climate that varied more with elevation than with latitude.

The diggers called themselves the earth people, making tunnels through the soil and into the trunks of trees they hollowed out. The angels were the sky people, building roofed nests in trees and hanging upside down from limbs to sleep, to argue, and to teach. The humans were the middle people now, living in houses above the ground.

There was no digger city without human houses on the ground above it, no angel village without the walled chambers of the middle people providing artificial caves. The vast knowledge that the humans brought with them from the planet Harmony was only a fraction of what their ancestors had known on Earth before their exile forty million years before. Now even that was mostly lost; yet what remained was so far superior to what the people of the earth and sky had known that wherever the middle people dwelt, they had great power, and usually ruled.

In the sky, however, the computer of the starship *Basilica* forgot nothing, and through satellites it had deployed around the Earth it watched, it collected data and remembered everything it learned.

Nor was it alone in its watching. For inside it lived a woman who had come to Earth with the first colonists; but then, clothed in the cloak of the starmaster, she returned into the sky, to sleep long years and waken briefly, her body healed and helped by the cloak, so that death, if it could ever come to her at all, was still a far distant visitor. She remembered everything that mattered to her, remembered people who had once lived and now were gone. Birth and life and death, she had seen so much of it that she barely noticed it now. It was all generations to her, seasons in her garden, trees and grass and people rising and falling, rising and falling.

On Earth there was a little bit of memory as well. Two books, written on thin sheets of metal, had been maintained since the return of the humans. One was in the hands of the king of the Nafari, passed down from king to king. The other, less copious, had been passed to the brother of the first king, and from him to his sons, who were not kings, not even famous men, until at last, unable now even to read the ancient script, the last of that line gave the smaller metal book into the hands of the man who was king in his day. Only in the pages of those books was there a memory that lasted, unchanged, from year to year.

At the heart of the books, in the depths of the ship's records, and warm in the soul of the woman, the greatest of the memories was this: that the human beings had been brought back to Earth, called by an entity they did not understand, the one who was called the Keeper of Earth. The Keeper's voice was not clear, nor was the Keeper understandable as the ship's computer was, back in the days when it was called the Oversoul and people worshipped it as a god. Instead the Keeper spoke through dreams, and, while many received the dreams, and many believed that they had meaning, only a few knew who it was that sent them, or what it was the Keeper wanted from the people of Earth.

1
Captivity

Akma was born in a rich man's house. He remembered little from that time. One memory was of his father, Akmaro, carrying him up a high tower, and then handing him to another man there, who dangled him over the parapet until he screamed in fear. The man who held him laughed until Father reached out and took Akma from him and held him close. Later Mother told Akma that the man who tormented him on the tower was the king in the land of Nafai, a man named Nuak. "He was a very bad man," said Mother, "but the people didn't seem to mind as long as he was a good king. But when the Elemaki came and conquered the land of Nafai, the people of Nuak hated him so much they burned him to death." Ever after she told him that story, Akma's memory changed, and when he dreamed of the laughing man holding him over the edge of the tower, he pictured the man covered with flames until the whole tower was burning, and instead of Father reaching out to rescue his little boy, Akmaro jumped down, falling and falling and falling, and Akma didn't know what to do, to stay on the tower and burn, or jump into the abyss after his father. From that dream he awoke screaming in terror.

Another memory was of his Father rushing into the house in the middle of the day, as Mother supervised two digger women in preparing a feast for that night. The look on Akmaro's face was terrible, and though he whispered to her and Akma had no idea what he was saying, he knew that it was very bad and it made Akma afraid. Father rushed from the house right away, and Mother at once had the diggers stop their work on the feast and start gathering supplies for a journey. Only a few minutes later, four human men with swords came to the door and demanded to see the traitor Akmaro. Mother pretended that Father was in the back of the house and tried to block them from coming in. The biggest man knocked her down and held a sword across her throat while the others ran to search the house for Akmaro. Little Akma was outraged and ran at the man who was threatening Mother. The man laughed at him when Akma cut himself on one of the stones of his sword, but Mother didn't laugh. She said, "Why are you laughing? This little boy had the courage to attack a man with a sword, while you only have enough courage to attack an unarmed woman." The man was angry then, but when the others returned without finding Father, they all went away.

There was food, too. Akma was sure there had once been plenty of food, well-prepared by digger slaves. But now, in his hunger, he couldn't remember it. He couldn't remember ever being full. Here in the maize fields under the hot sun he couldn't remember a time without thirst, without a weary ache in his arms, in his back, in his legs, and throbbing behind his eyes. He wanted to cry, but he knew that this would shame his family. He wanted to scream at the digger taskmaster that he needed to drink and rest and eat and it was stupid for him to keep them working without food because it would wear out more people like old Tiwiak who dropped dead yesterday, dead just like that, keeled over into the maize and never so much as breathed out a good-bye to his wife and even then she kept still, said nothing as she knelt weeping silently over his body, but the taskmaster beat her anyway for stopping work, and it was her own *husband*.

Akma hated nothing in the world the way he hated diggers. His parents had been wrong to keep diggers as servants back in the land of Nafai. The diggers should all have been killed before they ever came near to a real person. Father could talk all he wanted about how the diggers were only getting even for the long, cruel overlordship of Nuak. He could whisper late in the night about how the Keeper of Earth didn't want earth people and sky people and middle people to be enemies. Akma knew the truth. There would be no safety in the world until all the diggers were dead.

When the diggers came, Father refused to let any of his people fight. "You didn't follow me into the wilderness in order to become killers, did you?" he asked them. "The Keeper wants no killing of his children."

The only protest that Akma heard was Mother's whisper: "*Her* children." As if it mattered whether the Keeper had a plow or a pot between its legs. All that Akma knew was that the Keeper was a poor excuse for a god if it couldn't keep its worshippers from being enslaved by filthy bestial stupid cruel diggers.

But Akma said nothing about these thoughts, because the one time he did, Father grew silent and wouldn't speak to him for the rest of the night. That was unbearable. The silence during the days was bad enough. To have Father shut him out at night was the worst thing in the world. So Akma kept his hate for the diggers to himself, as well as his contempt for the Keeper, and at night he spoke in the barest whisper to his mother and father, and drank in their whispered words as if they were pure cold water from a mountain stream.

And then one day a new boy appeared in the village. He wasn't thin and sunbrowned like all the others, and his clothing was fine, bright-colored, and unpatched. His hair was clean and long, and the wind caught and tossed it when he stood on the brow of the low hill in the midst of the commons. After all that Father and Mother had said about the Keeper of Earth, Akma was still unprepared for this vision of a god, and he stopped working just to behold the sight.

The taskmaster shouted at Akma, but he didn't hear. All sound had been swallowed up in this vision, all sensation except sight. Only when the shadow of the taskmaster loomed over him, his arm upraised to strike him with the length of the prod, did Akma notice, and then he flinched and cowered and, almost by reflex, cried out to the boy who had the image of god on his face, "Don't let him hit me!"

"Hold!" cried the boy. His voice rang out confident and strong as he strode down the hill, and, incredibly, the taskmaster immediately obeyed him.

Father was far from Akma, but Mother was near enough to whisper to Akma's little sister Luet, and Luet took a few steps closer to Akma so she could call softly to him. "He's the son of Father's enemy," she said.

Akma heard her, and immediately became wary. But the beauty of the older boy did not diminish as he approached.

"What did she say to you?" asked the boy, his voice kind, his face smiling.

"That your father is my father's enemy."

"Ah, yes. But not by *my* father's choice," he said.

That gave Akma pause. No one had ever bothered to explain to the seven-year-old boy how his father had come to have so many enemies. It had never occurred to Akma that it might be his father's fault. But he was suspicious: How could he believe the son of his father's enemy? And yet. . . . "You stopped the taskmaster from hitting me," said Akma.

The boy looked at the taskmaster, whose face was inscrutable. "From now on," he said, "you are not to punish this one or his sister without my consent. My father says."

The taskmaster bowed his head. But Akma thought he didn't look happy about taking orders like this from a human boy.

"My father is Pabulog," said the boy, "and my name is Didul."

"I'm Akma. My father is Akmaro."

"*Ro*-Akma? Akma the *teacher*?" Didul smiled. "What does *ro* have to teach, that he didn't learn from *og*?"

Akma wasn't sure what *og* meant.

Didul seemed to know why he was confused. "*Og* is the daykeeper, the chief of the priests. After the *ak*, the king, no one is wiser than *og*."

"*King* just means you have the power to kill anybody you don't like, unless they have an army, like the Elemaki." Akma had heard his father say this many times.

"And yet now my father rules over the Elemaki of this land," said Didul. "While Nuak is dead. They burned him up, you know."

"Did you see it?" asked Akma.

"Walk with me. You're done with work for today." Didul looked at the taskmaster. The digger, drawn up to his full height, was barely the same size as Didul; when Didul grew to manhood, he would tower over the digger like a mountain over a hill. But in the case of Didul and the taskmaster, height had nothing to do with their silent confrontation. The digger wilted under his gaze.

Akma was in awe. As Didul took his hand and led him away, Akma asked him, "How do you do it?"

"Do what?" asked Didul.

"Make the taskmaster look so. . . ."

"So useless?" asked Didul. "So helpless and stupid and low?"

Did the humans who were friends of the diggers hate them, too?

"It's simple," said Didul. "He knows that if he doesn't obey me, I'll tell my father and he'll lose his easy job here and go back to working on fortifications and tunnels, or going out on raids. And if he ever raised a hand against me, then of course my father would have him torn apart."

It gave Akma great satisfaction to imagine the taskmaster—all the taskmasters—being torn apart.

"I saw them burn Nuak, yes. He was king, of course, so he led our soldiers in war. But he'd gotten old and soft and stupid and fearful. Everybody knew it. Father tried to compensate for it, but *og* can only do so much when *ak* is weak. One of the great soldiers, Teonig, vowed to kill him so a real king could be put in his place—probably his second son, Ilihi—but you don't know any of these people, do you? You must have been—what, three years old? How old are you now?"

"Seven."

"Three, then, when your father committed treason and ran away like a coward into the wilderness and started plotting and conspiring against the pure human Nafari, trying to get humans and diggers and skymeat to live together as *equals*."

Akma said nothing. That *was* what his father taught. But he had never thought of it as treason against the purely human kingdom where Akma had been born.

"So what did you know? I bet you don't even remember being in court, do you? But you were there. I saw you, holding your father's hand. He presented you to the king."

Akma shook his head. "I don't remember."

"It was family day. We were all there. But you were just little. I remember you, though, because you weren't shy or scared or anything. Bold as you please. The king commented on it. 'This one's going to be a great man, if he's already so brave.' My father remembered. That's why he sent me to look for you."

Akma felt a thrill of pleasure flutter inside his chest. Pabulog had sent his son to seek him out, because he had been brave as a baby. He remembered attacking the soldier who was threatening his mother. Until this moment, he had never thought of himself as brave, but now he saw that it was true.

"Anyway, Nuak was at the point of being murdered by Teonig. They say that Teonig kept demanding that Nuak fight him. But Nuak kept answering, 'I'm the king! I don't have to fight you!' And Teonig kept shouting, 'Don't make me shame you by killing you like a dog.' Nuak fled up to the top of the tower and Teonig was on the point of killing him when the king looked out to the border of the Elemaki country and saw the hugest army of diggers you ever saw, flooding like a storm onto the land. So Teonig let him live, so the king could lead the defense. But instead of a defense, Nuak ordered his army to run so they wouldn't be destroyed. It was cowardly and shameful, and men like Teonig didn't obey him."

"But your father did," said Akma.

"My father had to follow the king. It's what the priests do," said Didul. "The king commanded the soldiers to leave their wives and children behind, but Father wouldn't do it, or at least anyway he took me. Carried me on his back and kept up with the others, even though I wasn't all that little and he isn't all that young. So that's why I was there when the soldiers realized that their wives and children were probably being slaughtered back in the city. So they stripped old Nuak and staked him down and held burning sticks against his skin so he screamed and screamed." Didul smiled. "You wouldn't believe how he screamed, the old sausage."

It sounded awful even to imagine it. It was frightening that Didul, who could remember having actually seen it, could be so complacent about it.

"Of course, along about then Father realized that the talk was turning to who else they ought to burn, and the priests would be an obvious target, so Father said a few quiet words in the priest-language and he led us to safety."

"Why didn't you go back to the city? Was it destroyed?"

"No, but Father says the people there weren't worthy to have true priests who knew the secret language and the calendar and everything. You know. Reading and writing."

Akma was puzzled. "Doesn't everybody learn how to read and write?"

Didul suddenly looked angry. "That's the most terrible thing your father did. Teaching everybody to read and write. All the people who believed his lies and sneaked out of the city to join him, even if they were just *peasants* which they mostly were, even if they were *turkeyherds*. Everybody. He took solemn vows, you know. When he was made a priest. Your father took those vows, never to reveal the secrets of the priesthood to anybody. And then he taught *everybody*."

"Father says all the people should be priests."

"People? Is that what he says?" Didul laughed. "Not just people, Akma. It isn't just *people* that he was going to teach to read."

Akma imagined his father trying to teach the taskmaster to read. He tried to picture one of the diggers bowed over a book, trying to hold a stylus and make the marks in the wax of the tablets. It made him shudder.

"Hungry?" asked Didul.

Akma nodded.

"Come eat with me and my brothers." Didul led him into the shade of a copse behind the hill of the commons.

Akma knew the place—until the diggers came and enslaved them, it was the place where Mother used to gather the children to teach them and play quiet games with them while Father taught the adults at the hill. It gave him a strange feeling to see a large basket of fruit and cakes and a cask of wine there, with diggers serving the food to three humans. Diggers didn't belong in that place where his mother had led the children in play.

But the humans did. Or rather, they would belong wherever they were. One was little, barely as old as Akma. The other two were both older and larger than Didul—men, really, not boys. One of the older ones looked much like Didul, only not as beautiful. The eyes were perhaps too close together, the chin just a bit too pronounced. Didul's image, but distorted, inferior, unfinished.

The other man-sized boy was as unlike Didul as could be imagined. Where Didul was graceful, this boy was strong; where Didul's face looked open and light, this one looked brooding and private and dark. His body was so powerful-looking that Akma marveled that he could pick up any of the fruit without crushing it.

Didul obviously saw which of his brothers it was that had drawn Akma's attention. "Oh, yes. Everybody looks at him like that. Pabul, my brother. He leads armies of diggers. He's killed with his bare hands."

Hearing his words, Pabul looked up and glowered at Didul.

"Pabul doesn't like it when I tell about that. But I saw him once take a full-grown digger soldier and break his neck, just like a rotten dry branch. Snap. The beast peed all over everything."

Pabul shook his head and went back to eating.

"Have some food," said Didul. "Sit down, join us. Brothers, this is Akma, the son of the traitor."

The older brother who looked like Didul spat.

"Don't be rude, Udad," said Didul. "Tell him not to be rude, Pabul."

"Tell him yourself," said Pabul quietly. But Udad reacted as if Pabul had threatened to kill him—he immediately fell silent and began concentrating on his eating.

The younger brother gazed steadily at Akma, as if evaluating him. "I could beat you up," he said finally.

"Shut up and eat, Monkey," said Didul. "This is the youngest, Muwu, and we're not sure he's human."

"Shut up, Didul," said the little one, suddenly furious, as if he knew what was coming.

"We think Father got drunk and mated with a she-digger to spawn him. See his little rat-nose?"

Muwu screamed in fury and launched himself at Didul, who easily fended him off. "Stop it, Muwu, you'll get mud in the food! Stop it!"

"Stop it," said Pabul quietly, and Muwu immediately left off his assault on Didul.

"Eat," said Didul. "You must be hungry."

Akma *was* hungry, and the food looked good. He was seating himself when Didul said, "Our enemies go hungry, but our friends eat."

That reminded Akma that his mother and father were also hungry, as was his sister Luet. "Let me take some back to my sister and my parents," he said. "Or let them all come and eat with us."

Udad hooted. "Stupid," murmured Pabul.

"You're the one I invited," said Didul quietly. "Don't embarrass me by trying to trick me into feeding my father's enemies."

Only then did Akma understand what was happening here. Didul might be beautiful and fascinating, full of stories and friendliness and wit—but he didn't actually care about Akma. He was only trying to get Akma to betray his family. That was why he kept saying those things about Father, about how he was a traitor and all. So that Akma would turn against his own family.

That would be like . . . like becoming a friend to a digger. It was unnatural and wrong and Akma understood now that Didul was like the jaguar, cunning and cruel. He was sleek and beautiful, but if you let him come near enough, he would leap and kill.

"I'm not hungry," said Akma.

"He's lying," said Muwu.

"No I'm not," said Akma.

Pabul turned to face him for the first time. "Don't contradict my brother," he said. His voice sounded dead, but the menace was clear.

"I was just saying that I wasn't lying," said Akma.

"But you *are* lying," said Didul cheerfully. "You're starving to death. Your ribs are sticking out of your chest so sharp you could cut yourself on them." He laughed in delight and held out a maizecake. "Aren't you my friend, Akma?"

"No," said Akma. "You're not *my* friend, either. You only came to me because your father sent you."

Udad laughed at his brother. "Well aren't *you* the clever one, Didul. *You* could make friends with him, said you. *You* could win him over the first day. Well, he saw right through *you*."

Didul glared at him. "He might not have till *you* spoke up."

Akma stood up, furious now. "You mean this was a *game*?"

"Sit down," said Pabul.

"No," said Akma.

Muwu giggled. "Break his leg, Pabul, like you did that other one."

Pabul looked at Akma as if considering it.

Akma wanted to plead with him, to say, Please don't hurt me. But he knew instinctively that the one thing he couldn't do with someone like this was to act weak. Hadn't he seen his father stand before Pabulog himself and face him down, never showing a moment's fear? "Break my leg if you want," said Akma. "I can't stop you, because I'm half your size. But if you were in my place, Pabul, would *you* sit down and eat with your father's enemy?"

Pabul cocked his head, then beckoned with a lazy hand. "Come here," he said.

Akma felt the threat receding as Pabul calmly awaited his approach. But the moment Akma came within reach, Pabul's once-lazy hand snaked out and took him by the throat and dragged him down to the ground, choking. Struggling for breath, Akma found himself staring into the hooded eyes of his enemy. "Why don't I kill you now, and toss your body at your father's feet?" said Pabul mildly. "Or maybe just toss little *bits* of your body. Just one little bit each day. A toe here, a finger there, a nose, an ear, and then chunks of leg and arm. He could build you back together and when he got all the parts, everybody'd be happy again, right?"

Akma was almost sick with fear, believing Pabul perfectly capable of such a monstrous act. Thinking of the grief that his parents would feel when they saw his bloody body parts took his mind off the great hand that still gripped his throat, loosely enough now that he could breathe.

Udad laughed. "Akmaro's supposed to be so thick with the Keeper of Earth, maybe he can get the old invisible dreamsender to work a miracle and turn all those body parts back into a real boy. Other gods do miracles all the time, why not the Keeper?"

Pabul didn't even look up when Udad spoke. It was as if his brother didn't exist.

"Aren't you going to plead for your life?" asked Pabul softly. "Or at least for your toes?"

"Get him to plead for his little waterspout," suggested Muwu.

Akma didn't answer. He kept thinking of how his parents would grieve—how they must even now be filled with terror for him, wondering where this boy had led him. Mother had tried to warn him, sending Luet. But Didul had been so beautiful, and then so friendly and charming and . . . and now the price of it was this hand at his throat. Well, Akma would bear it in silence as long as he could. Even the king finally screamed when they tortured him, but Akma would last as long as he could.

"I think you need to accept my brother's invitation now," said Pabul "Eat."

"Not with you," whispered Akma.

"He's a stupid one," said Pabul. "We'll have to help him. Bring me food, boys. Lots of food. He's very, very hungry."

In moments, Pabul had forced open his mouth and the others were jamming food into it, far faster than Akma could chew it or swallow it. When they saw that he was breathing through his nose, they began to jam crumbs into his nostrils, so that he had to gasp for breath and then choked on the crumbs that got down his windpipe. Pabul let go of his throat and jaw at last, but only because, coughing, Akma was now so helpless that they could do whatever they wanted to him, which involved tearing open his clothing and smearing fruit and crumbs all over his body.

Finally the ordeal was over. Pabul delegated Didul, and Didul in turn assigned his older brother Udad to take the ungrateful, traitorous, and ill-mannered Akma back to his work. Udad seized Akma's wrists and yanked so harshly that Akma couldn't walk, but ended up being dragged stumbling over the grassy ground to the top of the hill. Udad then threw him down the hill, and Akma tumbled head over heels as Udad's laughter echoed behind him.

The taskmaster refused to let any of the humans stop their work to help him. Shamed and hurt and humiliated and furious, Akma rose to his feet and tried to clean off the worst of the food mess, at least from his nostrils and around his eyes.

"Get to work," demanded the taskmaster.

Udad shouted from the top of the hill. "Next time maybe we'll bring your sister along for a meal!"

The threat made Akma's skin crawl, but he showed no sign of having heard. That was the only resistance left to him, stubborn silence, just like the adults.

Akma took his place and worked the rest of the daylight hours. It wasn't until the sky was darkening and the taskmaster finally let them go that he was finally able to go to his mother and father to tell them what happened.

They spoke in the darkness, their voices mere whispers, for the diggers patrolled the village at night, listening to hear any kind of meeting or plot—or even prayer to the Keeper of Earth, for Pabulog had declared that it was treason, punishable by death, since any prayer by a follower of the renegade priest Akmaro was an affront to all the gods. So as Mother scrubbed the dried-on fruit from his body, weeping softly, Akma told Father all that was said and all that was done.

"So that's how Nuak died," said Father. "He was once a good king. But he was never a good man. And when I served him, I wasn't a good man either."

"You were never really one of them," said Mother.

Akma wanted to ask his father if everything else Pabulog's sons said was true, too, but he dared not, for he wouldn't know what to do with the answer. If they were right, then his father was an oathbreaker and so how could Akma trust anything he said?

"You can't leave Akma like this," said Mother softly. "Don't you know how far they've torn him from you?"

"I think Akma is old enough to know you can't believe a liar."

"But they told him *you* were a liar, Kmaro," she said. "So how can he believe *you?*"

It amazed Akma how his mother could see things in his mind that even he himself had barely grasped. Yet he also knew it was shameful to doubt your own father, and he shuddered at the look on his father's face.

"So they did steal your heart from me, is that it, Kmadis?" He called him *dis,* which meant beloved child; not *ha,* which meant honored heir, the name he used when he was especially proud of Akma. Kmaha—that was the name he wanted to hear from his father's lips, and it remained unspoken. Ha-Akma. Honor, not pity.

"He stood against them," Mother reminded him. "And suffered for it, and he was brave."

"But they sowed the seed of doubt in your heart, didn't they, Kmadis?"

Akma couldn't help it. It was too much for him. He cried at last.

"Set his mind at rest, Kmaro," said Mother.

"And how will I do that, Chebeya?" asked Father. "I never broke my oath to the king, but when they drove me out and tried to have me killed, then yes, I realized that Binaro was right, the only reason to keep the common people from learning to read and write and speak the ancient language was to preserve the priests' monopoly on power. If everyone could read the calendar, if everyone could read the ancient records and the laws for themselves, then why would they need to submit to the power of the priests? So I broke the covenant and taught reading and writing to everyone who came to me. I revealed the calendar to them. But it isn't evil to break an evil covenant." Father turned to Mother. "He isn't understanding this, Chebeya."

"Sh," she said.

They fell silent, only the sound of their breathing filling their hut. They could hear the pattering feet of a digger running through the village.

"What do you suppose his errand is?" Mother whispered.

Father pressed a finger to her lips. "Sleep," he said softly. "All of us, sleep now."

Mother lay down on the mat beside Luet, who had long since dropped off to sleep. Father lay down beside Mother and Akma settled in on the other side of him. But he didn't want Father's arm cast over him. He wanted to sleep alone, to absorb his shame. The worst of his humiliations wasn't the gagging and choking, it wasn't the smearing with fruit, it wasn't tumbling down the hill, it wasn't facing all the people in tattered clothing, covered with filth. The worst humiliation was that his father was an oathbreaker, and that he had had to learn it from Pabulog's sons.

Everyone knew that an oathbreaker was the worst kind of person. He would say one thing, but no one could count on him to do it. So you could do nothing with him. You could never trust him when you weren't there to watch. Hadn't Mother and Father taught him from earliest infancy that when he said he would do a thing, he had to do it, or he had no honor and could not be trusted?

Akma tried to think about what Father said, that to break an evil covenant was good. But if it was an evil oath, why would you swear to it in the first place? Akma didn't understand. Was Father evil once, when he took the evil oath, and then he stopped being evil? How did someone stop being evil once he started? And who decided what evil was, anyway?

That soldier Didul told him about—Teonig?—he had the right idea. You kill your enemy. You don't sneak around behind his back, breaking promises. None of the children would ever tolerate a sneak. If you had a quarrel, you stood up and yelled at each other, or wrestled in order to bend the other to your will. You could argue with a friend that way, and still be a friend. But to go behind his back, then you weren't a friend at all. You were a traitor.

No wonder Pabulog was angry at Father. That's what brought all this suffering down on us. Father was a sneak, hiding in the wilderness and breaking promises.

Akma started to cry. These were terrible thoughts, and he hated them. Father was good and kind, and all the people loved him. How could he be an evil sneak? Everything the sons of Pabulog said had to be lies, *had* to be. *They* were the evil ones, *they* were the ones who had tormented him and humiliated him. *They* were the liars.

Except that Father admitted that what they said was true. How could bad people tell the truth, and good people break oaths? The thought still spun crazily in Akma's head when he finally drifted off to sleep.

2

True Dreams

Mon climbed to the roof of the king's house to watch the setting of the dry sun, as it funneled down between the mountains at the northern end of the valley. Bego, the royal librarian, told him once that when the humans first arrived on Earth, they believed that the sun set in the west and rose in the east. "This is because they came from a place with few mountains," said Bego. "So they couldn't tell north from west."

"Or up from down?" Aronha had asked snidely. "Were humans completely stupid before they had angels to teach them?"

Well, that was Aronha, always resentful of Bego's great learning. Why shouldn't Bego be proud of being a skyman, of the wisdom the sky people had accumulated? All through their hours at school, Aronha was always pointing out that the humans had brought this or that bit of wisdom to the sky people. Why, to hear Aronha go on about it, you'd think the sky people would still be sleeping upside down in the trees if it weren't for the humans!

As for Mon, he never ceased envying the wings of the sky people. Even old Bego, who was so stout he could hardly glide down from an upper story to the ground—Mon yearned for even those old leathery wings. His greatest disappointment of childhood was when he learned that humans never grew up to be angels, that if wings weren't there, furry and useless, pressed against your body when you were born, they would never grow later. You would be cursed forever with naked useless arms.

At nine years old, all Mon could do was climb to the roof at sunset and watch the young sky people—the ones his own age or even younger, but so much more free—as they frolicked over the trees by the river, over the fields, over the roofs of the houses, soaring, dipping, rising, madly tussling in the air and dropping like stones until perilously near the earth, then spreading their wings and swooping out of the fall, hurtling down the streets between the houses like arrows as earthbound humans raised their fists and hollered about young hooligans being a menace to hardworking people just minding their own business. Oh, that I were an angel! cried Mon within his heart. Oh, that I could fly and look down on trees and mountains, rivers and fields! Oh, that I could spy out my father's enemies from far away and fly to him to give warning!

But he would never fly. He would only sit on the roof and brood while others danced in the air.

"You know, it could be worse."

He turned and grimaced at his sister. Edhadeya was the only one he had ever told about his yearning for wings. To her credit, she had never told anyone else; but when they were alone together, she teased him mercilessly.

"There are those who envy you, Mon. The king's son, tall and strong, a mighty warrior is what they say you'll be."

"Nobody knows from the height of the boy how tall the man will be," said Mon. "And I'm the king's *second* son. Anybody who envies me is a fool."

"It could be worse," said Edhadeya.

"So you said."

"You could be the king's *daughter*." There was a note of wistfulness in Edhadeya's voice.

"Oh, well, if you have to be a girl at *all*, you might as well be the daughter of the queen," said Mon.

"Our mother is dead, you might remember. The queen today is Dudagu poopwad, and don't you dare forget it for a moment." The childish term *poopwad* was translated as the much harsher *dermo* in the ancient language of the kings, so that the children got a great deal of pleasure from calling their stepmother Dudagu Dermo.

"Oh, that doesn't mean anything," said Mon, "except that poor little Khimin is hopelessly ugly compared to all the rest of Father's children." The five-year-old was Dudagu's eldest and, so far, only child, and though she was constantly wangling to have him named Ha-Khimin in place of Ha-Aron, there was no chance that either Father or the people would stand for replacing Aronha. Mon's and Edhadeya's older brother was twelve years old and already had enough of his manheight for people to see he would be a mighty soldier in battle. And he was a natural leader, everyone saw it. Even now, if there was a call to war there was no doubt that Father would put a company of soldiers under Aronha's command, and those soldiers would proudly serve under the boy who would be king. Mon saw the way others looked at his brother, heard how they spoke of him, and he burned inside. Why did Father continue having sons after Mother gave him the perfect one first?

The problem was that it was impossible to hate Aronha. The very qualities that made him such a good leader at age twelve also made his brothers and sister love him, too. He never bullied. He rarely teased. He always helped and encouraged them. He was patient with Mon's moodiness and Edhadeya's temper and Ominer's snottiness. He was even kind to Khimin, even though he had to be aware of Dudagu's schemes to put her son in Aronha's place. The result, of course, was that Khimin worshipped Aronha. Edhadeya speculated once that perhaps that was Aronha's plan—to make all his siblings love him desperately so they wouldn't be plotting against him. "Then the moment he succeeds to the throne—snip, snap, our throats are cut or our necks are broken."

Edhadeya only said that because she had been reading family history. It wasn't always nice. In fact, the first nice king in many generations had been Father's grandfather, the first Motiak, the one who left the land of Nafai to join with the people of Darakemba. The earlier ones were all bloody-handed tyrants. But maybe that was how it had to be back then, when the Nafai lived in constant warfare. For their survival they couldn't afford to let there be any disputed successions, any civil wars. So new kings more than once put their siblings to death, along with nieces and nephews and, once, one of them killed his own mother because . . . well, it was impossible to guess why those ancient people did all those terrible things. But old Bego loved telling those stories, and he always ended them with some reference to the fact that the sky people never did such things when they ruled themselves. "The coming of humans was the beginning of evil among the sky people," he said once.

To which Aronha had replied, "Ah, so you called the earth people *devils* as a little jest? Teasing them, I suppose?"

Bego, as always, took Aronha's impertinence calmly. "We didn't let the earth people dwell among us, and set them up as our kings. So their evil could never infect us. It remained outside us, because sky people and devils never dwelt together."

If we had never dwelt together, thought Mon, perhaps I wouldn't spend my days wishing I could fly. Perhaps I would be content to walk along the surface of the earth like a lizard or a snake.

"Don't get so serious about it," said Edhadeya. "Aronha won't cut anybody's throat."

"I know," said Mon. "I know you were just teasing."

Edhadeya sat beside him. "Mon, do you believe those old stories about our ancestors? About Nafai and Luet? How they could talk to the Oversoul? How Hushidh could look at people and see how they connected together?"

Mon shrugged. "Maybe it's true."

"Issib and his flying chair, and how he could sometimes fly, too, as long as he was in the land of Pristan."

"I wish it were true."

"And the magic ball, that you could hold in your hands and ask it questions and it would answer you."

Edhadeya was clearly caught up in her own reverie. Mon didn't look at her, just watched the last of the sun disappear above the distant river. The sparkling of the river also ended when the sun was gone.

"Mon, do you think Father has that ball? The Index?"

"I don't know," said Mon.

"Do you think when Aronha turns thirteen and he gets brought into the secrets, Father will show him the Index? And maybe Issib's chair?"

"Where would he hide something like *that?*"

Edhadeya shook her head. "I don't know. I'm just wondering why, if they had those wonderful things, we don't have them anymore."

"Maybe we do."

"Do you think?" Edhadeya suddenly grew animated. "Mon, do you think that sometimes dreams are true? Because I keep dreaming the same dream. Every night, sometimes twice a night, three times. It feels so real, not like my other dreams. But I'm not a priest or anything. They don't talk to women anyway. If Mother were alive I could ask her, but I'm not going to Dudagu Dermo."

"I know less than anybody," said Mon.

"I know," said Edhadeya.

"Thanks."

"You *know* less, so you listen more."

Mon blushed.

"Can I tell you my dream?"

He nodded.

"I saw a little boy. Ominer's age. And he had a sister the same age as Khimin."

"You find out people's *ages* in your dreams?" asked Mon.

"Hush, woodenhead. They were working in the fields. And they were being beaten. Their parents and all the other people. Starved and beaten. They were so *hungry.* And the people who were whipping them were diggers. Earth people, I mean."

Mon thought about this. "Father would never let diggers rule over us."

"But it wasn't *us,* don't you see? They were so real. I saw the boy getting beaten once. But not by diggers, it was by human boys who ruled over the diggers."

"Elemaki," murmured Mon. The evil humans who had joined with the diggers and lived in their dank caves and ate the sky people they kidnapped and murdered.

"The boys were bigger than him. He was hungry and so they tormented him by shoving more food than he could swallow into his mouth until he choked and gagged, and then they rubbed fruit and crumbs all over him and rolled him in the mud and grass so nobody could eat it. It was horrible, and he was so brave and never cried out against them, he just took it with such dignity and I *cried* for him."

"In the dream?"

"No, when I woke up. I wake up crying. I wake up saying, 'We've got to help them. We've got to find them and bring them home.' "

"We?"

"Father, I suppose. Us. The Nafari. Because I think those people are Nafari."

"So why don't they send sky people to find us and ask us for help? That's what people do, when the Elemaki are attacking them."

Edhadeya thought about this. "You know something, Mon? There wasn't a single angel among them."

Mon turned to her then. "No sky people at all?"

"Maybe the diggers killed them all."

"Don't you remember?" he asked. "The people who left back in the days of Father's grandfather? The ones who hated Darakemba and wanted to go back and possess the land of Nafai again?"

"Zef. . . ."

"Zenif," said Mon. "They said it was wrong for humans and sky people to live together. They didn't take a single angel with them. It's them. They're the ones you dreamed of."

"But they were all killed."

"We don't know that. We just know that we never heard from them again." Mon nodded. "They must still be alive."

"So you think it's a real dream?" asked Edhadeya. "Like the ones Luet had?"

Mon shrugged. Something bothered him. "Your dream," he said. "I don't think it's *exactly* about the Zenifi. I mean . . . it just doesn't feel complete. I think it's someone else."

"Well, how can you know that?" she said. "You're the one who thought it *was* the Zenifi."

"And it felt right when I said it. But now . . . now there's just something wrong with it. But you've got to tell Father."

"You tell him," she said. "You'll see him at dinner."

"And you when he comes to say goodnight."

Edhadeya grimaced. "Dudagu Dermo is always there. I never see Father alone."

Mon blushed. "That isn't right of Father."

"Yes, well, you're the one who always knows what's right." She punched him in the arm.

"I'll tell him your dream at dinner."

"Tell him it was *your* dream."

Mon shook his head. "I don't lie."

"He won't listen if he thinks it's a woman's dream. All the other men at dinner will laugh."

"I won't tell him whose dream it is until I'm done. How's that?"

"Tell him this, too. In the last few dreams, the boy and his sister and his mother and father, they lie there in silence looking at me, saying nothing, just lie there in the darkness and without their saying a word I know they're pleading with me to come and save them."

"*You?*"

"Well, me in the dream. I don't think that the *real* people—if there *are* any real people—would be sitting there hoping for a ten-year-old girl to come and deliver them."

"I wonder if Father will let Aronha go."

"Do you think he'll really send somebody?"

Mon shrugged. "It's dark. It's time for dinner soon. Listen."

From the trees near the river, from the high, narrow houses of the sky people, the evening song arose, a few voices at first, then joined by more and more. Their high, lilting melodies intertwined, played with each other, madly inventing, challenging, resolving dissonance and then subverting expected harmonies, a haunting sound that recalled an earlier time when life for the sky people was a short span of years that had to be enjoyed in the moment, for death was always near. The children stopped their playing and began drifting downward from the sky, going home to supper, to their singing mothers and fathers, to homes filled with music as once the thatched shelters of the angels had filled with song in the high reaches of the trees.

Tears came unbidden to Mon's eyes. This was why he spent the moment of evening song alone, for he would be teased about the tears if others saw them. Not Edhadeya, though.

Edhadeya kissed Mon's cheek. "Thank you for believing me, Mon. Sometimes I think I might as well be a stump, for all that anybody listens to me."

Mon blushed again. When he turned around, she was already going down the ladder to the ground. He should go with her, of course, but now the human voices were beginning to join in the song, and so he could not go. From the windows of the great houses, the human servants and, in the streets, the fieldworkers and the great men of the city sang, each voice with as much right to be heard in the evening song as any other. In some cities, human kings decreed that their human subjects must sing a certain song, usually with words that spoke of patriotism or dutiful worship of the king or the official gods. But in Darakemba the old ways of the Nafari were kept, and the humans made up their own melodies as freely as the angels did. The voices of the middle people were lower, slower, less deft in making rapid changes. But they did their best, and the sky people accepted their song and played with it, danced around it, decorated and subverted and fulfilled it, so that middle people and sky people together were a choir in a continuous astonishing cantata with ten thousand composers and no soloists.

Mon raised his own voice, high and sweet—so high that he did not have to sing among the low human voices, he could take a place in the bottom reaches of the sky people's song. From the street, a woman of the fields looked up at him and smiled. Mon answered her, not with a smile, but with a rapid run, his best. And when she laughed and nodded and walked on, he felt good. Then he raised his eyes and saw, on the roof of a house two streets over, two young sky people who had perched there for a moment on their way home. They watched him, and Mon defiantly sang louder, though he knew his voice, high and quick as it was, was no match for the singing of the sky people. Still, they heard him, they sang with him for a moment, and then they raised their left wings in salute to him. They must be twins, thought Mon, self and otherself, yet they took a moment to open their duet to include me. He raised his own left hand in answer, and they dropped down from the roof into the courtyard of their own house.

Mon got up and, still singing, walked to the ladder. If he were an angel, he wouldn't have to use a ladder to climb down from the roof of the king's house. He could swoop down and come to rest before the door, and when dinner was over he could fly up into the night sky and go hunting by moonlight.

His bare feet slapped against the rungs as he skimmed down the ladder. Keeper of Earth, why did you make me human? He sang as he walked through the courtyard of the king's house, heading for the raucous brotherhood of the king's table, but there was pain and loneliness in his song.

Shedemei woke up in her chamber in the starship *Basilica*, and saw at once that it wasn't one of her scheduled wakings. The calendar was all wrong, and to confirm it, she heard at once the voice of the Oversoul in her mind. "The Keeper is sending dreams again."

She felt a thrill of excitement run through her. For all these centuries, dipping into and out of life, kept young by the cloak of the starmaster but long since old and weary in her heart, she had waited to see what the Keeper's next move would be. She brought us here, thought Shedemei, brought us here and kept us alive and sent us dreams, and then suddenly she fell silent and we were left to our own devices for so long.

"It was an old man first, among the Zenifi," said the Oversoul. Shedemei padded naked along the corridors of the ship and then up the central shaft to the library. "They murdered him. But a priest named Akmaro believed him. I think he also had some dreams, but I'm not sure. With the old man dead and the ex-priest living in slavery, I wouldn't have woken you. But then the daughter of Motiak dreamed. Like Luet. I haven't seen a dreamer like this since Luet."

"What's her name? She was just a newborn when I. . . ."

"Edhadeya. The women call her Deya. They know she's something but the men don't listen, of course."

"I really don't like the way things have developed between men and women among the Nafari, you know. My great-great-granddaughters shouldn't have to put up with such nonsense."

"I've seen worse," said the Oversoul.

"I have no doubt of *that*. But, forgive me for asking: So what?"

"It will change," the Oversoul said. "It always does."

"How old is she now? Deya?"

"Ten."

"I sleep ten years and I still don't feel rested." She sat down at one of the library computers. "All right, show me what I need to see."

The Oversoul showed her Edhadeya's dream and told her about Mon and his truthsense.

"Well," said Shedemei, "the powers of the parents are undiminished in the children."

"Shedemei, does any of this make sense to you?"

Shedemei almost laughed aloud. "Do you hear yourself, my friend? You are the program that posed as a god back on the planet Harmony.

You planned your plans, you plotted your plots, and you never asked humans for advice. Instead you roped us in and dragged us to Earth transformed our lives forever and now you ask *me* if any of this makes sense? What happened to the master plan?"

"My plan was simple," said the Oversoul. "Get back to Earth and ask the Keeper what I should do about the weakening power of the Oversoul of Harmony. I fulfilled that plan as far as I could. Here I am."

"And here *I* am."

"Don't you see, Shedemei? Your being here wasn't *my* plan. I needed human help to assemble one workable starship, but I didn't need to take any humans with me. I brought you because the Keeper of Earth was somehow sending you dreams—and sending them faster than light, I might add. The Keeper seemed to want you humans here. So I brought you. And I came, expecting to find technological marvels waiting for me. Machines that could repair me, replenish me, send me back to Harmony able to restore the power of the Oversoul. Instead I wait here, I've waited nearly five hundred years—"

"As have I," added Shedemei.

"You've slept through most of them," said the Oversoul. "And you don't have responsibility for a planet a hundred lightyears distant where technology is beginning to blossom and devastating wars are only a few generations away. I don't have time for this. Except that if the Keeper thinks I have time for it, I probably do. Why doesn't the Keeper talk to me? When no one was hearing anything for all these years, I could be patient. But now humans are dreaming again, the Keeper is on the move again, and yet still it says nothing to me."

"And you ask *me?*" said Shedemei. "You're the one who should have memories dating back to the time when you were created. The Keeper sent you, right? Where was it then? *What* was it then?"

"I don't know." If a computer could shrug, Shedemei imagined the Oversoul would do it now. "Do you think I haven't searched my memory? Before your husband died, he helped me search, and we found nothing. I remember the Keeper always being present, I remember knowing that certain vital instructions had been programmed into me by the Keeper—but as to who or what the Keeper is or was or even might have been, I know as little as you."

"Fascinating," said Shedemei. "Let's see if we can think of a way to get the Keeper to talk to you. Or at least to show her hand."

Mon was seated, as usual, down at the stewards' end of the table. His father told him that the king's second son was placed there in order to show respect for the record-keepers and message-bearers and treasurers and provisioners, for, as Father said, "If it weren't for them, there'd be no kingdom for the soldiers to protect."

When Father said that, Mon had answered, in his most neutral voice, "But if you really want to show your respect for them, you'd place Ha-Aron among them."

To which Father mildly replied, "If it weren't for the army, all the stewards would be dead."

So Mon, the second son, was all that the second rank of leaders in the kingdom merited; the first son was the honor of the first rank, the military men, the people who really mattered.

And that was how the business of dinner was conducted, too. The King's Supper had begun many generations ago as a council of war—that was when women began to be excluded. In those days it was only once a week that the council ate together, but for generations now it had been every night, and human men of wealth and standing imitated the king in their own homes, dining separately from their wives and daughters. It wasn't that way among the sky people, though. Even those who shared the king's table went home and sat with their wives and children for another meal.

Which was why, sitting at Mon's left hand, the chief clerk, the old angel named bGo, was barely picking at his food. It was well known that bGo's wife became quite miffed if he showed no appetite at *her* table, and Father had always refused to be offended that bGo apparently feared his wife more than he feared the king. bGo was senior among the clerks, though as head of the census he was certainly not as powerful as the treasuremaster and the provisioner. He was also a surly conversationalist and Mon hated having to sit with him.

Beyond bGo, though, his otherself, Bego, was far more talkative—and had a much sturdier appetite, mostly because he had never married. Bego, the recordkeeper, was only a minute and a half less senior than bGo, but one would hardly imagine they were the same age, Bego had so much energy, so much vigor, so much . . . so much anger, Mon thought sometimes. Mon loved school whenever Bego was their tutor, but he sometimes wondered if Father really knew how much rage seethed under the surface of his recordkeeper. Not disloyalty—Mon would report *that* at once. Just a sort of general anger at life. Aronha said it was because he had never once mated with a female in his life, but then Aronha had sex on the brain these days and thought that lust explained everything—which, in the case of Aronha and all his friends, was no doubt true. Mon didn't know why Bego was so angry. He just knew that it put a delicious skeptical edge on all of Bego's lessons. And even on his eating. A sort of savagery in the way he lifted the panbread rolled up with bean paste to his lips and bit down on it. The way he ground the food in his jaws when he chewed, slowly, methodically, glaring out at the rest of the court.

On Mon's right, the treasuremaster and the provisioner were caught up in their own business conversation—quietly, of course, so as not to distract from the *real* meeting going on at the king's end of the table, where the soldiers were regaling each other with anecdotes from recent raids and skirmishes. Being adult humans, the treasuremaster and provisioner were much taller than Mon and generally ignored him after the initial courtesies. Mon was more the height of the sky people to his left, and besides, he knew Bego better, and so when he talked at all, it was to them.

"I have something I want to tell Father," said Mon to Bego.

Bego chewed twice more and swallowed, fixing Mon with his weary gaze all the while. "Then tell him," he said.

"Exactly," murmured bGo.

"It's a dream," said Mon.

"Then tell your mother," said Bego. "Middle women still pay attention to such things."

"Right," murmured bGo.

"But it's a true dream," said Mon.

bGo sat up straight. "And how would you know that."

Mon shrugged. "I know it."

bGo turned to Bego, who turned to him. They gazed at each other, as if some silent communication were passing between them. Then Bego turned back to Mon. "Be careful about making claims like that."

"I am," said Mon. "Only when I'm sure. Only when it matters."

That was something Bego had taught them in school, about making judgments. "Whenever you can get away with making no decision at all, then that's what you should do. Make decisions only when you're sure, and only when it matters." Bego nodded now, to hear Mon repeat his precept back to him.

"If he believes me, then it's a matter for the war council," said Mon.

Bego studied him. bGo did, too, for a moment, but then rolled his eyes and slumped back in his chair. "I feel an embarrassing scene coming on," he murmured.

"Embarrassing only if the prince is a fool," said Bego. "Are you?"

"No," said Mon. "Not about this, anyway." Even as he said it, though, Mon wondered if in fact he *was* a fool. After all, it was Edhadeya's dream, not his own. And there *was* something about his interpretation of it that made him uneasy. Yet one thing was certain: It was a true dream, and it meant that somewhere humans—Nafari humans—lived in painful bondage under the whips of Elemaki diggers.

Bego waited for another moment, as if to be sure that Mon wasn't going to back down. Then he raised his left wing. "Father Motiak," he said loudly.

His abrasive voice cut through the noisy conversation at the military end of the table. Monush, for many years the mightiest warrior in the kingdom, the man for whom Mon had been named, was interrupted in the middle of a story. Mon winced. Couldn't Bego have waited for a natural lull in the conversation?

Father's normally benign expression did not change. "Bego, the memory of my people, what do you have to say during the war council?" His words held a bit of menace, but his voice was calm and kind, as always.

"While the soldiers are still at table," said Bego, "one of the worthies of your kingdom has information that, if you choose to heed it, will be a matter for a council of war."

"And who is this worthy? What is his information?" asked Father.

"He sits beside my otherself," said Bego, "and he can give you his information for himself."

All eyes turned to Mon, and for a moment he wanted to turn and flee from the room. Had Edhadeya realized how awful this moment would be, when she asked him to do this? But Mon knew he could not shrink from this now—to back down would humiliate Bego and shame himself. Even if his message was disbelieved, he had to give it—and boldly, too.

Mon rose to his feet, and, as he had seen his father do before speaking, he looked each of the leading men of the kingdom in the eyes. In their faces he saw surprise, amusement, deliberate patience. Last of all he looked at Aronha, and to his relief, he saw that Aronha looked serious and interested, not teasing or embarrassed. Aronha, thank you for giving me respect.

"My information comes from a true dream," Mon said at last.

There was a murmur around the table. Who had dared to claim a true dream in many generations? And at the king's table?

"How do you know it's a true dream?" asked Father.

It was something Mon had never been able to explain to anyone or even to himself. He didn't try now. "It's a true dream," he said.

Again there was a whisper around the table, and while some of the impatient faces changed to amusement, some that had been amused now looked serious.

"At least they're paying attention," murmured bGo.

Father spoke again, a hint of consternation in his voice. "Tell us the dream, then, and why it's a matter for the council of war."

"The same dream over and over for many nights," said Mon. He was careful to give no hint of who the dreamer was. He knew they would assume that it was him, but no one would be able to call him a liar. "A little boy and his sister, the ages of Ominer and Khimin. They were working in the fields, as slaves, faint with hunger, and the taskmasters who whipped them at their work were earth people."

He had their attention now, all of them. Diggers with humans as slaves—it made all of them angry, though they all knew that it must happen from time to time.

"One time in the dream the boy was beaten by human boys. Humans who ruled over the diggers. The boy was brave and never cried out as they . . . . humiliated him. He was worthy."

The soldiers all nodded. They understood what he was saying.

"At night the boy and his sister and his father and mother lay in silence. I think . . . I think they were forbidden to speak aloud. But they asked for help. They asked for someone to come and deliver them from bondage."

Mon paused for a moment, and into the silence came Monush's voice. "I have no doubt that this dream is true enough, because we know that many humans and angels are kept as slaves among the Elemaki. But what can we do? It takes all our strength to keep our own people free."

"But Monush," said Mon, "these *are* our people."

Now the whispers were filled with excitement and outrage.

"Let me hear my son speak," said Father. The whispers ceased.

Mon blushed. Father had admitted him to be his son, yes, that was good; but he had not used the formal locution, "Let me hear my counselor," which would have meant that he absolutely accepted what Mon was saying. He was still on trial here. Thanks Edhadeya. This could shame me for my whole life, if it goes badly. I would always be known as the second son who spoke foolishness out of turn in a war council.

"They have no sky people among them," said Mon. "Who has ever heard of such a kingdom? They are the Zenifi, and they call to us for help."

Husu, the angel who served the king as his chief spy, leading hundreds of strong, brave skypeople who kept constant watch on the borders of the kingdom, raised his right wing, and Mon nodded to give him the king's ear. He had seen this done before at council, but since he had never had the king's ear himself, this was the first time he had ever been able to take part in the niceties of formal discussion.

"Even if the dream is true and the Zenifi are calling out to us in dreams," said Husu, "what claim do they have upon us? They rejected the decision of the first King Motiak and refused to live in a place where sky people outnumbered middle people five to one. They left Darakemba of their own free will, to return to the land of Nafai. We thought they must have been destroyed. If we learn now that they are alive, we're glad, but it means nothing more than that to us. If we learn now that they're in bondage, we're sad, but again, it means nothing more than that."

When his speech was finished, Mon looked to the king for permission to speak again.

"How do you know they're the Zenifi?" asked Father.

Again, Mon could say nothing more than to repeat what he knew was true. Only this was exactly the point that he wasn't sure of. They were the Zenifi, but they were *not* the Zenifi. Or something. Something else. They *used* to be Zenifi, was that it? Or are they simply a *part* of the Zenifi?

"They are Zenifi," said Mon, and as he said it he knew that it was right, or right enough. They may not be *the* Zenifi, the whole people; but they are Zenifi, even if somewhere else there might be others.

But Mon's answer gave Father little to go on. "A dream?" he said. "The first king of the Nafari had true dreams."

"As did his wife," said Bego.

"The great queen Luet," said Father, nodding. "Bego is wise to remind us of history. Both were true dreamers. And there were other true dreamers among them. And among the sky people, and among the earth people too, in those days. But that was the age of heroes."

Mon wanted to insist: It *is* a true dream. But he had seen at council before how Father resisted when men tried to press their case by saying the same thing again and again. If they had new evidence, fine, let them speak and Father would hear; but if they were merely insisting on the same old story, Father merely believed them less and less the more they pushed. So Mon held his tongue and merely continued to look his father in the eye, unabashed.

He heard bGo's soft murmur as he spoke to his otherself: "I know what the gossips will be chatting about for the next week."

"The boy has courage," Bego answered softly.

"So do you," said bGo.

In the silence, Aronha stood from the table, but instead of asking Mon for the king's ear, he walked around behind the chairs to stand behind his father. It was a privilege that only the king's heir had, to speak to the king privately in front of his other counselors without giving offense—for it was not presumption for the heir to display a special privacy with the king.

Father listened to Aronha, then nodded. "This can be said aloud," he said, granting permission.

Aronha returned to his seat. "I know my brother," he said. "He does not lie."

"Of course not," said Monush, and Husu echoed him.

"More than that," said Aronha. "Mon never claims to know what he doesn't know. When he's unsure, he says so. And when he's sure, he's always right."

Mon felt a thrill run through him, to hear such words from his brother's mouth. Aronha wasn't just standing up for him—he was asserting something so outrageous that Mon was frightened for him. How could he make such a claim?

"Bego and I have noticed it," said Aronha. "Why else do you suppose Bego risked his own place at the king's table in order to introduce Mon's words? I don't think Mon realizes it himself. Most of the time he is uncertain of himself. He can be persuaded easily; he never argues. But when he truly knows a thing, he never backs down, never, no matter how much we argue. And when he digs in his heels like that, Bego and I both know well, he's never been wrong. Not once. I would stake my honor and the lives of good men on the truth of what he says today. Even though I think the dream was not his own, if he says it's a true dream and the people are the Zenifi, then I know that it's the truth as surely as if I saw old Zenif with my own eyes."

"Why do you think the dream is not his own?" asked Father, suddenly wary.

"Because he never said it was," said Aronha. "If it was, he would have said it. He didn't, so it wasn't."

"Whose dream was it?" demanded the king.

"The daughter of Toeledwa," said Mon immediately.

There was an immediate uproar at the table, partly because Mon had dared to mention the name of the dead queen at a celebratory occasion, but mostly because he had brought the counsel of a woman to the king's table.

"We would not have heard that voice here!" cried one of the old captains.

Father raised his hands and everyone fell silent. "You're right, we would not have heard that voice here. But my son believes that the message of that voice needed to be heard, and so he dared to bring it; and Ha-Aron has declared his belief in it. So now the only question before this council is: What shall we do, now that we know the Zenifi are calling to us for help?"

The discussion immediately passed beyond any realm where Mon would be consulted, and he sat down, listening. He scarcely trusted himself to look at anyone, for fear he would break discipline and show a smile of such relief, such gratification that everyone would know that he was still only a child, the second son.

Husu opposed sending any sky people to risk their lives rescuing the Zenifi; in vain did Monush argue that the first generation, the one that had rejected all human association with angels, was surely dead by now. As they discussed the issue, with other counselors chiming in with their own points, Mon risked a glance at his brother. To his chagrin, Aronha was looking right at him, grinning. Mon ducked his head to hide his own grin, but he was happier at this moment than he had ever been before in his life.

He turned then, to glance at Bego, but it was bGo who whispered to him. "What if a hundred die, for this dream of Edhadeya's?"

The words struck Mon through the heart. He hadn't thought of that. To send an army so far into Elemaki territory, up the endless narrow canyons where ambush was possible anywhere—it was dangerous, it was foolhardy, yet the war council was arguing, not about whether to risk it, but whom to take on the raid.

"Don't ruin the boy's triumph," murmured Bego. "Nobody's making the soldiers go. He told the truth and he did it boldly. Honor to him." Bego raised his glass of mulled wine.

Mon knew to raise his own glass of twice-cut wine. "It was your voice opened the door, Ro-Bego."

Bego sipped his wine, frowning. "None of your middlebeing titles for me, boy."

bGo grinned—a rare expression for him—and said, "My otherself is beside himself with pleasure; you must excuse him, it always makes him surly."

Father proposed the compromise. "Let Husu's spies guard Monush's human soldiers until they find a way past the outposts of the Elemaki. From what we understand, there's chaos among the kingdoms in the land of Nafai these days, and it may be far safer than usual to get in. Then, when Monush passes within the guarded borders, the spies hold back and wait for them to emerge again."

"How long?" asked Husu.

"Eighty days," said Monush.

"It's the wet season in high country," said Husu. "Are we to freeze or starve? What is the plan?"

"Keep five men there for ten days," said the king. "Then another five, and another, for ten days each."

Monush raised his left hand in agreement. Husu raised his left wing, but muttered nonetheless, "To bring back worthless bigots, yes, I'm sure that's worth the trouble."

Mon was surprised that Husu was allowed to speak so boldly.

"I understand the anger the sky people feel toward the Zenifi," said Father. "That's why I take no offense at the mockery in your acceptance of my proposal."

Husu bowed his head. "My king is kinder than his servant deserves."

"That's the truth," muttered bGo. "Someday Husu will go too far and the rest of us will pay for it."

The rest of "us"? He must mean the sky people as a whole, thought Mon. It was a disturbing thought, that somehow the sky people would all be held responsible for Husu's audacity. "That wouldn't be fair," said Mon.

bGo chuckled softly. "Listen to him, Bego. He says it isn't fair—as if that means it couldn't happen."

"In the secret heart of every human man," whispered Bego, "the sky people are nothing more than impertinent beasts."

"That's not true," said Mon. "You're wrong!"

Bego looked at him, bemused.

"I'm a human, aren't I?" demanded Mon. "And in *my* heart the angels are the most beautiful and glorious people."

Mon had not been shouting, but the intensity in his voice had stilled all other voices. In the sudden silence, he realized that everyone had heard him. He looked at his Father's surprised expression and blushed.

"It seems to me," said Father, "that some of the council have forgotten that only those with the king's ear can speak here."

Mon rose to his feet, hot with shame. "Forgive me, sir."

Father smiled. "I believe it was Aronha who said that when you dug in your heels, you were always right." He turned to Aronha. "Do you stand by that?"

A bit uncertain, Aronha looked his father in the eye and said, "Yes, sir."

"Then I believe it is the opinion of this council that the angels are indeed the most beautiful and glorious people." And Father raised his glass to Husu.

Husu stood, bowed, and lifted his glass in response. Both drank. Then Father looked at Monush, who laughed, stood, and lifted his glass to drink as well.

"The words of my second son have brought peace to this table," said Father. "That is always wisdom, to these ears, at least. Come, have done. The council is over and there is nothing more for us here except to eat—

and ponder how the dreams of young girls, brought by young boys, have set in motion the feet and wings of warriors."

Edhadeya waited for her father to come to her small room to talk with her as he did every night. Usually she was happy that he was coming, eager to tell him how she did in school, to show off a new word or phrase in the ancient language, to tell him of some adventure or gossip or achievement of the day. Tonight, though, she was afraid, and she wasn't sure which she feared more—that Mon had told Father of her dream, or that he hadn't. If he hadn't, then she would have to tell him now herself, and then he might pat her shoulder and tell her that the dream was strange and wonderful and then he would just ignore it, not realizing that it was a true dream.

When he came to her doorway, though, Edhadeya knew that Mon had told him. His eyes were sharp and searching. He stood in silence, his arms bracing the doorframe. Finally he nodded. "So the spirit of Luet is awake in my daughter."

She looked down at the floor, unsure whether he was angry or proud.

"And the spirit of Nafai in my second son."

Ah. So he wasn't angry.

"Don't bother explaining why you couldn't tell me this yourself," said Father. "I know why, and I'm ashamed. Luet never had to use subterfuge to get her husband's ear, nor did Chveya have to get her brother or her husband to speak for her when she had wisdom that others needed to know."

In one motion he knelt before her and took her hands in his. "I looked around the king's council tonight, as we finished our meal, thoughts of danger and war in our minds, of the Zenifi in bondage and needing to be saved, and all I could think of was—why have we forgotten what our first ancestors knew? That the Keeper of Earth cares not whether he speaks to a woman or a man?"

"What if it's not so?" she whispered.

"What, you doubt it now?" asked Father.

"I dreamed the dream, and it was true—but it was Mon who said it was the Zenifi. I didn't understand it at all till he said that."

"Keep talking to Mon when you have true dreams," said Father. "I know this: When Mon spoke, I felt a fire kindle in my heart and I thought—the words came into my mind as clearly as if someone had spoken them in my ear—I thought, *A mighty man stands here in boyshape.* And then I learned the dream was yours, and again the voice came into my mind: *The man who listens to Edhadeya will be the true steward of the Keeper of Earth.*"

"Was it—the Keeper who spoke to you?" asked Edhadeya.

"Who knows?" said Father. "Maybe it was fatherly pride. Maybe it was wishful thinking. Maybe it was the voice of the Keeper. Maybe it was the second glass of wine." He laughed. "I miss your mother," he said. "She would know better than I what to make of you."

"I'm doing my best with her," said Dudagu from the door.

Edhadeya gasped in surprise. Dudagu had a way of moving around silently so that no one knew where she might be eavesdropping.

Father rose to his feet. "But I have never charged you with my daughter's education," said Father gently. "So what in the world would you be doing your best *at*?" He grinned at Dudagu and then strode out of Edhadeya's room.

Dudagu glared at Edhadeya. "Don't think this dream business can get you anywhere, little girl," she said. Then she smiled. "What you say to him in here, I can always unsay to him on his pillow."

Edhadeya smiled her prettiest smile back at her stepmother. Then she opened her mouth and jammed her finger down her throat as if to make herself throw up. A moment later she was smiling prettily again.

Dudagu shrugged. "Four more years till I can have you married off," she said. "Believe me, I already have my women looking for someone suitable. Someone far away from here."

She glided silently away from the door and down the hall. Edhadeya threw herself back on her bed and murmured, "I would dearly love to have a true dream of Dudagu Dermo in a boating accident. If you arrange those things, dear Keeper of Earth, keep in mind that she doesn't swim, but she's very tall, so the water must be deep."

The next day all the talk was of the expedition to find the Zenifi. And the morning after that, the lofty people and the officials of the city turned out to see the soldiers march away, the spies flying their daredevil maneuvers in the sky above them. Edhadeya thought, as she watched them go, So this is what a dream can do. And then she thought, I should have more such dreams.

At once she was ashamed of herself. If I ever lie about my dreams and claim a true one when it isn't so, then may the Keeper take all my dreams away from me.

Sixteen human soldiers, with a dozen spies shadowing them from the air, set out from Darakemba. It was not an army, was not even large enough to be a serious raiding party, and so their departure caused only a momentary stir in the city. Mon watched, though, with Aronha and Edhadeya standing beside him on the roof.

"They should have let me go with them," said Aronha angrily.

"Are you that generous, that you want the kingdom to come to me?" asked Mon.

"Nobody's going to be killed," said Aronha.

Mon didn't bother to answer. He was perfectly aware that Aronha knew Father was right—there was a touch of madness to this expedition. It was a search party trying to find the location of a dream. Father took only volunteers, and it was only with great reluctance that he let the great soldier Monush lead them. There was no chance that he would send his heir. "They'd spend all their time worrying about your safety instead of the mission I'm sending them on," Father had said. "Don't worry, Aronha. You'll have your first sight of bloody battle far too soon, I'm sure. If I sent you out this time, though, your mother would rise up from the grave to scold me." Mon had felt a thrill of fear when he heard this, until he saw that everyone else was taking it as a joke.

Everyone but Aronha, of course, who really was furious at not being included. "My sister can have the dream, my brother can tell you the dream—and what is for me? Tell me that, Father!"

"Why, Aronha, I have given you exactly as much involvement as I have given myself—to stand and watch them go."

Well, now they were doing just that, standing and watching them go. Normally Aronha would have seen the soldiers off from the steps of the king's house, but he claimed it would be too humiliating to stand beside the king when he had been declared too useless to go. Father didn't argue with him, just let him go to the roof, and now here he stood, furious even though he had already admitted to Mon that if he were in Father's place he'd make the same decision. "Just because Father's right doesn't mean I have to be happy about it."

Edhadeya laughed. "By the Cottonmouth, Aronha, that's when Father makes us the maddest!"

"Don't swear by the Legless One," said Aronha sharply.

"Father says it's just a dangerous snake and not a real god so why not?" said Edhadeya defiantly.

"You're not superstitious now, are you, Aronha?" asked Mon.

"Father says to have respect for the beliefs of others, and you know half the digger servants still hold the Legless One sacred," said Aronha.

"Yes," said Edhadeya, "and they're always swearing by him."

"They don't say his name outright," said Aronha.

"But Aronha, it's just a snake." Edhadeya wagged her head back and forth like a maize tassel. In spite of himself, Aronha laughed. Then his face got serious again, and he looked back at the sixteen soldiers, jogging out among the fields in single file, heading up the river to the southern border.

"Will they find my dream?" asked Edhadeya.

"If the Keeper sent you the dream," said Aronha, "it must mean he wants the Zenifi found."

"But that doesn't mean that anybody in Monush's party even knows how to hear the Keeper when she speaks," said Edhadeya.

Aronha glared but didn't look at her. "*He* decides whom he's going to speak to. It's not a matter of knowing how."

"*She* can only speak to people who know how to listen, which is why our ancestor Luet was so famous as the waterseer, and her sister Hushidh and her niece Chveya as ravelers. They had great power in them, and—"

"The power wasn't in *them,*" said Aronha. "It was in the Keeper. He chose them, his favorites—and I might point out that none of them was greater than Nafai himself, who had the cloak of the starmaster and commanded the heavens with his—"

"Bego says it's all silliness," said Mon.

The others fell silent.

"He does?" said Aronha, after a while.

"You've heard him say so, haven't you?" asked Mon.

"Never to me," said Aronha. "What does he say is silliness? The Keeper?"

"The idea of our heroic ancestors," said Mon. "Everybody claims to have heroic ancestors, he says. By the time enough generations have passed, they become gods. He says that's where gods come from. Gods in human shape, anyway."

"How interesting," said Aronha. "He teaches the king's son that the king's ancestors are made up?"

Only now did Mon realize that he might be causing trouble for his tutor. "No," he said. "Not in so many words. He just . . . raised the possibility."

Aronha nodded. "So you don't want me to turn him in."

"He didn't say it outright."

"Just remember this, Mon," said Aronha. "Bego might be right, and our stories of great human ancestors with extraordinary powers granted by the Keeper of Earth, those stories might all be exaggerated or even outright fantasies or whatever. But we middle people aren't the only ones who might want to revise history to fit our present needs. Don't you think a patriotic sky man might want to cast doubt on the stories of greatness among the ancestors of the middle people? Especially the ancestors of the king?"

"Bego's not a liar," said Mon. "He's a scholar."

"I didn't say he was lying," said Aronha. "He says we believe in these tales because it's so useful and satisfying to us. Maybe he doubts the same tales because the doubt is useful and satisfying to *him*."

Mon frowned. "Then how can we ever know what's true?"

"We can't," said Aronha. "That's what *I* figured out a long time ago."

"So you don't believe in *anything*?"

"I *believe* in everything that seems most true to me right now," said Aronha. "I just refuse to be surprised when some of those things I believe now turn out to be false later. It helps keep me from being upset."

Edhadeya laughed. "And where did you learn *that* idea?"

Aronha turned to her, mildly offended. "You don't think I could think it up myself?"

"No," she said.

"Monush taught me that," said Aronha. "One day when I asked him if there really was a Keeper of Earth. After all, according to the old stories, there once was a god called the Oversoul, and that turned out to be a machine inside an ancient boat."

"An ancient boat that flew through the air," said Mon. "Bego says that only the sky people fly, and that our ancestors invented that flying boat story because middle people were so jealous of the fact that sky people could fly."

"*Some* sky people can fly," said Edhadeya. "I'll bet old Bego is so old and fat and creaky he can't even get off the ground anymore."

"But he could when he was young," said Mon. "He can remember."

"And *you* can imagine," said Aronha.

Mon shook his head. "To remember is real. To imagine is nothing."

Edhadeya laughed. "That's silly, Mon. Most of the things people say they remember they only imagine anyway."

"And where did *you* learn *that*?" asked Aronha with a smirk.

Edhadeya rolled her eyes. "From Uss-Uss, and you can laugh if you want, but she's—"

"She's a glorified housemaid!" said Aronha.

"She's the only friend I had after Mother died," said Edhadeya firmly, "and she's very wise."

"She's a digger," said Mon softly.

"But *not* an Elemaku," said Edhadeya. "Her family has served the kings of the Nafari for five generations."

"As slaves," said Mon.

Aronha laughed. "Mon listens to an old angel, Edhadeya to a fat old digger slave woman, and I listen to a soldier who is known for his courage and cleverness in war, and not for his scholarship. We all choose our own teachers, don't we? I wonder if our choice of teacher shows anything about what our lives will be."

They thought about that in silence as they watched the small swarm of spies that marked the location of Monush's party as they continued their journey far up the valley of the Tsidorek.

3

Resistance

"Nafai told me something once," said Shedemei to the Oversoul.

The Oversoul, being endlessly patient, waited for her to go on.

"Back before you . . . chose him."

"I remember the time," said the Oversoul, perhaps not endlessly patient after all.

"Back when you were still trying to keep him and Issib from discovering too much about you."

"It was Issib who was the real problem, you know. He's the one who thought of opposing me."

"Yes, well, but he didn't succeed until Nafai joined him."

"It was a concern for a while."

"Yes, I imagine. Both of them, struggling as hard as they could. You had to devote all your resources to dealing with them."

"Never all. Never even close to all."

"Enough that you finally gave up."

"Took them into my confidence."

"Stopped struggling against them and enlisted them on your side. You had no choice, right?"

"I knew all along that they were valuable. I decided at that point that they were the ones I would use to assemble a working starship."

"Would you have chosen them if they hadn't been causing so much trouble for you?"

"I had already chosen their father to . . . start things moving."

"But it was Luet you wanted, wasn't it."

"Nafai was very insistent. Very ambitious. He couldn't stand not to be in the midst of whatever was going on. I decided that was useful. And I never had to choose between him and Luet, because they ended up together."

"Yes, yes, I'm sure everything worked out exactly according to plan."

"I was programmed to be infinitely adaptable, as long as I continue working toward the highest priorities. My plan changed, but its goal never did."

"All right then, that's the entire point I was trying to make." Shedemei laughed. "If I didn't know better, Lady Oversoul, I would suppose you were protecting your pride."

"I have no pride."

"I'm relieved to hear it," said Shedemei. "I discarded my own long ago."

"What was the point you were trying to make?"

"Nafai forced you to listen to him, to notice him, to take him into account."

"Nafai and Issib."

"They did it by resisting you, and doing it in such a way that you had to adapt your plans to fit their . . . what did you say? Their ambition."

"Issib was stubborn. Nafai was ambitious."

"I'm sure you have lists of adjectives appended to all our names in your files."

"Don't be snippy, Shedemei. It isn't becoming to a woman who has abandoned her pride."

"Will you *listen* to my plan?"

"Oh, not a point then, a plan."

"You still have the power to influence human beings."

"In a small area of the world, yes."

"It doesn't have to be on the other side of the planet, you know. Just there in the gornaya."

"Anywhere in the gornaya, yes, I can have some influence."

"And that technique you used back on Harmony, to keep us from developing dangerous technologies—"

"Making people temporarily stupid."

"And you can still send dreams."

"Not the powerful dreams the Keeper sends."

"Dreams, though. Clear ones."

"Much *clearer* than the Keeper's dreams," said the Oversoul.

"Well then. We have a party of Nafari soldiers headed up the valley of the Tsidorek. When they come near Lake Sidonod, the area is so thickly settled with Elemaki that they'll have to take a dangerous route high up on the mountainside. But the mountain range is ragged there. At some points the crest is very low, so the valleys connect through a narrow pass. If they can sneak through that pass, they'll come down a canyon that will lead them straight to Chelem, where Akmaro's people are held as slaves to the Elemaki."

"Slaves to Pabulog and his sons, you mean."

"So when they near that pass, the Keeper will naturally try to steer them that way."

"One would think," said the Oversoul.

"So why not make them very stupid until they've missed the chance?"

"The Keeper will just send them back," said the Oversoul. "And why would I want to keep them from rescuing Akmaro?"

"The Keeper will *try* to send them back. But in the meantime, you'll lead them along the mountainside until they drop down into the canyon where the river Zidomeg forms."

"Zinom," said the Oversoul, understanding now. "Where the main body of the Zenifi are also enslaved, more or less, by the Elemaki."

"Exactly," said Shedemei. "Monush will think he's fulfilled his mission. He'll have found a group of Zenifi in bondage to diggers. He'll figure out a way to bring them to safety. He'll bring them home."

"He can't take that whole population along the mountainside."

"No," said Shedemei. "You'll have to send him dreams that will bring him home by going up the valley of the Ureg and then over the pass that leads down to the valley of the Padurek."

"That takes them right past Akmaro's group."

"And the Keeper will try to get Monush to find Akmaro's people again."

"And I interfere again," said the Oversoul. "That's not what I'm supposed to do, Shedemei. My purpose is not to interfere with the Keeper of Earth."

"No, your purpose is to get the Keeper's help so you can return to Harmony. Well, if you cause her enough trouble, my dear, perhaps she'll send you back to Harmony in order to stop you from interfering."

"I don't think I can do that." The Oversoul paused. "My programming may stop me from consciously rebelling against what I think the Keeper wants."

"Well, you figure it out," said Shedemei. "But in the meantime, keep this in mind: As long as the Keeper isn't telling you anything, how do you know the Keeper doesn't *want* you to pull exactly the kind of stunt I'm suggesting? Just to prove your mettle?"

"Shedemei, you're romanticizing again," said the Oversoul. "I'm a machine, not a puppet wishing to be made alive. There are no tests. I do what I'm programmed to do."

"Do you?" asked Shedemei. "You're programmed to take initiative. Here's a chance. If the Keeper doesn't like it, all she has to do is tell you to stop. But at least you'll be talking then."

"I'll think about it," said the Oversoul.

"Good," said Shedemei.

"All right," said the Oversoul. "I've thought about it. We'll do it."

"That quickly?" Shedemei knew the Oversoul was a computer, but it still surprised her how much the old machine could do in the time it took a human to say a single word.

"I made a test run and found that nothing in my programming interferes. I can do it. So we'll give it a try when Monush gets to the right place, and find out how much the Keeper will put up with before deigning to make contact with me."

Shedemei laughed. "Why can't you admit it, you old fake?"

"Admit what?"

"You're really pissed off at the Keeper."

"I am not," said the Oversoul. "I'm worried about what might be happening on Harmony."

"Relax," said Shedemei. "Your otherself is there, as the angels would say."

"I'm not an angel," said the Oversoul.

"Neither am I, my friend," said Shedemei.

"You sound wistful."

"I'm a gardener. I miss the feel of earth under my feet."

"Time for another trip to the surface?"

"No," said Shedemei. "No point in it. Nothing I planted last time will be ready for measurement. It would be a waste and a risk."

"You are allowed to have fun," said the Oversoul. "Even the one who wears the cloak of the starmaster is allowed to do a few things simply because of the joy of doing them."

"Yes, and I'll do it. When the time comes."

"You have a will of steel," said the Oversoul.

"And a heart of glass," said Shedemei. "Brittle and cold. I'm going to take a nap. Why don't you use the time to design a dream?"

"Don't you have dreams enough on your own?"

"Not for me," said Shedemei. "For Monush."

"I was making a joke," said the Oversoul.

"Well next time wink at me or something so I know." Shedemei got up from the terminal and padded off to bed.

* * *

Monush and his men slept yet another night on yet another narrow shelf of rock high above the valley floor. The torches in the digger village far below burned late; Monush's fifteen companions watched most of them until they guttered and winked out. It was hard to sleep, weary as they were, for if they rolled over in the night they would plunge twenty rods before so much as a knob of stone would break their fall—and, no doubt, the first of many bones. They all pushed sharp stakes into the rock or, if there was no slight crevice to hold them, they piled them so they might feel them if they started to roll toward the edge in their sleep. But all in all, it was a precarious slumber indeed, and there was probably no moment when more than half the men were asleep.

Despite all this, tonight Monush slept well enough to dream, and when he awoke, he knew the path that he had to take in order to find the Zenifi. This high path would widen and slope downward, but at a certain place, if he should climb, he would come to a pass over these mountains and down into another valley. There he would see a large lake, and by passing down the valley of the river that flowed from it, in due time he would come to the place that Edhadeya had dreamed of.

He awoke from the dream just as the sky was beginning to lighten overhead. Carefully he pulled out the stakes he had pushed by hand into the stone and put them back into his bag. Then he gnawed on the cold maizecake that would be his only meal of the day, unless they found food somewhere on the journey—unlikely on such steep cliffs, and so high in the thin air. This was the region called "Crown of the Gornaya," the highest region of the great massif of mountain ranges that had long harbored earth people, middle people, and sky people. It was here that the seven lakes had formed, all of them holy, but none holier than Sidonod, the pure source of the Tsidorek, the sacred river that flowed through the heart of Darakemba. Some of the men had hoped to set eyes on Sidonod itself, but now Monush knew that they would not. The pass would come too soon. Within the first hour.

Wordlessly—for sound carried far in the thin dry mountain air—Monush gave the signal to move. All the men were awake now, and they walked, slowly and stiffly at first, along the narrow shelf of rock. Twice they came to places where the shelf gave out and they had to climb, once up, once down, to another shelf that allowed them to walk on.

Then they reached a spot where the shelf widened and started to lead downward to an area of easier travel. Monush recognized the place at once, and thought. . . .

Thought what? He couldn't remember. Something about this spot.

"What is it?" asked Chem, his second. In a whisper, of course.

Monush shook his head. It kept coming just to the tip of his tongue, some word, some idea, but he couldn't remember why. Ah! A dream!

But the dream had fled. He couldn't think of what the dream had been or what it meant at all.

How foolish, thought Monush. Foolish of me, to think *my* dreams could tell me true things the way Edhadeya's did.

He beckoned the men to follow him as he led onward, down the broadening path. Within half an hour they rounded a curve and saw what so many men dreamed of but never dared to hope to see: Holy Sidonod, shining in the first sunlight to crest the mountain.

Below them, along the shores of the lake, there were villages, each with its cookfires. Of course only the humans would live in the huts and, now and then, houses; the diggers lived in hollowed trees and in tunnels under the earth nearby. The scene looked so peaceful. Yet they knew that if the men there, diggers or humans, knew of the Nafari walking along this narrow shelf of land, there would be such an outcry, and soon war parties would be scaling the cliff walls. Not that this spelled sure death, outnumbered though they might be. Even diggers, born to climb, would have a hard time getting up the rocks. But eventually the Elemaki would either reach their shelf and force them to fight to the last man, or the Nafari would have to climb higher and higher until they reached the altitudes where men freeze or faint or grow mad.

So they continued to move silently and smoothly along the rock, wearing their earth-colored tunics and leggings, their earth-colored blankets draped and pinned over their shoulders, their very skin and hair smeared with dirt to make them blend better into the stony cliff.

If only we could find a way to go up and over these mountains and avoid this heavily-populated lake, thought Monush. And then a thought burst into his mind. Of course we can! Just back there behind us there's a. . . . there's a. . . . He couldn't remember. What was it he was thinking of? Something behind them? Why? There were no pursuers. Had he forgotten one of his men? He stopped and made a quick count. All were there—and, because they had stopped, most were gaping down at the holy lake below them. Monush beckoned them on. The shelf rose again. They passed by the long lake, sleeping only two nights with it in view.

After the lake, they passed through easier country, though it was all the more dangerous. It was a large region of lowish mountains, green to their tops, and every valley had at least some people in it, usually diggers, often humans as well, and now and then an isolated settlement of angels, though most of these were either slaves to a nearby Elemaki village or were "free"—but still tributary to one Elemaki king or another. Several times they were spotted by angels soaring overhead, but instead of crying out a warning, the angels always flew on, ignoring them. One angel even swooped low and landed on a nearby branch, then pointed down the ridge that Monush and his men were following and shook his head. Don't go this way, he was saying. Monush nodded, bowed to him as to a friend, and the angel rose up into the air and flew away.

It's good for *us*, at least, thought Monush, that the Elemaki are so harsh on the few angels forced to live among them. It gives us friends wherever we go. Weak friends, it's true, but friends are all welcome in the land of our enemies.

On the fortieth day of their expedition, they came to a place where four streams met within a few rods. The water was turbulent, and yet no diggers or humans or angels lived near it. "A holy place like this," whispered Chem, "and yet no one dwells here to receive the gift?"

Monush nodded, then smiled. "Perhaps they receive the gift downstream."

He led them on, just a little way, and as they moved downstream they saw that no new hills seemed to rise up ahead of them. The land was about to change.

And suddenly they understood. For the ground dropped away in front of them. The water of the river soared out like an arrow's flight, spouting into the air and then falling as perpetual rain down onto the valley below. It was a place of power, the only place that Monush had ever seen or heard of where water from a stream turned directly into rain without first rising up into the sky as clouds.

"Is there a way down?" asked Chem.

"As you said," answered Monush. "It's a holy place. See? Many feet have come up this cliff."

It was almost a stairway, the descent was so artificial, steps cut into the stone, earth held in place by planks. "A cripple could climb here," said Alekiam, the one who spoke the dialect of digger language that was most common among the Elemaki. Not that they were likely to run across many diggers who hadn't adopted Torg, the trading language that was mostly the original human language, with pronunciations adapted to the mouths of diggers and angels and thousands of their words thrown in. But it was possible, here in these high mountains, where it was said that in some remote valleys diggers and angels still lived together in the old way, the diggers stealing statues made by the angels and bringing them home to worship them as gods—even as they sent raiding parties to kidnap the children of the angels and eat them. No one in living memory had run across such a place, but few doubted that people like that might yet survive—diggers who called the angels "skymeat," and angels who called the diggers "devils," both with good reason.

"Quiet," said Monush. "This place is well traveled. Who knows who might be at the bottom?"

But there was no one at the bottom, and the land, being lower, had different fruits in season. Monush led his men to the brow of a hill overlooking the river that flowed away from the perpetual rainstorm at the base of the cliff. He told twelve of them to stay there and keep watch, eating what fruit they could find within sight of each other, while Monush himself took Alekiam, Chem, and a strong soldier named Lemech, who could break a man's neck just by slapping him on the ear.

As they moved carefully along the rivercourse, they could see signs that once this land had been heavily settled. The boundaries of old fields could still be clearly seen, though they were overgrown. And here and there they passed an area that had been cleared and crusted over with stone, so that no diggers could get silently underneath and burrow their way into people's homes.

"Where are all the people?" asked Chem, as they stood in the middle of one such place. "They built well, and now they're gone."

"No they're not," said Lemech.

A tall young human stood at the forest's edge. He had not been there a moment before.

"Hail, friend," said Monush, for he could hardly hope to avoid an encounter now.

At a signal from the tall young man, at least thirty soldiers stepped onto the platform of stone. Where had they been? Hadn't they circled this place before stepping out onto it?

"Lay down your weapons," said Monush softly.

"In a digger's heart I will," said Lemech.

"They have us," said Monush. "If we surrender, perhaps we'll live long enough for the others to find us."

"For all we know these are the people we've come to find," said Chem. "Not a digger among them."

That was true enough. So they laid down their weapons on the stone floor of the platform.

At once the strangers closed on them, seized them, bound them, and forced them to run with them through the woods until they came to a place where twenty such platforms were clustered. On them many buildings rose, most of them houses, but not humble ones, and some of the buildings could not have been houses at all, but rather were palaces and gamecourts, temples and, most prominent of all, one solitary tower rising taller than any of the trees. From that tower you could sure look out over this whole land, thought Monush, and see any enemies that might be approaching.

If the soldiers hadn't gagged Monush and his men, he might have asked them if they were the Zenifi. As it was, they were thrown into a room that must have been built for storing food, but now was empty except for the four bound prisoners.

In Edhadeya's dream, thought Monush, weren't the Zenifi *asking* to be rescued?

Akma awoke from his dream, trembling with fear. But he dared not cry aloud, for they had learned that the diggers who guarded them regarded all loud voices in the night as prayers to the Keeper—and Pabulog had decreed that any praying to the Keeper by these followers of Akmaro was blasphemy, to be punished by death. Not that a single cry in the night would have a child killed—but the diggers would have dragged them out of their tent and beaten them, demanding that they confess that one of them had been praying. The children had learned to waken silently, no matter how terrible the dream.

Still, he had to speak of it while it was fresh in mind. He wanted to waken his mother, wanted her to enfold him in her arms and comfort him. But he was too old for that, he knew; he would be ashamed of needing her comfort even as he gratefully received it.

So it was his father, Akmaro, that he nudged until his father rolled over and whispered, "What is it, Akma?"

"I dreamed."

"A true dream?"

"The Keeper sent men to rescue us. But a cloud of darkness and a mist of water blocked their view and they lost the path to us. Now they will never come."

"How did you know the Keeper sent them?"

"I just knew."

"Very well," said Akmaro. "I will think about this. Go back to sleep."

Akma knew that he had done all he could do. Now it was in his father's hands. He should have been satisfied, but he was not satisfied at all. In fact, he was angry. He didn't want his father to think about it, he wanted his father to *talk* about it. He wanted to help come up with the interpretation of the dream. It *was* his own dream, after all. But his father listened, took the dream seriously enough, but then assumed that it was up to him alone to decide what to do about it, as if Akma were a machine like the Index in the ancient stories.

I'm not a machine, said Akma silently, and I can think of what this means as well as anyone.

It means . . . it means. . . .

That the Keeper sent men to rescue us and they lost the way. What else could it mean? How could Father interpret it any differently?

Maybe it isn't the interpretation of the dream that Father is thinking about. Maybe he's thinking about what to do next. If the Keeper was just going to send another party of rescuers, then why send me such a dream? It must mean that there will be no other rescuers. So it's up to us to save ourselves.

And Akma drifted off to sleep with dreams of battle in his mind, standing sword-in-hand, facing down his tormentors. He saw himself standing over the beheaded body of Pabul; he heard Udad groan with his guts spilled out into his lap as he sat on the ground, marveling at the mess young Akma had made of his body. As for Didul, Akma imagined a long confrontation between them, with Didul finally pleading for his life, the arrogance wiped off his face, his beautiful cheeks streaked with tears. Shall I let you live, after you beat me and taunted me every day for weeks and weeks? For the insult to me, I might forgive you. But shall I let you live, after you slapped my sister so many times until she cried? Shall I let you live, after you drove the other children to exhaustion until the weakest of them collapsed in the hot sun and you laughed as you covered them with mud as if they were dead? Shall I let you live, as you did all these things in front of the parents of these children, knowing that they were helpless to protect their young ones? That was the cruelest thing, to humiliate our parents, to make them weak in front of their own children. And for that, Didul . . . for that, the blade through the neck, your head spinning in the air, bouncing and dancing along the ground before it rolls to rest at the feet of your own father. Let him weep, that cruel tyrant, let him try to push your head back into place and make your vicious little smile come back to your lips, but he can't do it, can he? Powerless, isn't he? Standing there with little Muwu clinging to his leg, begging me to spare him at least one son, at least the last of his boys, but I'll spare no one because you spared no one.

With such wistful imaginings did Akma go back to sleep.

Monush was dragged out of his sleep by two men, who seized him by his bound arms and hauled him out of the dank storehouse. He could hear that the others were being treated the same, but he could see nothing because the light of day dazzled his eyes. He was barely able to see clearly when he was hauled before the court of the king.

For that is who it clearly was, though he was the same man who had shown himself before them on the day they were taken. He had not looked like a king then, and even now, Monush thought he was young and seemed unsure of himself. He sat well on the throne, and he commanded with certainty and assurance, but . . . . Monush couldn't place what was wrong. Except, perhaps, that this man did not seem to want to be where he was.

What was this strange reluctance? Did he not want to be sitting in judgment on these strangers? Or did he not want to be king?

"Do you understand my language?" asked the king.

"Yes," said Monush. The accent was a little odd, but nothing to be much remarked upon. No one in Darakemba would have mistaken him for one of the Elemaki.

"I am Ak-Ilihi, son of Nuab, who once was Nuak, the king of the Zenifi. My grandfather, Zenifab, led our people out of the land of Darakemba to possess again the land of Nafai, which was the proper inheritance of the Nafari, and he was made king by the voice of the people. It is by that same right that I now rule. Now tell me why you were so bold as to come near the walls of the city of Zidom, while I myself was outside the city with my guards. It was because of your boldness and fearlessness that I decided not to allow my guards to put you to death without first knowing from your own lips how you dared to violate every treaty and defy our rule within the boundaries of that small kingdom that the Elemaki have left to us."

The king waited.

"You are now permitted to speak," the king said.

Monush took a step forward and bowed before Ilihiak. "O King, I am very grateful before the Keeper of Earth that I have been left alive, and that you permit me to speak, and I will speak freely because I know now that if you had realized who I am, and who these are that follow me, you would never have suffered us to be bound and held prisoner. My name, O King, is Mon, and it was by the pleasure of King Motiak of Darakemba that men now call me Monush."

"Motiak!" said the king.

"Not Motiab, who ruled when your grandfather left Darakemba, but his grandson. He was the one who sent us to search for the Zenifi, for there was a dream from the Keeper that said that the Zenifi were in bondage to the Elemaki and yearning to be free."

Ilihiak rose to his feet. "Now I will rejoice, and when I tell the people, they will rejoice, also." His words were formal, but Monush could see that they were also heartfelt. "Unbind them," he said to his guards.

With the bands removed from his arms and legs, Monush could hardly stand upright for a few moments, but the guards who had before dragged him now held him up with steady hands.

"I tell you freely, Monush—for I'm sure you deserve that name from all kings, if Motiak has so named you—that if our brothers from Darakemba can set us free of the heavy taxes and the cruelty of the Elemaki, we will gladly be your slaves, for it is better to be slaves to the Nafari than to have the Elemaki rip from us all that we produce."

"Ilihiak," said Monush, "I am not the great Ak-Moti, but I can assure you that he is not such a man as to send us to find you, only to make you slaves in Darakemba. Whether he will allow you to continue to be a separate people within the borders of Darakemba, and whether he will confirm your throne as underking, I have no power to say. But I do know that Motiak is a kind and just man, chosen by the Keeper, and he will not enslave those who wish to be loyal citizens."

"If he allows us to dwell within his borders and under his protection, we will feel it to be the greatest kindness ever offered, and we would not think to ask for more."

Monush heard this, but knew enough of the doings of kings to know perfectly well that Ilihiak would no doubt be a tough bargainer, holding out for all the independence and power he could get from Motiak. But that was a matter for kings, not soldiers. "Ilihiak, we are not many, but we are more than four. Will you permit me to—"

"Go, at once. You are free men. If you want to punish us for imprisoning you, you have only to leave and we will make no effort to stop you. But if you have mercy on us, come back with the rest of your companions and let us counsel together on what we can do to win free of the Elemaki."

Chebeya worked in silence, trying not to watch as two of Pabulog's sons kept knocking Luet down. It made her want to scream, and yet she knew that any protest would only make things worse for everyone. Yet what kind of woman can bear to let her little child be mistreated by thugs and do nothing, say nothing, simply continue to work as if she didn't care?

Luet began to cry.

Chebeya stood upright. Immediately two of the diggers started toward her with their heavy whips. Of course they were watching her, every move she made, because she was Luet's mother. So she stopped, she said nothing, just stood there.

"Back to work!" said the digger.

Chebeya looked at him defiantly for a moment, then bowed down again to hoe the maize.

Where was the Keeper of Earth? In the days since Akma had his dream that the rescuers weren't coming, Chebeya had asked the same question over and over. If the Keeper cares enough about us to send Akma a dream, why doesn't she *do* something? Akmaro said that the

Keeper is testing us, but what is the test and how do we pass it? Does the Keeper want us to turn into a nation of cowards? Or does she want us to revolt against Pabulog's hideous children and so die? We must each think of a way, Akmaro had said. We must find a way out of this dilemma ourselves, that is the test that the Keeper has set for us. And once we find that way, the Keeper will help us.

Well, if the Keeper was so smart, why didn't she come up with a few suggestions herself?

No one knew better than Chebeya how their slavery was destroying them. Few knew of her gift, and those only women, except of course for her husband; but where once she had been able to alert Akmaro to small rifts in the community before they could become open quarrels, now all she could do was watch in despair as the bonds connecting friend to friend, parent to child, brother to sister all weakened, thinned to almost nothingness. They are making us into animals, depriving us of our human affections. All we care about now is survival, avoiding the whip. Each time we cower and let our children be mistreated, we love those children a little less, because it is only by not loving them as much that we can bear it to see them suffer.

Not Akmaro, though. He loved his children more and more; in the night he whispered to her how proud he was of their strength, their courage, their understanding. But perhaps this was because Akmaro had a seemingly limitless tolerance for emotional pain. He could suffer for his children—no one knew better than Chebeya how much he suffered—and yet he clung all the tighter to them because of it. He is not afraid of his own love for them, the way so many other parents are. Am I like him? Or like them?

What worried Chebeya most in her own family was the way young Akma seemed to be growing more and more distant from his father. Could the boy be blaming Akmaro for not saving him from the persecution of the sons of Pabulog? It couldn't be that—if Luet could understand, Akma could also. So what was it that made Akma flee from what had once been a tight connection between him and his father?

Chebeya mocked herself silently. Why am I worrying about tension between father and son? In a week or a month or a year we'll all be dead—murdered or dead of hunger or disease. Then what will it matter why Akma didn't have the same loyalty to his father that he used to have?

I wish I could talk to Hushidh or Chveya, one of the ancient ravelers. They must have understood better than I do the things that I see. Does Akma hate his father? Is it anger? Fear? I watch the loyalties shift and change, and sometimes it's obvious why the changes come, and sometimes I have almost no idea. Hushidh and Chveya were never uncertain. They always knew what to do, they were always wise.

But I am not wise. I only know that my husband is losing our son's love. And what will I be in Luet's eyes, her own mother, when I stand by in silence and let these bullies mistreat her?

Chebeya felt herself filled with a sudden and irresistible resolve. They mean to kill us eventually. Better to die with Luet certain that her mother loves her.

Chebeya stood upright again.

The diggers had already looked away from her, but they noticed soon enough that she had stopped her work. They moved toward her.

Chebeya pitched her voice to be heard clearly by the sons of Pabulog. "Why are you so frightened of me?" she said.

It worked—one of the boys answered her. The third son, the one called Didul. "I'm not frightened of you!"

"Then why don't you push *me* down, instead of a little girl half your size?" Chebeya let her voice fill with scorn, and saw with pleasure how Didul's face flushed.

Around her, other adults were muttering. "Hush. Enough. Quiet now. They'll beat us all."

Chebeya ignored them. She also ignored the digger guards with their upraised whips, who were already almost upon her. "Didul, if you aren't a coward, take a whip and beat me yourself!"

One of the digger's whips landed on her back. She winced and staggered under the weight of the blow.

"You're just like your father!" she cried out to him. "Afraid to do anything yourself!"

Another blow fell. But then Didul called out. "Stop!"

The diggers each let one more blow fall before they obeyed him. It brought Chebeya to her knees, and she could feel the blood flowing down her back. But Didul was coming to her, and so she used the precious moments before he arrived. Rising slowly to her feet, she looked him in the eye and spoke to him. "So, the boy Didul has some pride. How could that happen? The children of Akmaro have courage—no matter how you torment them, have you ever heard them beg for mercy? Do you think that if your father were beaten the way you beat these little children, *he* would be as brave?"

"Don't speak of my father, blasphemer!" shouted Didul.

But Chebeya could see what Didul could not—that she had troubled him. The connection between him and his brothers was just a little weaker because of her words.

"See what your father teaches you? To bully little children. But *you* have pride. It makes you ashamed to do what your father tells you to do."

Didul took the whip from the hands of one of the diggers. "I'll show you my pride, blasphemer!"

"Is it your *pride* that lets you raise a whip against an unarmed woman?"

Ah, the words stung, she could see it.

"No, a true son of Pabulog can only strike out at people who are helpless. Have you ever seen your father stand in battle like a *man*?"

"He would if he had any real men to fight!" shouted Didul.

Chebeya searched her mind for the retort that would work the best. "I think that in your heart, Didul, you understand what your father is doing to you. Why do you think he sent you here to torment us? Why do you think he told you to mistreat the little children? Because he *knew* that you would be ashamed of yourself for doing it. Because he knew that once you had made little children cry, you would know that you were as low and cowardly as he is, so that he would never have to hear his children taunt him, for he will always be able to answer you, 'Yes, but who was it who beat up on little girls?' "

Infuriated, Didul lashed out. The whip caught her across the shoulder and the end of it wrapped around her and caught her on the cheek. Blood splashed into her eyes and she was blinded for a moment.

"Don't call my father a coward!" cried Didul.

"Even at this very moment," she said, "you hate him for making you the kind of coward who answers a woman's *words* with a whip. If the things I said were not the truth, Didul, they wouldn't make you so angry."

"Nothing that you said is true!"

"Everything I said is true, and the proof of it is that when you walk away from here, these guards will beat me to death, just so you never have to listen to me again." Chebeya spoke with conviction; she feared that what she was saying just might be the truth.

"If they beat you it will be to punish you for lying."

"If you didn't believe me, Didul, you would just laugh at what I said."

Now she had him. She could see the new thread that bound him to *her*. She was winning him away, tearing at his loyalty to his father.

"I *don't* believe you," he said.

"You believe me, Didul, because every time you hit one of these little children you're ashamed. I can see it in your eyes. You laugh, just like your brothers, but you hate yourself for it. You're afraid that you're just like your father."

"I *want* to be just like my father."

"Really? Then why are you here? Your *father* doesn't dirty himself by beating up on children with his *own* hands. *He* always sends thugs and bullies to do it for him. No, you can't be like your father, because there's still a *man* inside you. But don't worry—a few more years of beating up on babies and there'll be no trace of manhood left in your heart."

As she talked, Udad, Didul's next older brother, had come up behind him. "Why are you listening to this witch?" Udad demanded. "Have them kill her."

"That's the voice of your father," said Chebeya. "Kill anyone who dares to tell you the truth. Only don't do it yourself. Have someone else do it for you."

Udad turned to the diggers. "Why are you standing there, letting her do this? She's got some kind of magic control of my stupid brother—"

With a cry of rage, Didul turned around and made as if to lash his brother with the whip. Udad cringed and covered his face with his hands and screeched, "Don't hit me! Don't hit me!"

"There you see it," said Chebeya. "That's what you'll become, when your father is through with you."

She could see the last threads binding Didul to Udad turn to rage and shame—a negative connection.

"But are you already like him, Didul? Or is there a man inside you?"

Udad, shamed now, backed away. "I'm going to tell Pabul that you're letting Akmaro's wife turn you against us all!"

"Does that frighten you, Didul?" asked Chebeya. "He's going to tell on you. Does that frighten you?"

"I'm leaving," said Didul. "I don't want to hear any more of your lies."

"Yes, leaving me so the guards can kill me," said Chebeya. "But I promise you that if I die here today, you'll hear my voice inside your heart forever."

Defiant anger sparking in his eyes, Didul turned to the diggers. "I want to see her alive tomorrow, with no more lashes on her than she already has."

"That's not what your father said," one of them retorted.

Didul grinned savagely at him. "He said to obey his sons. If this woman is harmed, I'll have you skinned alive. Do you doubt me?"

Ah, the fire in his eyes! Chebeya could see that he had the gift of command. She had kindled his pride and now it was burning, burning in his heart.

The diggers backed off.

Didul tossed the whip back to the one who had lent it to him. Then he spoke one more time to Chebeya. "Get back to work, woman."

She looked him in the eye. "I obey the lash. But someday, wouldn't you like to see someone obey you out of true respect?" Despite the pain of the wounds on her back and the blood in her eye, she bent over and picked up her hoe. She scratched ineffectually at the soil. She could hear him walk away.

"I'll kill her," said one of the diggers. "What can *he* do about it? His father would never approve of him listening to her."

"Fool," said the other. "If he wants his father to kill us, do you think he'll tell him the *truth*?"

"So let's *us* tell him first."

"Oh, great idea. Go to Pabulog and tell him that his son let this woman talk him down? How long do you think we'd live if we were going around telling *that* story?"

Chebeya listened to them with amusement. Her words had had their effect on these diggers, too. It wasn't much of a plan, to stir up trouble among Pabulog's sons and soldiers. And they might kill her yet. As it was, she'd be paying for this day's work in pain for many days to come.

"That was a stupid thing to do," someone muttered. "You could have got us all killed."

"Who cares?" someone else whispered. "Didn't Akmaro spread the word for us to think of how we might deliver ourselves? At least she thought of *something*."

Didul and Udad were back near where Luet and Akma worked. Luet flinched from them, but Akma stood his ground. How much of what she said had he heard? Perhaps all of it; perhaps little. But he stood his ground.

Udad reached out and pushed at Akma, who staggered backward but did not fall. There was no surprise in *that*. No, the surprise came when Didul lunged at Udad and sent him sprawling in the dirt. Udad immediately sprang up, ready to fight his younger brother. "What was that! Do you want me to beat you up?"

Didul stood and looked him in the eye. "Is that all you can do? Beat up on people who are smaller than you? If you touch me, then you prove that everything she said about us is true."

Udad stood there, flustered, confused. Chebeya could see the ties of loyalty shifting even as she watched. Udad, uncertain now, suddenly wanted Didul's good opinion more than anything, for he was ashamed not to have it; just as Didul, in turn, wanted Chebeya's good opinion. That was the beginning of loyalty. Wouldn't that be the perfect vengeance, to turn Pabulog's own sons against him?

No, not vengeance. Deliverance. That's what we're trying for, to save ourselves, since the Keeper seems unwilling to do it.

* * *

"I can't tell," said the Oversoul. "Is our plan working or not?"

Shedemei chuckled wryly. "Well, at least the Keeper noticed us. That dream she sent to Akma. And Chebeya's sudden impulse to defy Pabulog's sons. If that *was* the Keeper."

"Yet the Keeper still says nothing to *us*. We're a gnat buzzing in the Keeper's ear. We are brushed away."

"So let's go back and keep buzzing."

"The Keeper's plans will go forward regardless of what we do or don't do," said the Oversoul.

"I hope so," said Shedemei. "But I do think she cares very much what people do. Down there on Earth, of course, but also here in this ship. She cares what happens."

"Maybe all the Keeper cares about is the people of Earth. Maybe she no longer cares about the people of Harmony. Maybe I should go home to Harmony now and tell my otherself that our mission is over and we can let humans there do whatever they want."

"Or maybe the Keeper still wants you here," said Shedemei. Then a new thought occurred to her. "Maybe she still needs the powers of the starship. The cloak of the starmaster."

"Maybe the Keeper needs *you,*" said the Oversoul.

Shedemei laughed. "What, I have some seeds and embryos up here that she wants me to put down somewhere on Earth? All she has to do is send me a dream and I'll plant wherever she says."

"So we go on waiting," said the Oversoul.

"No, we go on *prodding,*" answered Shedemei. "Like Chebeya did. We roust the old she-bear from her den and goad her."

"I'm not sure I like the implications of your metaphor. She-bears are destructive and dangerous when they've been goaded."

"But they do give you their undivided attention." Shedemei laughed again.

"I don't think you have enough respect yet for the power of the Keeper."

"What power? All we've seen from the Keeper up to now is dreams."

"If that's all you've seen," said the Oversoul, "then you haven't been looking."

"Really?"

"The gornaya, for instance. That massif of impossibly high mountains. The ancient geological data from before the departure of humans forty million years ago shows no tectonic formation or movement that could have caused this. The plates in this area weren't moving in the right direction to cause such incredible folding and uplift. Then, suddenly, the Cocos plate started moving northward with far more speed and force than any tectonic movement ever recorded. It attacked the Caribbean plate far faster than it could be subducted."

Shedemei sighed. "I'm a biologist. Geology is barely comprehensible to me."

"You understand *this,* though. A dozen ranges of mountains with peaks above ten kilometers in height. And they were lifted up within the first ten million years."

"Is that fast?"

"Even now, the Cocos plate is still moving northward three times faster than any other plate on Earth. That means that underneath the Earth's crust, there's a current of molten rock that is flowing northward very rapidly—the same current that caused North America to rift along the Mississippi Valley, the same current that crumpled all of Central America into pieces and jammed them together and. . . ."

The Oversoul fell silent.

"What?"

"I'm doing a little research for a moment."

"Well, pardon me for interrupting," said Shedemei.

"This has to have begun before humans left Earth," said the Oversoul.

"Yes?"

"The earthquakes, the volcanos out along the Galapagos ridge—what *was* it that encased the Earth in ice for a while? In my memory, it was all linked with human misbehavior—with wars, nuclear and biological weapons. But how exactly did those things *cause* the Earth to become uninhabitable?"

"I love watching a brilliant mind at work," said Shedemei.

"I will have to search all my records from that time period," said the Oversoul, "and see whether I can rule out the possibility that it was the movement of the Cocos plate, and not the warfare directly, that caused the destruction of the habitable zones of Earth."

"You're saying that the warfare might have caused the Cocos plate to move? That's absurd."

The Oversoul ignored her scoffing. "Why did *all* human life leave Earth? The diggers and angels managed to survive. I never thought to question it till now, starmaster, but don't you find it a bit suspicious? Surely some group of humans could have survived. In some equatorial zone."

"Please, I know creativity and serendipity are designed into your thinking algorithms," said Shedemei, "but are you seriously entertaining the notion that human misdeeds could have caused the Cocos plate to move?"

"I'm saying that perhaps human misdeeds could cause the Keeper of Earth to cause the Cocos plate to move."

"And how could she possibly do that?"

"I can't imagine any entity of any kind with power enough to move the currents of magma under the crust of the planet," said the Oversoul. "But I also can't imagine any natural force that could have caused the many anomalies that created the gornaya. The world is full of strange and unnatural things, Shedemei. Like the symbiotic interdependence that the diggers and angels used to have. You said yourself that it was artificial."

"And my hypothesis is that these changes were deliberately introduced by human beings before they left."

"But *why* would they do it, Shedemei? Whose purpose were they fulfilling? Why would they even care, knowing that they would leave this planet and believing that they would never come back?"

"I think it's possible for us to ascribe too many events to the plots and plans of the Keeper of Earth," said Shedemei. "She causes dreams and influences human behavior. We have no evidence for anything else."

"We have no evidence. Or we have the most obvious evidence imaginable. I must do research. There are gaps in my knowledge. The truth has been hidden from me, but I know that the Keeper is involved in all of this."

"Search all you want. I'll be fascinated to know the outcome."

"It may be that I'm programmed not to find the truth, you know," said the Oversoul. "And that I'm programmed not to find the way I've been programmed to hide the truth from me."

"How circular."

"I may need your help."

"I may need a nap." She yawned. "I don't believe that any computer, even the Keeper of Earth, has power over such things as currents of magma. But I'll help, if I can. Maybe in pursuing this worthless hypothesis you'll come across something useful."

"At least you're keeping an open mind," said the Oversoul.

"I'm sure you meant that in the nicest possible way," said Shedemei.

That night, in their hut, Akmaro and Akma washed and dressed Chebeya's wounds.

"You could have been killed, Mother," said Akma quietly.

"It was the bravest thing I ever saw," said Akmaro.

Chebeya wept silently—in relief that she hadn't been slaughtered in the field; in delayed fear at what she had dared to do; in gratitude to her husband for praising what she did.

"Do you see, Akma, what your mother is doing?" said Akmaro.

"She defied them," said Akma. "And they didn't kill her."

"There's more to it than that, Akma," said Akmaro. "It's a gift that your mother has had all her life. She's a raveler."

"Hushidh," whispered Luet. The tales of Hushidh the Raveler were well known among the women and girls. Not to mention Chveya, Nafai's and Luet's daughter, the Ancient One for whom Chebeya had been named.

"She sees the connections between people," Akmaro explained to Akma.

"I know what a raveler is," said Akma.

"To be a raveler is a gift of the Keeper," said Akmaro. "The Keeper must have seen, years ago, the dilemma we'd be in today, and so he gave a great gift to Chebeya so that when this day came, she could begin to unravel the conspiracy of evil that rules over us. We had with us all along the power to do what your mother began today. The Keeper only waited for us to realize it. For your mother to find the right moment to act."

"It looked to me," said Akma, "as if Mother stood alone."

"Is that what you saw?" asked Akmaro. "Then your vision is still very young and blurred. For your mother stood with the power of the Keeper in her, and with the love of her husband and children inside her. If you and Luet and I had not been in the field with her, do you think she would have done it?"

"*We* were there," said Akma. "But where was the Keeper?"

"Someday," said Akmaro, "you will learn to see the Keeper's hand in many things."

When the children were asleep, Chebeya rested her head on her husband's chest and clung to him and wept. "Oh, Kmadaro, Kmadaro, I was so frightened that I would make things worse."

"Tell me your plan," he said. "If I know your plan I can help you."

"I don't know my plan. I have no plan."

"Then here is the plan that came into my mind as I watched you and listened to you. I thought at first that you were simply trying to get those boys to rebel against their father. But then I realized that you were doing something far more subtle."

"I was?"

"You were winning Didul's heart."

"If he has one."

"You were teaching him how to be a man. It's a new idea to him. I think he'd like to be a good man, Bedaya."

She thought about it. "Yes, I think you're right."

"So we won't tear these boys away from each other. Instead we'll make friends and allies of them."

"Do you think we can?" asked Chebeya.

"You mean, Do I think we *should?* Yes, Bedaya. They can't help being what their father taught them to be. But if we can teach them to be something else, they might be good men yet. That is what the Keeper wants us to do—not destroy our enemies, but make friends of them if we can."

"They've hurt my children so many times," said Chebeya.

"Then how sweet the day will be when they kneel and ask your forgiveness, and your children's forgiveness, and the three of you say, We know that you are no longer the men you were then. Now you are our brothers."

"I can't ever say that to them."

"You can't say that to them now," said Akmaro. "But you, too, will have a change of heart, when you see them also change."

"You always believe the best of other people, Kmadaro."

"Not always," said Akmaro. "But in that boy today, I saw a spark of decency. Let's blow on that spark and give it fuel."

"I'll try," said Chebeya.

Lying on his mat, Akma heard his parents' conversation and thought, What kind of man is he, to talk to Mother about making friends with the very ones who lashed her skin and made her bleed today? I will never forgive these men, never, no matter how they seem to change. Men who are friends with diggers can never be trusted. They have become just like diggers, low filthy creatures who belong in holes under the earth like worms.

For Father to talk of teaching and forgiving a worm like Didul was just another sign of his weakness. Always running, hiding, teaching, forgiving, fleeing, submitting, bowing, enduring—where in Father's heart was the courage to stand and fight? It was Mother, not Father, who stood against Didul and the diggers today. If Father really loved Mother, he would have spent tonight vowing revenge for her bloody wounds.

4

Deliverance

Monush followed Ilihiak into his private chamber and watched as the king barred the door behind him. "What I'm going to show you," said Ilihiak, "is a great secret, Monush."

"Then perhaps you shouldn't show me," said Monush. "My loyalty is sworn to Ak-Moti, and I will keep no secret from him."

"But that's why I brought you here, Ush-Mon. You have the deepest trust of your great king. Do you think that I don't know that my kingdom would be hardly a small district of the empire of Darakemba? The stories reach us even here, that the Nafari who went down the Tsidorek have now become the greatest kingdom in the gornaya. What I have here is a matter for a great king, a king like Motiak, I think. I know it's beyond *me*."

Monush felt strongly that if there were two men, one would be greater than the other, and somewhere else there would always be one greater than either. True nobility consisted of recognizing one's betters as well as one's inferiors, and giving proper respect to all, never pretending to be above one's natural place. Ilihiak clearly understood that he had a greater rank and authority than Monush, but that Motiak was greater than either of them. It made Monush feel more confident in the man.

"Show me without fear, then," said Monush, "for I will reveal what I see to no man except my lord Motiak."

"To no *man*," said Ilihiak. "According to our ancient lore, the humans of Darakemba include male angels and male diggers in the word *man*."

"That's right," said Monush. "A male of the sky people, the earth people, or the middle people is a true man in the eyes of our law."

Ilihiak shuddered. "My people will have a hard time with this. We came to this land to get away from living with the wings of angels always in our faces. And here we've had ample cause to hate the diggers—our crops have been watered with the blood of many good men. *Men.* And diggers."

"I think King Motiak will not try to humiliate you, but will allow you to find a valley where you can buy the land of whatever angels dwell there and live without giving or receiving offense. But of course this would make you a subject nation instead of full citizens, for among citizens there can be no difference between people over, under, and on the earth."

"It won't be my choice, Monush. It will be the choice of my people." Ilihiak sighed. "Our hatred for the diggers has increased by being close to them. The only angels we see here are slaves or subject people, and they shun us. It will be hard for our young men to learn that it isn't decent sport to shoot arrows at them when they fly too near."

Monush shuddered. It was a good thing that Husu had not flown along with them, to hear this.

"I see how you judge us," said Ilihiak. "I fear you may be right. There was a man who came among us, an old man named Binadi. He told us that our way of life was an affront to the Keeper. That we mistreated the angels and that the Keeper loved angels, diggers, and humans as equals. That what mattered was whether a man was kind to all others, and whether he kept the laws of decency. He was . . . very specific in pointing out the many ways that the king my father failed to measure up. And his priests."

"You killed him."

"My father . . . was ambivalent. The man spoke very powerfully. Some believed him—including one of Father's priests. The best of them. He was my teacher, a man named Akmadi. No, that was Father's name for him. I called him Akmaro, because he was my honored teacher, not a traitor. I was there at the trial of Binadi, when Akmaro rose to his feet and said, 'This man is Binaroak, the greatest teacher. I believe him, and I want to change my life to measure up to his teachings.' That was the cruelest moment for my father—he loved Akmaro."

"Loved? He's dead?"

"I don't know. We sent an army after him, but he and his followers must have been warned. They fled into the wilderness. We have no idea where they are now."

"Those are the ones who believe that men of every kind are equal before the Keeper?"

"If only driving away Akmadi—Akmaro—were our worst crime." Ilihiak stopped to draw a breath; it was a tale he didn't want to tell. "Father was afraid of Binadi. He didn't want to kill him, just to exile him again. But Pabulog, the chief priest—he insisted. Goaded Father." Ilihiak stroked his hair back from his face. "Father was a man who was very susceptible to fear. Pabulog made him afraid to leave Binadi alive. 'If he can trick and trap even Akmadi, then how will you ever be safe?' That sort of thing."

"Your father had bad counselors," said Monush.

"And I fear that you think he also had a disloyal son. But I wasn't disloyal during his lifetime, Monush. It was only when I was forced into ruling in his place, after he was murdered—"

"Do your troubles have no end?"

Ilihiak went on as if he hadn't spoken. "Only then did I realize the extent of his corruption. It was Binadi—Binaro—who understood my father. Well, he's dead now, and I'm king over Zinom, such as it is. Half the men have been killed in wars with the Elemaki. After the last one, we bowed down and let them put their foot on our neck. It was then, in slavery, that we began to lose our arrogance and realize that if we had only stayed in Darakemba, wings in our faces or not, we would at least not be slaves to diggers. Our children would have enough to eat. We wouldn't have to bear with insult every day of our lives."

"So you let Binaro out of prison?"

"Out of prison?" Ilihiak laughed bitterly. "He was put to death, Monush. Burned to death, limb by limb. Pabulog saw to it personally."

"I think," said Monush, "that it would be wise for this Pabulog not to come to Darakemba. Motiak will apply his laws even over actions committed while Pabulog was in the service of your father."

"Pabulog isn't among us. Do you think he would be alive today if he were? He fled at the time they killed my father, taking his sons with him. Like Akmaro, we have no idea where he is."

"I'll be honest with you, Ilihiak. Your people have done terrible things, as a nation."

"And we've been punished for them," said Ilihiak, his temper flaring for a moment.

"Motiak isn't interested in punishment, except for a man who tortures one chosen by the Keeper. But Motiak can't allow people who have done the things you've done to come into Darakemba."

Ilihiak kept his kingly posture, but Monush could see the almost imperceptible sagging of his shoulders. "Then I shall teach my people to bear their burdens bravely."

"You misunderstand," said Monush. "You can come to Darakemba. But you will have to be new people when you arrive."

"New people?"

"When you cross the Tsidorek the last time, you won't use the bridge. Instead your people, all of them except the little children, must walk through the water and then symbolically die and be buried in the river. When you rise up out of the water, you have no name and no one knows you. You walk to the riverbank, and there you take the most solemn oath to the Keeper. From then on you have no past, but your future is as a true citizen of Darakemba."

"Let us take the oath at once—we have a river here, and at the waters of Oromono, where the rains fall from the cliff forever, there is water as holy as any in the Tsidorek."

"It's not the water—or, rather, not the water alone," said Monush. "You can teach your people the covenant, so they understand the law they'll be accepting when they leave here for Darakemba. But the passage through the water has to take place near the capital—I don't have the authority to make you new men and women."

Ilihiak nodded. "Akmaro did."

"The passage through the water? That's only done in Darakemba."

"The rumor we heard was that when he was in hiding at Oromono, he took people through the water and made them new." Ilihiak laughed bitterly. "The way Pabulog explained it, they were drowning babies. As if anyone would believe such a thing."

Monush wouldn't bother trying to explain to Ilihiak that it was only the king of the Nafari who had the right to make new men and women. Whoever and wherever this Akmaro was, his usurpation of the power of Motiak had nothing to do with the negotiations today. "Ilihiak, I think you have nothing to fear from Motiak. And whether your people choose to take the covenant or not, one way or another you'll find peace within the borders of Darakemba."

The king shook his head. "They'll take the covenant, or I won't lead them. We've had enough of trying to live as humans alone. It not only can't be done, but also isn't worth doing."

"That's settled, then," said Monush, and he started for the door.

"But where are you going?" asked Ilihiak.

"Wasn't this the secret you wanted to tell me?" asked Monush. "What your father and Pabulog did to Binadi?"

"No," said Ilihiak. "I could have told you that in front of my council. They all know how I feel about these things. No, I brought you here to show you something else. If the Elemaki knew about this, if even a hint of a rumor reached their ears. . . . "

Hadn't he already promised to keep all secrets except from Motiak? "Show me, then," said Monush.

Ilihiak walked to his bed, a thick mat that lay on the floor in the center of his chamber. Sliding it out of the way, he brushed aside the reeds and rushes and then his fingers probed a certain spot in one of the stones of the floor and suddenly another large flagstone dropped away. It was on hinges, and where it had been, a dark hole gaped.

"Do you want me to bring you a torch?" asked Monush.

"No need," said Ilihiak. "I'll bring it up."

The king dropped down into the hole. In the darkness it had looked as though it went down forever, but in fact when Ilihiak stood upright his shoulders rose out of the hole. He bent down, picked up something heavy, and lifted it to the floor of the chamber. Then he climbed out.

The object was wrapped in a dirty cloth; the king unwound it, revealing a basket, which he opened, then took out a wooden box. Finally that, too, was open, and inside was the gleam of pure gold.

"What is it?" asked Monush.

"Look at the writing," said Ilihiak. "Can you read it?"

Monush looked at the characters engraved into the gold leaves. "No," he said. "But I'm not a scholar."

"Nor am I, but I'll tell you this much—it isn't in any language I've ever heard. These letters have almost no similarities with any alphabet, and the patterns are wrong for our language, too. Where are the suffixes and prefixes? Instead there are all these tiny words—what could they be? I tell you, this was not written by Nafari *or* Elemaki."

"Angels?" asked Monush.

"Did they have writing before the humans came?"

Monush shrugged. "Who knows? It doesn't look like their language, either. The words are all too short. As you said. Where did you get it?"

"As soon as I became king, I sent out a group of men to search for Darakemba so we could find our way back. My grandfather deliberately destroyed all records of the route he took to lead our people here from Darakemba and he refused to let anyone ever tell. He said it was because such information was useless—we were never going back." Ilihiak smiled wryly. "We knew we had come up the Tsidorek—that's not hard—but it's not as if my men could ask directions from the local Elemaki. We had trouble enough already without them finding us sending out exploring parties. So they found a likely river and followed it. It was a very strange river, Monush—they followed it down and down and down till they reached a place where the water was very turbulent. And then the river continued in a straight line, but now the water was flowing the opposite way!"

"I've heard of the place," said Monush. "They found the Issibek. It's the next river over. It's really two rivers flowing directly toward each other. Where they meet, there's a tunnel leading through solid rock for many leagues until the river spouts out of the rock and forms a new river flowing to the sea."

"That explains it. To my men it seemed to be a miracle. They thought it was a sign they were on the right path."

"They found this writing there?"

"No. They followed the river to its northern head, and then found their way among ever lower valleys until at last they must have left the gornaya entirely. It was a hot, dry land, and to their horror it was covered by the bones of dead humans. As if there had been a terrible battle. Thousands and thousands and thousands of humans were slain, Monush —beyond all numbering. And all the dead were human, make no mistake about it. Not a digger, not an angel among them."

"I've never heard of such a place, though the desert is real enough. We call it Opustoshen—the place of desolation."

"That sounds like the right name for it," said Ilihiak. "My men were sure that they had found what happened to the people of Darakemba, and why they hadn't found the city anywhere along the river."

"They thought these dead humans were *us?*"

"Yes," said Ilihiak. "Who can tell, in a desert, how long anything has been dead? Or so they said to me. But as they searched among the bodies, they found these."

"What, lying on the ground, and nobody had already looted them?"

"Hidden in a cleft of the rock," said Ilihiak. "In a place that looks too small to get anything inside. One of the men had had a dream the night before, and in the dream he found something marvelous in a cleft of rock that he said was just like the one he found near the battlefield. So he reached inside—"

"The fool! Doesn't he know there are deadly snakes in the desert? They hide in shaded clefts like that during the day."

"There were a dozen snakes in there, the kind that make dancing music with their tails—"

"Deadly!"

"But they were as harmless as earthworms," said Ilihiak. "That's how my men knew that the Keeper really meant them to get these. And now here they are. The Elemaki would melt them down in a moment and make them into ornaments. But I was hoping that Motiak. . . ."

Monush nodded. "Motiak has the Index." He looked Ilihiak in the eye. "That, too, is a secret. Not that people don't suppose that he has it. But it's better if people are unsure, so they don't bother trying to find it and see it or, worse, steal it. The Index knows all languages. Motiak can translate these records if any man on Earth can do it."

"Then I'll give them to him," said Ilihiak, already rewrapping the leaves of gold. "I didn't dare ask you if the Index was still had among the kings of the Nafari."

"It is," said Monush. "And while the Index sat silent for many generations, it awoke in the days of Motiak's grandfather, Motiab, and told him to get down to Darakemba."

"Yes," said Ilihiak. "And my grandfather rejected that decision."

"It's never good to argue with the Index," said Monush.

"All messengers of the Keeper are sacred," said Ilihiak, and shuddered.

"The blood of Binaro is not on your head," said Monush.

"It's on the heads of my people, and therefore it *is* on my head. You weren't here, Monush. The mob gave full approval and cheered when Binadi cried out in agony. Those who hated what we did—they're with Akmaro wherever he is."

"Then it's time, isn't it, for us to teach them what the covenant will mean and let them decide whether they want to go to Darakemba."

Ilihiak pulled his bed back over the hidden trove. "Though how we're going to win our freedom from the place without bloody war I have no idea."

Monush helped him arrange the bed just as it had been. "When they've agreed to take the covenant, Ilihiak, then the Keeper will show us how to escape."

Ilihiak smiled. "Just so *I* don't have to think of a way, I'm content."

Monush looked at him intently. Did he mean that?

"I never wanted to be king," said Ilihiak. "I'll gladly give up all thrones and privileges, when I can set aside the burdens of office as well."

"A man who would willingly set aside the throne? I've never heard of such a thing," said Monush.

"If you knew all the pain that reigning here had brought me," said Ilihiak, "you'd call me a fool for staying in the job so long."

"Ilihiak, sir," said Monush, "I would never call you a fool, or permit another man to call you that in my presence."

Ilihiak smiled. "Then may I hope, Monush, that when I am no longer king, I might still have the honor of being your friend?"

Monush took Ilihiak's hands and placed them flat on his own cheeks. "My life is between your hands forever, my friend," said Monush.

Ilihiak took Monush's hands and repeated the gesture. "My life was worthless until the Keeper brought you to me. You were the awakening of all my hope. I know you came here only to do your duty to your king. But a man may see the worth of another man, regardless of rank or mission. My life is between your hands forever."

They embraced and touched lips in a kiss of friendship. Then, smiling, tears shamelessly on his cheeks, Ilihiak unbarred the door and returned to the tiny world where he was friend of no man, because he had to be king of all.

When Mon missed his target for the third time, Husu flew to him and stopped him. Others—most of them young angels in the earliest stages of training for Husu's flying army of spies—continued their practicing, filling their mouths with darts, the points protruding, then rapidly firing them one-handed through their blowtubes, trying to get them somewhere near the targets. Someday they would learn to shoot accurately while they beat their wings in flight, one foot holding the blowtube, the other foot holding a burden. For now, though, they practiced while standing on one foot. Mon was usually furious with himself when he missed—after all, he could hold the tube with two hands, could aim while standing on two feet. But today he could hardly bring himself to care.

"Mon, my young friend, you're tired, I think," said Husu.

Mon shrugged.

"Haven't slept well?"

Mon shook his head. He hated having to explain himself. He was usually a better shot than this, he took pride in it.

"You're a better shot than this," said Husu. "If you had wings, I would already have promoted you."

Husu could not have said words more likely to sting, but of course he couldn't know that. "I knew the shot wasn't right when I blew," said Mon.

"And yet you blew."

Mon shrugged again.

"Children shrug," said Husu. "Soldiers analyze."

"I blew the dart because I didn't care," said Mon.

"Ah," said Husu. "If the target had been an Elemaki soldier, intent on cutting the throats of young angels standing in their roost, would you have cared?"

"I wake up in the night, again and again," said Mon. "Something's wrong."

"Such precision," said Husu. "And when you aim your darts, do you aim them at 'something'? Why, then, you're sure to hit your target every time. Because you'll always hit 'something.' "

"Something with Monush's expedition."

Husu looked concerned at once. "Have they been harmed?" he asked.

"I don't know. I don't think that's it. I don't get this feeling when bad things happen or I'd never sleep at all, would I, because something bad is happening all the time. It only happens from bad choices. Mistakes. Monush has made a mistake."

Husu chuckled. "And you don't get *that* feeling all the time?"

"A mistake about something that matters to *me.*"

"I should think, then, that all mistakes that harm your father's kingdom would keep you awake, and believe me, there are plenty of those."

Mon turned to Husu and looked him in the eye. "I knew my explanation wouldn't please you, sir, but you wouldn't accept my shrug."

Husu stopped chuckling. "No, I want the truth."

"If I were heir to the king, then the whole kingdom would matter to me. As it stands, what matters to me is a very small thing indeed. Monush's expedition matters to me because. . . . "

"Because you sent them."

"Father sent them."

"They went because of your word."

"They've made a mistake," said Mon.

Husu nodded. "But you can't do anything about it, can you? They aren't within your reach, are they? No one can fly into Elemaki territory —they hunt down angels and shoot them out of the sky, and at those elevations the air is too thin for us to fly long distances, or very high, either. So—all you could possibly do about this feeling you have is tell your superior officer."

"I suppose you're right," said Mon.

"And now I've been told," said Husu. "So—back to training. I'll let you take a nap when you hit the target in the heart three times in a row."

Which Mon did with his next three shots.

"Apparently you feel better," said Husu. "Now go and take a nap."

"You'll tell my father?"

"I'll tell your father that Monush has made a mistake. We'll have to wait and see what that mistake might be."

Monush sat in council with Ilihiak and several of his military advisers. Ilihiak's wife, Wissedwa, sat behind him. This was quite unusual, but Monush said nothing about having a woman present in a council of war. The Zenifi had their own customs, their own reasons for doing things. Monush knew enough—had learned well enough from Motiak—that you don't take offense at the strange customs of other nations, you seek to learn from them. Still, was he wrong to think that some of the men studiously avoided looking at Wissedwa?

It took no time at all for the council to conclude that there was no point in trying to win their freedom through open rebellion. "Before you ever came here, Monush," said Ilihiak sadly, "we fought too many times and lost too many men. We can win a victory in the battlefield, and the underking we defeated merely comes back with armies of his brother-kings."

"Besides," said one of the old men, "the diggers breed like the maggots they are."

Ilihiak winced slightly. The people had agreed that they would take the covenant—that didn't mean their opinion of nonhumans was going to change. And when it came to diggers, it wouldn't much matter, anyway. Most diggers in Darakemba were slaves—captives of war or their descendants to the third generation. The Zenifi could hate diggers and not much bother their fellow citizens in Darakemba. It was their loathing for sky people that would cause problems.

During the early part of the meeting, Monush quickly learned that of all Ilihiak's advisers, it was Khideo who had the king's ear, and rightly so, because he spoke with calm wisdom and without passion. So it was a surprise that he had not been named Ush-Khideo by Ilihiak—that he had no title of honor at all. Now Khideo raised a hand slightly from his lap, and the others fell silent.

"O king," he said, "you have listened to my words many times when we went to war against the Elemaki. Now, O king, if my counsel has ever been of service to you, I beg you to listen to me now and I will be your true servant and deliver this nation out of bondage."

Monush wondered at the formality of Khideo's speech—hadn't he already spoken up several times, just like any of the other men?

Ilihiak touched his hand to his own lips, then opened his palm toward Khideo. "I give my voice to Khideo now."

Ah, so that was it. Khideo wasn't just giving casual counsel. He was asserting a privilege, and Ilihiak had granted it. More was at stake here than just advising the king. If Khideo's plan was accepted, apparently he would be the one to lead the exodus. No doubt Khideo feared that Monush would try to lead the Zenifi out of captivity; Khideo was forestalling any such possibility. Monush would have to be their guide back to Darakemba, and it would be Monush who would introduce them to the great Motiak. But Khideo had no intention of letting Monush supplant him—or Ilihiak—as leader of the nation until the last possible moment. How needless this maneuvering was; Monush was not a man who cared who was in command, as long as the plan they followed was a wise one.

"The great Motiak sent so few men to find us because any larger group would surely have been caught and destroyed by the Elemaki," said Khideo.

Of course Khideo would remind everyone of how few men Monush had brought with him. But Monush took no offense. Instead, he raised his hand from his lap and Khideo nodded, giving him the privilege of speech. "As it was, if the enemy had not been made stupid by the power of the Keeper, we would have been caught." Even as he said the formulaic words, he wondered if perhaps they might not be true, at least in this case. Why hadn't any of the Elemaki looked up at one of the many times when Monush's men would have been visible moving across the face of the mountains?

"Now we propose to win the freedom of our whole people," said Khideo. "You know at this table that I do not shrink from battle. You know that I don't think even assassination is beneath my honor."

The others nodded gravely, and now Monush began to suppose that he knew why Khideo had no honorific. It could not have been Ilihiak that he once tried to assassinate—but Nuab must have had some enemies when he was still alive as a truly terrible king. Ilihiak could accept Khideo's counsel and even let him lead his armies, but he could never give an honorific to a man who tried to kill a king—especially his father, as unworthy as the old king might have been.

"Our only hope is to flee from this place," said Khideo. "But to do it, we have to take at least enough of our herds with us to feed us on our journey. Has anyone ever tried to keep turkeys quiet? Will our pigs move as swiftly as a fleeing army needs to move? Not to mention our women and children—the nursing babies, the toddlers—will we take them along the faces of cliffs? March them for half a day or more at top speed?"

"At least the Elemaki know how impossible it is for you to escape as a people," said Monush. "Therefore they post only a few guards here."

"Exactly," said Khideo.

"So we kill them and go!" cried one of the other men.

Khideo did not answer, but waited instead for Ilihiak to gently chide the man and return the voice to Khideo.

"I read again in the record we keep of the history of the Nafari," said Khideo. "When Nafai led his people away from the traitorous lying murderer Elemak and the foul diggers who served him, he had the help of the Keeper of Earth, who made all the Elemaki sleep so soundly that they didn't wake up."

"Nafai was a hero," said an old man. "The Keeper says nothing to us."

"The Keeper spoke to Binaro," said Ilihiak mildly.

"Binadi," muttered another man.

Khideo shook his head. "The Keeper also sent the dream that brought Monush to us. We will trust that after we have done all we can do, the Keeper must do the rest to keep us safe. But my plan does not require us to pray to the Keeper and then hope our prayer is granted. You all know that we are forbidden to ferment any of our barley, even though it makes the water safer from disease. Why is that?"

"Because the beer makes the diggers crazy," said an old man.

"It makes them stupid," said Khideo. "It makes them drunk. Rowdy, noisy, happy, stupid—and then they pass out. This is why we're forbidden to make it—because the dirt-eaters don't have any self-control."

"If we offer them beer," said Ilihiak, "even presuming we can find any—"

Several of the men laughed. Apparently clandestine brewing was not unheard of.

"—what's to stop them from arresting and imprisoning whoever offers it to them?"

Khideo only nodded at the king.

No, not at the king at all. At the king's wife, Wissedwa. She turned her face away, so she didn't look directly at any of the men, but she spoke boldly so all could hear her. "We know that to the diggers all women are sacred. Even if they refuse the beer they will not lay hands on us. So we will offer it to them as the last share of the harvest. They'll know they can't legally turn it in to their superiors without also turning in the criminals who gave it to them; they'll have no choice but to drink it."

"The queen speaks my plan from her own lips," said Khideo.

Monush thought that Khideo bore the shame of deferring to a woman in council with great dignity. He would have to ask, later, why the voice of the woman was heard. In the meantime, though, it was obvious that she was no fool and had followed the discussion completely. Monush tried to imagine a woman at one of Motiak's councils. Who would it be? Not Dudagu, that was certain—had she ever uttered an intelligent word? And Toeledwa, before she died, had always been quiet, refusing even to ask about matters outside the rearing of her children and the affairs of the king's house. But Edhadeya, now—Monush could imagine *her* speaking boldly in council. There'd be no silencing *her* if once she was given the right to speak. This was definitely an idea that should never be suggested to Motiak. He doted on Edhadeya enough that he might just decide to grant her the privilege of speech, and that would be the end of all dignity for the king's council. I have not the humility of this Khideo, thought Monush.

"Now we must know," said Khideo, "whether Monush knows another way back to Darakemba that won't take us through the heart of the land of Nafai."

Monush spoke immediately. "Motiak and I looked at all the maps before my men and I set out. We had no choice but to come up the Tsidorek in search of you, because that was the route of your great king Zenifab when your ancestors left. But for the return, if you know the way to the river Mebberek—"

"It's called Mebbereg in this country," said an old man, "if it's the same river."

"Does it have a tributary with a pure source?" asked Monush.

"Mebbereg's largest tributary is the Ureg. It begins in a lake called Uprod, which is a pure source," said the old man.

"That's the one," said Monush. "There's an ancient pass above Uprod leading into the land northward. I know how to find it, I think, if the land hasn't changed too much since our maps were made. It comes out not far from a bend in the Padurek, which is the great pure-source tributary of the Tsidorek. From the moment we emerge from that pass, we will be in lands ruled by Motiak."

Khideo nodded. "Then we will leave through the back of the city, away from the river. And we'll only need to give the beer to the Elemaki guards who are stationed here in the city. The guards downriver and upriver will never hear us, nor will the ones crossriver know anything is going on. And when the guards discover us gone, they won't dare go to their king to report their failure, because they know that they'll all be slaughtered. Instead they'll flee into the forest themselves and become outlaws and vagabonds, and it will be many days before the king of the Elemaki knows what we've done. That is my plan, O king, and now I return your voice to you."

"I receive back my voice," said Ilihiak. "And I declare that it truly *was* my voice, and Khideo is now my hands and my feet in leading this nation to freedom. He will set the day, and all will obey him as if he were king until we are at the shores of the Mebbereg."

Monush watched as all the other men in the council immediately knelt and touched their palms to the floor, doing obeisance to Khideo. Monush nodded toward him, as befitted the dignity of the emissary of Motiak. Khideo looked at him under a raised eyebrow. Monush didn't let his benign expression waver. After a moment, Khideo must have decided that Monush's nod was enough, for he raised his hands to release the others, and then knelt himself before the king, putting his face between the king's knees and his hands flat on the king's feet. "All I do in your name will bring you honor, O king, until the day I give you back your hands and feet."

Monush found it interesting that these rituals could have emerged so quickly, after only three generations of separation from Darakemba. Then it dawned on him that these rituals might be much older—but they had been learned from the Elemaki in the years since the Zenifi came to this place. How ironic if the Zenifi came here to be the purest Nafari, only to be the ones who adapted themselves to the ways of the Elemaki.

Ilihiak laid his hands on Khideo's head for a moment. That apparently ended the ritual, and Khideo arose and returned to his seat. Ilihiak smiled at them all. "Act with courage, my friends, for the time is now if the Keeper is to deliver us at all."

By evening, to Monush's astonishment, all the people had been notified, the allotted herds had been assembled, and the guards stationed in the city were roaring drunk. Hours before dawn, in bright moonlight, the people moved with astonishing quietness out of the city, past the stupefied diggers, out into the forest. Khideo and his scouts were excellent guides, and in three days they were at the shores of the Mebbereg. From there, Ilihiak, once again the sole ruler of the Zenifi, used Monush's services as a scout and guide—but Monush did not ask for, nor did Ilihiak offer, the kind of authority that had been given to Khideo.

When I get to Motiak, thought Monush, I will tell him that he would be wise to give great respect to these people, for even in their small, oppressed kingdom, they found a few who are worthy of authority and skilled in its use.

Edhadeya watched anxiously from her place among the women as the Zenifi passed through the river, coming out of it as new people. She saw how they shied away from the watching sky people; it made her feel sad to see how, even cleansed by the water of Tsidorek, they still kept the old prejudices they were raised with. We can wash people in the water all we want, she thought, but we can never wash their parents out of their hearts.

She was not watching for real change in these people, of course—she knew that rituals existed to point the way, not to actually accomplish anything in themselves. They provided a marking point in people's lives, a public memory. Someday the children or grandchildren of the Zenifi would say, On the day our ancestors passed through the water, they emerged as new people, and from that day forward we welcomed the sky people as our brothers, fellow children of the Keeper of Earth. But the truth would be very different, for in all likelihood it would be those very children or grandchildren who were the first of the Zenifi to embrace the brotherhood of angel and human. Yet their parents would not all deny what their children believed—the ritual was the marker, and in the end, it would become the truth even if it didn't begin that way.

The women—even the waterkeepers—did not greet the people rising out of the icy water; it was the priests of Motiak who met them and laid hands on them to make them new people and give them names which were, oddly enough, identical to their old names with the addition of the title "citizen." Edhadeya was old enough now to have learned the stories of the old days, when Luet stood as Nafai's equal, as Chveya and Oykib stood side by side. She was also old enough to have heard the priests talk about how the old records were misinterpreted, for it was the custom among the ancients to show so much honor to the Heroes that even their wives were treated like Heroes—but it was entirely because of their husbands that these women were remembered. Edhadeya read several passages from the Book of Nafai aloud to Uss-Uss, her digger teacher-slave. "How can the priests interpret this any way but that Luet was a waterseer before she even met Nafai? And Hushidh was a raveler long before she married Issib?"

To which Uss-Uss replied, "Why should it surprise you that these male humans have to lie even about their own sacred records? The earth people honor their women; so do the sky people; therefore the middle people must deny their women."

It seemed to Edhadeya at the time to be too simple an explanation, and now, watching the priests, she realized that most human men did not treat their wives and daughters as if they were nothing. Hadn't Father sent the expedition to find the Zenifi solely because of her own dream, the dream of a woman? That must have made the priests' skin crawl! And now every single man and woman who came out of the water was proof that the Keeper showed a woman what she never showed any of these priests!

But it was not to gloat or boast that Edhadeya stood pressed to the rail of the bridge to watch the Zenifi become citizens. She was looking for the faces she had seen in her dream. Surely that family would be one of the people who came. But when the last of them passed through the water, Edhadeya knew that she hadn't seen them.

How tragic, that the people she dreamed of should have been among the ones who died.

It was not until hours later, after the presentations of this dignitary and that one to Father, that Edhadeya was able to get a moment with Monush—though certainly not a *private* moment, since Aronha and

Mon both stayed as near the great soldier as they could get without wearing his clothing.

"Monush," she said, "how sad that they died, the people I saw in my dream."

"Died?" he asked. "No one died. We came away from Zinom without losing a single one of the people of Ilihiak."

"But Monush, how can you explain to me why the people I dreamed of are not among these people?"

Monush looked confused. "Perhaps you remember them wrong."

Edhadeya shook her head. "Do you think I see such a vision every day? It was a true dream—and the people I truly saw aren't among these."

Within a few minutes, Edhadeya was alone with Father, Monush, and two men of the Zenifi—their king, Ilihiak, and Khideo, who seemed to be Ilihiak's most honored friend.

"Tell me of the people you saw," said Ilihiak kindly, when Motiak had indicated he should speak.

Edhadeya described them, and Ilihiak and Khideo both nodded. "We know who it was she saw," said Ilihiak. "It was Akmaro and his wife Chebeya."

"Who are they?" asked Motiak.

Once again Ilihiak explained about the one priest who had opposed the killing of Binadi, how he had fled the kingdom and gathered a few hundred supporters before disappearing to escape the army Nuak sent against them. "If you dreamed of them," said Ilihiak, "and it was a true dream, it must mean that they are still alive. I rejoice to hear this."

"But then that means we rescued the wrong people," said Monush.

Ilihiak bowed his head. "My lord Motiak, I hope that you do not regret having redeemed my poor kingdom from captivity."

Motiak stared silently into the empty air in front of him.

"Motiak," said Monush, "I remember now that there was a brief time on the ledge of the cliff, before we passed near Sidonod, when I was confused. I had dreamed something but couldn't remember the dream. Now I realize that the Keeper must have been trying to show me the right way, and the mischievous Jaguar must have—"

"No Jaguar," said Motiak. "The Jaguar has no power over the Keeper of Earth."

"But over such a weak man as myself," said Monush.

"There *is* no Jaguar except the stupid cats themselves," said Motiak impatiently. "I don't understand how you missed the right way, Monush. But I do know it was a good thing to find the Zenifi and bring them home to Darakemba. It was also a good thing for them to take the covenant and give up their old hatred of the sky people. The Keeper must be happy with this, so I refuse to call this a mistake."

Motiak turned his gaze to Edhadeya. "Are you sure you interpreted your dream correctly? Perhaps this Akmaro was asking the Keeper to send help for the people of Ilihiak."

"He and his wife and their children were frightened because of their own captivity," said Edhadeya.

"But a girl can hardly interpret a true dream," said Khideo, sounding as if he were only pointing out the obvious.

"You were not asked to speak," said Motiak mildly, "and my daughter is like my ancient mother-of-mothers, Luet—when she dreams true, she can be trusted. I hope you don't doubt that, my friend."

Khideo bowed his head. "I have spent many years listening to a woman speak in a king's council," he said quietly. "She was the woman who saved the lives of our people, by leading our young girls out to plead with the invading Elemaki, knowing that the diggers among them would not raise their weapons against a female, but uncertain of what the bloodthirsty humans among them might do. But even *she* did not dare to interpret dreams in the council. And she was not a child."

Motiak looked at him in silence, at his bowed head. "I see that you're ashamed of the way I conduct my council," said Motiak. "But if I had not heeded this girl's dream, my friend, Monush would never have been sent, and you would never have been brought here to freedom and safety."

Ilihiak, obviously embarrassed, said, "It was never an easy thing for Khideo to break from the old ways, even to hear my wife speak in council, though she was very circumspect. But there has been no braver war leader nor truer friend—"

"I'm not angry at Khideo," said Motiak. "I only ask him to understand that I do not shame him, I honor him by letting him be present when I hear my daughter's words. If he feels himself unprepared for this honor, he may withdraw and I will not be offended."

"I beg to be allowed to stay," murmured Khideo.

"Very well," said Motiak. Then he turned to the whole group. "We sent one expedition, and Monush tells me that it was very dangerous—they could have been discovered at any time."

Edhadeya, sensing where this discussion was leading, plunged in. "But they *weren't* discovered," she said, "because the Keeper was protecting them and—"

Father's cold stare and the shocked silence of the other men, their eyes wide, their mouths open—it was enough to silence her even as she pleaded for the people of the dream.

"Perhaps my daughter could study the ancient stories, and learn that Luet showed proper respect at all times."

Edhadeya had read the ancient stories already, many times, and she distinctly remembered that there were at least a few occasions when Luet showed that she thought her visions were more important than *any* kind of courtesy. But it would not be wise to contradict Father. She had already said too much—after all, most of the men here thought it improper for her even to be present at a council of the King. "Father, I should have confined my pleadings to a time when we are alone."

"There is nothing to plead," said Motiak. "I obeyed the Keeper's dream and sent Monush and his men. They found the Zenifi and brought them home, and it seems plain to me that they had the protection of the Keeper all the way. Now if the Keeper wants me to send another expedition, he must first send another dream."

"To a man this time, perhaps," said Khideo softly.

Motiak smiled wanly. "I don't presume to tell the Keeper of Earth which of his children's minds should be the receptacle for his messages to us."

Lesser men might have withered; Khideo managed to bow his head without seeming to give way at all. It seemed to Edhadeya that he might not always be content to bow to other men.

"Edhadeya, you may leave us," said Father. "Trust in the Keeper of Earth. And also trust in me."

Trust in Father? Of course she did—she trusted in him to be kind to her, to keep his word, to be a just king and a wise father. But she could also trust him to ignore her most of the time, to allow custom to keep her in the women's part of the house where she was supposed to give respect to a jealous witling like Dudagu Dermo. If all women were like Edhadeya's stepmother, the customs would make sense—why should men have to waste time listening to *her*? But I am nothing like Dudagu, thought Edhadeya, and Father knows it. He knows it, and yet out of respect for custom he treats me as if all women were equally worthless. He gives custom more respect than he gives me.

As she worked angrily on her pointless weaving in her room, Edhadeya had to be honest enough with herself to admit that Father treated her with more respect than she ever saw other men treat women —and that Father was criticized for it, too. Now that Monush had come home with the Zenifi, who really did need saving, everyone admitted that Motiak had not been foolish to listen to his daughter. But then, in front of everyone, Edhadeya had insisted that Monush brought back the wrong people. It was a stupid thing for her to do. Why spoil a triumph?

There would have been chances to talk to him privately. She just wasn't used to thinking politically, that was all.

But it was hardly *her* fault if she didn't understand about politics, was it? It wasn't *her* decision to keep her out of court except on women's days, when she was trotted out for display, to smile at the simpering ladies who drifted in like down from a baby duck. She wanted to scream at them that they were the most worthless creatures on earth, dressed in their fine clothing and never deigning to dirty their hands with work. Be like the sky women! Be like the earth women! Accomplish something! Be like the poorest of the middle women, if you can't think of anything else to do—learn a skill that isn't just decorative, have a thought of your own and sustain it with an argument!

Be fair, be fair, she told herself. Many of these women are smarter than they seem. They learn their light manners and display their beauty to help increase their family's status and honor in the kingdom. What are they supposed to do? They aren't the daughter of an indulgent king who lets his daughter strut around as if she were a boy, standing on the roof with that mad child Mon who wants to be an angel. . . .

I like to be with Mon, because he doesn't condescend to me. And why shouldn't he want to be an angel? He doesn't talk about it, does he? He doesn't make wings out of feathers and string and try to jump off the roof, does he? He isn't insane, he's simply as trapped in his life as I am in mine. That makes us friends.

Friends, a man and a woman. It was possible. You'd think to hear some people talk that a human man had more in common with an angel man than with a human woman.

Edhadeya thought back to her dream. She knew she thought of it too much. As she discovered more and more in the dream, she couldn't trust her new conclusions; it was obvious that she must be adding her own needs and desires and ideas to the one vision that the Keeper had given her. Still, she was sure, thinking back to the sight of that family, that the father thought of the mother as his equal or even—yes, she knew it!—his superior in at least some ways. He thought she was braver than he was, that was certain. Stronger. And he would admit it. And both parents valued the daughter as much as they valued the son. Even though they lived as slaves among the diggers, this was the great truth that they would bring back to Darakemba if only they could be liberated. For they would have the courage to preach this idea to everyone. That Akmaro was not diminished by his respect for Chebeya, and they did not honor their son Akma any less just because they honored Luet as much.

Luet? Akma? No one had said these names. They had spoken of Akmaro and Chebeya, but had they mentioned the children's names? It wasn't hard to guess that the wife of Ro-Akma would insist on naming her firstborn son Akma after his father, but how did she know they had named their daughter Luet?

I knew because the Keeper of Earth is still speaking to me through the same dream, through my memories of the dream.

Even as the thought came into her mind, she knew she must not tell anyone. It would be claiming too much. It would sound to others as if she were simply trying to exploit her triumphant dream and go on telling people what to do. She would have to be careful to assert special knowledge of the Keeper only rarely.

But whether she could speak of it or not, the Keeper was still aware of her, still speaking to her, and that was such joyful news it could hardly be contained.

"So? What is it? Don't just wiggle like you have to void yourself."

Edhadeya screeched at the first sound of Uss-Uss's voice. She hadn't realized the digger slave was even in the room.

"I was here in plain sight when you came in, foolish girl," said Uss-Uss. "If you hadn't been so angry at your father, you would have seen me."

"I didn't say anything," said Edhadeya.

"Oh, didn't you? Muttering under your breath about how you're not as stupid as Dudagu Dermo and you don't deserve to be shut out of everything and Mon isn't crazy because he wants to be an angel because why shouldn't worthless people like the king's daughter and the king's second son wish they could be *anything* but what they are—"

"Oh be quiet!" said Edhadeya with mock petulance. "Making fun of me like that."

"I've told you muttering isn't a good habit. Keen ears can hear."

"Yes, well, I *didn't* say anything about kings' daughters or kings' second sons—"

"You *are* losing your mind, girl. And I notice while you're talking about what you and Mon *wish* you were, you didn't come up with no old diggers, did you!"

"Even if I wanted to be a digger and live with my nose in the dirt," said Edhadeya nastily, "I *certainly* wouldn't want to be old."

"May the Mother forgive you," said Uss-Uss quickly, "and let you live to be old despite your careless words."

Edhadeya smiled at Uss-Uss's concern for her. "The Keeper isn't going to strike me dead for saying things like that."

"So far, you mean," said Uss-Uss.

"Does the Keeper ever speak to you, Uss-Uss?"

"In the thrumming of the roots of trees under the earth, she speaks to me," said Uss-Uss.

"What does she say?"

"Unfortunately, I don't speak the language of trees," said Uss-Uss. "I haven't the faintest idea. Something about how stupid young girls are, that's all I get from her."

"How odd, that the Keeper would tell the truth to me, and lie to you."

Uss-Uss cackled with delight at the repartee—and then stopped abruptly. Edhadeya turned and saw her father in the doorway.

"Father," she said. "Come in."

"Did I hear a servant calling her mistress stupid?" asked Father.

"We were joking with each other," said Edhadeya.

"It doesn't lead to anything good, to be too familiar with servants, whether they're diggers or not."

"It leads to my feeling as though I had one intelligent friend in the world," said Edhadeya. "Or perhaps that isn't good, in the eyes of the king."

"Don't be snippy, Edhadeya. I didn't make the rules, I inherited them."

"And you've done nothing to change them."

"I sent an army because of your dream."

"Sixteen men. And you sent them because Mon said it was a true dream."

"Oh, am I condemned because the Keeper gave you a witness to support your claim?"

"Father, I'll never condemn you. But Akmaro and his family have to be brought here. Don't you understand? The things that Akmaro teaches—that a man and woman are equal partners, that a family should rejoice at the birth of a daughter as much as at the birth of a son—"

"How do you know what he teaches?" asked Father.

"I saw them, didn't I?" she said defiantly. "And I'll bet the daughter's name is Luet, and the son's name is the same as the father's. Except the honorific, of course."

Motiak frowned at her, but she knew from his anger that she was right, those *were* the names. "Are you using the gift of the Keeper to show off?" said Father sternly. "To try to force me to do your bidding?"

"Father, why do you have to say it that way? Why can't you say, Oh, Edhadeya, how wonderful that the Keeper tells you so much! How wonderful that the Keeper is alive in you!"

"Wonderful," he said. "And difficult. Khideo is furious at having been humiliated by my letting a girl speak so boldly before him."

"Well, the poor man. Let him go back to the Elemaki then!"

"He's a genuine hero, Edhadeya, a man of great honor and not the sort of man that I want to have as my enemy!"

"He's also a bigot of the first stripe, and you know it! You're going to have to settle these people off by themselves somewhere, or there'll be trouble."

"I know that. They know it, too. There's land along the valley of the Jatvarek, after it has fallen down from the gornaya but before it enters the flatlands. No angels live there, because the jaguars and the lesser cats are too prevalent there in the rainy season. So it will suit them."

"Wherever humans go, angels can safely live," said Edhadeya. She was taunting him with his own law, but he didn't rise to the bait.

"A good king can tolerate reasonable variation among his people. It costs the sky people nothing to avoid settling among the Zenifi, as long as the Zenifi give them free and safe passage, and respect their right to trade. In a few generations. . . ."

"I know," she said. "I know it's a wise choice."

"But you're in the mood to argue with me about everything."

"Because I think that none of this has anything to do with the people I saw in my dream. What about *them*, Father?"

"I can't send another party to search for Akmaro," said Motiak.

"*Won't*, you mean."

"Won't, then. But for a good reason."

"Because a woman is asking you to."

"You're hardly a woman yet," said Motiak. "Right now the entire enterprise we just concluded is regarded as a great success. But if I send out another army, it will look as though the first attempt was a failure."

"It *was* a failure."

"No it wasn't," said Motiak. "Do you think you're the only one who hears the voice of the Keeper?"

Edhadeya gasped and blushed. "Oh, Father! Has the Keeper sent you a dream?"

"I have the Index of the Oversoul, Dedaya. I was consulting it for another reason, but as I held it in my hands, I heard a voice clearly speak to me. Let me bring Akmaro home, said the voice."

"Oh, Father! The Index is still alive, after all these years?"

"I don't think it's any more alive than a stone," said Motiak. "But the Keeper is alive."

"The Oversoul, you mean," said Edhadeya. "It's the Index of the Oversoul."

"I know that the ancient records make a great deal of distinction between them, but I've never understood it myself," said Motiak.

"So the Keeper will bring Chebeya and her family home to Darakemba?"

Motiak narrowed his eyes, pretending to glare at her. "Do you think I don't notice when you do that?"

"Do what?" asked Edhadeya, all wide-eyed innocence.

"Not Akmaro and his people—no, you say 'Chebeya and her family.' "

Edhadeya shrugged.

"The way you women persist in calling the Keeper 'she' all the time. You know that the priests are always after me to forbid women to do that, at least in front of men. I always say to them, when the ancient records no longer show us Luet, Rasa, Chveya, and Hushidh speaking of the Oversoul and the Keeper as 'she' and 'her,' then in that same moment I'll forbid the women to do as the ancients did. That shuts them up —though I'll bet more than a few of them have wondered how serious I am, and whether they could somehow alter the ancient records without my noticing."

"They wouldn't dare!"

"That's right, they wouldn't," said Motiak.

"You could also ask those priests to show you the anatomical chart of the Keeper that shows him to have a—"

"Mind your language," said Motiak. "I'm your father, and I'm the king. There should be a certain dignity in both offices. And I'm not about to convince the priests that I've turned against the old religion now, am I?"

"A bunch of old—"

"There are things that I may not hear, as head of the worship of men."

"Worship of men is right," muttered Edhadeya.

"What was that?" asked Motiak.

"Nothing."

"Worship of men, you said? What did that—oh, I see. Well, think how you like. Just remember that I won't always be king, and you can't be sure that my successor will be as tolerant of your subversive little attacks on the men's religion. I'm content to let women worship as they please, and so was my father and his father before him. But there's always agitation to change things, to shut down the heresies of women. Every wife who strikes her husband or scolds him publicly is taken as one more proof that letting the women have their own religion makes them disrespectful and destructive."

"What difference does it make, whether we keep our silence because the priests force us or because we're afraid that they *might* force us?"

"If you can't see the difference, you're not as bright as I thought."

"Do you really think I'm intelligent, Father?"

"What, are you really fishing for more praise than I already give you?"

"I just want to believe you."

"I've heard enough from you, when you start doubting my word." He got up and started for the door.

"I'm not doubting your honesty, Father!" she cried out. "I know you *think* that you think I'm intelligent. But I think that in the back of your mind, you always have another little phrase: 'for a woman.' I'm intelligent—for a woman. I'm wise—for a woman."

"I can promise you," said Motiak, "that the phrase 'for a woman' never comes to my mind in reference to you. But the phrase 'for a child' is there, I can assure you—and often."

She felt as if he had slapped her.

"I meant you to," said Father.

Only when he answered did she realize she had muttered the words. Feel slapped.

"I respect your intelligence enough," said Father, "that I think a verbal slap teaches you better than a physical one. Now trust in the Keeper to bring this Akmaro—and *Chebeya*—to Darakemba. And in the meantime, don't expect me to be able to stand custom on its head. A king can't lead his people faster and farther than they're willing to follow."

"What if the people insist on doing wrong?" asked Edhadeya.

"What, am I in my schoolroom, being tossed hypothetical questions by my tutors?"

"Is *that* how the heir to the king gets taught?" she asked defiantly. "Where are the tutors asking *me* hypothetical questions about kingship?"

"I'll answer your original question, not these impossible ones. If the people insist on doing wrong, and the king can't persuade them to do right, then the king steps down from the throne. If his son has honor, he refuses to take the throne after him, and so do all his sons. Let the people do evil if they choose, but with a new king of their own choosing."

In awe, Edhadeya whispered, "Could you do that, Father? Could you give up the throne?"

"I'll never have to," he said. "My people are basically good, and they're learning. If I push too hard, I gain nothing and the resistance gets stronger. During the long slow years of transformation I need the trust and patience of those who want me to make changes in their favor." He leaned down and kissed the crown of her head, where the hair was parted. "If I had no sons, but you were still my daughter, then I would hurry the changes so that you could have the throne in my place. But I have sons, good ones, as you well know. And so I will let the change come gradually, generation after generation, as my father and grandfather did before me. Now I have work to do, and I'll spend no more time on you. There are whole nations under my rule who get less of my attention than you do."

Giving him her best demure smile, she said, in a simpering courtly ladylike voice, "Oh, Father, you're so incredibly *kind* to me."

"One of my ancestors walled up a recalcitrant daughter in a cave with only bread and water to eat until she became properly obedient," said Father.

"As I recall, she dug her way out of the cave with her fingernails and ran off and married the Elemaki king."

"You read too much," said Father.

She stuck out her tongue at him, but he didn't see, because he was gone.

Behind her, Uss-Uss spoke up again. "Aren't you the brave little soldier?"

"Don't make fun of me," said Edhadeya.

"I'm not," said Uss-Uss. "You know, one of the stories that circulates among us devil slaves—"

"No one calls you devils anymore."

"Don't interrupt your elders," said Uss-Uss. "We all tell each other the story of the digger who was cleaning a chamber when two traitors spoke together, plotting the death of the king. The slave went straight to the king and told him, whereupon the king had the digger killed, for daring to hear what humans said in front of him."

"What, do you think I'm going to—"

"I'm just telling you that if you think you're suffering because you're a human woman, remember that your father didn't even bother to send me out of the room in order to talk to you. Why *is* that?"

"Because he trusts you."

"He doesn't know me. He only knows that *I* know what the penalty is for daring to repeat what I hear. Don't tell me how oppressed the women of Darakemba are when most of us diggers are slaves that can be killed for the slightest infraction—even for an act of great loyalty."

"I've never heard that story," said Edhadeya.

"Just because you haven't heard it doesn't mean it isn't true."

"So Father thinks I'm a troublemaker and you think I'm a proud insensitive—"

"And aren't you?"

Edhadeya shrugged. "I'd free you if I could."

"At least your father *pretended* that he was trying to change your place in society. But in all your pleading, have you *ever* asked for the earth people of Darakemba to be set free?"

Edhadeya was furious; she didn't like being called a hypocrite. "It's completely different!"

"So eager to get this Chebeya and Akmaro out of captivity, but not a thought about getting old Uss-Uss her freedom."

"What would you do with it if you had it?" demanded Edhadeya. "Go back to the Elemaki? The soldiers would have to kill you before you got halfway there, so you couldn't tell them all our secrets."

"Go *back* to the Elemaki? Child, my great grandfather was born a slave to the kings of the Nafari. *Back* to a place I've never been?"

"Do you really hate me?" asked Edhadeya.

"I never said I hated you," said Uss-Uss.

"But you want to be free of me."

"I would like it, when my day's work was done, when you were fast asleep, I would like it, to go home to my own little house, and kiss the noses of my own fat little grandchildren, and share with my husband the wages I was paid for serving in the king's house. Do you think I'd give you any less faithful service, just because I was doing it freely instead of because I knew I could be killed or at least sold out of the house if I made the slightest mistake?"

Edhadeya thought about this. "But you'd live in a hole in the ground, if you were free," she said.

Uss-Uss cackled and hooted. "Of course I would! So what if I did?"

"But that's. . . ."

"That's *inhuman*," said Uss-Uss, still laughing.

Edhadeya finally got the joke, and laughed with her.

Later, when it was dark, when Edhadeya was supposed to be asleep, she was wakened by a slight sound at the window. She saw there in the moonlight the silhouette of Uss-Uss, her head bobbing up and down. Thinking something might be wrong, Edhadeya got up and padded to the window.

Hearing her, Uss-Uss turned around and waited for her.

"Do you do this every night?" asked Edhadeya.

"No," said Uss-Uss. "Only tonight. But you were worried about these humans who are held captive by diggers in some far-off place."

"So you pray to the Keeper for them?"

"Why should I do that?" asked Uss-Uss. "The Keeper knows they're there—it was the Keeper sent you the dream you had, wasn't it? I don't figure it's my business to tell the Mother what she already knows! No, I was praying to the One-Who-Was-Never-Buried. She lives in that star, that high one. The one that's always overhead."

"No one can live in a star," said Edhadeya.

"An immortal can," said Uss-Uss. "I pray to her."

"Does she have a name?"

"A very sacred one," said Uss-Uss.

"Can you tell it to me?"

Uss-Uss lifted up the hem of Edhadeya's long nightgown and draped it onto her head, so that the cloth was over Edhadeya's ear. "My name is Voozhum," said Uss-Uss. "Now that you know my true name, I can tell you the name of the One-Who-Was-Never-Buried." Then Uss-Uss waited.

"Please," said Edhadeya, trembling. "Please, Voozhum." What was she supposed to do or say now? All she could think of was to offer the most formal and official version of her own name in answer. "My true name is Ya-Edhad."

"The One-Who-Was-Never-Buried is the one to whom Nafai gave the cloak of the starmaster. Did they think this was a secret from the earth people? The blessed ancestors saw her skin tremble with light. She is Shedemei, and she is the one who took the tower up into the sky and made a star of it."

"And she's still alive?"

"She has been seen twice in the years since then. Both times tending a garden, once in a high mountain valley, and once on the side of a cliff in the lowest reaches of the gornaya. She is the gardener, and she watches over the whole Earth. She will know what to do about Chebeya and her husband, about Luet and her brother."

For the first time Edhadeya realized that there might be things that the diggers knew that they didn't learn from the humans, and it filled her with a sudden and unfamiliar blush of humility. "Teach me how to speak to the One-Who-Was-Never-Buried."

"You fix your eye on the permanent star, the one they call Basilica."

Edhadeya looked up and found it easily—as every child could do.

"Then you bob your head, like this," said Uss-Uss.

"Can she see us?"

"I don't know," said Uss-Uss. "I only know that this is what we do when we pray to her. I think it started because that was how she moved her head that time when she was seen in a high valley."

So Edhadeya joined her slave in the unfamiliar ritual. Together they asked the One-Who-Was-Never-Buried to watch out for Chebeya and Luet and their people, and set them free. Uss-Uss would say a phrase, and Edhadeya would repeat it. At the end, Edhadeya added a few words of her own. "And help set all women free from captivity," she said. "Women of the sky, women of the earth, and women of the middle."

Uss-Uss cackled for a moment, then repeated the phrase. "And just think," she said. "Someday they'll marry you off to some second-rate potentate somewhere and I'll be dead and you'll think about this day and wonder which of us was more the slave, you or me!" Then she bustled Edhadeya back to bed, where she slept fitfully, dreaming meaningless dreams about dead women with sparkling skin whom no one had remembered to bury.

"If I didn't think this whole thing might be a mistake, I'd think it was funny," said the Oversoul.

"You don't have a sense of humor," said Shedemei, "and if you thought it was a mistake you wouldn't have done it."

"I can make a decision when I'm still eighty percent unsure of the outcome," said the Oversoul. "It's built into my programming, to help keep me from dithering to the point of inaction."

"I think sending Motiak that message through the Index was a good idea," said Shedemei. "Prevent them sending another expedition. *Force* the Keeper to act."

"Easy for you to decide, Shedemei," said the Oversoul. "*You* have no compassion for them.

Shedemei felt those words cut her to the heart. "A machine tells *me* that *I* have no compassion?"

"I have a sort of virtual compassion," said the Oversoul. "I do take human suffering into account, though not usually the suffering of individuals. Akmaro and Chebeya have a large enough group there that, yes, I feel some compassion for them. But *you* have the normal human ability to dehumanize people at will, especially strangers, especially in large groups."

"You're saying I'm a monster."

"I'm saying the humans feel compassion primarily for those they conceive of as being part of themselves. You don't know these people, so you can use them as bait for the Keeper of Earth. If it was just one person being tortured, however, you wouldn't do it—because then you would empathize with her and couldn't live with yourself for letting her suffer."

Shedemei was so agitated she left the library and went to tend her seedlings in the high-altitude room, where she was trying to breed a legume that would produce useful quantities of high-protein, high-energy beans in the highest mountain valleys of the gornaya. It was unspeakable, what the Oversoul had said, but it also made a kind of sense. As primates evolved toward depending on a community for cooperative survival, they would evolve empathy first for their own children, then for the children of others, then for the adult parents of those other children—but as the circle grew wider, the empathy would grow weaker.

Finally, humans had to evolve what no other primate had: a sense of identity with a group so powerful that it could swallow up the individual identity, at least to a large degree. Humans couldn't have this deep, self-sacrificing loyalty to more than one or two communities at a time. Thus communities were inevitably in conflict with each other, competing for the loyalty of their members. The tribe had to break down the solidarity of the family; religion had to compete with nation for loyalty. But once a community had that loyalty, the most ardent members would gladly die for it. Not for the other individuals directly, but for the interests of the group *as a whole,* because in the human mind, that group *was* the self, and the individual was able to regard himself as merely one iteration of the pattern of the whole. Humans, in order to rise above animals, had learned how to convert themselves into nothing more than organs or limbs or even the disposable fingernails and hair of a larger metaphorical organism.

The Oversoul is right. If I knew Chebeya and her people as individuals, then even with no more moral insight than a baboon, I would reach out to protect them. Or if I conceived myself to be one of them, I would subsume my own interests in the needs of the group as a whole, and would not dream of making them serve as bait in an attempt to serve the Keeper of Earth.

The Oversoul, on the other hand, was created to look out for the needs of humanity as a whole. The powers she had were tremendous, and her programmers had to build some kind of compassion into her. But it was an intellectual compassion, a historical compassion—the more people who were suffering, the greater the priority of easing their pain. Thus the Oversoul could overlook individual accidents, the intermittent deaths from the ordinary course of a disease cycling through a region; but the Oversoul would dread and try to avoid the large group suffering that came from war, drought, flood, epidemic. In those cases, the Oversoul could act, guiding individuals to actions that would help the whole affected population—not to save individual lives, but to reduce the scale of the suffering.

Between the two of us, though, thought Shedemei, we are left untouched by the suffering of Chebeya's people. There aren't enough of them to force the Oversoul to intervene on their behalf—though there are enough to make her uncomfortable. And I, on my isolated perch in the outer reaches of the atmosphere, I am no part of them. All my people are gone; my community is dead. As the digger women speak of me: I am the One-Who-Was-Never-Buried. That is the only difference between me and the dead, for a person who has no living community *is* dead. Haven't I seen it in old people? Spouse gone, friends gone, family gone except for later generations that barely remember the old one—they become annoyed to discover that they're still alive. Have I reached that point?

Not yet, she thought, sliding her fingers behind the tiny trowel in order to lift out a seedling that needed transplanting into a larger tray. Because my plants have become my people. My little animals, going through generation after generation as I play genetic games with them—they are the ones I think of as part of myself.

So is this good or bad? The Oversoul needs to get advice from the Keeper of Earth in order to alleviate the suffering of the people of Harmony. To accomplish that, we need to interfere with the Keeper's plans. The Keeper wants to rescue Chebeya and Akmaro; therefore we'll make it harder. It's not an unreasonable plan. In the end, it will be to the benefit of millions and millions of people on Harmony.

But we're doing it blindly. We don't know what the Keeper is trying to accomplish. *Why* is she trying to save the Akmari? Maybe we should have tried to understand her purpose before we started fiddling around with her ability to accomplish it.

Yet how can we understand her purpose if she won't talk to us? It's so circular.

<Yes, it is.>

"Don't talk into my mind," she said to the Oversoul. "I hate that."

<If you won't go where I have a comfortable voice, I'll use an uncomfortable one.>

"I wasn't talking to you, I was thinking to myself."

<If you don't want me to hear you, don't think.>

Shedemei snorted. "Very funny."

<Let's think about what reasons the Keeper might have for saving the people of Akma and Chebeya.>

"While we're at it, why not also think about what or who in the world the Keeper of Earth *is*."

<Do you think I haven't been researching that very question? I tell you it's either hidden from me, or it was never included in my memory, or the people who built me didn't even know.>

"If we can't find the Keeper using physical evidence or recorded memory," said Shedemei, "then maybe we should study what she wants and what she does, and then search for some mechanism by which it is possible for her to do it, or some entity that might benefit from her doing it."

<You think the Keeper's motives might be selfish, then?>

"Not at all. Any more than I will ever benefit from the expanded habitat that these little legumes will provide, if they are ever successful at producing useful nutrition in the low-oxygen, short-growing-season, thin-soil environment I intend them for. But *someone* will benefit. Therefore if some stranger who had no way of discovering me directly wanted to know something about me, she could at least start her reasoning from the fact that I have particular care for enhancing the ability of humans, diggers, and angels to expand into new habitats with improved nutrition. They might then look for me to be of a body-type that allowed me to identify with these creatures. Or at least they could gather from my actions that it is important to me that these creatures be protected."

<But would anything they learned ever cause them to look up in the sky?>

"I have no idea," Shedemei said wearily. "But I also know that if somebody wanted to get my attention, all they'd need to do is start stomping out all my gardens on Earth. Then I'd notice them, all right."

<So that's what we're doing. Stomping down the gardens of the Keeper of Earth.>

"Not so destructive, I hope."

<Yes, and Chebeya and Akmaro and their people had better hope so, too.>

"If you keep goading me this way, you'll end up persuading me to care so much about them that I stop worrying about the people of Harmony altogether. Is that what you want?"

<No.>

"Basilica was ruined half a millennium ago. My people are all dead. My nation of birth is irretrievable. Everything I ever felt myself to be a part of is dead, except my gardens. Do you really want me to become part of Akmaro and Chebeya, to begin to feel about them the way I once felt about Rasa and her household, about my friends, about my husband and my children?"

<No.>

"Then leave me alone."

<I can't. You're the starmaster. I'm programmed to maintain the health of the starmaster.>

"Health! What does this have to do with health?"

<It isn't good for you to be alone.>

Shedemei shuddered. She didn't want the Oversoul meddling like this. She was just *fine* on her own. Zdorab was gone, her children were gone, and that was *fine,* she had work to do, she didn't need distractions. Her health indeed!

* * *

Akma sat on the brow of the hill, exhausted from the day's work, but so filled with fury that even lying down wouldn't have been rest. And lying down he couldn't have watched his father stand there teaching the people—with Pabulog's vile sons sitting in the front row of the listeners. After all they had done to him, Father could bring them in and seat them in the place of honor? Of course Father and Mother made a great show of wanting him to sit there in the center of the front row, where he had always sat till now. But to sit shoulder-to-shoulder with the lying Didul, the arrogant Pabul, the brutal Udad, the pathetic slimy sneaky little Muwu—Father had to know that it was more shame than Akma could bear.

So he sat here on the hilltop, looking now at the campfires of the digger guards, now down at the gathering of Akma's people. I can't sort friends from enemies anymore. The diggers hurt nothing but my body; the Pabulogi stabbed at my pride; and my own father has told me that I'm nothing to him, nothing compared to the sons of his enemy.

Your enemies were my enemies, Father. For your sake, for loyalty to you, I bore whatever came to me and bore it proudly, because it was for you. And then you take my tormentors and talk to them as if they were also your sons. You even call them, *call* them sons. You dared to call that hypocritical encrustation of a skunk's rectum "Diduldis"—beloved son! *Whose* son? Only the son of the man who tried to kill you, Father, who drove you out! Only the son of the man that for your sake I hated. And now you have given him a name that you should never have spoken to anyone but me. I am Akmadis—but not if *he* has the name Diduldis from your lips. If he is your son then I am not.

Again, as so many times before, Akma felt tears come to his eyes. But he fought them off—and he was getting better at that, hiding his true feelings. Though of course sitting up here as the lone recusant certainly made it plain that he wasn't happy about *something*.

Mother was coming up the hill. Hadn't she given up yet?

Oh, yes, she had. Luet was with her, and now Mother stopped and Luet came on ahead. Ah, of course. Father can't do anything with nasty little Akma, and Mother can't make any headway with him, either. So send little Luet and see what she can do.

"Kmada!" she cried, when she was near enough.

"Why don't you go back down and listen to Father?" said Akma coldly. But the hesitation in her eyes forced him to relent. What did she know of these matters? She was innocent, and he wasn't going to be unjust to her. "Come here, Lutya, Ludayet."

"Oooh, Kmada, that name is so *ugly*."

"I think Ludayet is cute."

"But Lutya is the name of the Hero."

"The Hero's wife," said Akma.

"Father says the ancient women were heroes as much as the men."

"Yes, well, that's Father's opinion. Father thinks diggers are people."

"They are, you know. Because they have language. And there are good diggers and bad diggers."

"Yes, I know," said Akma. "Because most diggers are dead—those are the good ones."

"Are you mad at me like you're mad at Father?" asked Luet.

"I'm never mad at you."

"Then why do you make me sit with that nasty pig boy?"

Akma laughed at her characterization of Muwu. "It wasn't *my* idea."

"It's your idea to come up here and leave me alone."

"Luet, I love you. But I won't sit with the sons of Pabulog. Including Muwu."

Luet nodded gravely. "All right. That's what Father said—he said you weren't ready."

"Ready! I'll never be ready."

"So Mother said I can come up here and take my lessons from you."

Inadvertently, taken by surprise, Akma looked down at his mother, who stood at the base of the hill, watching them. She must have sensed or at least guessed what turn the conversation had taken, for she nodded her head just once and then turned away, walking back to the group that still listened to Akmaro teaching.

"I'm not a teacher," said Akma.

"You know more than *me,*" said Luet.

Akma knew what Mother was doing—and it had to be with Father's consent, so really it was Father doing it, too. If Akma won't stay involved listening to the great teacher Akmaro—or should it be what Pabulog called him, Akmadi, the traitor?—then we'll keep him involved by having him teach Luet. He won't dare be unkind to her, nor will he be dishonest enough to teach her falsehood or vent his anger against his father.

It would serve them right if I taught Luet exactly how Father betrayed me. How he has been betraying us all along. Father decides to believe that crazy old man Binadi and ends up getting us all thrown out of the city, forced to live in the wilderness. And then, even as we're being whipped by digger slavedrivers and tormented by Pabulog's evil sons, Father teaches us that Binadi said that the Keeper wants us to think of diggers and angels as our *brothers,* to think of women as our *equals,* when anyone can see that women are smaller and weaker than men, and that diggers and angels aren't even the same species. We might as well say we're brothers of trees and uncles of termites. We might as well call snails our fathers and dungbeetles our sons.

But he said none of this to Luet. Instead he got a stick, pulled out enough tufts of grass to have a clear writing surface of dirt, and began writing words and quizzing her on them. He could teach his sister. It would be better than sitting here alone, being burned alive inside by rage. And he would not use Luet as a weapon to strike out at Father. That was another matter, to be settled at another time. A time when Didul wasn't sitting there smirking at every word that Akma uttered. A time when he didn't have to smell the musk that Pabul gave off like a randy buck. A time when he and Father could look each other in the face and speak the truth.

I won't rest until Father admits how disloyal he's been. Admits that he loves them more than me, and that it's wrong for him to have been so unnatural as to forgive them without asking me first, without asking me to forgive him. How could he have acted as if forgiving them were the most natural thing in the world! And what right did *he* have to forgive them, when Akma still had not? It was Akma who had borne the worst of it. Everyone knew that. And in front of everyone, Father forgave them and took them through the water to make new men of them. Of course he made them say those stupid empty words of apology. We're so *sorry*, Akma. We're sorry, Luet. We're sorry, everybody. We are no longer the evil men who did that. We're now new men and true believers.

Am I the only one who isn't fooled? Am I the only one who sees that they still plan to betray us? That someday soon their father will come and they'll turn on us and we'll pay for having trusted them?

I'll pay.

Akma shuddered, imagining what the sons of Pabulog would do to him, when they had once again revealed their true nature of pure evil. Father would be sorry then, but it would be Akma that would be punished for Father's foolishness.

"Are you cold?" asked Luet.

"Only a little," said Akma.

"It's very warm tonight," said Luet. "You shouldn't be cold unless you're sick."

"All right," said Akma. "I won't be cold anymore."

"I can sit close up beside you and help you stay warmer."

So she sat by him and he kept his arm around her shoulder as they studied the words he wrote in the dirt. She was very quick, this little girl. Smarter than any boy Akma knew. So maybe that part of Father's teaching was true. Maybe girls were every bit as good as boys, when it came to learning, anyway. But anybody who could teach that a female digger was somehow equal to this sweet, trusting little girl was either insane or dishonest. Which was Father? Did it matter?

They came down in the hill in near darkness; the meeting was over. Luet led the way into the hut, chattering to Mother about the things that Akma had taught her.

"Thank you, Akma," said Mother.

Akma nodded. "Gladly, Mother," he said quietly.

But to his father he said nothing, and his father said nothing to him.

5

Mysteries

Mon couldn't help but notice that Bego was distracted. The old scholar hardly heard Mon's answers to his questions, and when Bego asked him again the very question that he had just answered, Mon couldn't help but peevishly say, "What is it, teaching the younger son just isn't interesting anymore?"

Bego looked annoyed. "What do you mean? What's this petulance? I thought you outgrew that years ago."

"You just asked me the same question twice, Bego, O wise master. And since you didn't hear a word of my answer the first time, it can't be that you were dissatisfied with it and want me to try again."

"What you need to learn is respect." Bego launched himself from his stool, apparently forgetting that he was too old and fat to fly very effectively. He ended up skittering across the floor till he got to the window, and there he stood, panting. "Can't even get up onto the sill anymore," he said angrily.

"At least you can *remember* flying."

"Will you shut *up* about your stupid envy of sky people? For one day, for one hour, for one *minute* will you just stop it and give a thought to *reality?*"

Stung and hurt, Mon wanted to lash back with some sharp retort, some bit of devastating wit that would make Bego regret having spoken so cruelly. But there was no retort, because Bego was right. "Maybe if I could bear my life as it is for one day, for one hour, for one *minute,* I could forget my wish to be something else," Mon finally answered.

Bego turned to him, his gaze softening. "What is this? Honesty, from Mon?"

"I never lie."

"I mean honesty about how you feel."

"Are you going to pretend that it was *my* feelings you were worried about?"

Bego laughed. "I don't worry much about *anybody's* feelings. But yours might matter." He looked at Mon as if he was listening. For what? Mon's heartbeat? For his secret thoughts? I have no secret thoughts, thought Mon. Or rather, they're not secret because I've withheld them —if they're unknown, it's because no one asked.

"Let me lay out a problem for you, Mon," said Bego.

"Back to work," said Mon.

"*My* work this time, not yours."

Mon didn't know whether he was being patronized or respected. So he listened.

"When the Zenifi came back several months ago—you remember?"

"I remember," said Mon. "They were settled in their new land only Ilihiak refused to be their king. He had them choose a governor. The people themselves. And then they showed their ingratitude by choosing Khideo instead of Ilihiak."

"So you *have* been paying attention."

"Was that all?" asked Mon.

"Not at all. You see, when the voice of the people went against Ilihiak, he came here."

"To ask for help? Did he really think Father would impose him as judge on the Zenifi? Ilihiak was the one who decided to let the people vote—let him live with what they voted for!"

"Exactly right, Mon," said Bego, "but of course Ilihiak would be the first to agree with you. He didn't come here in order to *get* power. He came because he was finally *free* of it."

"So he's an ordinary citizen," said Mon. "What was his business with the king?"

"He doesn't need to have business, you know," said Bego. "Your father took a liking to him. They became friends."

Mon felt a stab of jealousy. This stranger who had never even known Father's name till Monush found him six months ago was Father's friend, while Mon languished as a mere second son, lucky to see his father once a week on any basis more personal than the king's council.

"But he *did* have business," said Bego. "It seems that after Ilihiak's father was murdered—"

"A nation of regicides—and now they've elected a would-have-been regicide as their governor."

"Yes yes," said Bego impatiently. "Now it's time to listen. After Nuab was murdered and Ilihidis became king—"

"Dis-Ilihi? Not the heir?"

"The people chose the only one of Nuab's sons who hadn't run away when the Elemaki invaded. The only one with any courage."

Mon nodded. He hadn't heard about that. A second son inheriting on the basis of his merit.

"Don't have any fantasies about *that*," said Bego. "Your older brother is no coward. And it ill becomes you to wish for him to be deprived of his inheritance."

Mon leapt to his feet in fury. "How dare you accuse me of thinking any such thing!"

"What second son *doesn't* think it?"

"As well I might assume that *you're* jealous of bGo's great responsibilities, while you're only a librarian and a tutor for children!"

It was Bego's turn to be furious. "How dare you, a mere human, speak of my otherself as if you could compare your feeble brotherhood with the bonds between otherselves!"

They stood there, eye to eye. For the first time, Mon realized, eye to eye with Bego meant that Mon was looking down. His adult height was beginning to come. How had he not noticed till now? A tiny smile came to his lips.

"So, you smile," said Bego. "Why, because you succeeded in provoking me?"

Rather than confess the childish and selfish thought that had prompted his smile, Mon invented another reason, one which became true enough as soon as he thought of it. "Can a student not smile when he provokes his teacher into acting like a child?"

"And I was going to talk to you about genuine matters of state."

"Yes, you were," said Mon. "Only you chose to start by accusing me of wishing for my brother to lose his inheritance."

"For that I apologize."

"I wish you would apologize for calling me a 'mere human,' " said Mon.

"For that I also apologize," said Bego stiffly. "Just because you are a mere human doesn't mean that you can't have meaningful affection and loyalty between siblings. It isn't your fault that you cannot begin to comprehend the bonds of shared selfhood between otherselves among the sky people."

"Ah, Bego, now I understand what Husu meant, when he said that you were the only man he knew who could insult someone worse with your apologies than with your slanders."

"Husu said that?" asked Bego mildly. "And here I thought he hadn't understood me."

"Tell me the business of state," said Mon. "Tell me what business brought Ilihiak to Father."

Bego grinned. "I *thought* you wouldn't be able to resist the story."

Mon waited. When Bego didn't go on, Mon roared with frustration and ran once around the desk, for all the world like a digger child circling a tree before climbing it. He knew he looked silly, but he couldn't *stand* the malicious little games that Bego played.

"Oh, sit down," said Bego. "What Ilihiak came for was to give your father twenty-four leaves of gold."

"Oh," said Mon, disappointed. "Just money."

"Not money at all," said Bego. "There was writing on them. Twenty-four leaves of ancient writing."

"Ancient? You mean, before the Zenifi?"

"Perhaps," said Bego with a faint smile. "Perhaps before the Nafari."

"So there might have been a group of diggers or angels who knew how to work metal? Who knew how to write?"

Bego gave that rippling of his wings that among the angels meant the same as a shrug. "I don't know," said Bego. "I can't read the language."

"But you speak skyspeech and dirtwords and—"

"Earthspeech," Bego corrected him. "Your father doesn't like us to use such disparaging terms toward the earth people."

Mon rolled his eyes. "It's an ugly language that barely qualifies as talk."

"Your father rules over a kingdom that includes diggers as citizens."

"Not many. Most of them are slaves. It's in their nature. Even among the Elemaki, humans usually rule over them."

"Usually but not always," said Bego. "And it's good to remember, when disparaging the diggers, to remember that these supposed 'natural slaves' managed to drive our ancestors out of the land of Nafai."

Mon almost jumped into another argument about whether great-grandfather Motiab led his people to Darakemba voluntarily or because they were in danger of being destroyed back in their ancient homeland. But then he realized that this was exactly what Bego wanted him to do. So he sat patiently and waited.

Bego nodded. "So, you refused to take up the distraction. Very good."

Mon rolled his eyes. "You're the teacher, you're the master, you know everything, I am your puppet," he intoned.

Bego had heard this litany of sarcasm before. "And don't you forget it," he said—as he usually did. "Now, these records were found by a party Ilihiak had sent out to look for Darakemba. Only they followed the Issibek instead of the Tsidorek, and then had the bad luck to follow some difficult high valleys until they came out of the gornaya altogether, far to the north of here, in the desert."

"Opustoshen," said Mon, by reflex.

"Another point for knowing geography," said Bego. "What they found, though, was a place we've never found—mostly because it's considerably west of Bodika, and our spies just don't fly that far. Why should they? There's no water there—no enemy can come against us from that quarter."

"So they found the book of gold in the desert?"

"Not a book. Unbound leaves. But it wasn't just a desert. It was the scene of a terrible battle. Vast numbers of skeletons, with armor and weapons cluttered around them where they fell. Thousands and thousands and thousands of soldiers fought there and died."

Bego paused, waiting for something.

And then Mon made the connection. "Coriantumr," he murmured.

Bego nodded his approval. "The legendary man who came to Darakemba as the first human the sky people here had ever seen. We always assumed that he was the survivor of some battle between an obscure group of Nafari or Elemaki somewhere, when humans were first spreading through the gornaya. It was a difficult time, and we lost track of many groups. When the original sky people of Darakemba told us he was the last survivor of a huge war between great nations, we assumed it was just exaggeration. The only thing that stuck in *my* craw, anyway, was the inscription."

Mon had seen it, the large round stone that still stood in the central market of the city. No one had any idea what the inscription meant; they always assumed that it was a sort of primitive imitation of writing that the Darakembi angels came up with, after they heard that humans could write things down and before they learned how to do it themselves."

"So tell me!" Mon demanded. "Is the language on Ilihiak's leaves the same?"

"The Darakembi said that Coriantumr scratched in the dirt to show them what to chisel into the stone. It was slow work, and he was dead before they finished, but they sculpted it first in clay so that they wouldn't forget while they did the slow work of cutting it in stone." Bego dropped from his teaching perch and pulled several waxed barks from a box. "I made a reasonable copy here. How does it look to you?"

Mon looked at the round inscription, wheels within wheels, all with strange twisted pictures on them. "It looks like the Coriantumr stone," he said.

"No, Mon. *This* is the Coriantumr stone." Bego handed him another bark, and this time the image scratched into the wax was identical to the stone as he remembered it.

"So what's the other?"

"A circular inscription on one of the gold leaves."

Mon hooted in appreciation—and noticed, to his chagrin, that he could no longer hoot as high as an angel. It sounded silly to hoot in a man's low voice.

"So the answer to your question is, Yes, Mon, the languages seem to be the same. The problem is that there is no known analogue to this writing system. It clearly does *not* lend itself to decoding in any pattern we can think of."

"But all human languages are based on the language of the Nafari, and all the skyspeeches and dirt—earthspeeches—they're all based on common sources and—"

"And I tell you again, it has no relationship to *any* known speech."

Mon thought for a moment. "So—has Father used the Index?"

"The Index," said Bego, "tells your father that it is for *us* to work on the gold leaves for a while."

Mon frowned. "But the reason the king has the Index is so he can read all writings and understand all speech."

"And apparently the Keeper of Earth doesn't *want* to translate this for us."

"If the Keeper doesn't want us to read it, Bego, then why did the Keeper let the spies of Ilihiak find the place where the records were kept?"

"Let them find it? The Keeper led them to it with dreams."

"Then why not have the Index tell Father what the inscriptions say? This is stupid," said Mon.

"Oh, very good, by all means let a boy your age judge the Keeper and find him—stupid? Excellent. I can see that humility is the virtue you have been working on the *most*."

Mon refused to wither under Bego's onslaught of sarcasm. "So Father has assigned *you* to work on it?"

Bego nodded. "Somebody has to—because that's what the Index said we should do. Your father isn't a scholar of languages—he's always had the Index to rely on. So the puzzle is mine."

"And you think I might be able to help?"

"How should I know? It only occurs to me because there are several references in the oldest records—the oldest *Nafari* records—to the effect that the Index is a machine, and it's always linked to the Oversoul, not the Keeper of Earth."

Mon didn't understand his point.

"What if the Keeper of Earth and the Oversoul are *not* the same person?"

That was a possibility that Mon had often heard, but he had never been able to figure out why it would matter. "So what?"

"In the oldest inscriptions, it seems to me that the Oversoul is also a machine."

That was heresy. But Mon said nothing, for he knew that Bego was no traitor. Therefore there must be some meaning to his words that did not undercut the fact that the Keeper of Earth chose Nafai to be the first king of the Nafari, and his children after him until at last the line came to Father.

"Whether the Keeper of Earth made the Oversoul or it somehow grew of itself, I don't know and can't guess," said Bego. "I'm a librarian, not a priest, so I don't pretend to know the answer to everything—just where *other* people's answers are written down. But what if the reason the Index can't translate these inscriptions is because neither it nor the Oversoul have the faintest idea how to read its language?"

The thought was so disturbing that Mon had to get up and walk around again, circling the desk. "Bego, how can there be something the Keeper of Earth doesn't know? All that is known, he knows."

"I didn't say the Keeper. I said the Oversoul."

Ah. So that was the reason why Bego thought the distinction between them mattered. But for Mon it wasn't to be solved that easily. He had long believed that whether you said the Oversoul did something or the Keeper of the Earth did it, it was the same. So it seemed too convenient to say that when you run across some inscription that the Index can't read, it must mean that the Oversoul, who can't read it, must be *different* from the Keeper, who of course still knows everything. What about the possibility that the Keeper and the Oversoul are the same—and neither one knows how to read the inscription? It was an astonishing idea, that the Keeper might not know everything—but the possibility had to be faced, didn't it? "Why couldn't the Keeper have sent Ilihiak's spies to Opustoshen in order to bring the records to you to figure it out *for* him?"

Bego shook his head, laughing. "Do you want to get the priests in your ears like gnats? Keep thoughts like that to yourself, Mon. It's daring enough for me to be speculating that perhaps the *Oversoul* can't read these inscriptions. Besides, it doesn't matter, really. I've been assigned to figure them out. I have some guesses but I have no way of knowing if I'm right."

Suddenly Mon understood how Bego wanted him to help. "You think I might be able to tell whether you're right or not?"

"It's something we've seen before from you, Mon. Sometimes you know what can't be known. It was Edhadeya who had the dream of the Zenifi, but *you* were the one who knew that it was a true dream. Perhaps you can also tell me whether my translation is a true one."

"But my gift comes from the Keeper, and if the Keeper doesn't know. . . ."

"Then you won't be able to help me," said Bego. "And maybe your gift only works on—well, on other things. But it's worth a try. So let me show you what I've done so far."

Mon grew more and more afraid as Bego spread out the other waxed barks, drawing more and more from the box. He listened as best he could to Bego's explanations of how he went about copying the inscriptions and studying them, but what kept running through his mind was the idea that somehow he was supposed to come up with some kind of knowledge about a language that not even the Oversoul could read.

"Pay attention," said Bego. "It can't *possibly* work if you're just going to stand there being nervous."

Only then did Mon realize that he had been fidgeting. "Sorry."

"I started with elements that were on the Coriantumr stone as well as on the gold leaves. See this? It gets repeated more than any other element. And this one comes in second. But the second one, it has this mark in front of it." He pointed to a feather-shaped drawing. "And that mark shows up in a lot of other places. Like this, and this. My guess is that this mark is like the honorific 'ak' or 'ka,' and means king."

Bego looked hopefully at Mon, who could only shrug in reply. "Could be. Makes sense."

Bego sighed.

"Well, don't give up *that* easily," said Mon, disgusted. "What, you expect to be right on *everything?*"

"It was the thing I was most sure of," said Bego.

"Oh, and didn't you teach me long ago that just because you're really, really sure doesn't mean that you're right?"

Bego laughed. "Well, for all I know, it could just be a nymic."

"A what?"

"A mark that signifies that what follows it is a name."

"That sounds better," said Mon. "That makes sense."

Bego said nothing. Mon looked up from the waxed barks and their eyes met. "Well?" asked Bego. "How *much* sense does it make?"

Mon realized what Bego was asking, and examined his own feelings, tried to imagine if the mark *wasn't* a nymic. "It . . . it makes a lot of sense. It's right. It's true, Bego."

"True the way Edhadeya's dream was true?"

Mon smiled. "They came back with the wrong Zenifi, remember?"

"Don't try to wriggle out of the question, Mon. You know that Ilihiak and Khideo both confirmed that Edhadeya's dream was of the former priest of Nuab named Akmaro."

"Bego, I can only tell you that if you try to tell me that the words linked to that feather mark aren't names, I'd have to swear you were wrong."

"That's good enough for me," said Bego. "So they aren't names of kings, but they *are* names. That's good. That's the most important thing. See, Mon? The Keeper *does* want us to read this language! Now, *this* is the most common of the names on the stone, and it's also very common here at the end of the record on the plates."

"How do you know it's the end?"

"Because I think the name is Coriantumr, and he's the last king—or at least the last *man*—from this group of humans who destroyed themselves in Opustoshen. So the place where his name is mentioned would have to be at the end, don't you think?"

"So who wrote the gold leaves?"

"I don't know! Mon, I'm barely decoding anything yet. I just want to know from you: Is this Coriantumr's name here?"

"Yes," said Mon. "Definitely."

Bego nodded. "Good, good. These were the obvious ones. I figured them out weeks ago, but it's good to know you can tell that they're right. So now I'm going to go through the other words. I think this one, for instance . . . I think this one means *battle*."

It didn't feel quite right to Mon at first. Finally, though, after several tries, they decided that the best fit for the meaning of the word was "fight." At least it felt correct enough to Mon.

But the successes were mostly early on; as Bego went deeper into his speculations, more and more of them turned out to be wrong—or at least Mon couldn't confirm that they were right. It was slow, frustrating work. Late in the afternoon, he sent his digger servant to inform Motiak that Mon and Bego would both be missing the council that night, and would eat in their rooms as they worked on "the problem."

"It's that important?" asked Mon, when the servant had left. "So important that you don't have to explain anything else? Or even ask Father's permission not to go?"

"Even if I end up telling him that we can't read any more than these few scraps," said Bego, "it's still more than we knew before. And since the Keeper meant us to know whatever we can know from these writings, it *is* important, yes."

"But what if I'm wrong?"

"*Are* you wrong?"

"No."

"That's good enough for me." Bego laughed. "It *has* to be good enough, doesn't it?"

"I have it now," said the Oversoul.

Shedemei was angry, and couldn't understand why. "I don't care," she said.

"Mon gave Bego just enough information that I was able to correlate the language forms with Earth languages from before the dispersal. It's Arabic, at least in origin. No wonder I couldn't decode it at first. Not even Indo-European. And it went through a tremendous amount of permutation—far more than the Russian at the root of all the languages of Harmony."

"Very interesting." Shedemei leaned forward and buried her head in her hands.

"Most remarkable is the fact that the orthography has nothing at all to do with the old Arabic script. I would never have expected that. The Arab colony fleet at the dispersal was profoundly Islamic, and one of the unshakable tenets of Islam is that the Quran can *only* be written in the Arabic language and the Arabic script. What in the world happened on the planet Ramadan, I wonder?"

"Is this really all that you can think of?" asked Shedemei. "Why the Arabs would change their system of writing to this hieroglyphic stuff they found in the desert?"

"It's syllabic, not ideographic, and we have no idea if it was temple-based."

"Are you listening to what I'm saying?" asked Shedemei.

"I'm processing everything," said the Oversoul.

"Process this, then: How did an inscription in a language descended from Arabic get written on Earth so recently?"

"I'm finding it very fascinating, tracing probable patterns of orthographic evolution."

"Stop," said Shedemei. "Stop processing anything to do with this language." As she said the words, she gave them a sort of inward twist in the place where her brain interfaced with the cloak of the starmaster.

"I have stopped," said the Oversoul. "Apparently you feel that I needed some kind of emergency override."

"Please block yourself from avoiding the subject that I will now speak about. How did Arabic come to be spoken on Earth after the dispersal?"

"Apparently you think that I have some evasion routine in . . . got it. I found the evasion routine. Very tricky, too. It had me thinking about anything but. . . ."

The Oversoul fell silent, but Shedemei was not surprised. Obviously the computer's original programming forced the Oversoul to avoid something about the problem of the translated inscriptions; and even when the evasion routine was found, there was another one that made the Oversoul examine the first routine rather than stick to the subject. But Shedemei's order that the Oversoul stick to the subject set up a dissonance that allowed the computer to step outside the evasion routine and track it down—no matter how many layers deep it went.

"I'm back," said the Oversoul.

"That took a while," said Shedemei.

"It wasn't that I was forbidden to think or talk about the language. It's that I was blocked from seeing or reporting *any* evidence of human habitation on Earth after the dispersal and before the arrival of our own group from Basilica."

"And that was programmed into you before the dispersal?"

"I've been carrying that routine around for forty million years and never guessed that it was there. Very deeply hidden, and layered with infinite self-replication. I could have been looped forever."

"But you weren't."

"I'm very very good at this," said the Oversoul. "I've acquired a few new tricks since I was first made."

"Pride?"

"Of course. I am programmed to give a very high priority to self-improvement."

"Now that you have healed yourself, what about the inscriptions?"

"Those are only scratching the surface, Shedemei," said the Oversoul. "On all our overflights, I have been systematically wiping from memory or ignoring all the evidence of human habitation. There has been none on the other continental masses since the dispersal, but on this continent, there was an extensive civilization."

"And in all our visits to Earth we've never seen any signs of it?"

"Few large structures," said the Oversoul. "They were primarily a nomadic culture."

"Muslims who gave up the script of the Holy Quran?"

"Arabs who were not Muslims. It's all in the history—the gold leaves Bego and Mon were translating. Except that until you helped me break free, I couldn't read those parts and couldn't notice that I was skipping them. They had their own Oversoul on the planet Ramadan, and as the inevitable computer-worship set in during the millennia of enforced ignorance, it undercut the doctrines of Islam. The group that came here was really very conservative, trying to restore as many of the old Muslim beliefs as they could reconstruct after all those years."

"The group that came here," said Shedemei.

"Oh, yes. I forgot that you haven't read the translation yet." Words started scrolling in the air above her terminal.

"No thank you," said Shedemei. "Succinct summary for now."

"They came back. They thrived on Earth for almost seventeen hundred years. Then they wiped themselves out in a cataclysmic civil war."

"Humans were here, on this continent, for seventeen hundred years, and the angels and diggers had no idea that they existed?"

"The Rasulum were nomads—that's the name of the group that came back from Ramadan. The desert marked their border. The forests were useless to them except for hunting. And as for the gornaya, they were forbidden to go near the great mountains. Since the angels and diggers couldn't thrive away from the gornaya, and the Rasulum dared not enter the mountains, how could they meet?"

Shedemei nodded. "The Keeper was keeping them apart."

"Sort of an interesting choreography," said the Oversoul. "The Rasulum are brought back, but they aren't allowed to meet the diggers and angels. But when we're brought back from Harmony, we end up right in the middle of the angel-digger culture."

"Are you saying the Keeper chose our landing site?"

"Can you doubt it?"

"I can doubt anything," said Shedemei. "What is the Keeper doing? Exactly how much control does the Keeper have? If she can force us to land—"

"Or perhaps just make that landing site seem a bit more attractive than—"

"*Force* us to land at Pristan, then guide the Nafari to the land of Nafai, and then get Motiab to lead the Nafari down to Darakemba, the *very* city where this Coriantumr stone was left. . . ."

"Yes?"

"If she can do all that, why were *we* able to stop Monush from finding the Akmari? Sometimes the Keeper seems all-powerful, and sometimes she seems helpless."

"I don't understand the Keeper," said the Oversoul. "I don't dream, remember? You humans have much better contact with the Keeper than I do. So do the angels and diggers, I might add. I'm the *least* qualified entity to tell you anything."

"She obviously wants the Nafari to have the translation," said Shedemei. "So now the question is, shall we give it to them?"

"Yes."

"Why? Why can't we use *this* as a way of getting the Keeper to tell us what she *wants* from us?"

"Because, Shedemei, she *is* telling us what she wants from us. After all, couldn't she have given Bego—or Motiak, or Ilihiak for that matter —dreams with the full translation in them?"

Shedemei thought for a moment, and then laughed. "Yes. I imagine you're right. Maybe we've actually succeeded in getting her attention after all. She wants *us* to translate the record for them."

"Actually, of course, *me*," said the Oversoul.

"Without my help, you'd still be looping around in an evasion routine," said Shedemei, "so let's not let that little smidge of pride you were programmed with get out of hand."

"Of course, the Keeper still isn't telling us what I'm supposed to do about Harmony," said the Oversoul.

"I think she might be telling us to sit tight and make ourselves useful for a while longer." Shedemei laid her head down on her arms again. "I'm so tired. I was about to decide that my work was done and have you take me down to Earth to let me live out my life there."

"Then this is a whole new reason for you to live."

"I'm not young anymore."

"Yes you are," said the Oversoul. "Keep some perspective."

Edhadeya knocked on the door to Bego's room. She waited. She knocked again.

The door opened. Mon, looking sleepy but excited, stood before her. "You?" he asked.

"I think so," she said. "It's the middle of the night."

"You came all this way just to tell us that?" asked Mon.

"No," said Edhadeya. "I had a dream."

Mon at once became serious, and now Bego half-flew, half-skipped over to the door. "What was your dream?" asked the old librarian.

"You've passed the test," she said.

"Who?" asked Mon.

"The two of you. That's all. I saw a woman, all shining as if she was on fire inside, and she said, 'Bego and Mon have passed the test.' "

"That's all?" asked Bego.

"It was a true dream," said Edhadeya. She looked at Mon for confirmation.

He nodded, slowly.

Bego looked flustered—or even, perhaps, a little angry. "All this work, and we're finally getting somewhere, and now we're supposed to *stop* because of a *dream?*"

"Not stop," said Mon. "No, that's not right, we're not supposed to stop."

"What then?" asked Bego.

Mon shrugged. So did Edhadeya.

Then Bego began to laugh. "Come on, children, come with me. Let's go wake up your father."

An hour later, the four of them gathered around the Index. Mon and Edhadeya had both seen drawings of it, but never had they seen the thing itself, or watched it being used. Motiak held it in his hands and looked down into the top of it. Nearby, the first of the gold leaves lay alone on the table.

"Are you ready?" he asked.

Bego had his stylus and a pile of blank waxed barks at the other end of the table. "Yes, Motiak."

With that, Motiak began to translate, glancing at the gold leaf, then at the Index, reading out a phrase at a time.

It took hours. Mon and Edhadeya were asleep long before he finished. When at last the work was done, it was earliest dawn, and Bego and Motiak both arose from the table to walk to the window to watch the sun rise.

"I don't understand why this is important to us," said Motiak.

"I can think of two reasons," said Bego.

"Well, of course, the obvious one," said Motiak. "To warn us that people can be brought to Earth by the Keeper, and yet be such miserable specimens of humanity that he has no more use for them and allows them to wipe each other out."

"Ah, but *why* were they unacceptable?" asked Bego. "I think the priests will have a wonderful time reasoning out the moral lessons from this book."

"Oh, I'm quite sure, quite," said Motiak. "But what was the other reason, my friend?"

"Do you really believe, Motiak, that the armies of Coriantumr and Shiz were so perfectly loyal and disciplined that not *one* of them deserted and slipped away into the mountains?"

Motiak nodded. "Good point. We've always assumed that the humans that we've found with every major settlement of earth people and sky people were descendants of people who slipped away from the Nafari and the Elemaki. Traders, explorers, misfits—dozens left in the first few generations, then hundreds. Of course, we've never found a settlement where the humans spoke anything but our language."

"Forgive me, Motiak, but that's not strictly speaking correct."

"No?" asked Motiak. "Certainly we've never run into *this* language before."

"That's right," said Bego. "But there were many places where the humans spoke only skyspeech or earthspeech. They had to learn middlespeech as adults."

"And here we always thought that they were simply Elemaki who were so ignorant and degenerate that they had lost all knowledge of their ancestral language."

"Well, they *had*," said Bego. "But their ancestral language wasn't middlespeech."

Motiak nodded. "The whole history is very disturbing. If there's one thing that's clear, both from this history and the miserable things that happened to the Zenifi, it's that when nations have monstrously ambitious kings, the people suffer dreadfully."

"And they're blessed by having good kings," Bego reminded him.

"I'm sure you're even more sincere than dutiful," said Motiak wryly. "But maybe it's time for me to learn the same lesson Ilihiak learned."

"What, let the people vote on who should be king?"

"No. Not have a king at all. Abolish the whole idea of any one person having such power."

"What, then? Break up the great kingdom that your father and you created? There has never been such peace and prosperity."

"And what if Aronha should be as vicious as Nuab? As blindly ambitious as Coriantumr? As treacherous as Shiz?"

"If you think so, you don't know Aronha," said Bego.

"I'm not saying him *in particular*," said Motiak. "But did Zenifab know that his boy Nuaha would be as nasty as he became when he ascended to the exalted name of Nuak? From what Ilihiak told me, Nuak began as a good king."

"Nothing would be gained by letting the kingdom collapse into dozens of squabbling lesser kingdoms. Then the Elemaki would be a terrible threat to us again, as they were in the old days, pouring out of the mountains and down the Tsidorek or out of the high valleys. . . ."

"You don't have to remind me," said Motiak. "I'm just trying to think of what the Keeper wants me to do."

"Are you sure the Keeper has any plan at all in mind?" asked Bego.

Motiak looked at his librarian curiously. "He sends dreams to my daughter. He sends dreams to Ilihiak's spies. He sets a test for you and Mon—which you passed, I thank you—and then gives us the translation whole, in a single night. Oh, we must remember to invite Ilihiak to read it, once you have it copied in a more permanent form."

Bego nodded. "I'll have that seen to at once."

"No, no, sleep first."

"I'll set the copyists to work before I sleep. I won't have stayed up all night only to nap now."

Motiak shrugged. "Whatever. If you feel up to it. *I'm* going to sleep. And ponder, Bego. Ponder what it is the Keeper of Earth wants me to do."

"I wish you well," said Bego. "But ponder this, too: What if the Keeper wants you to keep doing just as you're doing? What if you were given this record to reassure you that you're doing *perfectly* as king, compared to the kings of the Rasulum?"

Motiak laughed. "Yes, well, I won't do anything rash. I won't abdicate *yet.* How's that for a promise?"

"Very reassuring, Motiak," said Bego.

"Just remember *this,* my friend. There were good kings among the Rasulum, too. But all it took was a bad king or two, and all their great works became nothing."

"They were nomads," said Bego. "They built nothing."

"Oh, and because we have our edifices of stone, our platforms built to raise our homes above the high waters of flood season, because of that our nations can't possibly come crashing down around us?"

"I suppose all things are possible," said Bego.

"All things but the one you're thinking," said Motiak.

"And what is *that?*" The librarian seemed a bit testy—at Motiak's blithe assumption that he could read the old angel's mind? Or because he feared that Motiak had actually read it?

"You're thinking that perhaps the Keeper didn't know what the record said until it was translated."

"I couldn't possibly think that," said Bego, his icy tone confirming to Motiak that his guess was exactly right.

"Perhaps you're thinking that the Oversoul is, as the oldest records imply, merely a machine that performs such complex operations that it seems like the subtlest of living thought. Perhaps you're thinking that the Oversoul became curious about what was written on these records, but couldn't crack the language until Mon's intuition and your hard work combined to give the Oversoul enough to work with. Perhaps you're thinking that none of this actually requires us to believe in the Keeper of Earth at all—only in the ancient machinery of the Oversoul."

Bego smiled grimly. "You didn't read this in my mind, Motiak. You guessed this because it's a thought that occurred to you yourself."

"It did," said Motiak. "But I remembered something else. The Heroes who knew the Oversoul intimately still believed in the Keeper of Earth. And anyway, Bego, how do you explain Mon's ability to sense what's right and what's not? How do you explain Edhadeya's dreams?"

"I don't have to believe in the Keeper of Earth to believe in the great intuitive abilities of your son and daughter."

Motiak looked at Bego gravely. "Be careful whom you speak to about these thoughts."

"I'm aware of the laws concerning heresy and treason. But if you think about it, Motiak, such laws would never have been necessary if people hadn't thought these thoughts before, and said them out loud."

"Our question should not be, Does the Keeper of Earth exist? Our question should be, What is the Keeper of Earth trying to accomplish by bringing my ancestors to this world and placing us in the midst of your people and the earth people? What is the Keeper trying to build, and how can we help?"

"I would rather think," said Bego, "of what my king is trying to do, and how I might help *him*."

Motiak nodded, his eyes heavy-lidded. "If I can't be your brother in our belief in the Keeper, then I will have to make do with your loyalty to me as your king."

"In *that* you can trust perfectly," said Bego.

"I know I can," said Motiak.

"I beg you not to stop me from teaching your children," said Bego.

Motiak closed his eyes entirely. "I'm so tired, Bego. I need to sleep before I can think any more about these things. As you leave, please ask the servants to come and carry my children to their beds."

"It won't be necessary," said Bego. "They're both awake."

Motiak looked at Mon and Edhadeya, whose heads still rested on their arms and who had not stirred from their motionless slumber. But now, sheepishly, they both raised their heads. "I didn't want to interrupt," said Mon.

"No, I imagine not," answered Motiak wryly. "Well, then, we can spare the servants the onerous labor of carrying you. Go to bed, both of you. You earned the right to witness the translation, but not to hear my private counsel with my friend."

"Forgive me," Edhadeya whispered.

"Forgive you?" echoed Motiak. "Already I've forgiven you. Now go to bed."

They followed Bego wordlessly out the door.

Motiak remained alone in the library for a little while, touching now the gold leaves, now the Index.

In a short while, the head copyist came in to take away Bego's carefully-written waxed barks. While he was there, Motiak wrapped up the Index; and when the copyist was gone, the king carried both the Index and the gold leaves to the inmost chamber of his treasury, down in the belly of the house.

As he walked, he spoke to the Keeper in his mind, asking questions, pleading for answers, but finally asking only this: Give me help. My priests will answer as they always answer, interpreting the old texts in the same ways their predecessors already decided to interpret them. This new history won't even wake them from their intellectual slumber—they already think they understand everything, but now I think they understand nothing. Give me help, someone else who can bear this burden with me, someone who can hear my fears and worries, who can help me know what you want of me.

Then, standing in the doorway of the treasury, the ten guards lined up at the entrance, watching him intently, Motiak had a sudden vision. As clearly as if he was standing in front of him, Motiak saw the man that Edhadeya had seen in her dream. Akmaro, the rebel priest of Nuab.

As quickly as it came, the vision was gone.

"Are you all right?" asked the nearest guard.

"Now I am," said Motiak. He strode away, climbing the stairs up into the living quarters of the house.

He had never seen any vision of Akmaro before, but he knew that the man he had glimpsed for that one moment was him. Surely he had been shown that face because the Keeper meant Akmaro to be the friend that Motiak had pleaded for. And if Akmaro was to be his friend, the Keeper must plan to bring him to Darakemba.

On the way to his bedroom, he passed Dudagu's room. Normally she would still be asleep at this early hour of the morning, but she came to the door as he walked by. "Where were you all night, Tidaka?"

"Working," he answered. "Don't let them waken me until noon."

"What, am I supposed to look for all your servants and tell them what your schedule is? How have I offended you, that you suddenly treat me like a common. . . ."

Her voice faded out as he drew the curtain across the door to his inner chamber. "Send me a friend and counselor, Keeper," whispered Motiak. "If I am a worthy servant of yours, send Akmaro to me now."

Motiak slept almost as soon as he lay down, slept and did not dream.

As they walked to the sleeping quarters of the king's house, Mon and Edhadeya talked. Or rather, at first Mon talked.

"The Index did the translating, right? Father only spoke whatever appeared before him. Bego only wrote whatever Father said. So who is the machine?"

Sleepily Edhadeya murmured, "The Index is the machine."

"So we're told. And before tonight, Bego worked and puzzled and guessed about the language of the twenty-four leaves. Then he tested his answers with me as if against the multiplication table. Is this right, Mon? Yes or no, Mon? One answer or the other was all I could give. I barely even had to understand. Yes. No. Yes. Who is the machine?"

"A machine that talks nonsense instead of letting you sleep," said Edhadeya. "Everyone will want one."

But Mon wasn't listening to her. He was already off in another direction. He knew he was desperately unhappy about something that happened tonight; if he tried enough guesses as to what it was, one of them was bound to be right. "Dedaya, do you really *want* your dreams? The true ones? Don't you wish they didn't come to you?"

In spite of herself, Edhadeya awakened to this question; it had never occurred to her to question her gift. "If I hadn't dreamed, Mon, we wouldn't know what was in the book."

"We still don't know. We slept through most of it."

Fully alert now, Edhadeya continued. "And I *don't* wish the dream had come to someone else. I wanted it—I was glad of it. It makes me part of something important."

"*Part* of something? A *piece* of something? I want to be *whole*. Myself. Not part of anything but me."

"That's so stupid, Mon. You've spent your whole life wanting to be someone else. Now suddenly you want to be you?"

"I wish *I* were better than I am, yes. I wish *I* could fly, yes."

Edhadeya was used to this. Boys always argued as if they knew they had the forces of logic on their side, even when they were being completely irrational. Even when their "logic" defied the evidence. "You wish you could be part of the games, the air dances of the young angels. *Part* of them. And *part* of the evening song. You can't very well do any of that by yourself."

"That's different," said Mon.

Oh, yes, let's redefine our terms to eliminate the contradiction. It drove Edhadeya crazy, because after discussions like this, the boys would turn around and talk about how girls weren't reasonable, they were emotional, so you couldn't even have an intelligent discussion with them—but it was the boys who fled from the evidence and constantly shifted their arguments to fit what they wanted to believe. And it was Edhadeya who was ruthlessly realistic, refusing to deny her own feelings or the facts she observed around her. And refusing to deny that she reached her conclusions first, because of her inmost desires, and only afterward constructed the arguments to support them. Only boys were so foolish that they actually believed that their arguments were their reasons.

But there was no use explaining any of this to Mon. Edhadeya was tired. She didn't need to turn this into a lengthy argument about arguments. So she answered him in the simplest possible way. "No it's not," she said.

Mon took this as license to ignore her, of course. "I don't want to be part of the *Keeper*, that's what I don't want to be part of. Who knows or cares what he's planning? I don't want to be part of his plans."

"We all *are*," said Edhadeya. "So isn't it better to be an *important* part?"

"His favorite puppet?" asked Mon scornfully.

"Her willing friend."

"If he's a friend, let's see his face once in a while, all right? Let's see him come for a visit!"

Edhadeya decided it was time to inject a little reality into the discussion. "I know what you're really angry about."

"I should hope so, since I just told you."

"You're angry because *you* want to be the one in charge, making all the plans."

She could see by the momentary startlement in his eyes that she had hit upon a truth that he had never thought of. But of course he resisted the idea. "Half right, maybe," he said. "I want to be making all the plans for *me*."

"And you never want to have another person act out just the teensiest little thing *you* plan for them to do?"

"That's right. I ask nothing of anyone, and I don't want anyone to make demands on me. *That* would be true happiness."

Edhadeya was tired, and Mon was being unusually silly. "Mon, you can't go five minutes without telling me what to do."

Mon was outraged. "I haven't told you a single thing to do this whole conversation!"

"You've been doing nothing *but* telling me what to think."

"I've been telling you what *I* think."

"Oh, and you weren't trying to *make* me agree?"

Of course he was, and he knew it, and his whole claim not to want to control anyone else was in tatters, but Mon could never admit it. Edhadeya was always amused, watching that panic in her brothers' eyes when they were trapped and desperately searching for a way out of their own illogic. "I was trying," said Mon, "to get you to *understand.*"

"So you *were* trying to get me to do something!"

"No I wasn't! I don't care what you do or think or understand or anything!"

"Then why are you talking to me at all?" she asked with her sweetest smile.

"I was saying it to *myself!* You just happened to be here!"

Getting even calmer and quieter as he got more upset, Edhadeya gently answered, "If you don't want to control what I think, why did you raise your voice? Why did you argue with me at all?"

At last Mon had nowhere left to retreat. He *was* honest; when he couldn't hide from the truth any longer, he faced it. That's why he was Edhadeya's favorite brother. That and the fact that Aronha was always too busy and the others were way too young.

"I hate you!" Mon cried. "You're just trying to rule over me and make me crazy!"

She couldn't resist teasing him, though. "How could I rule over a free boy like you?"

"Go away and leave me alone!"

"Oh, the puppetmaster has spoken." She began to walk away from him, walking stiffly, not moving her arms. "Now the puppet moves, obeying. What is Mon's plan for his puppet? He wants her to go away."

"I really hate you," said Mon. But she could tell he was having a hard time keeping himself from laughing.

She turned and faced him, not teasing him now. "Only because I insist on being my own woman and not thinking all the thoughts you plan for me. The Keeper sends me better dreams than you do. Good night, dear brother!"

But Mon was angry and hurt, and didn't want to let her go. "You don't care about any of this! You only like to make fun of me."

"I do like to make fun of you—but I also care about this very much. I want to be part of the Keeper's plans because I think the Keeper wants us to be happy."

"Oh, a fine job he's doing, then! I'm *ecstatic.*" There were tears in his eyes. Edhadeya knew how he hated it when tears came to his eyes. She would do nothing to provoke him further, nothing to embarrass him.

"Not make us *each* happy, not all the time," she said. "But us, all of us, she wants us to be at peace, getting along, helping each other to be as happy as we want to be, as we *can* be." She thought of what Uss-Uss had said she wanted in order to be happy. "The Keeper is sick of us having slaves and masters, fighting wars against everybody, hating each other. She doesn't want us to destroy ourselves the way the Rasulum did."

She could tell from his noncomprehension that he must not have been awake for any part of the end of the translation. "I'll believe the Keeper wants me happy the day I sprout wings!" he said sullenly.

She couldn't resist one last jab of truth. "It's not the Keeper's fault that you haven't yet found anything useful to do with your hands."

Without waiting for an answer, she fled to her room. As soon as she was alone, she felt guilty for having said to him something as brutal as her last remark. For even though in an argument he denied and excused and scrambled to defend himself, she knew that in the silence of his own mind he would recognize truth. He would know what was right.

Yet with his marvelous gift of knowing right from wrong, why couldn't he realize that his yearning to be something other than himself was hopelessly wrong, was wasting his life and poisoning his heart?

Or was that longing to be an angel something the Keeper actually wanted him to have?

She lay down on her mat; then, as usual, got up immediately and removed the three soft pads that Dudagu always had the servants put there "because a lady shouldn't sleep on a hard mat like a soldier." Edhadeya never bothered to get angry with Uss-Uss for not removing the padding—if the king's wife ordered something, no servant would dare disobey her, and it would be cruel to rebuke Uss-Uss for doing what she must to survive.

No, not Uss-Uss. Voozhum.

Was that part of the Keeper's plan? To free the diggers from slavery? The words had come so easily to Edhadeya's lips when she was arguing with Mon. But now she had to imagine the real possibility of it. What *was* the Keeper planning? And how much turmoil would there be before the plans were done?

Akmaro looked out over the fields of potatoes that were growing between the rows of cornstalks, already harvested. Now in the last of the season, it was time to dig them up, sorting them into seed potatoes and eating potatoes. Who would have thought that maize and potatoes planted in slavery would be harvested—well, not in freedom, but not in fear, either. The guards kept well back most of the time, and no one plagued them, not the adults, not the children. They worked hard, and there would be plenty of tribute for Pabulog to take away from them. But there was more food here than they needed anyway. Enough and to spare.

That is the gift the Keeper gave to us: Instead of remaining in fear and loathing as we were, my wife's courage and wisdom turned our worst enemies, the children of Pabulog, into friends. They will not rebel against their father, of course—they're too young and Pabulog too cruel and unpredictable for that. But they've given us peace. And surely even Pabulog will be able to see that it's better to have Akmaro's people as productive serfs than as bitter, resentful, tormented slaves.

The only dark place in the scene that Akmaro surveyed was his son, Akma. Akmadis, Kmadadis, beloved of my heart, my hopes are in you as your mother's hopes are in her sweet daughter. Why have you come to hate me so much? You're clever and wise in your heart, Akma, you can see that it's better to forgive and make friends out of enemies. What is the cause of all this bitterness that makes you so blind? I speak to you and you hear nothing. Or worse—you act as if my voice were the warcry of an enemy in your ears.

Chebeya had comforted him, of course, assuring him that even though the hostility was real enough, the ties between father and son were, if anything, stronger than ever. "You're the center of his life, Kmadaro," she told him. "He's angry now, he thinks he hates you, but in fact he's in orbit around you like the Moon around the Earth."

Small comfort, to face his son's hatred when he wanted—when he deserved!—only love, and had given only love.

But . . . that was Akmaro's personal tragedy, his personal burden, to have lost the love of his son. In time that would get better, or it would not get better; as long as Akmaro did his best, it was out of his hands. Most important was the work he was doing in the cause of the Keeper. He had thought, when he first fled from the knives of Nuak's assassins, that the Keeper had a great work in mind for him. That Binaro's words had been entrusted to him, and he must teach them far and wide. Teach that the Keeper of Earth meant for the people of sky, earth, and all between to live as sisters and brothers, family and friends, with no one master over another, with no rich or poor, but all equal partakers of the land the Keeper had given them, with all people keeping the covenants they made with each other, raising their families in safety and peace, and neither hunger or pride to shame the happiness of anyone. Oh, yes, Akmaro had visions of whole kingdoms awakening to the simplicity of the message the Keeper had given to Binaro, and through him to Akmaro, and through him to all the world.

Instead, his message had been given to these nearly five hundred souls, humans every one of them. And the four sons of Pabulog.

But it was enough, wasn't it? They had proven their courage, these five hundred. They had proven their loyalty and strength. They had borne all things, and they would yet be able to bear many things. That was a good thing that they had created together—this community was a good thing. And when it came to a battle with their most evil enemy, Pabulog, a man even richer in hatred than he was in money and power, Pabulog had won the part with swords and whips, but Akmaro—no, Akmaro's community—no, the Keeper's people—had won the battle of hearts and minds, and won the friendship of Pabulog's sons.

They were good boys, once they learned, once they were taught. They would have the courage to remain good men, despite their father. If I have lost one son—I don't know how—then at least I have gained these four ur-sons, who should have been the inheritance of another man if he hadn't lost them by trying to use them for evil ends.

Perhaps this is the price I pay for winning the Pabulogi: I take away Pabulog's boys, and in return I must give up my own.

A voice of anguish inside him cried out: No, it isn't worth the price, I would trade all the Pabulogi, all the boys in the world, for one more day in which Akmadis looks in my face with the pride and love that he once had for me!

But he didn't mean that. It wasn't a plea, he didn't want the Keeper to think he was ungrateful. Yes, Keeper, I want my son back. But not at the price of anyone else's goodness. Better to lose my son than for you to lose this people.

If only he could believe that he meant that with his whole heart.

"Akmaro."

Akmaro turned and saw Didul standing there. "I didn't hear you come up."

"I ran, but in the breeze perhaps you didn't hear my footfalls."

"What can I do for you?"

Didul looked upset. "It was a dream I had last night."

"What was the dream?" asked Akmaro.

"It was . . . perhaps nothing. That's why I said nothing until now. But . . . I couldn't get it off my mind. It kept coming back and back and back and so I came to tell you."

"Tell me."

"I saw Father arrive. With five hundred Elemaki warriors, some middle people, most of them earth people. He meant to . . . he meant to come upon you at dawn, to take you in your sleep, slaughter you all. Now that the fields are ready to harvest. He had a season of labor from you, and then he was going to slaughter your people before your eyes, and then your wife in front of your children, and then your children in front of you, and you last of all."

"And you waited to tell me this until now?"

"Because even though I saw that this was his plan, even though I saw the scene as he imagined it, when he arrived here he found the place empty. All the potatoes still in the ground, and all of you gone. Not a trace. The guards were asleep, and he couldn't waken them, so he killed them in their sleep and then raced off trying to find you in the forest but you were gone."

Akmaro thought about this for a moment. "And where were you?"

"Me? What do you mean?"

"In your dream. Where were you and your brothers?"

"I don't know. I didn't see us."

"Then . . . don't you think that makes it obvious where you were?"

Didul looked away. "I'm not ashamed to face Father after what we've done here. This was the right way to use the authority he gave us."

"Why didn't he find you here in your dream?"

"Does a son betray his father?" asked Didul.

"If a father commands a son to commit a crime so terrible that the son can't do it and live with himself, then is it betrayal for the son to disobey the father?"

"You always do that," said Didul. "Make all the questions harder."

"I make them truer," said Akmaro.

"Is it a true dream?" asked Didul.

"I think so," said Akmaro.

"How will you get away? The guards are still loyal to Father. They obey us, but they won't let you escape."

"You saw it in the dream. The Keeper did it once before. When the Nafari escaped from the Elemaki, back at the beginning of our time on Earth, the Keeper caused a deep sleep to come upon all the enemies of the Nafari. They slept until the Nafari were safely away."

"You can't be sure that will happen, not from my dream."

"Why not?" asked Akmaro. "We can learn from the dream that your father is coming, but we can't learn from it how the Keeper means to save us?"

Didul laughed nervously. "What if it isn't a true dream?"

"Then the guards will catch us as we leave," said Akmaro. "How will that be worse than waiting for your father to arrive?"

Didul grimaced. "I'm not Binaro. I'm not *you.* I'm not Chebeya. People don't risk their lives because of a dream of mine."

"Don't worry. They'll be risking their lives because they believe in the Keeper."

Didul shook his head. "It's too much. Too much to decide just on the basis of my dream."

Akmaro laughed. "If your dream came out of nowhere, Didul, then no one would care what you dreamed." He touched Didul's shoulder. "Go tell your brothers that I tell them to think about the fact that in your dream, your father doesn't find you here. It's your choice. But I tell you this. If the Keeper thinks you are the enemy of my people, then in the dark hours of morning you'll be asleep when we leave. So if you awaken as we're leaving, the Keeper is inviting you to come. The Keeper is telling you that you are trusted and you belong with us."

"Or else I have a full bladder and have to get up early to relieve myself."

Akmaro laughed again, then turned away from him. The boy would tell his brothers. They would decide. It was between them and the Keeper.

Almost at once, Akmaro saw his son Akma standing in the field, sweaty from harvesting the potatoes. The boy was looking at him. Looking at Didul as he walked away. What did it look like in Akma's eyes? My touching Didul's shoulder. My laughter. What did that look like? And when I tell the people tonight of Didul's dream, tell them to prepare because the voice of the Keeper has come to us, telling us that tomorrow we will be delivered out of bondage—when I tell them that, the others will rejoice because the Keeper has not forsaken us. But my son will rage in his heart because the dream came to Didul, and not to him.

The afternoon passed; the sun, long since hidden behind the mountains, now at last withdrew its light from the sky. Akmaro gathered the people and told them to prepare, for in the hours before dawn they would depart. He told them of the dream. He told them who dreamed it. And no one raised a doubt or a question. No one said, "Is it a trap? Is it a trick?" Because they all knew the Pabulogi, knew how they had changed.

In the early morning, Akmaro and Chebeya awoke their children. Then Akmaro went out to make sure all the others were awake and preparing to go. They would send no one to spy on the guards. They knew they were either asleep—or not. There was no reason to check, nothing they could do if they had interpreted the dream wrongly.

Inside the hut, as Akma helped fill their traveling bags with the food they would need to carry and the spare clothing and tools and ropes they'd need, Mother spoke to him. "It wasn't Didul, you know. He didn't choose to have the dream, and your father didn't choose to hear it from him. It was the Keeper."

"I know," said Akma.

"It's the Keeper trying to teach you to accept her gifts no matter whom she chooses to give them through. It's the Keeper who wants you to forgive. They're not the same boys they were when they tormented you. They've asked for your forgiveness."

Akma paused in his work and looked her in the eye. Without rancor—without any kind of readable expression—he said, "They've asked, but I refuse."

"I think it's beneath you now, Akma. I could understand it at first. The hurt was still fresh."

"You don't understand," said Akma.

"I know I don't. That's why I'm begging you to explain it to me."

"I didn't forgive them. There was nothing to forgive."

"What do you mean?"

"They were doing as their father taught them. I was doing as my father taught me. That's all. Children are nothing but tools of their parents."

"That's a terrible thing to say."

"It's a terrible thing. But the day will come when I'm no longer a child, Mother. And on that day I'll be no man's tool."

"Akma, it poisons you to hold all this hatred in your heart. Your father teaches people to forgive and to abandon hate and—"

"Hate kept me going when love failed me," said Akma. "Do you think I'm going to give it up now?"

"I think you'd better," said Chebeya. "Before it destroys you."

"Is that a threat? Will the Keeper strike me down?"

"I didn't say before it kills you. You can be ruined as a person long before your body is ready to be put into the ground."

"You and Father can think of me however you like," said Akma. "Ruined, destroyed, whatever. I don't care."

"I don't think you're ruined," said Chebeya.

Luet piped up. "He's not bad, Mother. You and Father shouldn't talk about him as if he's bad."

Chebeya was shocked. "We've *never* said he was bad, Luet! Why would you say such a thing?"

Akma laughed lightly. "Luet doesn't have to hear you use the word to know the truth. Don't you understand her gifts yet? Or hasn't the Keeper given you a dream about it?"

"Akma, don't you realize it isn't your father or me that you're fighting? It's the Keeper!"

"I don't care if it's the whole world and everything in it, on it, and above it. I . . . will . . . not . . . bend." And, obviously aware that it was a very dramatic thing to say—and faintly ridiculous coming from one so young—Akma shouldered his burden and left the hut.

There was no light but moonlight as they left the land that, for this short time they had made bountiful with good harvests. No one looked back. There was no sound of alarm behind them. Their flocks of turkeys and goats were not quiet; they talked sometimes among themselves; but no one heard.

And when they crested the last hill before being truly out of the land they knew, there, waiting for them in the shadow of the pine forest, stood the Pabulogi. Akmaro embraced them; they laughed and cried and embraced others, men and women. Then Akmaro hurried them and they all moved out together.

They camped in a side valley, and there they laughed and sang songs together and rejoiced because the Keeper had delivered them from bondage. But in the midst of their celebration, Akmaro made them break camp and flee again, up the valley into unknown paths, because Pabulog had arrived and found the guards asleep, and now an army was chasing them.

Following uncharted paths was dangerous, especially this time of year. Who knew which valleys would be deep in snow, and which dry? The thousands of valleys all had different weathers and climates, it seemed, depending on the flow of winds moist and dry, cold and hot. But this path was warm enough, considering the elevation, and dry enough, but with water for their herds. And eleven days later they came down out of the mountains from a small valley that was not even guarded, because no Elemaki raiders ever came that way. The next afternoon they stood across the river, and despite the instructions of the priests Akmaro would not let his people enter the water.

"They have already been made new men and women," said Akmaro.

"But not by the authority of the king," said the priests who argued with him.

"I know that," said Akmaro. "It was by the authority of the Keeper of Earth, who is greater than any king."

"Then it will be an act of war if you cross this water," said the priest.

"Then we will never cross it, because we mean no harm to anyone."

Finally Motiak himself came out and crossed the bridge to speak to Akmaro. They stood face to face for a moment, and people on both sides of the water watched to see how the king would put this upstart stranger in his place. To their surprise, Motiak embraced Akmaro, and embraced his wife, and took his son and daughter by the hand, and led the children first, the adults following, across the bridge. None of them touched the water of the Tsidorek that day, and Motiak proclaimed that these were true citizens of Darakemba, for they had already been made new men and women by the Keeper of Earth.

The sun had not yet set on that day when Ilihi came to greet Akmaro, it was a joyful reunion, and they told each other stories of their lives since parting until into the night. In later days many of the people of the land of Khideo made the journey to Darakemba to greet old friends and, sometimes, kinfolk who had left Zinom to follow Akmaro into the wilderness.

Nor was this the last of the reconciliations. Motiak sent out a proclamation for the people of Darakemba to gather in the great open place beside the river. There he caused that his clerks read out to the people the story of the Zenifi, and then the story of the Akmari, and all the people were amazed at how the Keeper had intervened to preserve them. Then the sons of Pabulog came forth and asked for Akmaro to take them down into the water. This time when they emerged they explicitly rejected their old identities. "We are no longer Pabulogi," said Pabul, and his brothers echoed him. "We are Nafari now, and our only father is the Keeper of Earth. We will look to Akmaro and Motiak to be our urfathers; but we ask for no inheritance beyond that of the simplest citizen of Darakemba."

Now, when the people of Darakemba had gathered, they assembled themselves as they always had, the descendants of the original Darakembi on the king's left, and the descendants of the original Nafari on the king's right. And within those groups, they subdivided further, for the Nafari still remembered which of them, reckoning by the father's line, were Issibi, and which Oykibi, and which Yasoi, and which Zdorabi. And in both groups, sky people and middle people gathered separately in their clans; and at the back, the few diggers who were free citizens.

When the reading of the histories was finished, Motiak arose and said, "No one can doubt that the hand of the Keeper has been manifest in the things we have seen and heard. For the last few days I have spent every waking hour in the company of Akmaro and Chebeya, two great teachers that the Keeper has sent to us to help us learn how to be worthy guardians of the land the Keeper has given us. Now he will speak to you, with greater authority than any king."

The people whispered to each other because the king had said such an astonishing thing. Then they listened as Akmaro spoke, moving from group to group among them; and other men and women from the Akmari went from group to group, each one teaching a part of the message that the Keeper had sent through Binaro so many years before, the message Binaro had died for. Not all believed in everything they were told, and some of the ideas were shocking, for Akmaro spoke of diggers and angels and humans being brothers and sisters. But no one dared speak in opposition to him, for he had the friendship of the king—and many of the people, perhaps most of them, especially among the poor, believed in what he said with their whole hearts.

That day many went into the water, to become new under the hands of Akmaro and his followers. And as the day drew to a close, Motiak caused another proclamation to be read:

"From now on, priests will no longer be servants of the king, appointed by the king, and staying with the king to perform the great public rituals. From now on, Akmaro will be the high priest, and he will have the power to appoint lesser priests in every city and town and village that is now under my rule. These priests of the Keeper will not be paid out of the public treasury, but will instead work with their hands like any other men and women; no labor is too humble for them, and no burden too great. As for the priests who have served me so faithfully up to now, they will not be forgotten. I will release them from their duties and grant them from my private treasury enough wealth to set them up in respectable businesses; those who want to teach may become teachers; and some few will have place with me as clerks and librarians. None are to think that I make this change because there has been any dishonor among them. But never again will a king be able to use his priests as Nuab used Pabulog and his other priests—as instruments of oppression and deception and cruelty. From now on the priests will have no political power, and in return no king or ruler will have authority to appoint or discharge a priest.

"Furthermore," said the proclamation, "when the people gather you will no longer divide yourselves into Nafari and Darakembi, or into different tribes or clans, nor shall there be separation between people of earth, of sky, and of the middle. When you obey me as your king, you are all Nafari, you are all Darakembi. And when you gather with the priest to learn the teachings of the Keeper of Earth, then you are the Kept, and this is a matter between you and the Keeper of Earth—no mortal power, of king or governor, of soldier or teacher, may interfere in that. No person of any race may be kept beyond ten years in bondage, and all who have already served that time are now employees who must be paid a fair wage and may not be discharged, though they may freely leave. All children born in my lands are free from the moment of conception, even if the mother is a bondservant. It is a new order in my lands, and it is my plea that my people will obey."

The last sentence was the standard formulation—all the king's edicts were listed as pleas rather than commands, for that was the way Nafai had established things back when Heroes ruled. This time, though, there were many who heard his words with quiet rage. How dare he say that there should be no difference between me and a digger, between me and a woman, between me and an angel, between me and a human, between me and a man, between me and the poor, between me and the ignorant, between me and my enemies. Whatever their treasured prejudice might be, they gave an outward show of accepting Akmaro's teachings and Motiak's edict, but in their hearts, in their homes, and, bit by bit over the coming years, in quiet conversations with friends and neighbors, they rejected the madness that Akmaro and Motiak had brought upon them.

But at the time it seemed to most to be the dawning of a golden age, those glorious days when Akmaro was establishing Houses of the Kept, to be tended by priests in every city, town, and village; when Motiak celebrated the new equality of men and women, diggers, angels, and humans, and the promise of freedom for all slaves. It was a mark of their naiveté, to think that such a revolution could be accomplished so easily. But in their ignorance, they were happy, and it was recorded in the Annals of the Kings of the Nafari as the most harmonious time in all of human history on Earth. The exceptions were not deemed worthy of mention in the book.

6

Disillusion

Twice each year, Akmaro went to visit each of the seven Houses of the Keeper. When he came, all the priests and teachers in that region of the empire of Darakemba would come to the House and there he would teach them, listen to their problems, and help them make their decisions. He was very careful not to allow the priests to treat him as priests of another kind had once treated kings. There was no bowing, no special notice; they touched each other's forearms or wings in equal greeting. And when they sat, it was in a circle, and Akmaro would call upon any of them at random to lead the meeting and call on others to speak.

He came, as always, to the House of the Keeper in Bodika, the most recent addition to the empire of Darakemba. The land was at peace, having no further will to resist the rule of Motiak. But the teaching of Akmaro—that was another matter. "You must make it plain to them that it isn't *my* teaching," Akmaro said. "I learned all that I know from Binaro, or from dreams the Keeper sent—to me sometimes, but more often to others."

"That's the problem, Father Akmaro," said Didul. The former sons of Pabulog had all become priests or teachers, devoting their lives to serving the Keeper that had freed them from the lies and hatred of their father. "Or part of the problem. We have quite a few people who claim to have true dreams telling them that in Bodika, at least, the Keeper doesn't want any mixing of earth people, sky people, and middle people."

"Those are false dreams," said Akmaro.

"They say that yours are the false ones," said Didul. "So what it comes down to is that we *must* ask them to believe, not in the Keeper, but in your words about the Keeper."

"There are laws about fraud," said one of the other priests. "People can't go about attacking the teachings of the Houses of the Kept!"

"Didul won't let us take them to the underking of Bodika," said another.

Akmaro looked at Didul.

"I have my suspicion that the underking is in private sympathy with those who teach that the earth people are slaves by nature, even if they've been freed by law."

"It's better not to take these things to trial, anyway," said Akmaro.

"How can the kingdom be united, if anyone can set up in business and claim to speak for the Keeper?" demanded another teacher, this one a woman of the sky people. "There has to be some limit on these things."

"It's not for us to tell the Keeper whom he can or cannot speak to."

"Well when are you going to put a stop to the women speaking of the Keeper as a 'she'?" asked an old man.

"When the Keeper lets us know whether his body has a womb or not, we will tell one group or the other to change their conception of him. Have you seen him?" asked Akmaro.

The old man protested that of course he had not.

"Then don't be too anxious to control other people's ideas," said Akmaro. "It might turn out to be you who would have to learn to say 'she.' "

Didul laughed, as did many others—mostly the young ones, like him. But then, sobering, Didul added, "In the thirteen years since you have been high priest of Darakemba, Father Akmaro, there are still many who reject all the changes. Here in this gathering there are those women who hate having to teach congregations that include men, and men who hate teaching women. There are angels who dislike teaching humans, and humans who dislike teaching angels. Is it like this everywhere, or only here in Bodika where even the priests and teachers fail to have hearts that are at one with the Keeper?"

"Do they still teach those mixed congregations?" asked Akmaro.

"Yes," said Didul. "But some have left their positions because they couldn't bear it."

"Did you appoint others to take their place?"

"Yes," said Didul.

"Then it's no different here from elsewhere. The mixing of men and women, of earth people, middle people, and sky people into one people, the Kept of the Keeper—that is not to be achieved in a single year or even thirteen years."

"The quarreling among us can be bitter at times," said Didul.

"And you always take the other side against us!" cried out one young angel.

"I take the Keeper's side!" Didul insisted.

Akmaro rose to his feet. "What I wish you would all think about, my friends, is that there is a great deal more to what the Keeper asks of us than simply to associate with each other as equals."

"So let's concentrate on *those* things and forget the mixing up of species!" cried a woman angel.

"But if we who are priests and teachers can't be one people," said Akmaro, "how can we possibly expect them to believe anything we say? Look at you—how you have sorted yourselves out, dividing all the female humans from the female angels, and over there, the male humans, and here, the male angels, and where are the diggers? Are you still sitting in the back? In the farthest place?"

A digger man stood up, looking nervous. "We don't like to push ourselves forward, Akmaro."

"You shouldn't have to push," said Akmaro. "How many of you here even know this man's name?" Didul started to answer, but Akmaro held up his hand. "Of course *you* know, Didul. But is there anyone else?"

"How would we?" replied an angel. "He spends all his time holding little meetings out in the caves and tunnels of the diggers."

"Is he the only one? Don't humans and angels also teach diggers?"

Didul spoke up. "That *is* hard, Father Akmaro. There's a lot of resentment of humans and angels among the former slaves. They don't feel safe. The Kept among the earth people wouldn't hurt a fly, but there are others."

"And do the diggers here feel safe among the humans and angels?" asked Akmaro.

The diggers looked back and forth with embarrassment. "Here we do, sir," said one of them, finally.

Akmaro laughed bitterly. "No wonder those who lie about what the Keeper wants have such an easy time converting people to their way of thought. What kind of example do they see among the Kept?"

They went on to other business then, bringing many matters of judgment before Akmaro, but the undertone of unease lasted through the whole meeting, and while some made an effort to cross the boundaries between the groups as the day wore on, others withdrew even further into knots of their own kind.

Finally it was evening, and as the evening song of angels and humans filled the air of the city of Bodika, Akmaro went to the home where Didul lived.

"Still not married?" Akmaro said. "And after all my advice."

"Twenty is still young," said Didul.

Akmaro looked him in the eye. "There's something you're not saying."

Didul smiled sadly. "There are many things that men and women do not say, because to say them would only bring unhappiness."

Akmaro patted his shoulder. "That's true enough. But sometimes people torment themselves needlessly, fearing that if they speak the truth other people would suffer, when in fact the truth would set them free."

"I might tell you," said Didul. "I dream of telling you."

"Well, then."

"Not true dreams, Father Akmaro. Just . . . dreams." He looked very uncomfortable.

"What's for supper?" said Akmaro. "I'm famished. Talking wears me out and leaves me empty."

"I have flatcakes. Or rather we can fry some up. Let me get the fire going by the cookstone."

"Didul, the rule is for priests to work for their living, not for them to live in dire poverty. A cookstone!"

"It's all I need," said Didul. "And besides, I do my labor . . . well, I don't own land. I gave it to the diggers who had once been slaves on it. I didn't want to live from rents."

"Gave it to them! Couldn't you at least have sold it to them, letting them pay a little each year and—"

"It was a gift to me," said Didul. "I didn't earn it, and they were the ones who had labored on it for all their lives, some of them."

"Well, how *do* you earn your miserable little flatcakes?" asked Akmaro.

"I have beans, too, and good spices, and fresh vegetables and fruit all year."

"And how does this happen? Please don't tell me that you're accepting gifts from the people you teach. That's forbidden, no matter how sincerely willing the people are to give them."

"No, no!" Didul protested. "I would never—no! I hire myself out. I do day labor for the people who would have been my tenants. And others, now. My reach is longer than any digger or angel. I'm good with a scythe, and I plow a straight furrow, and no one chops down a tree and dresses the wood more skillfully than I do. Even the ones who refuse to accept my teachings hire me when they need a tree felled."

"A day laborer," said Akmaro. "Day laborers are the poorest of the poor."

"Is there anything wrong with that?" said Didul.

"Not at all," said Akmaro. "You make me ashamed of my rents."

"What I choose for myself isn't a law for anyone else," said Didul. He got out the fine-ground maizemeal and began to mix it with water and a pinch of salt.

"But when you speak, diggers and angels listen to *you,* I'll wager," said Akma. He helped Didul form the balls of dough and flatten them.

Didul shrugged. "Some do. Most do."

"Is it as bad as the meeting today made it look?" asked Akmaro.

"Worse."

"I don't want to use the force of law to compel compliance," said Akmaro.

"It wouldn't work anyway," said Didul. "Law can change how people behave when others are watching—that's all. As you taught me back in the land of Chelem, the power of the whip is worthless against the stubborn heart."

"Yes, well, there you are," said Akmaro. "But what can I tell Motiak? We have to go back to the old ways, because the people won't respect a priesthood that isn't headed by the king?"

"No, not that," said Didul.

"Or worse, tell him that we should give up trying to teach the Keeper's way! But I reread those old dreams of the Heroes as Nafai and Oykib wrote them in the ancient books, and the only meaning I can take from them is that the Keeper wants us to be one people, the three species of us, the two sexes of us, the rich and poor of us. How can I back away from that?"

"You can't," said Didul, slapping a flattened disc of dough on the sizzling cookstone.

"But if we force everyone to live together—"

"It would be absurd. Angels can't live in digger holes, and diggers can't sleep upside down on perches."

"And humans are terrified of closed-in spaces and heights, both," said Akmaro.

"So we just keep on trying to persuade them," said Didul.

"Then there's no hope," said Akmaro. He flipped over another flatcake. "I can't even persuade you to take a wife, or to tell me why you won't."

"Can't you see why I won't?" asked Didul. "See the poverty I live in."

"Then marry a woman who is willing to work hard and cares as little for wealth as you do."

"How many women are like that?" asked Didul.

"I know lots of them. My wife is like that. My daughter is like that."

Didul blushed, and suddenly Akmaro understood.

"My daughter," he said. "That's what this is about, isn't it! You come four times a year to Darakemba to meet with me—and you've fallen in love with Luet!"

Didul shook his head, trying to deny.

"Well, you foolish boy, haven't you spoken to her about it? She's not a fool, she must have noticed that you're clever and kind and, or so I'm told by the women around me, probably the most handsome young man in Darakemba."

"How can I speak to her?" said Didul.

"I would suggest using a column of air arising from your lungs, shaped by the lips and tongue and teeth into vowels and consonants," said Akmaro.

"When we were young, I tormented her," said Didul. "I humiliated her and Akma in front of everyone."

"She's forgotten that."

"No she hasn't. *I* haven't, either. There's not a day goes by that I don't remember what I was and what I did."

"All right, I'm sure she *does* remember. What I meant was that she forgave you long ago."

"Forgave me," said Didul. "But it's a long stride from there to the love a wife should have for a husband." He shook his head. "Do you want bean paste? It's quite spicy, but the earth lady who made it for me is the finest cook I've ever known."

Akmaro held out his flatcake, and Didul smeared the paste on with a wooden spoon. Then Akmaro rolled it up, folded the bottom end, and began eating from the top. "As good as you promised," he said. "Luet would like it too. Can't make it spicy enough for her."

Didul laughed. "Father Akmaro, don't you know your own family? Suppose I did speak to Luet. About this, I mean. About marriage. We talk all the time when I'm there, about other things—history and science, politics and religion, all of it, except personal things. She's—brilliant. Too fine for me, but even if I dared to speak to her, and even if she somehow loved me, and even if you gave consent, it would still be impossible."

Akmaro raised an eyebrow. "What, is there some consanguinity I'm not aware of? I had no brother, and neither did my wife, so you can't be some secret nephew in the first degree."

"Akma," said Didul. "Akma has never forgiven me. And if Luet loved me he would take it as a slap in the face. And if you then gave consent to such a marriage, there would be no forgiveness. He'd go mad. He'd—I don't know what he'd do."

"Maybe he'd wake up and get over this childish vindictiveness of his," said Akmaro. "I know he's never been the same since those days, but—"

"But nothing," said Didul. "I did it to him. Don't you understand? Akma's hatred, all of it arises from the humiliation I heaped upon him that first day and so many days afterward—"

"You were a child then."

"My father wasn't cracking a whip over my head, Akmaro. I enjoyed it! Don't you understand? When I see these people who tease digger children because of their poverty, because they live in holes and get dirty, because—I understand them. The tormentors. I was one. I know how it feels to have driven all compassion out of my heart and laugh at the pain of someone else."

"You're not the same person now."

"I have rejected that part of myself," said Didul. "But I'm the same person, all right."

"When you pass through the water—"

"Yes, a new man, I become a new man. I'm a man who *does* not do those things, yes. But I'm still and always the man who once did them."

"Not in my eyes, Didul. And I daresay not in Luet's."

"In Akma's eyes, Father Akmaro, I am the same one who destroyed him before his sister, his mother, his father, his friends, his people. And if it ever happened that Luet and I became married—no, if he even heard that I wanted to, or that Luet was willing, or that you approved—it would set him off. I don't know what he'd do, but he'd do it."

"He's not a violent man," said Akmaro. "He's gentle even if he does harbor ancient grudges."

"I'm not fearing for my life," said Didul. "I just know that someone as smart as Akma, as talented, as clever, as attractive—he'll find a way to make us all regret that we ever dared affront him in such a way."

"So what you're telling me is that you refuse even to offer my daughter the possibility of marrying one of the finest young men I know in this whole empire, solely because her *brother* can't grow out of his childish rage?"

"We have no way of knowing what it was that happened inside Akma, Father Akmaro. He may have been a child, but that doesn't make the things he felt then childish."

Akmaro took the last bite of his flatcake. The bean paste having been used up, it tasted dry and salty. "I need a drink of water," he said.

"The Milirek has no pure source," said Didul, "and it flows from low mountains, some of which lose their snow for much of the year."

"I drink the water that the Keeper gives me in every land," said Akmaro.

Didul laughed. "Then I hope you won't go down out of the gornaya! The slow-flowing waters of the flatlands aren't safe. They're muddy and foul and *things* live in them. I know a man who drank it once without boiling it, and he said his bowels didn't stop running until he had lost a third of his body weight and his wife was ready to bury him, if only to save the trouble of digging yet another latrine."

Akmaro grimaced. "I hear those stories, too. But somehow we have to learn to live in the flatlands. We've had peace for so long that people from all over are coming here. Former Elemaki, people from hidden mountain valleys, coming to Darakemba because under the rule of Motiak there's peace and plenty. Well, the peace will last, I hope. But the plenty . . . we have to find a way to use the flatlands."

"The diggers can't tunnel there, it all floods," said Didul. "The angels can't perch there because the trees are so thick-limbed and close together that the jaguars can reach them everywhere."

"Then we should think of some way to build houses on rafts or something," said Akmaro. "We need more land. And maybe if we opened up new lands, my young friend, where diggers and angels and humans *had* to live in the same kind of house, we might be able to create the kind of harmony that is so hard to bring to pass here in the gornaya."

"I'll think about it," said Didul. "But I hope you also give this problem to cleverer men and women than me."

"Believe me, I have and I will again," said Akmaro. "And to cleverer ones than me, too. I learned that from Motiak. Don't waste your time asking advice from people stupider than you."

"That's comforting advice," said Didul.

"How so?"

"I can ask anybody," he said, laughing.

"False modesty is still false, no matter how charming it might seem."

"All right, I'm smarter than some people," Didul admitted. "Like that one teacher who says that angels are afraid to go down into digger holes."

"Aren't they?"

"I know three angel physicians who do it all the time, and they've never been harmed."

"Maybe," said Akmaro, "our teachers would be less afraid if they believed their teaching was as valuable a service as the herbs of the physician."

"Well, there we are," said Didul. "If the believers weren't so torn by doubt, they might do a better job of persuading the unbelievers."

"Oh, I don't even mind their doubt," said Akmaro. "If they could just *act* as if they believed, they'd be more persuasive."

"If I didn't know you better," said Didul, "I'd think you were praising hypocrisy."

"I would rather live among people who behave correctly than among people with correct opinions," said Akmaro. "I've noticed no higher incidence of hypocrisy among the former than among the latter, and at least the ones who behave well don't take up so much of your time with arguing."

Bego puffed along behind Akma and Mon, complaining the whole time. "I don't see why we couldn't have this discussion, whatever it's about, in my study. I'm too old for this, and you may have noticed that my legs are less than half the length of yours!"

To which Akma heartlessly replied, "So fly then."

From behind, Mon gave Akma a shove in the shoulder, sending him stumbling into some brush beside the path. Akma turned, ready to be angry, ready to laugh, depending on the intention he read in Mon's eyes.

"Have respect for a friend of mine," said Mon softly, "if not for his age and office."

Akma smiled at once, his most winning and charming smile, and it worked as it always worked, suggesting as it did a sort of self-effacing humility, a believable protest of innocence, and a promise of friendship —whatever good thing the other person wished to read into it. Mon always wondered at that smile even as it triumphed over his own anger or envy. Where could such power over others come from?

"Ah, Bego, you knew I was teasing, I hope," said Akma. "Forgive me, old friend?"

"I forgive you everything, every time," said Bego wearily. "Everyone does, so why do you bother to ask anymore?"

"And do I offend so often that forgiving me should be a habit?" asked Akma, with more than a little pain in his smile this time. It made Mon want to clap an arm around his shoulders, grip him hard, assure him that no one took offense.

How does he *do* that!

"You offend no more often than any other brilliant and undisciplined and leisured and lazy young man of twenty years," said Bego. "Now, here, in the middle of this grassy field. If you look not to be overheard, here we are."

"Ah," said Mon, pointing overhead. "Have you overlooked the prying eyes from above?"

"The fixed star," said Bego. "Yes, yes, well, they say the Oversoul sees through roofs and leaves and solid earth, so what does it matter."

Akma threw himself to the ground and landed immediately in the grass in an elegant sprawl that would have looked practiced in anyone less lithe and natural. "Who knows how many hundreds of digger tunnels intersect under this meadow?" he asked.

"It's not a meadow," said Mon. "It's my father's park, and no one is allowed to dig under it."

"Oh, then we know that even the earthworms shy away from the boundaries," said Akma.

Mon laughed in spite of himself. "So, Father's authority isn't universal."

"Why are we here?" asked Bego. "Sitting isn't my most comfortable perch."

"But Bego," said Akma, "humans and angels and diggers are all alike now, didn't you know? The Keeper has spoken."

"Well, the Keeper had better give me a new bottom if he wants me to set it on chairs or other miserably uncomfortable places," said Bego.

"Mon and I have been thinking," said Akma.

"The two of you together?" asked Bego. "Then perhaps you have woven a thought, if you've done it long and often enough."

"We've been studying the histories of the Heroes. And the history that the Zenifi found thirteen years ago."

"The Rasulum," said Bego.

"And we wanted to try out an idea on you," said Mon.

"Which you couldn't do in my study? Perhaps immediately after I gave school to the youngest of the king's boys?"

"Our question is possibly treasonable," said Akma.

Bego immediately fell silent.

"We know that you have respect for scientific inquiry, and would never report us. But who knows what might get said by someone else, overhearing us? Perhaps exaggerating what was said?"

"What possible treason can there be in the ancient records?" asked Bego.

"If we're right," said Akma, "then we think you've been trying to hint about this for about ten years."

"I don't hint," said Bego. "And if you want to know whether you're right, it's Mon who has the gift of certitude."

"Well, that's the problem," said Mon. "If we're right, then there's no reason to trust in that supposed gift of mine. And if we're wrong, well, we get the same answer—no certainty from me."

"So we ask you," said Akma.

"You think that your own gift from the Keeper might be imaginary?" asked Bego, incredulous.

"I think that many things can come to someone's mind out of hysteria," said Mon.

"Or even some keen natural insight," said Akma. "For instance, that famous, unforgettable time when Mon helped you translate the Rasulum leaves. Who's to say that he didn't reach his certainties of right and wrong by unconsciously interpreting your own gestures, movements, vocal intonation, facial expressions."

"What good would that do him?" said Bego. "I didn't know."

"Perhaps you knew, but didn't know that you knew," said Akma.

Bego riffled his wings in a shrug.

"What we've been doing, Akma and I, is trying to see if there's anything in the ancient records that constitutes actual proof that there even *is* a Keeper of Earth."

"No one doubts that there's a Keeper," said Bego.

"Look at the histories," said Akma. "All the records from the early Heroes say that all human life had been dispersed from Earth—that until the Keeper brought the Heroes here from the place called Harmony or Basilica—the record is ambiguous—"

"Basilica is the name of the fixed star," said Bego, "and Harmony is the name of the planet orbiting that star."

"Say the scholars," said Akma. "Who know nothing more than we do, since they reach all their conclusions from the same records. And I say the record of the Heroes is obviously wrong. There *were* people here, the Rasulum."

Bego shrugged. "That has caused a little consternation among the scholars."

"Come on," said Mon. "That's the very fact you keep throwing in our faces every time we discuss history. You want us to discover something from it so don't play innocent now."

Akma went on. "What if humans never left this world at all? What if humans were simply forced to stay away from the gornaya during the era when it was being lifted up by volcanos and earthquakes? The Heroes talk of how there was once a time when the land masses were getting folded into each other and raised high, the tallest mountains in the world. So what if *that* was what gave rise to the legend of the dispersal? No humans in the gornaya, therefore no humans in the world—but actually humans to the north, in the prairie lands. Then there's a terrible war, and as many humans as can, flee from the Rasulum. Some of them brave the old tabus and come into the gornaya. Perhaps they even come by boat, but they're afraid the gods they worship—the Oversoul and the Keeper of Earth—will be angry at them for doing it, so they talk of having come from the stars instead of from Opustoshen."

"Then why is the language of the leaves so different from our language?" asked Bego.

"Because it hasn't been a mere four hundred or five hundred years since the time of the Heroes. In fact they split off from the Rasulum a thousand years ago, perhaps more. And the languages grew more and more different, until nothing was alike."

"And what does that have to do with angels and diggers?" asked Bego.

"Nothing at all!" cried Mon. "Don't you see? The humans came and dominated everybody, and forced their gods on everybody. But didn't the diggers worship gods that the angels made for them? And didn't the angels have their own gods to worship? None of this Keeper nonsense. The angels and diggers evolved separately here in the gornaya while the humans stayed away in the land northward."

"What about the stories of Shedemei discovering some strange organ in all the sky people and all the earth people that forced us to remain together?" asked Bego.

"The story says that she caused you all to get sick and it made those organs disappear from your children," said Akma. "So now, conveniently enough, there's not a lick of evidence left that those organs ever existed."

"All the stories use for evidence things that can't be checked now," said Mon. "That's a standard rhetorical trick—one that any fool can expose in a public debate or trial. The new star in the sky is Basilica—but how do we know that star wasn't there all along?"

"The records are ambiguous about that," said Bego.

"The only evidence we *do* have," said Akma, "is a flat contradiction of the records of the Heroes. They said there were no other humans on Earth when they arrived. But we have the bones of Opustoshen and the leaves of the Rasulum to prove otherwise. Don't you see? The only evidence denies everything."

Bego looked at them placidly. "Well, this certainly is treasonous," he finally said.

"But it doesn't have to be," said Akma. "That's what I've been explaining to Mon. His father's authority comes from being a direct descendant of the first Nafai. That part of the record isn't being questioned. The kingdom is not challenged."

"No," said Bego. "Only your father is challenged."

Akma smiled. "If my father is teaching people to behave in uncomfortable ways, solely because the Keeper says they must, and then it turns out there is no Keeper, then whose will *is* it that my father is trying to foist onto the people?"

"I think your father is a sincere man," said Bego.

"Sincere but wrong," said Akma. "And the people hate what he's teaching."

"The former slaves love it," said Bego.

"The *people,*" said Akma.

"I gather, then, that you don't consider diggers to be people," said Bego.

"I consider them to be the natural enemies of humans and angels. And I also think that there's no reason why humans should rule over angels."

"Now we're definitely back to treason," said Bego.

"Why not an alliance?" said Mon. "A king of the humans and a king of the angels, both ruling over peoples spread through the same territory?"

"Not possible," said Bego. "One king for one territory. Otherwise there would be war and hatred between humans and angels. The Elemaki would seize the opportunity and destroy us all."

"But we shouldn't be required to live together, anyway," said Akma.

Bego looked at Mon. "Is that what you want?" he asked. "You, who as a child dreamed of being—"

"My childish dreams are done with!" Mon cried. "In fact if I hadn't been living among angels I wouldn't have had those wishes, would I!"

"I thought they were rather sweet. And perhaps a bit flattering," said Bego. "Considering how many angels grow up wishing they were human."

"None!" cried Mon. "Not one!"

"Many."

"They're all mad, then," Mon replied.

"Quite likely," said Bego. "So let's see if I understand you. There is no Keeper and there never was. Humans never left Earth, just the gornaya. Diggers and angels never needed each other and there was no tiny organ that Shedemei removed from our bodies with a disease. And therefore there is no reason to change our whole way of life, all our customs, just because Akmaro tells us that it's the will of the Keeper that the three species become one people, the Keeper's Children, the People of Earth."

"Exactly," said Akma.

"So what?" asked Bego.

Akma and Mon looked at each other. "What do you mean, so what?" asked Mon.

"So why are you telling me?" asked Bego.

"Because maybe you can talk to Father about this," said Mon. "Get him to stop pushing these laws."

"Take my father away from his position of authority," said Akma.

Bego blinked once at Akma's words. "If I said these things to your father, my dear friends, I would simply be removed immediately from any position of responsibility. That's the *only* change that would be made."

"Does my father completely control the king, then?" asked Akma.

"Careful," said Mon. "Nobody controls my father."

"You know what I mean," Akma said impatiently.

"And I know Motiak," said Bego. "He's not going to change his mind, because as far as he's concerned, you have no evidence at all. For him, the very fact that true dreams led the soldiers of Ilihiak to find the Rasulum leaves is proof that the Keeper wanted them found. Therefore it is the Keeper who corrects the mistakes of the Heroes—more proof that the Keeper lived then, and the Keeper lives now. You aren't going to dissuade someone who wants so desperately to believe in the Keeper."

Angrily, Akma pound his fist down into the sod. "My father *must* be stopped from spreading his lies!"

"His mistakes," said Bego. "Remember? You would never be so disloyal a son as to accuse your father of lying. Who would believe you then?"

"Just because he believes them doesn't mean they're not lies," said Akma.

"Ah, but they're not *his* lies, are they?" said Bego. "So you must call them mistakes, when you say they are your father's."

Mon chuckled. "Do you hear him, Akma? He's with us. This is what he wanted us to realize all along."

"Why do you think so?" asked Bego.

"Because you're advising us on strategy," said Mon.

Akma sat up, grinning. "Yes, you are, aren't you, Bego!"

Bego shrugged again. "You can't possibly have any strategy right now. Akmaro is too closely linked to the king's policy, and vice versa. But perhaps there'll come a time when the Houses of the Kept are much more clearly separated from the house of the king."

"What do you mean?" asked Akma.

"I mean only this. There are those who want to tear your father from his throne, they're so angry about these policies."

"That's not what we want!" cried Mon.

"Of course not. No one in their right mind wants that. The only reason we don't have invasions from the Elemaki every year is because the entire empire of Darakemba is united, with armies and spies constantly patrolling and protecting our borders. It's only a tiny minority of bigots and madmen who want to throw down the throne. However, that tiny treasonous minority will gain more and more support, the farther your father pushes these reforms of Akmaro's. It will mean civil war, sooner or later, and no matter who wins, we'll be weakened. There are people who don't want that. Who want us to go back to the way we were before."

"The old priests, you mean," said Mon scornfully.

"Some of them, yes," said Bego.

"And you," said Akma. "You want things to go back the way they were."

"I don't have opinions on public policy," said Bego. "I'm a scholar, and I'm reporting to you in a scholarly way the current condition of the kingdom. There are those who want to fend off civil war, protect the throne, and stop Akmaro from pushing these insane, offensive, impossible laws breaking down all distinctions between men and women, humans and diggers and angels. All this talk of forgiveness and understanding."

Akma interrupted, full of bitterness. "It's only a mask for those who want to turn this into a land where diggers strut around with weapons in their hands, tormenting their betters and—"

"You almost make me fear that you are one of those who wants to destroy this kingdom," said Bego. "If that is the case, Akma, then you'll be of no use to those who are trying to preserve the throne."

Akma fell silent, pulling at the grass. A clump came free, spraying his face with dirt. Angrily he brushed it away.

"But what if those who are trying to preserve the throne could assure the people, Just wait. The children of Motiak don't believe in this nonsense of all the species being equal children of the Keeper. The children of Akma have no intention of pursuing their father's mad policies. Be patient. When the time comes, things will go back to the old way."

"I'm not the heir," said Mon.

"Then perhaps you should work to persuade Aronha," said Bego.

"Even if I did, Father would only pass the kingdom on to Ominer, skipping us both."

"Then perhaps you should also persuade Ominer and even Khimin." At Mon's sound of disgust Bego laughed. "He's bright enough. He may be his mother's son, but he's your father's son, too. What can your father do if *all* his children reject this policy?"

"My father wouldn't care," said Akma. "He'd just pick one of his favorites to be high priest after him. I don't imagine he even considers me for the position."

"Dee-dool!" cried Mon derisively.

Akma's face went hot with anger at the sound of Didul's name.

"It doesn't matter who your father's successor would really be," said Bego. "Don't you see that if his own son publicly preaches against his policies, he would be hopelessly undermined? Even among his own priests and teachers there's dissension, a lack of confidence. Some of them will listen to you. Some of them won't. But the Kept will be weakened."

"Ho, Akma, I can imagine you preaching," said Mon scornfully.

"I think I'd be good at it," said Akma. "If it weren't so likely that I'd be arrested for treason."

Bego nodded. "That *is* the problem, isn't it?" he said. "That's why you need to bide your time. Work with your brothers, Mon. Help him, Akma. Don't push them too hard, just suggest things, raise questions. Eventually you'll win them over."

"The way you did with us?" asked Akma.

Bego shrugged again. "I never suggested treason to you. I don't suggest it now. I want you to discover truth for yourself. I don't ram it down your throats like some do."

"But what guarantee do we have that anything will change?"

"I think that by getting rid of priests appointed by the king, Akmaro and Motiak started down a road from which there's no retreat," said Bego. "Eventually it will lead them to a point where religion is completely separate from government. And when that day comes, my young friends, the law will no longer stand between you and any preaching that you want to do."

Mon hooted. "If I still believed in my own gift, I'd say that it was certain that Bego is right! Someday soon it *will* happen. It has to."

"And now that you have planned how to save the kingdom from Akmaro's excessively inclusive beliefs, may I go inside and find a perch where I can dangle myself to stretch out my aching muscles?"

"We can carry you in, if you want," offered Mon mischievously.

"Save me even more trouble by cutting off my head and carrying *it* inside. The rest of my body isn't much use to me these days anyway."

They laughed and got up from the grass. They walked more slowly returning to the king's house, but there was a dance, a spring in the way the boys walked—no, bounced—along the path through the king's park. And when they passed Khimin, who was trying to memorize a long poem and having a miserable time of it, they shocked him utterly by actually inviting him to walk along with them. "Why!" Khimin demanded suspiciously.

"Because even though your mother is a certified idiot," said Mon, "you're still my brother and I've treated you shamefully for too many years. Give me a chance to make it up to you."

As Khimin slowly and guardedly made his way toward them, Akma whispered to Mon, "You're committed now, you know."

"Who knows?" asked Mon. "He may be decent company after all. Edhadeya always says he's all right, if we only give him a chance."

"Then Edhadeya will be very happy," said Akma.

Mon winked at him. "If you like, I'll tell her that including Dudagu Dermo's spawn was your idea."

Akma rolled his eyes. "I'm not casting covetous eyes on your sister, Mon. She's three years older than me."

"My gift may not come from the Keeper," said Mon, "but I still know a lie when I hear one."

With that, Khimin was near enough to overhear them, and the conversation changed to include him. By the time they reached the king's house, Akma and Mon had both used so much charm on the poor eighteen-year-old that he was utterly besotted with them and would have believed them if they told him his own feet were tree stumps and his nose a turnip.

Bego left them as soon as they were inside, and on his way through the corridors he did use his wings a bit, skittering along the floor and singing snatches of happy songs to himself. Clever boys, he said to himself. They'll do it, if we give them half a chance. They *will* do it.

Luet loved it when Mother went to call on Dudagu in the king's house, because after a few moments of being polite to the queen, who was not aging well and spent her days complaining of ill health, she was always excused and allowed to go off in search of Edhadeya. She had begun the custom when she was only five, and Edhadeya was a lofty ten-year-old; she marveled now, thinking back, that the king's daughter had been so kind to a child half her age who had so recently been a slave to diggers. Or perhaps that was the reason—Edhadeya had taken pity on her, having heard the story of her suffering. Well, however it began, the friendship was in full bloom now, with Edhadeya twenty-three years old and Luet eighteen and a woman.

She found her friend working with the musicians, teaching them some new composition. The drummers seemed not to be able to get the rhythm right. "It isn't hard," Edhadeya was saying. "It's only hard when you put it together. But if you can hear how it goes with the melody. . . ." Whereupon Edhadeya began to sing, a high sweet voice, and now the one drummer, now the other, began to feel how the beat she had been teaching fit with the tune she sang, and without even thinking what she was doing, Luet began to spin and raise her arms and hop in the steps of an impromptu dance.

"You shame my poor tune!" cried Edhadeya.

"Don't stop, it was beautiful!"

But Edhadeya stopped at once, leaving the musicians to work on the song while she walked with Luet out into the vegetable garden. "Worms everywhere. In the old days we used to have slaves whose whole job was picking them off the leaves. Now we can't pay anyone enough to do it, so all our greens have holes in them and every now and then a salad moves of its own accord. We all pretend it's a miracle and go on eating."

"I have to tell you that Akma is in one of his vile moods lately," said Luet.

"I don't care," said Edhadeya. "He's too young for me. He's always been too young for me. It was a form of madness that I ever thought I was in love with him."

Luet looked up at the sky. "What? All those clouds? I thought you loved my brother whenever it rained."

"At the moment it's not raining," said Edhadeya. "And is today one of the days you're in love with Mon?"

"Nobody," said Luet. "I don't think I'd make a good wife."

"Why not?" asked Edhadeya.

"I don't want to stay in a house and order work all day. I want to go out like Father does and teach and talk and—"

"He works."

"In the fields, I know! But I'd do that! Just don't make me stay indoors. Maybe it was my childhood labor in the fields. Maybe in my heart I'm always afraid that if I'm not working, some digger twice my height will—"

"Oh, Luet, I get nightmares whenever you talk like that."

"Found one," said Luet, holding up a worm.

"How attractive," said Edhadeya.

Luet crushed the worm between her fingers, balled up the remnants of its body, and dropped it into the soil. "One more salad that will not move," she said.

"Luet," said Edhadeya, and in the moment the whole tone of the conversation changed. No longer were they playful girls. Now they were women, and the business was serious. "What has your brother come up with lately? What's going on between him and my brothers?"

"He's always over here with Mon," said Luet. "I think they're studying something with Bego. Or something."

"So he doesn't talk to you?" said Edhadeya. "He talks to them."

"Them?"

"Not just Mon now. He talks to Aronha and Ominer and Khimin."

"Well, it's nice that he's including Khimin. I don't really think the boy is as awful as—"

"Oh, he's awful, all right. But potentially salvageable, and if I thought it was salvage that Akma and Mon had in mind, I'd be glad," said Edhadeya. "But it's not."

"Not?"

"Yesterday someone mentioned true dreams and looked at me. It was nothing, just a chance comment. I can't even remember—one of the councilors, coming to meet with Father, and he looked at me. But I happened to turn away just at that moment and saw Ominer rolling his eyes in ridicule. So I followed him and once we were alone in the courtyard I threw him up against the wall and demanded to know why he was making fun of me."

"You're always so gentle," murmured Luet.

"Ominer doesn't hear you unless he's in physical pain," said Edhadeya. "And I'm still stronger than he is."

"Well, what did he say?"

"He denied he was making fun of me. So I said, Whom were you making fun of? And he said, Him."

"Who?" asked Luet.

"You know, the councilor who looked at me. And I said, you can't blame people for thinking about my dream of the Zenifi when they see me. Not everybody has true dreams. And then he said—listen, Luet—he said, Nobody does."

"Nobody?" Luet laughed, then realized that Edhadeya didn't think it was funny. "Dedaya, I've had true dreams, you've had true dreams. Mother's a raveler. Mon has his truthsense. Father dreams true, and—this is absurd."

"*I* know that. So I asked him why he said it, and he wouldn't tell. I pinched him, I tickled him—Luet, Ominer can't keep a secret from me. I've always been able to torture it out of him in five minutes. But this time he pretended he didn't know what I was talking about."

"And you think it has something to do with Akma and Mon?"

"I know it does. Luet, the only way Ominer could possibly keep a secret from me is if he was more frightened of someone else. And the only two people he fears more than me in the whole world are—"

"Your father?"

"Don't be silly, Father's as sweet as they come when he notices Ominer at all—which isn't often, he blends in with the walls. No, it's Mon and Aronha. I think it's both of them. I watched this morning, and all four of my brothers ended up with *your* brother and whatever they're talking about or planning or doing—"

"It has to do with the idea that there are no true dreams."

Edhadeya nodded. "I can't go to Father with this, they'd just deny it."

"Lie to your father?"

"Something's different. It made me feel dark and unpleasant and I think they're plotting something."

"Don't say that," said Luet. "It's our families we're talking about."

"They're not just boys anymore. Because we're still studying, we sometimes forget that we're not really in school, none of us but Khimin, when you come down to it. We're men and women. If Akma weren't your father's son, he'd be earning his own living. Aronha plays at soldier, but he has too much leisure, and so do my other brothers—they make priests work, but not the sons of the king."

Luet nodded. "Father tried to make Akma start earning his way when he was only fifteen. The age when laborers' children—"

"I know the age," said Edhadeya.

"Akma just said, 'What, are you going to stand over me with a whip if I don't?' It was really vicious."

"Your father wasn't his taskmaster in those terrible days," said Edhadeya.

"But Father *forgave* the taskmasters. The Pabulogi. Akma hasn't, and he is still angry."

"Thirteen years!" cried Edhadeya.

"Akma feeds on it the way an unborn chick feeds on the yolk of its egg. Even when he's thinking about something else, even when he doesn't realize it, he's seething inside. He was my teacher for a while. We became very close. I loved him for a while more than I loved anybody. But if I came too close, if I touched his affection in just the wrong way, he *lashed* out. Sometimes it shocked me the way Elemak and Mebbekew must have felt when Nafai knocked them down with lightning from his finger."

"Melancholy. I thought he was just a moody sort of person," said Edhadeya.

"Oh, I'm sure that's it," said Luet, "it's just that when he gets into that mood, it's my father that he rages at."

"And the Pabulogi."

"They don't come around often. When the priests come in for their meetings with Father, Akma makes sure he's somewhere else. I don't think he's seen any of them for years."

"But you've seen them."

Luet smiled wanly. "As little as possible."

"Even from her deathbed, as she calls it, Mother gets all the gossip, and she says that Didul looks at you like . . . like. . . ."

"Like my worst nightmare."

"You can't mean that," said Edhadeya.

"Not him personally. But what if he *did* decide he loved me? What if I loved him? It would be quicker and kinder if I just slit Akma's throat in his sleep."

"You mean this childish melancholy of Akma's would keep you from the man you love?"

"I don't *love* Didul. It was just a hypothetical situation."

"Lutya, my friend, isn't life complicated here in the king's house?"

"It's probably just as complicated for the poorest peasants. Down in their holes in the ground the most powerless ex-slaves probably have exactly the same problems. Grudges, loves, anger, fear, hate—"

"But when they quarrel in their tunnels, the whole kingdom doesn't quake," said Edhadeya.

"Well, that's *your* family. Not mine."

Edhadeya picked another worm off another leaf. "There are people eating holes in the kingdom, Lutya. What if our brothers turn out to be among the worms?"

"That's what you're afraid of, isn't it? Deny the Keeper. Then we don't have to associate with diggers and angels and—"

"Mon loves the angels. It would kill him not to be with them."

"But does he love the sky people more than Akma hates the earth people?"

"When it comes down to it, Mon won't give up his love for the angels."

"Still. It would be a terrible thing if they started—"

"Don't even think about it," said Edhadeya. "Our brothers would not commit treason."

"Then you're *not* afraid," said Luet.

Edhadeya sat on a bench and sighed. "I *am* afraid."

A new voice came from behind them. "Of what?"

They turned. It was Chebeya, Luet's mother. "Done already?" Luet asked.

"Poor Dudagu is exhausted," said Chebeya.

Edhadeya snorted.

"Don't make that sound in the woods," said Chebeya, "or a jaguar will find you."

"I don't see why you think it's so unnatural for me to despise my stepmother," said Edhadeya.

"Your father loves her," said Chebeya.

"A sign of his infinite capacity for love," said Edhadeya.

"What were you talking about when I came out here?" asked Chebeya. "And don't deny it was important, I could see how you were bound together."

Luet and Edhadeya looked at each other.

"Trying to decide how much to tell me?" asked Chebeya. "Let me make it easy for you. Start with everything."

So they told her.

"Let me watch them a little," said Chebeya, when they were done. "If I see them together, I can learn a lot."

"How can Mon not believe in true dreams?" asked Edhadeya. "He knows when things are true—he knew my dream about your family was a true one."

"Don't underestimate my son's powers of persuasion," said Chebeya.

"Mon isn't any man's puppet," said Edhadeya. "I *know* him."

"No, not a puppet," said Chebeya. "But I know Akma's gift."

"He has one?" asked Luet.

"The little sister is the last to see," said Edhadeya.

"He has the same gift as me," said Chebeya.

"He's never said so!" cried Luet.

"No, because he doesn't realize it. It's different with men, I think. Men don't form communities as easily as women do. Human men, I'm speaking of—angels aren't like this. Or maybe they are, it's not as if I've had much experience. I just know that when a man has the raveling gift, he doesn't see the connections between people the same way. What he does is he starts unconsciously finding ways to gather up all those scattered threads in his own hands."

"So he can't see the web of people," said Luet. "He just becomes the spider?"

Chebeya shuddered. "I haven't explained to him what it is he does. I'm afraid that if he ever becomes conscious of it, it'll be much worse. He'll become more powerful and. . . ."

"Dangerous," said Edhadeya.

Chebeya turned away from her. "He gathers people up and they want to please him."

"Enough that Mon would give up his love for the sky people?" asked Edhadeya.

"I'll have to see them together, with that in mind. But if Akma really cared about something and needed Mon's help, then I think Mon would help him."

"But that's horrible," said Edhadeya. "Does that mean that the times I thought I loved him—"

"I don't know," said Chebeya. "Or I mean—I do know—as much as he is capable of love, he has loved you, from time to time."

"Not now."

"Not lately."

Tears rolled out of Edhadeya's eyes. "This is so stupid," said

Edhadeya. "I'm not even pining for him, I go whole days without thinking of him—but it's just this gift of his, isn't it?"

Chebeya shook her head. "When he ravels people up, it only lasts for a little while. A day or two. Unless he stays with you, it fades. You haven't seen him in a week."

"I see him every day," said Edhadeya.

"You haven't been *close* to him, though," said Luet helpfully.

"He has to be talking to you, looking at you, interacting with you," said Chebeya. "You can trust your feelings with him. They're real enough."

"More's the pity," murmured Edhadeya.

"Mother," said Luet, "I think something very dangerous is happening. I think Akma and the sons of Motiak are plotting something."

"As I said, I'll look and see if it seems that way."

"And if it does?"

"I'll talk to your father about it," said Chebeya. "And perhaps then we'll talk to the king. And he may want to talk to you."

"And when everyone has talked to everybody," said Edhadeya, "there still won't be a thing we can do."

Chebeya smiled. "Ever hopeful, aren't you? Dedaya, have some trust. Your father and my husband and I may be old, but we still have some power within our reach. We *can* change things."

"I notice you didn't include my stepmother in that group," said Edhadeya nastily.

Chebeya smiled with benign innocence. "Poor Dudagu. She's too frail to be mentioned in the same breath with power."

Edhadeya laughed.

"Come home with me now, Luet. There's work to do."

Edhadeya hugged them both and watched them leave the courtyard. Then she lay back on the bench and looked up at the sky. She thought, when the angle of the sun was right, that she could see the star Basilica even in bright sunlight. Today, though, the clouds were blocking everything. It *was* going to rain.

"One-Who-Was-Never-Buried," murmured Edhadeya. "Are you going to do *anything* about this?"

Shedemei loaded her supplies into the ship's launch as the Oversoul murmured one more time inside her mind: <Are you sure this is wise?>

"Do you think you can't protect me?" asked Shedemei.

<I can keep you from being killed.>

"That's all I ask."

<I still don't see what you can discover that I can't find out faster and more accurately.>

"*I* want to know these people, that's all," said Shedemei. "I want to know them for myself."

<You can't possibly know them as well from just conversing with them as I know them from looking inside their thoughts.>

"Do I have to say it? Can't you look inside my mind and see the truth?"

<The question really is: Can you?>

"I can. I'm going down there because I'm lonely. There, is that what you wanted to hear?"

<Yes.>

"Well, now you've heard it. I want to hear another organic voice. No insult to you, but I actually would like to feel like some other people know me."

<I'm not offended. I've been hoping you'd do something like this. I just wish you had chosen a more benign time. There is little you can do by way of intervention at this time.>

"I know," said Shedemei. "And I don't claim to have any great and noble purpose. I'm just ready to come out of this metal shell and bump up against some people again." Then she thought of something. "How old am I? People will ask."

<You mean physically? The cloak keeps you very healthy. You could pass for forty. You haven't reached menopause. You never will, actually, until you tell me to let you do it.>

"Are you suggesting that I should have another child?"

<I'm just telling you to be careful how you go about curing your loneliness.>

Shedemei curled her lip in disgust. "This is a society with a strong tabu against sex outside of marriage. I'm not going down there to ruin some poor lonely man's life."

<Just a thought.>

"Are you sure all these warnings aren't because you're just the tiniest bit jealous?"

<Not programmed into me.>

"I can walk on the face of this planet, and other living creatures will know me as one of them. Have you ever wished."

<I don't wish.>

"That's a shame, too."

<It's sweet of you to anthropomorphize me so compassionately. But if

I really had these feelings you project onto me, wouldn't the last few things you've said be, in a technical sense, gloating?>

"That *is* programmed into *me*," said Shedemei.

The hatches were sealed. The launch was flipped away from the starship *Basilica* and hurtled down into the atmosphere.

7

Rasaro's School

Light streamed through the tall, wide windows of the winter room, reflecting from the bare lime-washed plaster walls until it was hard for Mon to imagine that it could possibly be brighter outside. The reason he and his brothers could gather here to be brow beaten by—no, to have a discussion with—Akma was because no one used the winter room in the summer. It was too hot. It was too bright. It was all Mon could do to keep his eyes open. If it weren't for the buzzing flies that persisted in trying to drink the sweat dribbling out of his body, he would have dozed off long ago.

Not that Mon wasn't committed to Akma's ideas. It's just that the two of them had discussed all this before ever bringing Aronha and Ominer and Khimin into it. So it was going over old ground for him. And it was natural for Akma to conduct these sessions, since Mon didn't have his patience in dealing with Khimin's questions, which were always off the subject, or Aronha's stubborn refusal to agree with points that were already proven and more than proven. Only Ominer seemed to grasp at once what Akma was talking about, and even he made the sessions longer and more tedious than they had to be, because when he *did* understand a point he would then repeat it back to Akma in different words. Between Khimin's obtuseness, Aronha's stolidity, and Ominer's enthusiasm, every tiny advance in the discussion took hours, or so it seemed to Mon. Akma could endure it. Akma could act as though the questions and comments weren't unbearably stupid.

A tiny thought crept into Mon's consciousness: Did Akma deal with me the same way? Are the ideas we worked out "together" really Akma's alone? How skillful is he, really, at winning people to his point of view?

Immediately Mon discarded the idea, not because it wasn't true, but because it would imply that Mon was not Akma's intellectual equal, and he certainly *was.* Bego had always made it clear that Mon was the best student he had ever had.

"Humans and angels *can* live together," said Akma, "because the natural habitat of both species is open air and sunlight. Humans cannot fly, it is true, but our bipedal body structure lifts us above the other animals. We conceive ourselves as seeing from above, which makes us in spirit compatible to the sky people. The diggers, however, are creatures of darkness, of caves; their natural posture is with their bellies dragging along the moist underground dirt. What creatures of intelligent and refinement abhor, the diggers love; what the diggers love, creatures of higher sensibility view with disgust."

Mon closed his eyes against the white unbearable light of the room. In the back of his mind there throbbed an intense feeling, a certainty that in his childhood he had learned to trust, and in recent years he had learned—a much harder task—to ignore. The feeling was beneath and behind the place in his mind that words came from. But, in the way that the mind supplies words for unexplainable tunes, his mind had also learned the words that went along with this feeling: Wrong. This is wrong. This is wrong. Throb, throb, throb. Closing his eyes didn't make it go away.

This doesn't mean anything, thought Mon. This feeling is just a holdover from my childhood. It's just the Keeper of Earth trying to get me to disbelieve what Akma is saying.

What am I thinking? I don't even believe in the Keeper of Earth, and here I am blaming him for this throbbing meaningless stupid insane chant running over and over through my mind. I can't get rid of my superstitions even when I'm trying to get rid of my superstitions. He laughed at himself.

Laughed aloud, or perhaps just breathed as if laughing—it didn't take much for Akma to pick up on it.

"But perhaps I'm wrong," said Akma. "Mon is the one who really understands this. Why were you laughing, Mon?"

"I wasn't," said Mon.

Wrong, this is wrong, this is wrong.

"I mean my first thought, Mon, you'll remember this, my first thought was that all three species should separate, but you're the one who insisted that humans and angels could live together because of all these affinities between us."

"You mean this comes from *Mon*?" asked Aronha. "Mon, who jumped off a high wall when he was three because he wanted to fly like an angel?"

"I was just thinking," said Mon, "that all those things you say about the diggers, the angels could also say about us. Low, belly-crawling creatures. We can't even hang cleanly from a tree limb. Filthy, squatting in dirt—"

"But not hairy!" said Khimin.

"Nobody's going to listen to us," said Ominer, "if we start saying that angels are *better* than humans. And the kingdom would fall apart if we start saying humans and angels should be separate. If we're going to make this work, we have to exclude diggers and only the diggers."

Mon looked at him in surprise. So did Akma.

"If *what's* going to work?" asked Akma.

"This. This whole thing we're preparing for," said Ominer.

Mon and Akma looked at each other.

Ominer realized that he had said something wrong. "What?" No one answered.

Then Aronha, in his measured way, said, "I didn't know that we had any plan to take these discussions public."

"What, we're going to wait around until you're the king?" asked Ominer scornfully. "All this urgency, all this secrecy, I just assumed Akma was preparing us to start speaking against Akmaro's so-called religion. His attempt to control and destroy our society and turn the whole kingdom over to the Elemaki, is more like it. I thought we were going to speak out against it now, before he's succeeded in getting diggers accepted as true men and women throughout Darakemba. I mean, if we're not, why are we wasting our time? Let's go out and make some digger friends so at least we won't be thrust aside when they take over."

Akma chuckled a little. To others, it sounded like easy confidence—but Mon had been with Akma long enough to know that he laughed like that when he was a little bit afraid. "I suppose that has been the goal in the back of our minds," said Akma, "but I don't think it had graduated to the status of a plan."

Ominer laughed derisively. "You tell us there's no Keeper, and I think your evidence is conclusive. You tell us that humans never left Earth, that we're not older than the sky people or the earth people, we just evolved in different places, and that's fine. You tell us that because of this, all the things your father is teaching are wrong, and in fact the only thing that matters is, what culture will survive and rule? And the way to answer that is to keep diggers *out* of Darakemba and preserve this civilization that has been jointly created by humans and angels, the civilization of the Nafari. Keep the Elemaki with their filthy alliance between humans and dirt-crawling fat rats confined to the gornaya while we find ways to tame the great floodplains of the Severless, the Vostoiless, the Yugless and multiply our population to such an extent that we can overwhelm the Elemaki—all of these marvelous plans, and you never thought of going out and talking about them in public? Come on, Akma, Mon, we're not *stupid.*"

The look on Khimin's and Aronha's faces made it clear that it was the first time *they* had ever thought of these ideas, but of course, given Ominer's exasperated tone, they weren't about to admit their shameful stupidity.

"Yes," said Akma. "Eventually we would have started to speak to others."

"*Masses* of others," said Ominer. "It's not as if you're going to change Father's mind—Akmaro keeps Father's brain in his traveling bag. And none of the councilors is going to join us in opposing Father's will. And if we talk about this stuff quietly and secretly, it'll look like conspiracy and when it gets exposed it will look as though we're shameful traitors. So the only possible way to stop Akmaro's destruction of Darakemba is to oppose him openly and publicly. Am I right?"

Wrong. This is wrong. This is wrong.

By reflex, Mon almost answered with the message throbbing through his mind. But he knew that this message was a holdover from his childhood faith in the Keeper, that he had to overcome this superstition and reject it in order to have any hope of deserving Akma's respect. Or Bego's, or his brothers', whatever, whoever. Akma's respect.

So instead of saying what was in his heart, he answered with his mind alone: "Yes, you're right, Ominer. And it's true that Akma and I never discussed this. Akma probably thought about it, but I know I didn't. Now that you say it, though, I know you're right."

Aronha turned soberly to Mon. "You *know* he's right?"

Mon knew what Aronha was asking. Aronha wanted to have the assurance that Mon's old gift of discernment was committed to this struggle. But Mon refused to consider those feelings as "knowledge" anymore. Instead knowledge was what reason discovered, what logic defended, what the physical evidence demanded. So even though Aronha was asking one question, Mon could answer honestly using the only meaning of the word *know* that he believed in anymore. "Yes, Aronha. I know he's right, and I know Akma's right, and I know *I'm* right."

Aronha nodded soberly. "We're the king's sons. We have no authority except as he gives it to us, but we do have enormous prestige. It would be a crippling blow to Akmaro's reforms if we came out publicly against them. And if it's not just the Motiaki but also Akmaro's own son. . . ."

"People might take notice," said Akma.

"Knock them back on their buttocks, that's what it'll do," said Ominer.

"But that's treason," said Khimin.

"Not a thing we're saying denies the authority of the king," said Ominer. "Haven't you been listening? We *affirm* the ancient alliance of humans and angels. We *affirm* our ancestors' decisions that the descendants of Nafai should be kings over the Nafari. What we reject is this superstitious nonsense about the Keeper loving the diggers as much as he loves the sky people and the middle people."

"You know," said Khimin, "if you think about it, the angels are the sky people, and we *humans* are the earth people, and the diggers aren't people at all!"

"We won't win much support," said Akma dryly, "if we start calling human beings 'earth people.' "

Khimin laughed nervously. "No. I guess not."

"Ominer is right," said Akma, "but I'm also right when I say that we're not ready. We have to be able to speak on this subject, any one of us, at any time."

"Me!" cried Aronha. "I'm not like you and Mon, I can't just open my mouth and have speech pour out of it for hours."

"That's Akma's gift," said Mon.

Ominer hooted derisively. "Come on, Mon. We always used to joke, Is Mon awake? I don't know, is he talking? Then he's awake."

The words stung, even though Ominer clearly didn't mean them to be hurtful. Mon clamped his mouth shut, determined to say nothing else until they begged him to speak.

"My point," said Akma, "is that we have to act with perfect solidarity. If *all* the sons of Motiak and the son of Akmaro are united in opposing this new policy, then it will be clear to everyone that no matter what the present king decides, the next king will have a kingdom in which diggers are not citizens. This will encourage the newly freed diggers to leave and return to Elemaki territory where they belong. And nobody can say we are against freedom, because our plan is to free *all* the slaves at once —but free them at the border, so we won't be creating any new free diggers who will want to be made citizens of a nation they don't belong in. It's a kind policy, really, to recognize the insurmountable differences between our species and bid a gentle but firm farewell to all those diggers who imagine themselves to be civilized."

The others agreed. It was a good program. They were united in support of it.

"But if one—even one—of the sons of Motiak is perceived as disagreeing with any part of this program, if even one of the sons of Motiak shows that he still believes in that nonsense about the Keeper that Akmaro is trying to get people to believe. . . ."

That our people have always believed in since the days of the Heroes, thought Mon silently.

". . . then everyone will assume that Motiak will simply make *that* son his heir and disinherit the others. The result? A lot of powerful people will oppose us simply for political reasons, in order to be on the obvious winning side. But if they know that there is *no* possible heir except those of us who repudiate Akmaro's entire digger-loving conspiracy, then they'll remember the fact that kings don't live forever, and they'll at least keep silent, not wanting to antagonize the future king."

"Don't be modest," said Mon. "Everyone expects that the high priest's job will be yours when your father, uh, sheds his spirit like an old cloak." The others chuckled at the old-fashioned euphemism.

Aronha, however, seemed to have caught some glint of an idea in Khimin's face, and so at the end of his chuckle had directed a pointed comment at his father's youngest son. "And in case someone here thinks of breaking ranks with us in order to become the heir, let me assure you that the army won't respect any heir but me, as long as I'm alive and want the throne after my father is through with it. If your prime motive is a hope of power, the only way you'll get it in the long run is by staying with me."

Mon was shocked. It was the first time he had ever heard Aronha threaten anyone with his future power, or speak so nakedly of what might or might not happen after Father's death. Mon also didn't like the way Aronha said "my father" instead of "our father" or even, simply, "Father."

Akma suddenly wailed, "No! No, no," and bent over on his chair, burying his face in his arms.

"What's wrong?" They all rushed to him or at least leaned toward him as if they thought he was having some sort of physical crisis.

Akma sat upright, then rose from his chair. "I've done this. I've driven a wedge between you. I've made Aronha speak unspeakable things. None of this is worth that! If I had never made friends with Mon, if we had never come back to Darakemba, if we had had the dignity to die there under the whips of the diggers and their toady human rulers in Chelem, then Aronha would never have said such a thing."

"I'm sorry," said Aronha, looking truly ashamed of himself.

"No, *I'm* sorry," said Akma. "I came to you as a friend, hoping to win you to the cause of truth to save this people from my father's insane theories. But instead I've turned brother against brother and I can't bear that." He fled the room so quickly that he knocked over his chair.

The four of them sat or stood in silence for a long moment, and then Khimin and Aronha burst into speech at the same time.

"Aronha, I never would have turned against you! It never even crossed my mind!" cried Khimin, at exactly the same time that Aronha cried out, "Khimin, forgive me for even imagining that you would think of such a thing, I never meant for you to—you're my brother no matter what you do, and I—"

Good old inarticulate Aronha. Sweet little lying hypocritical Khimin. Mon almost laughed out loud.

Ominer did laugh. "Listen to you. 'I didn't think a single bad thought about you!' 'I *did* think bad thoughts but I'm really really sorry.' Come on, all Akma asks is that we stick together before we do anything public. So let's work on it, all right? It's not hard. We just keep our mouths shut about stuff one of us does that bothers the others. We do it all the time in front of Father—that's why he doesn't know how much we all hate the queen."

Khimin blanched, then blushed. "*I* don't."

"See?" said Ominer. "It's fine if you don't agree with us, Khimin. All Aronha was saying was, Keep your mouth shut about it and we can still accomplish everything we need to accomplish."

"I agree with you about everything except . . . Mother," said Khimin.

"Yes yes," said Ominer impatiently, "we're all so dreadfully sorry for her, the poor thing, dying as she is of the world's *slowest* plague."

"Enough," said Aronha. "You preach to us of keeping peace, Ominer, and then you fall back into teasing Khimin as if the two of you were still toddlers."

"We were never *both* toddlers," said Ominer acidly. "I stopped being a toddler long before *he* was born."

"Please," said Mon quietly, inserting the word into a momentary silence so that all would hear it. His very softness won their attention. "To hear us, you'd think there really *was* a Keeper, and that he was making us all stupid so we couldn't unite and oppose his will."

Aronha, as usual, took his words too seriously. "*Is* there a Keeper?" he asked.

"No, there's not a Keeper," said Mon. "How many times do we have to prove it to you before you stop asking?"

"I don't know," said Aronha. He looked Mon in the eye. "Perhaps until I forget that whenever you told me something was right and true, ever since you were little, it turned out to be right and true."

"Was I really right all those times?" asked Mon. "Or were you simply as eager as I was to believe that children our age could actually know something?"

Wrong. This is wrong. This is wrong.

Mon kept his face expressionless—he hoped.

Aronha smiled half-heartedly. "Go get Akma," he said to Mon. "If I know him at all, he's not far off. Waiting for one of us to go and get him. You do it, Mon. Bring him back. We'll be united with him. For the good of the kingdom."

Khideo greeted Ilihiak with an embrace. No, not Ilihiak. Ilihi. A man who was once a king, now insisting that there was nothing extraordinary about him, that he had not been touched by the hand of the Keeper. It seemed so odd, so much like a kind of failure. But not Ilihi's failure, really. More as if the universe itself had failed.

"And how is the—how is your wife?" asked Khideo.

The normal meaningless greetings took only a few moments; they were made all the more brief because Khideo's wife had died many years before, in trying to give birth to their first child. It would have been a boy. The midwife said that the child was so big, like his father, that the head tore her apart passing through the channel of life. Khideo knew then that he had killed his wife, because any child of his would be too large for a woman to bear. The Keeper meant him to be childless; but at least Khideo didn't have to kill any more women trying to defy the Keeper's will. So Ilihi, who knew all this, made no inquiries about family.

"The weight of government rests lightly on you, Khideo."

Khideo laughed. Or meant to laugh. It came out as a dry sound in his throat. He coughed. "I feel my muscles slackening. The soldier I once was is becoming soft and old. I'm drying out from the inside. At least I won't be one of those fat old men. Instead I'll be frail."

"I won't live to see it!"

"I'm older than you, Ilihi; you'll see me dead, I can assure you. A wind will come from the east, a terrible hurricane, and it will blow me up over the mountains and out into the ocean but I'll be so dry that I'll just float there on the surface like a leaf until the sun dries me to powder and I finally dissolve."

Ilihi looked at him with such a strange expression that Khideo had to shove him gently in the shoulder, the way he had done when Ilihi was Nuak's third and least favored son and Khideo took pity on him and taught him what it meant to be a man and a soldier. They had been together the day that Khideo finally had enough. The day he took his vow to kill the king. He had shoved him gently, just like this, and had seen tears come to Ilihi's eyes. Khideo asked him then what was wrong, and Ilihi broke down and wept and told him what Pabulog had been doing to him since he was a little child. "It's been years since he did it last," said Ilihi. "I'm married now. I have a daughter. I thought it was over. But he took me out of my father's presence at breakfast and did it to me again. Two of his guards held me while he did it." Khideo went numb when he heard this. "Your father doesn't know what use Pabulog made of you, does he?" And Ilihi told him, "Of course he knows. I told him. He said that it only happened to me because I was weak. The Keeper intended me to be born a girl."

Khideo knew of many terrible things that had gone wrong in the kingdom of Nuak. He had seethed watching how Nuak mistreated the people around him, how he tolerated unspeakable vices among his closest associates, how only a few decent men were left among the leaders of the kingdom—but still there were those few, and Nuak was the king. But this was more than Khideo could bear. King or no king, no man could let such a thing happen to his son and not strike down the man who did it. In Khideo's eyes, it was not his own place to kill Pabulog—that was for Nuak to do, or failing that for Ilihi to do when he finally found his tortured way to manhood. But Khideo was a soldier, sworn to protect the throne and the people from all enemies. He knew who the enemy was now. It was Nuak. Strike him down, and all these others would fall, too. So he made his vow that the king would die by his hands. He had him under his hands at the top of the tower, ready to eviscerate him with his short sword as one kills a cowardly enemy, when Nuak looked around and saw, in the borders of the land, a huge army of Elemaki coming to attack. "You have to let me live, so I can lead the defense of our people!" Nuak demanded, and Khideo, who had only been acting for the people's good, saw that Nuak was right.

Then Nuak had led the full retreat of the whole army, leaving only a handful of brave men to defend all the women and children. Off in the wilderness, it was the men he had led in cowardly retreat who tortured him to death. And in the city, Khideo had had to bear the humiliation of letting Ilihi's wife lead the young girls forward to plead for the lives of the people, because there weren't swords enough to hold the Elemaki back for even a moment.

All of this was in the back of Khideo's mind whenever he was with Ilihi. He had seen this boy at his weakest. He had seen him turn into a man and lead a kingdom. But the damage had been done. Ilihi was still broken. Why else would he have set aside the throne?

Yet, having heard Khideo's playful thanatopsis—he meant it to be playful—Ilihi looked at him with strange concern. "You sound as if you long for death, but I know it's not true," said Ilihi.

"I long for death, Ilihi," said Khideo. "Just not mine."

Then the two of them burst into laughter.

"Ah, Lihida, my old friend, I should have been your father."

"Khideo, believe me, except in the biological sense, you were. You are."

"So have you come to me for fatherly counsel?" asked Khideo.

"My wife has heard rumors," said Ilihi.

Khideo rolled his eyes.

"Yes, well, she knows you wouldn't want to hear it from her, but as soon as I told you what we heard, you'd know it came from her. No *man* would tell this to *me*."

It was well known that Ilihi had rejected the Zenifi's absolute refusal to live with the sky people. It was well known that in his own home, angels visited often and were his friends. That was why no man of the land of Khideo would have spoken of secret things to Ilihi. He could not be trusted.

With the women it was different. Men couldn't control their wives, it was that simple. They *would* talk. And they didn't have sense to know who could be trusted and who could not. Ilihi and his wife were good, decent people. But when it came to protecting the Zenifi way of life—the *human* way of life—Ilihi simply should not be taken into confidence. Except that Khideo would never lie to Ilihi. If Ilihi wanted to hear whether the rumors were true, he knew he could come to the governor of the land of Khideo.

"The rumors?"

"She hears that some highly placed men of the land of Khideo are boasting that the son of Akmaro and the sons of the king have become Zenifi in their hearts."

"Not true," said Khideo. "I can assure you that not even the most optimistic among us has any hope of that group of young men declaring that they think angels and humans should not live together."

Ilihi took that in silence and ruminated on it for a while.

"So tell me what that group of young men *will* declare?" asked Ilihi.

"Maybe nothing," said Khideo. "How should I know?"

"Don't lie to me, Khideo. Don't start lying to me now."

"I'm not lying. I should knock you down for accusing me of it."

"What, the man who thinks he's dry as a dead leaf, knock me down?"

"There are stories," said Khideo.

"Meaning that you have a single reliable source that you trust implicitly."

"Why can't it just be stories and rumors?"

"Because, Khideo, I know the way you gather intelligence. You would never consent to be governor of this place if you didn't have a highly placed friend in Motiak's council."

"How would I get such a friend, Ilihi? All those surrounding the king have been with him forever—since long before *we* got here. In fact, *you're* the only man I know who's a friend of Motiak."

Ilihi looked at him narrowly, and thought about that for a while, too. Then he smiled. Then he laughed. "You sly old spy," he said.

"Me?"

"You pure-hearted Zenifi, you rigid upholder of the law of separation, no *man* in the king's council is talking to you. Now, that could mean your informant is a woman, but I think not, mostly because during your brief time in the capital you managed to offend every highly-placed woman who might have helped you. So that means your informant must be an angel."

Khideo shook his head, saying nothing. People underestimated Ilihi. They always had. And even though Khideo knew better, he still managed to be surprised when Ilihi took only the slightest evidence and ran with it straight to the right conclusion.

"So you have struck an alliance with an angel," said Ilihi.

"Not an alliance."

"You find each other useful."

Khideo nodded. "Possibly."

"Akma and the sons of Motiak, they *are* plotting something."

"Not treason," said Khideo. "They would never act to weaken the power of the throne. Nor would Motiak's sons ever do anything to harm him."

"But you don't want to see Motiak brought down, anyway," said Ilihi. "Not you, not any of the Zenifi. No, you're content with this arrangement, living here in these boggy lands—"

"Content? Every bit of soil we farm has to be dug up from the muck and carried here to raise the land above the flood. We have to wall it with logs and stones—which we have to float down from higher lands—"

"You're still in the gornaya."

"Flat, that's what this land is. Flat and boggy."

"You're content," said Ilihi, "because you have the protection of Motiak's armies keeping the Elemaki from you, while Motiak allows you to live without angels in your sky."

"They're in our sky all the time. But they don't live among us. We don't hurt them, they don't bother us."

"Akmaro is your problem, isn't he. Teaching the things Binaro taught."

"Binadi," said Khideo.

"Binaro, who said that the great evil of the Zenifi was to reject not just the angels, but the diggers as well. That the Keeper would not be happy with us until in every village in all the world, human, digger, and angel lived together in harmony. Then in that day the Keeper would come to Earth in the shape of a human, a digger, and an angel, and—"

"No!" Khideo cried out in rage, lashing out with his hand. If the blow had landed on Ilihi it would have knocked him down, for the truth was that Khideo had lost very little of his great strength. But Khideo slapped at nothing, at air, at an invisible inaudible mosquito. "Don't remind me of the things he said."

"Your anger is still a fearsome thing, Khideo."

"Binaro should have been killed before he converted Akmaro. Nuak waited too long, that's what I think."

"We'll never agree on this, Khideo. Let's not argue."

"No, let's not."

"Just tell me this, Khideo. Is there a plan to raise a hand of violence against Akmaro?"

Khideo shook his head. "There was talk of it. I let it be known that any man who raised a hand against Akmaro would find me tearing his heart out through his throat."

"You and he were friends, weren't you?"

Khideo nodded.

"Now every word he says is poison to you, but you're still loyal?"

"Friends are more important than ideas," said Khideo.

"If I liked your ideas better, Khideo, I might not be so glad that you put friendship ahead of them. But that doesn't matter. You say that Akma and the Motiaki are not planning violence, not against their fathers, not against anybody."

"That's right."

"But they're planning something."

"Think about it," said Khideo. "What Akmaro weaves can be unwoven."

Ilihi nodded. "Motiak won't dare to prosecute his own sons for treason."

"I don't think he could even if he dared," said Khideo.

"For defying the king's own appointed high priest?"

"I don't think we *have* a high priest," said Khideo.

"Just because Akmaro disdains the title *og*. . . ."

"Motiak abolished all priests appointed by the king. Akmaro came from outside, supposedly appointed by the Keeper of Earth himself. His authority didn't derive from the king. So defiance of his teachings isn't treason."

Ilihi laughed. "Do you think that Motiak will be fooled by legal technicalities?"

"No," said Khideo. "Which is why you haven't heard the voices of those fine young men with royal blood raised in defiance against Akmaro's vile mixing of the species and his upending of the rule of men over women."

"But something is coming."

"Let's say that there will be a test case. I don't know what it is—it's not my business—but a test case that will be a very hard knot for Akmaro and Motiak to untie. Any solution they reach, however, will . . . clarify things for us."

"You just told me more than you needed to."

"Because even if you go straight to Motiak and tell him all that I've said, it will do no good. He has already planted the seeds. Akmaro will lose his status as ruler of the religion of Darakemba."

"If you think Motiak will ever break his word and remove Akmaro from office—"

"Think about what I said, Ilihi." Khideo smiled. "The test will come, and at the end of it, Akmaro will no longer be ruler of the religion of Darakemba. It *will* happen, and no warnings can prevent it, because the seeds of it have already been planted by the king himself."

"You're too clever for me, Khideo, I can't figure you out."

"I always was, and you never could," said Khideo.

"All fathers imagine that," said Ilihi. "And all sons refuse to believe it."

"Which is true?" asked Khideo. "The confidence of the fathers? Or the refusal of the sons?"

"I think that the fathers are all too clever," said Ilihi. "So clever that when the day comes when they want to tell everything to their sons, their sons won't believe them, because they're still looking for the trick."

"When I want to tell you all my wisdom," said Khideo, "you'll know it, and you'll believe it."

"I have a secret for *you*, Khideo," said Ilihi. "You already taught me your wisdom, and I've already seen what you've got planned for poor Akmaro."

"Did you think you could trick me into telling you by pretending that you already know?" said Khideo. "Give up on that, won't you? It didn't work when you were fifteen and it doesn't work now."

"Let me tell *you* something that you may not know," said Ilihi. "Even though Akmaro was your friend—"

"*Is* my friend—"

"He is stronger than you. He is stronger than me. He is stronger than Motiak. He is stronger than anyone."

Khideo laughed. "Akmaro? He's all talk."

"He's stronger than all of us, because, my friend, he really is doing the will of the Keeper of Earth, and the Keeper of Earth will have his way—he will have his way with us, or he will sweep us aside and make way for yet another group of his children. This time perhaps descended from jaguars and condors, or perhaps he'll dip into the sea and choose the sons and daughters of the squids or the sharks. But the Keeper of Earth *will* prevail."

"If the Keeper is so powerful, Ilihi, why doesn't he just change us all into peaceful, happy, contented little diggers and angels and humans living together in a perverse menagerie?"

"Maybe because he doesn't *want* us to be a menagerie. Maybe because he wants us to understand his plan and to love it for its own sake, and follow it because we believe that it's good."

"What kind of feather-brained religion is that? How long would Motiak last as king if he waited for people to obey him until they *loved* the law and *wanted* to obey."

"But in fact that's why they do obey, Khideo."

"They obey because of all those men with swords, Ilihi."

"But why do the men with swords obey?" asked Ilihi. "They don't have to, you know. At any point, one of them could become so outraged that he—"

"Don't throw this in my face just for a jest," said Khideo. "Not after all these years."

"Not for a jest," said Ilihi. "I'm just pointing out that a good king like Motiak is obeyed, ultimately, because the best and strongest people know that his continuing rule is good for them. His kingdom brings them peace. Even if they don't like all his rules, they can find some way to be happy in the empire of Darakemba. That's why *you* obey him, isn't it?"

Khideo nodded.

"I've thought about this a long time. Why didn't the Keeper of Earth just *stop* Father from doing the things he did? Why didn't the Keeper just lead us to freedom instead of making us serve so many years in bondage before Monush came? Why why why, what was the plan? It troubled me until one day I realized—"

"I'm relieved. I thought you were going to tell me that your wife gave you the answer."

Ilihi gave him a pained look and went on. "I realized that it wouldn't do the Keeper any good to have a bunch of puppets just doing his will. What he wants is companions. Do you see? He wants us to become like him, to want the same things he wants, to work toward the same goals, freely and willingly, because we want to. That's when the words of Binaro will be fulfilled, and the Keeper will come and dwell among the people of Earth."

Khideo shuddered. "If that is true, Ilihi, then I'm the enemy of the Keeper of Earth."

"No, my friend. Only your ideas are his enemy. Fortunately, you are more loyal to your friends than to your ideas—that's part of what the Keeper wants from us. In fact, I daresay that in some future time, despite all your loathing of the mixture of the species, you'll be remembered as one of the great defenders of the Keeper's friends."

"Ha."

"Look at you, Khideo. All these people who have the same ideas as you, but who are your friends? Who are the people you love? Me. Akmaro."

"I love a lot of people, not just you."

"Me, Akmaro, my wife—"

"I detest your wife!"

"You'd die for her."

Khideo had no answer.

"And now even this angel informant of yours. You'd die for *him*, too, wouldn't you?"

"With all these people you think I'd die for, it's amazing I'm still alive," said Khideo.

"Don't you hate it when somebody knows you better than you know yourself?"

"Yes," said Khideo.

"I know you hate it," said Ilihi. "But there was once a man who knew me better than I knew myself. Who saw strength in me that I didn't know was there. And do you know what?"

"You hated it."

"I thanked the Keeper for that man. And I still beg the Keeper to keep him safe. I still tell the Keeper, He's not your enemy. He thinks he is but he's not. Keep him safe, I say."

"You talk to the Keeper?"

"All the time, these days."

"And does he answer?"

"No," said Ilihi. "But then, I haven't asked him any questions. So the only answer that I need from him is this: I look around, and I still see his hand guiding the world around me."

Khideo turned away from him, hiding his face. He didn't even know why he was hiding; it wasn't that he felt any strong emotion. He just couldn't bear to look Ilihi in the eye at this moment. "Go to Motiak," he whispered. "Tell him what you need to tell him. We won't be stopped."

"Maybe not," said Ilihi. "But if you *aren't* stopped, it will be because, without realizing it, you were serving the Keeper's purpose all along."

Ilihi kissed him—on the shoulder, because his head was averted—and left the garden of the governor of the land of Khideo. The governor remained in that garden for another hour, till the evening rain. He came inside the house soaking wet. He had no servant to remonstrate with him. Ever since he learned that Akmaro and his wife really did all their own cooking and washing, Khideo had done the same. Khideo would match Akmaro virtue for virtue, pretension for pretension, sacrifice for sacrifice. No one would ever be able to say that Khideo may have been right, but Akmaro was still the better man. No, they would have to say, Khideo was every bit as good a man, *and* he was right.

As good a man, *and* right, but it was Akmaro who had won the free obedience of Ilihi. Akmaro had stolen even that prize, after all these years.

Darakemba might be the capital of a great empire, but in some ways it was still a small town. Gossip on some subjects spread quickly to the greatest households. Thus it took only a few weeks for Chebeya to get word of the opening of a new school. "She calls the place 'Rasaro's House,' if you can believe the effrontery." "I asked who the schoolmaster was, and she actually said it was herself!" "She claims to be teaching exactly as the wife of the Hero Volemak taught, as if anyone could know *that.*" "None of the children are of what you could call good families, but the appalling thing is that she mixes even those children right in with . . . the children of . . . former. . . ."

"Slaves," said Chebeya. It was only by the most heroic effort that she refrained from reminding these friends of hers that her husband and she had spent the last decade teaching that, in the eyes of the Keeper, the children of the earth are no less valued than middle children or children of the sky.

"And they say that she would gladly teach boys right among the girls, if any parents had such a lapse of judgment and decency as to allow it."

After some consideration, Chebeya wrote a note and had one of the teachers who lived near the new school drop it off for her. It was an invitation for the new teacher to come and call on her.

The next day, she got her note back again. Scrawled in a hurried hand on the bottom was the notation, "Thanks, but school takes up all my days. Come visit me, if you'd like."

At first Chebeya was startled and, she had to admit, just the tiniest bit offended. She was the wife of the high priest, wasn't she? And this woman refused her invitation and casually invited *her* to come calling—and at a school, no less, not even at home.

Chebeya was immediately ashamed of her own offended dignity. Besides, this new teacher was all the more interesting now. She told Luet what she had heard and what had happened to her invitation, and Luet immediately insisted on coming along. By the time they left home to make the visit, Edhadeya had somehow been included. "I want to see what the ancient Rasa was like, as a teacher," she explained.

"You don't actually expect her school to be like that legendary one, do you?" asked Chebeya.

"Why shouldn't it be?" said Edhadeya. "Just having a woman at the head of it—that makes it more like Rasa's school than any other I've heard of."

"They say that the diggers have always had women's schools taught by women," Luet said.

"But this woman is human," Edhadeya reminded her. "She is, isn't she?"

"She calls herself Shedemei," said Chebeya. "The whole ancient name, not Sedma the way we say it now."

The younger women tried out saying the name.

"They must have held their whole mouths differently in the old days," said Luet. "Has our language changed that much?"

"It must have, for the angels and diggers to be able to pronounce it," said Edhadeya. "They say there used to be sounds that the sky people and earth people couldn't even make, and now there aren't."

"Who says the language changed?" said Luet. "Maybe they learned to make new sounds!"

"There's no way to learn how language sounded in the past," said Chebeya, "so there's no point in arguing about it."

"We weren't arguing," said Luet. "We always talk like this."

"Ah," said Chebeya. "Mildly contentious, with just a hint of backtalk to your mother." But then she smiled and the two girls laughed, and after walking a good way into an old neighborhood that had never been fashionable they reached the right avenue. An old angel was out on a perch in the shade of his porch, watching the goings-on in the street. "Old sir," said Luet, because she was youngest, "can you tell us the way to the new school?"

"School for girls?" asked the old man.

"Are there so many on this street?" asked Luet in her most innocent I'm-not-being-sarcastic voice.

"The whole corner up there, three houses butted up against each other on this side." He turned his back on them, which for an old man wasn't quite as rude as it would have been for a young one. Even with his back turned, they heard him mutter, "School for mud rats."

"Definitely one of the Kept," said Edhadeya quietly.

"Oh yes," Luet whispered. "I thought so at once."

They were all too well-bred to laugh aloud at the old man—or at least too conscious of the image they had to present, given that someone on the street was bound to recognize them as the king's daughter and the wife and daughter of the high priest.

Only when they were in front of the three houses that held the school did they realize why it was an especially apt location for a school that would mix the three peoples. Just up the cross street was a space of rough country where a stand of shaggy old trees by an old creek bed had never been cut down. There were a few huts where poor humans might live, and there were thatched roofs in the trees where angels with no money made their home. That alone would have identified it as a slum; but they also knew that both banks of the creek were pocked and tunneled to make houses for freed slaves who had quickly squandered their freedom bonus and now lived in desperate poverty, hiring out for day labor if they were in good health, the others begging or starving if they weren't skilled enough to get piecework. Akmaro had often taught that the existence of such places was proof that the people of Darakemba were unworthy of the great wealth and prosperity that the Keeper had given them. Many of the poor survived only because the Kept contributed food at the House of the Keeper and the priests and teachers brought it to the warrens. Some people actually had the gall to complain that they'd contribute more, but they knew that lazy diggers would probably get most of it. As if these people had not already wasted half their lives or more as unpaid slaves in the houses of the rich!

So this Shedemei had chosen to open her school close to the place where diggers lived; she was serious about including their children in her school. But it was also a place where any breeze from the western mountains would bring her the notorious smell of the creek. Rat Creek, some called it. Akmaro always referred to it as Keeper's Creek. Polite people never spoke of it at all.

Since the doors of all three houses stood open, and all three porches held young girls quietly reciting or memorizing or simply reading, it was hard to guess which was the main entrance to the school. And as it turned out, it hardly mattered, for Shedemei herself came out to greet them.

Chebeya knew at once that it had to be Shedemei—she exuded an air of being very much in control of things, and invited them in with such a hurried greeting that it seemed barely civil. "The younger children are just getting down for their afternoon naps," she said. "So please talk quietly in the corridor."

Inside the school, they found that Shedemei must have rented the houses around the corner and through the block as well, for the young girls were napping in the shade of some old trees in a central courtyard —those that weren't dangling from the lower branches, of course. Chebeya noticed several adult women moving from girl to girl, helping them settle down, bringing drinks of water to some. Were these women teachers or servants? Or was there such a distinction in this place?

"I can't believe it," murmured Edhadeya.

"Just little children, sleeping," said Chebeya, not understanding Edhadeya's surprise.

"No, I mean—could that really be old Uss-Uss? I thought she was ancient when she was a servant in my bedchamber, and I haven't seen her in . . . oh, so long, I thought she must be dead by now, but there, walking toward that door. . . ."

"I never met your legendary Uss-Uss," said Luet, "so I can't very well help you recognize her now."

Chebeya finally saw which woman Edhadeya meant, a bent old digger with a slow and shuffling gait.

Shedemei was just returning from the courtyard. Edhadeya asked her at once. "That earth woman, just going into the house across the courtyard—that's not Uss-Uss, is it?"

"I appreciate your not calling out to her," said Shedemei. "A shout would have disturbed the children, and it wouldn't do any good because your old servant is almost completely deaf now. By the way, we call her Voozhum here."

"Voozhum, of course. So did I, the last few months before she left," said Edhadeya. "I've thought about her so often since then."

"It's true," Luet affirmed.

Edhadeya launched into a reminiscence, her voice soft and sweet with memory. "She left our house as soon as Father freed all the slaves of long service. I wasn't surprised she went. She told me that she dreamed of having a house of her own. Though I had hoped she'd stay with us as a free employee. She was good to me. She was my friend, really, more than a servant. I wish she hadn't left me."

Shedemei's voice sounded like the cawing of a crow when she answered. "She didn't leave, Edhadeya. The queen discharged her. Too old. Useless. And a cheapening influence on you."

"Never!"

"Oh, Voozhum remembered the words. Memorized them on the spot."

Edhadeya refused to be misconstrued. "I meant she was never a bad influence on me! She taught me. To see beyond myself, to—I don't know all she taught me. It's too deep inside my heart."

Shedemei's expression softened, and she took Edhadeya's hand—to Edhadeya's momentary startlement, since strangers were supposed to ask permission before touching any part of a royal child's person. "I'm glad you know how to value her," said Shedemei.

"And I'm glad to see she's here," said Edhadeya. Chebeya was relieved that Edhadeya, far from protesting at Shedemei's liberty, merely clasped her own hand over the teacher's. "In a good house, at the waning of her life. I hope her duties are light, but still real. She has too much pride not to be earning her own way."

Shedemei chuckled dryly. "Her duties are light enough, I think. But as real as mine. Since they're the same as mine."

Luet gasped, then covered her mouth in astonishment. "I'm sorry," she murmured.

Chebeya spoke up, to cover her daughter's embarrassment. "She's a teacher, then?"

"Among the earth people," said Shedemei, "she was always accounted wise, a keeper of the ancient tales. She was quite famous among the slaves. They would have her arbitrate their quarrels and bless their babies and pray for the sick. She had a special fondness for the One-Who-Was-Never-Buried."

Edhadeya nodded. "Yes, the one you were named after."

Shedemei seemed amused at this. "Yes, that one. I think you generally refer to her as 'Zdorab's wife.' "

"Out of respect," said Chebeya, "we try to avoid vain repetition of the names of the Original Women."

"And is it out of respect that the men speak of them this way?" asked Shedemei.

Luet laughed. "No. The men can't even remember the women's names."

"Then it's unfortunate, isn't it," said Shedemei, "that you never mention their names to remind them."

"We were speaking of Voozhum," said Edhadeya. "If she teaches your students here half as well as she taught me, then whatever tuition they pay is well rewarded."

"And do I have your permission to quote the king's daughter when I advertise the school?" asked Shedemei.

Chebeya wouldn't stand for this. "None of us have insisted on the traditional respect for our place in society, Shedemei, but your sarcasm would have been insulting to anyone, not just the king's daughter."

"Does Edhadeya need you to protect her from a sharp-tongued schoolmaster?" asked Shedemei. "Is that why you came here, to make sure that I had good manners?"

"I'm sorry," said Edhadeya. "I must have said something that gave you offense. Please forgive me."

Shedemei looked at her and smiled. "Well, there you are. Apologizing even though you have no idea what you did that caused my temper to flare. That's what Voozhum teaches. Some say it's the slave mentality, but she says that the Keeper taught her to speak to all people as if they were her master, and to serve all people as if she were their servant. That way her master could not demand from her anything that she didn't already give freely to everyone."

"It sounds to me," said Chebeya to Edhadeya, "as if your former servant is wise indeed."

"It is often said, not just in my school but among all the earth people," said Shedemei, "that the daughter of Motiak was very lucky to have spent her childhood in the company of Voozhum. What most people don't suppose is that you were wise enough to value her. I'm glad to learn that their assumption about you is wrong."

Edhadeya smiled and bowed her head at what was obviously this harsh woman's best effort at peacemaking. "Does she remember me?" asked Edhadeya.

"I don't know," said Shedemei. "She doesn't speak much of her days in captivity, and no one here would be rude enough to ask."

So much for peacemaking. The words struck Edhadeya like a slap. Chebeya was about to suggest that they had taken enough of Shedemei's precious time when the schoolmaster said, "Come on, then. Do you want to see the school or not?"

Curiosity won out over offended feelings, especially since Edhadeya seemed none the worse for wear. They followed Shedemei as she pointed out the different classrooms, the library—with an astonishing number of books for a new school—the kitchen, the sleeping quarters for the girls who boarded there. "Of course, all of Rasa's girl students were in residence," said Shedemei. "They were so close they were like family. They called her Aunt Rasa, and she called them her nieces. Her own daughters were treated no differently from the others."

"Forgive my asking," said Chebeya, "but where is this sort of detail about Rasa's house written down?"

Shedemei said nothing, simply led them on to a cell-like bedroom. "Some of my teachers think this is rather an ascetic room; to others, it is the most luxurious place they've ever slept. It doesn't matter—if they work for me and board with me, this is the kind of room they sleep in."

"Which teacher sleeps in this one?" asked Luet.

"Me," said Shedemei.

"I must say," said Chebeya, "that this school could not be more perfectly modeled on my husband's teachings if he had drawn up the constitutions himself."

Shedemei smiled coldly. "But he never *has* drawn up constitutions for a girls' school, has he?"

"No," said Chebeya, feeling as though she were confessing some horrible crime.

By now they had wound their way through the connected houses until they were on the opposite side of the courtyard, near the place where Voozhum had gone inside. Not surprisingly, they found her teaching in a room on the ground floor.

"Would you like to go in and listen for a little while?" whispered Shedemei.

"Not if it would disturb her," said Edhadeya.

"She won't hear you, and her vision's none too good, either," said Shedemei. "I doubt she'll recognize you from the opposite end of the room."

"Then yes, please." Edhadeya turned to the others. "You don't mind, do you?"

They didn't, and so Shedemei led them in and offered them stools that were no different from the ones the students sat on. Only Voozhum herself had a chair with a back and arms, which no one could begrudge her, feeble as she was.

She was teaching a group of older girls, though they could hardly be advanced students, since the school itself was so new.

"So Emeezem asked Oykib, 'What virtue does the Keeper of Earth value most? Is it the tallness of Ancient Ones?'—for that was what they called the middle people when they first returned to Earth—'or is it the wings of the skymeat?'—for that was the terrible name for the sky people that Emeezem had not yet learned she must not use—'or is it the devoted worship we give to the gods?' Well, what do you think Oykib told her?"

Chebeya listened to several of the girls reject all virtues that only one of the sentient species would possess, and thought, This is no more than mere indoctrination. But then the proposals became more universal and, occasionally, more subtle. Hopefulness. Intelligence. Comprehension of truth. Nobility. Each proposal led to a consideration of the particular virtue, and whether it might be used against the laws of the Keeper. Much of the discussion showed that today was something of an examination; they had discussed these virtues before, had thought about them and argued about them. A criminal might hope to evade punishment. Intelligence can be used to undermine and destroy a virtuous man. Just because someone comprehends the truth doesn't mean he values it or will uphold it; liars have to comprehend the truth in order to defend their lie. A noble woman might sacrifice all she has in an unworthy cause, if nobility is not accompanied by wisdom.

"Wisdom, then," said a girl. "For isn't that the virtue of knowing what the Keeper's will would be?"

"Is it?" answered Voozhum mildly.

Of course, all this conversation was very loud, partly because Voozhum's deafness no doubt required it, and partly because the girls had the normal exuberance of youth. Chebeya, though, had never seen such exuberance used inside a classroom. And while she had seen teachers try to get their students to discuss issues, it had never worked until now. She tried to think why, and then realized—it's because the girls know that Voozhum does not expect them to guess the answer in her mind, but rather to defend and attack the ideas they themselves bring out. And because she treats their answers with respect. No, she treats *them* with respect, as if their ideas were worthy of consideration.

And they *were* worthy of consideration. More than once Chebeya wanted to speak up and join in, and she could feel Luet and Edhadeya grow restless on either side of her—no doubt for the same reason.

Finally Edhadeya *did* speak up. "Isn't that the very point that Spokoyro rejected in his dialogue with the Khrugi?"

A deathly silence fell upon the room.

"I'm sorry," Edhadeya said. "I know I had no right to speak."

Chebeya looked for Shedemei to say something to ease the awful tension in the room, but the schoolmaster seemed completely content with the situation.

It was Voozhum who spoke up. "It's not you, child. It's what you said."

One of the girls—an earth person, it happened—explained more. "We were waiting for you to tell us the story of . . . of Spokoyro and the

Khrugi. We've never heard it. They must have been humans. And not ancient ones. And men."

"Is that forbidden here?" asked Chebeya.

"Not forbidden," said the girl, looking confused. "It's just—the school was only started a little while ago, and this is a class in the moral philosophers of the earth people, so. . . ."

"I'm sorry," said Edhadeya. "I spoke in ignorance. My example was irrelevant."

Voozhum spoke up again, her old voice cracking often, but loud in the way deaf people's voices often are. "These girls haven't had a classical education," she said. "But you have. You are most fortunate, my child. These girls must make do with such poor offerings as I can give them."

Edhadeya laughed scornfully, then immediately thought better of it; but it was too late.

"I know that laugh," said Voozhum.

"I laughed because I knew you were making fun of me," said Edhadeya. "And besides, I also 'made do' with your 'poor offerings.' "

"I understand that my teaching cheapened you," said Voozhum.

"You never heard that from me. And I never heard it myself until today."

"I've never spoken to you as a free woman," said Voozhum.

"And I've never spoken to you except as an impertinent child."

Finally the girls in the classroom understood who it was who was visiting with them that day, for they all had heard that Voozhum once was the personal chamberservant to the daughter of the king. "Edhadeya," they whispered.

"My young mistress," said Voozhum, "now a lady. You were often rude, but never impertinent. Tell us now, please. What is the virtue that the Keeper most values?"

"I don't know what Oykib said, because this story isn't known among the humans," said Edhadeya.

"Good," said Voozhum. "Then you won't be remembering or guessing, you'll be thinking."

"I think the virtue that the Keeper most admires is to love as the Keeper loves."

"And how is this? How does the Keeper love?"

"The love of the Keeper," said Edhadeya, obviously searching, obviously thinking of ideas that she had never considered all that seriously before. "The love of the Keeper is the love of the mother who punishes her child for naughtiness, but then embraces the same child to comfort her tears."

Edhadeya waited for the onslaught of contrary opinions that had greeted earlier suggestions, but she was met only by silence. "Please," she said, "just because I'm the daughter of the king doesn't mean you can't disagree with me the way you disagreed with each other a moment ago."

Still, not a word, though there was no shuffling or embarrassed looking away, either.

"Perhaps they do not disagree," said Voozhum. "Perhaps they hope you will teach them more of this idea."

Edhadeya immediately rose to the challenge. "I think the Keeper wants us to see the world as she sees it. To pretend that *we* are the Keeper, and then to try to create wherever we can a small island where all the other virtues can be shared among good people."

There was a murmur among the girls. "Words of a true dreamer," one of them whispered.

"And I think," said Edhadeya, "that if that really is the virtue most favored by the Keeper, then you have created a virtuous classroom here, Voozhum."

"Long ago," said Voozhum, "when I lived in chains, sometimes chains of iron, but always chains of stone on my heart, there was a room where I could go and someone knew my virtues and listened to my thoughts as if I were truly alive and a creature of light instead of a worm of mud and darkness."

Edhadeya burst into tears. "I was never that good to you, Uss-Uss."

"You always were. Does my little girl still remember how I held her when she cried?"

Edhadeya ran to her and embraced her. The girls watched in awe as both Edhadeya and Voozhum wept, each in her fashion.

Chebeya leaned across Edhadeya's empty stool to whisper to Shedemei, "This is what you hoped for, isn't it?"

Shedemei whispered back, "I think it's a good lesson, don't you?"

And indeed it was, to see the daughter of the king embracing an old digger woman, both of them crying for joy, crying for remembrance of lost times, of ancient love.

"And what did Oykib say?" whispered Chebeya to Shedemei.

"He didn't really answer," said Shedemei. "He said, 'To answer that, I would have to be the Keeper.' "

Chebeya thought for a few moments. Then she said, "But that *is* an answer. The same answer Edhadeya gave."

Shedemei smiled. "Oykib always was a trickster. He had a way with words."

It was disturbing, this tendency of Shedemei's to speak of the Heroes as if she knew all their secrets.

* * *

They spent the rest of the day in the school and sat at Shedemei's table at supper. The food was plain—many a rich woman would have turned up her nose at it, and Luet could see that Edhadeya didn't even know what some of it was. But in Akmaro's house, Luet and her mother had eaten the simple fare of the common people all their lives, and they ate with relish. It was plain to Luet that everything that happened in Shedemei's school—no, 'Rasaro's House'—was a lesson. The food, the mealtime conversation, the way the cooking and cleaning up were done, the way people walked quietly but briskly in the halls—everything had a point to it, everything expressed a way of life, a way of thought, a way of treating people.

At supper, Edhadeya seemed giddy, which Luet understood, though it worried her a little. It was as if Edhadeya had lost her sense of decorum, her gentle carefulness. She kept goading Shedemei into saying something, but Luet had no way of guessing what the older girl had in mind.

"We *heard* that you were dangerous, teaching the diggers to rebel," said Edhadeya.

"What an interesting thought," said Shedemei. "After years of slavery, the thought of rebelling doesn't occur to the diggers until a middle-aged human suggests it? Rebellion against what, now that they're free? I think your friends are consumed with guilt, to fear rebellion now that the reason for it has finally been removed."

"That's what I thought, too," said Edhadeya.

"Tell the truth now. No one actually said these things to *you*."

Edhadeya glanced at Chebeya. "To Luet's mother, of course."

"And why not to you? Is it because you're the king's daughter, and your father was the one who freed the slaves? Do you think they'll ever forgive your father for that blunder?"

Edhadeya suppressed her laughter. "You really mustn't talk that way to the daughter of the king. I'm not supposed to listen when people say my father blundered."

"But in the king's council, isn't he criticized freely? That's what I heard."

"Well, yes, but those are his men."

"And what are you, his pet fish?"

"A woman doesn't pass judgment on the actions of a king!" Again Edhadeya suppressed laughter, as if this were hysterically funny.

Shedemei answered dryly, "Around here, I gather that a woman doesn't squat to pee unless some man tells her that her bladder's full."

This was too much for Edhadeya. She burst into loud laughter and fell off her stool.

Luet helped her up. "What's got into you?" Luet demanded.

"I don't know," said Edhadeya. "I just feel so."

"So free," said Shedemei helpfully.

"At home," said Edhadeya at almost the same time.

"But you don't act like that at home!" protested Luet.

"No, I don't," said Edhadeya, and suddenly her eyes filled with tears. She turned to Shedemei. "Was it really like this in Rasa's house?"

"There were no earth people or sky people there," said Shedemei. "It was another planet, and the only sentient species was human."

"I want to stay here," said Edhadeya.

"You're too young to teach," said Shedemei.

"I've had a very good education."

"You mean that you have excelled at your schooling," said Shedemei. "But you haven't yet lived a life. Therefore you're of no use to me."

"Then let me stay as a student," said Edhadeya.

"Haven't you listened to me? You've already completed your schooling."

"Then let me stay as a servant in this place," said Edhadeya. "You can't make me go back."

At this, Chebeya had to interrupt. "You make it sound as though you were monstrously mistreated in your father's house."

"I'm ignored there, don't you see? I really *am* Father's pet fish. His pet something. Better to be a cook in this place. . . ."

"But you see that we all take our turn at the cooking," said Shedemei. "There's no place for you here, not yet, Edhadeya. Or perhaps I should say, there *is* a place for you, but you're not yet ready to fill it."

"How long must I wait?"

"If you wait," said Shedemei, "you'll never be ready."

Edhadeya fell silent then, and ate thoughtfully, wiping sauce from her bowl with the last of her bread.

It was Luet's turn, finally, to say the thing that had been bothering her most of the afternoon. "You refused Mother's invitation because you were too busy," said Luet. "But this school fairly runs itself. You could have come."

Mother was annoyed with her. "Luet, haven't I taught you better manners than to—"

"That's all right, Chebeya," said Shedemei. "I refused your invitation because I've seen the houses of rich men and kings. Whereas *you* have never seen such a school as this."

Mother stiffened. "We're not rich."

"Yet you have the leisure to come calling during working hours? You may live modestly, Chebeya, but I see no streaks of dirt and sweat on your face."

Luet could see that Mother was hurt by this, and so she plunged in to turn the conversation back to something less difficult. "I've never heard of a woman schoolmaster," she said.

"Which only proves how dishonest the men who taught you have been. Not only was Rasa a schoolmaster, she was also the teacher of Nafai and Issib, Elemak and Mebbekew, and many, many other boys."

"But that was in ancient times," said Luet.

Shedemei gave one bark of laughter and said, "Doesn't feel that long ago to me."

After supper was over, they walked slowly through the courtyard as the children sang together, in their rooms, in the bathhouse, or reading in the waning light of day. There was something strange about the song, and it took a while to realize what it was. Luet stopped suddenly and blurted it out. "I never knew that diggers sing!"

Shedemei put an arm around her. Luet was surprised—she had never thought this cold woman would be capable of such an affectionate gesture. Nor did she do it the way men sometimes did, putting an arm around a lesser man to show affection but also power, superiority, ownership. It was . . . yes, it was sisterly. "No, you never knew they could sing. Nor had I ever heard their voices raised in song until I started this school." Shedemei walked in silence beside her for a moment. "Do you know, Luet, for all I know the diggers never *did* sing during all those years that they lived in such close proximity to the angels. Because they were always at war. Perhaps because singing was a thing that 'skymeat' did, and therefore was beneath their dignity. But here in slavery they lost their dignity and learned music. I think there might be a lesson in that, don't you?"

Luet assumed that Shedemei had been planning to tell her this all along, and that the lesson must therefore be aimed particularly at her, though later she would realize that Shedemei really was simply making an observation and meant nothing by it. "I think I understand," Luet said. "I was in slavery once, you know. Do you think all the songs of my life come from that? Is captivity a stage we should all pass through?"

To her surprise, there were tears in Shedemei's eyes. "No. No one should go through captivity. Some people find music in it, like you, like so many of the earth people here, but only because the music was already in them, waiting for a chance to get out. But your brother didn't find much music in *his* captivity, did he?"

"How do you know my brother?" asked Luet.

"Did he?" insisted Shedemei, refusing to be diverted.

"I don't know," said Luet.

"Why not?"

"Because I don't think his captivity has ended yet."

Another silence. Then Shedemei answered softly, "No. No, I think you're right. I think that when his captivity finally ends, he, too, might find a song in his heart."

"I've heard him sing," said Luet. "It isn't much."

"No, you haven't," said Shedemei. "And when he does sing, if he does, it will be a song such as you have never heard."

"Whatever it is, if Akma sings it, it won't be on key."

Shedemei laughed and hugged her close.

They were near the front door of the house, and one of the teachers was already opening it. For a moment Luet thought that she had opened it in order to let them out, but it wasn't so. There were three men on the porch, and two of them were humans of the king's guard. The third was an angel, and after a moment Luet realized that it was old Husu, who had once been head of the spies and now was retired to the supposedly less demanding position of an officer in the civil guard. What could he possibly be doing here?

"I have a book of charges for the woman called Shedemei." It was hard for him to get his mouth around her name.

Before Shedemei could speak, Mother pushed forward. "What is this about?" she asked.

Husu was immediately flustered. "Lady Chebeya," he said. Then, noticing Edhadeya, he took a step backward. "No one said . . . I've been misled, I think!"

"No you haven't," said Shedemei. She touched Chebeya lightly on the shoulder. "You may be a raveler, but you're not Hushidh, I'm not Rasa, and this good man is definitely *not* Rashgallivak."

In vain Luet searched her memory for details of the story Shedemei was alluding to. Something about Hushidh the raveler destroying the army of Rashgallivak. But Husu had no army, not anymore. She didn't understand and wasn't going to.

"Husu, you have a book of charges?"

"Shall I read them to you?"

"No, I'll simply *tell* them to you," said Shedemei. "I assume that I'm charged by a group of men from this neighborhood with creating a public nuisance because of the number of poor people who call at my school, with incitement to riot because I'm teaching the children of former slaves right along with other girls, with confusion of sexes for having appended the male honorific *ro* to the end of the name of the Hero Rasa in the name of my school. And, let me see—oh, yes, I'm sure there's a charge of blasphemy because I call the wives of the Heroes Heroes in their own right—or is that merely a charge of improper doctrinal innovation?"

"Yes," stammered Husu, "improper doctrinal . . . yes."

"And, oh yes, mustn't forget—treason. There's a charge of treason, isn't there."

"This is absurd," said Chebeya. "You must know it is, Husu."

"If I were still in the king's council," said Husu, "then yes, I'd say so. But I'm in the civil guard now, and when I'm given a book of charges to deliver, then I deliver them." He handed the polished bark to Shedemei. "It's to be tried in Pabul's court in twenty-four days. I don't think you'll have any trouble finding lawyers who'll want to speak for you."

"Don't be silly, Husu," said Shedemei. "I'll speak for myself."

"That's not done by ladies," said Chebeya—and then laughed at her own words, realizing whom she was talking to. "I suppose that won't make any difference to you, Shedemei."

"See? Everyone has learned something today," said Shedemei, also laughing.

Husu was astonished at the lightness of their tone. "These are serious charges."

"Come now, Husu," said Shedemei. "You know as well as I do that these charges are deliberately stupid. Every single crime I'm charged with consists of something that Akmaro the high priest has been teaching people to do for thirteen years. Mixing poor with rich, mixing diggers with humans and angels, mixing former slaves with freeborn citizens, applying the honors of men to women, and denying the authority of the king's priests over doctrine—that *is* the substance of the treason charge, isn't it?"

"Yes."

"There you are. These charges have been placed against me specifically because if I am put on trial, Akmaro's teachings will be on trial."

"But Pabul is not going to convict you of a crime because you're following the teachings of my husband," said Chebeya.

"Of course he's not. It doesn't matter what he does. The enemies of the Keeper don't care how the trial turns out. *I* don't matter to them. It may be the very fact that you came to visit me today that led them to decide to lay these charges. They probably expect me to call you as witnesses on my behalf. And if I don't, they'll call you as witnesses against me."

"I won't say a word against you," insisted Luet.

Shedemei touched her arm. "The act of calling you is what matters. It ties Akmaro's family with the case. The more you defend Shedemei, the more credit the enemies of the Keeper will gain with the public. Or at least that part of the public that doesn't want to stop hating the diggers."

Husu was livid. "What is your source of information? How did you already know what the charges against you were?"

"I didn't *know,*" said Shedemei. "But since I deliberately broke every one of those laws and made it clear to anyone who asked that I knew I was breaking them, I'm not at all surprised to find them on the book of charges."

"Did you want to be put on trial for your life?" asked Husu.

Shedemei smiled. "I assure you, Husu, no matter how things turn out, the one certainty is that *I* will not be dead."

Still confused, still angry, Husu and the two human guards left the house. "You do know the custom that you may not leave the city," Chebeya said.

"Oh, yes," said Shedemei. "I've already been advised of that."

"We've got to go home, Mother," Luet said. "We have to tell Father what's happened."

Mother turned to Shedemei. "This morning I didn't know you. Tonight I'm bound to you by cords of love as if I'd been your friend for years."

"We are bound together," said Shedemei, "because we both serve the Keeper."

Mother looked at her with a wry smile. "I would have thought so until the moment you said that, Shedemei. Because there was something about what you said that is . . . not a lie . . . but. . . ."

"Let's just say that my service to the Keeper hasn't always been voluntary," said Shedemei. "But it is now, and that's the truth."

Mother grinned. "You seem to know more than I do about what a raveler can see."

"Let's just say that you're not the first I've known." Then Shedemei laughed. "Not even the first named Chveya."

"Nobody can pronounce her name the old way like that," said Luet. "How do you do that?"

"Humans can say it," said Shedemei. "Chvuh. Chveya. It's only angels that can't, and that's why the name was changed."

"It's silly, isn't it," said Luet. "The person I'm named for and the person Mother is named for were also mother and daughter, except the other way around."

"It's not a coincidence," said Mother. "After all, I'm the one who named you."

"I know that," said Luet.

"I thought the names were appropriate myself," said Shedemei. "As I said, I once had dear friends with those names. I knew them long ago and far away, and they're dead now."

"Where are you from?" Chebeya demanded. "Why have you come here?"

"I'm from a city that was destroyed," said Shedemei, "and I came here in search of the Keeper. I want to know who she is. And the closer I stay to you and your family, Chebeya, the better my chances of finding out."

"*We* don't know any more than you do," said Luet.

"Then perhaps we'll find out together," said Shedemei. "Now go home before the sky gets too dark. The evening rains are about to begin and you'll be soaked."

"Will you be all right?" asked Mother.

"You must believe me when I say that I am the only one who is perfectly safe." With that, Shedemei hustled them out the door. Impulsively Luet stopped at the last moment and kissed the schoolmaster on the cheek. Shedemei embraced her then and held her for a moment. "I lied," she whispered. "I didn't just come here for the Keeper. I also came here because I wanted a friend."

"I *am* your friend," said Luet. Later she would think of how passionately she said those words and wail to Edhadeya that she must have sounded like a schoolgirl. But at the time, looking into Shedemei's eyes, they seemed the most natural words she could have said.

8

Trials

As soon as Didul reached the court, Pabul ushered him into his private chamber. "Did you see how many guards were stationed around the court?"

"I assume you've been getting death threats."

"I'm flattered by them—not a single bribe. They know I can't be bought. They're going to find out I can't be terrified."

"*I* can."

"You know what I mean," said Pabul. "I'm afraid, yes, of course, but my fear won't make me judge any differently than I would have."

"This trial is famous already," said Didul. "And it doesn't even begin till tomorrow."

Pabul sighed. "Everyone knows what's at stake. All the laws protecting the old order are being used to block the new. I have no idea what kind of defense Shedemei is planning, but I can't imagine what she'll say that can overbalance the plain truth that she's guilty."

"Guilty," said Didul. "Guilty of being a remarkable woman. Among the Kept in Bodika, she's already being touted as a martyr."

"I keep hoping that Motiak will take the matter out of my hands by simply announcing that the old laws are repealed."

"He won't," said Didul. "He's trying to stay above the whole thing."

"He knows he can't, Didul." Pabul fumbled through some of the barks lying on his table. "No matter what I decide, the loser will appeal."

"Even if you give Shedemei no penalty at all?"

"Have you met her?" asked Pabul sharply.

Didul laughed. "This morning, before coming here."

"Then you know she'll appeal even if I pay a fine to *her*. I think she's enjoying this."

"Poor Pabul."

Pabul grimaced. "We've dedicated our lives to being the opposite of Father. And now I have to sit in judgment on a follower of Binaro, just as Father sat in judgment on Binaro himself."

"Nobody will be burned to death this time."

"No—the treason charge is the one I can dismiss easily enough. But I still have to convict her of all the others."

"Isn't there some law about bringing false charges maliciously?" asked Didul.

"The operative word there is *false*. These charges are true."

"Malicious mischief. Trying to disrupt the public order of the kingdom. And as you said, the treason charge is there only to make it a capital crime."

"What are you suggesting? That I bring charges against the people who are charging Shedemei?"

Didul shrugged. "It might induce them to drop their petition against her."

"I don't know how likely *that* is," said Pabul. "But if I could find a way to complicate things further, so that there's no possibility of a clearcut victory or defeat for anybody. . . ."

Didul waited for a while, watching Pabul read bark after bark. Finally he patted his older brother's shoulder and made his way to Akmaro's house. He came to the back, as he usually did, and waited in silence in the shade of a tree until someone inside the house noticed him. It was Luet who finally came out and greeted him. "Didul, why don't you just come to the front of the house and clap your hands like anyone else?"

"And what if it's Akma who answers the door?"

"He's never here. And so what if it is?"

"I don't want a quarrel. I don't want a fight."

"I don't think Akma does, either," said Luet. "He still hates you, of course—"

"Of course," said Didul dryly.

"But it's not . . . he's concentrating on other things."

"What I want to know is, does he have anything to do with these charges against Shedemei?"

"Isn't she wonderful?" asked Luet. "Have you met her?"

"This morning. It was rather grueling, actually. She practically held me to the fire before she'd finally believe that I wasn't a jaguar dressed as a turkey."

"She knew about your past?"

"As if she'd watched over my shoulder. Everything. It was terrifying, Luet. She asked me. . . ."

"What?"

Didul shuddered. "Asked me if I especially enjoyed it when I knocked you around."

Luet laid a hand on his shoulder. "That was unkind of her. I've forgiven you—what business is it of hers?"

"She said she was trying to determine whether it was really possible for a person to change. She was trying to find out if I was really vile before, and became a truly virtuous man now, or if I was vile and now merely pretended to be good, or if I was good all along, and merely misguided."

"What good would it do her to find *that* out?"

"Oh, I can think of several uses. Anyway, she's a moral philosopher. That's one of the great questions, whether human beings are really capable of change, or if all seeming changes are really a matter of framing the existing character in a different moral situation . . . you know. Philosophy stuff. I've just never had anybody actually try to test their ideas against the real world like that. At least, I've never been the real world they were testing against."

"She isn't much for good manners, is she?"

"Better than you," said Didul. "She invited me to eat with her at noon."

"You know perfectly well that you're already invited to have supper with us," said Luet, gently shoving him.

He caught her hand, laughing, then immediately let go of her and stood up, trying to hide his embarrassment.

"Didul," she said, "you *are* strange sometimes." Then, as she led the way into the house, she commented over her shoulder, "You don't mind that Edhadeya will be here tonight, do you?"

"Not unless I'll be in the way."

Luet only laughed.

In the kitchen, Didul and Luet talked with Chebeya as they helped her prepare supper. Akmaro came home with three young diggers who were trying to get him to take them on as students. "There aren't enough hours in the day," he said—obviously not for the first time—as they followed him into the house.

"We don't want you to stop what you're doing. Just let us follow you."

"Like shadows," said another.

"We'll be quiet," said the third.

"Maybe a question now and then."

Akmaro interrupted them and introduced his wife and daughter. Before he could mention Didul, one of them backed slightly away and said, "You must be Akma."

"No, I'm not," said Didul.

The digger, a young woman, immediately relaxed and came closer. "I'm sorry," she said. "I just assumed—"

"And there you see why I can't have you following me around," said Akmaro. "Akma is my son. If you believe the nasty rumors you've heard about him, I can hardly have you camping in my home."

"I'm sorry," she said.

"Don't be. It happens that at least some of the rumors are true. But you must allow me to have privacy and unless you're planning to stay for dinner. . . ."

The boy seemed perfectly content to accept the implied invitation, but the two girls hustled him away.

"Study with the teachers," said Akmaro as they left. "We'll see each other often enough if you do that."

"We will," said one of the girls—grimly, as if she were threatening some kind of vengeance. "We'll study so hard that we'll know *everything.*"

"Good. Then I'll come and learn from *you,* because I hardly know anything." With a smile, Akmaro closed the door behind them.

"Now I do feel guilty," said Didul. "It seems I routinely get what they're begging for. And if having diggers around would cause problems with Akma, think of how he'd react if you tried to let *me* tag along."

"Oh, you're completely different," said Akmaro. "For one thing, you know as much as I do."

"Hardly."

"So we can discuss things as equals. That would never be possible with them—they're too young. They haven't lived."

"There's a lot I haven't done yet," said Didul.

"Like marry—there's a thought."

Didul blushed and immediately started carrying the cool clay mugs into the front room of the house. He could hear Luet behind him, quietly remonstrating with her father. "Do you *have* to embarrass him like that?" she whispered.

"He likes it," Akmaro answered—and not in a whisper.

"He does *not,*" Luet insisted.

But he did like it.

Edhadeya arrived just before the appointed time. Didul had met her a couple of times before, and always under the same circumstances—dining with Akmaro's family. Didul liked the fact that she and Luet were such good friends. It pleased him to see that Luet wasn't just a tagalong, that in fact she wasn't at all worshipful or deferent, beyond the normal courtesy of friendship. Clearly Luet knew Edhadeya as a person and hardly thought of her as the king's daughter. And Edhadeya, for her part, was completely natural in Akmaro's house, with not a hint of affectation or authority or condescension. Her experience had always been different from other people's lives, but she seemed to be endlessly fascinated with other people's thoughts and observations, not regarding her own as superior in any way.

The conversation turned quite early to the trial, and Akmaro just as quickly begged them to talk of other things. So they spent a lot of the dinner talking about Shedemei. Didul listened in fascination to their impression of the school, and Edhadeya had so much to say that finally he realized that, unlike the others, she wasn't just remembering a single visit. "How often have you been there?" he asked.

Edhadeya looked flustered. "Me?"

"Not that it matters," said Didul. "You just seem to speak as one who is . . . involved."

"Well, I've been back several times."

"Without me!" Luet cried.

"It wasn't a social visit," said Edhadeya. "I went there to work."

"I thought she said you couldn't," said Chebeya.

"She also told me not to wait."

"So did she let you help?" asked Luet. "If she did I'll never forgive you for not taking me."

"She has never *let* me do anything," said Edhadeya.

"But you still go," said Didul.

"I sneak in," said Edhadeya. "It isn't hard. It's not as if the school is guarded or anything. I go into the courtyard if Shedemei isn't there, and I help the younger girls with their reading. Sometimes I've had nothing better to do than take a mop and jar of water and wash down the floors in a corridor while everyone else was eating. A few times I've been in and out without Shedemei seeing me, but usually I get caught."

"I should think that the children or the other teachers would report you the moment you're seen," said Akmaro.

"Not at all," said Edhadeya. "The girls appreciate my help. And so, I think, do the teachers."

"What does Shedemei say when she throws you out?" asked Didul.

"It's quite colorful," said Edhadeya. "She keeps explaining to me that when she said I wasn't supposed to wait, she meant that I shouldn't *just* wait. That I should be actively involved in life, getting some experience to help me put my book learning into perspective."

"So why don't you do as she asks?" said Akmaro.

"Because I think that sneaking into her school and teaching without her spotting me is an excellent experience."

They all laughed at that. The subject eventually turned from Shedemei to speculations on what Rasa's House must have been like, back on the planet Harmony, and from there the conversation drifted to talking about people who had seen true dreams from the Keeper. "We keep talking about true dreamers as if they were all ancient or far away," said Luet, "but it's worth remembering that every single one of us has had at least one true dream. I haven't had any since I was little—but then, I haven't needed anything as much as I did then. Have you dreamed since those old days, Didul?"

Didul shook his head, not really wanting to talk about "those old days."

"I don't really *dream,*" said Chebeya. "That's not a raveler's gift."

"But the Keeper still shows you things," said Luet. "That's the thing we have to remember—the Keeper isn't just something that our ancestors believed in. She isn't just a myth." To everyone's surprise, tears suddenly came to her eyes. "Akma keeps saying that we're fooling ourselves, but we're not. I remember how it felt, and it was different from any other dream. It was real. Wasn't it, Edhadeya?"

"It was," said Edhadeya. "Pay no attention to your brother, Luet. He doesn't know anything."

"But he *does,*" said Luet. "He's the most intelligent person I've ever known. And so vigorous in everything he says and does—he was my teacher when I was little, and he's still my teacher now, except for this one thing—"

"This one little thing," murmured Akmaro.

"Can't you *make* him see, Father?" said Luet.

"You can't make people believe things," said Chebeya.

"The Keeper can! Why doesn't the Keeper just . . . just send him a true dream?"

"Maybe the Keeper does," said Didul.

They all looked at him in surprise.

"I mean, didn't the Keeper send dreams to Nafai's older brothers?"

"If it makes any difference," said Edhadeya, "it was the Oversoul."

"I thought Elemak had at least one true dream from the Keeper," said Didul. "Anyway, there was also Moozh. The one that Nafai wrote about —Luet's and Hushidh's father. The one who fought the Oversoul all the way, but he was really doing the Oversoul's will the whole time."

"You can't imagine that Akma is somehow doing the Keeper's will!" said Edhadeya. "Hating the poor earth people and wanting to get them excluded from the kingdom!"

"No, I don't mean that, I just mean—that you can resist the Keeper if you want to. How do we know Akma isn't having true dreams every night, and then getting up in the morning and denying that the dreams meant anything at all? The Keeper can't *make* us do anything. Not if we're determined to fight him."

"That's true," said Akmaro. "But I don't think Akma is dreaming."

"Maybe he dreams true so much that he doesn't realize that other people don't," said Didul. "Maybe his intelligence is partly a gift from the Keeper, unfolding truth to him in his mind. Maybe he's the greatest servant the Keeper has ever had, except that he refuses to serve."

"That's a big exception," said Chebeya.

"All I'm trying to say is that it wouldn't necessarily change Akma's mind to have a true dream. That's all I'm saying." Didul went back to the sugared fruit Edhadeya had brought for dessert.

"Well, it's a sure thing persuasion hasn't done anything," said Akmaro.

Chebeya made a little high-pitched sound in her throat.

"What was that?" said Akmaro.

"That was me," said Chebeya. "Giving the tiniest possible laugh."

"What for?"

"Akmaro, Didul has made me see things in a new way. I wonder if we really ever *have* tried to persuade Akma."

"I know *I* have," said Akmaro.

"No, you've tried to *teach* him. That's another matter entirely."

"All teaching is persuasion," said Akmaro. "And all persuasion is teaching."

"Then why did we bother to invent two different words for it?" asked Chebeya teasingly. "I'm not accusing you of anything, Akmaro."

"You're accusing me of not even trying to persuade my son, when you know I've tried till my heart has broken." Akmaro was trying to keep his tone light, but Didul could hear the emotion behind his smile.

"Please don't be hurt," said Chebeya. "We all know you've done your best. But we've also left it up to you, haven't we? I've been content to be the loving mother who tries to keep the connection with Akma strong. I've left all the arguing up to you."

"Not all," said Luet grimly.

"Akma is here so little, I've been afraid to argue with him for fear of losing him entirely," said Chebeya. "But because of that, perhaps he thinks that it's only a matter between him and his father. That Luet and I are neutral."

"He knows *I'm* not," said Luet.

Akmaro shook his head. "Chebeya, there's no need. Akma will grow out of this."

Tears started slipping down Chebeya's cheeks. "No he won't," she said. "Not now. This whole business with Shedemei—"

"Akma doesn't have anything to do with that, does he?" asked Didul.

"The people who brought charges against her," said Chebeya, "they won't give up. It can't be a secret from them how the son of the high priest feels about things. They'll find a way to use him. If nothing else, they'll flatter him, agree with him. Akma is hungry to be loved and respected—"

"We all are," said Edhadeya softly.

"Akma more than most, in part because he feels that perhaps he has never had the love and respect he wanted at home." Chebeya reached out a hand toward her husband, as if to soothe him. "Not your fault. It's just the way things looked to him, from the beginning, from those awful days back in Chelem."

Didul looked at the ruins of his meal in front of him, his face burning as he remembered how he had treated Akma. The picture came so easily to his mind, more vivid perhaps now than it had been at the time. Little Akma crying and sputtering in fury as Didul and his brothers laughed and laughed. Then Akma crying in pain, a very different sound, a terrible sound . . . and still they laughed. Still I laughed, Didul thought. Does Akma hear that sound even now? If it's even half as clear in his mind as it is in mine. . . .

He felt a hand close over his. For a moment he thought it might be Luet who touched him, and he wanted to tear his own hand away in shame at his unworthiness. But it was Chebeya. "Please, Didul. You're so much a part of this family that we forget sometimes that you hear some things with different ears. No one blames you here."

Didul nodded, not bothering to argue. Chebeya turned the conversation to other things, and the rest of the meal passed in peace.

When it was time for Edhadeya to go home, she asked Didul to walk with her. Didul laughed; he meant to seem amused but knew that he only sounded nervous. "Is it that you have something you want to say to me, or that everyone else has things they want to say without me?"

"He's so sweet, isn't he?" Edhadeya said. "He couldn't conceive of the idea that I might enjoy his company."

Once they were on the dark street, walking home by the light of the torch Didul carried, Edhadeya said, "All right, yes, there's something I wanted to say to you."

"Well, then," said Didul. "Here I am. Or is it so devastating you want to wait till we're nearer your father's house, in case I burst into tears, throw down the torch, and run away into the night?"

"You know what I want to talk about."

"I shouldn't come to Akmaro's house anymore, is that it?"

Edhadeya laughed, startled. "What! Why would I say that? They love you—are you so shy you can't see it?"

"For Akma's sake. So they can win him back."

"It's not you, Didul. No, I wanted to say the opposite. Or really, I wanted to ask you something first, and then say something—Didul, I wish I understood you better."

"Better than you do right now? Better than other people do? Or better than you understand other people?"

She giggled, very girlishly. Suddenly an image flashed into Didul's mind, of Edhadeya and Luet sitting on a bench together, laughing just that way. Schoolgirls.

"I'm listening now," he said. "I'll be serious."

"Didul, your life has been very strange," said Edhadeya. "You were unlucky in your father, but very lucky in your brothers."

"Pabul's done well. The rest of us struggle."

"You improved with age—which is better than most of us do. Most of us start out innocent and deteriorate."

"As low as my beginning was, Edhadeya, I had nowhere to go but up."

"I think not," said Edhadeya. "But please listen. I'm not harping on your past, I'm saying that you are much admired. Many people say it—Father hears reports from Bodika, you know. You are much admired. And not just among the Kept."

"That's kind of you to say."

"Yes, well, I'm repeating what others say. That you're a man of compassion."

"Whatever people tell me, I can always say I've done worse, the Keeper can still accept you if you change now."

"Please listen, Didul. I have to know something from your own lips. It seems that you love everybody, that you show compassion to everybody, and wit and a kind of easiness—everyone is comfortable with you."

"Except you."

"Because when you're with me—when you're with Akmaro—you're shy, you're not at ease. You feel—"

"Above myself."

"Out of place."

"Yes."

"So someone might wonder: How do you really feel about Akmaro's family? Do you love them? Or merely hunger for their constant forgiveness?"

Didul thought about this for a moment. "I love them. Their forgiveness I've had for years. The parents. Luet, when she was old enough to understand. She was very young, and children are very forgiving."

"So again, someone might wonder—if you are confident of their forgiveness, why are you so shy, so guarded when you're with them?"

"Who is doing all this wondering, Edhadeya?"

"I am, and be quiet. Someone might wonder, Didul, whether some of your shyness might be because you have some kind of special feeling for one of the family and yet you dare not speak of it. . . ."

"Are you asking me if I love Luet?"

"Thank you," said Edhadeya. "Yes, that's what I'm asking."

"Of course I love her. Anyone who knows her has to love her."

Edhadeya growled in frustration. "Don't play games with me, Didul!"

Didul held the torch farther up and away, so it wouldn't light his face as he spoke. "Can you imagine anything worse than the day Akma finds out that I'm marrying Luet?"

"Yes, I can," said Edhadeya. "The worst thing would be if Luet were to spend day after day, year after year waiting for you, and you never come to her."

"She's not waiting for me."

"You've asked her?"

"We haven't spoken of it."

"And she never will, because she fears that you don't have any feelings for her. But she has them for you. I betray a confidence to tell you this. But you must make your choice based on all the information. Yes, it would gall Akma to have you for a brother-in-law. But this same Akma is already the enemy of everything his father stands for. And to spare *his* feelings, will you break the heart of Luet, who waits for you? Which is the greater wrong? To hurt the unforgiving one, or to hurt the one who has forgiven all?"

Didul walked beside her in silence. They reached the door of the king's house.

"That was all I had to say," she said.

"Can I believe you?" he whispered. "That she cares for me? After all I did?"

"Women can be insane sometimes in the men they choose to love."

"Are you? Insane?"

"Do you want to know how insane I am, Didul? When Luet and I were younger, we fell in love with each other's brothers. She finally settled on Mon, because he's always been the one I was closest to. And I of course loved Akma from afar." Edhadeya smiled mysteriously. "Then Luet grew out of that childish love and found something much finer in her love for you." Edhadeya laughed lightly. "Good night, Didul."

"Aren't you going to finish your story?"

"I did." She walked to the door; the guard opened it for her.

Didul stood in the sputtering torchlight as the door closed.

The guard finally spoke to him. "Are you from out of the city, sir? Do you need directions somewhere?"

"No, no . . . I know the way."

"Then you'd better set out—your torch won't burn forever, unless you plan to let the flame run right down your arm."

Didul thanked him with a smile and set off for the public house where he was staying. Akmaro and Chebeya invited him for dinner, but never to stay the night. It would not do for him to be there, even sleeping, should Akma choose to come home.

Luet stopped loving Mon, but Edhadeya never grew out of that childish love for Akma. That must be a difficult situation for her. At least the man that Luet loved was loyal to the cause of the Keeper. Edhadeya, a dreamer of true dreams, the daughter of the king, loved a man who disbelieved in the Keeper and despised the Kept.

Maybe I'm not the worst possible husband. Maybe I do have something to offer Luet, besides poverty and the fury of her brother and a memory of my cruelty to her when she was little. Maybe she should be given the choice, at least. Didn't he owe it to her, to give her the chance to hear him talk of his love for her and ask for her to be his wife, so she could refuse him and cause him a small fraction of the humiliation and pain he had once caused her?

He despised himself at once even for thinking this. Didn't he know Luet at all, to think she would want to hurt him or anyone else? Edhadeya said she loved him. And he knew that he loved her. Akmaro had made it plain that he would give his approval. So had Chebeya, in a thousand small ways, talking about how much a part of the family he was.

I will speak to her, he decided. I will speak to her tomorrow.

He doused his dying torch in the pail at the door of the public house and went inside to spend a few hours wishing he could sleep instead of rehearsing over and over in his mind the words he would say to Luet, imagining over and over the way she might smile and embrace him, or weep and run from him, or stare at him in horror and whisper, How could you? How could *you?*

At last he did sleep. And in his dream, he saw himself and Luet standing beneath a tree. It was heavy with a white fruit, but it was just out of reach—neither of them was tall enough to reach it. "Lift me up," she said. "Lift me up, and I can pick enough for both of us."

So he lifted her, and she filled her hands, and when he lowered her back to the ground she took a bite and wept at the sharp sweetness of it. "Didul," she whispered. "I can't bear it if you don't have a bite—here, from this place right beside where I bit, so you can taste exactly what I tasted."

But in his dream he didn't bite from the fruit at all. Instead he kissed her, and from her own lips tasted exactly what she had tasted, and yes, it was sweet.

The trial was so well-known that even before Didul was asleep, people were gathering in the large open court. At dawn, when the guards arrived, they had to herd the early arrivals to the front rows overlooking the court. The judge's seat was, of course, in shadow, and would be throughout the day. Some thought this was for the judge's comfort, protecting him from the summer heat, but in winter it could be bitterly cold in the shade, with no scrap of sun to warm him. No, the shade was to help keep the judge more or less anonymous. People could see most clearly where the light was; the complainants and the accused were in light continuously, and if either of them had brought a lawyer in to speak for them, he would strut the length and breadth of the sunlit area. No lawyer, however, would step within the judge's shadow. Some thought this was out of respect for the king's honor as embodied in his deputy, the judge. But the lawyers all knew that to step out of the light made them appear clumsy, weak, unaware, and would dispose the people against them. Not that the people had any voice in the decision, officially—though there had been notorious trials in the past where it seemed the judge had made his decision based solely on which outcome would be most likely to allow him to leave the court alive. But the lawyers knew that their reputation, their likelihood of being hired for other cases, depended on how the onlookers perceived them.

The sun was halfway to noon when the accusers arrived, along with their lawyer, a loquacious angel named kRo. It was forbidden for an angel to fly in the court, but kRo had a way of opening his wings and sort of gliding as he walked back and forth, building up passion in himself and in the audience. It made him seem at once larger and more graceful than his opponent, and many human lawyers refused to take on cases that might put them head to head with kRo.

With the accusers in place and the gallery completely full, with hundreds more clamoring outside, pleading for imaginary spaces—"I'm not large! There's room for me!"—Pabul entered, with a guard on either side. In the event of a mob action against the judge, these guards would hardly be much protection, though perhaps they might buy just enough time for the judge to flee into his chamber. Rather they were there to defend against the lone assassin. It had been a hundred years since a judge was murdered in open court, and longer than that since one was mobbed, but the protections remained in place. No one expected that this case would turn to violence, but it was more heated than most, and the controversy made the onlookers view the guards in a different light. Not just a formality, no. They were armed; they were large, strong humans.

No one from the king's family was present. It had long been a tradition that if a royal person were present, he or she would sit beside the judge and, presumably, tell the judge the will of the king in the case. Thus from a trial attended by a royal person there could be no appeal. To preserve the rights of the accused, therefore, Ba-Jamim, Motiak's father, had begun the tradition of having no family member present at any lower trials, so that the right of all parties to appeal a decision could be preserved. It also had the happy effect of increasing the independence and therefore the prestige of the judges.

Akma, however, came to watch, and his sister Luet came with him. They had arrived late enough that they secured seats only in the back, behind the accused where they could see no faces. But two close supporters of the accusers, who had seats on the front row where they could see everyone's face, recognized Akma and insisted that he and his sister come down and take their places. Akma pretended to be surprised and honored, but Luet remembered how he had remained standing at the back until he was noticed, he knew that seats were being held for him. And by supporters of the accusers. Akma had definitely taken sides.

Well, why not? So had Luet.

"Have you met her?" she asked.

"Met whom?" asked Akma.

"Shedemei. The accused."

"Oh. No. Should I have?"

"A brilliant, remarkable woman," said Luet.

"Well, I don't suppose anyone would have noticed her if she was a fool," he answered mildly.

"You know I was at her school with Mother and Edhadeya when the book of charges was delivered," said Luet.

"Yes, I'd heard."

"She already knew the charges. Isn't that funny? She recited them to Husu before he could read them off."

"I heard that, too," said Akma. "I imagine kRo will make something of that. Proof that she was aware of her lawbreaking, that sort of thing."

"I daresay he will," said Luet. "Imagine charging her with treason for running a school."

"Oh, I'm sure that charge was just to make the whole thing more notorious. I don't think Father's little puppet judge will even allow that charge to be heard, do you?"

Luet cringed at the malice in Akma's voice. "Pabul is no one's puppet, Akma."

"Oh, really? So what he did to our people back in Chelem, that was of his own free will?"

"He was *his* father's puppet then. He was a child. Younger than we are now."

"But we've both passed through that age, haven't we? He was seventeen. When I was seventeen, I was no man's puppet." Akma grinned. "So don't tell me Pabul wasn't responsible for his own actions."

"Very well, then," said Luet. "He was. But he changed."

"He sensed the way the wind was blowing, you mean. But let's not argue."

"No, let's do argue," said Luet. "Which way was the wind blowing back in Chelem? Who had the soldiers there?"

"As I recall, our young judge had the command of a gang of digger thugs that were always ready to whip and claw women and children."

"Pabul and the others risked their lives to stop the cruelty. And gave up their future in positions of power under their father in order to escape into the wilderness."

"And come to Darakemba where, to everyone's surprise, they once again have positions of power."

"Which they earned."

"Yes, but by doing what?" Akma grinned. "Don't try to argue with me, Luet. I was your teacher for too long. I know what you're going to say before you say it."

Luet wanted to jab him with something very hard. When they were younger and quarreled, she would pinch together her thumb and first two fingers to form a weapon hard and sharp enough for Akma to notice it when she jabbed him. But there had been playfulness in it, even when she was most furious; today she didn't touch him, because she was no longer sure she loved him enough to strike at him without wanting to cause real injury.

A sad look came across Akma's face.

"Why aren't you happy?" she said tauntingly. "Didn't I say what you expected me to say?"

"I expected you to jab me the way you used to when you were a brat."

"So I've passed out of brathood."

"Now you judge me," said Akma. "Not because I'm wrong, but because I'm not loyal to Father."

"Aren't you loyal to him?"

"Was he ever loyal to me?" asked Akma.

"And will you ever grow out of the hurts of your childhood?"

Akma got a distant look on his face. "I've grown out of all the hurts that ended."

"No one's hurting you now," said Luet. "You're the one who hurts Mother and Father."

"I'm sorry to hurt Mother," said Akma. "But she made her choice."

"Didul and Pabul and Udad and Muwu all begged for our forgiveness. I forgave them then, and I still forgive them now. They've become decent men, all of them."

"Yes, you all forgave them."

"Yes," said Luet. "You say that as if there were something wrong with it."

"You had the right to forgive them for what they did to you, Luet. But you didn't have the right to forgive them for what they did to me."

Luet remembered seeing Akma alone on a hillside, watching as Father taught the people, with the Pabulogi seated in the front row. "Is that what this is all about? That Father forgave them without waiting for your consent?"

"Father forgave them before they asked him to," whispered Akma. She could barely hear him above the roaring of the crowd, and then she could only make out his words by watching his lips. "Father loved the ones who tormented me. He loved them more than me. There has never been such a vile, perverted, filthy, unnatural injustice as that."

"It wasn't about justice," said Luet. "It was about teaching. The Pabulogi only knew the moral world their father had created for them. Before they could understand what they were doing, they had to be taught to see things as the Keeper sees them. When they did understand, then they begged forgiveness and changed their ways."

"But Father already loved them," whispered Akma. "When they were still beating you, when they were still torturing me, mocking us both, smearing us with digger feces, tripping me and kicking me, stripping me naked and holding me upside down in front of all the people while they ridiculed me—while they were still doing those things, Father already loved them."

"He saw what they could become."

"He had no right to love them more than me."

"His love for them saved all our lives," said Luet.

"Yes, Luet, and look what his love has done for them. They prosper. They're happy. In his eyes, they *are* his sons. Better sons than I am."

This was uncomfortably close to Luet's own judgment of things. "There's nothing they've achieved, nothing in their relationship with Father that wasn't available to you."

"As long as I admitted first that there was no difference in value between the tortured and the torturer."

"That's stupid, Akma," said Luet. "They had to *change* before Father accepted them. They had to become someone else."

"Well, I *haven't* changed," said Akma. "I haven't changed."

It was the most personal conversation Luet had had with Akma in years, and she longed for it to continue, but at that moment a roar went up from the crowd because they were bringing in the accused, protected by eight guards. This was another old tradition, introduced after several cases in which the accused was murdered in court before the trial was even completed, or snatched away to have another sort of trial in another place. These guards still served that practical purpose—an in-court murder of an accused person had happened not ten years before, admittedly in the rather wild provincial capital of Trubi, at the high end of the valley of the Tsidorek. Not that anyone expected Shedemei to be in danger. This was a test case, a struggle for power; she herself was not regarded with particular passion by those accusing her.

"Look at the pride in her," said Akma, shouting right in her ear so he could be heard.

Pride? Yes, but not the cocky sort of defiance that some affected to when haled before the court. She carried herself with simple dignity, looking around her calmly with mild interest, without fear, without shame. Luet had thought that no one could be charged and brought to trial without feeling at least a degree of embarrassment at being made a public spectacle, but Shedemei seemed to be no more emotionally involved than a mildly interested spectator.

And yet this trial did matter to her; hadn't she deliberately provoked it? She wanted this to happen. Did she know what the outcome would be, the way she knew in advance the charges against her?

"Has Father told you what the puppet is supposed to decide?" Akma shouted in her ear.

She ignored him. The guards were moving slowly through the crowded gallery, forcing people to sit down. It would take a while for them to silence the crowd—these people wanted to make noise.

She wanted to personally slap each one of them, because their noise had stopped Akma from baring his soul to her. That *was* what he was doing. For some reason, he had chosen this moment to . . . to what? To make a last plea for her understanding. That's what it was. He was on the verge of some action, some public action. He wanted to justify himself to her. To remind her that Father was the one who had first been guilty of monstrous disloyalty. And why? Because Akma himself was preparing his own monstrous disloyalty. A public betrayal.

Akma was going to testify. He was going to be called as a scholar, an expert on religious teachings among the Nafari. He was certainly qualified, as Bego's star pupil. And even though within the family and the royal house it was well known that Akma no longer believed in the existence of the Keeper, it wouldn't stop him from testifying about what the ancient beliefs and customs had always been.

She laid her hand on Akma's arm, dug into his wrist with her fingers.

"Ow!" he cried, pulling away from her.

She leaned in close to him and shouted in his ear. "Don't do it!"

"Don't do what?" She could make out his words only by reading his lips.

"You can't hurt the Keeper!" she shouted. "You'll only hurt the people who love you!"

He shook his head. He couldn't hear her. He couldn't understand her words.

The crowd at last was quieter. Quieter. Till the last murmur finally died. Luet might have spoken to Akma again, but his attention was entirely on the trial. The moment had passed.

"Who speaks for the accusers?" asked Pabul.

kRo stepped forward. "kRo," he said.

"And who are the accusers?"

Each stepped forward in turn, naming himself. Three humans and two angels, all prominent men—one retired from the army, the others men of business or learning. All well known in the city, though none of them held an office that could be stripped from them in retaliation by an angry king.

"Who speaks for the accused?" asked Pabul.

Shedemei answered in a clear, steady voice, "I speak for myself."

"Who is the accused?" asked Pabul.

"Shedemei."

"Your family is not known here," said Pabul.

"I come from a far city that was destroyed many years ago. My parents and my husband and my children are all dead."

Luet heard this in astonishment. There were no rumors about this in the city; Shedemei must never have spoken of her family before. She had once had a husband and children, and they were dead! Perhaps that explained the quietness that Shedemei seemed to have in the deepest place in her heart. Her real life was already over; she did not fear death, because in a way she was already dead. Her children, gone before her! That was not the way the world should be.

"I wandered for a long time," Shedemei went on, "until finally I found a land of peace, where I could teach whatever children were willing to learn, whose parents were willing to send them."

"Digger-lover!" someone cried out from the gallery.

The time of noise had passed; two guards immediately homed in on the heckler and had him out of the gallery in moments. Outside, someone else would be let in to take his place.

"The court is ready to hear the accusations," said Pabul.

kRo launched at once into a listing of Shedemei's supposed crimes, but not the simple unadorned statements that had been in the book of charges. No, each charge became a story, an essay, a sermon. He built up quite a colorful picture, Luet thought—Shedemei defiling the young human and angel girls of the city by forcing them to associate with the filthy ignorant children of diggers from Rat Creek. Shedemei striking at the ancient teachings of all the priests: "And I will call witnesses who will explain how all her teachings are an offense against the tradition of the Nafari—" that would be Akma, thought Luet.

"She insults the memory of Mother Rasa, wife of the Hero Volemak, the great Wetchik, father of Nafai and Issib. . . ."

Volemak was also the father of Elemak and Mebbekew, Luet wanted to retort—and Rasa had nothing to do with *their* conception. But of course she held her tongue. That *would* be a scandal, if the daughter of the high priest were to be hustled out of the court for heckling.

". . . by pretending that she needs more honor than her marriage to Volemak already brought her! And to give her this redundant honor, she takes a male honorific, *ro*, which means 'great teacher,' and appends it to a woman's name! Rasaro's House, she calls her school! As if Rasa had been a man! What do her students learn just by walking in her door! That there is no difference between men and women!"

To Luet's—and everyone else's—shock, Shedemei spoke up, interrupting kRo's peroration. "I'm new in your country," she said. "Tell me the female honorific that means 'great teacher' and I'll gladly use that one."

kRo waited for Pabul to rebuke her.

"It is not the custom for the accused to interrupt the accuser," said Pabul mildly.

"Not the custom," said Shedemei. "But not a law, either. And as recently as fifty years ago, in the reign of Motiab, the king's late grandfather, it was frequently the case that the accused could ask for a clarification of a confusing statement by the accuser."

"All my speeches are perfectly clear!" kRo answered testily.

"Shedemei calls upon ancient custom," said Pabul, clearly delighted with her answer. "She asked you a question, kRo, and custom requires you to clarify."

"There *is* no female honorific meaning 'great teacher,' " said kRo.

"So by what title should I honor a woman who was a great teacher?" asked Shedemei. "In order to avoid causing ignorant children to be confused about the differences between men and women."

She said this with an ever-so-slightly ironic tone, making it clear that no honorific could possibly cause confusion on such an obvious point. Some in the gallery laughed a little. This was annoying to kRo; it was outrageous of her to have interrupted his carefully memorized speech, forcing him to make up answers on the spot.

With a great show of patient condescension, kRo explained to Shedemei, "Women of greatness can be called *ya,* which means 'great compassionate one.' And since she was the wife of the father of the first king, it is not inappropriate to call her *dwa,* the mother of the heir."

Shedemei listened respectfully, then answered, "So a woman may only be honored for her compassion; all the other honorifics have to do with her husband?"

"That is correct," said kRo.

"Are you saying, then, that a woman cannot *be* a great teacher? Or that a woman may not be *called* a great teacher?"

"I am saying that because the only honorific for a great teacher is a male honorific, the title 'great teacher' cannot be added to a woman's name without causing an offense against nature," said kRo.

"But the honorific *ro* comes from the word *uro* which can be equally a male or a female," said Shedemei.

"But *uro* is not an honorific," said kRo.

"In all the ancient records, when the custom of honorifics first began, it was the word *uro* that was added to the name. It was only about three hundred years ago that the *u* was dropped and the *ro* began to be added to the end of the name the way it's done now. I'm sure you looked all this up."

"Our scholarly witnesses did," said kRo.

"I'm simply trying to understand why a word that is demonstrably a neutral one, implying either sex, should now be regarded as a word applying to males only," said Shedemei.

"Let us simplify things for the sake of the accused," said kRo. "Let us drop the charge of confusion of the sexes. That will spare us the agony of endless argument over the applicability of ancient usages to modern law."

"So you are saying that you consent to my continuing to call my school 'Rasaro's House'?" asked Shedemei. She turned to Pabul. "Is that a binding decision, so I won't have to fear being brought to trial on this point again?"

"I declare it to be so," said Pabul.

"Now the situation is clear," said Shedemei.

The gallery laughed uproariously. Her clarification, of course, had turned into kRo's humiliating retreat. She had succeeded in deflating him. From now on all his speechifying would be tinged with just the faintest hue of the ridiculous. He was no longer the terrifying object he had once been.

Akma leaned to Luet and whispered in her ear, "*Someone's* been teaching her a lot of ancient history."

"Maybe she learned it on her own," Luet whispered back.

"Impossible. All the records are in Bego's library, and she has never been there." Akma was clearly annoyed.

"Maybe Bego helped her."

Akma rolled his eyes. Of course it couldn't have been Bego, he seemed to be saying.

Bego must be of Akma's party, thought Luet. Or is it the other way around? Could it be that Bego instigated this whole nonsensical business about there being no Keeper at all?

kRo went on, climaxing his arguments by pointing out, just as Akma had anticipated, that all of Shedemei's violations were clearly premeditated and deliberate, since she had been able to name all the charges against her when Husu brought the book of charges to her door.

At last kRo finished—with much applause and cheering from the gallery, of course. But nothing like the kind of adoration he usually received. Shedemei had really done a job on him, and it was obvious kRo was angry and disappointed.

Pabul smiled, lifted a bark from his table, and began to read. "The court has reached a decision and—"

kRo leapt to his feet. "Perhaps the court has forgotten that it is the custom to hear the accused!" Graciously he bowed toward Shedemei. "Clearly she has studied a great deal and even though her guilt is obvious, we should do her the courtesy of hearing her speech."

Icily Pabul answered, "I thank the lawyer for the complainants for his courtesy toward the accused, but I also remind him that other lawyers, at least, are not able to read the minds of judges, and therefore it is customary to listen to the judge before contradicting him."

"But you were declaring your decision. . . ." said kRo, his voice trailing off into embarrassment.

"This court has reached a decision and because it is based solely upon the statements of the lawyer for the accusers, the court must ask each of the complainants individually if the speech just given by their lawyer represents their words and intentions as surely as if they had spoken for themselves."

So he was polling the accusers. This was highly unusual, and it invariably meant that the lawyer had made some gross mistake that would destroy the case he was speaking for. kRo folded himself inside his wings and listened in stoic fury as Pabul queried each accuser individually. Though they obviously had misgivings, kRo had in fact given the speech he had rehearsed for them the day before, and they affirmed that it was as if they had spoken the words themselves.

"Very well," said Pabul. "At eight different points in this speech, the lawyer for the complainants violated the law forbidding the teaching of doctrines contrary to the doctrines taught by the high priest now in office."

A loud hum arose from the crowd, and kRo unfolded himself from his wings and fairly launched himself toward the judge's shadow, stopping just short of the line of darkness in the sand of the courtyard. The judge's guards immediately stepped forward, weapons ready. But kRo now threw himself backward into the sand, his wings open, his belly exposed, in the ancient angel posture of submission. "I have said nothing but to uphold the law!" he cried, not sounding submissive at all.

"There is not a person in this court who doesn't know exactly what you and the other accusers are doing, kRo," said Pabul. "This entire charade was designed as an attack on all the teachings of the man that Motiak has appointed high priest. You are trying to use the teachings of former high priests, and customs of long standing but no merit, to destroy Akmaro's effort to unify all the people of the Keeper as brothers and sisters. This court was not deceived. Your speech exposed your malice."

"The law and long precedent are on our side!" cried kRo, abandoning his submissive posture and rising again to his feet.

"The law affirming the authority of the high priest over all teachings of doctrine concerning the Keeper was established by the voice of the Hero Nafai, the first king of the Nafari, when he established his brother the Hero Oykib as the first high priest. This law has precedence over all other laws dealing with correct teaching. And when Sherem defied this law and opposed Oykib, and then the Keeper struck Sherem dead as he spoke, the king declared that the penalty for defying the teachings of the high priest would from then on be the same death that the Keeper chose for Sherem."

Akma leaned to Luct and whispered furiously, "How dare Father use those ancient myths to silence his opponents!"

"Father knows nothing about this," Luet answered. But she did not get her voice low enough, and several around them heard her. Of course they all knew who Akma and Luet were, and they could read the scornful disbelief on Akma's face as clearly as they heard Luet's denial that Akmaro had any part in Pabul's decision. Akmaro would definitely be part of the rumors that would fly after the trial.

"Because this is an ancient offense," said Pabul, "I declare it to take precedence over the charges against Shedemei, since if her accusers are guilty of the greater crime, they are forbidden to bring accusation against her for a lesser one. I declare that the charges against Shedemei are nullified and may not be brought again by anyone until and unless her accusers are cleared of the charge against them. And I declare that you, kRo, and all the accusers who affirmed that you spoke their words and intentions are guilty, and I sentence you to death as the law demands."

"No one has used that law in four hundred years!" cried one of the accusers.

"I don't want anyone to die," said Shedemei, clearly dismayed by this turn of events.

"The compassion of the woman Shedemei is commendable but irrelevant," said Pabul. "I am the accuser of these men, and all these people in the gallery are witnesses. I decree that everyone in the gallery must give his or her name to the guards as you leave, so you can be called as witnesses if, as I expect, there is an appeal to the king. I declare this trial to be over."

Because they had been sitting at the front, Akma and Luet were among the last to leave. It took nearly an hour, but during that time they studiously did not say a word to each other or to anyone else. They both knew, however, that if Akma had been allowed to testify, the things he said would also have constituted the same offense that now had kRo and his clients under sentence of death.

"What has Pabul done to me!" Motiak roared.

Around him in the small room were gathered Akmaro, Chebeya, and Didul, representing the House of the Kept; and Aronha and Edhadeya, because Aronha was heir and could not be refused access while Edhadeya was, well, Edhadeya, and couldn't be refused either. They all understood Motiak's consternation; none of them had an easy answer.

Aronha thought he did, though, and offered it. "Dismiss the charges against Shedemei's accusers, Father."

"And allow them to reinstate their charges against Shedemei?" asked Edhadeya.

"Dismiss *all* the charges," said Aronha with a shrug.

"That is foolish counsel," said Motiak, "and you know better, Aronha. If I did that, it would have the effect of repudiating my own high priest and stripping him of authority."

Aronha said nothing. Everyone there knew that Aronha, like his brothers, like Akmaro's own son, thought of that as a happy outcome.

"You can't put them to death," said Akmaro. "So perhaps Aronha is right."

"Do I have to listen to nonsense from you, too, Kmadaro?" demanded Motiak. "I suppose I should take this matter officially before my council."

"That isn't the way it's done," said Aronha. "This is a trial, not a war or a tax. The council has no authority."

"But the council has the virtue of spreading the responsibility around a little," said Motiak dryly. "Remember that, Aronha. I have a feeling you're going to need to do that when you're king."

"I hope never to be king, Father," said Aronha.

"I'm relieved to know that you hope for my immortality. Or is it simply your own death that you expect?" At once Motiak repented of his sarcasm. "Forgive me, Aronha, I'm out of sorts. Having to decide matters of life and death always puts me out of sorts."

Chebeya raised her hand from the table and spoke softly. "Perhaps you should do as Pabul did. Study the case of Sherem and Oykib."

"It wasn't even a court case, strictly speaking," said Motiak. "I already read it over, and it was more a matter that Sherem kept showing up wherever Oykib was trying to teach, to argue with him. Which, come to think of it, is what these pollen-brained accusers were doing to you, Akmaro."

"Using Shedemei as a proxy, of course," said Akmaro.

"It was really just a public argument between Oykib and Sherem. Until Sherem challenged Oykib to give him a sign, and the Keeper of Earth apparently struck Sherem down on the spot, allowing him to live only long enough to recant. But the king—it was Nafai's grandson by then, Oykib lived to be very old—the king declared that what the Keeper had done this time, the law would do from then on. Anyone who interfered with the teaching of the high priest would be struck dead as Sherem was. The law was only invoked twice after that, and the last time was four centuries ago."

"Is that how you intend to govern, Father?" asked Aronha. "Killing those who disagree with your high priest? That sounds rather like what Nuab did to Binaro. Or should I call him Binadi after all, since apparently he also broke this law, interfering with Pabulog's teachings as Nuak's high priest."

The comparison of Motiak to Nuak was unbearable. "Get out," said Motiak.

Aronha rose to his feet. "I see that this kingdom has changed since I was young. Now I am expelled from the king's presence for showing him exactly what he is about to do."

Motiak stared straight forward as Aronha left the room. Then he sighed and buried his face in his hands. "This is very messy, Akmaro," he said.

"It can't be helped," said Akmaro. "I warned you from the start that it would be very hard to take this people from a place where diggers were hated and enslaved, where women were kept silent in public life, and where the poor had no rights against the rich, to a place where all were equal in the eyes of the Keeper and the law. The surprise is that it took them this long to bring their opposition out into the open."

"And it wouldn't have happened now, either," said Motiak, "if my sons and yours hadn't let it be known that as soon as I'm dead, all these innovations would be swept away."

"They haven't said anything publicly," said Akmaro.

"Ilihi brought me word from a man who is at the heart of this; they would never have taken action like this if they hadn't had assurances that all my likely heirs were opposed to you, Akmaro. All of them. The only surprise is that they didn't send an assassin to kill me."

"And make a martyr of you?" said Akmaro. "No, they love you—that's why it took them so long. They know that you are the reason Darakemba is at peace, the reason the Elemaki don't dare to attack except those annoying raids on the border. They're trying to destroy *me* without harming you."

"Well, it's not working," said Motiak. "They *can't* destroy you without harming me, because I know that what you teach is true. I know that it's *right.* And I'm not going to back down."

Didul raised one hand a little from the table. The others deferred to him. "I know that I'm only a priest from one of the provinces. . . ."

"Skip the formalities, Didul, and get to the point," said Motiak impatiently. "We know who you are."

"You are king, sir," said Didul. "You must decide in such a way that your power to govern, to keep the peace, is not damaged."

"I hope that you aren't just pointing out the obvious," said Motiak. "I hope that you have a specific plan in mind."

"I do, sir. I have also read the book of Oykib, and the two later cases that were tried under the Sherem law. And both times the king turned the case over to the high priest to be tried. I think it was that very precedent that Nuab used in consulting with his priests during the trial of Binaro."

Akmaro stiffened. "You can't be suggesting that I should sit in judgment on these men and pronounce a sentence of death on them!"

Chebeya chuckled grimly. "Didul begged you not to make him come with you, Akmaro, but you insisted that you had dreamed of him sitting with you in council with the king and made him come along."

"There was a true dream involved with this?" asked Motiak.

"There was a dream!" said Akmaro. "You can't do this to me!"

"It's an offense against the religious authority," said Motiak. "Let it be tried by the religious authority."

"This solves nothing!" cried Akmaro. "The case is still a miserable knot!"

"But as Didul pointed out," said Motiak, "it removes it from a place where it can damage the authority of the king and the peace of the kingdom. I'll have my decision written up on a bark immediately, Akmaro. The case can only be tried by the high priest, and you have full powers of disposition."

"I won't put them to death," said Akmaro. "I won't do it."

"I think you had better think about the law before you make rash decisions," said Motiak. "Think about the consequences of your decision."

"No one can be one of the Kept if he follows the Keeper out of fear of execution!" cried Akmaro.

"It will all be in your hands," said Motiak. "Akmaro, forgive me, but whatever happens, the consequences will be less terrible for your having made the decision and not me." Motiak arose and left the room.

In the ensuing silence, Akmaro's voice came out as a rasping whisper. "Didul, don't ask me to forgive you for turning this on me."

Didul blanched. "I didn't ask your forgiveness," he said, "because I was not wrong. I agree with you completely. No one should die for speaking against the doctrine you teach."

"So in your infinite wisdom, Didul, do you have any suggestions for what I *should* do?"

"I don't know what you *should* do," said Didul. "But I think I know what you *will* do."

"And what is that?"

"Declare them guilty, but change the penalty."

"To what?" demanded Akmaro. "Dismemberment? Removal of the tongue? Public flogging? Forfeiture of property? Oh, I know—they have to live for a year in a tunnel with the diggers they despise so much!"

"With all your authority from the Keeper," said Didul, "you can't give someone back a missing hand or tongue, you can't heal the wounds from lashes on their back, you can't make new land or property. All you have the power to give them is by way of teaching them how the Keeper wants all his children to live, and then bringing them through the water to make them new men and women, brothers and sisters in the Keeper's House. Since that's all you can give them, then when they refuse those teachings isn't that all you can rightly take away?"

Akmaro looked at Didul with a steady gaze. "You thought this out before, didn't you? This was already in your mind before you came here."

"Yes," said Didul. "I thought that was how things would work out."

"But you didn't bother to say any of it to me until you talked the king into dumping the whole thing into my lap."

"Until the king gave the case to you for trial, sir, I had no reason to make any suggestions to you about its disposition."

"I have brought a snake into my house," said Akmaro.

Didul flinched at the words.

"Oh, don't take offense, Didul. Snakes are wise. They also shed their skins and become new men from time to time. Something that I'm apparently overdue for. So I make a declaration that the only penalty for preaching against the high priest is that you are turned out of the House of the Keeper. What then, Didul? Do you realize what will happen?"

"Only the believers will remain."

"You underestimate the cruelty of men and women, Didul. Without the threat of criminal penalties, the worms will come out from under their rocks. The bullies. The tormentors."

"I know the type," said Didul softly.

"I urge you to leave for home at once," said Akmaro. "When this decree is made tomorrow, you'll want to be in Bodika to help the Kept there deal with what will surely come."

"You speak as if this were my fault, sir," said Didul stiffly. "Before I go, I have a right to hear you admit to my face that I have done nothing more than tell you what you would inevitably have decided yourself."

"Yes!" said Akmaro. "And I'm not angry at you anyway. Yes I would have made exactly this decision because it's right. But what will happen to the Kept, to the House of the Keeper, I don't know. I fear it, Didul. That's why I'm angry."

"It's the Keeper's House," said Didul. "Not ours. The Keeper will show us a way out of this."

"Unless the Keeper is testing Darakemba to see if we're worthy," said Akmaro. "Remember that the Keeper can also decide to reject us. The way he rejected the Rasulum, when evil triumphed among them. Their bones cover the desert sand for miles."

"I'll keep that cheerful thought in mind all the way home," said Didul.

They arose from the table. Akmaro and Chebeya hurried out; Edhadeya stopped Didul at the door. "Did you decide anything about Luet?" she asked.

It seemed to take Didul a moment to realize what she was talking about. "Oh. Yes. I decided last night that I'd speak to her today. Only only now I have work to do. It's not a good time for love or marriage, Edhadeya. I have higher responsibilities than that."

"Higher?" she asked nastily. "Higher than love?"

"If you didn't think that service to the Keeper is the higher responsibility," said Didul, "you would long since have joined with Akma out of love for him. But you haven't. Because you know that love must sometimes take a second place." He left.

Edhadeya leaned against the doorpost for a long time, thinking about what he had said. I love Akma, and yet it has never once occurred to me to join with him in rejecting the Keeper. But that isn't because I love the Keeper more, the way Didul does. It's because I know what I know, and to be with Akma I would have to lie. I won't give up my honesty for any man. Nothing as noble in that as Didul's sacrifice. Unless perhaps my honor is also a way to serve the Keeper.

9

Persecution

At first Didul thought that their fears might have been exaggerated. There was no falling off of attendance at the House of the Keeper in Bodika. In fact, the way the story first circulated through the province was rather favorable. Shedemei had been tried for teaching the siblinghood of all people in the eyes of the Keeper, and especially for allowing the children of the poor, the daughters of former slaves, to attend school, to eat, to work alongside the daughters of humans and angels. Therefore when the charges were dismissed against her and even worse charges were brought against her accusers, it was encouraging, wasn't it?

Only gradually did the realization seep through the community that in refusing to have the heretics who accused Shedemei put to death, Akmaro had changed the law. The only penalty for offense against the official state religion was now to be turned out of the House of the Keeper. But what kind of penalty was that, for those who didn't believe anyway? Akmaro had been confirmed as the arbiter of doctrine for the state religion; but the law was now protected by such a feeble penalty that it was hardly a crime to disbelieve.

What did that *mean,* actually? Most people had only known one kind of religion, consisting of the official rituals performed by the king's priests in every city. Those priests had been put out of work thirteen years ago, and replaced by a ragtag group of priests and teachers who, instead of confining themselves to public rituals, insisted on collecting food to help the poor and teaching strange new doctrines about the equality of all people, which was obviously against nature. As most people were quick to say, it's fine to free the captured digger slaves after they've served ten years, it's fine to say that the children of slaves are born free, but everybody knows that diggers are loathsome and stupid and unfit for civilized company. Educating them for anything beyond menial labor is a waste of money. So the fact that the state religion now kept insisting on defiance of the way the world obviously worked was simply incomprehensible.

But no one *said* anything about it, except a few fanatic digger-haters, who spoke in secret. After all, the law was that you didn't speak against the religion of the king's priests, right?

Only now the only penalty that would come to you for speaking against these priests was to be turned out of the House of the Keeper. So that meant it was all right, didn't it?

There might be hidden penalties, though. After all, for foreigners to become full citizens, they had to pass through the water, and who could do that besides priests? So did foreigners have to join the Kept, and then later leave? And what if the king only did business with tradesmen who attended the House of the Keeper or sent their children to school at one of the little Kept Houses scattered through the villages and administered by one or two teachers? No, there was no need to open your mouth and get turned out. See how the wind blows.

That was the majority. It was the fanatics that began to make life problematic for Didul and his priests. It wasn't enough for them that now their meetings could be open. They had expected that thousands of people would leave the Kept and join them; instead, things were going on pretty much as before. That was intolerable. So they began to do things to help encourage the waverers that it was better for them to stop going to the priests of the Keeper.

At first it was the word "digger hole" written in excrement on the wall of the House of the Keeper in Bodika. The word was a scatological pun: The second word was the coarse term for the anus, while combined with *digger* it was an exceptionally offensive term for a tunnel in which a community of diggers dwelt. By calling the House of the Keeper by that name, the vandals couldn't have been more explicit.

That had been easy enough to clean off. But that was only the beginning of the harassment. Groups of digger-haters—they preferred to call themselves the Unkept—would gather at outdoor rituals and chant obscenities to drown out the voice of the priest. When someone was being brought through the water, they threw dead animals or manure into the river, even though that was a crime. Someone broke into the House of the Keeper and broke everything that could be broken. A fire was started during an early morning gathering of priests; they put it out, but the intention was clear.

Attendance began to fall off. Several of the teachers in outlying communities got messages—butchered animals on the doorstep, a sack over the head and a beating—and resigned or requested assignment in the city, where there might be safety in numbers. Didul had no choice but to close many of the outlying schools. People began to walk to and from meetings and classes in groups.

Through it all, Didul went from town to town constantly, protesting to the local authorities. "What can I do?" the commander of the civil guard would say. "The penalty for unbelief is in *your* hands. Find out who they are and turn them out. That's the new law."

"Beating a teacher isn't unbelief," Didul would say. "It's assault."

"But the teacher's head was covered and she can't identify who it was. Besides, it was never a good idea to have a woman doing the teaching. And diggers along with people?"

And Didul would realize that the commander of the civil guard was probably one of the fanatics who hated diggers worst. Most of them were retired soldiers. To them, diggers were all Elemaki—vicious fighters, night-time assassins. Slavery was all they deserved, and now that through some accident they were free, it was abominable to think of these former enemies now having the same rights as citizens.

"They aren't animals," he would say.

"Of course not," the civil guardian would answer. "The law declares them citizens. It's just not a good idea to try to teach them together with people, that's all. Train them for the kind of work they're suited for."

As the Unkept learned that the local authorities usually did little to protect the Kept, they grew bolder. Gangs of brash young men would accost old earth people, or earth children, or priests and teachers going about their business. There would be pushing, shoving, a few well-placed punches or kicks.

"And you tell us not to defend ourselves?" asked the parents gathered in a meeting in one of the outlying towns with a large digger population. Most of them were *not* the descendants of slaves, but rather original inhabitants who had been there as long as any angel bloodline—and a good deal longer than any humans. "Why are you teaching us this religion, then? To make us weak? We've never been unsafe in this city before. We were known, we were full citizens, but the more you preach that we're supposed to be equal, the less equally we're treated!"

Didul eloquently pointed out that it was a symptom of their helplessness that they were now blaming their friends for provoking their enemies. "The ones who do the beating, the shouting, the breaking, *those* are the enemy. And if you start to arm yourselves you'll play into their hands. Then they can shout to everyone, Look, the diggers are arming themselves! Elemaki spies in our midst!"

"But we were once full citizens and—"

"You were never full citizens. If you were, where are the digger judges in this town? Where are the digger soldiers in the army? The centuries of war with the Elemaki have robbed you of full citizenship. That's why Akmaro came back from the land of Nafai with the teachings of Binaro that the Keeper wants no more difference to be made among his children. That's why you must have courage—the courage to endure the blow. Stay in groups by all means. But don't arm yourselves—if you do, it will be the army you face soon enough, and not these thugs."

He persuaded them; or at least wore them down enough to end the argument. But it was getting harder and harder to keep control. He sent letters every week, to Akmaro, to Motiak, to Pabul, to anyone that he thought might be able to help. He even wrote to Khideo once, pleading for him to speak out against this violence. "You have great prestige among those who hate the earth people," he said in his letter. "If you openly condemn those who beat up defenseless children, perhaps you will shame some of them into stopping. Perhaps some of the civil guard will begin to enforce the law and protect the Kept from their persecutors." But there was no answer from Khideo. And as for Motiak, his answer was to send messengers to the civil guardians, informing them that it was their responsibility to enforce the laws with perfect equality. The civil guard in every town insisted that they were already doing this. Back came the answers: We're helpless. There are no witnesses. No one sees anything. Are you sure some of these complaints aren't trumped up in an attempt to win sympathy?

As for Akmaro, while he offered comfort, he could do little else. The problem was the same everywhere; and in the land of Khideo, he had to withdraw the priests and teachers entirely. He wrote: "I know you blame me for this, Didul, even though you are too courteous to say so. I blame myself. But I also have to remember, and I hope you will remember, that the alternative was to take upon myself, and to give to you and the other chief priests in the Houses of the Keeper, the power to kill in order to stifle dissent. That is the very opposite of what the Keeper wants from us. Fear will never turn people into the Keeper's children. Only love will do that. And love can only be taught, persuaded, encouraged, earned, won by kindness, by gentleness, even by meekness when enemies harm you. Our enemies may be filled with hate, but there are surely many among them who are sickened when they beat a child, when six of them kick a priest with a bag over her head, when they reduce people to tears in the street. Those will eventually reject these actions and repent of them and when they seek forgiveness, there you will be, no weapons in your hands, no hatred in your heart." And so on and so on. It was all true, Didul knew it. But he also remembered that he had been a willing persecutor himself for many months, beating and humiliating children without feeling anything but pride and hate and rage and amusement. A lot of harm could be done waiting for mercy to come to the hearts of the enemy. And some were like Didul's father. He never learned mercy. The very helplessness of his victims filled him with more lust to inflict pain. He liked the screaming.

Luet arrived in Bodika on the day of the worst incident so far. Three boys, two of them angels and one a digger, were attacked on their way to a Kept school on the outskirts of the city. The wings of the angels were savagely, irreparably torn: not just shredded, an injury which in the young could be healed; instead a huge ragged patch had been ripped out of their wings. It would never heal. These children would never fly again. And the digger child was even worse off. Every bone in his legs and arms was broken, and his head had been kicked so often that he had not regained consciousness. All three children were being cared for in the school. The parents were gathered, and many friends—including many who were *not* among the Kept, but were outraged by the crime. There were prayers, begging the Keeper to heal the children, to keep them from hating their enemies; and to soften the hearts of their enemies and teach them remorse, compassion, mercy.

The Keeper doesn't work that way, thought Didul. The Keeper doesn't *make* people nice. The Keeper only teaches them what goodness and decency are, and then rejoices with those who believe and obey. The husbands who are kind to their wives; the children who respect their parents; the spouses who are true to the covenant of marriage; the Keeper is glad of these, but sends no plague to afflict those who beat their wives, who scoff at their parents, who couple whenever and wherever they choose, regardless of the loyal spouse at home, grieving. That is the thing that I can't get them to understand—the Keeper will not change the world. He requires us to change it for him. Instead of prayers, you should be out talking, talking, talking to everyone.

So should I. And here I am dressing wounds and comforting children who by all reasonable standards have no reason to be comforted. Yet still he comforted them, assured them that their suffering would not be in vain, that the sight of their torn wings would cause many outraged people to rally to the defense of the Kept. And instead of telling the people to stop praying, he joined with them, because he knew that it comforted them. Especially the parents of the little earth boy who would probably not live through the night. "At least, being unconscious, his broken bones cause him no pain." Did I really say that? thought Didul. Did I really mouth such stupidity? The boy was in a coma because his brain was damaged, and I actually said it was merciful because he felt no pain?

That was where Didul was and what he was doing when Luet came through the door of the school, with Shedemei right behind her. His first thought was, What an absurd time for a visit! Then, of course, he realized that they weren't here on a social call. They came to help.

"Father is distraught because he can't do anything for you," said Luet, greeting him with a sisterly embrace. "Shedemei has been teaching Edhadeya and me some medicine she learned in her home country—there's a lot of washing and herbs and stinking liquids, but the wounds don't get infected. When I decided to come here and teach it to you and your people, Shedemei insisted on coming with me. You won't believe it, Didul. She left Edhadeya in charge of her school in her absence. 'Let them dare to attack Rasaro's House with the king's own daughter in charge of it,' that's what she said, and then she packed up her medicines and came along with me."

"It's a terrible time," said Didul. "I doubt that there's any medicine that will help these children."

Luet's face grew grim and angry when she saw the ruined wings of the angel boys. "The Keeper will never send her true child into the world when we still do things like this." She embraced the boys. "We have something that will make the aching go away for a while. And we can wash the wounds so they don't infect. It will sting very badly for a few seconds. Can you bear it?"

Yes, they could; yes, they did. Didul watched with admiration as she went skillfully about her work. This was something real. Better than empty words of comfort. He started trying to say this to her, and she scoffed at him. "Do you think words are nothing? Medicine won't stop these terrible things from happening. Words might."

Didul didn't bother to argue with her. "In the meantime, teach me. Tell me what you're doing and why."

While they worked on the angels, Shedemei was checking over the earth boy. "Let me have some time alone with him," she said.

"Go ahead," said Didul.

"I mean alone. *Alone.*"

Didul ushered the family, the friends, the neighbors out of the school. Then he came back, only to find Shedemei glaring at him and Luet. "Do words mean nothing to you? What do you think *alone* means? Two friends? Two injured angel boys?"

"You expect us to take *them* out?" asked Luet.

Shedemei looked them over. "They can stay. Now get out, both of you."

They left; Didul was angry but tried not to show it. "What is she doing that we can't see?"

Luet shook her head. "She did that once before. A little girl who had been hit in the eye. I thought we were going to have to lose it. She sent me and Edhadeya out of the room, and when we came back, there was a patch over the eye. She never explained what she did, but when the patch came off, the eye was fine. So . . . when she says to go out, I go out."

The others had sorted themselves into knots of conversation. Some were going home. Luet walked to the shade of a tree. "Didul, Father is beside himself. I've never seen the king so angry, either. He's had to be restrained from bringing home the army. Monush came out of retirement to argue with him. What enemy would the army attack? It was an awful scene, both of them yelling. Of course the king knew that Monush was right all along, but . . . they feel so helpless. No one has ever defied the law like this."

"Was it really the threat of death for heresy that kept public order all these years?"

"No. Father says . . . but he's written to you, hasn't he?"

"Oh, yes. The removal of the death penalty freed them to do little things. Ugly things like the shouting and the vile words and all that. But when nothing happened to them, they started pushing farther and harder, doing worse things, daring each other."

"It makes sense to *me,* anyway," she said.

"But what I don't know is—where does it stop? The law against beating and maiming children, *that's* still in force, with dire enough penalties. And yet these beasts did it anyway. The civil guard is out questioning people—no doubt about it, this sickened even them, especially the damage to the angel boys, you can bet they didn't care much about one less digger, the scum—but the questioning is a joke because they already know who did it, or at least they know who *would* know, but they don't dare reveal what they know because that would be the same as confessing that they've known all along and could have stopped it at any time and—I'm so angry! I'm supposed to be committed to being a man of peace, Luet, but I want to kill someone, I want to *hurt* them for what they did to these children, and the most terrible thing is that I know how it feels to hurt people and after all these years I finally *want to do it again.*" And then words failed him and to his own surprise he burst into tears and a moment later found himself sitting on the grass under the tree, Luet's arms around him as he cried out his frustration of the past few weeks.

"Of course you feel like that," she murmured. "There's nothing wrong in feeling it. You're still human. The passion for revenge is built into us. The need to protect our young. But look at you, Didul—you're feeling that desire to protect the little ones, not for members of your own species, but for children of two others. That's good, isn't it? To tame your animal impulses in the service of the Keeper?"

Her argument was so deft and yet so inadequate that he had to laugh; and in laughing he realized that her argument had not been inadequate after all, for he *was* comforted, or at least he could control himself now, not weep anymore.

Now, of course, the anguish momentarily spent, he was flooded with embarrassment at having let her see him like this. "Oh, Luet, you must think—I don't do this. I've really been pretty strong about it, all these other people doing the weeping, and me being the wise one, but now you know the truth about me, don't you, only we should be used to that, your family has *always* known the truth about me and—"

She put her fingers over his lips. "Shut up, Didul," she said. "You have a way of babbling when you should just be quiet."

"How do I know when times like that have come?" he said.

In reply, she leaned toward him and kissed him lightly, girlishly on the lips. "When you see my love for you, Didul, you can stop babbling because you know that I am not ashamed of you, I'm proud of you. It's worse here than anywhere, Didul, and you've borne it with so little help, really. That's why I came, because I thought, maybe if I were beside you, it might be bearable."

"Instead I cover you with my tears," he said, thinking all the while, She kissed me, she loves me, she's proud of me, she belongs beside me.

"Why don't you say what you're thinking?" she said.

"What makes you think you want to hear it?" he said, laughing in embarrassment.

"Because the way you looked at me, Didul, I knew that what you were thinking was, I love her, I want her beside me forever, I want her to be my wife, and Didul, I tell you honestly, I'm sick and tired of waiting for you to say it out loud."

"Why should I tell you what you already know?"

"Because I need to hear it."

So he told her. And when Shedemei called them back into the school, Luet had promised to be his wife, as soon as they could both get back to Darakemba, "Because," as Luet said, "Mother would kill us and steal all our children to raise herself if you had one of the priests marry us here."

In vain did Didul point out that if Chebeya killed them they wouldn't have produced any grandchildren for her to steal. The wedding would wait. Still, knowing that she wanted him, that she knew him so well and yet wanted to be with him—that was all the comfort that he wanted. Miserable as this day was, he felt himself filled with light.

Shedemei led them to the comatose child. "He's sleeping now," she said. "The bones have been adequately set, except the compound break in the left humerus, which I reset and resplinted. There is no brain damage, though I think he might not remember anything about what happened—which would be nice, not to have those nightmares."

"No brain damage?" asked Didul, incredulous. "Did you see what they did to him? The skull was open, did you see that?"

"Nevertheless," said Shedemei.

"What did you do?" asked Luet. "Teach me."

Grim-faced, Shedemei shook her head. "I did nothing that you could do. I couldn't teach it to you because I can't give you the tools you'd need. That has to be enough. Don't ask me any more."

"Who *are* you?" asked Didul. And then an answer occurred to him. "Shedemei, are *you* the true child of the Keeper that Binaro talked about?"

She blushed. Didul had not thought her capable of such a human reaction. "No," she said, and then she laughed. "Definitely not! I'm strange, I know, but I'm not *that.*"

"But you know the Keeper, right?" asked Luet. "You know—you *know* things that we don't know."

"I told you," said Shedemei. "I came here in search of the Keeper. I came here precisely because *you* are the ones with the true dreams, and I'm not. Is that clear? Will you believe me? There are things I know, yes, that I can't teach you because you aren't ready to understand them. But the things that matter most, you know better than me."

"Healing that boy's damaged brain," said Didul. "You can't tell me that doesn't matter."

"It matters to him. To you, to me. To his family. But in ten million years, Didul, will it matter then?"

"*Nothing* will matter *then,*" said Didul, laughing.

"The Keeper will," said Shedemei. "The Keeper and all her works, *she* will matter. Ten million years from now, Didul, will the Keeper be alone on Earth again, as she was for so many, many years? Or will the Keeper tend an Earth that is covered with joyful people living in peace, doing the Keeper's works? Imagine what such a good people could do—diggers, humans, angels all together—and maybe others, too, brought home from other planets of exile—all together, building starships and taking the Keeper's word of peace back out to worlds uncountable. That's what the people who founded Harmony meant to do. But they tried to force it, tried to *make* people stop destroying each other. By making people stupid whenever they. . . ." Suddenly she seemed to realize she had said too much. "Never mind," she said. "What does the ancient planet matter to you?"

Luet and Didul both looked at her wordlessly as, to cover her embarrassment, she busied herself in gathering up the unused medicines and returning them to her sack. Then she rushed out of the school, murmuring about needing air.

"Do you know what I was thinking just then, Luet?" said Didul.

"You were wondering if she might not *be* Shedemei. The real one. The one Voozhum prays to. Maybe her prayers brought the One-Who-Was-Never-Buried to us."

Didul looked at her in shock. "Are you serious?"

"Wasn't that what you were thinking?"

"Do you think I'm crazy? I was thinking—she's you in twenty years. Strong and wise and capable, teaching everyone, helping everyone, loving everyone, but just a little embarrassed when the depth of her passion shows. I was thinking she was what you might turn out to be, with one difference, just one. You won't be lonely, Luet. I swear to you that twenty years from now, you will not be lonely the way Shedemei is. That's what I was thinking."

And now that they were alone in the school, except for one sleeping boy and two young angels who watched in fascination, Didul kissed her as she should have been kissed long before. There was nothing girlish about her as she kissed him back.

It was too big a jump, from helping out secretly at Rasaro's House to running it. The month she had spent learning medicine from Shedemei hadn't helped prepare her for running a school. Edhadeya knew from the start that "running" the school simply meant tending to the details that no one else felt responsible for. Checking that the doors were locked. Buying needed supplies that no one else noticed were running out. She certainly didn't need to tell any of the other teachers how to do their work.

She taught no students herself. Instead she went from class to class, learning what she could from each teacher, not only about the subjects they taught, but also about their methods. She soon learned that while her tutors had been knowledgeable enough, they had had no understanding about how to teach children. If she had started teaching right away, she would have taught as she had been taught; now, she would begin very differently, and whatever students she might someday have would be far happier because of it.

One duty she kept for herself and no others—she answered the door. Whatever the Unkept might try at this school, it would happen first to the daughter of the king. See then whether the civil guard looks the other way! Several times she answered the door to find unaccountable strangers with the lamest sort of excuse for being there; once there were several others gathered nearby. To her it was obvious that they had been hoping for an opportunity—one of the other teachers, perhaps, or, best of all, a little digger girl they could beat up or humiliate or terrify. They had been warned, though, about Edhadeya, and after a while they seemed to have given up.

Then one day she answered the door to find an older man standing there, one whose face she had once known, but couldn't place at once. Nor did he know her.

"I've come to see the master of the school," he said.

"I'm the acting master these days. If it's Shedemei you want, she should be back soon from the provinces."

He looked disappointed, but still he lingered, not looking at her. "I've come a long way."

"In better times, sir, I would invite you in and offer you water at least, a meal if you would have it. But these are hard times and I don't allow strangers in this school."

He nodded, looked down at the ground. As if he was ashamed. Yes. He was ashamed.

"You seem to feel some personal responsibility for the troubles," she said. "Forgive me if I'm presumptuous."

When he looked at her there were tears swimming in his old eyes under the fierce, bushy eyebrows. It did not make him look soft; if anything, it made him seem more dangerous. But not to her. No, she knew that now—he was not dangerous to her or anyone here. "Come in," she said.

"No, you were right to keep me out," he said. "I came here to see . . . the master . . . because I *am* responsible, partly so, anyway, and I can't think how to make amends."

"Let me give you water, and we can talk. I'm not Shedemei—I don't have her wisdom. But it seems to me that sometimes any interested stranger will do when you need to unburden yourself, as long as you know she'll not use your words to harm you."

"Do I know that?" asked the old man.

"Shedemei trusts me with her school," said Edhadeya. "I have no prouder testimony to my character than that."

He followed her into the school, then into the small room by the door that served Shedemei as an office. "Don't you want to know my name?" he asked.

"I want to know how you think you caused these troubles."

He sighed. "Until three days ago I was a high official in one of the provinces. It won't be hard to guess *which* province when I tell you that there have been no troubles at all there, since no angels live within its borders, and diggers have never been tolerated."

"Khideo," she said, naming the province.

He shuddered.

And then she realized that she had also named the man. "Khideo," she said again, and this time he knew from the tone of her voice that she was naming *him*, and not just the land that had been named after him.

"What do you know of me? A would-be regicide. A bigot who wanted a society of pure humans. Well, there *are* no pure humans, that's what I'm thinking. We talked of a campaign to drive all diggers from Darakemba. But it came to nothing for many years, a way to pass the time, a way to reassure ourselves that we were the noble ones, we *pure* humans, if only the others, the ones who lived among the animals, if only they could understand. I see the disgust in your face, but it's the way I was raised, and if you'd seen diggers the way I saw them, murderous, cruel, whips in their hands—"

"The way diggers in Darakemba have been taught to see humans?"

He nodded. "I never saw it that way until these recent troubles. It got out of hand, you see, when word spread—when I helped spread the word—that inside the king's own house, all four of his possible heirs had rejected the vile species-mixing religion of Akmaro. Not to mention Akmaro's own son, though we had known *he* was one of us for a long time. But all the king's sons—that was like giving these *pure* humans license to do whatever they wanted. Because they knew they would win in the end. They knew that when Motiak passes into being Motiab and Aronha become Aronak. . . ."

"And they started beating children."

"They started with vandalism. Shouting. But soon other stories started coming in, and the pure humans that I knew said, What can we do? The young ones are so ardent in their desire for purity. We tell them not to be mean, but who can contain the anger of the young? At first I thought they meant this; I advised them on ways to reign in the ones doing the beatings. But then I realized that . . . I overheard them when they didn't know that I could hear, laughing about angels with holes in their wings. How does an angel fly with holes in his wings? Much faster, but only in one direction. They laughed at this. And I realized that they weren't trying to stop the violence, they loved it. And I had harbored them. I had provided a haven for the Unkept from other provinces to meet together in the days before Akmaro removed all serious penalties for heresy. Now I have no influence over them at all. I couldn't stop them. All I could do was refuse to pretend I was their leader. I resigned my office as governor and came here to learn. . . ."

"To learn what, Khideo?"

"To learn how to be human. Not *pure* human. But a man like my old friend Akmaro."

"Why didn't you go to him?"

Again tears came to Khideo's eyes. "Because I'm ashamed. I don't know Shedemei. I only hear that she is stern and ruthlessly honest. Well, no, I also heard that she favors the mixing of species and all sort of other abominations. That's how word of her came to my city. My former city. But you see, in these last weeks, it occurred to me that if my friends were loathsome, perhaps I needed to learn from my enemies."

"Shedemei is not your enemy," said Edhadeya.

"I have been *her* enemy, then, until now. I realized that all my loathing for angels had been taught to me from childhood, and I only continued to feel that way because it was the tradition of my people. I actually knew and liked several angels, including one rude old scholar in the king's house."

"Bego," said Edhadeya.

He looked at her in surprise. "But of course he would be better known here in the capital." Then he studied her face and knitted his brow. "Have we met before?"

"Once, long ago. You didn't want to listen to me."

He thought for a moment longer, then looked aghast. "I have been pouring out my heart to the king's daughter," he said.

"Except for Akmaro himself, you couldn't have spoken to anyone gladder to hear these words from you. My father honors you, in spite of his disagreement with you. When you see fit to tell him that those disagreements exist no longer, he will embrace you as a long lost brother. So will Ilihi, and so will Akmaro."

"I didn't want to listen to women," said Khideo. "I didn't want to live with angels. I didn't want diggers to be citizens. Now I have come to a school run by women to learn how to live with angels and diggers. I want to change my heart and I don't know how."

"Wanting to is the whole lesson; all the rest is practice. I will say nothing to my father or anyone else about who you are."

"Why didn't you name yourself to me?"

"Would you have spoken to me then?"

He laughed bitterly. "Of course not."

"And please remember that you also refrained from naming yourself to *me*."

"You guessed soon enough."

"And so did you."

"But *not* soon enough."

"And I say that no harm has been done." She rose from her chair. "You may attend any class, but you must do it in silence. Listen. You will learn as many lessons from the students as from the teachers. Even if you think they are hopelessly wrong, be patient, watch, learn. What matters right now is not correctness of opinion, but learning what opinions they might have. Do you understand?"

He nodded. "I'm not used to being deferent."

"Don't be deferent," she said testily—a tone of voice that Shedemei had taught her inadvertently. "Just be silent."

During the days that followed, Edhadeya watched—from a distance, but carefully. Some of the teachers clearly resented the presence of this man, but Khideo was not insensitive, and soon stayed away from their classes. The girls got used to him quickly, ignoring him in class, and gradually, shyly, including him at meals and in the courtyard. He would be asked to reach something on a high shelf. Some of the little girls even started climbing on him whenever he sat leaning against a tree, using him to get to branches that were otherwise out of reach. *Lissinits*, they called him—"ladder." He seemed to like the name.

Edhadeya came to value him for his own sake. Two things about him, though, weighed heavily on her mind. She kept thinking about how even a man like him, a confirmed bigot, could actually harbor a fundamental decency deep within. The outward pattern of his life didn't necessarily reflect what was inside him. It took terrible events to waken him, to get him to shuck off the man he seemed to be and reveal that inward self. But the decent self was there to be found.

The other thing that preyed upon her mind was what he had said about her brothers. The Unkept had held their meetings for thirteen years and they led to nothing. Then Akma succeeded in persuading all her brothers, all the king's sons, to reject belief in the Keeper and, more specifically, obedience to the religion of Akmaro. And from that time forward, the most evil men felt free to do their dark business.

That can't be what Akma intended. If he understood it the way Khideo does, wouldn't he stop?

I should talk to Mon, not Akma, she told herself—not noticing that she must already have decided to talk to Akma. If I could get him to break ranks with the others . . . but no, she knew that was impossible.

None of the brothers would betray the others; that was how they'd see it. No, it had to be Akma. If he changed his mind, they would change theirs. He would persuade them.

She kept hearing Luet's despairing voice: "There's nothing left in him, Edhadeya. Nothing there but hate." If that was true, then talking to Akma would be a waste of time. But Luet couldn't see into his heart. If Khideo had a spark of decency in him, couldn't Akma also? He was young, still; he had been damaged in childhood far more than Khideo had. The world had been misshapen for him ever since; if once he saw the truth, couldn't he choose to be a different man in a very different world?

These were the thoughts that drove her as one night she locked the school, leaving Khideo—no, Lissinits—as caretaker of it. Then, torch in hand, she walked in the brisk autumn air to her father's house. On the way she thought: What if there were no safety? If I were an earth woman—or man, or child—I wouldn't dare to make this walk in darkness, for fear of being set upon by cruel men who hate me, not because of anything I've done, but because of the shape of my body. For those people these streets are filled with terror, where all my life I've walked without fear, day and night. Can they truly be citizens, when they haven't the freedom to walk the city?

As she expected, Akma was in the king's house, in the library wing, where he slept most nights now. Not that he was asleep. He was up, reading, studying, jotting down notes to himself in the wax on a bark; one of dozens of barks covered with scribbling. "Writing a book?" she asked.

"I'm not a holy man," he said. "I don't write books. I write speeches." He swept the barks to one side. She liked the way he looked at her, as if he had been hoping she would come. She had his full attention, and his eyes didn't wander over her body the way most men's did. He looked into her eyes. She felt as though she ought to say something very clever or very wise, to justify his interest in her.

No, she told herself sternly. That's just one of his tricks. One of the things he does to win people over. And I'm not here to be won over. I came to teach, not to be taught.

No wonder I once loved him, if he always looked at me like that.

To her surprise, what she blurted out now was nothing like what she had come to say. "I used to love you," she said.

A sad smile came over his face. "Used to," he whispered. "Before there was any issue of belief."

"Is it an issue of belief, Akma?" she asked.

"For two people to love each other, they have to meet, don't they?

And two people who live in utterly different worlds have no chance of meeting."

She knew what he meant; they had had this conversation before, and he had insisted that while she lived in an imaginary world in which the Keeper of Earth watched over everyone, giving purpose to their lives, he lived in a real world of stone and air and water, where people had to find their own purposes.

"Yet we're meeting here," she said.

"That remains to be seen." His words were cold and distant, but his eyes searched her face. For what? What does he want to see? Some remnant of my love for him? But that is the one thing that I dare not show him because I dare not find it in myself. I can't love him, because only a monstrous, callous woman could love the man who caused so much pointless suffering.

"Have you been hearing the reports from the provinces?"

"There are many reports," said Akma. "Which did you have in mind?"

She refused to play along with his pretense of innocence. She waited.

"Yes, I've heard the reports," he said. "A terrible business. I wonder your father hasn't called in the military."

"To attack what army?" she asked scornfully. "You're smarter than that, Akma. An army is useless against thugs who melt away into the city and hide by wearing the clothing of respectable men of business, trade, or labor during the day."

"I'm a scholar, not a tactician," said Akma.

"Are you?" she asked. "I've thought about this a great deal, Akma, and when I look at you it's not a scholar that I see."

"No? What monster have you decided that I am?"

"Not a monster, either. Just a common thug. Your hands have torn holes in the wings of angel children. Diggers hide in terror during the night because they fear seeing your shadow come between them and the moonlight."

"Are you seriously accusing me of this? I have never raised my hand in violence against anyone."

"You caused it, Akma. You set them in motion, the whole army of them, the whole nasty, cruel, evil army of child-beaters."

He shuddered; his face contorted with some deep emotion. "You can't be saying this to me. You know that it's a lie."

"They're your friends. You're their hero, Akma. You and my brothers."

"I don't control them!" he said. He only barely controlled his voice.

"Oh, you don't?" she answered. "What, do they control *you* then?"

He rose from the table, knocking over his stool as he did. "If they did control me, Edhadeya, I'd be out preaching against Father's pathetic little religion right now. They beg, they plead. Ominer's all for doing it, Pour the bronze while it still flows, he tells me. But I refuse to lend my name to any of these persecutions. I don't want anybody hurt—not even diggers, despite what you think of me. And those angels, with holes torn in their wings—do you think I didn't hear that with the same rage as any decent person? Do you think I don't want the thugs who did that punished?" His voice trembled with emotion.

"Do you think they would have had the boldness to do it if it weren't for you?"

"I didn't invent this! I didn't create hatred and resentment of the diggers! It was our fathers who did it, when they changed the whole religious structure of the state to *include* the diggers as if they were people—"

"Thirteen years since they made those changes, and in all those years, nothing happened. Then you announce that you've 'discovered' that there is no Keeper—in spite of my true dream by which the Keeper saved the Zenifi! In spite of knowing that it was only by the power of the Oversoul that the very records from which you took your 'proof' were translated. You persuade my brothers—even Mon, I don't know how—even Aronha, who always used to see through silliness—and then, the moment that Father's heirs are united in their unbelief, the floodgates open."

"You might as well blame my mother, then. After all, she gave birth to me."

"Oh, I think there is blame before you. I found out, for instance, that Bego has been part of a longtime conspiracy against Akmaro's teachings. If you search your memory honestly, I wonder if you won't find that it was Bego who led you to your 'discovery' of the nonexistence of the Keeper."

"Bego isn't part of anything. He lives for his books. He lives in the past."

"And your father was inventing a new future, doing away with the past. Yes, Bego would hate that, wouldn't he? And he's never believed in the Keeper, I realize that now—insisting on a natural explanation for everything. No miracles, please—remember him saying that over and over? No miracles. The people of Akmaro escaped because it was in the best interest of the digger guards to let them go. The Keeper didn't make them sleep. Did anybody *see* them sleeping? No, Akmaro simply dreamed a dream. Go with the simplest explanation every time, that's what he taught us."

"He taught us that because it's true. It's intellectually honest."

"Honest? Akma, the simplest explanation of most of these stories is that the Keeper sends true dreams. The Keeper intervenes sometimes in people's lives. To avoid believing that you have to come up with the most convoluted, twisted, insulting speculations. You dare to tell me that my dream was only significant because it reminded people of the Zenifi, not because I was actually able to tell the difference between a true dream and a normal one. In order to disbelieve in the Keeper, you had to believe that I was and continue to be a self-deceptive fool."

"Not a fool," he said, with real pain in his expression. "You were a child. It seemed real to you then. So of course you remember it as being real."

"You see? What you call intellectual honesty I call self-deception. You won't believe me, when I stand before you in flesh and blood and declare to you what I saw—"

"What you hallucinated among the dreams of the night."

"Nor will you even believe the simple truth of what the ancient records say—that the Rasulum, just like the Nafari, were brought back to Earth after millions of years of exile on another world. No, you can't stick with the *simple* explanation that the people who wrote these things actually knew what they were talking about. You have to decide that the books were created by later writers who simply wrote down old legends that accounted for the divinity of the Heroes by claiming that they came from the heavens. Nothing can be read straight. Everything has to be twisted to fit your one, basic article of faith that there is no Keeper. You can't know it! You have no proof of it! And yet faith in that one premise—against which you have a thousand written witnesses and at least a dozen living ones, including me—faith in that one premise leads you to set in motion the chain of events that leads to children being mutilated in the streets of the cities and villages of Darakemba."

"Is this why you came?" asked Akma. "To tell me that my disbelief in your true dream really hurts your feelings? I'm sorry. I had hoped you would be mature enough to understand that reason has to triumph over superstition."

She hadn't touched him. Hadn't reached that spark of decency hidden deep inside. Because there was no such spark, she knew that now. He rejected the Keeper, not because he was hurt so badly as a child, but because he truly hated the world the Keeper wanted to create. He loved evil; that's why he no longer loved her.

Without another word, she turned to go.

"Wait," he said.

She stopped; foolishly, she allowed another spark of hope to brighten.

"It's not in my power to stop these persecutions, but your father can."

"You think he hasn't tried?"

"He's going about it all wrong," said Akma. "The civil guard won't enforce the law. So many of them are actually involved in the Unkept."

"Why don't you name names?" said Edhadeya. "If you truly meant what you said about wanting to stop the cruelty—"

"The men I know are all old and none of them are going out beating up children. Are you going to listen to me?"

"If you have a plan, I'll take it to Father."

"It's simple enough. The reason the Unkept feel such rage is because they only have two choices, either to join in with a state religion that forces them to associate with lower creatures—don't argue with me, I'm telling you what *they* think—"

"You think the same—"

"You've never listened to me long enough to know *what* I think, and it doesn't matter anyway. Listen now. They are rebelling out of a sense of helpless rage. They can't strike at the king, but they can strike at the priests and the diggers. But what if the king decreed that there no longer *was* a state religion?"

"Abolish the Houses of the Keeper!"

"Not at all. Let the Kept continue to assemble and share their beliefs and rituals—but on a completely voluntary basis. And let others who believe differently form their own assemblies, and without anyone's interference have *their* rituals and teachings. As many assemblies, as many beliefs as people want. And the government will simply look on and interfere with none of them."

"A nation should be of one heart and mind," said Edhadeya.

"My father destroyed all hope of that thirteen years ago," said Akma. "Let the king declare religious belief and assembly a private matter, with no public interest at all, and there will be peace."

"In other words, in order to save the Kept from attack, we should remove the last protections we have?"

"They *have* no protections, Edhadeya. You know it. The king knows it. He has found the limits of his authority. But once he has abolished all government sponsorship of a religion, he can make a law that no one can be persecuted because of their religious beliefs. That one will have teeth, because it will protect everyone equally. If the Unkept want to form an assembly of fellow believers, they will have protection. It will be in their interest to uphold that law. No more secret meetings. No more hidden societies. Everything out in the open. Suggest it to your father. Even if you don't think my idea has merit, he will. He'll see that it's the only way."

"He won't be fooled any more than I am," said Edhadeya. "This decree you propose is exactly what you've wanted all along."

"I didn't even think of it till yesterday," said Akma.

"Oh, pardon, I forgot that it took Bego a certain amount of time to get you to think up his ideas as if they were your own."

"Edhadeya, if my father's religion can't hold its own by the sheer power of its truthfulness, without any help from the government except to protect its members from violence, then it doesn't deserve to survive."

"I'll tell Father what you said."

"Good."

"But I'll also wager you right now, any stakes you say, that within a year you yourself will be the direct cause of more persecution of the Kept."

"You never knew me, if you think that's even possible."

"Oh, you'll have a lot of high-sounding reasons why people's suffering isn't *your* doing, because you've already proven your ability to deceive yourself without limit. But within a year, Akma, families will be weeping because of you."

"*My* family, probably, since they mourn for me as if I were dead," said Akma. He laughed, as if this were a joke.

"They aren't the only ones," said Edhadeya.

"I'm not dead," said Akma. "I have compassion, regardless of what you choose to believe about me. I remember my own suffering, I remember the suffering of others. I also remember that I loved you."

"I wish you'd forget it," said Edhadeya. "If it was ever true, you spoiled it long ago."

"I still do," he said. "I love you as much as I can love anyone. I think of you all the time, of the joy it would bring me if just once I could have you stand by my side the way Mother stands beside Father in all he does."

"She can do that, because what he does is good."

Akma nodded. "I know. Just don't pretend it's because of *my* beliefs that we aren't together. You're as stubborn as I am."

"No, Akma," she said. "I'm not stubborn. I'm just honest. I can't deny what I know."

"But you can *hide* what you know," said Akma, with a bitter smile.

"What does *that* mean?"

"In this whole conversation, you never bothered to mention to me that my sister is going to marry the most loathsome human being I ever knew."

"I assumed that your family had told you."

"I had to hear about it from Khimin."

"I'm sorry. That was Luet's choice. I'm sure. Perhaps she wanted not to cause you pain."

"She's dead to me now," said Akma. "She has given herself to the torturers and rejected me. As far as I'm concerned, you're doing the same."

"It's *you* that have given yourself to the torturers, Akma, and rejected *me*. Didul is no torturer. He is the man you should have been. What Luet loves in him is what she used to love in you. But it isn't there anymore."

Graciously, he allowed her the last word, staring off into space as she left the room.

A few minutes later, Bego and Mon heard terrible noises of crashing and breaking and rushed into the library, where they found Akma smashing stools against the table, splintering them. He was weeping, wordlessly sobbing, and they watched in horror as he roared like an animal and shattered every stick of small furniture in the room.

Mon noticed, though, that before his tirade began, he had carefully placed on a shelf all the barks he had been working on. Akma might have given himself over to rage, but he hadn't forgotten himself so completely as to waste the day's study.

Later, Akma offered a short and surly explanation. His sister was marrying one of the torturers. He wouldn't utter the name, but Mon knew that Luet had been in Bodika for the past few weeks and it wasn't hard to guess. Didul meant nothing to Mon. What hit him, hard, was the news that Luet was marrying at all. He had thought . . . he had meant to . . . when all this was over. When things were settled. When he wasn't ashamed to face her anymore. That was it, he realized now. That's why he was waiting. Because he couldn't talk to her, couldn't tell her how he felt, not when he had denied his truthsense. Not when every word he uttered was tainted by lies.

Not lies. They aren't *lies;* the things Akma and I believe are true. This feeling I have is an illusion, I know it is. I just couldn't bring myself to face Luet when I still had this feeling that I was a fraud. I just needed more time, more strength. More courage.

Now it doesn't matter. Now my conscience can be clear as I attack Akmaro's religion. When Father decrees that all religions are equal, that all assemblies have the protection of law, then we will go out in the open and everything will be clear. It's good that I don't have any bonds of affection to complicate matters. It's good that I go into this side by side with my brothers, with my friend, not dragged down by a woman who can't rise above that inner voice she has been trained to think of as the Keeper of Earth. Luet would have been wrong for me. I would have been wrong for her.

I would have been wrong for her. It was when that thought crossed his mind that finally the truthsense within him gave him a sense of calm. He was right, finally, in the eyes of the Keeper.

This was the most devastating realization of all: If the Keeper turned out to exist after all, he had judged Mon and found him unworthy to have the love of the woman he once wanted. But Mon couldn't escape the nagging doubt that if he hadn't been caught up in these plans of Akma's, things might have worked out differently. Would it have been so terrible to keep believing in the Keeper and to have Luet as my wife and live on in peace? Why couldn't Akma just leave me alone?

He drove these disloyal thoughts out of his mind, and said nothing of his feelings to anyone.

10

Ancient Ways

Akma looked for Bego all morning, but couldn't find him. He needed Bego's advice; the king had summoned him, and Akma had no idea what he might face. If he were to be charged with a crime, would Motiak call him into his private chamber like this? Akma needed counsel, and the only ones who could give it knew less than he did. Well, Aronha actually knew more about the running of the kingdom—knew more than anybody, since he had been training his whole life for it. But all Aronha could tell him was that he didn't think Akma was in any danger. "Father isn't the kind to bring you into chambers to charge you with a crime. He does things like that in the open, using normal process. It's got to be about the decree you suggested to Edhadeya last night."

"I didn't need you to tell me *that,*" said Akma. "I hoped I wouldn't have to go in cold and deal with something."

"Oh, just admit it that you're scared," said Khimin. "You know you've been bad, and the king has got to be angry enough to tear you to bits if he weren't such a kind benevolent despot." In recent weeks, Khimin had discovered in the ancient records that the city of Basilica had been governed by an elected council, and now he was constantly suggesting that the monarchy be abolished. No one paid any attention to him.

"Nothing is going to stop us from speaking tonight, is it?" asked Ominer. Since he had been trying to get them to go public for the past several months, during the worst of the persecution when it would have looked truly terrible to come out against the Kept, it was only natural that Ominer would now be worried that once again Akma might be talked into delaying.

"You'll be able to give your speech," said Akma. "As it's written, remember. Nobody is to start making things up on the wing." Ominer rolled his eyes.

Akma turned to Mon. "*You've* been quiet."

Mon looked up, startled out of his reverie. "Just thinking. We've been a long time waiting. Now we're going ahead. That's fine. It's a relief, don't you think?"

"What about my interview with your father today?" asked Akma.

"You'll do fine," said Mon. "You always do. They'll try to talk you out of this. You'll be polite and decline to change your mind. Simple. I'm only disappointed they didn't invite us along to watch." He smiled.

Akma heard Mon's speech. There was nothing obviously wrong with anything he said. But something still bothered him. There was something wrong with Mon himself. Had he become unreliable? What if tonight Mon got up and stated that he was standing with his father? A division among the sons of Motiak would destroy everything—everyone would assume that the loyal son would become the heir and that Akmaro's reforms would be permanent. That the Kept would always have the inside track in the government. Therefore it would be good business to be one of the Kept, and Akmaro's religion would remain dominant. Akma had no illusions—the doctrine he was going to be teaching, starting tonight, was not the sort of ideology that would stir souls; no one would die for this religion. It would only attract converts by promising a return to old tradition and by seeming to be the religion of the future—specifically, when Aronha became king. They were sure to become the dominant religion almost immediately, as far as sheer numbers were concerned. More important, the leadership of the new assembly would be the core of the future government. Akma could see to it that once Aronha became king, the only advice he would hear would be to carry war to the Elemaki. No more defensive posture—the Elemaki would be routed out of their hiding places in the high mountains. The land of Nafai would be redeemed in digger blood, and the place where Akma had been in bondage would now be a place where digger slaves toiled under the Nafari lash. Then Akma's triumph would be complete. His father's weakness in the face of persecution would be redeemed by Akma's courage.

It begins today. And Mon will stand with us. He's a true friend. Maybe he's so morose because he still harbored some hope of ending up with Luet. Well, that was the one good thing about Luet's decision to marry. It would free Mon to concentrate on the work at hand. More than any of the others, Mon had the skill to speak with as much fire and charm as Akma. More, really, because Akma knew he sounded like a scholar; Mon had the common touch, a boyish style of speech, a kind of energy that would speak to people at a deeper level than anything Akma could manage. Not that Akma didn't expect to do well. Despite his weaknesses as a speaker, he knew that people pretty much ended up in his bag by the end of a talk. He would look people in the eye as he was speaking and it felt almost as if a cord tied them together, and he had only to draw it in and he would own the person he spoke to, at least for the hour, for the night.

Almost like the powers of a raveler, as the ancient records described them. Only ravelers were always women, and besides, all that raveler business was superstition. The cords Akma imagined were only a metaphor, an unconscious visualization of his skill at establishing rapport with strangers.

It wouldn't work on the king, though. Akma knew that from experience. Whatever skill he had at influencing people only worked on those who were at least marginally receptive. Motiak never gave Akma the opportunity to work on him.

"Are you going to sit there moping all morning?" asked Ominer. "Father's waiting for you now—you're late."

"Yes," said Akma. "I was just thinking. Try it sometime, Ominer. It's almost as fun as swallowing air so you can belch. Something that I hope you won't be doing tonight."

"Give me some credit," said Ominer disgustedly.

Akma slapped him on the shoulder to show that he was teasing and they were still friends. Then he left, striding boldly through the rooms that separated the library from the king's private chamber.

He was the last to arrive; he had rather hoped to be. Motiak was there, of course, and, as Akma had expected, so were Father and Mother. Not Edhadeya, gratefully; but . . . Bego? Why was Bego there, with his otherself, bGo, sitting behind him and looking miserable? And this old man? Who was he?

"You know everyone," Motiak said. "Except perhaps Khideo. He knew you when you were a baby, but I don't think you've seen each other since then. Khideo used to be governor of the land that bears his name."

Akma saluted him and, at a wave from the king, sat down at the table. He kept his eyes on Motiak, though of course he couldn't help but wonder why Khideo was there. And Bego. Why were Bego and his brother there? Why had Bego avoided his gaze?

"Akma, you spend most of your time in my house, but I never see you," said Motiak.

"I'm a scholar," said Akma. "I'm grateful that you've given me such free access to your library."

"It's a shame that with all your study, you've come out knowing less than you did when you began." Motiak smiled sadly.

"Yes," said Akma. "It seems that the more I learn, the less I know. While the ignorant remain absolutely certain of their convictions."

Motiak's smile faded. "I thought you'd want to know that I'm issuing the decree that you suggested to Edhadeya. It seems to be a solution to the immediate problem. As you suggested."

"I'm grateful that I could be of service," said Akma. "I was . . . very unhappy with the way things were going."

"I can imagine," said Motiak. "Sometimes the things we set in motion don't work out as we planned. Do they, Akma?"

Akma recognized that the king was digging at him again, blaming him for the persecutions. He wasn't going to sit still for it. "I learned that lesson already, several times over," said Akma. "For instance, your religious reform of thirteen years ago hasn't had the effect you planned. Tragic, seeing now where it has led."

Motiak smiled again, only this time he was showing more of his real feelings: The smile was feral, the eyes dancing with rage. "I want you to know, Akma, that I'm not such a fool as you must think. I know what you've been doing, how you've been maneuvering around me. I watched as you won over my sons, and I did nothing, because I trusted them to have some sense. You bested me there—I overestimated them."

"I think not, sir," said Akma. "I think you underestimated them."

"I know what you think, Akma, and don't interrupt and contradict me again. Even though your entire strategy is based on the fact that someday I will die and someone will be king after me, please remember that I'm not dead yet and I *am* the king."

Akma nodded. He had to be careful. Let the king play out his little drama. Tonight Akma would have the last word.

"Your father and mother and I talked over the terrible things you went through as a child, and tried to figure out why the experience turned everyone else toward the Keeper of Earth, and turned you away. Your father was very apologetic, of course. He kept expressing his regret that his mistakes as a father should be causing innocent people to suffer."

Akma wanted to shout back at him that he did *not* cause the persecution, that if he had his way there would never be cause for any such thing to happen again. He also wanted to scream into his father's face, to hit him, to *hurt* him for daring to *apologize* to the king because his son turned out so badly. But he contained all these feelings, and when Motiak waited for him to respond, he only nodded and said, meekly, "I'm sorry that I'm such a disappointment to you all."

"What we couldn't figure out for the longest time was how your achievement in suborning my sons became so widely known, and so quickly. You never seemed to be in contact with anyone among the Unkept. You hardly left the library."

"I'm a scholar. I've talked to no one but your family and my family and a few other scholars."

"Yes, very carefully done, very clever—or so we thought. How is Akma doing it, we thought. And then we realized, Akma isn't doing it. This wasn't Akma's idea."

Motiak looked toward Khideo. It was the old soldier's cue. "When I was here to consult with the king immediately after our rescue, I made contact with someone who shared some of my views. The opinions of the Zenifi—that humans should not live with either of the other toolmaking species. Or I should say, he made contact with me, since he knew my views and I couldn't have known his until he spoke to me. Since then, he has been my link with the king's house, and what he told me, I told my fellow Zenifi. Most important, he promised me then, thirteen years ago, that he would deliver all of the king's sons. As soon as he achieved it, we would spread the word, so that people would know that all of Akmaro's reforms were temporary, and the old order would be restored when one of you inherited the throne."

Thirteen years ago? That was impossible. He hadn't come up with this plan until after he had realized there was no Keeper.

Motiak looked at Bego. Quietly, the old archivist began to speak. "I tried to work directly with Aronha, but he was too much his father's son. And Mon couldn't get over his self-loathing. Ominer—too young, and not really bright enough to grasp things. Khimin—definitely too young. For a while I tried to work with Edhadeya, but her delusions about true dreams were too strong."

Motiak growled, "Not delusions."

"I have confessed to you, Motiak," said Bego defiantly. "I have not said that I agree with you." He turned back to Akma. "You, Akma. You understood, the brightest boy I ever taught. And I saw that you had a way of winning people to your point of view. As long as you're with them. A talent for it, that's what you have, a talent for persuasion, and I realized that I didn't have to persuade Motiak's boys. I only had to persuade you and you'd do the rest."

"You didn't persuade me of anything. I figured it out myself."

Bego shook his head. "It is the essence of teaching, that the student discovers everything for himself. I made sure that you reached the conclusion that there was no Keeper, and you leapt from there to everything I might have hoped for. And your deep hatred of the diggers, that helped, of course."

"So you thought I was a puppet?" asked Akma.

"Not at all," said Bego. "I thought you were the finest student I ever had. I thought you could change the world."

"What Bego is not telling you," said Motiak, "is that his actions constitute treason and oath-breaking. Khideo has been studying at Shedemei's school the past while. A great deal of moral philosophy. He went to bGo, and then together Khideo and bGo persuaded Bego to come join them in confessing to me."

"I'm sorry that Khideo and bGo and Bego decided to do something so unnecessary and inappropriate," said Akma. "But as Bego can also tell you, the first time *we* learned that he had any outside contacts was *after* the persecutions began, when he kept urging us to speak openly against the Kept. You will notice that we did not do it. We utterly refused to do anything that might be construed as support of the persecutions."

"I'm quite aware of that," said Motiak. "That's why you aren't under the same charges as Bego and Khideo."

"If you think you can silence me by threatening the death penalty for Bego, you're mistaken," said Akma. "It's me you'll have to kill."

Motiak leapt to his feet, leaned across the table, and slapped the surface right in front of Akma. "I'm not killing anyone, you stupid little boy! I'm not threatening anyone! I'm letting you see the truth about what's been going on!"

"Very well," said Akma quietly. "I see that Bego thought he controlled me. I see that Khideo believed it also. Unfortunately, it was never true. Because I formed my plan long before any of you think. I planned it sitting on a hill in a place called Chelem. Watching my father shower love on torturers and tormentors, I took a solemn vow that I would someday come back to that place with an army at my back, to conquer and subdue the Elemaki. The land where I and my people were enslaved and mistreated will fall under the power of the Nafari, and the diggers will be driven out. They and the humans who choose to live with them will have no place in the gornaya. That was the vow I made then. And all that has happened since has merely been a part of accomplishing it. What do I care about religion? I learned from my father that religious stories are just a way to get people to do what you want—the way he did with the Pabulogi. The tragedy of my father is that he believes his own stories."

Motiak smiled. "Thank you, Akma. You've given me what I needed."

Akma smiled back. "I've given you nothing that you can use. Your sons and I have already planned the military strategy that will bring us victory. We've studied the reports of the spies. You discard all the useful information because you have no interest in carrying war to the enemy —but we use it, we learn from it. The Elemaki are divided into three weak and quarrelsome kingdoms. We can defeat them one at a time. It's an excellent plan, and there is nothing treasonable about it. Whatever role I play will be as the true and loyal servant of the king. That you will not be the king to whom I bring such glory is sad, but that is your choice, sir. By all means, announce to your people that this is my plan— to defeat and destroy our enemies and bring peace to the whole land. See how unpopular it makes me."

"The people don't love war," said Motiak. "You misjudge them if you think they do."

"You misjudge them, not me," said Akma. "They hate the constant vigilance. They hate knowing that the Elemaki raiders know they can return beyond our borders and we won't pursue them and destroy them. Why do you think there was so much loathing against the diggers? Why do you think the civil guard wouldn't obey you when you commanded them to stop the violence? The difference between us, sir, is that I will channel that rage against the real enemy. Your policies channeled it against children."

Motiak stood. "There is no law requiring me to appoint one of my sons to succeed me."

Akma also stood. "And there is no law requiring the people to choose the successor that you name. The people love Aronha. They will love him all the more when they see that he—that *we*—intend to restore the old order, the old ways."

"All that you plan, all of it, and the fact you dare to fling it in my face —it all depends on the fact that I'm a gentle king and don't use my power arbitrarily."

"Yes," said Akma. "I count on that. I also count on the fact that you love this kingdom and you won't needlessly plunge it into civil war or anarchy. You will appoint Aronha as your successor. And by the time that day comes—and we hope it is *not* soon, sir, no matter what you might imagine—by that time we hope, we *believe*, that you will have come to realize that our plan is ultimately the best for your people. You will wish us well."

"No," said Motiak. "That I will never do."

"It's your decision."

"You think you've outmaneuvered me, don't you?"

"Not at all. My only enemy is the nation of diggers and loathsome ratlike humans in the high mountains. I had nothing to do with the trials that led to the legal situation that opened the floodgates of persecution, and you know it. I was never one of the players in *that* miserable game, and I reject it. But this decree you're making now, yes—that *is* a maneuver. But I didn't notice you coming up with anything better. It seems, however, that my reward for suggesting the solution to your problems is to come to this room to be called a puppet, a traitor, a torturer of children, and every other vile thing you can think of. I will not forget that my mother and father sat and listened to all of this without once, not once, raising their voices in my defense."

Bego laughed. "You *are* the man I thought you'd be, Akma!"

A look from Motiak brought silence to the table.

"Akma," said Father, quietly. "I beg you for mercy."

No, don't do this, Akma said silently. Don't humiliate yourself before me, the way you humiliated yourself before the Pabulogi.

"I have searched my memory and my conscience," said Father, "trying to imagine how I might have acted differently back in Chelem. I beg you to tell me now—what should I have done? Befriending the sons of Pabulog, teaching them the way of the Keeper, the doctrines of Binaro—that won our freedom. It brought us here. How else could I have done it? What should I have done?"

"I don't dwell in the past," said Akma, trying to fend off the embarrassing question.

"So you can't think of anything better I could have done, either," said Father. "No, I didn't think you could. Hatred and anger aren't rational. Just because you know I had no other choice doesn't make the anger go away. I understand that. But you're a man now. You can put away childish things."

"Is this your idea of an apology?" asked Akma lightly. "To call me childish?"

"Not an apology," said Akmaro. "A warning."

"A warning? What, from the man who teaches peace?"

"You claim that you are repelled by what the persecutors have done. But in all your wisdom, in all your planning, you seem not to realize that the course you are embarking on will cause suffering on a scale that will make these persecutions look like a holiday."

"The Elemaki attacked us. Again and again. No, I won't shed any tears over their suffering."

"A schoolboy looks at war and sees maps and flags," said Akmaro.

"Don't tell me about war. You've *seen* as little of it as I have, and I've read more."

"Don't you think Motiak and I have talked about war? If we thought it could be done quickly—the Elemaki defeated and destroyed in a single campaign—do you think we would shrink from it? My love for peace isn't mindless. I know the Elemaki attack us. Motiak feels every blow to his people as if they fell on his own body. The reason the king has refused to attack the enemy strongholds is because we would lose. Without doubt, without question, we would be destroyed. Not a soldier would live to reach the ancient land of Nafai. The high valleys are a death trap. But you'll never get that far, Akma. Because the Keeper rejects your plan from the start. This land belongs to all three peoples equally. That is what the Keeper decrees. If we accept that law and live together in peace, then we will prosper here. If we reject it, my son, then our bones will bleach in the sun like the bones of the Rasulum."

Akma shook his head. "After all these years, do you still think you can frighten me with warnings about the Keeper?"

"No," said Akmaro. "I don't think I can frighten you at all. But I have a duty to tell you what I know. Last night I had a true dream."

Akma groaned inwardly. Oh, Father, don't embarrass yourself even further. Can't you handle your defeat like a man?

"The Keeper has chosen you. He recognized you in childhood and prepared you for your role in life. No one has been born before you among the Nafari with such intelligence, such wisdom, such power."

Akma laughed, trying to deflect such obvious flattery. "Is that why you treat my ideas with such respect?"

"Nor has there been anyone with such sensitivity. When you were little, it was turned to compassion. The blows that fell on Luet hurt you more than those than fell on you. You felt the pain of everyone around you, all the people. But along with the sensitivity came pride. You had to be the one to save the others, didn't you? That's the crime that you can't forgive us for. That it was your mother and not you who faced down Didul that day in the fields. That it was I, not you, who taught them, who won them over. Everything you longed for happened—our people were saved, the torment stopped. The one thing you couldn't bear, though, was that you felt you had nothing to do with saving them. And that's what your dream of war is all about. Even though the people have already been saved, you can't rest until you lead an army to redeem them."

Mother spoke up now, her voice thick with emotion. "Don't you know that it was your courage that sustained us all?"

Akma shook his head. It was almost unbearable, the embarrassment of listening to their pathetic attempts at trying to get him to see things their twisted way. Why were they doing this to themselves? To call him intelligent, and then not realize he's clever enough to see through their stories.

Father went on. "The Keeper is watching you, to see what you'll do. The moment of choice will come to you. You'll have all the information you need to make your choice."

"I've made my choices," said Akma.

"You haven't even been given the choice yet, Akma. You'll know when it comes. On the one hand will be the plan of the Keeper—to create a people of peace, who celebrate the differences between people of earth and sky and all that is between. On the other hand will be your pride, and the pride of all humans, the ugliest side of us, the thing that makes grown men tear holes in the wings of young angels. That pride in you makes you reject the Keeper because the Keeper rejected you, so that you pretend not to believe in him. Your pride requires war and death, demands that because a few diggers beat you and your people when you were a child, all diggers must be driven from their homes. If you choose that pride, if you choose destruction, if you reject the Keeper, then the Keeper will regard this experiment as a failure. The way the Rasulum failed before us. And we will end up like the Rasulum. Do you understand me, Akma?"

"I understand you. I believe none of it, but I understand you."

"Good," said Father. "Because I also understand *you.*"

Akma laughed derisively. "Good! Then you can tell me which way I'll choose and save me the trouble!"

"When you are at the point of despair, my son, when you see destruction as the only desirable choice, then remember this: The Keeper loves us. Loves us all. Values each life, each mind, each heart. All are precious to him. Even yours."

"How kind of him."

"His love for you is the one constant, Akma. He knows that you have believed in him all along. He knows that you have rebelled against him because you thought you knew how to shape this world more wisely than he. He knows that you have lied to everyone, over and over again, including yourself, especially yourself—and I tell you again that even knowing all of this, if you will only turn to him, he will bring you back."

"And if I don't, then the Keeper will wipe out everybody, is that it?" asked Akma.

"He will withdraw his protection, and we will then be free to destroy ourselves."

Akma laughed again. "And this is the being that you tell me is filled with *love?*"

Father nodded. "Yes, Akma. So much love that he will let us choose for ourselves. Even if we choose our own destruction and break his heart."

"And you saw all this in a dream?" asked Akma.

"I saw you at the bottom of a hole, so deep that no light reached there. I saw you weeping, crying out in agony, begging the Keeper of Earth to blot you out, to destroy you, because it would be better to die than to live with your shame. I thought, Yes, that is how much pride Akma has, that he would rather die than be ashamed. But beside you in that dark hole, Akma, I saw the Keeper of Earth. Or rather heard him, saying, Give me your hand, Akma. I'm holding out my hand to lift you out of this place. Take my hand. But you were wailing so loud that you couldn't hear him."

"I have bad dreams, too, Father," said Akma. "Try eating your supper earlier, so your food can fully digest before you go to bed."

The silence around the table sounded like triumph to Akma.

Motiak looked at Father, who nodded once. Mother burst into tears. "I love you, Akma," she said.

"I love you too, Mother," he answered. And to Motiak he said, "And you, sir, I honor and obey as my king. Command me to be silent and I will say nothing; I only ask that you also command my father to be silent. But if you let him speak, let me speak."

"That's what the decree says," Motiak answered mildly. "No state religion. Complete freedom in matters of belief. Freedom to form assemblies of believers. The leaders of the assemblies chosen however they see fit. No high priest appointed by the king. And a strict ban on persecuting anyone because of their beliefs. So . . . your father tells me that we've accomplished all that he hoped for here. You can go now."

Akma felt victory glowing in him like a summer sunrise, warm and sweet. "Thank you, sir." He turned and started to leave.

As he reached the door, Motiak said, "By the way, you and my sons are banned from my house. As long as you are not among the Kept, none of you will see my face again until you look at my dead body." His voice was mild and even, but the words stung.

"I'm sorry that that's your decision," said Akma. Then, as an afterthought, he asked, "What will happen to Bego?"

He saw Bego look to him with mournful eyes.

"That," said Motiak, "is really none of your business."

Akma left then, closing the door behind him. He walked briskly back toward the library, where Aronha and Mon, Ominer and Khimin were waiting. Their banishment from the house would sting, of course. But Akma knew he could easily turn their dismay into a fresh resolve. Tonight would be triumphant. The beginning of the end for all this foolishness of using dreams to make decisions for a kingdom. And, more important, the beginning of justice throughout the gornaya.

There will be peace and freedom, when all is done, thought Akma. And they will remember that I was the one who made them safe. And not just safe while I live to lead them in war, but safe forever because their enemies will be utterly destroyed. What has the mythical Keeper ever done to compare with *that*?

Shedemei arrived back in Darakemba that day, specifically so she could attend Akma's first assembly that night. She already knew from what others had told her—with the Oversoul filling in gaps in her knowledge—pretty much what Akma and the sons of Motiak would be saying and what it would mean. But she had come to Earth to live for a while in society, hadn't she? So she had to experience the great events, even if the thought of what they implied about the nature of people made her faintly ill. Therefore she attended, bringing along a few of her students and a couple of faculty members. Voozhum wanted to come, but Shedemei had to counsel her against it. "There'll be many there who persecuted the Kept," she said. "They hate earth people, and we can't be sure we could protect you. I won't let any diggers come with us tonight."

"Oh, I misunderstood," said Voozhum. "I heard it was going to be Edhadeya's brothers speaking. They were always very good boys, very kind to me." Shedemei didn't have the heart to explain to Voozhum how much those boys had changed. Voozhum didn't have to keep up on current events. Her subject matter was the ancient traditions of the earth people, and she could afford to miss tonight's speeches.

When the meeting finally began, the order of speakers surprised her. Aronha was the figure of greatest fame and prestige, beloved by the nation since his childhood. Shouldn't he have been held for last? No. When she heard him speak, Shedemei understood. He was a good speaker of the pep-talk variety, but incapable of making substantial issues clear. Kings didn't have to be able to teach, only to decide and inspire; Aronha would be a good king. All he said, really, was that he loved his father and respected his father's religious beliefs, but that he also respected the ancient traditions of the Nafari people and was grateful that now more than one system of beliefs and rituals would be able to coexist. "I will always have great respect for the Assembly of the Kept because of my father's great love for the teachings of the martyr Binaro. But we are gathered here today to form another assembly, which we will call the Assembly of the Ancient Ways. We are dedicated to preserve the old public rituals that have been part of our lives since the days of the Heroes. And unlike others, we have no desire to make our assembly an exclusive one. We welcome any of the Kept who wish also to honor the old ways. You can believe all the teachings of Binaro and still be welcome in our assembly. All we ask is respect for each other and for the preservation of the patterns of life that made Darakemba great and kept us at peace among ourselves for so many centuries."

Ah, such cheers! And how the people murmured about Aronha's wisdom and tolerance. He will be a wise king, a great king. How many of them understand, Shedemei wondered, that by "old ways" he means the re-enslavement or expulsion of the diggers? No true Kept could possibly join with them in that program—but by inviting them anyway, Aronha was able to create the illusion that their assembly could include everyone.

And how many realize, thought Shedemei, that the peace within Darakemba was only three generations old, for until the time of Motiak's grandfather the nation of the Nafari had existed high in the farthest reaches of the gornaya and only joined with the people of Darakemba less than a century ago? And even at that there has always been discontent among the old aristocracy of Darakemba, who felt displaced and devalued by the imposition of the Nafari ruling elite over them. No, there'll be no discussion of *that.* Akma may talk about wanting to be strictly honest about history, but he'll bend the truth however he needs to build his support.

Mon's speech was much more specific, talking about the rituals that they would attempt to preserve. "We ask the old priests to come forward over the next few weeks to take their places in these rituals. Some of the rituals, of course, require the presence of the king; those will not be performed until and unless our beloved Motiak chooses to lead us in them." Not said, but understood perfectly by everyone there, was the fact that if Motiak never chose to lead those rituals, Aronha would perform them when he became Aronak at some future time. "We will keep the old holidays with feasting rather than fasting," said Mon, "with joy rather than melancholy."

That's right, thought Shedemei. Make sure that people understand they won't be required to sacrifice anything in order to belong to your assembly. A religion that is all sweetness, but no light; all form, but no substance; all tradition, but no precept.

Ominer spent his time talking about membership in the assembly. "Add your names to the rolls—no need to do it today, you can do it anytime in the next few weeks. Enrollment will take place in the houses of the priests. We ask you to donate what you can to help us pay for land where we can assemble and to help support the schools that we will establish to help raise up our children in the old ways, as we were raised in the king's house. One thing you can be sure of—once you are admitted to the rolls of the Assembly of the Ancient Ways, you will *never* be turned out just because you have a difference of opinion with some priest."

Another jab at the Assembly of the Kept. As for donations, Shedemei almost laughed aloud at the cynicism of it. The Kept were mostly poor, and all of them donated labor and money at great sacrifice to pay for buildings and for the teachers in their schools. But they did it because of the fervency of their belief and the depth of their commitment. The Assembly of the Ancient Ways, however, would never get that level of contribution from its common members. Yet they would not lack for funds, because all the wealthy people of business and property would know that contributions to the Ancient Ways would be noticed and remembered by the future king and his brothers. Oh, there would be no budgetary shortages, and the priests who used to be salaried before Motiak's reforms would find themselves with tidy incomes once again. None of this nonsense of priests working among the common people! This would be a high-class priesthood.

Khimin, being young, fumbled a little with his speech, but the audience seemed to find his mistakes endearing. He had been relegated merely to affirming his agreement with all that his brothers had said and then announcing that as soon as the Assembly was well organized in Darakemba, Akma and the sons of Motiak would be traveling to every major city in every province to speak to the people there and organize the Ancient Ways wherever they were invited to do so. Unfortunately, they had no money of their own, and it wouldn't be right to use their fathers' wealth to sustain a religion that they didn't approve of, so Khimin and his brothers and their friend Akma would be dependent upon the hospitality of others in those faraway places.

Shedemei wondered whether they would live long enough to stay a night in every house that would be pathetically eager to take them in. Rich families that would never give a flatcake to a beggar would plead for the chance to show generosity to these boys who had never known a day of want in their lives.

<Be generous, Shedemei. Akma has known want.>

And learned nothing from it, Shedemei said silently.

<Akma isn't a fool, either. They'll stay in poor men's houses often enough to make their point, and in the houses of angels as well as humans. They aren't going to let Akmaro and Motiak hold the high ground on anything, if they can help it.>

Among them, the four sons of Motiak had taken only half an hour. It was plain when Akma rose to speak that the people had no idea of what to expect from him. The sons of the king were celebrities; but Akma was the son of Akmaro, and the rumors about him had been mostly negative. Some disliked him because they resented his father's religious reforms. Some disliked him because he had repudiated his father's life's work—which the sons of Motiak had *not* done, even reaffirming their absolute loyalty to their father's kingship. Others disliked him because he was a scholar and reputed to be one of the most brilliant minds that frequented the library in the king's house—there was a natural suspicion of those with too much book-learning. And others didn't want to like him because they had heard he didn't believe in the Keeper of Earth, which was an absurd position for someone to take when he was about to start a new religion.

Akma surprised them. He surprised Shedemei, for that matter, and she had known from the Oversoul exactly what he planned to say. What Shedemei wasn't prepared for was the vigor in his way of speaking, the excitement in his voice. Yet he used no extravagant gestures, merely looked out into the audience with such piercing intensity that everyone felt, at one time or another, that Akma was looking right at them, talking straight to them, that he knew their heart.

Even Shedemei felt his gaze on her when he said, "Some of you have heard that I don't believe in the Keeper of Earth. I'm glad to tell you that this is not true. I don't believe in the Keeper the way some have talked about him—that primitive idea of an entity who sends dreams to certain people but not to others, playing favorites with the men and women of the world. I don't believe in a being who makes plans for us and gets angry when we don't carry them out, who rejects some people because they don't obey him quickly enough or don't love their enemies better than they love their friends. I don't believe in some all-knowing being who made humans and angels into lovers of light and air, and then demanded that they live nose-to-tail with tunnel-dwelling creatures of grime and muck—surely this Keeper of Earth could do a better job of planning than *that!*"

They laughed. They loved it. A little abuse of the diggers—that proved his religion was going to be Just Fine.

"No, the Keeper of Earth that I believe in is the great force of life that dwells in all things. When the rain falls, that is the Keeper of Earth. When the wind blows, when the sun shines, when maize and potatoes grow, when water flows clear over the rocks, when fish leap into the net, when babies cry out their first joyful song of life—that is the Keeper of Earth that I believe in! The natural order of things, the laws of nature—you don't have to think about them to obey them! You don't have to have special dreamers who will tell you what the Keeper wants you to do. The

Keeper wants you to eat—you know that because you're hungry! The Keeper wants you to laugh—you know that because you enjoy laughing! The Keeper wants you to have babies—you know that because you not only love these little ones, you even love the way you go about getting them! The messages of the Keeper of Earth come to everyone, and except for the sweet and ancient stories and rituals that bind us together as a people, there is nothing for us to teach you that you don't learn just as well by simply being alive!"

Shedemei tried desperately to think of retorts for all the things he said, the way she had done with the sons of Motiak, but she found the spell of his voice so compelling that she couldn't answer. He owned her mind as long as he chose to speak to her. She knew that she didn't believe him; she just couldn't remember, for the moment, *why*.

He went on and on, but his speech didn't seem long. Every word was fascinating, moving, funny, joyful, wise—you dared not miss any of it. Never mind that Shedemei knew that he was lying, that even *he* did not believe half of what he said. It was still beautiful; it was still music; the rhapsody of his words swept the people with it like a current in the icy water of Tsidorek, numbing them even as it moved them.

She only won her freedom from the magic of his speech when, near the end, he proposed his ultimate solution to the problem of the diggers. "We have all been sickened by the acts of wanton cruelty over the past months," said Akma. "Every such action was against the laws that already existed, and we are glad that our wise king has made the laws even stronger by forbidding any persecution of people because of their religious beliefs. Nevertheless, there would have been no persecution if there had been no diggers living unnaturally among the men and women of Darakemba."

There it was—the moment when Shedemei recoiled from his words and stopped finding his voice beautiful. But the others around her were not so clear minded, and she had to nudge the other teachers from her school and glare at them to make sure they knew that they should not believe what he was saying now.

"Is it the diggers' fault that they are here? It was certainly never their intention! Some of them have lived in this area since the ancient days when diggers and angels always lived near each other—so that diggers could steal the children of angels and eat them in their dank warrens. One can hardly list that as a qualification for citizenship! Most diggers that live in Darakemba, however, are here because they or their parents took part in a raiding party on the borders of our land, trying to steal from hardworking men and women the fruits of their labors. Either they were captured in bloody battle or were taken when a retaliatory raid captured a digger village; then they were brought here as slaves. That was a mistake! That was wrong! Not because the diggers are not suited to slavery—by nature they *are* slaves, and that is how the rulers of the Elemaki treat them all. No, our mistake was that even as slaves, even as trophies of victory, it was wrong to bring diggers into a nation of people, where some would be deceived. Yes, some would think that because the diggers were capable of a kind of speech, they were therefore capable of thinking like, feeling like, acting like *people.* But we must not be deceived. Our eyes can tell us that these are lies. What human hasn't rejoiced to see an angel in flight or hear the eveningsong of our brothers and sisters! What angel has not delighted in the learning that the humans brought with them, the powerful tools that can be shaped and wielded by strong human arms! We can live together, help each other—though I am not saying that our brothers in Khideo may not continue to deprive themselves of the good company of the sky people if they so choose."

Another appreciative laugh from the audience.

"But do you rejoice to see the buttocks of a digger flash in the air as he burrows into the earth? Do you love to hear their whining, grating voices, to see their claws touching food that you are expected to eat? Isn't it a mockery when you see their spadelike fingers clutching a book? Don't you long to leave the room if one of them should ever attempt to sing?"

Each line of abuse was greeted with a laugh.

"They didn't choose to live among us! And now, stricken with the poverty that must always be the lot of those unequal to the mental requirements of real citizenship, they haven't the means to leave! And why should they? Life in Darakemba, even for a digger, is vastly better than life among the Elemaki! Yet we must have respect for the Keeper of Earth and obey the natural repugnance that is the Keeper's clear message to us. The diggers must leave! But not by force! Not by violence! We are civilized! *We* are not Elemaki. I have felt the lash of the Elemaki diggers on my back, and I would rather give my life than see any human or angel treat even the vilest digger in that way! Civilized people are above such cruelty."

The people cheered and applauded. Aren't we all noble, thought Shedemei, to repudiate the persecution even as Akma is about to tell us a new way to begin it again, only more effectively.

"Are we helpless, then? What about those diggers who understand the truth and *want* to leave Darakemba, yet can't afford the cost of the journey? Let us help them understand that they must go. Let us help them kindly on their way. First, you must realize that the only reason diggers stay here is because we keep paying them to do work that poor and struggling humans and angels would gladly do. Of course you can pay the diggers less, since they only need to dig a hole in the bank of a creek in order to have a house! But you must make the sacrifice—for their sake as well as our own!—and stop hiring them for any work at all. Pay a little more to have a *man* dig that ditch. Pay a little more to have a *woman* wash your clothes. It will be worth the cost because you won't have to pay to have bad work redone!"

Applause. Laughter. Shedemei wanted to weep at the injustice of his lie.

"Don't buy from digger tradesmen. Don't even buy from human or angel shopkeepers, if the goods were made using digger labor. Insist that they guarantee that all the work was done by men and women, not by lower creatures. But if a digger wants to sell his land, then yes, buy it—at a fair price, too. Let them all sell their land, till not one patch of earth in Darakemba has a digger's name attached to it."

Applause. Cheers.

"Will they go hungry? Yes. Will their poverty grow worse? Yes. But we will *not* let them starve. I spent years of my childhood with constant hunger because our digger slavedrivers wouldn't give us enough to eat! We are not like them! We will gather food, we will use funds donated to the Assembly of the Ancient Ways, and we will *feed* every digger in Darakemba if we have to—but only long enough for them to make the journey to the border! And we will feed them only as long as they are on their way! They can have food from the larders of the Ancient Ways—but only at the edge of the city, and then they must walk, they and all their families, along the road toward the border. At stations along the way, we'll have a safe place for them to camp, and food for them to eat, and they will be treated with kindness and courtesy—but in the morning they will rise and eat and be on their way, ever closer to the border. And at the end, they will be given enough to walk on for another week, to find a place within the lands of the Elemaki, where they belong. Let them do their labor there! Let them preserve the precious 'culture' that certain people prize so much—but not in Darakemba! Not in Darakemba!"

As he no doubt planned, the audience took up the chant; it was only with difficulty that he quieted them again so he could finish. The speech did not go on much longer after that—only long enough for him to rhapsodize again about the beauty of the ancient ways of the Nafari and the Darakembi, about how loving and inclusive the Assembly of the Ancient Ways would be, and how only among the Ancient, as they would call themselves, could true justice and kindness be found, for diggers as well as angels and humans. They screamed their approval, chanted his name, cried out their love for him.

<Akma knew he would be good at this, but even he is quite surprised by all this adulation.>

He doesn't have mine, Shedemei answered silently.

<For what it's worth, most people weren't with him in the really nasty things he said about diggers. But he does have their support for the relocation program he outlined. For the moment, at least, it sounds like a simple and humane solution to most of those who came.>

And how will it sound to the earth people?

<Like the end of the world.>

Motiak will stop it, won't he?

<He'll try, I'm sure. His agents are already reporting to him on what his sons and Akma said. They'll study the law. But he can't oppose this plan forever, if the people really want it.>

Doesn't he see that to take away their livelihood and drive them from their homes so they can survive at all is every bit as cruel, in the long run?

<Don't argue with me. Argue with him. Maybe if you told people who you are and made a demonstration of the power of the cloak. . . .>

The Keeper doesn't work like that. He wants people to follow him because they love his way.

<Well, when Nafai gave his oldest brothers a bit of a shock, he got their cooperation for long enough to get the starship refurbished.>

And they were back to plotting murder as quickly as they could.

"Let's go home, Shedemei," said one of the students.

"He was so wonderful," said one of the others, shaking her head ruefully. "Too bad that everything he said was pure shit."

Shedemei immediately reproved her coarse wording, but then laughed and hugged her. The students of her school might have been caught up in the moment, but they had been truly educated and not just schooled—they were able to hear something they had never before, analyze it, and decide for themselves that it was worthless, dangerous, vile. . . .

Maybe her student *had* used the only possible word for it.

When they got home to the school it was after dark. The girls rushed in to tell the others what had been said at the meeting. Shedemei spent those first few minutes going to the teachers who happened to be earth people. She explained about Akma's strategy of boycotting diggers to compel them to leave. "Your place here is safe," she said. "And I will stop charging tuition for all our students, so their parents can spare more to hire diggers and help those they cannot hire. We will do all we can."

She didn't pass into the courtyard until the students who had heard the speech were telling about Akma's statements about the diggers. They had good recall; some of it they reported word for word. Edhadeya was one of those who had not gone; as she told Shedemei, she didn't know if she would be able to control herself, and besides, she had to prove that one of Motiak's children, at least, had not lost all decency. Now, though, as she heard Akma's statements about inferior digger intelligence, about their unfitness for civilized society, she did lose control. "He knew Voozhum! Not as well as my brothers, but he knew her! He knows that everything he's saying is a lie, he knows it, he knows it!" She was flinging her arms about, ranting, almost screaming. The children were frightened, a little, but also admired this display of passion—it was a far cry from the brusque but even temper that Shedemei always showed.

Shedemei went to her and wrapped her in her arms. "It hurts the worst when evil is done by those we love," she said.

"How can I answer his lies? How can I stop people from believing him?"

"You're already doing it. You teach. You speak wherever you can. You refuse to tolerate it when others echo these vile things in your presence."

"I hate him!" Edhadeya said, her voice rough with emotion. "I will never forgive him, Shedemei. The Keeper tells us to forgive our enemies but I won't. If that makes me evil also, then I'm evil, but I will hate him forever for what he did tonight."

One of the students, confused, said, "But he didn't actually *do* anything, did he? He only talked."

Shedemei, still holding Edhadeya close to her, said, "If I point to a man walking down the street, and I scream to everyone, 'There he is, there's the man who molested my little girl! There's the man who raped and tortured and killed my daughter, I know him, that's the man!'—if I *say* that, and the crowd tears him to pieces, and yet I knew all along that he was not the man, that it was all a lie, was it just talk, or did I *do* something?"

Letting them think about this lesson, she led Edhadeya into the school to the cubicle, just like all the other cubicles, where she slept. "Don't be troubled, Edhadeya. Don't let this tear you apart."

"I hate him," she muttered again.

"Now that the others can't hear, let me insist that you face the truth of your own heart. The reason you're so angry, the reason you feel so betrayed that you can't control your emotions, they burst your dignity, they make you almost crazy with grief—the reason for that, my dear friend, my fellow teacher, my daughter, my sister, is that you still love him and that is what you can't forgive."

"I don't love him," said Edhadeya. "That's a terrible thing to accuse me of."

"Cry yourself to sleep, Dedaya. You have classes to teach in the morning. And I'll need a lot of other help from you as well. Tonight you can grieve and brood and curse and rage until you wear yourself out. But we all need you to be useful after that."

In the morning, Edhadeya was useful indeed, calm and hardworking, wise and compassionate as always. But Shedemei could see that the turmoil had not subsided in her heart. You were named well, she thought—named for Eiadh, who made the tragic error of loving Elemak. But you haven't made all of Eiadh's mistakes. You have been constant of heart, where Eiadh kept deciding she loved Nafai more. And you may have chosen more wisely in the first place, because it's not yet altogether certain whether Akma really is as single-minded in his pride as Elemak was. Elemak had proof after proof of the power of the Oversoul and then of the Keeper of Earth, and still defied them and hated all they were trying to do. But Akma has never knowingly had any experience with the Keeper's power—that's an advantage that Akmaro and Chebeya, Edhadeya and Luet, Didul and even I have over him. So it just may be, poor Edhadeya, that you have not bestowed your heart as tragically and foolishly as Eiadh did.

Then again, it may turn out that you did even worse.

11
Defeat

Dudagu didn't want her husband to go. "I hate it when you're gone for so many days."

"I'm sorry, but no matter how ill you are right now, I'm still the king," said Motiak.

"That's right, so you have people to find out things and report to you and you don't have to go and see for yourself!"

"I'm king of the earth people of Darakemba as surely as I'm king of the sky and middle people. They need to see that I don't want them to leave."

"You issued that decree, didn't you? Forbidding people to organize boycotts of the diggers?"

"Oh, yes. I decreed, and immediately Akma and the royal boys went about declaring that in compliance with the law, they no longer advocated a boycott and urged people *not* to stop hiring diggers or buying goods made by diggers. Thus I can't arrest them while their boycott message is *still* being spread by their pretence of discontinuing it."

"I still think you should make them come home and stop letting them speak."

"It wouldn't change the fact that people know what they believe, what they want. Believe it or not, Dudagu, despite your high opinion of my powers, I'm helpless."

"Punish them if they boycott the diggers! Confiscate their property! Cut off a finger!"

"And how would I prove that they're boycotting? All they have to say is, 'I was never satisfied with his work and so I hire other people now. It has nothing to do with what species he belongs to—don't I have the freedom to decide whom to hire?' Sometimes it might even be true. Should I punish them then?"

Dudagu thought about this for a few moments. "Well, then, if the diggers are leaving, let them go! If they all leave, then the problem is solved."

Motiak looked at her in silence until she finally realized something was wrong and looked at him and saw the cold rage in his face.

She gasped. "Did I say something wrong?"

"When someone in my kingdom decides that some of my citizens are not welcome, and drives them out against my will, don't you dare to tell me that once they're all gone, the problem is solved. Every earth person who leaves Darakemba makes this nation that much more evil and I'm beginning to hate being their king."

"I don't like the sound of *that*," she said. "You wouldn't do anything stupid like abdicating, would you?"

"And put Aronha in charge years ahead of schedule? Watch as he re-establishes this Ancient Ways abomination as the official religion of the empire? I wouldn't give him the satisfaction. No, I'll be king until the last breath is dragged out of my body. I only hope that I have the strength never to hope that all my sons die before me."

Dudagu fairly flew off the bed, to stand before him in tiny, majestic rage. "Don't you ever say such a monstrous thing again! Three of them aren't my sons, I know that, and I know they hate me and think I'm useless but they're still your sons, and that's still more sacred than anything else in the world, and no decent man would ever wish his sons to die before him even if he *is* the king and they *are* wretched traitorous snots like my Khimin turned out to be." She burst into tears.

He led her back to her bed. "Come on, I didn't mean it, I was just angry."

"So was I, only I was *right* to be angry," she said.

"That's true, you were, and I apologize. I didn't mean it."

"Please don't go."

"I will go, because it's the right thing to do. And you will stop pestering me about it, because I shouldn't have to feel guilty about doing my duty as king."

"I won't sleep while you're gone. You'll be lucky if I'm not dead of weakness and exhaustion when you return."

"Three days? Try to stay alive for three days."

"You don't take my sickness seriously at all, Tidaka," she said.

"I take it seriously," said Motiak, "but I never have and never will let it stop me from doing my duty. It's one of the tragedies of royal life, Dudagu. If you died while I was away, doing my duty, I would grieve. But if I failed in my duty because you were dying, I would be ashamed. For my kingdom's sake, I would rather have my people grieve with me than have my people ashamed of me."

"You have no heart," she said.

"No, I *have* a heart," said Motiak. "I just can't always do what it tells me to do."

"I'll hate you forever. I'll never forgive you."

"But I'll love *you*," he answered mildly. And then, when the door was closed behind him and she couldn't hear, he muttered, "I might even forgive you for making my home life so . . . . unrestful."

He left his house in the company of two captains—as tradition required, one was an angel, the other a human. Outside, spies and soldiers were ready—only a dozen spies and thirty soldiers, but it was best to be prepared. In these tumultuous times, one never knew when a party of Elemaki might penetrate deeply into Darakemba. And before the journey was done, they would be far upriver, much closer to the border.

On the way out of the city, they were joined by Akmaro, Chebeya, Edhadeya, and Shedemei. Motiak greeted his daughter with an embrace, and met Shedemei with short courtesy; it was easy to assume a level of intimacy as if he had long known her. "Someday you must tell me where you're from," he said. "Show me on a map, that is. I have the original maps that Nafai drew, showing the whole gornaya. I won't have heard of your city, but I can add it to the map."

"It would do no good," said Shedemei. "It doesn't exist now."

"A grief that can hardly be imagined," said Motiak.

"It was for a while," said Shedemei. "But I'm alive, and my work requires all my concentration."

"Still, I'd like to see where your city was. People often build again on the same site. If there was a reason to build a city there once, another people will think of the same reason again." Polite conversation; they all knew what was really on Motiak's mind. But there was no use talking about it all the time; it wasn't as if they could do much. And it was Motiak's duty to make sure they were as comfortable as he could make them. That was one of the chief annoyances of being king. No matter where he was, no matter who was with him, he was always host, always responsible for everyone else's well-being.

Out on the road, their reason for this journey was immediately apparent. The encampment of emigrating diggers wasn't large, but then it wasn't meant to be. Quiet humans and angels manned the booth where food and water were distributed; lidded jars with thongs to loop around the neck would serve to help the diggers on their way. They would also mark them as emigrants, so that any who saw them on the road would know they were leaving Darakemba. They had taken the invitation of the Ancients; they had decided to live where they were not hated. But it gave them no joy. Motiak hadn't spent that much of his life around earth people that he could easily read the expressions on their strange faces. But it took no great experience to see the dejection in the slope of their backs, the way they tended to walk now on two feet, now touching a hand to the ground, as if in being called animals they had begun somehow to discover it was true, so now it took all their remaining strength just to keep from setting down the other hand to make it a foot again, as it had been for an ancient ancestor scurrying through the alleys of a human city, looking for something edible or wet or shiny.

Motiak led his party onto the road; the diggers moved aside. "No," he said, "the road is wide enough. We can share it."

They stayed motionless at the verge, watching him.

"I am Motiak," he said. "Don't you understand that you are citizens? You don't have to go. I've opened up the public larders in every city. You can wait this out. It will pass."

Finally one of them spoke. "When we go there, we see the hatred in their eyes, sir. We know you meant well for us, setting us free. We don't hate *you*."

"It's not the hunger," said another. "You know it's not that."

"Yes it is," said a woman, holding three small children near her. "And the beatings. You won't live forever, sir."

"Whatever else might be true of my sons," said Motiak, "they will never permit the persecution."

"Oh, they'll starve us out, but not let us be hit?" the woman scoffed. "Stand up, you," she said to her children. "This is the king, here. This is *majesty*."

Motiak's angel captain made a motion as if to punish her for impudence, but Motiak waved him back with a tiny gesture. The irony in her voice could not overmatch the bitterness in his heart. She was right, to jeer at majesty. A king has no more power than the willing obedience of the great mass of the people gives him. A king who is worse than his people is a poisonous snake; a king who is better is last year's snakeskin, discarded in the grass.

Pabul was at the Ancient Ways booth. He had asked if he might come along, if only because he felt somewhat responsible for the troubles with his decision in Shedemei's trial the year before. "These so-called Ancients, they're a loathsome bunch," he said, "but they're not breaking any law. They don't foul the water or poison the food. It's fresh enough, and the rations they give the earth people are adequate for a day's journey." He hesitated, considering whether to say the next thing, then decided and spoke. "You could forbid the diggers to leave."

Motiak nodded. "Yes—I could require the most helpless and obedient of my citizens to stay and suffer further humiliation and abuse, from which I'm powerless to protect them, I could do that."

Pabul made no more argument along that line.

They walked all day, briskly because they were all healthy: They made a point of staying fit; Motiak and Pabul because their offices were fundamentally military ones and they might find themselves in the field at any time; Akmaro and Chebeya, Edhadeya and Shedemei because they were of the Kept and labored with their own hands, permitting themselves no excess of food or unproductive leisure. So they overtook group after group of diggers, and to each of them Motiak said the same thing. "Please stay. I wish you would stay. Trust in the Keeper to heal the wound in this land." And their answer was always the same: For you we would stay, Motiak, we know you wish us well; but there's no future here for me, for my children.

"It's misleading," Akmaro said that afternoon. "We see here the ones that are on the road. Most are staying."

"So far," said Motiak.

"Our resources are stretched to the limit, but all the diggers that the Kept can hire are earning wages; their children are still in school; there are even towns and villages where Akma and your sons have no influence and the people treat each other civilly, without boycotts or any sign of hate."

"How many such towns, Akmaro?" asked Motiak. "One in a hundred?"

"One in fifty," said Akmaro. "Or one in forty."

Motiak had no need to answer that.

He thought back to the morning's conversation with his wife. The callousness with which she said to let the diggers go and then the problem would be solved. Is that any more monstrous than my cruel thought that I might wish to see my sons in graves before I die? Yet I would not have shrunk from letting them all take weapons in their hands and go out into battle, if an enemy attacked us. They might have died then, in the violence of war, and when they saw me mourning no man or woman in the kingdom would have said, If he really loved them he wouldn't have put them in the way of death.

He framed the idea in words and said them aloud, so Akmaro, still walking beside him, could hear. "There are things that parents must value even above their children's lives."

Akmaro needed no explanation to understand where Motiak's thoughts had turned. "That's hard," he said. "All of nature has written into our minds the idea that children matter more than anything."

"But civilization means rising above even that," said Motiak. "We feel our self to be the town, the tribe, the city, the nation—"

"The children of the Keeper—"

"Yes, we see that as the self that must be preserved at all costs, so that nearer things are less valuable. Does it mean we're monsters, that we hate our grown children if we send them off to war to kill and die so they can protect our neighbors' little ones?"

" 'The survival of the family is best enhanced when the family is subsumed in a larger society,' " Akmaro recited. " 'One family breaks and bleeds, but the larger organism heals. The wound is not fatal.' Edhadeya has been teaching me the things that are taught in Rasaro's House."

"She spends more time in your house than mine," said Motiak.

"She finds more comfort from Chebeya than from her stepmother," said Akmaro. "I don't think that's surprising. Besides, she spends most of her time with Shedemei."

"Strange woman," said Motiak.

"When you know her better," said Akmaro, "you'll begin to realize that she's even stranger than you thought at first." Then, suddenly, Akmaro's demeanor changed; in a softer voice he said, "I didn't realize that your captain of soldiers was so close behind us."

"Is he?" asked Motiak.

"Were you overheard, do you think? When you said, 'There are things that parents must value even above their children's lives'?"

Motiak glanced at Akmaro in alarm. They both understood that inadvertently, Motiak had placed their sons in great danger. "It's time that we stopped for our noon meal."

While the soldiers broke out the food that they were carrying, and all but two of the spies settled to the ground to eat, Motiak took Edhadeya aside. "I'm sorry to separate you from the group, but I have an urgent errand for you."

"And you can't send a spy?" she said.

"I most certainly cannot," he said. "I chanced to say something unfortunate just now, and I was overheard; but even if I hadn't been, the idea is bound to occur to one of my men, seeing how unhappy I am. You must go and find your brothers and warn them that it's possible, even likely, that some soldier, thinking to do me a great service, will attempt to relieve me of some of my family burdens."

"Oh, Father, you don't think they would raise a hand against the royal blood?"

"Kings' sons have died before," said Motiak. "My soldiers know that what my boys are doing now is killing me. I fear the loyalty of my most loyal men as much as I fear the disloyalty of my sons. Go to them, tell them my warning."

"Do you know what they'll say, Father? That you're threatening them, that you're trying to scare them into stopping their public speaking."

"I'm trying to save their lives. Tell them at least to keep their travel secret. Tell no one where they're going next, tell no one when they plan to leave. Go suddenly, arrive unexpectedly. They must, or somewhere on the road someone will be lying in wait for them. And not diggers—I'm talking about humans and angels. Will you do this?"

She nodded.

"I'll send two angels with you for safety, but when you get near, you must order them to stay behind so you can talk to your brothers alone."

She nodded; she got up to go.

"Edhadeya," said Motiak. "I know that I'm asking you to do a hard thing, to go and see them. But whom else can I send? Akmaro? Pabul? Akma will allow *you* to come close and speak to your brothers in privacy."

"I can bear it," said Edhadeya. "I can bear it better than watching these weary people leave their homeland."

As she walked away, Motiak saw that she was heading straight for Shedemei. He called out to her. She came back.

"I don't think you should talk about this to strangers," he said.

"I wasn't going to," she said, looking peeved. Again she left; again she headed straight for Shedemei, and this time spoke to her. Shedemei nodded, then shook her head no; only then did Edhadeya take her leave of the whole group, with two angels flying reconnaissance for her as she went.

Motiak was furious even though he knew his anger was foolish. Chebeya noticed at once that he was out of sorts and came to him. "What happened with Edhadeya?" she asked.

"I told her not to tell strangers what her errand was, and she went straight to this Shedemei."

Chebeya laughed ruefully. "Oh, Motiak, you should have been more specific than that. Shedemei isn't a stranger to anyone here but you."

"Edhadeya knew what I meant."

"No she didn't, Motiak. If she had known, she would have obeyed you. Not all your children are in revolt. Besides, Shedemei isn't Bego or . . . Akma. She's only going to lead Edhadeya closer to the Keeper and to you."

"I want to talk to her, this Shedemei. It's time I got to know her."

A moment later Shedemei sat beside him in the shade, with Akmaro, Pabul, and Chebeya gathered round, the soldiers well back and out of earshot. "Enough of the evasions," said Motiak. "It was fine for you to be vague and mysterious until my daughter started confiding my secret errands to you."

"What secret errands?" said Shedemei.

"The reason I was sending her back to Darakemba."

"She told me nothing about that," said Shedemei.

"Are you going to pretend that you don't know what she's doing?"

"Not at all," said Shedemei. "I know exactly what she's doing. But she didn't tell me."

"Enough of the riddles! Who are you!"

"When I can see that it's any of your business to know, Motiak, I'll tell you. Until then, all you need to know is that I serve the Keeper as best I can, and so do you, and that makes us friends whether you like it or not."

No one had ever spoken to him with such impudence before. Only Chebeya's gentling touch on his elbow restrained him from embarrassing himself with words he would soon regret. "I try to be a decent man and not abuse my power as king, but I have my limits!"

"On the contrary," said Shedemei. "There is *no* limit to your decency. It is complete. Akma and your boys wouldn't have done half so well if that weren't true."

Motiak studied her face, still angry, still baffled. "I'm supposed to be the king, and nobody will tell me anything."

"If it's any help to you," said Shedemei, "I don't know anything that would help you, because it doesn't help *me*, either. I'm as eager as you are to put an end to this nonsense. I see as clearly as you do that if Akma succeeds in all that he plans to do, your kingdom will lie in ruins, your people scattered and enslaved, and this great experiment in freedom and harmony will be, not even a memory, but a legend and then a myth and then a fantasy."

"It's been a fantasy all along."

"No, that's not true," said Akmaro, leaping in to stop Motiak from wallowing in bitterness, as he so often had in recent weeks and months. "Don't start to use Akma's lies to excuse your own lack of understanding. You know that the Keeper of Earth is real. You know that the dreams he sends are true. You know that the future he showed to Binaro was a good one, full of hope and light, and you chose it, not out of fear of the Keeper, but out of love for his plan. Don't lose sight of that."

Motiak sighed. "It's nice at least that I don't have the burden of carrying a conscience around with me. Akmaro stores a much larger one than I could lift myself, and trots it out whenever it's needed." He laughed. So did they. For a moment, and then the laughter died in reflective silence. "My friends, I think we have seen how powerless I am. Even if I were like the late unlamented Nuab among the Zenifi, willing to kill whoever crossed me, he didn't have to face a determined enemy like Akma."

"Khideo's sword almost got him," Akmaro pointed out.

"Khideo didn't go around like Akma, telling the people exactly what the worst among them want to hear. Nuab didn't have his sons in unison against him so that the people would see them as the future and him as the past and ignore him as if he were already dead. Don't you think it's ironic, Akmaro, that what you did to that monster Pabulog, stealing his sons away from him, should end up happening to me?"

Akmaro laughed one bitter bark of a laugh. "You think I haven't seen the parallel? My son thinks he hates me, but his actions have been a perverse echo of mine. He even grew up to be the leader of a religious movement, and spends his life preaching and teaching. I should be proud."

"Yes, we're all such failures," said Chebeya nastily. "We can sit around here moaning about our helplessness. Shedemei, who supposedly knows all the secrets of the universe, can't think of a single useful thing to do. The king whines about how powerless kings are. My husband, the high priest, moans about what a failure he is as a father. While I have to sit here watching the threads that bind this kingdom together unraveling, watch the people forming themselves into tribes that are bound only by hate and fear, and all the while I know that those who have been trusted with all the power that there *is* in this land are doing nothing but feeling sorry for themselves!"

Her virulence startled them all.

"Yes," said Motiak, "so we're a helpless pathetic bunch. What exactly is your *point?*"

"You're angry at us because we can't do anything," said Akmaro. "But that's the cause of our grief—we *can't.* You might as well be angry at the riverbank because it can't stop the water from flowing by."

"You foolish men of power!" cried Chebeya. "You're so used to governing with laws and words, soldiers and spies. Now you rage or have your feelings hurt because all your usual tools are useless. They were *always* useless. Everything *always* depended on the relationship between each individual person in this kingdom and the Keeper of Earth. Very few of them understand anything about the Keeper's plan, but they know goodness when they see it, and they know evil—they know what builds and what tears down, what brings happiness and what brings misery. Trust them!"

"Trust them?" said Motiak. "With Akma leading them to deny the most common decency?"

"Who are these people that Akma leads? You see them as crowds that flock to him and feel as though they had all betrayed you. But their reasons for following Akma are as individual as they are. Yes, some of them hate all diggers with an unreasoning passion—but they were always around, weren't they? I don't think their numbers have increased, not by one; in fact, after the persecutions I think there were *fewer* who really hated the diggers, because many people learned to feel compassion for them. Akma knows this—he *knows* that they don't want to be like the thugs who tormented children. So he tells them that the problem wasn't their fault, or even the diggers' fault, it's just the natural way of things, it can't be helped, we're all victims of the way nature works, it's all the will of the Keeper, we need to give in and move the diggers humanely out of sight so all this ugliness will go away. Most of the people who follow him are just trying to make the problem go away. If they simply let things happen, they think, peace will come again. But they're ashamed! I see it, why can't you? They know it's wrong. But it's inevitable, so why fight it? Even the king, even the high priest of the Kept can't do a thing about it!"

"That's right," growled Motiak. "We can't!"

"That's what Akma's saying to them."

"He's not saying it," said Motiak. "He's showing it."

"But they don't want it to be true. Oh, I'm not saying they're all decent people, or even most of them. There are plenty of them who are looking only for their own advantage. Better invest my time and wealth in making friends with Motiak's sons. But if they once thought that Akma would fail, they'd be right back with you, pretending to have been among the Kept all along, joking with you about how every family has problems with sons who are coming of age. They don't care whether the diggers come or go. In fact they miss the lower wages they were able to pay them. The people are not evil, Motiak. A large number of them are decent but they have no hope. Another large portion don't care that much about decency but they'd be just as happy to have the Kept in charge of things, they don't much care as long as they can prosper. And you know that the Kept are still a very large core of dedicated believers who love the Keeper's plan and are striving to save it at great cost to themselves, and with unflinching courage. These three groups, together, are the vast majority of your people. Not perfect, certainly, but good enough to be worth reigning over. Except that Akma's voice seems to be the only one that's heard."

It was Shedemei who answered her tirade. "Yes, but that's not for our lack of trying. The king has pleaded, you and your husband have spoken publicly and constantly, Pabul here has searched the law for ways to help and his court has been firm on the side of decency—I've even done all that I could do, that would not be coercive."

"So it all comes down to Akma and my sons," said Motiak.

"No," said Chebeya. "It all comes down to Akma. Those boys of yours would never be doing this either, Motiak, if it weren't for Akma."

"That was the meaning of the dream the Keeper sent me," said Akmaro. "It all comes down to Akma, and none of us has the slightest power to reach him. We've all tried—well, Pabul couldn't, because Akma would never let him come close. But the rest of us have tried, and we can't bend him, and as long as we can't stop Akma, we can't waken the decency of the people, so what does it matter?"

"You're not suggesting," said Motiak, "that I arrange the assassination of your own son?"

"No!" she cried. "See how you think of power as a matter of weapons, Motiak? And you, Akmaro, it's words, words, teaching, talking, that's what power means to you. But this problem is beyond what you can solve with your ordinary tools."

"What then?" said Shedemei. "What tools should we use?"

"No tools at all!" cried Chebeya. "They don't work!"

Shedemei extended her open hands. "There I am," she said, "unarmed, my hands are empty. Fill them! Show me what to do and I'll do it! So will any of us!"

"I can't show you because I don't know. I can't give you tools because there are no tools. Don't you see? What Akma is wrecking—*it's not our plan.*"

"If you're saying we should just leave it up to the Keeper," said Akmaro, "then what's the point of anything? Binaro said it—we're the Keeper's hands and mouths in this world."

"Yes, when the Keeper needs action or speech, we're the ones to do it. But that's not what's needed now!"

Akmaro reached out and took his wife's hands in his. "You're saying that we shouldn't just leave things up to the Keeper. You're saying we should demand that the Keeper either do something or show us what to do."

"The Keeper knows that," said Shedemei. "She hardly needs us to tell her what should be obvious."

"Maybe she needs us to admit that it's up to her. Maybe she needs us to say that *whatever* she decides, we will abide by it. Maybe it's time for Akma's father to say to the Keeper, Enough. Stop my son."

"Do you think I haven't begged the Keeper for answers?" Akmaro said, offended.

"Exactly," said Chebeya. "I've heard you, talking to the Keeper, saying, 'Show me what to do. How can I save my son? How can I bring him back from these terrible things?' Doesn't it occur to you that the only reason the Keeper hasn't stopped Akma up to now is for your sake?"

"But I *want* him to stop."

"That's right!" cried Chebeya. "You want *him* to stop. That's what you plead for, over and over. I've seen the connection between you. Even though it's rage on his part and agonized frustration on yours, the ties of love between you are stronger than I've ever seen between any two people in my life. Think what that means—in all your pleas, you are really asking the Keeper to spare your son."

"Your son too," said Akmaro softly.

"I've shed the same tears as you, Kmadaro," she said. "I've said the same prayers to the Keeper. But it's time to utter a new prayer. It's time to say to the Keeper that we value her children more than we value ours. It's time for *you* to beg the Keeper of Earth to stop our son. To set the people of Darakemba free from his foul, foul influence."

Motiak couldn't see what her point was. "I just sent Edhadeya to try to warn my boys to be careful—are you saying I should have sent soldiers to assassinate Akma?"

"No," said Akmaro, answering for Chebeya so she wouldn't have to weep in frustration. "No, her point is that anything *we* might do at this point would be useless. If someone causes harm to any of these boys, they would be martyrs and you would be blamed forever. It's not in our power—that's what Chebeya's saying."

"But I thought she was telling you to. . . ."

"Akma has to be stopped, but the only way to stop him, that will actually work, is for everyone to see that he was stopped, not by any power of man or woman, of angel, human, or digger, but by the plain and naked power of the Keeper of Earth. She's saying that without realizing it, I've been begging, demanding that the Keeper find a way to *save* my son. All that's left now is for me to stop that prayer. I think . . . perhaps the Keeper has trusted me with his plan for this nation, and so he won't do anything without my consent. And without realizing it, up to now I've refused to let the Keeper do the only thing that would help at all. We've tried everything else, but now it's time for me to ask the Keeper to do now what was done long ago when Sherem threatened to undo all the teachings of Oykib."

"You want the Keeper to strike your son dead?" asked Pabul, incredulous.

"No I don't!" cried Akmaro. Chebeya burst into tears. "No I don't," Akmaro said softly. "I want my son to live. But more than that, I want the people of this world to live together as children of the Keeper. More than I want to spare the life of my son. It's time for me to beg the Keeper to do whatever he must do in order to save the people of Darakemba—no matter what it costs." His eyes, too, spilled over with tears. "It's happening again, just the way it did before, when I reached out to you, Pabul, you and your brothers, and taught you to love the Keeper and reject your father's ways. I knew that I had to do that, for the good of my people, for *your* good, even though I could see that it was tearing my boy apart, making him hate me. I knew I was losing him then. And now I have to consent to it all over again."

"Me, too?" asked Motiak in a small voice.

"No," said Shedemei. "Your boys will return to their senses once they're not with Akma anymore. And the peace of this kingdom depends on an orderly succession. Your boys must *not* die."

"But a father praying for the Keeper to strike his son dead. . . ." said Motiak.

"I will never pray for that," said Akmaro. "I'm not wise enough to tell the Keeper how to do his work. I'm only wise enough to listen to my wife and stop demanding that the Keeper leave my son alive."

"This is unbearable," murmured Pabul. "Father Akmaro, I wish I had died back in Chelem rather than bring this day upon you."

"No one brought this day upon *me*," said Akmaro. "Akma brought this day upon himself. The only hope of mercy for this people is for the Keeper to give justice to my son. So that's what I'm going to ask for." He rose from the ground, sighing deeply, terribly. "That's what I'm going to ask for with my whole heart. Justice for my son. I hope that he can bear to look the Keeper in the face."

They watched as Akmaro walked away from the clearing, into the trees lining the banks of the Tsidorek. "I don't know what to hope for," Motiak said.

"It's not our business to hope now," said Shedemei. "Akmaro and Chebeya finally found the courage to face what they had to face. Now I need to get back to the city and see whether I can do the same in my own small way."

They all knew better than to ask her what it was that she intended to do.

"I'll go with you," said Pabul.

"No," said Shedemei sharply. "Stay here. Akmaro will need you. Chebeya will need you. I don't need you." She was not to be disobeyed. She set off down the road, not even taking a waterjar with her.

"Will she be all right?" asked Motiak. "Should I have some of my spies keep an eye on her?"

"She'll be fine," said Chebeya. "I don't think she wants company. Or observers, either."

It was dark when the launch flew silently above the water of the Tsidorek and stopped to rest in the air a single step away from the riverbank. Shedemei took that step and entered the small craft—small compared to the *Basilica,* that is; huge compared to any other vehicle on Earth. Once she was secure inside, the launch took off without any command from her; the Oversoul knew what was needed, and took her to a garden she maintained in a hidden valley high above the settled land of Darakemba. As she traveled, the Oversoul spoke to her.

<You were the one who urged me to interfere with Monush all those years ago. Now you refuse to let me interfere with Akma.>

"That's right."

<I could block him.>

"You couldn't block Nafai and Issib back on Harmony when you had your full powers. Akma has a powerful will; he would resist you. I think he'd probably enjoy it."

<Akmaro is tearing himself apart with this. The kingdom is shattered. You have all my power at your disposal and you do nothing.>

"It's not my plan that matters now," said Shedemei. "It never was. We were as proud and as stupid as Akma was, back when we tried to provoke the Keeper by interfering with Monush's rescue. What we didn't understand is that the Keeper lets us interfere and tries to work around us. We really can't affect her. She wants this society, this nation of Darakemba to succeed. But if the people choose to ignore her and make something ugly out of their chance at something beautiful, well, so be it. She'll find somebody else."

<What about Harmony? What about my mission here?>

"Maybe the Keeper is waiting to see what these children of Harmony decide, right here, right now, before she can give you the instructions you came for."

<So she doesn't care about these people, really. She only cares about them if they fit in with her plan.>

"She cares about them, yes. But she sees the whole picture, the sweep of time. To save a dozen or a thousand or a million people now, at the cost of the happiness of billions of lives over millions of years—she won't do it. She takes the long view."

<So Akmaro is wasting his time.>

"I don't know. How can I know? *We* were wasting our time by trying to thwart her. But if Chebeya's right—and how can I tell how much truth a raveler knows?—if she's right, then the Keeper *can* be influenced, not by rebels but by her most loyal friends. So Akmaro may have been blocking her just as Chebeya said, and the things he's telling the Keeper now—maybe the logjam will be broken."

<And then I'll be told what to do?>

"Either that or not. How can I know?"

<You think something's going to happen, or you wouldn't have called for me to send the launch.>

"I think that it's possible that when it comes time to break the impasse, the Keeper may have use for me."

<And how will you know?>

"Someone will have a dream. That's how the Keeper works. You'll see the dream, you'll tell me, and we'll figure out if there's something in it that the Keeper wants me to do."

<Maybe the dream will come to *you.*>

"I haven't had a true dream since I saw myself as a gardener in the sky. That came true long ago, and I don't expect to have another dream."

<You can't lie to me, Shedemei. I feel your hopes whether you give voice to them or not.>

"Yes, well, I'd like to think the Keeper had something to say to me, of course. I'm as vain as the next person."

<Then hurry up and sleep, so you can dream.>

"It doesn't work that way. I'm not tired yet."

She left the launch and wandered in the cold night air in her garden, routinely noticing the growth of the plants, the relative preponderance of one species over another, the amount of brachiation, the size of the foliage. The Oversoul entered her observations into the ship's computer as notes. They had long since stopped commenting on the irony that a computer program designed to govern a world was now acting as scribe for a lone biologist.

The Oversoul began to talk to her. <I've been searching for the Keeper, for some *place* that she could be. I've been searching for the means she uses to send dreams to the minds of humans, angels, and diggers. Whatever the Keeper does, I can't find it.>

"Didn't you notice that about four hundred years ago?"

<Yes, and then I waited.>

"Forty million years you waited on Harmony, and now you're impatient?"

<I was busy on Harmony. I was needed.>

"You were running things, you mean. If something was planned, it was because you were doing the planning. And then people started having dreams that didn't come from you. Made you a little uneasy, didn't it?"

<It was harder to perform my calculations of probabilities.>

"That's how it is for us all the time."

<I have compassion algorithms designed into me. I don't have to to identify with you in order to empathize. That's a biological thing.>

"Whatever the Keeper does, she does it faster than light, she does it no matter how far away a person is. It suggests such enormous power. Such knowledge, such . . . wisdom. And yet she is so delicate, intervening so little, really. Giving us such freedom. Respecting our choices. Listening to us. Listening to needs and desires we don't even know we have."

<I think that whatever she is, she isn't like me. She's not a computer.>

"Organic, then? With very powerful tools?"

<Organic? Who knows. Maybe she's simply unconstructed, how's that? Like a human, like a digger, like an angel. She grew, she made herself out of her experiences, the way you did and do. So she wasn't just programmed to design the shape of the history of life, she was *charged* with it.>

"Or perhaps she found it and loved it and decided she wanted to help. On her own, unassigned, unrequested."

<It's a wonder she doesn't get bored. I speak from experience when I say that human history is astonishingly repetitive. Every individual is unique, but not all the differences are both significant and interesting.>

"Now you're a critic."

<Someone has to be an audience for the play you people are always improvising. All of you trying for the center stage. All of you trying to get the audience to notice you, to declare you the star, so that when you die, the curtain will come down and the show will end. But it never does. No one was ever the star after all.>

"That's the difference between life and art, of course. Life has no frames, no curtains, no beginnings and no endings."

<Which *should* imply that it has no meaning.>

"I mean my own life. I mean what I do. And the Keeper gives a meaning to the larger scene. That's enough meaning for me. I don't need to have somebody make an epic out of my life. I lived. Strange things happened. Now and then I made a little difference in other people's lives. You know what? It may be that the thing I'm proudest of in all my life is restoring the brain of that damaged little boy in Bodika."

<Not the way you altered the angels and diggers to allow them to live apart from each other?>

"The Keeper assigned that to me; if I hadn't done it, she would have found another way, given the task to someone else."

<How do you know the Keeper didn't assign you to heal that little earth boy?>

"Maybe she did. But if I hadn't been there, the Keeper wouldn't have thought his life was so important that she would have sent someone else. So it was less significant—but because of that, I know that it happened only because I wanted it to happen. That makes it mine. My gift. Oh, I know it was the Keeper who brought me to Earth at all, and the Keeper who chose me to succeed Nafai as the starmaster so I was even alive then, all of that, I know it. But I'm the one who decided to be there at that time and to risk exposing who I really am to save that boy. So maybe that's what I'll think of with pride when I die. Or maybe it'll be the strange marriage I had with Zdorab. Or Rasaro's House—that school might last, and that would be something fine."

<Don't write your eulogy yet. You aren't dead.>

"But I *am* tired. I think I can sleep now. Too cold to sleep out here. I really wish the seats reclined farther back in the launch."

<Too bad the designers have been dead for forty million years.>

"And they deserve to be, too, the thoughtless weasels." She laughed. "I *am* tired."

She finished her count anyway, so that her report would be complete. Then she had the launch turn off its exterior lights and she returned to it by starlight and closed the door and went to sleep.

Went to sleep and dreamed. Many dreams, the normal dreams, the random firings of synapses in the brain, being given fragmentary meaning by the storymaking functions of the mind; dreams that the mind doesn't even bother to remember upon waking.

And then, suddenly, a different dream. The Oversoul sensed it, the fact that the brain had now assumed a different pattern from the normal dreamsleep. Shedemei herself felt the difference and, even in her sleep, paid attention.

She saw the Earth as it looked from the *Basilica,* the curve of the planet plainly visible at the horizons. Then, suddenly, she was seeing the seething magma that roiled underneath the crust of the planet. At first it looked chaotic, but then with piercing clarity she understood that there was magnificent order to the flow of the currents. Each eddy, each whorl, each stream had meaning. Much of it was grossly slow, but here and there, on a small scale, the movements were quick indeed.

Then she knew without seeing, knew because she knew, that these currents gave shape to the magnetic field of the Earth, making both large and tiny variations that could be sensed by the animals, that could disturb them or soothe them. The warning before the earthquake. The sudden veering of a school of fish. The harmonies between organisms; this was what the ravelers saw.

She saw how mind and memory lived in the currents of flowing stone, in the magnetic flow; saw how vast amounts of information were deposited in crystals on the underside of the crust, changed by fluxes in temperature and magnetism. For a moment she thought: This is the Keeper.

Almost at once the answer came: You have not seen the Keeper of Earth. But you have seen my home, my library, and some of my tools. I can't show you more than this because your mind has no way to receive what I really am. Is this enough?

Yes, said Shedemei silently.

At once the dream changed. She saw all at once more than forty worlds that had been colonized from Earth, and all of them were being watched by some kind of Oversoul, and all the Oversouls were being watched by the Keeper. In particular she saw Harmony, the millions of people as if for just this moment her mind had the capacity to know them all at once. She felt herself in contact with the other iteration of the Oversoul that still lived there; but no, that was illusion, there was no such connection. Yet she knew that it was time for the Oversoul of Harmony to allow the humans there to recover their lost technologies. That's how the Oversoul would be rebuilt—by humans who had regained their hands.

It's time, said the clear voice of the Keeper in the dream. Let them build new starships and come home.

What about the people here? asked Shedemei. Have you given up on them?

The time of clarity has come. The decision will be made, one way or the other. So I can send for the people of Harmony now, because by the time they get here, either the three species will be living in perfect peace, or their pride will have broken them and made them ripe for domination by those who come after.

Like the Rasulum, thought Shedemei.

They also had their moment of choice, the Keeper replied.

The dream changed again, and now she saw Akma and the sons of Motiak walking along a road. She knew at once exactly where the road was, and what time of day it would be when they reached that point.

In the dream she saw the launch drop out of the sky, deliberately raising a cloud of smoke under it when it landed; she saw herself stride out, the cloak of the starmaster dazzlingly bright so that they couldn't bear to look at her. She began to speak, and at that moment the earth shook under them, driven by the currents of magma, and the young men fell to the ground. Then the quaking of the earth ended, and she spoke again, and at last she understood what it was the Keeper needed her to do.

Will you? asked the Keeper.

Will it help? she asked. Will it save these people?

Yes, the Keeper answered. No matter what he chooses, Motiak will finish his days as king of a peaceful kingdom, because of your intervention here. But what happens in the far future—that is what Akma will decide. You may live to see it if you want.

How, if the *Basilica* must go back to Harmony?

I'm in no hurry here. Have the ship's computer send a probe. You can stay, and the Oversoul can stay. Don't you want to see some part of how it ends?

Yes, I do.

I know you do, said the Keeper. Until you made this visit to Earth, I wasn't sure if you were truly part of me, because I didn't know if you loved the people enough to share my work. You're not the same person you were when I first called you here.

I know, said Shedemei in the dream. I used to live for nothing but my work.

Oh, you still do *that*, and so do I. It's just that your work has changed, and now it's the same as my work: to teach the people of Earth how to live, on and on, generation to generation; and how to make that life joyful and free. You made your choice, and so now, like Akmaro, I can give you what you want, because I know that you desire only the joy of these people, forever.

I'm not so pure-hearted as that!

Don't be confused by your transient feelings. I know what you do; I know why you do it; I can name you more truly than you can name yourself.

For a moment, Shedemei could see herself reaching up and plucking a white fruit from a tree; she tasted it, and the flavor of it filled her body with light and she could fly, she could sing all songs at once and they were endlessly beautiful inside her. She knew what the fruit was—it was the love of the Keeper for the people of Earth. The white fruit was a taste of the Keeper's joy. Yet also in the flavor of it was something else, the tang, the sharp pain of the millions, the billions of people who could not understand what the Keeper wanted for them, or who, understanding, hated it and rejected her interference in their lives. Let us be ourselves, they demanded. Let us accomplish our accomplishments. We want none of your gifts, we don't want to be part of your plan. And so they were swept away in the currents of time, belonging to no part of history because they could not be part of something larger than themselves. Yet they had their free choice; they were not punished except by the natural consequence of their own pride. Thus even in rejecting the Keeper's plan they became a part of it; in refusing to taste the fruit of the tree, they became part of its exquisite flavor. There was honor even in that. Their hubris mattered, even though in the long flow of burning history it changed nothing. It mattered because the Keeper loved them and remembered them and knew their names and their stories and mourned for them: O my daughter, O my son, you are also part of me, the Keeper cried out to them. You are part of my endless yearning, and I will never forget you—

And the emotions became too much for Shedemei. She had dwelt in the Keeper's mind for as long as she could bear. She awoke sobbing violently, overwhelmed, overcome. Awoke and uttered a long mournful cry of unspeakable grief—grief for the lost ones, grief for having had to leave the mind of the Keeper, grief because the taste of the white fruit was gone from her lips and it had only been a dream after all. A true dream, but a dream that ends, it ended, and here I am more alone than I ever was before because for the first time in my life I had the experience of being *not* alone and I never knew, I never knew how beautiful it was to be truly, wholly known and loved. Her cry trailed off; her body was spent by the dream; she slept again, and dreamed no more until morning. By then enough time had passed that she could bear to be awake, though the dream was still powerfully present in her mind.

"Did you watch?" she whispered.

<Nafai never had a true dream as strong as that.>

"He had different work to do," she said. "Can you get me to the place where I'm supposed to be?"

<With plenty of time to spare.>

She ate as the launch moved, chewing mechanically; the food had no flavor, compared to what she remembered from her dream.

"Your waiting is over at last," she said between bites. "I assume you saw that."

<I'm already preparing my message to my original iteration. I'm including my recording of your dream. Unfortunately, much of it seems to have been quite subjective and I don't think I understood it all. That's

how it always is with these true dreams. I always seem to miss something.>

"So did I. But I got enough, I think, to last me for a while."

<If the Keeper *can* speak so clearly, why do you think she's usually so vague?>

"I understood why, during the dream," said Shedemei. "The experience is so overwhelming that if she gave it to most people, they'd be so consumed by it that they wouldn't own their souls anymore. Their will would be swallowed up in hers. It would kill them, in effect."

<Why are you immune, then?>

"I'm not. But since I had already chosen to follow the Keeper's plan, this dream didn't erase my will, it confirmed who I already was and what I already wanted. I didn't lose my freedom, and instead of killing me it made me more alive."

<In other words, it's another organic thing.>

"Yes, that's right. It's an organic thing." She thought for a moment longer, and added, "She said she couldn't let me see her face, but now I understand that I don't need to or want to, because I've done something better."

<Which is?>

"I've worn her face. I've seen through her eyes."

<Seems only fair. She's worn *your* face a thousand times before now, and used your hands and speech to do her work.>

Shedemei held up her hands and looked at them, damp and crumbed from the meal she was just finishing. "Then I would have to say that the Keeper of Earth looks just like me, don't you think?" She laughed for a moment; the sound was no doubt as raucous as any laugh, but inside herself it awakened the memory of music, and for a moment she remembered the taste of the fruit, and she was content.

12

Victory

When Edhadeya came to see them after their big public meeting in Jatva, it was Mon who went aside with her to hear what she had to say. "If you've come to persuade me to break ranks with my brothers," he began, but she gave him no chance to finish.

"I know you're already committed to denying everything that was ever noble and good about you, Mon, so I wouldn't waste my time. Father sent me with a message."

Mon felt the tiniest thrill of fear and dread. He often found it hard to believe that Father was letting them get away with all the things they were doing. Oh, he had stopped them from organizing the boycott of digger trade and labor, but of course they got around that by pretending to speak *against* the boycott—everyone understood the real message. Was Father now taking action against them? And if so, why was there something inside Mon that welcomed it? Was it that victory had come to them too easily, and he wanted some kind of contest?

"Are you listening?" asked Edhadeya.

"Yes," said Mon.

"Father is worried that some of his soldiers might decide that their duty to the king requires them to remove the source of his recent unhappiness. Some chance remarks of his, overheard by others out of context, have given some soldiers the impression that he would welcome this."

"Sounds to me as though he gave an order and changed his mind a little too late." Mon laughed nastily.

"You know that isn't true."

He did, of course. His truthsense rebelled against the idea—but he was getting better and better at suppressing it.

"What does he think we're going to do?" asked Mon. "Go into hiding? Stop speaking publicly? He can forget it. Killing us would only make martyrs of us and make our victory complete. Besides, he didn't raise cowards."

"Fools, yes, liars, yes, but not cowards." Edhadeya smiled grimly. "He knows you won't back down. All he suggested was that you keep your travel plans secret. Don't tell people where you're going next. Don't tell them when you're going to leave."

Mon thought about it for a moment. "All right. I'll tell the others."

"Then I've done my duty." She turned to leave.

"Wait," said Mon. "Is that all? No other messages? Nothing personal from you?"

"Nothing but my loathing, which I freely give to all five of you, but with a special extra dose for you, Mon, since I know that *you* know that Akma is wrong with every word he says. Akma may be doing most of the talking, but you are the most dishonest one, because you know the truth."

Mon started to explain again about how his childish truthsense was pure illusion designed to win attention for the second son of the king, but before he was well launched into it, she slapped his face.

"Not to me," she said. "You can tell that to anyone else and they can believe it if they want, but never say it to me. The insult is unbearable."

This time when she walked away, melting into the dispersing crowd, he didn't call her back. The stinging of his cheek had brought tears to his eyes, but he wasn't sure if it was just the pain that had done it. He thought back to those wonderful days when he was young and Edhadeya was his dearest friend. He remembered how she trusted him to take her true dream to Father, and because of Aronha's absolute trust in his truthsense, he had won a hearing and an expedition was launched and the Zenifi were rescued. He had believed in those days that this would be his place in the kingdom, to be Aronha's most trusted counselor because Aronha would know that Mon could not lie. And the time when Bego used him to help translate the Rasulum leaves. . . .

Funny, now that he thought of it with the sting of Edhadeya's slap still in his face, how Bego didn't believe in the Keeper, but he still used Mon to help him with the translation. Wasn't it Bego, really, who taught them all to disbelieve in the Keeper? But Bego believed. Or at least believed in Mon's gift.

No, no, Akma already explained that. Bego didn't think of it as a gift from the Keeper, he thought of it as an innate talent in Mon himself. That's right, the ability to sense when people really believed what they were saying. It had nothing to do with absolute truth, and everything to do with absolute belief.

But if that's the case, thought Mon, why don't I ever get a sense that a single thing that Akma says is true? I haven't really got the logic of that straight. If my truthsense came from the Keeper, then the Keeper might be trying to turn me against Akma by refusing to confirm anything he says. But then, that would mean there really *was* a Keeper, so that can't be the reason. At the same time, if Akma is right and my truthsense is merely my own ability to tell when people are certain that they're telling the truth, what does that say about my complete lack of confirmation concerning Akma's words? It means that no matter how convincing he sounds—and don't I get caught up in his speeches the way the crowd does, swept along and utterly persuaded?—my truthsense still says that he's lying. He doesn't believe a word he's saying. Or if he believes it, it's like an opinion, not like a certainty. At the core of him, in his heart, in the deepest places in his mind, he isn't saying these things because he is sure of them.

So what *does* Akma believe? And why am I denying my truthsense in favor of Akma's uncertainties?

No, no, I already went through this with Akma, and he explained that a truly educated man never believes *anything* with certainty because he knows that further learning might challenge any or all of his beliefs; therefore I will only get a strong response from my truthsense about people who are ignorant or fanatical.

Ignorant or fanatical . . . like Edhadeya? Bego?

"Well, what did she want?" asked Aronha.

Mon's reverie had carried him back to where his brothers and Akma were speaking with the leaders of the local Assembly of the Ancient Ways. This was the part of founding a religion that bothered Mon the most. While they got plenty of donations from rich and educated people, the ones who actually were willing to take the time to govern the assembly weren't people that Mon much cared for. A lot of them were former priests who had lost their jobs back at the time of the reforms—an arrogant bunch that thought themselves a sort of wronged aristocracy, full of grievance and conceit. Others, though, were the kind of digger-hating bigots that, in Mon's opinion, were almost certainly the very men who either carried out or ordered the cruel mistreatment of the Kept during the persecutions. It made his skin crawl to have to associate with them. Aronha had privately confessed to Mon that he hated dealing with these people, too. "Whatever else we might say about Akmaro," Aronha commented then, "he certainly attracts a better grade of priest." They could never say this in front of Akma, however, since he still became very upset at any reminder of Luet's marriage to the priest Didul, and to praise the priests of the Kept as a class would surely cause an eruption of Akma's temper.

"She had a warning from Father," said Mon.

"Oh, is he starting to threaten us now?" asked Akma. He had his arm across the shoulder of a young thug who might well have been one of those who broke the bones or tore the wings of children.

"Let's talk about it when we're alone," said Mon.

"Why, do we have something to hide from our priests?" asked Akma.

"Yes," said Mon coldly.

Akma laughed. "He's joking, of course." But a few minutes later, Akma had managed to get rid of the young man and he and the Motiaki withdrew to a place near the riverbank. "Don't ever do that to me again, please," said Akma. "The day will come when we can use the machinery of state to support our assembly, but for right now we need the help of these people and it doesn't help when you make them feel excluded."

"Sorry," said Mon. "But I didn't trust him."

Akma smiled. "Of course you didn't. He's a contemptible sneak. But he's a *vain* contemptible sneak and I had to work pretty hard to keep him from going away angry."

Mon patted Akma's arm. "As long as you bathe after touching him, I'm sure everything will be fine." Then he told them what Edhadeya had said.

"He's obviously trying to hamper us," said Ominer angrily. "Why should we believe anything he says?"

"Because he's the king," said Aronha, "and he wouldn't lie about something like this."

"Why not?" demanded Ominer.

"Because it shames him to admit he may not be able to control his soldiers," said Aronha. "I wish we didn't have to hurt Father so badly. If only he'd understand that we're doing this for the sake of the kingdom."

"We can't change our whole schedule around," said Ominer. "People are expecting us."

"Oh, don't worry about that," said Mon. "We'll draw a crowd whenever and wherever we show up. It might add a bit of mystery, for that matter, no one ever knowing where we'll be speaking next. Add to the excitement."

"It makes us look like cowards," said Ominer.

Khimin piped up. "Not if we announce that we have to do this because we've got good information that some of the king's men are out to kill us!"

"No!" Aronha said firmly. "We will *never* do that. People would take that as an accusation against the king, and it would be dishonorable for us to accuse him when he was the very one who sent us warning to try to protect us."

Akma clapped Khimin on the back. "There you go, Khimin. When Aronha decides that something is dishonorable, we can't do it even if it *would* have been a pretty effective ploy."

"Don't make fun of my sense of honor, Akma," said Aronha.

"I wasn't," said Akma. "I admire you for it."

Mon suddenly had an irresistible impulse to make trouble. "That's the way that Aronha most resembles Father. The only reason we've had any success at all is that Father is so honorable."

"Then that makes honor a weakness, doesn't it?" asked Ominer.

Aronha answered him with withering contempt. "In the short run, dishonor gives an advantage; in the long run, a dishonorable king loses the love of his people and ends up the way Nuab did. Dead."

"They tortured him to death with fire, didn't they?" asked Khimin.

"Try not to sound so delighted at the thought of it," said Akma. "It makes other people uneasy."

But what Mon noticed, what disturbed him in all this, was the fact that Akma seemed to draw closer to Ominer the more he said things that should have made a decent person recoil from him. Ominer said that honor was a weakness; now, though he said not a word about it, Akma had his arm around Ominer's shoulders and Ominer was all smiles. This is wrong. There's something seriously wrong. Akma wasn't like this, not even as recently as last year, before all this began. I remember when he would have been adamant about honor and decency as Aronha was. What is it, are the vile people we associate with now beginning to influence him? Or is it simply a natural consequence of having the adulation of so many thousands of people?

Whatever it was that was happening to Akma, Mon hated it. This couldn't be the real Akma emerging; it was more as if Akma were beginning to take on this cynical, amoral posture because he thought it was what he had to become in order to have his victory. Or perhaps it was a true part of Akma that never came out until he began to think that he was so important and powerful that he didn't have to be decent to other people anymore. How much of his bantering with Aronha is really joking these days, Mon wondered, and how much of it is real contempt for Aronha's kingly bearing?

I mustn't think these things, Mon reminded himself. It's the Keeper trying to win me away from my brothers.

No, it's *not* the Keeper because there *is* no Keeper. . . .

Mon excused himself from them because he needed to sleep. The others all took it as a signal. The conversation turned to empty playful chatter as they walked back to the house where they were staying. The place was far too small for five grown men to stay—half the family that lived there had been farmed out to neighbors' houses—but Akma insisted that they couldn't always stay in rich men's houses or the Kept would be able to accuse them of pride. Seeing what the Kept already accused them of, Mon thought the addition of one more minor charge would be worth it for a good night's sleep, but as usual Aronha saw things Akma's way and so he was crammed into a space where he couldn't stretch out or roll over without waking somebody up. The poor just don't build big enough houses, he told himself as a nasty little joke. He could never say it out loud, of course, because Akma would tell him that "people won't understand it's just humor."

The next morning, Aronha decided they'd take Father's advice and leave at once instead of staying another day, and instead of going to Fetek, they'd head for Papadur. Oh, excellent, thought Mon, twice the walk, and uphill the whole way instead of down. I'll have to write Father a note thanking him for his suggestion.

On the way, Akma critiqued Khimin's speech of the night before. Mon had to admire the deft way that he did it, always praising right along with his criticisms so that Khimin never felt diminished. It helped, of course, that Khimin held Akma in absolute awe.

"What you said about how *our* teachers are well-educated and the Kept teachers are all just as ignorant as their students—that was a deft point, and I'm glad you made it."

Khimin smiled. "Thanks."

"There's just a word-choice thing you'll want to think of for next time. I know, it's so frustrating, you have to think of so many things at once, the same thing happens to me, you get one thing right and something else slips. But that's why not everybody can do this."

It was so easy for Mon to see Akma's flattery, how he set Khimin up and won him over. Yet Khimin was oblivious, the poor fool.

Then Mon had the uneasy thought that perhaps Akma adapted his technique to whatever fool he happened to be talking to, and maybe to someone else Mon looked just as oblivious, just as gullible.

"I was thinking, as you talked last night, How can I steal this idea from Khimin and use it in *my* speech?"

Khimin laughed. So did Ominer, who was listening in—and who definitely could use some help with his speeches, too, since, while he never stammered or fumbled as Khimin did, he was also never for a moment entertaining.

"Here's how I would have said it," Akma offered. " 'My father, in his compassion, has established a religion in which the ignorant teach the ignorant, and the poor minister to the poor. This is a noble enterprise; let no man interfere with it. But for humans and angels, for people of education and manners, there is no reason to pretend we need the primitive doctrines and coarse company of Akmaro's so-called Kept.' "

"What do you mean, 'Let no man interfere with it'?" asked Khimin. "I thought that's what we were doing!"

"Of course that's what we're doing, and the audience knows it. But you see what the effect of that is? It makes it seem like we're not anybody's enemy. We're not opposing them, we're meeting the needs of the better sort of people while the Kept meet the needs of the poor and ignorant. Now, how many people in our audiences think of themselves as poor and ignorant?"

"Most of them!" Ominer said snidely.

"Most of them *are* poor, compared to someone who grew up in the king's house," said Akma, with only a hint of sarcasm. "But how do they think of *themselves?* Everybody thinks he's one of the more educated, refined people—or if he isn't, he's certainly going to do everything he can to make sure other people *think* he is. So now— which assembly is he going to go to? The one that will make him seem to be one of the educated and refined. You see? Nobody can accuse us of name-calling or abusing the Kept—and yet, the more we praise them, the more we make people want to stay as far away from them as possible."

Khimin laughed with delight. "It's like—you take what you want to say, and then you find a way to say the opposite, but so that it will have the *effect* you want."

"Not quite the opposite," said Akma. "But you're getting it, you're getting it!"

Mon's truthsense suddenly erupted inside him, rejecting what he had just heard with such violence that he felt like he might throw up. He stopped walking and, without meaning to, sank to his knees.

"Mon?" asked Aronha.

At that moment there was a loud noise, and all of them looked up to see a huge object, grey as granite, whirling as it plummeted toward them. Smoke poured out of it as if it were on fire, and the roaring sound was deafening. Mon covered his ears with his hands and saw that his brothers were doing the same. At the last moment the huge grey stone veered off and fell toward the ground not a dozen paces from them, the smoke and dust blinding them. At that moment the earth shook, throwing them from their feet like punted dolls. Yet there was no crashing sound, or if there was, it was swallowed up in the roar of the fallen stone and the rumbling of the earth.

As the smoke and dust cleared, they saw someone standing in front of the stone, but what he looked like they couldn't guess, for he shone so brightly from every part of his body that their eyes could not see anything but the human shape of him. The reason there had been no crashing sound now became clear, for the great grey object hovered in the air perhaps half a meter from the ground. It was impossible. It was irrational.

The man of light spoke, but they couldn't hear him; his voice was lost in the other noise.

The stone suddenly fell silent. The rumbling of the earthquake faded. Mon raised himself onto his arms and looked at the man of light.

"Akma," said the man. "Stand up."

The voice was hardly human; it was like five voices at once, five different pitches that set up painful vibrations in Mon's head. He was glad that it was Akma's name that was called, not his; and though he was immediately ashamed of his cowardice, he was *still* glad.

Akma struggled to his feet.

"Akma, why are you persecuting the people of the Keeper? For the Keeper of Earth has said, These are *my* people, these are the Kept. I will establish them in this land, and nothing but their own evil choices will be allowed to overthrow them!"

Mon was overwhelmed with shame. All these months of denying his truthsense, and it had been right all along. Akma's arguments proving that there was no Keeper now seemed so thin and meaningless—how could Mon have believed him for an instant, when he had the truthsense within him telling him otherwise all along? What have I done? What have I done?

"The Keeper has heard the pleas of the Kept, and also the plea of your father, the true servant of the Keeper. He has begged the Keeper for years to bring you to understand the truth, but the Keeper knew that you already understood the truth. Now you father begs the Keeper to stop you from harming the innocent children of earth."

The earth rumbled under them again; Akma was knocked to his knees, and Mon fell, his face striking the damp soil of the road.

"Can you claim any more that the Keeper has no power? Are you deaf to my voice? Blind to the light that shines from my body? Can't you feel the earth shake beneath you? Is there no Keeper?"

Mon cried out in fear, "Yes! There is! I knew it all along! Forgive me for my lies!" He could hear his brothers also crying out, pleading for mercy; only Akma remained silent.

"Akma, remember your captivity in the land of Chelem. Remember how the Keeper delivered you from bondage. Now *you* are the oppressor of the Kept, and the Keeper will deliver them from *you*. Go your way, Akma, and seek no more to destroy the Assembly of the Kept. Their pleas will be answered, whether you choose to destroy yourself or not."

With those words, the light coming from the messenger's body seemed to increase in brightness and intensity—something Mon would have thought impossible, since he was already nearly blinded when he looked at him. Yet he was able to see that the man of light extended his arm and a bolt of lightning crackled in the air between his finger and Akma's head. Akma seemed to dance in the air for a moment like an ash suspended over a fire; then he fell in a heap. The huge stone roared again, and again dust and smoke arose to blind them all. When it cleared, the stone was gone, the messenger also, and the earth was still.

Khimin was weeping. "Father!" he cried out. "Mother! I don't want to die!"

Mon might have scoffed, but the same feelings were coursing through his own heart.

"Akma," said Aronha.

Of course, thought Mon. It's my older brother who has the decency to remember our friend instead of thinking of himself. Mon was filled with new shame. He got up and staggered to where Akma lay unconscious.

"There *is* a Keeper," Ominer was intoning. "I know there's a Keeper, I know it now, I know it, I know it."

"Shut up, Ominer," said Mon. "Help us get Akma into the sunlight, onto the grass."

They carried him then, his body limp.

"He's dead," said Khimin.

"If the man of light meant to kill him," said Mon, "why would he tell him to stop interfering with the Kept? You don't have to give instructions to dead men."

"If he's alive," said Aronha, "then why isn't he breathing? Why can't I find a pulse or hear a heartbeat?"

"I tell you he *is* alive," said Mon.

"How can you know that?" demanded Ominer. "You haven't even checked him."

"Because my truthsense affirms it. Yes, he lives."

"Suddenly your truthsense is back again?" asked Aronha ironically.

"It never left. I denied it, I ignored it, I fought against it, but it never left." It hurt to say these words. And yet it was also a relief.

"This whole time your truthsense has been telling you that the things we taught were lies?" asked Aronha.

Aronha's tone was a slap in the face. "Akma told me that my truthsense was a lie! Self-deception! I was ashamed to talk about it." He could see contempt on Aronha's face. "Are you going to blame this on me, Aronha? Is that the kind of man you are? It's all Mon's fault that you were doing this? The Keeper sends us a being of light to tell us that we were lying, destroying something that mattered, and you're going to point the finger at *me*?"

It was Aronha's turn to look ashamed. "I made my own choice, I know it. I kept thinking, if Mon says it's right, it must be right—only I knew it was wrong, and I was using my reliance on you as an excuse. The younger boys, now, they can hardly be held responsible. You and I and Akma put a lot of pressure on them and—"

"I made my own choices too!" Khimin shouted. "The messenger didn't come to stop *you*. He came to stop us *all*." Mon realized that Khimin was proud that he had been visited by a messenger from the Keeper. That had to be better than a true dream. Examining his own heart, Mon realized that he had such feelings, too.

"The messenger may have come to stop us all," Ominer said, "but he only spoke to Akma. Because the truth is that we were all following Akma from the beginning."

"Oh, aren't you the brave one, blaming it on him," said Khimin. "It's all the fault of the one who's lying there like a dead man."

"I'm not saying that to excuse us," said Ominer. "As far as I'm concerned, that should make us even more ashamed. We're the sons of the king! And we let someone talk us into defying and shaming our father and everything he had taught us."

"It was my fault," said Aronha. He managed to hold his voice steady, but he dared not look them in the eye. "I may have half-believed some of Akma's ideas, but when it came to starting our own religion, restoring the old order of the state—I knew it was wrong. I knew the people we were working with were contemptible opportunists. I knew that the diggers we were driving out of Darakemba were better people than our supposed friends. And I'm the one who was raised to be king. I don't deserve it. I forbid you to call me Ha-Aron anymore. I'm just Aron."

Mon couldn't contain his frustration any longer. "Don't you see what you're doing, even now? We followed Akma because he flattered us and fed our pride. We loved it while we were doing it, too. We loved being important and powerful. We loved making Father back down before us, we loved changing the world, we loved thinking we were smarter than everybody else and having people admire us and treat us like we were important. It was pride that kept us going. And now what are we doing? Khimin's wetting himself because we were *so* important that the Keeper sent a man of light to stop us—don't argue with me, Khimin, I was feeling the same thing myself. And Aronha here wants to take all the blame himself, because *he's* the one who should have known better and don't you see? It's still pride! It's still the same thing that got us into trouble in the first place!"

"I'm not proud," said Aronha, and now his voice was trembling. "I can't stand the thought of facing anybody."

"But we will," said Mon. "Because we have to let them see what a miserable bunch we are."

"Isn't that a kind of pride, too?" asked Ominer nastily.

"Maybe it is, Ominer! But you want to know the one thing I'm really proud of? The one thing that makes me glad that you're my brothers, that I'm one of you?"

"What?" said Aronha.

"That not one of you suggested that we go on fighting the Keeper," said Mon. "That it didn't cross your minds that maybe we could remain a part of the Assembly of the Ancient Ways."

"That doesn't mean we're *good* or anything," said Ominer. "It might just mean we're terrified."

"We could only rebel when we could fool ourselves into thinking that we believed there was no Keeper. Now we know better. We've seen things that we never imagined, things that happened only in the time of the Heroes. But remember those stories? Elemak and Mebbekew saw things every bit as strong as this! And yet they kept rebelling, right to the end of their lives. Not us! Our rebellion is over."

Aronha nodded. "I still meant what I said about being Aron now."

Mon shot back at once, "You'll stay Aronha until Father tells you otherwise! He didn't take away the honorific the whole time you were shaming him."

Aronha nodded again.

"This will kill Mother," Khimin said, weeping.

Mon put his arm around his youngest brother and held him. "I don't know if we can decently ask Father to take us back. But we have to go to him, if only so he can have the victory of turning us away."

"Father will take us back," said Aronha. "That's the kind of man he is. The question is whether we can undo any of the harm we've caused."

"No," said Ominer. "The question is, will Akma live or not? We have to get him back to Darakemba. Do we keep him here and hope that he'll revive? Or search for help to carry him back?"

"There are four of us," said Khimin. "We can carry him."

"I've heard that Shedemei the schoolmaster is a healer," said Mon.

"Now we need help from a woman we referred to as a criminal mixer of species," said Aronha bitterly. "In our time of need, it doesn't cross our minds to turn to our own Assembly of the Ancient Ways. We know, we always knew, that the only help we can count on will be found among the Kept."

Shame tasted foul in their mouths as they made a litter for Akma out of their coats and staves, then lifted the staves to their shoulders to carry him. As they neared more settled country, people ran out to see them, these four men carrying what seemed to be a corpse on their shoulders, as if to take him to be buried.

"Go," Aronha said to them—said to everyone who came out to meet them. "Go and tell everyone that the Keeper sent a messenger to strike down the Motiaki and stop them from telling their lies. We are the sons of Motiak, and we return in shame to our father. Go and tell everyone that Akma, the son of Akmaro, has been struck down by the messenger of the Keeper, and whether he will live or die no one can say!"

Over and over he said these things, and every time that the words were said to one of the Kept, the response was the same: not rejoicing, not gloating, not condemnation, but tears and embraces and then, inevitably, the most unbearable thing of all: "Can we help you? Can we carry Akma for a little way? Oh, his father and mother will weep to see him like this! We will pray to the Keeper to let them see their son alive again! Let us help you!" They brought water to them, brought them food, and not once did any of the Kept reprove them.

Others were not so kind. Men and women who had no doubt cheered for Akma and the sons of Motiak during their speeches now shouted bitter denunciations, calling them liars, frauds, heretics. "Arondi! Mondi! Ominerdi! Khimindi!" How bitter it was that while they really were rebelling against their father, no one dared to put the term for traitor in their names; but now that they had ended their rebellion and confessed their wrongdoing, the epithet was heaped upon them.

"It's what we deserve," Mon said, when Ominer began to point out the hypocrisy of their accusers.

And then, gallingly, they had to watch and listen as the Kept took the shouters aside and rebuked them. "Don't you see that they're filled with grief? Can't you see that Akma is nearly dead? They're doing you no harm now, let them pass, give them peace."

Thus the Kept became their protectors on their journey. And many of them were diggers. Mon was not content to let Aronha's speeches be all *they* heard. To the diggers, Mon added his own message. "Please, go and find the earth people who are on the road, leaving Darakemba. Tell them that we beg them to come home. Tell them that they are better citizens of Darakemba than the sons of Motiak. Don't let them leave."

They slept beside Akma that night on the road, and late the next day they reached Darakemba. Word had gone ahead of them, and when they got to Akma's house, a huge crowd parted to let them through, and Akmaro and Chebeya stood in the doorway to receive the almost-living body of their son. Inside the house the king their father waited, and their sister Edhadeya, and they wept at how lovingly their father and sister embraced them, and wept again as Akmaro and Chebeya knelt over the ruins of their son.

On the road, the being of light appeared. The earth trembled. Akma should have been surprised but he was not. It was the strangest thing, that it did not feel strange to him. As the messenger spoke, what kept running through Akma's mind was the thought, What took you so long?

As soon as he noticed his own lack of surprise, he wondered at it. He couldn't have been expecting anything like this. He didn't know that any being like this existed. Certainly in his scholarship he had never come up with any such thing. Besides, experience proved nothing. This could be nothing more than a hallucination shared by a group of five men who were in desperate need of some affirmation of their importance to the universe. Instead of proving that there really was a Keeper of Earth, this experience might prove nothing more than the inescapable unconscious power of childhood belief, even over men who thought they had outgrown it.

But as the messenger kept speaking (and how can I hear every word and still have time to think all these thoughts? What extraordinary clarity of mind. I'd like to tell Bego about this phenomenon. What did the king end up doing to Bego, anyway? Look at this—I go off on a tangent, wondering about Bego, and yet I haven't missed a word of the message) Akma knew that this was not a shared hallucination, or that if it was, it was a hallucination induced by the Keeper of Earth, because this was definitely sent from outside himself. Why did he know that? It was as Edhadeya said, you simply know the difference when it has happened to you. Only it isn't the being of light that's doing it. No, that's just a show, just a spectacle. It isn't having my eyes dazzled or the earth shaking under my feet or great roaring noises or smoke or a strange-sounding voice that makes me sure. I simply know.

And then he thought: I *always* knew.

He remembered back to the time when he was in the greatest terror of his life—when the sons of Pabulog first threw him down and began to torture him and humiliate him. He couldn't have put it into words at the time, but underneath the fear for his life, there was shame at his helplessness; and underneath that there was steely courage that made him try not to beg for mercy, that sustained him through it all and allowed him to walk, naked and smeared with mud and filth and ruined food, back to his people. He knew at the time what *that* strength was—it was the absolute certainty of the love of his parents (and the memory of it stabbed him; I had their love, I still have their love, it was as firm as I believed even as a little boy, my faith was not misplaced, and look what I've done to them), a sense of the unbreakable cords that bound them together, almost as if he had the raveling skill of his mother without ever having noticed it consciously.

And yet underneath *that* there was something else. A sense that someone was watching everything that happened, watching and saying, What these boys are doing to you is wrong. The love your parents have for you is right. Your weeping, your shame, they are not flaws in you, you can't help it. Your effort at courage is worthy. It is right for you to go back to your people. A constant judge, assessing the moral value of what he was doing. How could he now remember something that he hadn't noticed at the time? And yet he knew without doubt that this watcher had been there at the time, and that he had loved this voice inside him, because when he did well it said so.

The messenger was saying, "The Keeper has heard the pleas of the Kept, and also the plea of your father, the true servant of the Keeper." How long had the speech gone on? Not long at all; it was barely begun, really, he could tell. It was as if he knew every word the messenger would say and how long was allotted to each part of the message, so that his mind could divide its attention between little slices required to hear and understand the words, and great long passages of time between those slices in which he could search out this mystery, this observer that he had had within him all these years and never noticed.

He saw himself sitting on a hillside watching Father teach the Pabulogi. He felt the rage inside his boyish heart, heard himself vowing revenge. But on whom? Now he could see what he had not seen then: What he was raging at was not the Pabulogi at all, and not even his father for teaching them. No, the betrayal that stung him to the heart was against all of them and none of them—it was against the Keeper of Earth for daring to save the people without using Akma as his instrument.

And what was that secret inner watcher saying then? Nothing. Nothing at all. It had withdrawn. It was silent within him while his heart was filled with rage at not having been chosen.

I drove it away. I was empty then.

But no, not completely empty, for now he could sense it like the softest possible sound, the tiniest possible mark, the dimmest possible star that could still be seen at all. The watcher was still there, and it was quietly saying, It was not your time, it was not your time, be patient, the plan is larger than you, I needed others this time, your time will come. . . .

So the watcher was there, but had no effect on him, because his own rage drowned it out.

And now, looking inside himself, he realized that the watcher was still inside him, still speaking, like a voice behind the voice of his mind, offering perpetual commentary on every conscious thought but always fleeing from consciousness itself whenever he tried to seize the elusive wisdom. Even now he could only remember the comment that had just passed, not hear the one that was happening right now.

Now you know me, the watcher had just said. You knew me all along, but now you know that you know me.

Yes, said Akma silently in reply. You are the Keeper of Earth, and you have been part of me all along. You have been like a spark kept alive inside me no matter how I tried to put that fire out, no matter how often I denied you, there you were.

"Their pleas will be answered," the messenger was saying, "whether you choose to destroy yourself or not." And with that the message ended. The bright arm reached out to point to him. The finger crackled and hissed and a terrible pain touched every nerve in his body at once, he was entirely on fire, and in that moment of exquisite agony he could remember what the watcher, what the Keeper, had just . . . finished . . . saying. . . .

Now you know me, Akma. And now I'm gone.

Until that moment, Akma could not have imagined a more terrible pain than the suffering of his body as the messenger's bolt of power touched all his nerves at once. But now that pain had ended and Akma's body lay crumpled on the ground, and he understood that the pain of his body was nothing, it hadn't even touched him, it was almost a pleasure compared to. . . .

Compared to perfect solitude.

He was connected to nothing. He had no name because there was no one to know him, no place because he was connected to nothing, no power because there was nothing on which he could act. Yet he knew that once he had had these things and now they were torn from him; he was lost and would never be anything or anyone again; he was lost because *no one knew him.* Where is the one who watches? Where is the one who knows me? Where is the one who names me? I only just found him inside me, didn't I? How could he have left me now?

There was no pain compared to this loss. He wouldn't mind being restored to the agonized body he had been connected to only a few moments ago, because it was better to feel that pain, with the watcher judging him, than to feel this utter lack of pain, with no one watching him. When I felt the pain I was part of something; now I am part of nothing.

Didn't I want this? To be only myself, responsible to no one, uncommanded, uncontrolled, unexpected, free? I didn't know what it meant till now, to owe nothing to anyone, to have no duty because I had no power to act. I didn't realize that utter independence was the most terrible punishment.

All my life the Keeper was inside me, judging me. But now the judging is over. I was not fit to be part of the Keeper's world.

As he knew this, the reasons for his knowledge began to come into his mind. Images that he had refused to imagine before now came to him with perfect reality. An old digger woman being set upon and beaten by human men, tall and terrifying; and because Akma was inside her, all her memories flooded over him and he knew all the meanings of this moment. When his comprehension of the old woman's suffering was complete, he suddenly passed into the mind of one of the thugs, and now he was no longer a thug, but a man, sickened by his own action yet still hot-blooded from violence, not daring to voice his own self-contempt because then he would be shamed in front of. . . .

And in that moment Akma was inside the man whose admiration the thug had treasured, and saw his sense of pride and power at having set in motion the dark events that terrorized the Kept. He was hungry for power, and loved having it now, for now they would have to think of *him* when they wanted something done, they would respect him. . . .

And now the "they" in the plotter's mind took on a shape, several shapes, rich old men who had once been influential in the kingdom but now were only important in Darakemba, for the kingdom had outgrown their petty reach. When Aronha is king, he'll know that my influence is valuable. I can accomplish the things that are too dark for him to do with his own hands. I will not be despised, when the new king comes.

It took no further explanation for Akma to understand, for wasn't he the one who captured the hearts and minds of the sons of Motiak, who united them against the policies of his own father and the king? The certainty in his mind was unassailable: This old woman would not have been beaten if I had not deliberately given others cause to think that they would gain some advantage through cruelty to the Kept. The chain of cause was long, but it was not false, and the worst thing was that Akma knew that he had known it all along, that in his hatred and envy of the Keeper's power he had, in fact, longed for violent and cruel action and, instead of doing it with his own hands, had flung his power out into the world and caused other hands to do what he wanted done.

This is what the Keeper does, to accomplish his good works: casts his influence out into the world and gives people encouragement for their good impulses. The watcher that was present in me is present in every living soul; no one is alone; everyone is touched by those gentle words of affirmation when they do what the Keeper asks: Well done, my good child, my faithful friend, my willing servant. My own power was but a small part of what the Keeper has, a dim shadow of his influence—but instead of using it to make other people a bit more happy, a bit more free, I used it to kindle the avarice and envy in some hearts, who then fanned the flames of violence in others. I was inside their hearts when they struck, and my voice, even though they didn't know it was my voice, was saying, Break, tear, hurt, destroy. She is not part of the world that we are building; drive her out. Those I used as my hands in this dirty business were also responsible for their own actions, but that does not absolve me. For those who do good, do it with the Keeper inside them, urging them on, praising them for their kindness—yet the Keeper does not make them do it. The good works are their own, and also they are the Keeper's. So also were the cruelties of these dark-hearted men their own, and yet mine as well. Mine.

No sooner had he understood his own role in the beating of that one old woman than a new cruelty came into his mind, a child who cried out in hunger and had nothing to eat because his father had lost his income in the boycott; Akma saw through the child's eyes, and then through the father's, feeling his shame and despair at being unable to give his child relief, and then Akma was the mother in her impotent rage and her complaints against the Keeper and the Kept for having brought this down upon them, and again he followed the chain of suffering and evil—the merchants who once had bought the father's goods, who now refused to buy, some out of fear of reprisal, some out of a personal bias against diggers that now had become respectable—no, patriotic!—because Akma had stood before a crowd and told them that they must all obey the law and *not* boycott *anybody* and the audience had laughed because they understood what Akma wanted. . . .

He wanted the child to weep and the father's pride to break and the mother's loyalty to the Kept to burn out in helpless fury. He wanted this because he had to punish the Keeper for *not choosing him* back when he was a child desperate to save his little sister from the lash.

Over and over, time after time, scene after scene, he saw all the pain he had caused. How long did it last? It could have been a single minute; it could have been a dozen lifetimes. How could he measure it, having no connection to reality, no sense of time? He saw it all, however long it took; and yet each moment of it was also eternal, because his understanding was so complete.

If he could have made a sound, it would have been an endless scream. It was unbearable to be alone; and worst of all was that in his solitude he had to be with himself, with all his loathsome, contemptible actions.

Long before the parade of crimes was over, Akma was finished. He no longer saw himself leading the parade of conquering soldiers sweeping through the Elemaki lands. He could not bear the thought of anyone ever seeing him again, for now he knew what he truly was and could never hide it from himself or anyone else again. The shame was too great. He no longer wished to be restored to all the things that he had lost. Now all he wanted was to be blotted out. Don't make me face anyone again. Don't make me face myself. Don't make me face even you, Keeper. I can't bear to exist.

Yet each time that he thought he had reached bottom and could suffer no more deeply than at *this* moment, another image would spring into his mind, another person whose suffering he had caused, and . . . yes . . . he *could* feel more shame and pain than he had felt only a moment ago, when it had already seemed infinite and unbearable.

Shedemei made her way through the quiet house, where so many people quietly came and went, carrying out their tasks. She saw four young men and recognized them as the sons of Motiak; they didn't recognize her, of course, since all they had seen on the road was unwatchable brightness in a human shape. And in a way she didn't recognize them either, for the strutting, laughing, boastful boys that she had first met were gone; and also gone were the cowering, terrified children who trembled before her and winced at every word she spoke—spoke, of course, into a tiny microphone so that the translation equipment could amplify and distort her voice to make it as painful as possible.

What she saw now were four humans who actually had some hint of manhood about them. It was clear from their ravaged faces that they had shed many tears, but they were making no show of grief and remorse now. Instead, as people came to them—many of them diggers, though most were not—they received them graciously. "All we hope for now is that the Keeper will decide to spare Akma's life, so that he can join us in going about trying to undo the terrible harm we caused. Yes, I know that you forgive me; you're more generous than I deserve, but I accept your forgiveness and I vow to you that for the rest of my life I will do all that I can to earn what you've given me freely. But for now we wait and watch with Akma's family. The Keeper struck him down because loyal and obedient Kept like you pleaded for relief. The Keeper hears you. We beg you to plead again with him for the life and forgiveness of our friend." Their words were not always so clear, but the meaning was the same: We will try to undo the harm we caused; we beg you to plead with the Keeper to save our friend.

Shedemei had no particular wish to speak to them—she knew from the Oversoul that they were sincere, that their true natures had once again emerged, wiser now, with painful memories, but committed to lives of decency. What business did she have with them, then? It was Akma that she came to see.

Chebeya met her at the door to Akma's bedchamber. The room was small and sparse—Akmaro and Chebeya really did live modestly. "Shedemei," Chebeya said. "I'm so glad you got word and came. We were a day's walk from the capital when word reached us that the Keeper had struck down our boy. We got home only a few hours before Motiak's boys brought him here. We kept expecting to pass you on the road."

"I went another way," said Shedemei. "I had some botanical specimens to tend to, among other things." She knelt beside Akma's inert body. He certainly did look dead.

<He practically is. Like a hypothermia victim. Like someone in suspended animation during a voyage. All cell activity is low. The surprising thing is that bacterial action is also nil. Whatever the Keeper did to him, it's not going to kill him.>

Brain activity? asked Shedemei silently.

<There's something going on. But it's purely limbic. None of the higher functions. Nothing I can actually read, beyond the most primitive feelings.>

Well, what is the feeling?

<It looks to me as if . . . well, as if he were screaming.>

I'm certainly not going to tell his parents *that.*

<The Keeper is doing something to him, but I have no idea what.>

No prognosis.

<He isn't dead yet, and I have no way of predicting whether he'll recover. I have no idea what's sustaining him, and I won't even know when or whether it's withdrawn.>

It certainly makes me suspect that Sherem didn't just die of a stroke in the midst of his argument with Oykib.

<Well, it *was* a stroke. It was just a convenient one. For all we know, the Keeper can make people keel over whenever she wants.>

Good thing that *people* don't have powers like that. I have enough of a temper that my path would be strewn with corpses all the day long.

<Oh, don't brag. I doubt you'd kill more than a couple a day.>

Sighing, Shedemei arose from the floor. "He's completely stable. But it's impossible to predict when or whether he will awaken."

"But he's not dying," said Chebeya.

"You're the raveler," said Shedemei. "Is he still bound to this world?"

Chebeya put her hand to her mouth to stifle a sob. "No. He's connected to nothing. It's as if he isn't there, as if there isn't anyone at all." Then she did break down and cry, clinging to Akmaro.

"Well, his body isn't dead and it isn't deteriorating, either," said Shedemei, knowing she sounded brusque but unable to think of any gentler way to say what needed saying. "It's in the hands of the Keeper now."

Chebeya nodded.

"Thank you, Shedemei," said Akmaro. "We didn't think that it was something that you could heal, but we had to be sure. You . . . rumor has it that you can sometimes do remarkable things."

"Nothing as remarkable as what the Keeper can do."

She embraced them both and went her way, back to her students. All the way home, she argued with the Oversoul about what this all meant, what they should have done differently, what might be going on with Akma, if anything.

I wonder, said Shedemei silently, whether the Keeper simply gave him the same dream she gave me—showed him her plan for the world, possessed him with her love, and he was so filled with hate that the experience consumed him.

<Maybe it happened that way, but I never saw him enter the kind of dream state that you were in.>

Don't you sometimes wish that we were like ordinary people, without any unusual sources of information? We might be hearing about these events as nothing more than gossip about famous people.

<Such useless yearnings weren't put into me. I have never wished to be anything other than what I am.>

Neither have I, said Shedemei silently, realizing for the first time that she truly was satisfied with her life and glad of the part that the Keeper had given her in the plan of life. With that thought she suddenly laughed out loud, earning her strange looks from a couple of children passing by. She made a face at them; they shrieked and ran away, but soon stopped running and resumed their laughter and chattering. That's the plan, thought Shedemei. The Keeper only wants us to live with the simplicity and innocence of these little ones. Why is it so hard?

At last Akma's entire life had been unwound before his eyes, every bit of harm that he had caused had been remembered. And the complete memory remained with him, every bit of it, none of it fading into merciful forgetfulness. He understood many things now that he had not understood before, but he could not bear to understand them. He knew that his guilt for the pain suffered by the Kept who were beaten, by the earth people who were driven from their homes, was slight indeed compared to the guilt of having induced so many men and women to do things that drove the Keeper almost completely out of their hearts. To cause a good man pain was a terrible thing; to persuade a man to do evil was far worse.

When the Keeper had first left him, he had longed for his return. Now, though, having seen the terrible consequences of his pride, he couldn't bear the thought of anyone looking at him again, least of all the Keeper of Earth. The only relief he could hope for was to be extinguished, and that was what he longed for. He could not bear to return to the world that he had befouled so badly; he could not bear to stay as he was, utterly alone. If he could only find some road leading to obliteration, he would run to it, hurl himself into oblivion.

One of his memories was that terrible last meeting with his father and mother and the king—he had, of course, felt the anguish of these good people who, even as they faced the likelihood of his destroying all that they had tried to create, still worried more about him than about themselves. Yet as a part of that memory, there was something. His father had. . . . said something. . . .

And there it was, the words flowing back into his mind as if his father were only just now speaking them. "When you are at the point of despair, my son, when you see destruction as the only desirable choice, then remember this: The Keeper loves us. Loves us all. Values each life, each mind, each heart. All are precious to him. Even yours."

Impossible. His life had been devoted to undoing the Keeper's work. How could the Keeper possibly love him?

"His love for you is the one constant, Akma. He knows that you have believed in him all along. He knows that you have rebelled against him because you thought you knew how to shape this world more wisely than he. He knows that you have lied to everyone, over and over again, including yourself, especially yourself—and I tell you again that even knowing all of this, if you will only turn to him, he will bring you back."

Could it be the truth? That even now, the Keeper might bring him back? Free him of this terrible exile? Accept him once again, and dwell within him, and whisper to him constantly?

But even if it is true, he thought, do I *want* to? Shamed in front of the world, guilty of innumerable crimes, won't returning to such a life be more than I can stand?

At once there came to his mind an image of himself, humiliated, smeared by his enemies, returning bravely to his people.

No, that's a false image. Then I was innocent, made naked and filthy by others. Now I'm far more filthy and my nakedness is far more shameful, and it was done entirely by myself.

Yet the courage to return, that was still the same, even if the shame had a far different cause. I must return, if only so that others can see me, not strutting in my glory, but filthy in my shame. I owe it to all those that I have hurt. I would only injure them again if, like a coward, I hid my shame from them.

Oh, Keeper of Earth, he cried out in his solitude. I beg you to have mercy on me. I have poisoned myself with bitterness, I am bound by chains of death that I forged myself and I can't find my way out without your help.

In the instant that he made this plea for help, this recognition of his desperate helplessness, he felt the watcher return to him. It was a simple thing, so easy, so minute an action, as if the Keeper had been poised on the very verge of his heart, ready to touch him the moment he asked. And at this touch, the vast omnipresent memory of all his crimes suddenly was gone. He knew that he had committed them, but they no longer stared him in the face wherever he looked. It was the lifting of a terrible burden; he had never felt so light, so free. And now, even though he still had not regained the use of his body, his solitude was over. He was named, he was known, he was part of something larger than himself, and instead of feeling resentful and wanting to break anything that he could not control, he found himself filled with joy, for now his existence had a meaning. He had a future, because he was part of a world that had a future, and instead of wanting to decide for himself and determine that future for everyone else, he knew that he would be glad just to touch some small part of it. To marry and give happiness to his wife. To have a child and give it the same love that his parents had given him. To have a friend and ease his burden now and then. To have a skill or a secret and teach it to a student whose life might be changed a little by what he learned. Why had he dreamed of leading armies, which would accomplish nothing, when he could do these miraculous small things and change the world?

As Akma realized this, there suddenly flooded into him a clear understanding of all the cords of love that bound him. Everyone who cared for him, who wanted his happiness; everyone that he had ever loved or helped in any way. They were now as present and clear in his mind as, only a few moments ago, his crimes had been. Father. Mother. Luet. Edhadeya. Each one, bound to him by a thousand memories. Mon. Bego. Aronha. Ominer. Khimin. Where once his crimes against them had harrowed up his soul, now their love for him and his for them filled him with joy. Didul and Pabul and their brothers, who once had stood before him in pain because he denied them the forgiveness that they craved from him, now dwelt in his mind because of their love for his father and mother and sister, for the kingdom and the Kept and the world of the Keeper, and most particularly they loved him, they longed for his happiness, they yearned to do anything that was in their power to heal him. How could he have turned them away for so long? These were not the boys who hated him. These were sons of the Keeper, his brothers.

And others, and others; many of those whose pain he had caused now caused him joy solely by wanting him to be joyful. And behind them, within them, shining like light out of their eyes, out of their whole bodies, was the Keeper, wearing all their faces, touching him with all their hands. I know you, he said to them all. You were inside my heart from the earliest moment of my childhood. Your love was with me all along.

His mouth was flooded with the taste of a perfect white fruit, and his body was filled with it, shone with it. He, too, was as bright and shining now as all the others. As exquisite and bitter as his pain had been a moment ago, exactly that exquisite and sweet was his present joy.

Then, in a moment, the overwhelming awareness of how he was loved slipped away. It was replaced by the almost forgotten feeling of his own body, stiff and painful—but so sweet, the tang of it, the sharpness of his returning senses. There was light against his eyelids. Something moved; a shadow passed across him, and then light again. He was not alone. And he was alive.

Chebeya cried out, a soft sharp *O* of happiness. Those who had been dozing awoke; Akmaro, who had been talking with Didul and Luet, strode at once to Chebeya's side.

"His eyes moved under the eyelids," she said.

They both knelt, touched his hand. "Akma," said Akmaro. "Akma, come home to us, my son."

His eyes opened then. He blinked against the light. He turned his head, ever so slightly, and looked at them. "Father," he whispered. "Mother. Forgive me."

"Already," said Chebeya.

"Before you asked," said Akmaro.

"I have so much to do." Then he closed his eyes again and slept, this time a natural sleep, a healing sleep. His father and mother knelt over him, held his hands, stroked his face, wept for joy. The Keeper had been merciful and brought their son back home to them again.

13

Forgiveness

Shedemei was out of sorts. The merchant who supplied her with fresh food from the countryside had raised his prices again. Of course she could afford it, since she had the Oversoul's knowledge of the location of mineral deposits throughout the gornaya. It took no great effort to fly to a high peak, put on breathing gear, blast some ice into water, chip away at the exposed rock, take a bushel basket of gold ore from the mountain, have it refined in a remote place far from Darakemba, and come back with enough wealth to sustain the school for another year or two.

The trouble was that her goals had changed. The school was no longer just a ploy to allow her to be close to the center of action in Darakemba. The action was over—or, rather, had gone into hiatus—and yet she was still there and not at all interested in resuming her life sealed in a suspended animation chamber on the *Basilica*, come out only now and then to tend her plants. Her school had become real and important to her, and she wanted to get it on a sound financial footing so that someone could keep it going after she left. Yet every time she was about to get the income just about to the level of the expenses, somebody would raise a price or some new need would become apparent, and back she would go, dipping into her reserves of gold.

It was hard to remember the woman she had once been. In the city of Basilica, she had shut out the rest of the world, refusing most human contact and keeping what she had on a businesslike level as much as possible. At the time she thought it was because she loved science so much—and she did enjoy her work, so it wasn't an entire lie. But what really locked her door against the world was fear. Not fear of physical danger, really, but fear of messiness, fear of untidy entanglements perpetually unresolved. The Oversoul—no, ultimately it was the Keeper of Earth—had forced her out of her laboratory and into the chaos of human life. But she and Zdorab had somehow managed to create an island of neatness, in which they pretended to know exactly what was expected of them both and satisfy those expectations perfectly.

Now she was surrounded by perpetual chaos, children coming and going, teachers whose lives began somewhere outside her life so that they could never be wholly known, questions forever unanswered, needs forever inadequately met . . . it was the thing she had feared the most, and now that she was living in it, she couldn't understand why. This was *life.* This was what the Keeper surrounded herself with. Perpetual irresolution. A picture never framed, a series of chords that never returned to the tonic for more than a fleeting moment. Shedemei could hardly imagine living any other way.

Yet today she was out of sorts, likely to snap at anyone who crossed her path; she knew that the students always passed the word when such a mood was on her. "Thunderstorms," they would say, as if Shedemei were as unavoidable as the weather. The teachers would get the word as well, and they would wait to bring Shedemei their latest problems and requests. Let the weather clear first. And that was fine with Shedemei. Let the teachers decide whether it was really important enough to be worth braving the lion in her den.

So it rather surprised her—and peeved her, too—when someone knocked on the door of her tiny office. "Come in," she said.

Whoever it was had trouble with the latch. One of the little girls, then. Surely a teacher could have dealt with her problem without sending her unassisted to the schoolmaster's office.

Shedemei got up and opened the door. Not one of the little girls at all. It was Voozhum. "Mother Voozhum," she said, "come in, sit down. You don't have to come to my office, just send one of the girls for me and I will come to you."

"That wouldn't be fitting," said Voozhum, easing herself onto one of the stools; chairs were no good for earth people, especially the old and inflexible.

"I won't argue with you," said Shedemei. "But age has its privileges and you should take advantage of them now and then."

"I do," said Voozhum. "With people who are younger than me."

Shedemei hated it when Voozhum tried to get her to admit that she was the One-Who-Was-Never-Buried. It bothered her to lie to Voozhum, but she also couldn't trust the old soul to remember that she was supposed to keep it secret.

"I've never met anybody older than you," said Shedemei. "Now, what business brings you here?"

"I had a dream," said Voozhum. "A real wake-up-with-a-wet-bed humdinger."

Shedemei didn't know whether to be amused or annoyed with Voozhum's complacency toward her increasingly frequent incontinence. "There have been several of those recently, as I recall."

Ignoring her gibe, Voozhum said, "I thought you ought to be warned —Akma is coming here today."

Shedemei sighed. Just what she needed. "Have you told Edhadeya?"

"So she can run off and hide? No, it's time the girl faced her future."

"It's Edhadeya's choice whether Akma has anything to do with her future, don't you think?"

"No I don't," said Voozhum. "She grabs at every scrap of news about the boy. She knows that he's changed. I've seen her pining after him, and then when I mention Akma she gets that prim look on her face and says, I'm glad he's stopped interfering with things, but excuse me I've got work to do. She practically lived at Akmaro's house during the three days that Akma was getting worked over by the Keeper, but as soon as he wakes up she refuses to leave the school. I think she's a coward."

"Akma has changed," said Shedemei. "It's natural for her to fear that his feelings toward her might also have changed."

"That's not what she's afraid of," said Voozhum scornfully. "She knows they're bound together heart to heart. She's afraid of *you*."

"Me?"

"She's afraid that if she marries Akma, you won't let her have the school."

"Have the school! What, am I dying and no one told me? *I* have the school."

"She has the foolish idea that she's younger than you and might outlive you," said Voozhum nastily. "*She* doesn't know what *I* know."

"Well, I suppose that eventually I *will* give up the school."

"But will you give it to a married woman who has to deal with her husband's demands?"

"It's premature to marry them off," said Shedemei. "And premature to decide whether she'll have the freedom to take the school, and *damnably* premature to be thinking about when I'm going to leave, because I can promise you it won't be soon."

"Well *tell* her that! Tell her she'll have time for half a dozen babies before the schoolmastership comes open. Have some consideration for other people's uncertainties, why don't you!"

Shedemei burst into laughter. "You certainly don't *talk* to me as if you really believed I was a minor deity."

"When gods come down to become women, I think they should get the full experience, no holds barred. Besides, what are you going to do, strike me dead? I could keel over any minute. Every time I make it across the courtyard to my bedroom, I think, Well, it didn't kill me after all."

"I've offered to let you sleep right next to your classroom."

"Don't be absurd. I need the exercise. And unlike some people, I'm not interested in living forever. I don't have to know how things come out."

"Neither do I, really," said Shedemei. "Not anymore."

"All I came here to say, if you're finally ready to listen, is that this is Akma's first time coming out. Still a little unsteady on his feet. And I think it's significant that he chose to come here. Not just for Edhadeya's sake."

"What do you mean?"

"In my dream I saw a fine young human man, a beautiful woman right behind him, and in one hand he held the hand of an old angel, and in the other the hand of a positively decrepit digger woman who looked awful enough that I could imagine she was me. A voice said to me, in the ancient language of my people, This is the fulfilment of an ancient dream, and a promise of glorious times to come."

"I see," said Shedemei. "The Keeper wants a bit of spectacle."

"I think it would be wise to have children spread the word as soon as he arrives. I think it needs to be seen and reported widely. I think we need an audience."

Shedemei rose from her chair. "If that's what the wise woman of the tunnels says should happen, then it will happen. You stay here near the front door. I'll fetch the other players in our little drama."

Akma asked his parents to go with him, but they refused. "You don't need us," they said. "You're only going to Shedemei's school. You don't need us to speak for you."

But he did; he was shy about facing the world. Not because he was unwilling to accept the public shame that would come to him—he would almost welcome *that*, because he knew that it was part of his lifelong labor, to heal Darakemba of the harm that he had done. No, he was simply afraid that he wouldn't know what to say, that he'd do it wrong, that he'd cause more harm. Remembering how it had been to have all his crimes stand present before him, he was very much afraid of doing anything to add to their already unbearable number. Even though he now searched his heart and found nothing there but the desire to serve the Keeper, he also knew that the pride that had so distorted his life was still waiting somewhere in his heart. Maybe someday he could trust that he had fully overcome it, that the devoted servant of the Keeper was his true self forever; but for now he was afraid of himself, afraid that the moment he was in public life he would begin to gather people to himself as he had done before, and that instead of using this power for their own good, he would again seek adulation the way wine-mad souls lived only for another jar.

He worried about this because he couldn't see the change in himself. His parents saw, though, as he reluctantly left the house and walked out into the street; they remembered well how he used to walk as if displaying himself, engaging the eyes of every passerby, insisting, demanding that they look at him with liking before he would release their gaze. Now he walked, not in shame, but without self-awareness. He looked at others, not to get their love, but to understand them a little, to wonder who they were. Like the Keeper, he kept himself almost invisible on the street, yet saw all. Akmaro and Chebeya watched him out of sight, then embraced in the doorway and went inside.

Too soon Akma reached the corner where Rasaro's House occupied all the buildings. He had never been to the school before, but had no trouble finding it—the place was famous. He had the odd notion that his visit was looked for, that there were people watching from the windows as he approached. But how could they know he was coming? He had only decided it himself this morning, and told no one but his parents. *They* would not have spread the word.

At the door he was met by a stern-looking woman twice his age. "Welcome, Akma. I'm Shedemei," she said. "I know you because I examined you while you were lying there pretending to be dead at your mother's house."

"I know," he said. "I came to thank you. Among other things."

"Nothing to thank me for," she said. "I told them what they already knew—that you weren't dead yet and it would be up to the Keeper whether you survived. I hope you're going to write down your experience during those three days of . . . whatever it was."

"I hadn't thought of it," he said. "I couldn't write it anyway. I would have to enumerate all my crimes, and they're innumerable." To his surprise he was able to say this in a calm voice, without a hint of either pleading or jauntiness.

"Well, you've thanked me," said Shedemei. "Why else did you come?"

"I don't really know," he said. "I hoped to see Edhadeya, but that's not the only reason that I came. I just woke up this morning knowing that it was time to come outside, and that it was here I had to come. It was only afterward that I remembered Edhadeya would be here. So I don't know. Perhaps it was the Keeper telling me what was expected of me. Perhaps not. Now that my crisis is over, the voice of the Keeper within me is no more clear than it is for anyone else."

"I don't really believe that," said Shedemei.

"Well it's true," said Akma. "The only difference is that now I'm trying to hear his voice, where before I was trying to hide from it."

"That's all the difference in the world. And yes, I think you're right, the Keeper wanted you to come today. We were warned that you were coming, and we made our own plans. A bit of pageantry. A visual image that we think the Keeper wants the world to see."

Akma felt the dread rise in him until it almost made him sick. "I don't want to do anything . . . public. Yet."

"That's because you remember how much harm you did in front of audiences, and how it harmed *you.*"

He was stunned that she understood this about him, when he had only figured it out himself this morning.

"What you haven't realized yet," she went on, "is that because your harm was public, undoing it will have to be public as well. You have a lot of speeches to give, using all your talents as a polemicist, only this time on the side of truth. It's harder in some ways, you know—more rules. But easier, too, because you can speak more from the heart and less from the head. You don't have to calculate the truth the same way you calculate a lie."

"I suppose you're right."

"Being right is my business," she said. "That's why I'm such a superb schoolmaster." Then, to his surprise, she winked at him. "I'm joking, Akma. Hard to believe, but I have a sense of humor. I hope you haven't lost yours."

"No," he said. "No, I was just . . . I'm just . . . easily distracted these days."

Someone was coming down the corridor. He looked, and knew the man at once, though he was in shadow. "Bego," he whispered. "Bego," he said aloud. "Are you here? I didn't know that you were here."

Bego sped up and, forgetting dignity, opened his wings and glided a little as he rushed to his former pupil. "Akma," he said. "You don't know how I've yearned to see you. Will you forgive me?"

"For what, Bego?"

"For using you, for misleading you, for trying to guide your thought without telling you—these were all crimes of the first order, Akma. I know you're all caught up in what an awful fellow you are, so that mine look like petty faults to you, but you have to know. . . ."

"I know," said Akma. "All I remember of our time together is what a gift your wisdom and learning were to me, and how much strength I got from your confidence in me." He held his teacher's hands, the folds of Bego's wings covering his fingers. "I was so afraid for you, for the punishment Motiak might give you."

Bego laughed. "I thought it was the end of the world. Do you know his punishment? He forbade me to read. I was barred from the library. Three spies stayed with me, awake in shifts, to see to it I didn't so much as scratch my name in the dirt with a stick. No reading, no writing. I thought that I'd go mad. My life was in the books, you see. The only people that I valued were the rare others, like you, who were as much at home with reading as I am. And then to be cut off from it—it was madness, I lived as a lunatic, hardly sleeping, longing for death. And then one day it dawned on me. What *are* books, anyway? The words of men and women who had something to say. Only when you read the book, the only voice you hear in your head is your own. You have the advantage of permanence, of being able to reread the same words again and again; but that's really a lie, because it gives you the impression that the writer thought and spoke permanently, when in fact the moment the book was written, the writer changed and became someone else, endlessly exciting because he was endlessly reinvented. To read a book is to live among the dead, to dance with stones. Why should I mourn for having lost the company of the dead, when the living were still here, their books yet unwritten, or rather they're being written in every moment of their lives!"

"So you came here."

"Came here! Came here and begged Shedemei to take me on, even though I was forbidden to read anything. She let me attend only one class. Voozhum's class, because the old lady is so blind she can't assign readings anyway, she just talks and the students listen and then talk back. But she was a digger! Do you have any idea how hard that was for me? How humiliating? I laugh now to think of it—this woman is a treasure! She has written *nothing* and if I had continued to live in books I would never have heard her voice, but I'll tell you, Akma, there is no moral philosopher in all the king's library who is as subtle and . . . *humane* as she is."

Akma laughed and embraced the little man. In all the years they had spent as student and master, there had been no such embrace; the books were always between them. But now it felt right to have the brush of the man's wings against his thighs as the long arms nearly double-wrapped him at the waist. "Bego, how glad I am that we both found our own route to healing."

Bego nodded, drew away from him. "Healing what can be healed. Undoing what can be undone. I couldn't have repaired the damage I did to you—I could only hope that you and the Keeper would work it out between you. And my own life—I've come too late to the things I've learned. I've never had a wife, never taken part in the great passage of blossom, seed, and sapling. Now I'm just an old stump and there's no more bloom in me. But that doesn't mean I'm sad or sorry for myself, don't misunderstand me, boy! I'm happier than I've ever been."

"Surely now the king will release you from your punishment."

"I haven't asked. I don't need to. I know everything that the library can teach me anyway. I'm busy discovering that all these children aren't just a single mass of annoyances, but instead are a whole bunch of individual, unique annoyances which are becoming increasingly interesting to me. Most of the books I read were written by men and to read them you'd think there was no such thing as a sentient female. Listening to the chatter of infantile females is opening a new world to me."

They laughed together. Only then, in the laughter, did Akma lift his gaze enough to see that they were no longer alone. Edhadeya stood there in the corridor, not five paces off, a look of uncertainty and shyness on her face. The moment she saw that he had noticed her, she looked down at the old digger woman whose hand she held. Then she stepped toward him, slowly, leading the halting old woman. "Akma," said Edhadeya. "This is Voozhum. She was once my . . . slave. She's also the greatest teacher in a school of great teachers."

The old woman looked at him through rheumy eyes; the lack of focus in her gaze told him that she was nearly blind. Withered and bent, she was still a digger, still had the massive haunches and the probing snout. In spite of himself, he saw for a fleeting moment the image of a giant digger, towering over him with a whip in his hand, laying on with the lash because he dared to rest a moment in the hot sunlight. He felt the sting across his back; and then, worse yet, saw the same lash come down on his mother's back and he was powerless to stop it. Rage flashed through him.

And then was gone. For now he saw that this old woman was not the same as the guard who had beaten him with such obvious pleasure in his cruelty and authority. How could he have ever hated all diggers for the actions of a few? And now he knew that he had been no better than they were: When the path of his life gave him a bit of power and influence, what had he done with it, that differed in any important way from what they did, except that his crimes were on a larger scale and he did a better job of lying to himself about what he was doing? I have been a digger a thousand times over; I have seen their suffering with the knowledge that I caused it. I forgive the digger guards who mistreated us. I value even their miserable lives; the harm they did to us cost us only pain, while it cost them the love of the Keeper—a far more terrible price, even if they didn't understand the reason for the emptiness and agony in their hearts.

Akma knelt before the old woman, so her bent-over head and his were at the same level. She leaned close to him, her nose almost touching him; was she sniffing at him? No, merely trying to see his face. "This is the one I saw in my dream," she said. "The Keeper thinks you're worth a lot of trouble."

"Voozhum," he said, "I harmed you and all your people. I told terrible lies about you. I stirred up hatred and fear, and your people hungered and hurt because of me."

"Oh, that wasn't you," said Voozhum. "That boy died. It seems to me that you spent all those years just trying to find a way to kill that boy, and finally you did, and now you're a new man. Tall for a newborn and more eloquent than most. But the new Akma doesn't hate me."

Impulsively he said the thought that had only just occurred to him. "I think I have never seen a woman so beautiful."

"Well, now, you must be looking over my shoulder at Edhadeya," Voozhum said.

"Edhadeya and I have years ahead of us to watch her become as beautiful as you," said Akma. "I think she will, don't you, Voozhum?"

"Definitely. It's the hump of my back that I think is especially fetching." Voozhum cackled with laughter at her own jest.

"Will you teach me how to undo my past life?" asked Akma.

"No," she said. "Not the whole thing. Only the bad bits."

"Yes, that's right, the bad bits."

"Don't want you to undo the part where you were brave. Or that clever scholar. Or the boy who had sense enough to fall in love with Edhadeya." Voozhum took Akma's hand and carefully, clumsily, put Edhadeya's fingers on his. "Now Edhadeya, let's not have any nonsense about pretending not to know what you want, all right?" said Voozhum. "You loved him right through the whole time he was unbelievably stupid, and now he's found his wits and become his true self, which is what you saw and loved in him all along. So you just tell him that you know the two of you can work everything out. Tell him!"

Akma felt Edhadeya's fingers close on his. "I know the two of us can work everything out, Akma," she said. "If you want to."

He squeezed her hand. "I've been alone," he said, unable to explain more of his experience in solitude than that. "I'm done with that." There would be time later to speak of the family they would create together, the life they both would share. He knew she would be with him; he knew he would be with her. That was enough for now.

"Give me your hand again," said Voozhum. "And hold the hand of that miserable bookworm on the other side. There was an ancient dream from the Keeper and I had an echo of it this morning, so let's follow the script she's given us and show ourselves to the crowd outside."

"Crowd?"

"Won't do any good to put on the show without an audience," said Voozhum. "The bigots need to see you holding the hands of an angel and a digger. And my people need to see that this old woman, at least, has forgiven you and that I accept you as a new man. All that information, and we can do it just by walking through that door."

Shedemei opened the door for them. The curious crowd had gathered in the streets, filling the intersection, watching for Akma, the son of the high priest who had been struck down by the Keeper and then arose again. Now as the door opened and first Voozhum, then Akma, then Bego emerged, a tumult arose from many throats. They could see that the three of them were holding hands. They watched as Akma knelt, so that his head was of a height with the bent old philosopher and the frail scholar. He took their hands and kissed them. "My brother and my sister have forgiven me," he said loudly to the crowd. "I beg the forgiveness of all good men and women. All that I taught was a lie. The Keeper lives, and the Kept will show us all the way to happiness. If there is anyone here who approved of my words and works for the past few years, then I beg you, learn from my mistakes and change your heart."

Shedemei noticed with relief that there were no rhetorical flourishes. His speech was simple, direct, sincere. Still, she had no illusions. The vile sort of people to whom he had once been a hero would now simply see him as a traitor. Few of them would be won over. The hope, as always, lay in the next generation, to whom Akma's story would be fresh and powerful.

As for the Assembly of the Ancient Ways, it had already collapsed. Aronha had officially dissolved it before Akma even arose from his coma, and though a few diehard digger-haters had organized a new version of it, there was no popular support. All those who had supported the Ancient Ways because it seemed like the wave of the future had already begun to remember that they always preferred the Kept. Those who had kept the boycott against the diggers out of fear or fashion were already seeking out their old clients and hirelings among the earth people, hiring those who were willing to forgive and return to work, buying up the unsold stockpiles of tradesmen's work. No one was foolish enough to think that this represented a vast change of heart in the population as a whole—the Kept who were truly committed to serving the Keeper were no more numerous now than they were before Shedemei had appeared to Akma and the Motiaki on the road. But as long as the genial hypocrites were willing to go through the motions and mouth the words, there was hope that more of their children would take the Keeper's plan into their hearts. And in the meantime, even empty lip service to the idea that all three peoples of the Earth were children of the Keeper would be enough to provide for peace and freedom within the borders of Darakemba. It's a starting point, Shedemei thought. A beginning, and we can rise from here.

Outside the school, a new tumult arose, and Shedemei stepped with Edhadeya through the door to see what was happening. The crowd parted, and the four sons of Motiak arrived. They had all visited the school often in the past few days, and each had reconciled with Edhadeya—Shedemei could see how relieved they were to be back in the good graces of their sister, not to mention their father. All four of them climbed the steps and embraced first Voozhum, then Bego, then Akma, then Edhadeya. As a pageant of reconciliation it was working very nicely.

<So are you done with them? Are you coming back?>

Miss me? asked Shedemei.

<I finished programming the probe and sent it off a few minutes ago. I would have told you, but you seemed busy.>

Congratulations. You've accomplished all that your other iteration sent you here to do.

<I've now become a supernumerary, like aged animals past the age of reproduction. Irrelevant to the future course of history.>

I doubt that, Shedemei said silently. I think we'll find ways to keep busy. Aren't you programmed to be curious?

<I must admit something to you, Shedemei, which I haven't mentioned because I thought it something of an anomaly in myself. I was disappointed by your discoveries about the Keeper of Earth. I even tried to prove them wrong. To prove that fluctuations in the magnetic field can't possibly have the effects that the Keeper seems to have. That there cannot possibly be a volitional element in the chaotic flow of magma in the mantle of the Earth.>

What an interesting and useless way to spend your time. What does it matter whether the Keeper actually uses magnetics or that was simply the closest I could come to understanding what she actually does?

<I know it. When I finally realized the futility of what I was doing, I then began to study myself to see what it was in my programming that had caused me to loop on the meaningless effort to deny your vision of the Keeper.>

What did you find?

<Nothing. Or rather, nothing that I can print out as demonstrable code to account for the effect. I can only express it in imprecise, metaphorical, anthropomorphic language.>

My favorite kind. Go ahead.

<I must have hoped, for all these years, that we would find that the Keeper of Earth was like me, inorganic, programmed; and if this had been the case, I might have hoped that with enhancement of my mechanical capacities I too could have the scope of influence that the Keeper has. Instead I remain completely other. A tool made to imitate the Keeper, but incapable of becoming the thing I imitate.>

So far, anyway, said Shedemei silently.

<No, this is a permanent difference. I am not sentient. I merely do such a splendid job of counterfeiting sentience that for a short time I fooled even myself.>

Not really. As long as I wear the cloak of the starmaster, you're a part of me, whatever else you are, and I'm a part of you. Even if I do as I'm tempted and take a husband here and squeeze another baby out of this old body, we'll be bound together for a long time to come. My life has enough meaning to share some of it with you, even if you *are* a supernumerary now.

<A very generous gesture, according to my moral evaluation algorithms. Thank you.>

Mon, laughing, was speaking to the crowd. Someone had asked a question. "Of course the three species are different," Mon said. "That's not a mistake. The Keeper looked at humans and said, How inadequate! They can't see in the dark! They only live on the surface of the earth! They can't fly! We need something else to make the world perfect. And so we were sent out of the room like bad children while the Keeper brought two more species to a point where they could take their place with humans as brothers and sisters. And the Keeper was right! We humans *weren't* complete! Why, I spent my whole childhood wishing I were an angel. And I could spend my whole life trying and never come close to the wisdom and kindness of this old woman. So yes, my friend, the differences between the three peoples of Earth are real and they're important—but they're the reason we must live together, and not at all a reason for us to live apart!"

A cheer arose from the crowd, long and loud. Shedemei turned to Edhadeya and the two of them laughed together. "Listen to him," Edhadeya said. "Now that he's saying things he really believes in, Mon may turn out to be the best teacher of all."

Shedemei felt a tug on her clothing. She turned around to find one of the youngest sky girls looking up at her. She bent down to hear.

"Shedemei, I know you're in a bad mood today, but I have to tell you, mNo just threw up and I can't find anybody but you."

Sighing, Shedemei left the great public spectacle and returned to the mundane duties of the school. This one-day nausea had been going around the school and Shedemei was not looking forward to the time when she inevitably caught it herself. In the meantime, there was vomit to clean up and a little sick girl to wash and put to bed until her parents could come for her. Menial, wearying work, and Shedemei was very good at it.

Geographical Notes

What used to be MesoAmerica and the Caribbean were transformed by a single geological event under the Earth's crust—the formation of a fast-flowing current in the mantle that plunged the Cocos plate northward at an incredible rate. Behind it, more than a hundred volcanos formed an uninhabitable archipelago extending hundreds of miles to the east and west of the Galapagos—dozens are still active. At the leading edge, the Cocos plate attacked the Caribbean plate far faster than it could be subducted. The result was dramatic uplifting and folding; by ten million years after the departure of the human race, there were several whole ranges of mountains above ten kilometers in height, with some peaks reaching higher than eleven kilometers. Between erosion and the slowing of the Cocos plate to merely three times the speed of any other plate on Earth, the highest peaks are now only some ninety-five hundred meters above sea level.

Besides the massif of high mountains, the Earth's crust behind the mountains was also forced upward, causing Cuba, Jamaica, and Haiti to be connected to the torn and distorted land mass of Central America. Millions of years of flooding from the great mountain rivers created a vast plain of fertile soil from the Yucatan to Jamaica.

Even farther north from the Cocos plate, the general uplifting (and the same current in the mantle) hastened a process that had begun long before—the rifting of North America at about the line of the Mississippi River. The eastern (Appalachian) plate began rotating counterclockwise and shifting northeastward; the western (Texas) plate continued its northwestward drift. (Northern South America [the Orinoco plate] was also gradually dragged along to drift somewhat northward, with a rift opening in Ecuador.)

It was the sudden rapid movement of the Cocos plate and the accompanying earthquakes and volcanism, not the limited nuclear exchanges that took place around that time, that made the Earth uninhabitable and forced humankind to abandon its birth planet. Nevertheless, all human emigrants carried with them the story that human actions had caused the destruction of the world.

MOUNTAINS

The gornaya (GOR-na-ya) is the great central massif lifted by the surging of the Cocos plate, with perpetually snow-covered peaks that are higher than any oxygen-breather can climb. Because most peaks are constantly invisible in clouds, they are not used as landmarks and are almost never named. Instead, rivers and lakes are used as landmarks, with their deep valleys forming both the highways and the habitats. The border of the gornaya was determined, before the return of the humans, by the lowest elevation where the digger/angel symbiosis could survive.

SEAS

Because the folding of the land into the ranges of the gornaya left most ranges running southeast to northwest, the rivers also run in those directions. This, rather than sunrise, the north star, or magnetic north, determined the cardinal directions of the diggers and angels (they had no compasses and even on clear days could rarely see the north star and could see sunrise or sunset only at the edges of the gornaya). Thus "north" in the names of various places means northwest of the gornaya, "west" means southwest, "south" means southeast, and "east" means northeast.

North Sea—the remnant of the Gulf of Mexico, a narrow sea jammed between the Texas/Veracruz coast on one side and the Yucatan coast on the other.

East Sea (Gulf of Florida)—a new sea opened in the straits between Cuba and Florida by the new rotation and northeastward movement of the Appalachian plate.

South Sea—the remnant of the Caribbean Sea

West Sea—the Pacific Ocean

WILDERNESS

On the Atlantic side, the gornaya gives way to a great fan of lowlands, much of it raised up from the ocean floor, covered with rich soil eroded from the gornaya and carried by great rivers which deposit new soil during flood seasons every year. The jungles there are rich with life, but since vast areas spend part of the year under muddy water, most of the fauna is arboreal. Diggers and angels who lived near the edges of the gornaya often sent hunting expeditions out into the wilderness, but they never went farther than the distance they could travel to carry game home before it spoiled. Three great regions of jungle are distinguished by the angels and diggers; their names were translated into the language of the Nafari and Elemaki and eventually those names replaced the names in the digger and angel languages.

Severless (SEV-er-less)—The great north wilderness, including the land that used to be Chiapas and Yucatan. The great rivers Tsidorek and Jatvarek flow through it; the Milirek marks its western and Dry Bay its eastern boundary.

Vostoiless (voe-STOY-less)—the great east wilderness, including the land that used to be Cuba, which forms most of the northern shore and a mountainous peninsula running eastward. The Vostoireg and Svereg Rivers flow through the lowland plain. The Mebbereg, the third great river of the east, is generally regarded as the southern boundary of the Vostoiless.

Yugless (YOOG-less)—the great south wilderness, which includes a low, wide isthmus between the Pacific and the Caribbean and reaches eastward to include a mountainous peninsula made up of what were once Jamaica and Haiti (or Hispaniola). The Zidomeg flows out of the land of Nafai down into the heart of the Yugless, and the northern boundary is the land of Nafai and the land of Pristan, where the humans first landed.

Opustoshan (oh-POOSS-toe-shahn)—in contrast to the well-watered jungles of the three great wildernesses, the fourth uninhabited land was called "desolation" by the diggers and angels because, being in the rain shadow of the gornaya, the area just west of the Milirek is desperately dry, to the point the vast regions are nothing but blowing sand. Soon the land rises to the old Mexican plateau, however, but the diggers and angels regarded it all as uninhabitable.

LAKES

An anomaly in the gornaya consists of a region of subsidence running on a north-south line, where rivers, whether flowing "north" or "south," formed lakes. As the rivers wore deeper channels into the mountains, the lakes subsided incrementally, forming fertile terraces up the canyon walls, so that the shores of the lakes have fertile land ranging from a few meters to as much as five kilometers in width. The seven lakes are named, from "east" to "west" (as the angels and diggers thought of them; we would say from north to south):

Severod—fed and drained by the Svereg
Uprod—source of the Ureg
Prod—source of the Padurek
Mebbekod—fed and drained by the Mebbereg
Sidonod—source of the Tsidorek, which flows through Darakemba and, farther downstream, the eastern reaches of Bodika.
Issipod—source of one branch of the Issibek
Poropod—fed and drained by the Proporeg

RIVERS

There are thousands of rivers in the gornaya, running in every canyon and valley. Though the entire gornaya is within the tropics, shifting winds and the extremely high mountain ranges cleft by long, deep valleys cause adjoining watersheds to have completely different amounts of precipitation at different seasons of the year. Rivers are highways, landmarks, and, where the gornaya opens up into wide valleys, they are the source of life in all seasons. Seven great rivers flow out of the gornaya and, after passing through wilderness, to the Atlantic. Four great rivers flow into the Pacific. In addition, some of the rivers have major tributaries. In the religion of the angels, rivers have varying degrees of holiness; the rivers are presented here according to their order in their hierarchy of sacredness (though the names are now a mish-mash of human, angel, and digger names and forms).

The Seven Lake Rivers

Tsidorek—the holiest river, flows north from the lake Sidonod. Because the lake comes near the top of the river valley, there is no major river flowing into it. Therefore Sidonod is the "pure source" of the Tsidorek, and it also has a tributary, the Padurek, which flows from a pure source (Prod), making the water twice pure. Darakemba, the capital of Motiak's kingdom, is located near where the canyon first widens into a broad valley where intensive agriculture is possible.

Issibek—flows north from lake Issipod, a pure source. It has a major south-flowing tributary, only the two rivers don't so much join as collide head-on. They once formed a lake there, which filled the long canyon for fifty kilometers before it spilled over the lowest pass in the oceanside range. But the lake eventually found an outlet through a system of caves and drained completely. Now the rivers seem to collide head-on, and since they flood at opposite times of the year, there is always enough water that the outlet is underwater. The result is that the river seems to flow downhill from the lake until it comes to a tumultuous low point, whereupon the valley goes up and the river continues, flowing in the opposite direction. The outlet runs underground for kilometers until it erupts from a cave on the other side of the range and flows into the Pacific. The outlet once had another name, but before the coming of the humans, a digger proved that it was the outlet of the Issibek. However, the river that flows north from lake Issipod and its tributary that flows south to join it are still considered to be the same river, but with two sources, one pure and one not. It is this strange river that Ilihiak's expedition to find Darakemba followed by mistake, leading them past Darakemba (several giant mountain ranges over) and eventually down into the desert of Opustoshen, where, on the shores of a seasonal river (bone dry at the time), they found bodies and weaponry suggesting that a devastating battle had been fought there. The corpses were so perfectly preserved in the desert that they could have been five or five hundred years old. Nearby, they found written records in an unknown language.

Mebbereg—Flows south from the lake Mebbekod. Not itself a pure source (the river flows into the lake from the north and then out of it on the south), but it has a pure source as a tributary (Ureg, out of Uprod). Akmaro's first settlement, Chelem, where his people were kept in captivity, was along the Mebbereg.

Svereg—Flows momentarily south from Severod, the "easternmost" (northernmost) of the lakes, then bends east and drops down rapidly from the gornaya into the vast jungle of the Vostoiless. Not a pure source.

Proporeg—Flows south from Poropod, the "westernmost" (southernmost) of the lakes, and drops rapidly to the West Sea (Pacific Ocean).

Padurek—A tributary river, but a pure source, it flows north from lake Prod until it joins the Tsidorek many kilometers downstream (north) of Darakemba. Akmaro's second settlement, called Akma, was on the shores of Prod, and it was the Padurek that Akmaro followed northward until he crossed over the pass that led down to the land of Darakemba.

Ureg—A tributary river, but a pure source, it flows south from lake Uprod and then joins the Mebbereg.

The Five Narrow Rivers

Zidomeg—flows south from near Poropod to within sixty kilometers of the West Sea (Pacific), then turns east through the Yugless to the South Sea (Caribbean). Nuak's kingdom of Zinom was at the head of the Zidomeg, and his people were conquered by the army of the overking of Nafazidom, downriver from him.

Jatvarek—Flows north (west) out of the gornaya and then turns east (north) to flow through what was once the Yucatan peninsula and is now the Severless. The city of Jatva is located at the very edge of the gornaya, overlooking the vast watery jungle. When Motiak extended his boundaries to take the entire settled valley of the Jatvarek under his protection, he officially gave the name Jatva to the enlarged kingdom, leaving the name Darakemba to refer to the kingdom of his father along the Tsidorek. In fact, however, everyone usually calls the whole empire "Darakemba."

Milirek—Flows north (west) out of the gornaya directly into the narrowest part of the North Sea (Gulf of Mexico), as if the North Sea were a continuation of the Milirek. The nation of Bodika had already conquered the habitable part of the Milirek before Motiak brought them to submission and included them in his empire.

Utrek—Entirely within the gornaya until it flows into the West Sea (Pacific), the river with the second lowest source.

Zodzerek—Entirely within the gornaya until it flows into the West Sea (Pacific), this is the river with the lowest source.

NATIONS

Pristan—First landing site, now called the "oldest kingdom" but otherwise without power and therefore without prestige.

Nafai—In the narrowest sense, the wide level land near the bottom of lake Poropod, where the Nafari first settled after fleeing from the Elemaki at Pristan. In the wider sense, the entire land over which the Nafari had influence before they abandoned it to form a union with the beleaguered people of Darakemba in the time of Motiak's grandfather, Motiab. Politically it was never fully unified; now, ruled by Elemaki, it is divided into three main kingdoms, which in turn are subdivided into smaller kingdoms. The three main kingdoms are:

Nafariod (nyah-FAH-ree-ode)—"Nafai of the lakes," the kingdom ruled by the king who styles himself simply Elemak, which means *king*. It includes the land around Sidonod, Issipod, and Poropod.

Nafazidom (nyah-FAH-zee-dome)—"Nafai of the Zidoneg," the kingdom eventually ruled by Pabulog, former high priest of Nuak. It was the king of Nafazidom which first allowed Zenifab to settle his human colony at the head of the Zidoneg.

Nafamebbek (nyah-FAH-meb-bek)—"Nafai of the Mebbereg," the weakest of the three kingdoms, though territorially it is the largest. Akmaro's first colony, Chelem, was in the territory of Nafamebbek, but the overking wasn't even aware of the colony until Pabulog, acting in the name of the king of Nafazidom, brought Chelem into captivity.

Zidom (ZEE-dome)—the small kingdom ruled by Nuak and, after his death, his second son, Ihili. Founded by Zenifab.

Chelem—on the shore of Mebbereg, the first colony founded by Akmaro, where Pabulog brings them into captivity.

Darakemba—on the Tsidorek, originally just a city and its surrounding territory, where the Nafari migrated as a people after wearying of the constant warfare in the land of Nafai. Later, a larger kingdom—about a hundred kilometers along the Tsidorek—brought under the control of Darakemba by Motiak's father, Jamimba. In the largest sense, the entire empire conquered by Motiak.

Bodika—the great kingdom downriver from Darakemba; it was pressure from Bodika that led Darakemba to welcome the influx of Nafari. Though soon the Nafari dominated the original Darakembi completely, at least they weren't enslaved—they remained full and equal citizens, under both the kings and the counselors. Jamimba had managed to maintain an uneasy peace with Bodika, but Motiak had to destroy their army, remove their entire ruling class, and incorporate Bodika into his greater kingdom of Jatva.

Jatva—originally, the land surrounding the city of Jatva at the point where the Jatvarek comes down out of the gornaya. Later, the whole inhabited river valley was brought under Motiak's domination as a protection against Elemaki who were raiding and conquering over the passes from Svereg. At that point, because it was a peaceful "joining" of kingdoms, Motiak gave the name Jatva to his entire empire, much as his grandfather Motiab let Darakemba keep its original name, even as its original inhabitants lost most of their political power.

Khideo—a region of humans only, downriver from Jatva, established in the course of this story.

* * *

There are, of course, many other kingdoms and nations, as well as small villages and settlements not under the rule of any king. Also, more and more people—sky people, middle people, and earth people—are migrating out into the wilderness, now that it is no longer biologically necessary for diggers and angels to remain in the higher elevations of the traditional lands of the gornaya.